MANCHU

An epic journey into the rich and exotic past
of seventeenth-century China by the bestsell-
ing author of DYNASTY.

MANCHU

A masterful re-creation of the intrigues, decadence, corruption, and private passions that led
to the demise of the Ming Dynasty and the rise
of the conquering Manchus.

MANCHU

An unforgettable love story of a daring young
Englishman and three beautiful women—a
story marked by passion, tragedy, and triumph.

Also by Robert Elegant:

DYNASTY   23655 $3.50

MANCHU

A NOVEL BY

Robert Elegant

FAWCETT CREST • NEW YORK

MANCHU

Published by Fawcett Crest Books, CBS Educational and Professional Publishing, a division of CBS Inc., by arrangement with McGraw-Hill Book Company

ISBN: 0-449-24445-8

Featured Alternate Selection of the Book-of-the-Month Club
Main Selection of the Playboy Book Club

Printed in the United States of America

10   9   8   7   6   5   4   3   2   1

For Julian and Beverly

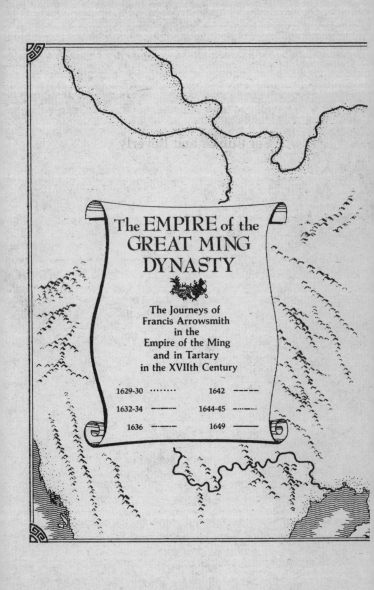

The EMPIRE of the GREAT MING DYNASTY

The Journeys of
Francis Arrowsmith
in the
Empire of the Ming
and in Tartary
in the XVIIth Century

1629-30 ········   1642 ‒ ‒ ‒ ‒

1632-34 ‒‒‒‒‒   1644-45 ·‒·‒·‒

1636 ‒·‒·‒·‒   1649 ‒‒‒‒‒

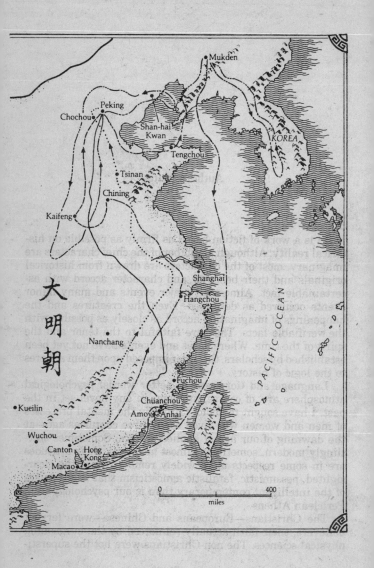

大明朝

Mukden

Peking
Chochou
Shan-hai
Kwan
KOREA
Tengchou

Tsinan
Chining

Kaifeng

Shanghai
Hangchou

PACIFIC OCEAN

Nanchang

Fuchou

Chüanchou
Amoy Anhai

TAIWAN

Kueilin

Wuchou

Canton Hong
Kong
Macao

0   400

miles

Author's Note

THIS is a work of fiction based as firmly as possible on historical reality. Although a number of the chief characters are imaginary, most of the characters are drawn from historical originals and their behavior and character accord with ascertainable fact. Almost all major events and many minor events occurred as described. Even the creatures and the happenings of imagination accord as closely as possible with the verifiable facts. They are faithful to the tenor and the spirit of the time. Where dates and events have not yet been established by scholars, the order imposed upon them adheres to the logic of history.

Language and (for want of better words) psychological atmosphere are, of course, problems in any novel set in the past. I have sought to depict faithfully the mental processes of men and women who lived some three centuries ago—at the dawning of our age of applied science. Sometimes startlingly modern, sometimes almost medieval, their attitudes are in some respects more widely removed from the clearsighted, pessimistic, fatalistic agnosticism that is the opiate of the intelligent contemporary than is our psychology from Periclean Athens.

The Christians—Europeans and Chinese—were fervent believers, their faith actually reinforced by the burgeoning physical sciences. The non-Christians were not the superstitious pagans their European contemporaries considered them. They were, however, untouched by the Renaissance, and they were by and large secure in the Confucian morality that had governed the personal and public lives of their forebears for almost twenty centuries. The minds of neither Christians nor non-Christians worked like our own.

Those observations, of course, apply not only to their thoughts but also to their speech. The dialogue is semiformal, seasoned only lightly with colloquialisms, since it is impossible to reproduce in modern English seventeenth-century Chinese or Portuguese. I have tried to avoid both self-conscious archaicism and gratingly anachronistic modernism.

Finally, a word regarding the sources. Though no individual could possibly digest all the rich material available on the period, both original and scholarly sources in English, Latin, Chinese, Japanese, German, French, and Portuguese were consulted. Travel in search of information led to Portugal, France, Germany, Macao, Hong Kong, Taiwan, Japan, and China.

June 1980
Greystones, County Wicklow
Eire

The Artillery of Heaven

June 1624–February 1632

St. Omer, the Spanish Lowlands

JUNE 20, 1624—OCTOBER 15, 1624

THE lead gutter trembled on the high-peaked roof, and the orange-throated robin fluttered into the morning haze. Twittering anxiously, she flew tight circles over the gaping beaks of the late fledglings in her nest of moss and feathers. Suspended between russet roof tiles and sandstone walls, the gutter quivered again. The fledglings cawed in raucous chorus, their incessant hunger displaced for an instant by fear.

Fifty feet below, smoke billowed from the cellar doorway. The leaded panes in the high-arched windows of the first floor vibrated violently when a second and a third explosion shook the monumental building. A fog of black-powder fumes lay over the quadrangle enclosed by the sheer walls. As a fourth explosion shattered the cloistered serenity of the English College of St. Omer at dawn on June 20, 1624, a lanky youth wearing a black clerical robe erupted from the cellar doorway.

Gasping and coughing, the youth doubled over with nausea. His brown eyes, streaming with tears, peered from his soot-blackened face like holes in a mask. His robe was torn and scorched, but his grimy hands clung to a broad-brimmed shovel hat more fitting to a staid middle-aged parish priest than a frightened seventeen-year-old.

"Francis! Francis Arrowsmith!" The Headmaster's bellow

transfixed the culprit. "What have you done this time? Is there *never* to be an end to your deviltry?"

"Nothing, Father...really nothing at all." There was something foreign about the youth's accent despite the elided vowels and metallic consonants of the Duchy of Lancaster, three hundred miles distant across the English Channel. "That is...hardly anything. I was just experimenting with..."

"Francis, my dearly beloved son, what *am* I to do with you?" The Headmaster's exasperation gave way to concern as he advanced, the winglike sleeves of his Jesuit cassock flying behind him. "What *is* to become of you?"

"I don't know, Father. Really I don't. I'm sorry...very sorry. I thought this time..."

The youth settled his black shovel hat on his head with both hands. Filmed by smoke, his long blond hair was spotted with scorch marks.

"I blame myself, Francis, not you." The Headmaster glared at the faces of boys and masters gaping through the windows, and they vanished. "An orphan delivered to my care, and I have failed miserably. Where have I erred? How have I failed to touch your soul?"

"I do not know, Father. But it was only a small explosion. I promise it won't happen..."

"You were making gunpowder again, Francis?"

"Yes, Father!"

"When you should have been in Father Pearson's class in homiletics. I've told you. Everything in its time and place....And never attempt alchemy without supervision. Next time, the Lord knows, you could blow up the whole College. How many times have I told you?"

"Many times, Father. Quite a number, I know."

The Jesuit glanced sharply, but read neither insolence nor defiance on the youth's features. Francis Arrowsmith appeared disarmingly repentant because tears had traced broad runnels in the soot on his cheeks.

"Francis, I fear you may have no true vocation for the priesthood. Your classmates, those who are not called, will return to England. Even in a kingdom ruled by heretics, they will be Catholic gentlemen....They have their families and their lands. But you have no kin and no property. If you are not a priest, what will you be?"

"I *will* be a priest, Father. I promise you I'll study harder. I want only to be a priest of the Society of Jesus."

"I doubt that, Francis. You are stirred more by the trum-

14

pet's blare than by plainsong. The sword's hilt fits your hand far better than the chalice. Caesar you love, but Cicero, even Vergil, you muddle. Though I must admit you speak Latin not badly."

"Thank you, Father." Again that elusive false note. "I am not utterly hopeless, then?"

"We are men of peace, not war," the baffled Jesuit persisted. "You are not meant to be a priest. Remember your mother's wishes and put aside this martial nonsense. . . . Put it out of your head entirely."

"I'll try, Father." Francis saw a glint of amused compassion in the dark blue eyes beneath the Jesuit's frowning brows. "I'll try hard. I promise."

His Headmaster was suspicious, but Francis Arrowsmith's promise was utterly sincere. Not only gratitude bound him to the Society of Jesus, but all his hopes for the future. If he were not a priest of the Society, he would be nothing in this world.

Francis again swore he would strive to fulfill the expectation his mother had impressed upon him eight years earlier when she gave him into the care of the Jesuit Fathers of the English College of St. Omer, some fifty miles from Calais in the Spanish Provinces of France. A year later Marie Dulonge Arrowsmith had joined her beloved husband Peter in the grave, not loath to depart from a world that had held no joy for her since his death in battle against the Protestants. Francis could still hear her voice in his ear: "Be a priest, my son, a man of God, not a man of blood like your father."

Francis idolized the father he had never known, for Peter Arrowsmith had died in June 1607, only four months after the birth of his only child. Francis had adored his mother, so gravely loving in her widow's dress.

For his Dulonge grandparents, who dutifully visited him once a year, Francis felt nothing, though he cherished the crude miniature portrait of his auburn-haired mother that was their only gift to him. Those stodgy burghers of the Spanish Lowlands had never been reconciled to their daughter's marriage to a penniless English exile. They grudgingly acknowledged Peter Arrowsmith's outstanding devotion to the True Faith, which had driven him from Lancashire after his yeoman family was stripped of its lands because of its staunch Catholicism. But the Dulonges had despised Peter Arrowsmith for his poverty, and they were delighted to be rid of the headstrong grandson their wayward daughter had foisted upon them.

Only one Englishman did the stolid Dulonges praise: Father Edmond Arrowsmith, who lay at that moment in a cell in London awaiting the headsman's axe. The Fathers of St. Omer's had taken Francis in chiefly because Edmond, the son of his uncle Robert, was a Jesuit in the secret mission to heretical England. They had accepted Francis gladly, though the Headmaster soon declared that he regretted his decision.

But his cousin's hand was no longer over Francis. Dead or alive, Edmond Arrowsmith could not abate the storms the youth's unruly temperament called down on his own head. Alone in the world, Francis knew that he must make his own way—and the Jesuits' way was the only way open to him.

His high forehead was wrinkled in contrition beneath its film of soot, and his eyes were repentantly veiled by his thick brown lashes. Nonetheless, his finely arched nose appeared assertive in his slender face. Though he wolfed the College's substantial midday meals, he had just attained his full height of almost six feet and his frame had not yet filled out. The quasi-cassock of a scholar of St. Omer's hung loose on his spare body.

Struck again by the unlikely combination of light brown eyes and blond hair, the Headmaster pondered again his pupil's inherent contradictions. Wholly open and honest, Francis was also stubborn and rebellious. Almost despairing of making the youth a good priest, the Headmaster wondered if it were wise to persist. A priest who was too handsome could be a curse to himself—and his flock. If Francis's boyish arrogance, untempered by female affection for many years, should persist, he would be far too attractive to the ladies. Perhaps, the Headmaster mused, it would be better for the boy to be a soldier. But he had promised Marie Dulonge Arrowsmith he would make Francis a priest.

"All right, my son, let me have your hand. This time I'll let you off easy. But, I promise you, next time..."

The leather ferrula—a foot long, three inches wide, and thick as a bootsole—lashed Francis's palm twenty times. Dismissed, he scurried toward the main gate, blowing on his swollen hand. Pride kept him from running to the horse trough whose water would cool the pain. Just before he reached the gate, the Headmaster's voice halted him.

"Francis, tomorrow is the month's holiday. But you won't be playing rounders at Blandyke. You will attend upon our

16

guest, that young priest from Rome, Father Giulio di Giacomo. And, Francis, you will speak Latin to him."

TWO days later, the green flag bearing the double-barred white Cross of St. Omer fluttered in the afternoon breeze over the College. The school's premises had expanded manyfold in the four decades since the fugitive English Jesuits had gratefully accepted the hospitality of St. Omer. Visitors from England, where the great properties of the Roman Catholic Church had been confiscated by the Crown, would sometimes stand stock-still on first seeing the massive sandstone edifice and breathe: "By God, it's more like a palace than a school."

Keeping alight the flame of English Catholicism in Spanish-ruled France by educating English Catholic gentlemen had, however, been no light task. The priests had been harassed not only by the heretical British monarchy but also by the local authorities until His Most Catholic Majesty, King Philip of Spain and Portugal, extended his personal protection and his personal patronage to the exiles. In the summer of 1624, some one hundred fifty boys from ten to nineteen years old pursued a rigorous classical curriculum leavened with mathematics and the new physical sciences that piqued the intellectual curiosity of their Jesuit masters. Seven to eight years of study uninterrupted by any vacation was hardly long enough for all they had to learn.

His black robe newly darned and his fair skin glowing after vigorous scrubbing, Francis Arrowsmith sat in the front row of the somnolent assembly in the Great Hall of the College. Neither his age nor his standing entitled him to that eminence. Still mired at seventeen in the middle grade, called Poetry, he was usually banished to the last row for inattention to religious studies. Neither his erratic charm nor his enthusiastic participation in the three-hour-long Latin dramas the College loved could excuse his frequent truancy to visit the nearby barracks of the Spanish Guards. But he was allotted a place of honor that afternoon because of his leading role in the pageant that had belatedly celebrated the fortieth anniversary of the College and also because he had discharged so well the task the Headmaster had imposed upon him as punishment.

Francis had waited with exemplary care upon the twenty-nine-year-old Italian priest who came to tell the College of the enterprise that was the glory of the militant Society of

Jesus. Father Giulio di Giaccomo, ordained only a year earlier, was himself destined for the Mission to the Great Ming Empire, where a few score supernally dedicated priests carried the light of the True Faith to some one hundred fifty million pagans.

While awaiting embarkation on the two-year voyage to the Portuguese settlement of Macao on the edge of China, Father Giulio di Giaccomo had been assigned a task the Father General in Rome considered almost as important. With a score of others, he brought news of the brilliant progress of the China Mission to the chief Catholic burghers, noblemen, and princes of Europe—and to the Jesuit colleges that would provide recruits for the Holy Mission. *Propaganda Fidei* the Church called the sacred task of propagating the Faith. The Jesuits vigorously publicized their successes in order to draw from the laity essential financial and spiritual support. Confusing the two endeavors, men also called the work of publicization propaganda.

Almost alone among the schoolboys, Francis was not distracted by the buzzing of the honeybees or the shouts of the herdsmen in the green fields that surrounded the College. He intently watched the plump Italian priest, who looked on the world through round, dark eyes like those of tan-and-white Friesian cattle. Despite his indolently genial manner, Giulio di Giaccomo was inspired by soaring enthusiasm for the China Mission. He had that morning displayed his treasures to Francis, lifting them as reverently as sacred relics from a leather box carved with scarlet-and-gilt patterns.

"A Mandarin's traveling casket," he explained. "They use them to hold their papers when away from home."

"Mandarin?" Francis asked. "*Qui est hoc?*...What is that?"

"Ah, yes." The priest's full red lips smiled. "You don't know, of course. The name comes from *mandar,* Portuguese for command. So we call the learned officials of the Great Ming Empire, who are as like to Plato's ideal of the perfect philosopher-king as any mortal can be."

"Mandarin...Mandarin." Francis rolled the sounds dubiously on his tongue. "A strange word, I think."

"But no more strange than many things in that wondrous Empire. Even more wonderful...this."

The Jesuit uncoiled a roll of paper from a wooden cylinder. Francis saw an ink drawing of two middle-aged men standing before an altar. The altar cloth bore the familiar inscription

IHS, *In Hoc Signo*, while a painting of the Madonna and Child hung on the wall behind them between placards with angular symbols. The man on the left wore a full white beard, and his nose was long between large eyes. The chin of the other was adorned by a pointed goatee, and his eyes were peculiarly tilted. Both wore flowing robes and tall black hats unlike any Francis had ever seen.

"Father Matthew Ricci, the holy pioneer of the Mission to China, now gathered unto the Lord," Father di Giacomo explained. "And, beside him, Dr. Paul Hsü, the great Mandarin who is the chief pillar of Holy Church in the Empire of China."

Francis felt a proprietary attachment to that scroll drawing, now displayed on an easel beside the young Italian. Two quite different pictures flanked it. One was a highly realistic painting of Matthew Ricci with the great sun of the Orient ablaze behind him and a Latin inscription reading *Father M. Ricci of Macareta in Italy who, first of all the Society of Jesus, preached the True Gospel in China*. The other was a charcoal sketch of a Jesuit missionary in the full dress of a Chinese gentleman with high-peaked hat and voluminous sleeves.

Francis's eyes strayed to the glowing colors of the altarpiece done by the same Peter Paul Rubens who had sketched the missionary. Gazing at the swelling bosoms of the ladies attending the Blessed Virgin Mary he felt a thrill of guilty pleasure. But he was drawn back to the charcoal sketch.

The painting was—he struggled to formulate his thought—Holy Church in Europe, Christendom already mature and complete. The sketch represented Holy Church in the mysterious Empire of the Ming, where the Jesuits had begun their endeavors some four decades earlier. Was it not more worthy—and more exciting—to be at the beginning, rather than the fruition?

"...many things in China more wondrous than anything ever dreamed of in Europe." The Italian priest's eloquence was Ciceronian, as were the rolling cadences of his Latin address. "Only by becoming one with the Chinese...only by first adopting their customs and imbibing their learning could the Society bring the True Faith to the Chinese. That is why the priests wear the robes of Chinese Mandarins and assiduously study both the spoken tongue and the classical writings of China.

"The pioneer and the guide in this difficult adaptation was Father Matthew Ricci, whose journal is today the most widely read book in all Europe. Yet the holy Father Matthew, who now lies buried in Peking, the capital of the Ming Empire, did but make a beginning. The greater work is still to be done ... to bring more than a hundred million souls to Christ's salvation."

The priest paused to sip beer from a pewter cup. The English were truly different, he reflected with an involuntary grimace. Who else would drink thin beer when he could drink rich wine? Still, he had won the attention of both the English schoolboys and their cool masters who were, perforce, his brothers in the Society. But none was as raptly attentive as the gawky Francis Arrowsmith, his guide at the College. Giulio di Giaccomo decided to offer them a jest in return for their courtesy.

"Father Matthew Ricci himself declared shortly before he was gathered unto the Lord that the greater tasks remained. He said: 'I have done all I could to make myself Chinese, learning their difficult tongue and their intricate writing, adopting all their customs, and clothing myself after their fashion. If only I could make this long, thin nose of mine short and flat, if only I could make these great staring eyes of mine small, oblique, and dark, then I should be perfectly Chinese. But that boon the Lord has denied me.'"

Laughter rippled through the assembly. Some boys tittered; others forced guffaws. Even the aloof masters smiled. Looking directly at Francis Arrowsmith, Father Giulio began the summation he had found equally effective with elderly noblemen and raw schoolboys:

"The Lord God has given our generation the greatest challenge in history: the opportunity to implant Christianity among tens of millions of pagans. The Great Emperor of the Ming is harassed by the barbarian tribesmen from the north called Tartars or, sometimes, Manchus. The Emperor has appealed to the Portuguese of Macao through the Jesuit Fathers at his capital. He has invited the Portuguese, who are our Catholic brothers, to send him cannon and artillerymen. He knows that the green-bronze cannon of Portugal are the most powerful ordnance in the world and Catholic artillerymen the finest soldiers."

Francis Arrowsmith flung his head back, automatically brushing away the blond hair that lay like folded wings on his forehead. He glanced surreptitiously to see whether the formidable Headmaster had noted his unseemly excitement. But that priest was studying their visitor, his eyebrows quirked quizzically. Francis cupped his pointed chin in his hands and gazed intently as the Italian concluded:

"The Fathers were, at first, reluctant to assist the Emperor in obtaining European arms. They were, they said, men of the Holy Book, not the sword. But the great Mandarin Dr. Paul Hsü pointed out that the Lord had given them a unique opportunity. By facilitating the Emperor's request and winning the Emperor's favor they could end the persecutions that have on several occasions virtually halted the propagation of the True Faith in the Empire. The Fathers in Peking therefore resolved to obtain ordnance and artillerymen from Macao.

"More are needed, many more to serve God in China. There are many ways to serve the Lord. Not all men are chosen to serve Him with book and bell and candle. Some... many... are chosen to serve him with the sword!"

FATHER Giulio di Giaccomo left the next morning for Antwerp, where he would exhort solid merchants to support the Mission to China with their guilders. The Headmaster was not sorry to see the Italian go, though he had been moved by the account of the Mission to China. He felt the volatile Southerner had upset and muddled the schoolboys.

There was, the Headmaster believed, only one way for the flower of Catholic England to serve God. That was as consecrated priests of the Society of Jesus. Too many soldiers walked the earth in the third decade of the seventeenth century, too many men of blood. But too few stalwart servants of the Prince of Peace, too few Jesuits sworn to propagate the True Faith throughout the non-Christian world by pacific means—meekly enduring martydom if that were the Lord's will. No good, the Headmaster felt, could come of muddling the Cross and the sword as the excitable Latins did.

At the end of the summer term, the Headmaster assessed all his pupils and wrote of Francis Arrowsmith: "The boy was diligent in his studies for some months after Father Giulio di Giaccomo's visit. He was so well-behaved I feared he was ill. My anxiety was, however, dispelled. Afterward, the boy was as unruly as ever."

FOR almost three months Francis Arrowsmith had been bemused by a vision. Reminded by the Headmaster of his

21

mother's exhortations to become a priest, he had been inspired by Giulio di Giaccomo's message.

Looking up from his schoolbooks, he would see himself, ascetic in a black robe of strange cut, features gravely composed beneath a tall hat that concealed a priestly tonsure, preaching the Gospel of the Lord to the Chinese in their own liquid tongue. He saw himself always as a Jesuit who fearlessly faced the swords the pagans unsheathed to turn him from his Holy Mission. It was more noble, he told himself, to die for the Living Christ in the Empire of the Ming, if need be, than to slay other men—even in His cause. He honored his father's memory, but reflected with unbelieving horror upon his former self, who had longed to be a soldier for Holy Church and the Catholic sovereigns of Europe.

The fogs of winter came early to the Spanish Lowlands that year, and the long, sweet afternoons of September were succeeded by the short, gruff days of October. The resolution that had flourished in the sunlight withered in the storms that swept across the Channel to pelt St. Omer's College. Francis Arrowsmith longed for the company of other men than his withdrawn Jesuit masters—and he dreamed of the unattainable warmth of women. The rough good fellowship of the campfire again seemed far more congenial than the lonely piety of the priesthood.

On a Saturday afternoon in late October, Francis slipped away from the College just after the sparse meal that preceded evening prayers at six. Too restless to lie obediently on his straw-stuffed mattress when the candles were snuffed at eight, he assured himself he would be back long before the assistant masters shook the sleeping boys awake at five for Sunday Mass. Abandoning stealth when he left the College grounds, he strode through the mist lying on the road to the barracks of the Spanish Guard.

He hoped the sergeants would again lend him clothing to replace the distinctive black robe of a scholar of St. Omer. He looked forward to drinking full-bodied Spanish wine and to conversing in mixed dog Latin and broken Spanish. However reckless he might feel, he would not lay his hands on the serving wenches whose breasts lolled provocatively in their low-cut blouses. But he would look hard at those full-blooded wenches and jest with them as the guardsmen did. And soon, perhaps, more. He was, after all, almost eighteen, no longer a timorous boy foolishly obedient to every prohibition prattled by his schoolmasters.

22

The Color Sergeant welcomed Francis uproariously, shouting that the English priestling had at last come back to his friends. Other sergeants crowded around, encouraging him with bawdy jests as he put on a doublet and breeches. Delighted to entertain again the son of the Englishman who had died fighting his heretical countrymen in the service of the King of Spain, they pressed bumpers of the red wine of Rioja on him. When they set off for the tavern called the Three Ravens, Francis's head was reeling—but his valor was high.

For some time thereafter, Francis tried to recall that evening. But he could remember clearly only entering the crammed taproom arm-in-arm with sergeants of the Spanish Guard. His further memories were forever fragmentary: slopping pewter beakers of wine and pewter cups of raw brandy; the rank female odor of the buxom serving wenches; the local farmhands glaring across the dim-lit tap-room; and, finally, a blur of kicking feet and pounding fists as good fellowship dissolved in a furious fight. He could not remember the constables who carried him back to the College, happy to do him that good turn rather than leave him to sleep off his drunkenness.

He always remembered the brief, decisive encounter when the Headmaster summoned him after Holy Mass the next morning. His stomach heaving and his head trembling, Francis gingerly fingered the bruises on his face.

"I'll not waste reproaches on you." The Headmaster did not raise his voice. "I see no point in spending passion on one who is lost, irredeemably lost. I thought for a time...but you clearly have no vocation for the priesthood. Your vocation may be for the Devil's service. That question is debatable. It is not debatable that you must leave the College. I can keep you no longer."

"But, Father, is one lapse to mean that I..." The words that could touch the Headmaster's heart did not come to Francis's thick tongue. "Father, you said you promised my mother..."

"Enough, boy!" Francis had never before heard steel-cold anger in the Headmaster's voice. "I promised your mother I would try.... And I have tried. But I can try no longer. You *must* go away from us."

"Father, what is to become of me?" In despair, Francis blinked away traitor tears.

"Lad, th'art no good to us," the Headmaster lapsed for a

23

moment into his own childhood's broad Lancashire accent. "I must cast you out of the College. Last night's work is but the final straw...the final proof. It would be spitting in God's own face to persist in trying to make a priest of you. I cannot bring you into the Society."

"What can I do, Father?" Francis pleaded. "There is no other who cares for me or would help..."

"I know that, lad. And you've lived among us too long for us ever to forget you—or you to forget us. I'll give you a letter to my beloved brother in Christ, Father Antonio D'Alicante, who stands high in the favor of King Philip in Madrid. Perhaps he can make something of you. Perhaps you are meant to be a soldier. God knows you carouse like a soldier!"

Macao

THE luminous sunset of the fourth day of June in the year of Our Lord 1628 trailed its spangled skirts over the red-tiled roofs of Macao, the minuscule European enclave on the edge of the Great Ming Empire. The pure light touched the pastel houses with the intense clarity only seen just before dusk closes a rain-washed day. Rays glinted on the narrow windows of the Residence of the Captain-General, the settlement's chief official, and lit the red-and-green flag that fluttered over the bronze cannon gaping from the white-limed Guia Fort. The declining sun gilded the broad Pearl River where it broke free of its chain of islets to flow rust-brown through the green waters of the South China Sea.

Impervious to the drizzle, four coolies wearing black tunics and baggy trousers squatted among the puddles. Their spatulate feet were planted a foot apart, and their lean haunches hung from high-flexed knees scant inches above the cobblestones. A heavy-shouldered yellow dog watched them cast carved bones and gather in copper coins. Weathered skin stretched taut over broad cheekbones, the gamblers' ocher features grimaced in exaltation or despair when the dice fell. But the mahogany eyes glinting through oblique slits were secretive and withdrawn. The gamblers acknowledged by

25

neither a word nor a glance the tumult rising from the foreshore, where revelers were congregating around bonfires.

The sweet smell of roasting pig hung heavy in the still air. The acrid stench of drying fish drifted from the fishing junks swinging offshore to contend with the pungent reek of frying garlic from food stalls. Sweating cooks turned crackling noodles from fire-blackened woks into coarse porcelain bowls and topped the tawny strands with tidbits of orange octopus and scarlet pigs' intestines, so that the faintly saline sea scent mingled with the musty smell of earth. Above all the other odors, the fruity richness of the red wine of Europe contended with the salty savor of the soy sauce of the Extreme East.

"They eat, by God, they eat like wolves.... And they gamble like fiends." The stocky Portuguese Captain grinned. "When they find time to fornicate like rabbits only God knows. But, otherwise, Francis, why so many of these Chinese?"

"Why, indeed, Miguel?" The slender English Lieutenant forced a laugh.

At twenty-one, Francis Arrowsmith was still uncomfortable with soldiers' obsessive sexual jesting. The decorum instilled by his Jesuit teachers had not been submerged by the licentiousness he had seen during some four years as a Spanish officer and a working passenger on caravels making the long voyage from Lisbon to remote Macao. As his tender conscience reminded him, his own behavior was hardly prudish. But he was reserved in speech, detesting the contempt for women that lay under the soldiers' jests. His reverence for the Blessed Virgin and his own saintly mother forbade his mocking their sex as if they were only vessels shaped for men's pleasure.

The young Englishman prudently kept his own counsel regarding the so-called gentlemen who ruled Macao. If they could not restrain their inordinate lust for gold and women's flesh, they could, at least, draw over it a veil of decent dissimulation. He despised Macao's hundred or so Portuguese ladies equally—but for their calculated hypocrisy. They made great show of their piety and even greater show of their impregnable virtue. Yet he himself had already been approached several times, and he knew of a dozen who lay indiscriminately with Japanese *ronin,* with African slaves, and with common soldiers, paying them well. There were ten females to every male in Macao.

The men of Macao were no more true gentlemen than the

women were true ladies. They were called *hidalgos,* "sons of someone." Most were manifestly sons of nobody, if their lewd behavior was the measure of their worth. Most appalling, however, were the licentious Dominican and Franciscan friars who had been corrupted by Oriental laxness. Many lived in open concubinage, while their drunkenness and greed shocked even the Portuguese laymen.

Francis was not repelled by the frank coarseness of the Portuguese Captain-Sergeant who bore the imposing name Miguel Gonsalves Texeira Correa. On his arrival in Macao a week earlier, the bluff Captain-Sergeant had welcomed Francis generously. Since then Miguel Texeira had given the latest recruit as much of his time as had Father Giulio di Giaccomo of the Society of Jesus, his sponsor in the colony. Francis already felt a strong liking for the man he hoped would soon be his commanding officer.

The Portuguese had served in the Extreme East for more than a decade, almost a quarter of his life. Having voyaged to Japan, Taiwan, and the Philippines, Miguel Texeira was as much at home in the East as the ubiquitous Jesuits. Having fought the Dutch, the English, and the Spanish as well as the swarming pirates of the China Seas, he had perfected the warcraft first learned in the battles of Europe.

Even in his loose sailor's smock over white-duck trousers, Texeira carried unchallengeable authority. Even when his square, black-furred hand groped instinctively for the hilt of the sword he had been forbidden to wear that evening, the Portuguese was formidable. Though his features were neatly planed, the wide-flared nostrils of his short nose and the set of his broad mouth hinted at a certain ferocity. But the lines engraved on his swarthy-gray cheeks vanished when he laughed, and he laughed often.

"There, just at the foot of Mount Guia, Francis, mark it well." Miguel Texeira pointed. "There we defeated the Dutch invasion in twenty-two, the same year we sent the first cannon to Peking. Turned the heretics back and kept Macao as the bastion of Holy Church and our trade in the Extreme East."

"You fought in that battle, Miguel, did you?" Francis brushed his side to reassure himself that he had not lost the dirk he, like the Captain, wore under his smock.

"I did, Francis. But we few regulars weren't really in it. That battle was won by drunken black slaves and the fighting Jesuits. The good Fathers fought like demons. One young

27

priest...a German...trained a great mortar on the Dutch and blew up their powder magazine. He waded into the fray swinging a pike and shouting like a wild Teuton."

"Adam Schall, was it, Miguel?" Francis asked. "I've heard from Father Giulio..."

"Yes, by God, Adam Schall was his name. He's now in Peking—and I pity anyone who....But we must hurry, Francis my boy."

The June day that began with drizzle weeping from gray clouds was ending with the incandescent blaze of the sun settling behind the rounded hills of South China. The spectacle did not move the nine thousand residents of the territory ceded to Portugal by the Ming seven decades earlier to keep European merchants safely distant from the trading metropolis of Canton. The Macanese were inured to the heavens' abrupt transition from leaden pallor to pyrotechnic grandeur.

All were, however, jubilant because two weather-stained caravels had completed the two-month voyage from Goa in Portuguese India just before the sunset gave way to velvet night. Black slaves from Angola and Mozambique; geishas from Shimabara and their protectors, the outlawed warriors called *ronin* from Edo; stout Dominicans from the Algarve and hard-handed seamen from Java—all rejoiced at the break in their normal isolation.

Soldiers roistered with slaves and bondservants around the bonfires blazing on the Praya Grande, the esplanade along the shore. They capered, drank, and gorged under sputtering torches. Their oiled skin reflecting the flames like polished jet, twenty stick-thin black slaves clothed only in breech-clouts leaped in a Dahomey war dance and screamed shrill war chants. Seamen sprawled around the dancers, clicking a rhythmic accompaniment with the stripped ribs of roast piglets. A sozzled Franciscan friar swaying atop a winebarrel led a hymn of thanksgiving to a merciful and tolerant God who so loved His creatures that He bestowed upon them the twin boons of fermented grapes and carnal congress.

Francis eyed the geishas kneeling on straw mats on the edge of the light. Twin sword hilts bristling in their sashes, two *ronin* stalked bandy-legged toward him. Seeing their flat cheeks dyed crimson by *saké*, he stepped out of their way. The Japanese warriors were insanely belligerent when wine inflamed their yearning for the home islands and the perished feudal lords they would never again see.

28

A geisha wearing a lotus-flowered kimono, her face caked with white powder, beckoned with a sinuous movement of her wrist. Francis paused irresolute. The feral odor of the prancing Blacks had stirred him profoundly.

"Move along, my boy," Miguel Texeira commanded in rough Portuguese. "We have other work to do this night. First work, then fornicate."

Francis hurried after the Captain, vividly aware that deviating from Giulio di Giacomo's instructions could alienate the Italian. The good will of the Jesuits had brought him to Macao. Only the Jesuits' continuing good will could admit him to China. The only foreigners who could reside and travel in the Ming Empire, the black priests held the key to China. And only China could offer Francis the opportunity to amass the fortune needed to reclaim the Arrowsmith lands in Lancashire. Deprived of Jesuit patronage, he would be derelict on the China coast, no more than another sword for hire.

The officers moved out of the torches' glare into the shadows the half moon cast on the hillside below the graveyard. Since tropical fevers scourged Macao, its headstones were more numerous than houses in the town. Though the demand for firewood was denuding the peninsula, shrubbery still clustered around tall cypresses. Only the foolhardy cut those funereal groves, where, the Chinese warned, disconsolate spirits preyed on living men. All the subject races were terrified of malevolent ghosts. The Portuguese, too, avoided Cemetery Hill, though most priests laughed at their fears. Even the Jesuits did not necessarily comprehend the ways of either Chinese ghosts or Christian spirits stranded on the alien shore.

Francis followed Texeira's white figure through the moonlight. He smiled uneasily, thinking he would himself appear a restless spirit to the Chinese. His arched nose, his fair hair, and his slender height—those, the Chinese said, were the characteristics of maneating ghosts. He laughed with bravado and suppressed a shudder. Ghosts, of course, walked the earth, but ghosts at least he did not fear. He was a cool-headed Englishman, not a superstitious Oriental.

Two white forms, incorporeal and flowing drapery, appeared above the dense shrubbery a few yards ahead. Their heads glowed yellowish in the moonlight, and their mouths emitted ululating wails.

"You will see strange sights, but they will mean all is proceeding well," Giulio di Giacomo had warned. "I cannot...no priest can be present. You must be our deputy, as Texeira is the Captain-General's. You are not to interfere, but only to observe—and report to me."

Recalling those instructions to steady his nerves, Francis followed the stolid captain. The specters whined pitifully, and their draperies fluttered. Most unghostlike, they bobbed quick bows and touched pallid hands to their foreheads when the officers stood before them.

Beneath the coating of flour paste Francis recognized the features of two of the Jesuits' loyal African bondservants who were, he saw, draped in old sails. He knew that a number of bondservants had been persuaded with silver and consecrated medals to frighten away interlopers by playing the ghost.

Miguel Texeira and Francis Arrowsmith followed the mock specters to the far corner of the cemetery. Two mottled figures were insubstantial in the watery moonlight that splattered through the foliage. Their shapes wavered eerily when the wind stirred the branches. Coming closer, Francis saw that two Portuguese infantrymen in black uniforms splotched with red were leaning on long shovels beside an open grave. A pine coffin lid lay against the heaped red earth they had dug up.

A figure in a gray shroud climbed stiffly out of the coffin. Hooked fingers clawing at the crumbling soil, the figure slipped back twice before the soldiers offered their hands.

"*Mas mais con pres, homer!*" one said contemptuously. "Move your feet, man! You should've thought of this before you killed the damned Chinaman."

"They should've shot you," the second added. "Waste of time all this mummery!"

"Any other Captain-General would've shot you. You should thank God this one's too proud to give you to the Chinks."

After fifteen hours in the grave, the apparition croaked: "Water! For...love of God, give...water!"

The first gravedigger dangled a pewter water bottle from a leather thong. But the cramped fingers of the man from the grave slipped on its slick sides. The bottle cradled between his palms, he finally drank, and inrushing air gurgled through the silent night.

The life of that creature, Francis reflected with disgust, had cost Macao five weeks of deprivation. Chinese pride had demanded that he be delivered to the Mandarins of Canton for execution after he stabbed a Chinese servant who was slow to bring a fifth bottle of wine. Portuguese pride—and Portuguese policy—maintained that no Portuguese subject could be punished under Chinese law. The Viceroy of Canton had therefore imposed an absolute embargo on all trade goods and food for the enclave.

Despite the embargo, the Captain-General had remained firm. Only when convinced by the Jesuits that the Viceroy would deny Macao food indefinitely had he sanctioned the mock garroting, followed by burial in a coffin supplied with air through a bamboo tube. Ignorant of the deception, the Viceroy had then declared Chinese honor satisfied.

The murderer grunted witlessly when the soldiers thrust his limbs into a black uniform and drew a hood over his head. While the murderer stumbled through the dark groves surrounding the spectral tombstones among which he had lain, the Englishman thanked God he had not suffered the same ordeal.

Unspeaking, the two officers followed the three dark figures along the hill paths to the Cacilhas Beach, where a caravel lay at anchor far from the revelers' bonfires. When they had seen the culprit embarked in a skiff, their task was done. Light-hearted, the Captain and the Lieutenant returned to the town. Texeira made for the Captain-General's Residence. Francis climbed to the Jesuit College to report to Father Giulio di Giaccomo that the criminal had embarked on his secret journey to Goa.

THE Church of St. Paul thrust its baroque intricacy into the ashen Sunday dawn, its tawny stone façade almost obscured by the profuse handiwork of Chinese masons and European metalworkers. Bronze doves soared among the four tiers of white pillars that framed bronze statues of the Christ, the Blessed Virgin, and their attendant saints. A stone cross reached into the clouds above the Greek pediment of the belltower. From ponderous wooden doors broad stone steps swept downhill toward the mist-veiled shore.

In the sitting room of the small house perched beside the plaza at the head of those steps, Father Giulio di Giaccomo returned his goose quill to its pewter inkwell and poured blotting sand on the paragraph he had just written. Distracted by the tumult resounding through the open shutters, he looked up at Francis Arrowsmith.

"What is that awful din?" he asked. "The ambassadors already?"

"Not yet, as far as I can tell," Francis replied. "But come see for yourself, Father Giulio."

The priest pushed back his chair and joined the young Englishman at the window. A voluminous black cassock cut in the Chinese style with flowing sleeves draped his plump body. Francis was vivid beside the somber Jesuit. The watery sunlight glinted on the gilt piping of his full green knee breeches and lit the gilt festooning the balloon sleeves of his scarlet-velvet doublet. Side by side they leaned out the window.

A flood of wanton color was cascading down the broad steps beneath them, slowing momentarily at each landing before plunging earthward again. Gaily clothed women were the waves of that bright tide.

The scarlet headscarves of Chinese boat women bobbed among streaming dark tresses. Purple Indian saris trailed beside Japanese kimonos girdled by silver obis. Sable Africans in gaudy dashikis elbowed tan Javanese whose bony ankles were hobbled by serpentine-batik sarongs.

The tattoo of the women's feet reverberated from the houses lining the steps. The leather soles of Bombay *chuplis* slapped the wet pavement. Three-inch-high *geta* pounded beside the shuffling sandals of the Indies. Chinese cloth shoes sighed amid the thud of broad bare feet.

The torrent of women poured down the hill into the lane leading to the cobblestone crescent of the Praya Grande on the seafront, where the hawkers spread their wares on straw mats. They chattered breathlessly in their own languages and the broken Portuguese that was their common tongue.

*"Yau yok, choi, gai-dan....Carne, pinto, pato....Ada da-geng babi, ayam, telor....Joldi! Joldi!...*There's pork and eggs....Chicken, duck, and vegetables....Hurry! Hurry!"

Giulio di Giaccomo stood smiling reminiscently at the window until the last woman had vanished into the lane. The tumultuous street life of Macao recalled the vivacity of his native Portofino. The narrow pastel houses stacked side by side on the hillside were a vista from the Gulf of Genoa transported to the South China Sea. Turning reluctantly to his desk, he clapped Francis Arrowsmith on the shoulder.

"Mulieres gaudeant..." he said in rapid Latin. "At least

32

the ladies are happy. If nothing else, our deceit has made them happy. The embargo was a great trial to them."

"And to us, Father Giulio," Francis replied. "I've lost pounds."

"I wish I had."

The Jesuit glanced ruefully at his paunch as he seated himself and reclaimed his goose quill from its inkwell. Before Francis had opened his Chinese grammar, di Giaccomo was again engrossed. Although he complained that it was dull, he enjoyed compiling the notes for the Father Provincial's Annual Letter to Rome. Already self-exiled for two years, the Italian felt some contact with the world he had renounced when he wrote up those notes. The Annual Letter for 1628 would be circulated throughout Europe to inform both clerics and laymen of the continuing progress of the Mission to China—and to solicit their continuing support:

Late in May of this year [he wrote] there came to Macao a young English soldier called Francis Arrowsmith to assist us as he could in our Sacred Task. Although hardly 21 years of age, he was already a veteran warrior for Holy Church, having served His Most Catholic Majesty King Philip for some two years before the Society granted his plea to assist the Mission to China. He is reputedly a skilled artilleryman and a competent maker of cannon. Precisely what use we shall make of him remains to be seen. But Giulio di Giaccomo, S.J., who abides still in Macao perfecting his knowledge of the Chinese language, is confident that the Lieutenant's unruly spirit is now under better control. He has been tempered by his disappointment of ordination and his subsequent hardships.

The Jesuit drew a line under the entry and poured sand on the wet ink. He looked up at the subject of his note, who had let his grammar book fall and drifted back to the window.

"Father Rodriguez has come into the plaza," Francis reported. "He is looking around anxiously."

"I suppose we must join him, though I've never known a Chinese to be punctual."

Giulio di Giaccomo set a stiff black hat of woven horsehair on his head and emerged resignedly into the plaza before St. Paul's. Francis followed, ignoring the raindrops trickling from the marble arch above the church's wooden doors to splash his only good clothing.

The Portuguese Father Juan Rodriguez, older by several

decades than his Italian colleague, irritably twitched his sleeves, which hung two feet below his fingertips.

"A beastly climate," he grumbled, removing his high-crowned hat to mop his seamed forehead. "Edo, even Nagasaki, was better than this Macao. The weather never changes."

"Assuredly it does, Juan," Giulio di Giaccomo answered. "It is sometimes cold and wet, rather than hot and wet like today."

"Yet they call Macao the City of the Name of God in China," Father Rodriguez said. "If Heaven is anything like this Holy City, what must Hell be like?"

"That which one fears most, I tell my converts." The Italian smiled. "They find hellfire and brimstone and imps with red-hot tridents no different from the Buddhist hells. In truth, less frightening...and less credible."

"Beware, Giulio, of your Italian levity." The throaty Portuguese they spoke enhanced Juan Rodriguez's natural gravity. "The Holy Inquisition likes not such jesting."

"What would you have me say, Juan? We are not dealing with naked savages wonderstruck by a handful of glass beads. We must present Holy Doctrine cleverly...convincingly ...to these Chinese. They are the most intelligent, the most learned people the Society has ever encountered."

"Nonetheless, the Inquisition likes sophistication not, Giulio....But where are our ambassadors? I cannot delay Mass much longer."

"They'll appear," the Italian laughed. "Chinese are never on time....No more than Italians."

Two Chinese were striding uphill against the tide of chattering women. The elder's eyes darted inquisitively behind his black-rimmed spectacles. The silk square on the breast of his vermilion robe was embroidered with a pair of white geese in flight among scrolled clouds, the insignia of a Mandarin of the Fourth Grade. The younger displayed the silver pheasants of a Mandarin of the Fifth Grade on his sapphire-blue robe. Like the priests, the Mandarins wore rimless black hats rising to a triangular peak. The white silk strips outlining their shawl collars were ascetic, almost clerical. But their black hair hung over their collars in a worldly manner, and their long-nailed fingers clutched jaunty umbrellas of green oiled paper stretched on bamboo ribs.

"*Ta-men-di hsi-kuan chi-kuai, Michael*..." The senior Mandarin spoke in the softly sibilant Officials' Language of China. "Their customs are very strange, Michael. Hordes of women racing about...daring to jostle us. They should be decorously locked behind high walls."

"*Ta-men shih chi-nü, Paul,*" the junior Mandarin answered. "They are women of pleasure, Paul. Here there are no other kind. And they cannot know it is we who gave them the fresh food they hungered for."

"Not we directly," Paul Sung objected.

"As good as," Michael Chang pointed out. "Let us not disclaim the credit. We may require it."

"From one viper's nest to another, you think, Michael? From Peking to Macao? But the barbarians cannot possibly be split into as many factions as the Imperial Court."

"Let us hope not...But Father Adam Schall did warn us."

The ambassadors ignored the mud that seeped through the felt soles of their black-cloth shoes. Comfort was less than decorum and decorum far less than dignity to the Mandarins. They were determined to impress upon their hosts the limitless power and the uncountable wealth of their master, the young Chung Chen Emperor who had ascended the Dragon Throne of the Great Ming Dynasty only a year and four months earlier. They were charged to win from the monkey-clever Europeans a favor their master could not, this once, demand.

To that end, the ambassadors would truly accept the Portuguese claim to sovereignty over the Macao Peninsula, a wart on the southeastern flank of the vast land mass of China. They would behave as if they were actually envoys to a monarch the equal of their own monarch, which was a preposterous proposition. They would pretend that minuscule Macao was actually an overseas province of the minuscule kingdom of Portugal, though the outlanders, all Chinese knew, occupied it at the pleasure of the Emperor.

The ambassadors' position was therefore powerful, though they came as supplicants. Macao had been the richest prize in Asia for Europeans since it was settled in 1556 by the Portuguese creeping up the China Coast in the wake of the holy missionary Francis Xavier. With Macao as their base, the Jesuits had performed near-miracles for the Lord God, for the King of Portugal, and for Portuguese commerce. *Cidade do Nome de Deos na China,* they called Macao, the City of the Name of God in China, for it had always been a holy city. A-ma-cao, the Chinese name, dedicated the peninsula to A-ma, the Goddess of the Sea, whose red-pillared temple stood by the shore. Possession of the only European-ruled territory on the mainland of the Extreme East virtually guaranteed a monopoly of the lucrative China trade. It also conferred a monopoly of the even more lucrative trade between China and Japan, because the Imperial Court in Peking had long forbidden its subjects to trade directly with the Japanese.

As the ambassadors approached the white-stone steps, a flood of crockery poured from the window of a pink-shuttered house. An eagle-emblazoned platter hurled a duck carcass onto the pavement, the yellow bill of its intact head flapping. A shattered azure soup tureen splashed grease on the ambassadors' robes. Teacups skidded amid clattering knives, and green wine bottles sprayed fountains of glass shards.

The Ming ambassadors traced the Sign of the Cross on their chests, and Paul Sung whispered a *Pater Noster*. But their grave expressions did not alter and their regular pace did not hasten.

The Jesuits and the English lieutenant watched from the high plaza of St. Paul's. The tall, grizzled Portuguese priest rumbled in annoyance, but his sleek, vivacious companion grinned.

"Now we must meet them more than halfway," Father Juan Rodriguez directed. "But what is this nonsense?"

"It's only Lobo de Sarmiento, Father," Francis Arrowsmith volunteered. "He always rids himself of his breakfast dishes through the window."

"That scamp Lobo surely has slaves and bondservants to wash his dishes," Rodriguez grumbled.

"Of course, Father," Francis answered. "But this way's less trouble. After all, trade is good."

"Not that good," said Giulio di Giaccomo. "If it were, the Senate would not be so favorable to our enterprise."

"The Senate is not that favorable," Rodriguez chided. "We must still obtain approval."

"They *must* come around," Francis's cool amusement gave way to fervor. "They *must*. It is the opportunity of a lifetime."

"So hot, Francis, for this enterprise of Father Juan's?" Giulio di Giaccomo asked mischievously. "Is it so desperately important to you?"

"It is my purpose, Father Giulio, my *sole* purpose now." Intense emotion choked Francis's clumsy Portuguese, and he slipped into Latin. "How else can I serve the Lord's purposes and also honorably advance my own worldly state?"

"And also serve your patron lady, Saint Barbara," the

Italian laughed. "I hear the cannon thunder in your throat. But put aside your dreams and greet our guests."

The young Englishman wore his air of deference awkwardly. His hands were clenched, and his mouth was clamped tight. His eyes veiled by his thick brown eyelashes, Francis followed the priests. On the central landing, the vermilion Mandarin and the sapphire Mandarin ascending met the black Jesuits descending. The scarlet-and-green Lieutenant halted respectfully four paces behind them.

"Huan-ying! Wo-men teng-che...," Juan Rodriguez said in fluent but heavily accented Chinese. "Welcome! We have awaited you eagerly for some time."

"We rejoice at paying our respects to you in the Holy City of the Name of God, Father Juan Rodriguez," Paul Sung, the senior Mandarin, declared. "It is a wondrous city."

"I apologize profoundly for our lack of decorum," Rodriguez continued. "We do not all hurl our dirty dishes out our windows."

"We did hear some slight clatter," said Michael Chang, the junior Mandarin. "But we hardly noticed it."

"Your courtesy is overwhelming, though you have every right to be affronted," the priest replied with ornate Chinese courtesy. "I must also apologize abjectly for our simple welcome. It is totally unworthy of your high rank and your great condescension. You do us profound honor by coming alone, without an entourage, as if to a family gathering."

"We have come today to hear Mass in your magnificent new church, Father Juan." Paul Sung ignored the barb. "This is not an official meeting."

"We are thrice honored. I gather the embargo has been lifted and food is coming into the city."

Rodriguez relaxed his formality. The ambassadors were, after all, fellow Christians, members of the minute elite within the Ming Empire that sought the same goals as the alien Jesuits. They proudly bore the saints' names bestowed at baptism, which set them apart from all their compatriots.

"We heard the women's shouts." Giulio di Giacomo's Chinese was not as fluent as Juan Rodriguez's, but it was unaccented and more precisely grammatical. "You have been generous to a fault."

"We did what we could," Michael Chang answered. "The Emperor is not niggardly, as you must know."

"Now, when he requires a trifling service of your esteemed country, he will be exceedingly lavish," Paul Sung made his

37

colleague's hint explicit. "It is also a unique opportunity for the propagation of the True Faith."

"Even out of the cannon's mouth?" Rodriguez mused. "Nonetheless, if it were up to us alone, the Expeditionary Force would march northward tomorrow with a hundred cannon."

"To smash down Tartars," Francis spoke in broken Chinese. "For God's great glory."

"Our zealous English friend is a master artilleryman," Giulio di Giaccomo interposed. "He yearns to join the great expedition. May I present Francis Arrowsmith?"

"Ar-ow-ssu-mi-ssu—" Paul Sung's tongue stumbled on the alien syllables.

"The name is difficult, too, for us to say," Rodriguez explained. "But it is a good omen. It signifies that his family were for many generations master makers of arrows."

"He should be called Ai Shih-jen, Ai the Arrowmaker," Michael Chang suggested. "Ai is a proud surname and sounds like his own."

The courtesies, warmed by genuine affection, continued as they entered the vaulted nave of St. Paul's. The Emperor's ambassadors had ostensibly come only to hear Father Rodriguez sing Mass. Though they were known as devout Christians, no one in Macao believed that tale. Everyone knew the Mandarins would later confer with the Jesuits regarding the proposed Expeditionary Force. Juan Rodriguez had himself recently returned from a journey to China whose purpose was patently diplomatic rather than religious. And he had chosen his text for the day from Luke: "I bring you not peace, but a sword."

What men believed mattered little in the shadow-play atmosphere of Macao. What men said was all-important. Themselves not the most straightforward of men, the Jesuits had learned much from those masters of illusion, the Chinese— perhaps even more than they had taught the Great Ming Dynasty of the theology and the science of a resurgent Europe.

THE Loyal Senate of the Holy City of the Name of God in China welcomed the Ming Emperor's ambassadors the next morning. Paul Sung and Michael Chang sat on ebony chairs set near the sixteen-foot walnut table that rested on scrolled wooden pedestals stayed by wrought-iron bows. Father Juan

Rodriguez sat beside the ambassadors—to interpret for them and to speak for the Society of Jesus. A second row of chairs was provided for Father Giulio di Giaccomo, Captain-Sergeant Miguel Texeira Correa, and Lieutenant Francis Arrowsmith, whom the spiteful Dominicans already called "the Jesuits' puppy." Around the table sat the three senators elected by Macao's freemen and their secretary.

Though fellow Catholics, the first Chinese gentlemen Francis had met were the most alien human beings he had ever seen. He studied them with veiled intensity.

Paul Sung, the senior Mandarin, wore bland benevolence like a mask on his narrow face with its sparse goatee. That mask slipped when his interest was fully engaged, and his eyes glinted behind his heavy spectacles. Michael Chang, the junior Mandarin, was thick-set, flamboyantly bearded, and enthusiastic in speech and gesture. Yet both appeared to Francis almost inhumanly restrained. Even beside the grave Juan Rodriguez, they were too obviously self-disciplined, too stringently inhibited.

No more than the Mandarins' thick silk robes or the priests' heavy cassocks did the senators' velvet doublets and starched linen ruffs concede a jot of dignity to the damp heat within the teak-paneled room. The men of Iberia believed somber opulence must honor portentous occasions like this session of the Loyal Senate. The red-brocade curtains covering the high windows trapped the heavy air, and King Philip of Spain and Portugal looked gravely down from the wall. Opposite His Most Catholic Majesty, an emaciated Christ was impaled by rusty iron nails on a great crucifix. His eyes had been shaped to Oriental obliqueness by the Chinese woodcarver, and a rictus of agony twisted His thin lips.

Nonetheless Francis Arrowsmith discerned a certain trumpery, playhouse atmosphere, which was unfitting to the epochal deliberations. The Loyal Senate could alter the destiny of two nations by voting to provide Portuguese military aid and technical assistance to the Ming Empire. Although Mediterranean histrionics had combined with Chinese ostentation to contrive a pinchbeck theatricality, the Loyal Senate was truly all-powerful.

Since Portuguese noblemen did not deign to settle in Macao, no aristocrats dominated the citizens' representatives. Besides, the Captain-General was concerned more with his commercial dealings than with his limited political power.

The unruly Portuguese freemen of Macao ruled themselves untrammeled, though they did not rule themselves peaceably or well. Their Loyal Senate would decide the vital issue that should properly have been referred to the Viceroy in Goa or the King in Iberia.

Great pressure had already been exerted on the Senate. The Dominicans and the Franciscans, who hated the Jesuits for excluding them from China, opposed any measure that would benefit the Society of Jesus—regardless of its benefits to Macao and the Faith. Those friars conspired with the Spanish of Manila, who seethed at their exclusion from the China trade by the Portuguese their own king ruled. The Jesuits were allied with the nationalistic Portuguese faction, which was aggressively pro-Chinese. The senators had already pocketed lavish bribes from both factions—and then reserved judgment for eight months.

The Secretary of the Senate, Antonio Castro, was presumed to be disinterested. The tall, thin man with the hooded black eyes was acknowledged to possess the best brain among the laymen of Macao, a group not celebrated for intellectual acuity. Because his shrewd understanding of the intricate network of their commerce throughout Asia and Europe protected their profits, the freemen of Macao overlooked his dubious origins.

Antonio Castro was foremost among Macao's Marranos, the epithet meaning "swine" applied to those Jews who had accepted conversion to Catholicism. Properly though rarely called *Christãos novos*, new Christians, the Marranos were not acknowledged by old Catholic families as brothers in religion. Antonio Castro was at least as alien to his countrymen as was an English Catholic gentleman. Francis Arrowsmith felt neither particular warmth nor particular coldness toward the crypto-Jewish Secretary because of his origins. But he had high regard for the Marrano's sardonic intelligence and cool humor.

"We are met today, gentlemen, to consider a matter of profound importance." Antonio Castro's dark mien was grave. "His Imperial Majesty of the Ming has sent an unprecedented invitation to this Holy City. He will receive a battalion of musketeers supported by four batteries of ordnance. That is sixteen cannon.... More if feasible. He asks our soldiers to campaign against the Tartars, who are a persistent irritant on his northern border.

"We are uniquely honored by the opportunity to serve as

the militant ally of the Empire by whose grant we hold Macao. For the first time in the two thousand years since that Empire was established, a Monarch of China has condescended to invite the troops of another sovereign to fight beside his own forces."

Ambassador Paul Sung, who had listened to Juan Rodriguez's whispered translation, spoke urgently to the priest.

"On behalf of the ambassadors I would add two additional points," Father Rodriguez addressed the Senate. "The Emperor has marked the good-heartedness of the Portuguese in this Holy City and the virtue of the Jesuit Fathers who reside in China. His Majesty wishes to offer further gifts and concessions to Macao. Moreover, he would be happy to receive a detachment even somewhat larger."

"On behalf of the Loyal Senate," Antonio Castro answered, "I acknowledge the further honor the Emperor offers us—and express deep thanks for whatever bounty it may please His Majesty to confer upon us."

"The nature of those gifts and concessions will unfold in time." Rodriguez again translated for Paul Sung. "And no citizen of Macao will be disappointed. However, as to the number of troops, what is the Senate's feeling?"

"May I remind the Ambassador that the expedition is not yet approved?" Castro answered. "But, in deference to the Ambassador's question, we might consult our master of war. Captain-Sergeant Miguel Gonsalves Texeira Correa, how many troops can you raise? How many can you maintain in the field?"

"As to that, Master Secretary, no more initially than a battalion of, say, two hundred Portuguese and two hundred other races," the Captain-Sergeant replied.

"Even before it's begun, the Chinese want more men," a dark senator of the Spanish party interjected. "We've already sent guns—both cannon and arquebuses. We've sent men to teach the Chinese their use. Apparently those weapons have done little good. Otherwise, why ask for Portuguese troops? And what possible use is a single battalion against the Tartar hordes?"

"Much use, Senators," Miguel Texeira responded hotly. "Though small, a disciplined force armed with modern weapons and practicing scientific warcraft could be decisive."

"I acknowledge the Captain's experience and commend his pride in his troops," the senator riposted. "But I ask again:

41

What could Portuguese troops accomplish when Portuguese weapons have had so little effect?"

"Not so little," Juan Rodriguez objected. "On several occasions our cannon have routed the Tartars."

"Then why not just more cannon?" the swarthy senator demanded. "Why commit troops?"

"Troops can be decisive for the Empire—and for ourselves." The senator who replied was a partisan of the Chinese. "This is a unique opportunity to win good will—and to expand trade. The interior of China has been closed to us too long. Visiting the Canton Trade Fair twice a year isn't enough. The riches of a continent will recompense this trifling service."

"I was promised in China that rich new trade would reward our cooperation." Juan Rodriguez spoke in his own right.

"Promises again!" the swarthy senator insisted. "We've had too many promises from the Chinese."

"This is a wondrous opportunity to advance the Faith, a Heaven-sent opportunity." Father Rodriguez appealed to the consciences of all good Catholics who knew the Jesuits were indispensable to trade as intermediaries and interpreters. "The Society of Jesus has toiled for half a century to bring the Word of the Lord to the most populous realm on earth. Would you gentlemen extinguish that Holy Light? Would the Loyal Senate do the work of the anti-Christ? Would you impede the glorious opportunity for Holy Church to win the souls of one hundred fifty million Chinese?"

"But what of Canton?" The senator of the Spanish party would not yield. "Will the Viceroy diminish his own profits by letting us communicate directly with Peking? The Viceroy, not the Emperor, determines whether we prosper or fail...whether we live or die."

Paul Sung spoke softly to Juan Rodriguez for a full minute.

"The Viceroy is, after all, the Emperor's creature, Ambassador Paul Sung reminds us," the Jesuit translated. "The Viceroy can interpose obstacles but cannot crush us. The Emperor *can* crush us. So the Ambassador, a man of our own faith, points out.... Not as a threat, but to emphasize the reality."

"Suppose the Tartars win?" the stocky senator persisted. "Where would we stand then?"

"What? The Tartars take Peking—conquer the Great Empire?" Rodriguez laughed. "Can you really imagine that happening? The Tartar tribes are an irritant, no more than a swarm of mosquitoes to the Emperor. And we are no more than a convenience to him. His Majesty would see how well we fight. He would amuse himself and rid himself of the Tartar mosquitoes with our aid. Dare we refuse him that aid? Dare we serve the anti-Christ?"

"For that matter, Father Rodriguez, we cannot in good commercial sense refuse," Antonio Castro interposed. "We cannot earn the enmity of the Emperor when we could win his good will. Macao could not live if we mortally offend the Ming."

Castro's appeal to commercial self-interest reinforced Rodriguez's exhortation to religious duty. The stocky senator of the Spanish party was silent when the Loyal Senate agreed to send troops north to fight the Tartars. Father Giulio di Giaccomo grasped Francis's arm to cut off his triumphant shout.

Later, in his small room, the young Englishman toasted the Expeditionary Force in brandy and danced the sailor's jig the Iberian gravity of his hosts forbade him in public. He paused briefly to set straight on the table the miniature portrait of his mother his stamping had knocked over, but he did not meet the accusing gaze of Marie Dulonge Arrowsmith's gray eyes.

Francis Arrowsmith felt himself hardened by experience, far removed from the callow schoolboy who had four years earlier listened avidly to Giulio di Giaccomo's account of the Mission to China. But the exuberance of youth flung him once more into the gyrations of the jig. He rejoiced over the Loyal Senate's approval of the Expeditionary Force and his certain place in its ranks. The Jesuits wanted their own man on the expedition, an officer who owed primary allegiance to them rather than to Portugal or to Macao. He was well qualified for that role by the military skills he had acquired.

Recommended by his Headmaster's friend, Father Antonio D'Alicante, Francis had been commissioned a sublieutenant in the Spanish service shortly after his arrival in Madrid, still shaken by his expulsion from St. Omer's College. He had spent the next two years fighting the battles of King Philip's wars. The haughty Iberian gentlemen who were his brother officers disdained both the mechanics and the mathematics of the artilleryman's craft—and above all, the sweaty casting of cannon. Natural inclination, as well as the interest in physical science awakened by his modern-minded Jesuit schoolmasters, had impelled him to learn all he could of the manufacture and the employment of ordnance.

Nonetheless, the arduous campaigning had finally appeared no more than a succession of marches and countermarches leading nowhere. Convinced that England would soon return to the True Faith, Francis was determined to accumulate sufficient wealth to reclaim the Arrowsmith lands. Frustrated and impatient, he had appealed again to Father D'Alicante. After much deliberation, the Society of Jesus had sponsored his passage to Macao.

The Loyal Senate's approval of the Expeditionary Force had now made the Englishman's hopes certainties. He knew he would find great riches in the Ming Empire.

Francis Arrowsmith cavorted exultantly, his feet pounding on the yellow-and-blue floor tiles. The whitewashed walls rang with his war cry: "St. George and England!"

No reservation marred Francis's rejoicing when he finally subsided and brushed the thick blond hair off his forehead with a casual hand. He had not heard Ambassador Michael Chang's whisper to Father Juan Rodriguez as they left the senate chamber.

"*Wo hsi-wang . . . ,*" Michael Chang had said. "I hope it will be as the sage Mencius said: 'Seizing the moment and triumphing!' Though I am glad, this is but the first small step. The Expedition still faces many perils. . . . Not only the perils of the battlefield but the intrigues of those who oppose it—in Macao, I fear, and, in China, I know."

Chochow—Peking, North China

JANUARY 11–FEBRUARY 13, 1630

THE slick white ice on the square paving blocks was melting three hours after daybreak of the eleventh of January 1630. Impervious to the sun's warmth, black ice lay solid in the ruts engraved deep into the stone face of the road by almost five centuries of turning wooden wheels. Today, the Great Post Road was a decaying vestige of the order once imposed upon the Empire by the great men whose bones were locked in the frozen earth.

The web of post roads had been laid out by the Mongols in the thirteenth century to bind every province of conquered China to the Northern Capital. Warning bells jingling on their horses' bridles, imperial couriers had carried the edicts of the Khan of Khans to his distant Mandarins and returned with reports on the state of the realm. The couriers had taken precedence over all other travelers; only an Imperial Progress could slacken their pace. Hearing the tinkling of bells and the tattoo of unshod hooves, all men had known that the world's most powerful empire remained peaceful and prosperous. The same signals had proclaimed the stability of the Great Ming Dynasty until the Chung Chen Emperor, newly seated on the Dragon Throne, abolished the post service for economy's sake in 1628.

45

Less than forty miles from Peking two years later, the Great Post Road was only a whisper from the past, wistfully recalling imperial grandeur. Most of the massive stones had been lifted by farmers to build houses or pigpens. Those remaining were cracked; the verges were crumbling; and the post stations were deserted. Only during the last ten days had the carts, the mounts, and the feet of tens of thousands fleeing southward tramped the road clear between ten-foot snowdrifts. For the first time since the Mongol invasions, a barbarian horde from the steppes of Inner Asia had penetrated the Great Wall to threaten Peking and send refugees streaming down the Great Post Road.

Lieutenant Francis Arrowsmith teetered in his saddle when his pony slipped on the black ice. The yellow plume of his long hair whipped in the wind above the vertical snowbanks that palisaded the road. Filtered through those white cliffs, the morning sun played with pitiless clarity on the mass of humans and animals struggling in the ice canyon. It had taken him almost two years, Francis reflected sadly, to cover the less than two thousand miles that lay between Macao and this abject misery, which touched him more deeply because it was more pitiful than any he had seen in Europe.

Matrons in padded-silk coats trimmed with fur peered through the curtains of their palanquins at other palanquins abandoned by their bearers. Their cheeks plump with decades of good living, tottering old gentlemen leaned on blackwood walking sticks. They ignored the outlandish foreigners, not really seeing them because they were beyond human comprehension. But the old gentlemen glanced apprehensively at the gnarled farmers who sat beside wives swaddled in gray coats on two-wheeled carts pulled by shaggy mules. Toddlers swarmed on those flat-bed carts. Their cheeks were polished to shiny red horn by the wind, and green slime streamed from their nostrils.

The poor of North China clung to the land like barnacles to a pier in the last decades of the Great Ming Dynasty. They had little else left to lose. Roving bandits, who claimed they fought for the poor, had virtually stripped them. What the bandits left was stolen by the Emperor's soldiers, who declared that they protected the people from the bandits. But those monsters of rapacity were, at least, Chinese.

Poor and rich were now fleeing from an alien word: "Tartars! Tartars! The Tartars are coming to rape and kill and burn!" They plodded south beside their oxen to beg shelter of villages that cared as little for them as for stray dogs, villages themselves poised for flight.

Francis recovered his seat in the saddle and patted his pony's neck. When the people looked through him as if he were invisible, he felt himself a heartless intruder upon their grief. A river of terrified Chinese flowed unseeing around the Portuguese Expeditionary Force.

Almost eleven months earlier, the Expedition had set out from the southern metropolis of Canton after many wearisome months of the Viceroy's procrastination. Their progress northward had been impeded equally by the hospitality and the obstruction of the district magistrates along their route. Almost all those Mandarins were loath to permit such alien penetration of the Motherland; most extorted large bribes for finally allowing the outlanders to proceed.

The slothful pace was merely irksome until they came to Tsinan, the capital of Shantung Province, five days before Christmas 1629. Francis had reveled in discovering the wonders of a land abundantly blessed by God. Wealth of all kinds abounded: tempting food and fine clothing; a myriad of boats and innumerable dwellings; thick forests and fertile fields; rich wines and fiery spirits; even silver, gold, and jewels. No Chinese appeared ill-fed or poorly dressed. Reports of the ravages of distant brigands were hard to believe. Only once as their barges moved on rivers and canals had he seen a burned-out house, a commonplace sight in warring Europe.

The rivers froze after Christmas in Tsinan, and snowdrifts smothered the roads. Yet messages from Peking almost daily urged haste. The Tartars were closing on the Northern Capital.

The Expedition plodded through the snowbound countryside, dragging its cannon behind it. Making at best twenty miles a day, the Portuguese came on the tenth of January to the district capital called Chochow, some forty miles southwest of Peking. An injunction to even greater haste awaited them. It was signed by the Mandarin Hsü Kwang-chi, whom Father Juan Rodriguez affectionately called Dr. Paul. Francis remembered the scroll painting of Dr. Paul Hsü he had seen at St. Omer's. The Jesuit did not explain why the Senior Vice-Minister of the Ministry of Rites, which was responsible for the Empire's spiritual welfare, should be so concerned with military matters. He said only: "Dr. Paul is a great man and a splendid Christian."

"We must be mad," Captain-Sergeant Miguel Gonsalves

47

Texeira Correa shouted above the groaning of the refugees, an endless sigh more terrible than screams. "Madder than Basques or Gascons."

"But not as mad as the Irish, I hope!" Francis's forced jest fell flat. "Yet how so?"

"Mad to think we can stem the Tartar tide." Texeira's wry smile corrugated the flat planes of his gray cheeks. "Five officers, sixty artillerymen, another sixty slaves—finally a priest and a Mandarin. There are more Chinese on this road alone than there are soldiers in all Portugal."

"Would you be happier if we had two Mandarins...if Paul Sung had not remained in Canton?"

"It wouldn't make much difference, would it?" Texeira laughed. "Ambassador Michael Chang is a good lot. He comes down hard on the officials who hold us up. But a hundred Mandarins wouldn't help. I'm not optimistic."

"You did not speak so to the Loyal Senate."

"More fool I, then! But I hadn't seen this mass of men and beasts when I waxed so confident."

"You think the Tartars will be too much for us? Wait till the bronze muzzles roar. Saint Barbara can perform greater miracles than all the other Holy Saints together."

"Fear the Tartars? Not I, by Our Lady. I fear we will never come to grips with the Tartars. A battalion of Saint Christophers couldn't carry us through this frozen land. This is no place to fight a war. Too many civilians."

"Dr. Paul Hsü's last message reports the road to Peking still open," Francis said. "But for how long?"

"I would not be trapped on the plains outside Peking. Even Saint Barbara's little darlings couldn't save us from the Tartars in the open. But we need a miracle to reach Peking."

"In three hours we've moved hardly four miles. I'm afraid, my Captain, miracles are not available on demand....Not even to you."

"Yes, by God, they are! A miracle! Father Juan Rodriguez must invoke a miracle!"

Francis smiled when Texeira turned his dappled pony back toward the litter that bore the aged priest. After six years' association, the Englishman was still amused by the volatile Latins.

Five minutes later, still skeptical, he watched a conclave assemble around the red-curtained litter. After hearing Texeira's plea, the priest had summoned Ambassador Michael Chang and the Major commanding the Imperial Infantry, who had joined the Expeditionary Force in Chochow. Ten minutes later Francis allowed himself to hope that nightfall would not catch them in the open country after progressing only a few additional miles against the torrent of refugees. Initially dubious, the Major had obeyed a brusque command from Ambassador Michael Chang.

"They weren't eager," Texeira told Francis after returning to the head of the column. "Father Juan says they'd much rather march south than north. But they'll do the job."

Led by a lieutenant astride a white horse with black mane and tail, a tide of Imperial Infantry flowed past the stranded Portuguese. Shaped like the bell dome of a mosque, the Lieutenant's steel helmet framed his smooth white features. Flexible steel plates armored him, while his men were protected by padded blue coats bordered with green-and-orange stripes. Like his men, the Lieutenant wore on his back a red square embroidered with the yellow ideogram Francis knew to be *yung,* meaning brave. Because of that symbol, the Portuguese called Ming soldiers Braves.

His cheeks carmine with anger, the Lieutenant flourished a triangular blue pennant bearing the vermilion ideogram *ling,* meaning command. That symbol proclaimed that he was engaged on the Emperor's personal service.

The driver of the two-wheeled cart blocking the road stared in stolid incomprehension at the swearing officer. His hands were locked on the reins that guided a fawn donkey beside two piebald horses harnessed abreast. Next to the gape-mouthed farmer, two young women twittered in alarm, while six red-faced children perched on the cartload of bamboo baskets and cloth-wrapped bundles. Behind the cart, sedan chairs, litters, oxcarts, and pedestrians had coagulated to halt all movement.

"Much good he's doing!" Francis announced. "Now, we'll never get through."

"Oh, to be twenty-two and so certain of everything—good fortune or disaster." A flush mantled Texeira's swarthy-gray cheeks, and his short nose wrinkled irritably, displaying its cavernous nostrils. "Just wait, youngster, and you'll learn."

The Ming Lieutenant gestured abruptly and six infantrymen seized the animals' bridles. Twisting the bits with hard fingers, the soldiers forced the kicking beasts over the road's broken edge into the stony quagmire at the foot of the snow cliff. The leading-pole cracked explosively under the strain, and the refugees' groaning stopped for an instant. The cart

49

tilted high, then toppled slowly. The women screamed as their children and their belongings slid beneath their broken cart.

"Make way in the name of the Emperor!" the Lieutenant screamed into the appalled silence. "Make way for the ocean barbarians and their cannon."

The knotted mass of refugees remained immobile, stunned by the cart's destruction.

"What says the wisdom of thirty-eight years to that?" Francis gibed. "He's built a dam of flesh and wood. Never move it now."

"A little patience, young man. You underestimate our Chinese allies—badly."

The Lieutenant shouted again, eight high-pitched syllables shattering the frozen crystal air: *"Ta, ta ta-men! Tung, tung ta-men! ...* At them! At them! Move them! Move them!"

A file of gaudy Braves thrust into the massed refugees like a spear fluttering bright ribbons. They flailed short battle-axes and spike-studded maces called *ku-tuo,* bonecrunchers.

An elderly merchant leaned out from his gilded palanquin. His plump face was flushed beneath a glossy sable cap, and his lips were a red circle of astonished indignation. His protests halted in midsyllable when a crescent axeblade trailing gay yellow streamers sliced through the fur to split his round head in half.

A red-cheeked young farmer tugged the nose ring of the slate-gray bullock carrying his wife, whose arms cradled a purple-swaddled infant. As the phlegmatic bullock began to move, a bonecruncher like a steel hedgehog snapped the farmer's wrist. Dumb with horror, he watched the bonecruncher smash the infant's skull and hurl its mother under the bullock's hooves.

"Never...never have I seen...," Francis gasped unbelieving. "Not even a chance to move."

"Not like Europe, is it? More like the Red Sea opening before Moses. I told you." No triumph sounded in Texeira's rumble, only the settled melancholy that lay beneath his Mediterranean vivacity. "If only they were as fierce against the Tartars."

The refugees' shocked inertness dissolved into frenzied movement. Rushing for safety beside the road, men bowled over women and youths trampled children. The slow-moving elderly and those who tried to shift their carts fell under the flailing battle-axes and bonecrunchers. Sunlight flashing on their weapons' steel heads, the Braves cut a path through the

50

throng. A second file thrust abandoned carts and litters into the mass of humans and animals lining the roadside.

"And we now go like the Israelites through the bloody sea?" Francis asked in horror.

Texeira waved his arm in answer, and the Expeditionary Force began lumbering through the shambles created by the Imperial Braves. The short-legged ponies of the Portuguese officers pranced daintily around the broken bodies of men and animals. Flesh crunched under the enormous ironbound wheels of the drays bearing the ponderous cannon.

The first gun, incongruously dedicated to the gentle Saint Francis of Assisi, weighed more than four tons, and thirty-six horses hauled it over the broken road. Behind the St. Francis gun trundled nine other cannons. Swearing Chinese drovers goaded the skittish horses through the blood-stench, their short whips on long bamboo shafts cracking a constant fusillade.

The first European military unit to march through China must, Francis reflected, appear even more outlandish to the cowed refugees than the Imperial Braves were to his eyes. The Portuguese, like their Indian and Negro slaves, wore padded Chinese coats against the knife-edge cold. When those coats opened, they revealed doublets slashed to show their gaudy linings. Such vandalism of good cloth had already provoked shocked questions from their Chinese hosts.

The Europeans' complexions, Francis had overheard, appeared to the Chinese either spectrally pale or cholerically flushed with blood under their coarse skin. The slaves looked like devils from the Buddhist hells: stocky Negroes so black their skin glowed purple in the sunlight and slender Indians, tan and sickle-nosed under white turbans. White or ruddy, brown or black, all the foreigners were terrifying to the Chinese, who knew of no other peoples except gibbering barbarians—and those barbarians all as dangerous as tigers.

Amid the carnage wrought by their Chinese allies, the slaves blew flourishes on their bronze trumpets and drew dark baritone notes from their ebony hautboys. Not only the melodies but the instruments as well were outlandish to the Chinese, particularly the hautboys with their curling double bells and globular mouthpieces. If the Expedition appeared invaders from another world, their cacophony sounded like the Devil's own anthem. Measured European harmonies were as discordant to Chinese ears as were disjointed, tinkling Chinese melodies to Francis's.

The Expeditionary Force crept northward, pausing frequently to adjust slipping loads and halting for two hours to lever back a culverin that fell into the mud when a dray axle snapped. Francis dismounted to join Father Juan Rodriguez, who lay haggard in a litter borne by six coolies. At sixty-eight the Jesuit should not have undertaken the arduous journey, but he had insisted that his gift of tongues was essential to its success.

Francis had come to love the old man—for his tart wisdom and for the innate goodness his brusque manner concealed. Continuing his own study with the amiable Ambassador Michael Chang, the Englishman knew how extraordinary was the priest's command of the Chinese language. Each time he himself scaled a towering peak of new understanding, he gazed up at a new range of peaks rather than across a plateau. Juan Rodriguez stood already on those far peaks.

Uneasiness lay on the Jesuit's seamed face like the shadow of a cloud on a ruffled pond. His blue eyes were filmed, and the creases incised between his long nose and his small mouth where white. Blue veins were gnarled knots under his hands' crepe skin. His body had been reduced to its essential stringy muscles by the rigors of the past months. He still suffered the bloody flux of dysentery, but Francis sensed the Jesuit's discomfort this early afternoon was not primarily physical.

"Father Juan, I've never seen anything as cruel...as barbaric," Francis exclaimed in horror. "To savage their own people wantonly...as a horseman might ride down a chicken."

"They do such things. I warned you." The Jesuit's tone was distant and abstracted. "Some might say it was necessary."

"Necessary, Father? A few minutes' grace...and the people would have moved of themselves. How could it be necessary...even to clear our path? We must reach Peking before the Tartars close the roads, but this was *not* necessary."

"Francis, my son, the Chinese are not as we are." Responding to the young man's distress, the priest accepted his duty of instruction. "The officers mortally fear their superiors....And the soldiers fear their officers more than they fear God. The act had no human or spiritual meaning to them. It was mere military necessity."

"It was *not* necessary, I tell you, Father Juan."

"Perhaps not, Francis. I must, however, concern myself with efficacy. Tell me. Will it be efficacious, what we are doing?"

"If we can come to grips with the Tartars, assuredly,

52

Father." Detesting his allies' atrocity, Francis missed the priest's deeper meaning. "But how justify this alliance with these savages? If it were necessary, truly necessary, I could..."

"I've told you, Francis, they fear not God....They know not God. We must bring them to God. Only then will they renounce wanton cruelty."

"Bring them to God by abetting their cruelty...even by provoking such barbarity?"

"That, too, if necessary, though Captain Texeira did not provoke the slaughter. He merely asked the Chinese officer to clear the road—never dreaming. But you, my son, have stressed the necessity—or lack of necessity—for the deed ...rather than the deed itself."

"And you as well, Father." Francis gripped the side of the priest's litter. "Regardless of necessity, the deed was foul."

The priest laid his emaciated hand on the young Englishman's white knuckles. Since Juan Rodriguez never paraded his emotions, his fellow Jesuits believed him little inclined toward human affection. He appeared dominated by his passion for great affairs, his influence over Chinese Mandarins and Japanese Daimyo, his Babel-tongued ability to sway Grand Chancellors and Shoguns. But his blue pupils looked up with fleeting fondness under wrinkled lids, which were so long from brows to lashes and so deeply pouched beneath that his eyes appeared to be set vertically in his narrow face.

"The deed was, of course, foul." The Jesuit's voice quavered with the reedy stubbornness of age. "But it may yet prove efficacious."

Francis's full lips drew taut, and his pointed chin thrust out. Incongruously Mediterranean under his yellow hair, his brown eyes glinted in protest. The next instant, his features reassumed the mask of compliance a disinherited orphan had early learned to wear. The flush receded from his cheeks, which had been burnished russet by sun and wind. The lines vanished from his high forehead, and his dark eyebrows unknotted above his arched nose.

"Efficacious, Father? How so?" Though it was impolitic, Francis persisted. "I was taught we must sometimes do distasteful deeds to advance the Faith. But this...this is not merely distasteful. It is detestable!"

"There are many mansions in thy Father's house, Francis. And there are many ways to advance the Faith. May not this be the way the Lord meant for us...and the Chinese? May not such cruel deeds...barbaric, you say...be the burden the Lord has laid upon our shoulders—to test us and, in His own time, to bring the Chinese to salvation? As long as it is efficacious..."

"I still do not see..."

"Francis, let it be for the time!" the priest's edged tone commanded. "Do you truly believe that I—that any of us—enjoy or desire this burden...this manner of propagating the Faith?"

Abashed, Francis was shaping an apology when the Lieutenant of the vanguard cantered past the horn-playing Negroes perched on the cart before the litter. The Ming officer leaned over the sweat-streaked withers of his white horse to speak urgently: "*Shen-fu, ching yüan-liang wo kan-jao ni....*"

Understanding imperfectly, Francis felt he was listening to the mellifluous syllables in a high wind that snatched half away: "Spiritual Father, I regret...disturb you....My scouts report...Tartars...many Tartars...thousands riding from Lianghsiang."

The Jesuit merely nodded. Only when the Lieutenant rode off to report to his commanding officer did the hooded eyes open fractionally wider in alarm.

"Francis, ride as fast as you can to Texeira," the priest directed. "Tell him the Tartars are at Lianghsiang, no more than twenty miles to the north—and pelting south in force. The Chinese will withdraw to Chochow. How can we defend ourselves if they desert us? Ride and tell the Captain-Sergeant. He must decide. And he must decide quickly!"

"By God, is it all to be done over again?" Francis's fiery indignation had burned down to ashen disgust. "Are we to repeat the carnage...the better to prove our Faith? The ways of the Lord are truly mysterious, are they not, Father?"

"Do not blaspheme, Francis!" The priest's patience was at its end. "Do not blaspheme! Just do as you're told! Just ride!"

THE Imperial Braves' reluctance to march north toward the Tartars was transmuted into a passion to march south to the shelter of Chochow. Their twelve-mile progress from the walled city had taken eight hours. Their return required only three. Axes, maces, and swords again carved a path through the refugees as if again opening a path through the Red Sea, as Francis had already observed in horror.

The Braves' eagerness to reach Chochow was diluted by other desires. Too campaign-wise to burden themselves on the outward march, they felt no such constraint on the return march. Time after time, until repetition numbed his anger, transforming the horrible into the grotesque, Francis watched Imperial Infantrymen strip refugees of their possessions. They commandeered carts to pile up clothing and food, excluding not even small pieces of furniture from their avarice. The stolen carts were heavy with the red-leather trunks in which the refugees carried their clothing, the folding vanity chests in which the farm women kept their ornaments, and the black-lacquered jewelry boxes of the prosperous.

"Soldiers always loot," Texeira said heavily. "I see our new allies are no exception."

"But not despoil their own people?" Francis said. "Only mercenaries loot indiscriminately."

"Well, they say this Ming Empire is very advanced."

Only one object of value was abandoned. The Chinese Major insisted that its recovery would delay the retreat too long. The troublesome culverin, two and a half tons of verdigrised bronze, rolled into the mud when the rear axle of its new dray snapped under a weight it had never been meant to bear. Resignedly, the Portuguese artillerymen stripped off their padded coats and began to rig lifting tackle. Summoned by his Lieutenant, the Major rode back from the head of the retreating column to expostulate with Texeira in rough Chinese Francis had no difficulty interpreting.

"Tell him we *never* abandon our guns," Texeira directed. "If he'll lend us a hundred men, we'll have the culverin remounted in twenty minutes."

"*Pu hsing! Ta-ta chien-chin-la hen kwai...*" the Major interrupted. "It won't do! The Tartars move too fast. Leave the gun!"

"All soldiers loot, but this is utter folly," the powerless Texeira observed, watching the infantrymen roll his culverin into the quagmire beside the road.

This day, Francis reflected, boded little good for collaboration between Portuguese artillerymen and Imperial Braves. He was soon to learn he had gravely underestimated Chinese guile, Chinese courage, and Chinese resourcefulness—as he was consistently to misassess the Chinese because their actions did not match his expectations. His arrogant assumption that they should behave as he would was to mislead him for some years.

Cantering toward Chochow through the gray afternoon of the following day, the Tartars found the abandoned culverin. Astonished by its size, they gingerly tested its rough green contours with their callused hands. Their fear of the demon in the gun was inflamed by the information they wrung from a young farmhand who had foolishly delayed his flight too long. At first too terrified to speak, the farmhand gushed words when the Tartar Captain held a dagger to his throat.

"They just left it behind," the farmhand gabbled. 'The ocean barbarians came in thousands...each seven feet tall. And that...that's the smallest of their hundred guns. They didn't bother to salvage it....Said they had so many more and it was practically a toy."

Instructed to be lenient to those Chinese who cooperated, the Tartar Captain released the farmhand. He promptly trotted cross-country toward Chochow to report to his Major, who had ordered him to stay behind in civilian clothing. The infantryman obeyed because, as Father Juan Rodriguez observed, he feared his officer even more than he feared the Tartars. The Major's classic deception was inspired by Sün Tzu, the great strategist who wrote five centuries before the birth of Christ.

Captain-Sergeant Miguel Gonsalves Texeira Correa had assiduously studied the writings of the wily Niccolò Machiavelli, who wrote fifteen centuries after the birth of Christ. He was delighted when the Major instantly agreed to his design for the defense of Chochow. The Portuguese captain and the Chinese major worked in perfect understanding. Chochow was crammed with seventy thousand refugees in addition to its normal population and its garrison. Since food stocks were wholly inadequate for more than one hundred thousand, the fortress could not endure a siege. Only by swiftly repelling its assailants could Chochow survive.

Miguel Texeira and Francis Arrowsmith looked down from the forty-foot-high city wall upon waves of gray-tiled roofs. The narrow streets and narrower alleys flowed with streams of diminutive figures. The city appeared an inland sea frozen by winter just beginning to thaw with spring.

"The walls could stand forever, even against cannon." Texeira's gray lips drew back in a lupine smile. "But these refugees would devour all provisions long before the Tartars withdrew. Damn all civilians."

"They do interfere with wars, don't they, Miguel?" Francis regretted his pert reply almost instantly.

Driven by swearing Imperial Braves, columns of civilians climbed ramps to the broad path atop the wall. Wearing red helmets inscribed with the ideogram *yung,* brave, and carrying spears, they marched back and forth between the watchtowers. The besiegers would not see a sparse garrison, but a fortress crammed with troops.

At the Double Hour of the Monkey, just before sunset at five o'clock, the Tartar vanguard cantered through the gray January dusk toward Chochow. Their yellow banners flapping, the scouts trotted cautiously across the arched stone bridge spanning the Chüma River. All had heard the farmhand tell of the monstrous armament of the gigantic ocean barbarians.

Torches flared on the walls and groves of moving spears bristled above the battlements as the Tartar vanguard drew close. Their captain had already been fooled twice by the crude deception of torches and spears in the hands of civilians. He would not, he swore, be deceived again. But he halted when thunder rumbled from the walls and lightning flashed.

The Tartar Captain knew how long it took to reload the crude iron cannon of the Chinese. Laying his finger on his wrist, he counted the deep reports. A gun fired each time his heart reached its eightieth beat. The ocean barbarians must truly possess a hundred cannon to fire one every minute.

From the wall, Miguel Texeira peered delightedly into the descending curtain of night. Double crews were toiling at his nine guns. Loading no shot, their drill was extraordinarily fast: powder and wadding; fuse to touch hole; wet sponges extinguishing sparks; and loading again.

"Fire! Swab! Powder! Fire! Swab! Powder!" The swift commands echoed in the darkness, climaxed by the roars of guns. Only one gun fired cannonballs from time to time.

Just out of range, the Tartar commander waited to satisfy himself that the ocean barbarians had not devised some devilish new trick. The regular detonations continued fiercely, and he heard the swish of occasional roundshot. After an hour he gave the order to withdraw. Chochow was too heavily defended; the prize was not worth the cost in time and casualties. Rashness, the Tartar Captain's orders stressed, was as grave a fault as cowardice—and would be punished with equal severity.

The blank fusillades roared throughout the night. Texeira wanted lingering Tartar scouts to report his ammunition so abundant he used it with prodigious lavishness. Cautious as he was crafty, he waited twenty-four hours while the cannon fired irregularly and the spears bristled on the walls.

"The easiest victory I've ever won," the Portuguese Captain-Sergeant exulted when the second day ended and no Tartars appeared. "And the quickest. The Tartars are as timorous as the Chinese—and even more credulous. Give me three infantry battalions with ten more batteries—and I'll defend the Empire alone. Give me ten battalions with twenty more batteries and I'll conquer the Empire."

Father Juan Rodriguez smiled thinly, his confidence in modern arms vindicated.

"The guns of the Lord have driven back the hosts of Baal," he said. "Now I know that our efforts will be efficacious—in every way."

Swept up by their enthusiasm, Francis Arrowsmith repented of his earlier misgivings and reproached himself for opposing his ignorance to the siegecraft of the Captain-Sergeant and the wisdom of the Jesuit. Rededicating himself to the Lord's cause, he swore he would unhesitatingly heed the Lord's will—and the counsel of the Lord's priests—so that he could wholeheartedly serve the Lord's purpose of converting the Chinese.

Peking, the center of that Holy Endeavor, lay only a few score miles to the north—and the road to Peking was open.

Peking

FEBRUARY 8, 1630

THE strains of Frescobaldi's *Third Toccata* twined around
the golden phoenixes on the cypress pillars of the Hall of the
Intellect in the Forbidden City of Peking. Two slight figures
in flowered aquamarine gowns peeped through the open door
of an antechamber at the tall man crouched over the harpsichord.

No more than twelve, those boys had been castrated three
years earlier to qualify them for the Imperial Corps of Eunuchs, which not only controlled the Emperor's household
but exercised great power throughout the Empire. Still curious children, they stared in wonder at the blond hair falling
over the collar of the musician. The elder mocked with raised
arms the man's great height; rubbing his own golden skin,
the younger smiled derisively at the yellow hair. The giggles
of the novice Court Eunuchs were drowned by the crashing
chords from the elongated keyboard instrument.

A string twanged, reverberating shrilly for an instant before snapping and curling above the fine-grained wooden top
of the Baffo harpsichord.

"*Verfluchte Maschine!*" the musician exclaimed in the soft
German of the Rhineland. "Blasted device!"

Father Johann Adam Schall von Bell of the Society of

Jesus resignedly hitched up his black cassock and crawled under the instrument, which had suffered badly during its long voyage from Naples. The young Emperor would have his toys, and the mechanical dexterity Adam Schall sometimes cursed condemned him to keep those toys in repair. He preferred tinkering with the music boxes, the timepieces, and the clockwork playthings to tuning the temperamental harpsichord presented to the Ming Emperor by the Hapsburgs.

"*Hsiao peng-yu-men*," the priest invited in the Officials' Language marked by the broad consonants of distant Sian, once the capital of the Empire. "My little friends, I know you're there. Come and chat while I work."

His gentle tone, tinged with pity, would have surprised his brother Jesuits. They respected Adam Schall for his spacious intellect, his scientific attainments, and his resolute nature. Most liked his generous spirit and his intermittent gaiety, but all were wary of his habitual sarcasm. If he could learn to control his tongue, which cut in anger, and his impatience with less agile minds, the older priests predicted, the Rhinelander would rise high in the Holy Mission to China, to which he was committed for a lifetime of voluntary exile from Europe. But none trifled with the thirty-seven-year-old son of a noble family of Cologne that traced its ancestry back to the legionaries who had conquered Germany for Julius Caesar.

"*Shen-fu, wo-men...*," the older Eunuch said timidly. "Spiritual Father, we have been watching you for some time."

"I know that, my friends," the priest spoke from under the harpsichord. "Can I tell you something?"

"We were wondering, Spiritual Father, why...," the younger Eunuch answered.

"Ask what questions you will. I am glad of your company."

Since Adam Schall remained crouched under the harpsichord, to the ribald delight of the young Eunuchs his voice seemed to issue from his black-covered posterior.

"Why do you do this work, Spiritual Father?" the smaller Eunuch asked. "You act like a Mandarin, and you wear a robe like a Mandarin's. But the job you're doing is a common workman's."

"It takes skill, my friends, particular skill," the priest rumbled. "And in my country, we obey the command of the Lord of Heaven to employ the skills He has given us."

"The Lord of Heaven, Spiritual Father? Who is that?"

"The One True God, who sent His Only Son to save us

sinful humans." Adam Schall drew the boys into the discussion that had already resulted in conversion of several vulnerable Eunuchs. "We are all his children, men and women, girls and boys, even the Emperor and all his Eunuchs."

"All the children of one father?" the older boy wondered.

"That is true. One Heavenly Father whom we call the Lord of Heaven. He has commanded me to carry his message to his Chinese children, who have been too long deprived of His Word. Knowing the Lord of Heaven makes us happy in this world and is the salvation of our immortal souls in the next world...in Heaven."

"*Ni-men Shen-fu...*" The younger Eunuch's curiosity overflowed. "You Spiritual Fathers here are all from the Society of Jesus, are you not? What is this Society?"

"Some eighty years ago, a Spanish soldier called Ignatius Loyola was touched by the Lord of Heaven." Adam Schall spoke simply so that the boys might understand. "He founded the Society of Jesus. Like soldiers, we Jesuits go where we are ordered by our General..."

"But you are not soldiers, Spiritual Father, are you?"

"No, we are not, though sometimes the Emperor commands us to do soldiers' work...and we can. We are, however, men of peace, who go out to the entire world."

"Why do you not stay among your own people?" The older Eunuch's question gratified the priest, whom experience had taught to guide such conversations unobtrusively.

"Because our holy Father Loyola taught it was selfish to keep the Word of the Lord for ourselves alone...to lock it within our own world, which we call Christendom. He ordered the Society of Jesus to carry the True Word to the Lord's children everywhere. He also directed all Jesuits to perfect skills like mechanics, star-watchers—what you call heaven-learning-scholars—physicians, teachers, and the like. We are charged to be of use to God's children on earth...to bring them the new learning of Europe as well as to show them the way to Heaven."

Cloth-soled shoes sighed across the marble floor of the anteroom, and the little Eunuchs looked at each other in horror. They darted behind the long harpsichord, trying vainly to hide.

"*Shih Tsao Chun-hua,*" the younger Eunuch whispered. "Is it Tsao Chun-hua? He's everywhere—the Black Premier! He'll beat us unmercifully for loitering."

"No, boys, it's not Senior Court Eunuch Tsao Chun-hua."

A portly Mandarin in a scarlet robe entered the music chamber and reassured the quivering Eunuchs. "It's only old Hsü Kwang-chi, the Vice-Minister of Rites. I have no host of spies, and I command no army of Flamboyant Cloaks. But run away now. Eunuch Officer Tsao will soon be coming."

The little Eunuchs scampered from the chamber, their aquamarine gowns swishing. They had come from utterly different backgrounds to the Imperial Palaces, which required a constant influx of novices to fill the ranks of some twenty thousand Court Eunuchs. After months of agonizing, the impoverished father of the elder boy had agreed to sell him to the procurer who bound him and cut off his immature testicles with a kitchen knife. The younger was the son of a wealthy minor nobleman, who had planned since his sixth son's infancy to castrate him so that the family would possess an influential advocate at the Imperial Court when the boy inevitably attained great power in the Corps of Court Eunuchs, who were in the decadence of the Great Ming Dynasty the virtual rulers of China. The Black Government, the common people called them.

His exalted rank as Mandarin of the First Grade proclaimed by the white crane with outspread wings on his chest, the Vice-Minister watched the little Eunuchs' flight and sighed sadly. His open features curled in a grimace of distaste before resuming their habitual half-smile. The Mandarin's goatee was white, but his luxuriant mustaches and eyebrows were glossy black—perhaps by nature, more likely by artifice at his age. His eyes alone revealed the extraordinary forcefulness behind his commonplace appearance. Large and round because the epicanthic fold was only a vestige, they were lustrous and commanding.

Having been drawn to Father Matthew Ricci by the new secular learning the Jesuit pioneer brought from Europe, the Mandarin Hsü Kwang-chi had been struck by the Italian's spirituality as much as by his knowledge. Distressed by the vice of the Ming Dynasty, by the corruption of Chinese society, and by the Tartar threat, Hsü Kwang-chi sought remedies in European science. The Jesuit's spiritual message had for a time seemed irrelevant. The Mandarin lived by the precepts of the Sage Confucius, whose pronouncements on government, morality, and manners governed the life of all Chinese.

Rising one afternoon after dispensing justice to petty criminals while he was still no more than a district magistrate,

Hsü Kwang-chi had been struck by a transcendent revelation: only the blessings of Christianity could redeem the Ming—and illuminate his own discontent with saving grace. Since his enlightenment was a shattering revelation like that vouchsafed Paul of Tarsus on the road to Damascus, he had taken the Apostle's name when he was baptized at the age of forty-one.

"Adam, it is you, is it not? I should have known." Addressing the faceless black form under the harpsichord, the Vice-Minister spoke the Officials' Language with the buzzing sibilants of Shanghai. "Who else would be repairing the foreign zither and, at the same time, preaching to children?"

"Not preaching, Dr. Paul, just conversing." The Jesuit awkwardly backed out from under the harpsichord to stand respectfully before the Mandarin, though they were obviously on familiar terms. "Children's souls are purer...far more easily saved. Besides, most children are more sensible than adults, even those poor corrupted geldings."

Though Father Adam Schall, almost six feet tall, stood a head higher than Dr. Paul Hsü, he did not stoop condescendingly. His hair shone yellow in the sunlight filtered through the latticed window, and his deep-set blue eyes glowed with energy. The sardonic air imparted by his spatulate nose and hollow cheeks dissipated when he smiled at Paul Hsü.

"You should really be at the Department of Astronomy, Adam," Paul Hsü chided gently. "The new calendar must be ready next week."

"Dr. Paul," the Jesuit lowered his voice. "I was summoned by the Black Premier to repair this blasted instrument. What else could I do?"

"You are right, Adam." The Mandarin, too, spoke softly. "We cannot flout the Eunuchs, though by right I as your superior in the Bureau should..."

"But you will not order me back to my astrolabes and my telescopes, Dr. Paul, will you?"

"Would that I could! But I cannot at this moment offend the Court Eunuch Officer Tsao, whom you call the Black Premier."

"Everyone in Peking does, Dr. Paul, as you well know. After all, he exercises greater power than the Emperor himself. Who else holds all the threads of the Divine Skein: evil spies, secret police, and those ruffians of the elite guard, the Flamboyant Cloaks?"

"I am aware of that, Adam. My poor country suffers not

only the cruelty but also the depredations of these half-men and their millions of agents. I sometimes wonder why the Lord of Heaven permits.... And they don't even take the Civil Service Examinations..."

"Unlike you industrious Mandarins, Dr. Paul, they could never pass. A Eunuch study for fifteen years? Unthinkable. They qualify not by what is inside their heads, but by what is missing beneath their penises."

"Father Adam Schall!" After years of close association, the Mandarin was still not habituated to the German Jesuit's occasional coarse levity. "Let us talk of other things while I await His Majesty's summons."

"I am sorry if I give offense, Dr. Paul." The Jesuit was contrite before the man he respected more than any other. "But you know we priests are only men.... And I have a regrettable tendency to say what I think, as my superiors constantly remind me."

"It does not matter, Adam. You are still very young to me. The thirty years that separate us sometimes seem an eternity and..."

"You still plan a small reception for our military friends, Dr. Paul, do you not?" The Jesuit diverted the elderly Mandarin from the brooding unease that simmered beneath his serene demeanor.

"When they arrive, Adam. *If* they arrive in Peking."

"Why should they not? They are not a score of miles distant."

"I am summoned today to the Emperor, Adam, as you know. He may still withhold permission for the Expedition to enter Peking. I fear I must repeat all my arguments again."

"Despite their victory? Despite the Tartar threat?"

"We shall see, Adam, whether I find His Majesty in a good mood. He may be jolly or he may be lowering. It all depends on who last spoke..."

The Vice-Minister stopped in midsentence, though his voice was already so low he almost whispered. An infinitesimal stirring in the inner chamber had alerted either his preternaturally keen hearing or the sixth sense that had enabled him to survive the vicious intrigues of the Imperial Court for many years.

A moon door opened in its frame of bright tiles embossed with mythical unicorns, lions, and phoenixes. The Senior Court Eunuch who stepped through the round opening was lean for a castrato. He lacked the folded chins common among the Eunuchs, his features were regular and attractive, marred only by his mottled complexion.

"*Ah, Fu-pu-chang gen Shen-fu.*" The baritone voice of the spymaster men called the Black Premier was surprisingly deep for a castrato. "Well, both the Vice-Minister and his friend the Spiritual Father. We bid you welcome."

Startled by the lordly *we* the Eunuch used to demonstrate his closeness to the Emperor, the Christians returned his perfunctory bow in silence. Adam Schall marveled at the gorgeousness of his scarlet-silk robe, which displayed blue five-clawed Imperial dragons on its breast, its shoulders, and the frieze below the knees.

"I have come to conduct you into the presence of His Imperial Majesty, Vice-Minister Hsü. The Emperor impatiently awaits your attendance."

"Perhaps you will be here when I return, Adam." Dr. Paul Hsü ignored the Eunuch's menacing implication that he had kept the impatient Emperor waiting.

"I'll still be here, Dr. Paul," the Jesuit replied. "There is much more to be done for this temperamental instrument."

Paul Hsü, Senior Vice-Minister of Rites, followed the Black Premier through corridors brilliant with inset tiles illuminated by crystal lamps. The silken rugs of Persia and the gaudily patterned carpets of Khotan muffled their tread. Nonetheless, the murmur of respectful greetings preceding them warned the Court Eunuchs and Palace Women who pressed themselves against the walls to avoid impeding their progress.

Paul Hsü's disciplined mind dismissed futile speculation regarding the Emperor's purpose in summoning him. Instead, he thoughtfully reviewed the personal history of the Black Premier, assessing again the danger that Eunuch posed to the welfare of both Christianity and the Ming Dynasty.

Though he held no position in the hierarchy of the government, that individual was the most powerful—and the most corrupt—man in the Empire because he commanded the Emperor's personal secret police and secret service. The man therefore called the Black Premier, Paul Hsü recalled, was in his early forties. He had begun his career of debauchery so early that he was at eighteen compelled to a loathsome expedient. After he was cast out by his family for his profligacy, strong-arm men threatened him with maiming if he did not pay his enormous gambling debts. Penniless, he chose self-maiming. He castrated himself to escape his pursuers by becoming a Court Eunuch in the impregnable citadel of the Imperial Palaces of the Forbidden City.

Behind their hands, a somewhat different tale was told by the Court Ladies. The Black Premier, they whispered, was a mock castrato. They had plucked out his scanty beard hair by hair and cauterized the roots with burning needles, producing his curiously mottled complexion. After enticing a young man of the people to a night of homosexual debauchery, the ladies added, the future Black Premier had stupefied him with opium drops. He had then cut off the young man's testicles, put out his eyes, and ripped out his tongue.

Taking life was abhorrent to the Tantric Buddhism the Black Premier practiced, though that creed forbade neither torture nor sexual orgies, which were justified as "spiritual exercises to strengthen the fiber of the soul." He therefore released his blind-and-dumb victim, perhaps to live, but more likely to die. Regardless of the young man's fate, there would be no charge for taking life against his tormentor's account in Heaven. Later, the Black Premier was to discard his Buddhist scruples against killing.

The young man's testicles, pickled in spirits, the new candidate for the Imperial Corps of Eunuchs presented as the essential "relicts" to prove that he was neutered. Well bribed with stolen silver, the examining board was too delicate to demand that the well-born youth display his own body.

Insinuating himself into the service of the First Concubine of the Heir-Apparent as her *chef de cuisine*, he made himself indispensable to that favorite. Some Court Ladies insisted he was also her lover, but others said he had been too prudent. He was beyond doubt the lover of the Lady Nursemaid of the son of the First Concubine, the child who was to become the Chung Chen Emperor.

The mock castrato was not sated by her favors, but lay indiscriminately with Eunuchs, Court Ladies, and military officers. Nor, when he came to the peak of his career, was he satisfied with the power he wielded as chief of both the Secret Police and its Armed Security Force, the forty thousand men who were called Flamboyant Cloaks because they wore gaudy uniforms and richly embroidered rust-yellow mantles. The Black Premier himself initiated the young Heir Presumptive into the pleasures of male lovemaking. When the boy attained puberty, the Black Premier urged—and watched—his initiation into female lovemaking by the Lady Nursemaid.

Since the youth's accession, the Black Premier had encouraged him to unrestrained indulgence with females, with males, and (it was whispered) with animals. Smoking opium and carousing late into the night over bowls of wine left the nineteen-year-old Emperor with little energy or inclination for his Imperial duties. That feebleness, Paul Hsü's mental review concluded somberly, precisely suited the Eunuch, who could usually dispose of affairs of state as he pleased. It usually pleased him to quash any reforms that might imperil the vast bribes he routinely garnered. He was usually supported by the powerful conservative faction among the Mandarinate, which loathed all change that might diminish its privileges.

Senior Vice-Minister of Rites Paul Hsü, life member of the Han Lin Academy, the Empire's primary intellectual institution, steeled himself as the Eunuch scratched on the door of the Emperor's Minor Audience Chamber. The petulant youth who sat on the Dragon Throne did occasionally assert his own feeble will. Only such fitful Imperial self-assertion had enabled the Christian Mandarin to bring the Portuguese Expedition into China over the Black Premier's objections. Perhaps he would again find the Emperor agreeable.

The Audience Chamber was deserted except for the portraits of His Imperial Majesty's predecessors staring impassively in full court regalia, painted in brilliant detail. No figure sat on the Minor Dragon Throne, which was a broad armchair with stepped arms covered with a cushion embossed with coiled Imperial dragons. Nor did any figure lean against the glowing five-foot porcelain jar whose domed lid was crowned by a stylized jade lion, its right paw on the ball that symbolized the earth. The openwork screen that concealed the further door was unmoving.

Nonetheless Paul Hsü dropped to the cream-and-blue carpet bordered with a geometrical scroll to perform the *kowtow*, the touching of the forehead to the ground nine times all subjects rendered the Emperor. A slight back clothed in Imperial-yellow silk leaned out the latticed window. As the elderly Mandarin kowtowed, he heard a high piping. The Emperor, he knew, was watching the doves released with whistles attached to their legs to celebrate the coming lunar New Year.

The Chung Chen Emperor of the Great Ming Dynasty turned from the window and languidly seated himself on the Minor Dragon Throne. Still kneeling, his Vice-Minister of Rites studied the Emperor through the incense smoke and the mist of cloying jasmine perfume so thick it was palpable.

67

Since he was totally without self-discipline, the Emperor's features invariably revealed his mood.

The querulous mouth of the youth who ruled the world's largest empire was drawn up in a half-smile, and Paul Hsü sighed in relief. Despite his youth, the Emperor's face was puffy with self-indulgence. His complexion was already marred by the broken blood vessels the Chinese called wineflowers, and violet half moons disfigured the skin beneath his small eyes. Under brows raised as if in perpetual astonishment, his pupils were the pinpoints of the habitual opium smoker and his black irises were dull. Under his informal headdress, crowned only by a golden scroll, his pendulous ears hung beside his beardless cheeks. The Emperor rested his head on his slender hand, one long-nailed forefinger scratching his scalp beneath his headdress.

Paul Hsü was delighted that the Emperor had received him in a casual robe, its breast displaying a single rampant dragon, unlike the embroidered robes of state worn for formal audiences. His Emperor's temper, the Mandarin judged was, this once, equable.

"Rise, Minister, rise!" The Emperor commanded in the light-timbred voice of youth. "You may seat yourself."

As Paul Hsü took an octagonal stool near the throne, the Court Eunuch moved sinuously to the side of the throne. There he hovered obsequiously. No Eunuch, his glare over the Emperor's head said to the Mandarin as plainly as words, might sit in the Emperor's presence, though an aged Vice-Minister was granted that privilege.

"We are pleased to see you looking well, Minister," the Emperor continued. "Of course, there is cause for rejoicing, is there not?"

"I rejoice to see Your Majesty so sprightly and vigorous." Paul Hsü no longer despised himself for the courtier's essential flattery. "That is the greatest cause for rejoicing I know."

"We thank you, Minister. But there is even greater cause for rejoicing. The Tartars are in full retreat, we are reliably informed. There will therefore be no need for the ocean barbarian soldiers to come to Peking. We direct you to send them back whence they came."

"Your Majesty, I submit most humbly that it would appear ungracious if the Sacred Dynasty dispatched the Portuguese to Macao without, at least, allowing them to come to Peking so that Your Majesty's ministers can express gratitude. Dismissing them peremptorily would appear to the people the act of small-minded men."

"His Majesty knows you only want those soldiers to back up your beloved barbarian priests." The Black Premier was boldly assertive. "You want them to compel all His Majesty's subjects to accept this outlandish sprinkling with water."

"That is not true, Esteemed Eunuch Officer," Paul Hsü replied shortly, assuming the Emperor's permission. "How could a hundred-odd men and a few cannon possibly compel multitudes to baptism? The Portuguese have come at His Majesty's invitation...not to intimidate his subjects but to fight the Tartars."

"Oh, stop your squabbling," the Emperor commanded irritably. "Tsao, the Minister makes an important point. We would not appear ungrateful. We shall let these barbarian soldiers come to the Capital, and We shall give them an honorable welcome. We shall decide afterward what is to become of them."

Paul Hsü rose to bow his thanks, but the Emperor impatiently motioned him to be seated again. As he resumed his stool, the Mandarin glimpsed a pair of eyes peering through the openwork screen. The eyes retreated, and a shadow moved behind the screen. The heavy fragrance of attar of roses drifted to his nostrils. The Emperor, Paul reflected in annoyance, would have a concubine in secret attendance to admire his power when he conducted state discussions.

"I thank Your Majesty profoundly."

Paul Hsü became aware that the sliding door behind the screen was ajar. He heard a rustle but could not see the two novice Eunuchs who had a few minutes earlier been watching Adam Schall with equal curiosity. Nowhere in the vast complex of Imperial Palaces could anyone, even the Emperor, be secure from prying eyes.

"As to the Jesuits, Your Imperial Majesty...," the Eunuch prompted malevolently.

"Yes, Minister," the Emperor said silkily. "It has come to Our attention that these outlanders who call themselves Spiritual Fathers nowadays even more ape the ways of our Mandarins, wearing similar robes and conducting themselves as if they were great officers of state. That must stop."

The youth wearing the Imperial robes glanced at his trusted Eunuch Officer, who nodded approvingly.

"Your Majesty, the Spiritual Fathers study as hard as any

69

Mandarin. They are qualified by their learning to wear robes like Mandarins. Besides, they wear robes without insignia. Yet they know not only China's Sacred Classics, but their own foreign Classics. And their practical skills are enormously helpful to the Realm."

"Nonetheless, Minister, they should not be so obtrusive," the Emperor commanded. "We have it in mind, after consultation with our faithful advisers, to consider expelling them from the Empire."

"I shall instruct the Spiritual Fathers to be less obtrusive, Your Majesty." Having already been confronted with the same threat several times, Dr. Paul Hsü was not unduly alarmed. "But expelling the Jesuits would be a violation of the Sacred Practices of the Great Ming Dynasty. Your Majesty will recall that Your Majesty's grandfather, the long-lived Wan Li Emperor, gave the priests permission to settle in Peking. Li Ma-tao...Matthew Ricci...was judged worthy of a state funeral by Your Majesty's sacred grandfather. It would be ungracious to expel his successors summarily. Instead, test them as you will. Let them debate theology and doctrine with the Buddhists and the Taoists. Besides, Your Majesty, the Jesuits are not only priests, but practical men who are of enormous service in so many..."

"Enough, Minister, enough." The Emperor was clearly bored. "Perhaps we were hasty. Send me a memorial on that matter, setting out your arguments."

Paul Hsü groaned to himself at the necessity to compose yet another lengthy justification for the Jesuits' presence in the Empire. But he relaxed, knowing the Emperor had merely repeated the words dinned into his ears by the wily Court Eunuch, who did not always find his master a wholly responsive puppet.

"One other matter concerns Us, Minister. And it is Our command."

"I hear and obey Your Majesty," Paul Hsü uttered the obligatory formula of compliance on hearing the word *command* from the Emperor's lips. "Pray give me your august instructions, Your Majesty."

"By Heaven's Grace...and, perhaps, the thunder of the barbarian cannon...the Tartars are retreating everywhere. But we are dissatisfied with the performance of Our Field Marshal in Manchuria. He allowed the Tartars to approach close to Our Capital. He was drawn away by a feint and left the road to the Northern Capital free. And he...and he..."

"...accepted bribes from the Tartars to behave in that craven, treasonous manner, His Majesty would say," the Eunuch prompted. "The reports of His Majesty's agents under the direction of his humble slave prove the Field Marshal's treachery irrefutably."

"Yes, Minister. Quite irrefutably. The Field Marshal must die. We have ordered him beaten to death in the Eastern Market by Our faithful Flamboyant Cloaks."

"Your Majesty, I implore you not to be hasty. I pray Your Majesty to remember that it was the Field Marshal who reconquered Manchuria from the Tartars. He reclaimed the vast territories your Sacred Predecessors colonized over the centuries. Besides, he is the Dynasty's greatest field general. His death would be an irreparable loss to the Dynasty. I implore..."

"His Majesty has given you a command, Vice-Minister," the Eunuch interjected. "You have sworn to obey."

"Let Us speak for Ourself, Tsao," the Emperor said irritably. "Our decision is irrevocable, Minister. You are required only to prepare a proper funeral for the Field Marshal, a funeral befitting his former services. We are not vindictive."

"I hear and obey, Your Imperial Majesty."

Sick at heart, Paul Hsü repeated the self-abnegating formula. He realized that the Black Premier, who was grinning in evil triumph, had trailed the expulsion of the Portuguese Expedition and the banishment of the Jesuits as decoys. The shrewd Eunuch had expected the Emperor to concede those points to Paul Hsü's pleading. His true objective had been the death of the Field Marshal, and he had attained that objective by playing to the Emperor's vindictive nature.

When the Emperor did not speak again but glanced expectantly at the screen concealing his concubine, Paul Hsü rose. The Emperor remained silent while he kowtowed, only calling after him as he withdrew: "Minister, you may tell your foreign soldier friends that We are well pleased with them. We but jested when We talked of not receiving them in Peking."

The two little Eunuchs scurried down the corridor to the interior of the Hall of the Intellect. No longer distracted, the Senior Eunuch might discover their presence.

"You know old Tsao, the old Black Premier, got two hundred thousand silver taels for the Field Marshal's head," the elder breathlessly confided. "I heard it from his steward. Oh to be grown up...and very rich."

As Dr. Paul Hsü trudged dispiritedly down the corridor to the antechamber, the Senior Eunuch turned to the Emperor.

"That was well done, my little Lord," he said familiarly. "And now, perhaps, we can, as you intimated earlier..."

"No, Tsao, not today," the Emperor commanded. "Buckle up your belt again and get yourself away. We are too tired today for a Threefold Entwining Dragon. Just send Our Opium Ladies and leave Us with Our Willow Concubine. We will amuse Ourselves adequately...but gently."

FATHER Adam Schall was washing his hands in violet-scented water proffered in a porcelain basin by a kneeling novice Eunuch when Dr. Paul Hsü returned to the music chamber.

"Well, Dr. Paul, I hope your time was as well spent as mine," the Jesuit said. "Though why I must keep this blasted harpsichord in perfect tune when no one ever plays it but myself..."

"Because it pleases the Emperor, Adam," Paul Hsü said shortly. "We must all please the Emperor in every way."

"Was it that bad, Sir?" the Jesuit lowered his voice.

"Worse than you can imagine, Adam. But come walk with me to my sedan chair."

Paul Hsü was silent until they reached the long avenue leading to the Meridian Gate, the boundary of the Forbidden City. Quickening his pace with a perceptible effort so that they could not be overheard by the passing Court Eunuchs and Palace Women, the portly Mandarin finally spoke to the German priest.

"Sometimes, Adam, I am close to despair," he said wearily. "How we can ever overcome the sloth and the avarice of these pestilential Eunuchs and their allies, I do not..."

"Come, Dr. Paul, you've mentioned only two of the deadly sins," Adam Schall joked. "Are they so guiltless of the remaining five?"

"Hardly, Adam. Pride, lust, gluttony...they practice all."

"We can but strive and pray, Dr. Paul. The Lord will not let his Chinese children..."

"I shall strive harder and pray harder, Adam. You must promise me to pray very much harder."

"I shall, Dr. Paul, most devoutly. But can we talk of pleasanter matters for a moment? Your young ladies are pressing me..."

"Yes, I know. Both Candida and Marta are anxious to see this foreign...English, is that right? Both at any rate are anxious to see this foreign lieutenant who speaks Chinese."

"And you have decided?"

"They may, I believe. I see no harm. You will be there...as shall I and Father Juan, as well as Ambassador Michael Chang. Certainly enough old wise heads for propriety's sake."

"Candida will be delighted, Dr. Paul."

"And Marta?"

"I am not so sure. Marta generally does as Candida wishes. But she will certainly be pleased."

"I wish I could make everyone happy as easily, Adam. Tell me, you know the concept of *Tien Ming*, the Mandate of Heaven, do you not? Is it a blasphemous...a pagan concept solely?"

"By no means, Dr. Paul. You know we Europeans speak of the Divine Right of Kings. Our monarchs are anointed by God."

"It's not quite the same thing, Adam, you know. The Mandate of Heaven cuts deeper. Once bestowed, it sanctifies a dynasty, which rules, my pagan countrymen say, by Heaven's Express Will. God's Will, you and I would say. But the Mandate endures only as long as the dynasty is worthy. I fear the Ming may lose the Mandate of Heaven because of its crimes and its follies."

"How can you tell, Dr. Paul? What signs are there?"

"Beyond the deadly sins we were just discussing, many signs. The Tartar thrust to conquer the Empire is only the greatest. Constant rebellions, famines, plagues, floods, and droughts—all warn that the Mandate of Heaven may be slipping from the Ming."

"We can, as I said, only strive and pray, Dr. Paul. Only when Christianity peacefully conquers the Ming Empire will these afflictions cease."

When the dignified Mandarin stopped, the hurrying courtiers respectfully walked around him. Standing stock-still, he peered into the Jesuit's blue eyes and smiled wryly.

"Tell me, Adam," he asked almost fiercely, "are there no fools or traitors or wars in Christian Europe?"

Peking

WOMEN'S laughter floated through the open door when a manservant carried in the tureen of *suan-la tang*, sour-and-hot soup, the last dish Vice-Minister Paul Hsü offered his foreign guests. Francis Arrowsmith stared under lowered lids. When another manservant entered with a platter of roasted chestnuts, he saw a ripple of tangerine silk and a golden hairpin glowing above upswept black hair. Reluctantly, he resumed his frowning attention to the male company's conversation.

"*Tao-ti wo-men hui shou-hsiang...*" Dr. Paul Hsü smiled to deprecate his fondness for the pleasures of the table. "Crowning our blessings, we can enjoy again the sweet chestnuts of Lianghsiang."

"The Lord's bounty!" Father Adam Schall's smile was faintly acerbic. "All things come to him who waits—and believes."

"True enough, Father Adam," Paul Hsü replied. "The Lord of Heaven sent His soldiers from across the seas to hold Chochow.... But above all to take back Lianghsiang—and its chestnuts—from the Tartars."

Joining the general laughter, Francis was somewhat surprised by his host's humor and by his sharing the Chinese

74

passion for cuisine. During the long journey north, he had learned that district magistrates, regimental commanders, and wealthy merchants avidly discussed the ingeniously varied dishes their chefs prepared. He could not imagine a Portuguese colonel or a Spanish grandee, much less an English knight, comparing the olives of Provence to those of Catalonia. But powerful Mandarins hotly debated the rival claims of the yellowfish of Hunan and the icefish of Shantung.

Having heard his Jesuit mentors talk so reverently of Dr. Paul, Francis had expected a virtual saint who was grave in demeanor, profound in discourse, and bowed with learning. Instead, the first Christian gentleman of the Great Ming Empire was jolly and plump as a favorite uncle. The Vice-Minister's paunch swelled against his blue long-gown, which was quilted with raw silk against the damp chill four glowing charcoal braziers on bronze tripods did not dispel.

The Portuguese Expedition had arrived in Peking two days before Shrove Tuesday, which fell on February 13 in 1630, to be accommodated in spacious guesthouses and to find a note from Paul Hsü: *Be sure to bring the English Lieutenant to dinner* [the Vice Minister had written after apologizing that duty prevented his welcoming them personally]. *I understand he speaks Chinese. To dine with us, might, however, be onerous for the Captain-Sergeant, who, I am told, does not.*

"He might have kept you newcomers waiting for days—to show his own importance," Father Adam Schall had remarked. "But not Dr. Paul. Though I wonder why he is so eager to meet you, my son."

Self-importance was obviously alien to Paul Hsü. Francis was struck by the simple furnishings of his mansion just inside the Hsüan Wu Gate near the Department of Astronomy. Conveniently close was the former pagan Temple of Benevolence an earlier Emperor had given the Jesuits in 1610 to consecrate as a church—and to bury Father Matthew Ricci, the pioneer of the Mission to China. The Vice-Minister's mansion was austere beside the ostentation Francis had seen in South China.

Despite his rank, Paul Hsü was amiable and warm. He possessed the same genius for friendship that had enabled that other towering intellect, his friend and teacher Matthew Ricci, to penetrate Chinese society. It was, perhaps, natural that the aged Father Juan Rodriguez should chat familiarly with the elderly convert. But the far younger Father Adam

Schall was clearly at ease, as was Ambassador Michael Chang, who was markedly inferior in age and rank.

Paul Hsü was laden with responsibilities. Already the Senior Vice-Minister of Rites, he was designated to succeed the enfeebled Minister who supervised the ceremonial, moral, and religious life of the Empire. Because he was a Christian, he was also occupied with manufacturing Christian firearms and with training infantrymen in Christian tactics.

Because he was responsible for the spiritual welfare of the Chinese people, Paul Hsü had been designated director of the bureau established eight months earlier to correct the Sacred Calendar. The sophisticated Chinese still sacrificed to the spirits of the earth. If those observances were awry by even a few hours, they believed, catastrophe would follow. But a mystical union would bind man and nature, ineluctably making all men happy and prosperous, if their devotions harmonized perfectly with the seasons. The absolute accuracy of the calendar was essential to that accord. Otherwise, the Emperor, addressing the spirits on behalf of his people, would invoke disasters rather than blessings.

Incongruously, a devout Christian for twenty-six years was rectifying the Sacred Calendar that governed those pagan observances. Even more incongruously, Paul Hsü had appointed a foreign priest to oversee the adjustment of the calendar. Father Adam Schall accepted that appointment because his superiors remembered that Matthew Ricci had been allowed to settle in the Northern Capital due to his mathematical and astronomical knowledge, which was so immediately useful. In order to preach the Gospel, the Jesuits were still compelled to demonstrate the utility of their learning. In the most recent formal competition, they had precisely predicted the solar eclipse of July 21, 1629, while both traditional Chinese and pseudomodern Moslem astronomers erred grandly. Most incongruously, the Jesuit Mission could flourish only by fixing the time of pagan rites.

"There's an excellent chance Dr. Paul will become Grand Secretary," Adam Schall had remarked while they walked from the Jesuit House. "Think of it, a Christian Chancellor, second only to the Emperor himself—except for the Eunuch spymaster they call the Black Premier."

"A Christian Chancellor for a pagan Empire?" Francis asked.

"Very likely. Power in the Empire is open to talent, far more than in Europe. All Mandarins must pass arduous ex-

76

aminations to qualify for the Civil Service, even ministers and grand secretaries."

Francis was dazzled by the knowledge of the energetic German priest, but he was charmed by the elderly gentleman whose cheeks glowed ruddy with the yellow rice wine of Shaohsing.

"Not only the sweet chestnuts of Lianghsiang." Dr. Paul gestured expansively. Soon we'll again drink the *pai-kar* of Manchuria. It smells foul, but a cup of *pai-kar* made from Manchurian sorghum would warm my old bones tonight."

"You expect a miracle, perhaps, Dr. Paul?" Adam Schall's sarcasm was velvet. "The Tartars to be driven from Manchuria, as well as China, by sixty Portuguese, sixty slaves—and ten cannon?"

"Peking is secure again," Paul Hsü replied. "Why should we not drive the Tartars north of the Great Wall—and, later, from Chinese Manchuria?"

"It's a daunting task," Ambassador Michael Chang warned. "The Portuguese are few...too few."

"I pray for a miracle every day," Dr. Paul insisted. "And I beg you all to pray. Pray to the Lord God to crush the Tartars. Pray also for the young Emperor to employ wise counselors who understand modern weapons and modern tactics."

"Sir, you make great demands on the Lord of Heaven." Ambassador Michael Chang's square face was animated. "But I saw a miracle at Chochow."

"Truly a miracle," Francis echoed. "Thousands of Tartars fleeing from nine unshotted cannon."

"A greater miracle than you think, Arrowmaker," Paul Hsü admonished. "The Lord of Heaven also afflicted the invaders with the heavenly flower disease, what you call the smallpox. I know he loves the Chinese people as he loved the Children of Israel."

"I shall pray to Him to keep the Emperor constant." Juan Rodriguez's age sanctioned his frankness.

"The Son of Heaven is still young, hardly nineteen, Father Juan." Dr. Paul remonstrated. "If only the Black Premier and his Court Eunuchs can be restrained, better times will come. I know it."

"The Eunuchs are still all-powerful," Adam Schall interjected fiercely. "What of the execution of the Field Marshal? The Emperor will soon have no generals left."

"The Lord of Heaven will provide," Paul Hsü avowed. "Sün

Yüan-hua, Ignatius Sün, is still in service. A Christian general who understands modern weapons. You know Ignatius planned the Field Marshal's strategy for reoccupying Manchuria."

"He'd better plan another reoccupation," Schall commented dourly. "Those few troops still in Manchuria will have to come south to flush all the Tartars from the home provinces."

"And to crush the rebel, One-Eyed Li," Ambassador Michael Chang said. "Otherwise the Ming could fall from within."

"How can we defend Peking without a buffer zone north of the Great Wall?" Francis was the only professional soldier in the company. "On my map, Peking is no more than fifty miles south of the Wall. At most, three days' march for infantry...much less for Tartar cavalry, so..."

"*Na chiu shih-la...*," Schall interrupted. "That's it. The Wall is indefensible. Perhaps it was different when the First Emperor completed the Great Wall two millennia ago."

"Not even then. The Great Wall was never meant to be impregnable." Dr. Paul's honesty compelled him to admit that unpalatable truth. "The Mongols did not find the Great Wall a major obstacle to conquering China centuries ago."

"All Chinese must realize that fact," Adam Schall insisted, "or the Empire will perish."

"My countrymen must also choke down the bitter truth about the bandit-rebels," Dr. Paul agreed sadly. "Unless the Great Ming rises in new vigor and new virtue, One-Eyed Li or another such rapscallion could soon sit on the Dragon Throne."

"Yet you were so optimistic a moment earlier," Juan Rodriguez probed. "How can you reconquer Manchuria again for the third time? You must learn to live with the Tartars on your doorstep—failing a miracle!"

"The miracle will occur," the Vice-Minister asserted. "I know it."

"Dr. Paul, a word on doctrine." Adam Schall's mild sarcasm gave way to earnestness. "We sinners can *pray* for a miracle. We cannot *demand* a miracle."

"A miracle has already occurred...a series of miracles," Paul Hsü insisted. "I therefore expect—not demand—further miracles."

"Do I understand you correctly, Dr. Paul?" Francis ventured. "Many miracles already?"

"Of course, Arrowmaker. But even the learned Fathers do not fully comprehend those sublime miracles. How could you?"

"And those miracles were?" Adam Schall asked.

"The Jesuits' coming into China was the first." Paul Hsü meditated aloud on the great mercy of his Christian God. "China was a sealed country. The Ming Dynasty had excluded all outsiders for two centuries. Only a miracle permitted foreign scholars who are also teachers of religion to reside in the Empire. Another miracle: My colleagues, the Mandarins, accepted those outlanders as equals."

"That's all past," Francis objected. "Four decades since Father Ricci came to Peking. I cannot doubt God's Grace. But what further miracles make you so confident?"

"*You* are the latest miracle, the most convincing. For us Chinese to use foreign weapons...your cannon and your arquebuses...is unusual, but not extraordinary. We adopted the bows of the Huns and learned the horsemanship of the Mongols. We have enrolled individual foreign officers, but never before an entire foreign unit. A high tide of enlightenment is rising in China. Christian guns and Christian cannon are the outward signs of profound spiritual change."

Grandfather Paul, the Lord of Heaven has given us a greater sign...Christian charity toward *all*. For the first time, some Chinese give alms and comfort to those who are not kinsmen or dependents. Christian charity to men and women and children who have no claim other than common humanity..."

The first Chinese female voice Francis had heard in equal conversation was high-pitched, self-assured, and faintly histrionic. If the sentiments it expressed had not been so pious, it might have seemed shrill to him, even assertive.

A lady stood at the head of the three steps leading down into the reception chamber. Her eyes were cast down to contemplate a platter heaped with deep-yellow segments of *chin-kua,* gold melon from South China. The ivory fingers curled around the platter in sinuous, almost boneless curves. But their pearly nails were cut short, a style more suited to a serving wench than the great lady her rich costume and her self-assurance proclaimed her. Like Paul Hsü's, her eyes were large and round. Family resemblance was also apparent in her long nose and her small mouth. Unlike the wanton women of pleasure Francis had seen in Macao, the lady's makeup was restrained. Her lips and cheeks were touched with rouge and her lashes with kohl, but no white mask of powder obscured her features.

A slightly taller female figure was half revealed in the dimness of the doorframe. The red-wax candles in sconces beside the door flared in a draft to light a blue-and-white platter of flaky pastries. The hands supporting the platter were concealed by the black shadows cast by the sudden glare.

"Ah, *chin-kwa* and *hung-tsao ping*," Paul Hsü beamed. "We are still capable of great feats, we Chinese. The gold melon comes on ice from Canton in barges on the Grand Canal. The ice is cut from frozen northern lakes and shipped south wrapped in straw. The *hung-tsao ping* are a Shanghai delicacy, an old family recipe, filled with pounded dates, jujubes, brown sugar, and hazelnuts."

"Grandfather, the Fathers and the Lieutenant are not interested in our kitchens," the lady chided.

"Perhaps not, my dear, though they have honored us by consuming our poor fare with gusto," Paul Hsü laughed. "More important... most important... may I present my own private miracle, my granddaughter Candida?"

"Grandfather, please do not make me feel small by paying me too much honor." The lady's smile was pained. "I'm a perfectly ordinary woman."

"Hardly that, my dear. A wonder of God's grace... tireless in Christian charity. Gentlemen, Candida is the only daughter of my only son. Only twenty-two, she has already given me two great-grandsons and two great-granddaughters. Another is soon to come."

A scarlet flush flowed from Candida's neck, which was framed by the crossed blue lapels of her pearl-gray gown, to dye scarlet her sharp chin and high cheekbones. She drew an arm protectively across her swollen abdomen and teetered down the stairs as if balanced on miniature stilts.

"Please, Grandfather Paul, that's enough about me. You have not presented my niece Marta."

"Quite right, my dear," Paul Hsü smiled. "How could I forget our faithful Marta?"

The second lady stepped into the light and teetered down the stairs. Candida's curious gait, Francis realized, was not due to the weight of her unborn child, but to her bound feet. Like all Chinese women of good family, her feet had at the age of five been tightly bound with bandages to inhibit growth, the distorted toes and heel forced together so that the instep became far narrower and far higher.

Two gold-embroidered slippers peeped like timorous mice under Candida's tangerine underskirt, which flowed beneath the blue-girdled tunic that ended just below her knees. Those slippers, Francis saw with revulsion, would nicely fit a seven-year-old European girl.

The origin of bound feet, Francis had been told, was lost in antiquity. Today they served to keep a wife, commonly called "the one within the house," from straying—and to impart a sensuous gait. They were called golden lilies. The Chinese habitually adorned the unpleasant with ornate language. The pox they named the "plum poison sickness" and smallpox the "heavenly flower disease," while the Emperor did not die but "ascended the Dragon."

"Gentlemen, this is Marta Soo, the daughter of Candida's husband's younger brother, who was baptized James." Paul Hsü's concern with the precise relationship was characteristic of the family-obsessed Chinese.

The Europeans rose awkwardly from their white stools carved with red-and-green swallows in shallow bas-relief. Paul Hsü objected heartily, and the ladies offered embarrassed protests to the alien courtesy.

Francis was delighted to stretch his cramped legs, for the orange-lacquered table was hardly two feet high. He murmured the courtly greetings that were the first Chinese phrases he had learned. Those *ke-chi hua,* guest phrases, did not include the polite terms used on meeting ladies, since Chinese gentlemen met few ladies outside their own families.

Juan Rodriguez was heaping heavy gallantries on the ladies in *Kwan-hwa,* the Officials' Language, so called because all Mandarins, whatever their native dialects, spoke that tongue of North China. For the first time since he had fallen ill at Tsinan, the elderly Jesuit appeared relaxed and free of pain.

"I have asked Candida and Marta to join us because this is a family party," Dr. Paul said complacently. "Among ourselves we Christians can put aside ceremony. But they are reluctant to sit with us at table."

"Ladies, please do." Adam Schall's deep-set blue eyes sparkled with uncharacteristic courtliness. "The Christian ladies of Europe sit at table with their guests. Why not the Christian ladies of China?"

"Men and women, male and female alike, we are all God's children," Juan Rodriguez smiled. "He values us all equally, though He requires different virtues of males and females."

Dr. Paul Hsü's black eyebrows knotted in annoyance. He had with some difficulty accepted the extraordinary concept that Chinese were no more than the equals of foreigners, rather than their manifest superiors. He could flout traditional etiquette by inviting the ladies of his family to join outsiders at table. But he *knew* that men and women were *not* equal. To assert otherwise was to deny the fundamental order of mankind delineated by the Sage Confucius. Since it would have been discourteous to dispute with his guests, he let the remark pass without comment.

With hierarchical Confucian courtesy, Marta waited until Candida, her senior and, therefore, her superior, was seated on a six-legged stool before perching herself with nervous grace on its neighbor. Preoccupied with the byplay in swift Chinese, Francis had not really looked at the younger woman until she came to rest.

He was drawn by the mingled fragrances of jasmine and sandalwood when her azure underskirt swirled like a matador's cape. The reception chamber dissolved from his sight; the red-painted walls with their geometrical gilt moldings and the scroll landscapes vanished. He saw only the slender young woman with glossy black hair tied in an intricate knot transfixed by a long hairpin in the shape of a golden dragon. He no longer heard the rapid trilling of the Officials' Language.

Delivered to the monastic discipline of the Jesuits at eleven, Francis Arrowsmith had rarely met virtuous European women of good family. His experience of common women and the bawds of the camp had also been tenuous. Reinforced by his masters' warnings of Hellfire, a certain fastidiousness kept him from his brother officers' drunken revels. Despite some carnal passages, he was, at twenty-three, still an innocent in spirit.

Trained since childhood for marriage, Marta Soo had been thoroughly instructed in all the nuances of relations between men and women. She no longer blushed at the exquisitely colored and meticulously explicit pictures in the pillow books that prepared a young woman for her bridal night and the nights thereafter. But the realities were wholly unknown to the cloistered Chinese maiden.

Eminently marriageable since her sixteenth birthday eight months earlier, Marta was, quite remarkably, not betrothed. Though her mother fretted, her father had allowed her a voice in her own fate. That much tolerance, he felt, he owed to his Christian principles. James Soo had readily agreed to break off the betrothal he had contracted for his daughter at the age of three to a four-year-old boy. He had with increasing reluctance bowed to her insistence that he reject three successive suitors proposed by Peking's most eminent marriage broker. The Mandarin was moved by his love for his daughter—and by his fear of her displeasure.

Marta knew that her marriage must be arranged by her father and that she would not speak to her bridegroom until their wedding day. She was, however, determined that her husband would not be an elderly Mandarin and that she would be his only wife—as Holy Church prescribed. Even the domineering Candida steeled herself before telling her independent niece what was unquestionably best for her welfare. Her Chinese name, Mei-lo, meaning Roseate Joy, was somewhat more appropriate than the Christian name Marta she had chosen to exemplify the meek obedience she professed but did not invariably practice.

The tendrils of smoke drifting from the tobacco pipes in the mouths of the priests and the Mandarins wreathed the flaring candles and the charcoal braziers. Francis and Marta watched each other under lowered eyelids. She ostentatiously studied her silver-paper fan painted with stylized lotus flowers. He gazed into the eggshell cup of sweet, white grape wine Paul Hsü had served to gratify his foreign guests' presumed taste. When their glances crossed, they hastily looked away.

Francis felt clumsy in the red-velvet jacket and the bulbous green-velvet breeches that were his only formal wear. His stockinged calves seemed ungainly and his clothes tawdry beside the somber elegance of the Jesuits' sinified black cassocks and the Mandarins' pale-blue long-gowns. His tanned features tightened in derogatory self-appraisal, and his callused fingers self-consciously pushed the dark-yellow hair off his high forehead.

It was, he knew, presumptuous even to look at Marta Soo, while it was preposterous to dream of seeing her again. Until the red bridal palanquin delivered her to the bridegroom chosen by her parents, she would remain as closely sequestered as a novice in a convent. This evening, only Dr. Paul's liberality—and the priests' reassuring presence—had released her from the seclusion of the women's quarters. Nonetheless his eyes were drawn by the mystery—and the beauty—of the first nubile Chinese maiden he had ever met.

The women of the Ming, Francis reflected, docilely accepted a deprivation that would enrage their European sisters. Except for the color, their garments were virtually uniform. Marta's underskirt was turquoise, contrasting with Candida's tangerine. The turquoise shawl-collar of her primrose overtunic revealed only a small triangle of her soft throat beneath her rounded chin. Even her slender fingers, glowing with jade-and-pearl rings, darted from flowing, concealing sleeves. But the wide lavender sash that girdled her tunic thrust her high, small breasts forward; and the fragile silk outlined her rounded hips and legs. Francis had never been as stirred by the form within a European dress that displayed half the bosom.

Marta's face, he rhapsodized to himself with Elizabethan lyricism, was a soft petaled flower amid the glossy foliage of her hair. Her dark eyes, set aslant above delicate cheekbones, glowed within the thicket of her black-kohled eyelashes when she smiled. Her nose was short and delicately arched above a generous mouth. Her molded lower lip, slightly open even in repose, displayed small white teeth. Her skin glowed translucent pink-and-gold, matte-smooth and almost poreless. From her perfect earlobes dangled three-inch pendants, each made of four pink pearls encircled by golden hoops.

"Francis, are you asleep?" Adam Schall's bass whisper reverberated in his ear. "This is no time to vanish into a brown study."

". . . is young, but has great knowledge of the military arts." Michael Chang was speaking slowly to ensure that the young foreigner understood. "If the Fathers will release him, he might be useful to you, Dr. Paul."

"We should be happy to lend you his services," Juan Rodriguez agreed. "If Captain Texeira can spare the Lieutenant. But the decision is his own."

"My young friend," Paul Hsü asked, "would you like to help me?"

"In every way I can." Francis pulled his bemused wits together. "How can I be of service?"

"My troops need training in musketry and tactics. I myself need military advice."

"It would be the greatest pleasure, Sir."

"Then the Fathers must have a word with Captain Texeira," Paul Hsü directed. "The sooner the better."

"We ladies, too, might benefit from the Lieutenant's knowledge." Candida Soo again startled Francis by her directness, at odds with everything he had heard about reserved

84

Chinese ladies. "We have never seen a European who wasn't a Spiritual Father. And my son Basil is clamoring to meet the English officer who speaks Chinese. Sometimes, I fear, he wants to be a soldier, though that would never do."

"My child, we must forgo our ancient prejudices against soldiers," Dr. Paul admonished. "Only soldiers can save the Empire. Why, I myself am virtually becoming a soldier."

"Then it's settled, Grandfather?" Candida preened herself on winning her grandfather's consent by playing on his passion for modernization. "The Lieutenant may come to see us?"

"We are not only anxious to hear about Europe and Macao. We would be better Christians if we learned how other Christian ladies lived."

Heard for the first time, Marta's voice was husky and slightly breathy. Abashed by her own forwardness, she colored and raised her silver fan. She was, however, deeply curious about the first European young man she had ever met. The unvarying pattern of life in the secluded women's quarters was tedious, and it must end with the brief excitement of a grand wedding followed by much the same tedium. Unlike Francis, Marta was not stirred by intense sensual speculation, since he was not—and never could be—part of her world. Nonetheless, she wondered a little.

"And what they wear and how they live." Candida, too, was frankly curious. "How they raise their children...and how they worship the Lord of Heaven."

"There are so many things the Fathers have no time to talk about." Marta spoke behind her fan. "Things the foreign Lieutenant could tell us about."

"Better if you could meet a Christian lady," Paul Hsü said severely. "On second thought, I'm by no means sure your meeting is a good idea."

Dr. Paul Hsü's hauteur was restrained by the presence of the Christian priests. Nonetheless he glanced quizzically at his great-grandniece by marriage. But oil and water never mixed. It was inconceivable that a Chinese lady could feel any interest in the young barbarian—aside from his tales of the outside regions.

"We only want to learn about the Christian world," Candida pleaded. "Surely, Grandfather, there's nothing wrong with that."

"And also Christian fashions and Christian adornment." Paul Hsü frowned. "I've never known you so frivolous, my dear Candida."

"It's not that," Marta cajoled. "This is our only chance to speak with a Christian gentleman who is our own age. We must not bother the venerable Fathers."

Marta quailed under Paul Hsü's reproving glance. She knew the ruthlessness beneath his amiable manner, and she feared his displeasure as she feared no other's. Adam Schall, who was only thirty-seven, bridled in silence.

"If you are properly chaperoned," Paul Hsü mused. "Your mother, Marta, or another suitable older lady, perhaps..."

"We should be very grateful, Grandfather," Candida promised, "and not take too much of his time."

The Senior Vice-Minister looked speculatively at the young officer. He had great need of the barbarian soldier's skills. He wished to bind the Arrowmaker's loyalty to himself, to make him, above all, Paul Hsü's obedient lieutenant, rather than the Jesuits' and Captain Miguel Texeira's. The first scheme that burgeoned unbidden in his mind the Mandarin rejected impatiently. It was inconceivable. But he could, at least, lure the barbarian with a silken skirt and smiling eyes. Many precedents hallowed by China's history sanctioned that stratagem—and the military situation was grave.

"Well...perhaps," he finally conceded. "It is not, at any rate, entirely impossible."

"I am at your service, Sir!" Francis assayed a gallantry in Chinese: "And a Christian officer is always at the service of charming and virtuous ladies."

"Then, Master Arrowmaker, you will call upon my humble household again?" The Mandarin winced inwardly at the barbarian's presumption, but his self-deprecating invitation was a command. "To discuss military matters...and, perhaps, to satisfy the ladies' curiosity."

"When, Sir, may I have that honor?" Francis saw approval glint in Father Adam's blue eyes.

"Tomorrow is Ash Wednesday, and Lent begins," Paul Hsü pondered. "We must give ourselves to prayer until Easter Sunday. But the matter is pressing. Shall we say Monday, then?"

Near the Nankou Pass between
Peking and the Great Wall

JUNE 21, 1630

THE smoldering ends of the slow fuse each soldier gripped in his left hand glowed orange against the luminescent twilight of the year's longest day. The black loops appeared to Francis Arrowsmith's heightened awareness to writhe in agony like two-headed snakes consumed by fire. He thrust away the image, which impaired his concentration. The tedious loading drill was dangerous if not properly executed, and his Ming soldiers had seen firearms for the first time only a week earlier.

He looked away from the two red-and-gilt palanquins, actually small houses on wheels standing beside the parade ground. Dr. Paul Hsü sat alone on the veranda of the nearer palanquin, having permitted his entourage to disperse. Some of his attendants were strolling northwest along the paved road to the Nankou Pass, halfway between Peking and the Great Wall. Others wandered east toward the Valley of the Tombs, where the former emperors of the Great Ming Dynasty lay in magnificent mausoleums. Somehow, Francis felt, the holiday atmosphere was inappropriate to the inspection of a battalion of arquebusiers by the Minister who was its sponsor.

Determinedly martial, the young officer deplored his eyes' tendency to stray toward the second palanquin. Candida Soo and her niece Marta sat on its veranda, modestly enveloped in light-blue cloaks against the soldiers' glances. The dry heat of day lingered, and the ladies fluttered their silk fans.

"I think he's fascinating...even if he is very strange to us," Candida whispered. "He's so tall and so earnest."

"But his hair..." Marta shielded her lips with her fan, though Francis could not possibly overhear them. "His hair is such a peculiar color...like goose grease. And his face, it's so red...as if he'd drunk too much rice wine."

"Perhaps he'd look better with a beard."

"That same color? I don't think so. Anyway, you heard him say he wouldn't grow a beard."

"Except for the beard, he's not so different from the Spiritual Fathers, though," Candida mused. "Only much younger."

"I don't think of the Spiritual Fathers as men...not really."

"The backs of his hands! Have you..."

"Yes, I have." Marta shuddered delicately. "Covered with hair the same color...like a yellow monkey."

"It's hard to say whether he's attractive or hideous. Isn't it?"

"Really hard to say, Candida. He's so outlandish. But he *is* interesting, I suppose."

Having overheard similar comments from men who did not know he understood their language, Francis would not have been surprised at the tenor of their conversation. He would have been shocked that the ladies whose reticent good manners he admired should discuss him so frankly. But he was absorbed in his task.

The Chinese troops he commanded were no more awkward than European pikemen just learning to fire the cumbersome arquebus. Some five hundred recruits were mastering the routine with surprising ease, though impeded by voluminous coats so different from the baggy breeches of European arquebusiers. The glowing two-headed snakes of their match fuses traced fiery arabesques against the pastel sky.

Francis wished he could arm his men with the ingenious new wheel-lock musket, whose steel disk struck sparks from a flint to ignite the priming powder. But even in Europe, the wheel-lock was reserved for officers because it was so costly.

Still, the matchlock fired every time the glowing fuse dropped onto the flash pan. Since Chinese artisans were already making matchlock arquebuses, they would serve—at least until the Tartars mastered them.

"*Chün-pei wu-chi!*" Francis's company commanders echoed his high-pitched command: "Prepare weapons!"

Each soldier clutched his forked firing-rest with the same left hand that held his glowing fuse.

"*Chia huo-yao!*" Again the command was repeated: "Load!"

Transferring the crooked stock of his arquebus to his overburdened left hand, each soldier drew a wooden cartridge from his bandolier.

A ramrod drove home wadding above the powder and the lead balls. Each arquebusier planted his long firing-rest in the ground and laid the heavy barrel in the fork.

"Prime pieces."

The soldiers opened horns of fine-grained priming powder and filled their flash pans. Although they had been repeatedly warned to keep the fuses well away, a volley of premature shots rattled.

"Fix matches." Obscenities rolled across the parade ground as the soldiers painstakingly inserted glowing fuses into serpentine trigger assemblies and secured them with thumbscrews.

"Aim!" The long barrels wavered in their forked rests, then steadied.

"*Kai huo!*" Francis bellowed. "Fire!"

A tattoo from the more alert soldiers preceded the roar as the majority fired and closed with scattered tardy shots.

Francis was satisfied for the moment. Only six minutes had elapsed between the preparatory command and the last shot. Two days earlier it had taken ten minutes, and drill would bring it down to four minutes. Few European troops could consistently do better.

He strode through the twilight toward the row of targets at the far end of the parade ground. They were painted with the villains of the plays-with-music the Chinese adored, the costumes gaudy and the faces black to symbolize evil. The lead balls had shredded the villains and toppled half the butts. His men could already shoot straight.

Dr. Paul Hsü had mustered an elite unit, which included a number of Christians, for this first experiment in training under a European officer. The dedicated soldiers could be rapidly forged into a shock battalion that would terrify—and shatter—attacking Tartars. Other Chinese soldiers, Francis felt, could not be wholly different from his intelligent troops.

Having spent more than a year in the Empire, which was forbidden to the Portuguese of Macao, Francis dismissed their spiteful calumny of the Chinese as "pitifully unwarlike, men properly dressed in women's skirts." Those boredom-racked exiles occupied themselves with vicious intrigues and with facile derogation of the Great Empire. He knew from direct experience the quality of the Chinese.

The declining sun burnished the troops' scarlet helmets, glowing on the golden *yung* ideograms that proclaimed their wearers' courage. *Yung* meant more than brave; it pledged total loyalty to their Emperor and their officers. The battalion, Francis realized exuberantly, was becoming a single entity responsive to his single will. It would triumph or fail as he determined. If he commanded the battalion wisely, it would overwhelm the Emperor's enemies on the battlefields of China and Tartary. If he should err, it would perish in defeat.

His exultation was clouded by awe. Just twenty-three, he was old for his first command by European standards, though youthful by Chinese. He had already fought a dozen battles, but always as a subordinate whose fate was not his own to command. For the first time, he recognized his absolute responsibility not only for his own life, but for the lives of five hundred subordinates as well. The silver lynx of a major of the Great Ming Dynasty embroidered upon the breast of his padded red-and-blue coat required of him fealty, courage, and wisdom.

When the rising wind toyed with the white plumes of his helmet, Francis lifted its heavy weight and mopped his brow. His hair was dark gold against the dove-gray sky.

The slopes of the horseshoe hills to the east were already black, though their peaks glowed with pale fire. Lying in the embrace of those hills, the Valley of the Tombs was an oblong pool from whose dark surface reared the massive arches and rounded tumuli marking the mausoleums of the Great Ming Dynasty. The setting sun gilded the past and the present. The future would be shaped by the arquebusiers of his battalion.

Resuming his burden of responsibility, Francis Arrowsmith clapped his helmet on his head. His Adjutant, the Christian Captain Simon Wu, stood at attention, his thick spectacles misted. Francis nodded, and Simon Wu bellowed a dismissal. The soldiers scattered toward the tents pitched beside a narrow stream that had gnawed deep into the ocher soil.

Francis strode eagerly toward the gilded horse-drawn palanquins beside the parade ground. His full lips rehearsed a greeting, and his light brown eyes were lit with anticipation beneath his dark brows. The stern Major of Arquebusiers was in an instant transformed into an ardent youth.

The outriders and drivers had lit their own campfires some distance away, but Candida and Marta sat on the veranda of the farther palanquin beneath a serpentine-grained cross of persimmon wood. Their forms were indistinct in their light-blue capes, and their high collars were drawn up. Alone on the veranda of the nearer palanquin, Paul Hsü was imposing in a scarlet robe embroidered with five-inch chrysanthemums. His blue-leather belt was clasped with a buckle of green jade. Blue-gray smoke from the slender bamboo tobacco pipe in his cupped hand drifted before the white crane embroidered on his breast.

That crane, his jade buckle, even the size of the chrysanthemums proclaimed Dr. Paul Hsü a Mandarin of the highest among the ten grades of the Empire's rigid hierarchy, just as the title *Doctor* signified that he had excelled in the highest of the three Civil Service examinations. Nowhere else, Francis reflected, were men so rigidly classified as they were by the Great Ming Dynasty. Not only military officers, but civilian officials invariably wore their insignia of rank in public.

That outward display expressed the inner order of a society precisely stratified by power and privilege. The people accepted that stratification, since it was designed to ensure their tranquil prosperity—and normally did so. Titles of nobility were largely ceremonial, and each generation declined one degree until the family was once again untitled. Noble rank did not automatically confer power, as it did in Europe. All power in the Ming Empire flowed directly from the Emperor to his Mandarins, who were qualified by the rigorous Civil Service Examinations in the Sacred Classics of China.

Such was the ideal structure of the Great Empire, and such was normally its actual structure. But the nobility and the commonalty unhesitatingly accepted the divine authority of the Emperor and his Mandarins only when all went well. Insubordination, rebellion, and usurpation burgeoned when natural disasters and human malevolence shook the Confucian State—as they did in the year 1630. Francis's own position testified to the disarray of the realm. Barbarian officers had served the Emperor in the past. But only in a time of acute disorder—and acute danger—would a barbarian officer command a battalion of the Imperial Guard.

Dr. Paul Hsü revealed no perturbation at the disorder that required his presence at a military encampment on a pleasant midsummer evening. His strong features were composed, and his luminous eyes were unclouded, though squinted against his pipe's smoke. His world had, after all, been greatly disturbed since he embarked on his official career shortly before the turn of the century, when the Tartars began to challenge an Empire already racked by natural disasters, by rebellions, and by the intrigues of a corrupt court dominated by rapacious Eunuchs.

"*Chiu-yang!*" The Mandarin spoke softly, deliberately excluding the ladies, who sat silent like actresses awaiting their cue. "Well met! I've looked forward to seeing with my own eyes the results of your endeavors, Major. It goes well, does it? What are your problems? How can I assist you?"

"*Hsien-sheng, huan-ying nin lai...*" Francis was pleased by his growing command of the language. "Sir, I welcome your inspection. All goes well, Sir, very well. The soldiers learn rapidly, and I am profoundly grateful for your constant support."

"That is as it should be. We all do the Lord's work as best we can. How may I assist you further?"

"At this stage, Sir, I have few problems," Francis replied. "Later, perhaps."

"Later, certainly," Dr. Paul laughed.

"I was told I would have trouble getting supplies, that they'd be stolen or diverted. But I've had no such trouble."

"It won't always be that way." Paul Hsü laughed again. "I've done what I could, but some of my countrymen..."

"I shall, if I may, appeal to you when necessary, Sir. Can you tell me what has been happening elsewhere? We hear little of the Tartars."

"Our spies' reports are confused, but the Tartars are clearly withdrawing north of the Great Wall. I believe they are re-forming for a new invasion, though not just yet."

"And Miguel Texeira and Juan Rodriguez?"

"The Captain-Sergeant is ordered to Tengchou on the Gulf of Pohai, where General Ignatius Sün commands. As surely as the Great Wall itself, those straits are our front line."

"And Texeira's cannon?" Francis presisted. "I could use cannon."

"All the cannon have gone to Tengchou with Texeira and his men. But Father Juan Rodriguez departed for Macao four days ago to secure more cannon and two battalions of Portuguese infantry."

"More troops are not necessary. I can...we can train Chinese as arquebusiers. Only secure more cannon...and skilled cannoneers to train Chinese soldiers."

"Your enthusiasm does you credit," Paul Hsü replied. "But we can use more Portuguese troops as a cutting edge. We cannot depend on Chinese troops. They are not all as biddable and diligent as the men I picked for you."

"I bow to your wisdom, Sir. But...I recall now...a boon I'd beg."

"And that is?"

"A banner. The battalion needs a flag of its own and a name of its own. Men fight better when they are an elite unit under their own banner."

"*Tien-chu-di Ying*...the Battalion of the Lord of Heaven, God's Own Battalion. What of that name? And the banner, what have you in mind?"

"God's Own Battalion is splendid," Francis answered. "And the banner. What, Sir, of the double-barred cross, St. Omer's Cross white on a green field as it was for St. Omer's College where I was a schoolboy?"

"Why not? Why not, indeed? It will please the Fathers...the emblem of a Jesuit college. St. Omer's Cross by all means!"

"My men will know they fight in God's cause..."

"Father Adam will no doubt consent to bless the banner," Paul Hsü added. "These two useless women can embroider it. A better occupation than badgering a foolish old man to take them places they don't belong. Women are not needed when an aged Mandarin inspects God's Own Battalion of Arquebusiers."

Having earlier followed Dr. Paul's example and ignored the ladies, Francis now offered them a sweeping bow. By finally alluding to their presence, the Mandarin had indicated that the business of the day was over and that he might address them.

Francis's half smile acknowledged the old man's peppery self-deprecation and greeted Candida and Marta. Paul Hsü would always flout conventions when necessary. Yet he would not have brought the ladies with him unless he felt their presence would, somehow, be useful. But Francis could not see how gratifying their desire to see a military camp would advance the two causes to which the Mandarin had dedicated his remaining years: propagating the True Faith and strengthening the Empire against the Tartars.

"*Shih-jen Ying-chang hau ma?*" Candida greeted him formally. "Major Arrowmaker, are you well?"

"Very well, Madame Soo," he replied with equal formality. "I trust that you and your lady niece are also well."

"We are both very well, though, I must confess, we have this past month missed your company. We have missed our talks and your Latin lessons...greatly."

"I too have felt deprived." Chinese courtesy sometimes imposed a stilted formality. "I have greatly missed your wise comments...and Marta's Chinese lessons, of course."

"We were both eager to see your battalion." Marta's face was half-hidden by her green-silk fan. "We finally persuaded Dr. Paul to allow us to accompany him."

"Still, Arrowmaker, it was hard work persuading my esteemed grandfather," Candida said forthrightly. "Some Mandarins of great age and great wisdom are as stubborn as Shansi mules."

"But Grandfather Hsü," Marta said, "finally condescended to permit us to observe the great work you are doing."

"And it was not too soon, Madame Candida?" He put the question delicately. "Should you be traveling so soon after the coming of your little son?"

"Why, Arrowmaker, the baby was born in March, almost three months ago. Besides, his wetnurse has plenty of milk—and leaves me free to travel."

"Then the Young Lord is well?" Francis dropped the words into the vacuum of his embarrassment at the sheltered Chinese lady's forthrightness.

"Very well indeed," Candida answered. "A veritable marvel, if his great-grandfather is to be believed."

"Truly a miracle," Paul Hsü laughed. "Though it was a greater miracle when his mother stopped instructing her betters long enough to produce him. Francis, I know Marta is anxious to see your fire-belching arquebuses. Will you be good enough to show her?"

"And, Francis, do lend her your arm," Candida instructed. "You cannot know what it is to walk across a broken field on golden lilies."

Supported by Francis's outstretched hand, Marta descended the curved wooden stairway from the palanquin, which was complete in miniature even to a carved red-and-gilt balustrade. Dr. Paul's offhand remark was her first knowledge of her keen desire to see the arquebuses. Resigned to pretending interest in the weapons that had fouled the twilight with their black-powder fumes, she picked her way among the stones, leaning on Francis's arm.

Happily bearing that slight burden, Francis looked down with pleasure at the golden-dragon pin that impaled the intricate knots of her glossy black hair. He marveled at the thick eyelashes that shaded her downcast eyes, and he delighted in the pink flush that mantled her cheekbones, accentuating the porcelain translucence of her skin. He could not summon a single phrase to enliven the sudden intimacy Dr. Paul had forced upon them.

Impelled by Candida's enthusiasm, they had met once or twice a week since mid-February to exchange Latin for Chinese lessons and to discuss their wholly different worlds. But they had never before that moment been together beyond the hearing of any other person.

Walking for the first time in her life on a rough surface, Marta studied the ground at their feet. Her sheltered girlhood had never before that moment taken her away from soft carpets, level floors, and rolled paths. Despite her care, her crippled feet stumbled on the broken turf. She clutched Francis's arm, though she feared the gesture would give him a wholly false impression.

No more than Francis could Marta cope with the predicament into which Dr. Paul Hsü had thrust her. Strolling through the twilight of Midsummer's Day with a strange man was not only unprecedented but faintly scandalous. Though her Aunt Candida and the Minister of Rites himself watched over their progress, she felt subtly cheapened. No more than Francis could she think of a single pleasantry to ease their mutual confusion.

She did not know what Paul Hsü intended, if indeed he had not merely yielded to a whim. But she wished herself a hundred miles away from that boot-scarred field. The black-powder fumes stung her eyes, and she was embarrassed by her dependence on Francis's support.

The answer to Candida's earlier question came to Marta abruptly: The barbarian was not at all attractive. Having been alternately intrigued and repelled by his curious appearance and his clumsy manners, she concluded that she

95

found him grotesque. An oddity like a carp with two tails was interesting, but it was still a monstrosity. A carp should no more have two tails than a man have a jutting beak like a bird and grease-colored yellow hair. Marta shuddered and wondered whether to pretend to turn an ankle so that he would take her back to the security of the palanquin.

"They are striking together, aren't they?" Candida asked insensitively. "It's a pity that..."

"We are accountable to her parents," Paul Hsü said. "A girl of good family walking alone with a young man, even worse a young barbarian.... But what were you saying, Candida?"

"Nothing in particular, Grandfather, I fear. Though it is a pity..."

"Perhaps it is," he mused. "But perhaps it need not be. Candida, are you aware of the decision Hung Wu, the Founding Emperor of the Ming Dynasty, took when he found many Mongols and Westerners within China's borders?"

"Grandfather, you know I'm no great scholar. Besides, I don't see what that has to do..."

"I shall soon come to the point. Meanwhile, let us ponder the symbolism of a name. The Founding Emperor adopted the reign-name Hung Wu when he ascended the Dragon Throne after driving out the Mongols. As you know, Hung Wu means a torrent of arms, the preponderance of military force..."

"Grandfather," Candida interrupted, "I am not a ten-year-old to be instructed in history."

"Nonetheless, instructing is good for an old man's soul. Hung Wu's son took the reign-name Chien Wen, which was not very filial. *Wen*, letters, is the opposite of *wu*, arms. The Second Ming Emperor placed the preponderant emphasis on the arts of peace."

"Grandfather, the sages counsel women to patient obedience. But I grow impatient with your digression."

"My meaning is clear: Gentle civilization will prevail over the rough war." The Mandarin smiled. "The *Yin*, the female principle, will prevail over the *Yang*, the male principle."

"In the case of our young friends? You can't mean..."

"Perhaps I can. The first Ming Emperor, as I began to tell you, found many outlanders within the realm. He would have preferred none—and he forbade others' entering the Empire. It was, however, impractical to expel so many who were already resident."

"Grandfather, I really don't see.... What has that to do with our time centuries later, when the Emperor invites Westerners to fight the Tartars?"

"Patience, you said, was a feminine virtue," Paul Hsü chided. "The wise Founding Emperor decreed that Mongols and Westerners might not marry among themselves. Since they could *not* intermarry, but *could* marry Chinese, the outlanders would soon vanish into the general population. Thus a grave internal threat to the Empire was removed."

"That's very interesting historically, but..."

"The law has never been altered. Despite the general belief that it is forbidden, outlanders *are* permitted to marry Chinese. As Minister of Rites, I see no bar to marriage between a Chinese and a Westerner—providing no disagreement on religion impedes it."

"Grandfather, you are a sly old fox. But.... No, it cannot be. Marta would be appalled."

"Appalled she may be. But obedient she will be, if I so decide."

"That is detestable, Grandfather. How can you possibly..."

"Detestable, perhaps. Nonetheless, it may prove necessary. And, if it is necessary, it will be done."

"I don't understand. Why necessary?"

"Candida, I can confide in you...as in no one else. I must keep the young barbarian by me, bind him to China and to myself. His skills could help save the Empire from the Tartars—and assist greatly in spreading the Faith. How better can I bind him?"

"But Marta would hate it."

"I imagine the Arrowmaker will not be wildly enthusiastic. He still dreams of returning to England with a great fortune. But he, too, can be managed."

"I see the advantage, Grandfather. For China and the Faith. But I cannot like it...any more than Marta will."

"You are not required to like it. No more is Marta. You will both do as you are told when—if—the time comes. Meanwhile, you may hint to Marta. Begin to prepare her very gently, but no more just yet."

Peking

SUNDAY, AUGUST 26, 1630

INCENSE smoke wreathed the red eaves and clung to the yellow-brick walls of the octagonal chapel of the Jesuit House in the Northern Capital of the Great Ming Dynasty. The closing chords of the Mass by the Spanish composer Tommaso Vittoria swelled from the organ loft into the alien air. The melody was achingly familiar and the sonorous instrument was quintessentially European, but the organist was a Chinese lay brother.

Tears prickled Francis Arrowsmith's eyelids, and a dark cloud drifted across the normally sunny terrain of his emotions. He yearned for Europe, which lay two years' journey distant, and he wondered whether he would ever again see the English College of St. Omer.

Vittoria's music was wholly European, but the European priests' green-and-white Mass vestments were ornately embroidered and cut with wide sleeves in the Chinese manner. An unpriestly beard framed Adam Schall's sardonic features, and his blue eyes looked out under a tall black hat. The Fathers wore horsehair hats even when saying Mass because the Mandarins, to whose status the Jesuits successfully aspired, never doffed their own hats in public. Papal dispensation also permitted the Fathers to wear their untonsured hair flowing over their collars, because that was the style of the Mandarins.

The Christian priests aped the pagan Mandarins in all ways, lest they be despised as were the beardless, shaven-pated Buddhist monks. Father Matthew Ricci had himself ordained that the Jesuits should win all Chinese to the Universal Truth by first winning acceptance as equals of the lordly Mandarins.

Even the Liturgy had been altered with Rome's reluctant sanction. Instead of the familiar Latin, Holy Mass was celebrated in the Officials' Language. It was, Francis chafed, like the heretical services recited by false priests in English, French, or German. The Mass seemed neither holy nor universal, indeed, hardly Catholic, when Father Adam released the congregation. He intoned *Hsien-tsai li-pai chiu wan-la!* instead of the *Ite missa est!* that had concluded Holy Mass in all Christendom for a millennium and a half.

The facile Chinese maxim, characteristically culinary, justified "Changing the soup's water while retaining the essential seasoning!—*Huang tang, pu huan yao!*" The Jesuits would reply with that self-justifying adage when the Dominicans of Macao charged them to consider whether their laxness did not nurture heresy. A homely English maxim straightforwardly refuted that Chinese sophistry. The Jesuits, Francis feared, were "throwing out the baby with the bath water."

Nonetheless, he was only slightly more troubled by such doubts than any other healthy young soldier would be. His stomach rumbled to remind him that theology was fit meat for elderly dyspeptics, but not for himself. Having drunk too much rice wine with his Adjutant before riding to Peking the preceding evening, he was eager for the breakfast Father Adam Schall had promised.

Francis was relieved when he saw that Adam Schall had put on the silk robe he wore in public rather than the cotton cassock he preferred at home. He had not looked forward to the ascetic company of the Jesuit's colleagues, whose heads seemed always to revolve among the heavenly spheres that were their own particular sphere in Dr. Paul Hsü's Bureau of the Calendar.

The burly German was exuberant—almost boisterous—for a man who, bound by the rules of the Church, had taken no food for twelve hours. His long blond hair swung like a shimmering curtain, and his normally saturnine features were lit by a broad smile.

Too often immersed in his own complex thoughts, when he hid behind a wall of wry humor, the priest from the Rhineland was, almost as often, childlike in his gaiety. Aware of the contradictory aspects of his own nature, the man who was childless by vocation was especially fond of children, with whom he was invariably gentle.

Today Adam Schall was almost manic in his exuberance, glorying in the respite from the strict self-discipline he normally imposed upon himself. He had, he recalled, always found it hard to submit to discipline, even as a boy at the Jesuit College of the Three Crowns in Cologne. The wild blood of his warrior ancestors ran so strong that he still had to struggle to force himself to bow meekly to the strict rule of the Society of Jesus. But, he consoled himself, Ignatius Loyola, the founder of the Society, had been similarly tormented, even after he broke his sword to take up the breviary. The deeply spiritual Ignatius, too, had been torn between his philosophic inclination and his delight in the clash of arms.

Recruited for the Mission in 1614, Adam Schall had not entered China until early 1623. He had chafed at the delay imposed by the persecution of Christianity in the Empire at that time. Although one side of him still resented the prolongation of his apprenticeship, Adam Schall's other side was thankful. If he had not been forced to linger in Macao, he would not have fought against the Dutch invasion on Midsummer's Day 1622.

When he recalled that mad battle, his hand groped involuntarily for the shaft of the halberd he had swung against a Dutch captain, almost decapitating him. Between elation and chagrin, the priest remembered the blood lust that had gripped him when he charged into the fray shouting a hoarse Teutonic war cry. He acknowledged ruefully that he had enjoyed the hand-to-hand combat, actually enjoyed it. He had also trained the gaping mortar on Mount Guia that blew up the Dutch powder magazine. But that detached mathematical exercise had not stirred him as had the clatter of swords.

His deep friendship with Dr. Paul Hsü, Adam Schall mused, had probably burgeoned because the older man's nature also displayed two distinct sides, the scholarly and the military. The Mandarin had recognized him as a kindred spirit when he first arrived in Peking, and they had composed a monograph on lunar eclipses together. Sent to Sian, the former capital in Shensi Province, to survey a possible overland route to Europe, the German had not only continued his compulsive study of the Chinese language and the Chinese Classics, but had also written a book of simplified lives of the saints with a great Christian Chinese author. He had returned to Peking just a year earlier because the death of the leading Jesuit in the Bureau of the Calendar urgently necessitated a replacement. Although he was noted even in the learned Society for his profound knowledge of astronomy, renewing his friendship with Dr. Paul Hsü was Adam Schall's greatest delight in that hurried return.

All the while, he had continued his study of Chinese. Some twelve years of concentration had finally placed his feet, he felt, on the lower rungs of the ladder he, like a conscientious Mandarin, would climb all his life toward the perfect learning he could never attain. Meanwhile, he found his association with the young English soldier refreshing to his spirit, because, he acknowledged, it released the madcap side of his nature. Today, he felt as reckless as a boy unburdened by any learning whatsoever.

"Francis, my good lad, we shall not breakfast with sour pedants today." Adam Schall's gaiety enlivened his precise Portuguese. "We are off to a feast at *Lao Chiao Wang*, the Old Dumpling King."

"And we eat old dumplings... very old dumplings?" Francis rose to Schall's mood.

"No, my son, young dumplings, very young dumplings sweet and tender as baby clouds. Come along now. I am hungry, even if you are not."

Clasping Francis's arm, the priest led him through the gates of the former pagan Temple of Benevolence into a street swirling with movement. Sunday was no different from any other day to the Chinese, who called it simply Day Seven and took their holidays at other times—any and all other times, according to Adam Schall. The priest's sarcasm contended that every day was Sunday in Peking "because the people refrain from laboring—every day."

One wearing the dress uniform of a major, the other a black-silk Mandarin's robe, the tall foreigners were immediately surrounded by gawking Chinese. That circle moved with them, constantly changing its composition but never diminishing. Their alien presence did not otherwise affect the kaleidoscopic movement of men and boys intent on their own pursuits. Except during the bitter North China winter, the people of Peking carried out all but their most intimate affairs before all eyes in the streets. August was high summer, the atmosphere so close most males fled their dwellings for the somewhat less oppressive heat of the thoroughfares.

Women and girls were secluded behind the blank walls that lined both the broad *malu,* the horse roads, and the narrow alleys called *hutung.* Despite the claustrophobic heat, they pursued their female concerns in sealed courtyards or under gray-tile roofs. From time to time a door opened a crack to reveal a brightly flowered sleeve hastily withdrawn or a pair of curious eyes hastily averted. The occasional slave girl or maidservant was ignored as she strode among the shops on lewdly unbound feet. Despite the heat, drawn curtains distinguished the sedan chairs of ladies.

Coming to Peking for the first time, an outlander might believe he had stumbled upon a race composed exclusively of males, a race that imported females for procreation as the Amazons of Trebizond briefly entertained captured enemy soldiers. Of course, the analogy was not quite appropriate. As the Chinese said to justify their polygamy: "One teapot can fill many cups, and one rooster can serve many hens. But one teacup to a single teapot, one rooster to one hen is pointless waste."

The constant bustle of the street was even more free and animated because it was almost exclusively masculine. The colorful life revealed by the open mat-shutters and the furled bamboo screens of shops, restaurants, and shrines flowed into the activity on the roads.

A stone-gray bullock released from its shafts sprawled in the yellow dust beside a cart heaped with white-wrapped bales before a shop whose fluttering awning boasted OUR CUS-TOMERS CAN CHOOSE FROM ALL THE MAGNIFICENT CLOTHS OF SUNGKIANG. In the shaded interior, an indecisive customer served by a wearily patient clerk was entwined in a rainbow's hoard of fabrics. Intent on his choice, he was oblivious to the bleating of five matted sheep in the frail wooden pen next door. Those terrified animals were the stock in trade of the adjoining shop, where an abundantly bearded butcher offered red chunks of mutton to an elderly gentleman whose white hair was tied in a neat bun. On the other side of the shoulder-high, plaited-bamboo partition that divided the shop length-wise a second butcher, shaded by a tall yellow-paper umbrella, carved strips of blush-pink pork for a youth dangling a cylindrical shopping basket.

No one revealed his awareness that the sunny afternoon was rent by a sow's unearthly squeals. Two red-armed butchers kneeled in the dust under the terrified stare of a second sow to saw at that sow's throat with long knives. No more did the elderly Moslem gentleman at the mutton counter display any concern that, on the other side of the flimsy partition, men were trafficking in pork, whose mere presence was proscribed as defiling by the Koran. Both customers and butchers were practical Chinese. It was only common sense to ignore the unholy juxtaposition—just as it was only common sense to ignore the high-pitched swearing of two beggars contending with clenched fists and flying feet for an advantageous corner. Though their gyrations were grand entertainment for idlers, respectable citizens walked wide of the affray, lest they become involved.

A penetrating stench floated over the streets: rich brown soy sauce, ammoniacal animal urine, pungent incense burning before street shrines, acrid human sweat, sharp vinegar, and the musty smell of the powdered soil borne by the winds from Inner Asia.

Supercilious mules, haughty Bactrian camels, patient donkeys, and glossy horses pushed through the throng. They harked neither to the falsetto oratorio of a historical play-with-music nor to the shouts of children skipping after a toy salesman whose wares dangled from the ribs of an orange umbrella. Beasts and men alike seemed deaf to the ceaseless din: the shouts of hawkers and the exasperated curses of teamsters; the wailing violins and the pounding drums that accompanied the singers; the clatter of metalworkers and the hammer blows of carpenters. Yet that cacophony was as palpable as the golden dust floating in the sunlight.

"A quiet Sunday afternoon in Peking." Adam Schall grinned. "Have you seen their festivals yet? Now, they are *really* noisy."

"Not yet, but I suppose there's time." To Francis's surprise his conversational tone was audible. "I'll probably sit on the outskirts of Peking forever... still trying to whip my battalion into shape."

"Trouble with your troops? You told me a month or so ago that Dr. Paul was running everything as smooth as silk."

"But there are others. I sometimes think I'm being deliberately thwarted—and constantly spied on into the bargain. But, I suppose, that's moon-madness, just fantasy."

"I would be surprised if you were *not* spied on. We all are,
103

and we're easy to watch because we're so obtrusive. But deliberate frustration, you say? That's likely. Tell me about it?"

"Later, Father Adam. It's a dull little tale, after all."

A barrow heaped with firewood rolled imperiously between them, its single wooden-spoked wheel, as tall as a man, alternately squeaking and wailing. The villainously bearded barrowman squinted benignly under lids encrusted with black-and-yellow scabs.

"Father Adam, something else is troubling me," Francis ventured when they walked side by side again. "And it's more your province than my military problems. They'll be solved. It's just a matter of time."

"I am not so confident," Adam Schall observed dryly. "In China time can make problems worse."

"I know this isn't the best place or time," Francis continued. "You'll think I'm simple...perhaps presumptuous. But it has troubled me, this..."

"What is it then, my lad?"

"What is the limit, Father? How far can you stretch the Liturgy and the practices of Holy Church before something snaps? Already your Mass seems to me less a Christian service to God than..."

"*Huan tang, pu huan yao!*" Adam Schall spontaneously offered the Jesuits' facile justification. "We've changed the broth, but not the essence. Mass celebrated in Chinese? What makes you think Latin is either sacred or sacrosanct? Did Our Lord and His Apostles converse in Latin or in Aramaic? You must know adopting Latin was a political expedient. It enabled Holy Church to reach more potential converts and to placate the civil authorities. That's only what we're doing."

"Is nothing sacred?" Francis protested.

"Vestments? The early Fathers of the Church adopted the costumes of different regions, just as we're doing. Candles, incense, holy water, and oil—all were used in pagan rites before Holy Church took them up. The externals matter greatly, but they are *not* all-important. The Church lives and grows and endures by adapting."

"And the spiritual essence?" Francis insisted hotly. "Matters like ancestor worship?"

"That...those important matters...are truly interesting questions, even debatable." The Jesuit offered that minute concession as grudgingly as he might surrender a splinter of the True Cross. "They merit discussion. But not now. Not here. Another time we can discuss those matters."

Rejected for the time being, Francis was silent as they passed an open-fronted guard post. Constables wearing short blue tunics, baggy white knee-length trousers, and high felt boots lounged, playing cards in their hands, on long platforms beneath the armory of curved swords and twin-pronged spears hanging on the wall. A placard enjoined those guardians to ZEALOUSLY PROTECT THE CITY'S LIVES AND TREASURES. Adjoining the police post either by design or by happy chance, a rush-shuttered facade displayed the discreet advertisement CHUAN-MEN CHIEH-KE...SPECIALIST IN SETTING BROKEN BONES. Such exclusive expertise was unknown in Europe, where barber-surgeons followed the armies, crudely ministering to the wounded.

A fringe of red curtains printed with virtually illegible ideograms in the scrawled grass-script hung limp beneath the high-propped shutters of the next shop. The fringe was intended to keep out insect pests with its flapping, but no wind stirred the dense air. An armada of metallic-green flies, each as large as a date, swooped through the spice-heavy atmosphere within. The blowflies alighted on time-rubbed pine tables, on patrons shoveling food into their mouths with bamboo chopsticks, and on uncooked dumplings arrayed on large wooden trays.

Two sweaty cooks standing over a boiling cauldron mechanically waved off the flies. They wore only wooden clogs and once-white trousers cut off above the knee. A crimson placard was inscribed with three golden ideograms LAO CHIAO WANG...OLD DUMPLING KING, but Francis already knew they had come to their destination.

Stooping to keep his square horsehair hat from brushing the lintel, Adam Schall preceded Francis into the eating-shop. He grinned broadly, waved his arms expansively, and inquired loudly: *"Chin-tien yo mei-yo tung-hsi chih?*...Do you have anything worth eating today?"

"Ah, Shen-fu lai-la." The cooks' bare pot bellies quivered when they laughed, and they displayed garlands of gold teeth. "The Spiritual Father is here. The good old Spiritual Father has come. Naturally, we have every possible thing."

The Jesuit settled upon a rickety bench with the air of an habitué. Ignoring the menu scrawled in black ideograms on paper slips tacked to the walls, he gave his order to the waiter. That pimpled youth wore a generously stained white coat over a ragged singlet and calf-length trousers. Scuffed straw sandals clung to his grimy feet by leather thongs.

"Tou-pi tang yu-tiao, se-gen..." The German priest's rapid Chinese was unaccented. "Bean-curd-skin soup; four fried bread sticks; small-steamer dumplings, four orders; and steamed dumplings, six orders. That's about it, and we'll drink tea."

"Hsierh-hsierh, Shen-fu...," the uneducated youth answered in the same thick Peking accent. "Thank you, Spiritual Father. The cooks'll prepare something specially good for you."

"Ni kai wan-hsiaerh ma?" Adam Schall replied in an even thicker brogue, rolling the final *erh* sounds of the Peking dialect. "Are you joking? Everything here is exactly the same. There's never anything specially good."

The chuckling youth shouted the order and repeated the jest to the appreciative cooks. The patrons joined their astonished laughter to the uproar. Two sleek merchants at a corner table looked at each other in incredulous speculation; four sweat-stained coolies wiping their faces with grimy hand towels gaped open-mouthed; and three thin youths, candidates for the Civil Service Examinations by their strained look, black-rimmed spectacles, and heavily patched scholar's gowns, stared frankly.

"They're used to me here," Schall observed needlessly. "But they're all the same, even if they know you well. They think of all foreigners as clever monkeys. If the monkey speaks a few words of Chinese, it's a wonder. If he makes a joke, it's six miracles rolled into one."

Sipping tea from a cracked cup, Francis nodded. His mouth was full of the boiled peanuts offered as an appetizer.

"I wanted to get you alone," Schall explained. "So I brought you here. The food is good....Simple, robust *pien-fan*. How do you say it? Yes, plain food. But, first, tell me about your troubles, your military problems, not your theological problems. I'm off duty just now."

"I cannot understand the Chinese, not at all." Francis was passionate in his perplexity. "They appeal for Portuguese troops, then allow only a handful to enter the country—and send those few off to Tengchou. Tengchou is hardly the front line when Peking itself is still threatened. They order me to train arquebusiers and provide everything I need. Then, just as I'm succeeding, a thousand obstacles appear. Almost it seems, deliberately contrived, as if they didn't want me to succeed...as if they didn't want the most formidable battalion in the Extreme East."

"Perhaps they don't really. But what kind of obstacles?"

"Little things, Father Adam. Perhaps it sounds like straining at gnats. I can't come to terms with the Chinese. They're so far ahead of us in so many ways. I never saw an expert in mending broken bones in Europe, but there's one next door in this middling neighborhood. Their agriculture, their canals, and their cuisine are centuries ahead of Europe, like their education and their communications. But they are so backward in some ways you would think they were expelled from the Garden of Eden only last year."

"What kind of obstacles, Francis?"

"They invented gunpowder, everyone says." Relieved by unburdening himself, Francis still disregarded the priest's question. "I believe that when I see their fireworks...so ingenious and so refined. But I must teach my soldiers time and time again how to mix saltpeter, sulfur, and charcoal for gunpowder. And they still blow themselves up!"

"Granted they've lost their touch in the martial arts. But, Francis, what are these deliberate obstacles?"

"I cannot get an arquebus mended properly, though they have many cunning artisans. As soon as I train a man for the task, he is transferred. Needed elsewhere, they tell me. Or his mother dies, and he must go off to bury her, never returning."

"They do mourn a parent for three years, you know."

"Sixty-four men out of five hundred? More than one in ten suffering the same loss in a few months?"

"Perhaps not," the priest conceded. "But what else?"

"Uniforms, tenting, and staples are short. Flour fails to arrive...or salted vegetables. Now they can't find fresh cabbage in August. A prohibition on firing practice for ten days because of a festival no one ever heard of. It goes on and on, Father Adam. I think I'm going moon-mad."

"Moon-mad you are not, Francis. The pattern is clear enough. The obstacles are deliberate."

"But why, Father Adam, why? I'm only trying to train *their* troops to defend *them* against the Tartars. How can any Chinese object? The entire court isn't in the pay of the Tartars, is it?"

"Only a few courtiers, not all. But the Court party doesn't want you to become strong. You, of course, meaning Dr. Paul, the Christian Mandarins, and the reformers, and us Jesuits. Thus your obstacles...undoubtedly deliberate."

"I still cannot understand it. How can *any* Chinese want

107

his country...his Emperor's troops...to be weak when *all* Chinese are threatened by the Tartars?"

"It's really quite simple. The Court Eunuchs, the diehard conservative Mandarins, and the old gentry believe China is invincible...dismiss the Tartar threat. They are far more worried that you and Dr. Paul may succeed. If you do, their power, their wealth, their Confucian doctrine—all will be mortally imperiled."

"But how? Why?" Virtually incoherent, Francis persisted.

"Look you, Francis, they believe there are worse things than an impossible Tartar conquest of China."

"Worse than a Tartar conquest?"

"Unquestionably! Even if the Tartars triumph, they believe, the Confucian system will endure. But the followers of that evil Eunuch, the Black Premier, cannot allow Christian doctrines and Christian weapons to prevail. Our triumph would fatally undermine the sacred Confucian system."

"That's ridiculous. We...you don't seek to..."

"*We* know that, but *they* won't believe it. A few years ago, Dr. Paul was almost exiled because he dared train a few soldiers with modern weapons. Only the Lord's Grace, giving us a new Emperor, preserved him to become Minister of Rites."

"But Dr. Paul is now powerful. Why can he not..."

"He does all he can. But he contends with the dead weight of custom and with myriads of little men terrified for their privileges."

"Then it's hopeless, is it? My task, perhaps yours as well."

"I did not say that. I do not believe that at all. If I did, I would....But here is the food."

"I could eat a horse."

"You may yet in China. But not at the Old Dumpling King."

The pimpled youth slapped down two bowls in which strips of the crisp skin of hard bean curd floated on steaming white soup. He returned balancing four split-bamboo sieves of steamed dumplings, miniature purses of translucent dough stuffed with minced shrimp and vegetables. A saucer of light-brown vinegar and shaved fresh ginger accompanied them.

"These are *hsiao-lung pao,* the little steamer packets," Schall said. "One dips them in the vinegar."

The youth returned with six blue-and-white platters, each holding twelve *chiao-tze,* boiled dumplings like plump half

108

moons. Soy sauce, vinegar, sesame oil, and hot-pepper oil in small jugs accompanied that prime North China dish.

Their conversation gave way to companionable grunts from full mouths. The merchants at the corner table, great trenchermen themselves by their rotundity, laid down their chopsticks to gape at the foreigners' prowess.

"Look," one said loudly. "They not only speak Chinese, but can even use chopsticks. And each eats enough for three starved coolies."

Adam Schall spluttered into his soup like a beached walrus. His first hunger satisfied, he wiped his mustaches with a damp cloth, laid his chopsticks on the oilslick table, and said: "I'll have a little rest. Now tell me about the spying."

"Do you know my secretary Joseph King?" Francis asked. "A Christian slave, condemned for his father's purported treason."

"A Christian slave? Outrageous!"

"Nonetheless, Dr. Paul presented Joseph to me.... Said I could depend upon him in all things."

"Well, that's different, of course. But what of this Joseph King?"

"Joseph King first warned me. You may know my adjutant. He is called Simon Wu. Since Joseph warned me, I have four times seen Simon in conversation with unknown horsemen. Joseph has twice seen him pass over written messages. New harassment followed each time. It looks like spying to me."

"Assuredly it is. Spying and sabotage!" The priest's verdict was certain. "First, I do know Simon Wu. His family is notorious for its connection with the Black Premier's secret police. Second, everyone, as I said earlier, is watched by the (I do not exaggerate) four million spies of the Eunuchs. Third, the Black Premier commands not only the Flamboyant Cloaks, the uniformed shock troops of the state police, but also the Eastern Chamber, which controls its secret agents. Finally, your battalion could rival the Flamboyant Cloaks in the Emperor's affections. *Quod erat demonstrandum!*"

"It is not my imagination, then?"

"Certainly not. Fear and intrigue, suspicion and trickery rule China. The closer to the Court, the worse the stench."

"What can I do, Father Adam?"

"Guard your Faith and consult your Faith. If the Lord God did not wish it, we would not be at the heart of the Empire."

"And beyond faith?"

"Persist, spurning despair and trusting in the Lord. Another related matter I shall discuss in a moment. And use their own devices against them. Set loyal soldiers and your secretary to watch Simon Wu. Inform Dr. Paul and myself, so that we can anticipate his designs. Above all, study Sün Tze."

"Sün Tze? Who is that?"

"Sün Tze is memorized by every educated man. He is China's Xenophon, Caesar, and Machiavelli all in one. A great general in the fourth century before the birth of Our Lord, he was the author of *Thirteen Strategic Precepts*. The thirteenth deals with secret agents."

"That, too?"

"That, too! Nothing new under the Chinese Heaven. Regarding what he calls 'doubled agents,' Sün Tze advises: 'It is essential to discover the enemy agents who spy on you. You must then turn them to your service by granting them their lives—and by offering lavish rewards.' Food for thought?"

"Food for thought, indeed—and action, perhaps. I hadn't thought China so complex."

"All Mandarins read Sün Tze...and shape their actions accordingly. That is the reality you must face. You must read Sün Tze, understand Sün Tze, and follow Sün Tze! Otherwise you cannot be a successful Ming officer."

They had abstractedly eaten their way through the *chiaotze* while they talked. The priest asked the waiter to go to the public market for persimmons from Kwangtung Province in the southeast and grapes from Kansu Province in the northwest to round out the meal. In Europe, men could enjoy the delicacies of distant lands only smoked, pickled, or preserved with the spices merchant-adventurers brought from Asia. But those exotic fruits, brought by swift barges and caravans, were sold at the open market near the Hsüan Wu Gate for modest prices.

"Now, as to the other matter I mentioned earlier," the Jesuit said.

"Yes," Francis acknowledged drowsily. "I remember your mentioning..."

"Dr. Paul came to me yesterday to discuss a proposed marriage. He has asked me to play the father of the bridegroom because the bridegroom is fatherless."

"That is an honor for you, isn't it? Though why you're telling me..."

"I approve heartily." The priest was emphatic. "The proposal is as dear to my heart as it is to the Minister's. Like him, I see great benefits...not only for the principals and their families, but for the Faith and the Empire."

"Then why not talk to this prospective bridegroom?" Francis asked. "Why waste your eloquence on me?"

"I *am* talking to the prospective bridegroom....And I shall be very eloquent."

"You're jesting!" Francis was alert. "They warned me in Macao your humor was wicked."

"I am *not* jesting. The Mandarin James Soo has proposed his daughter Marta as *your* bride. Blessed by Heaven, your marriage will be a bridge between European Christians and Chinese Christians. If I were the father of your flesh, I would agree immediately. Since I am only your spiritual father, I must ask you."

"It's ridiculous...ludicrous!" Francis exploded. "I'm a soldier, not some metaphysical bridge-builder. Besides, Chinese cannot marry barbarians. The Court will not permit it."

"Paul Hsü is Minister of Rites....And he will permit it."

"Preposterous!" Francis sputtered. "What did Marta say when they talked such nonsense to her?"

"I have no idea. But Dr. Paul would not come to me if it were not feasible."

"Preposterous, Father Adam, absolutely preposterous. For one thing, I shall only stay another year or two."

"I think you will find that your life is here for the most part, the better part," the priest observed coolly. "That is clearly the Lord's Will. Besides, you have already given too much to wooing China to desert China."

"Be that as it may, Father Adam, there is no reason to marry in haste." Francis's stubborn Lancashire blood asserted itself. "And I will not be told to marry this Miss or that Miss by strangers...virtual strangers."

"Then you will never marry as long as you remain in China. That is how marriage is arranged here—by parents and marriage brokers."

"And would that be so bad, my not marrying?"

"*You* are not vowed to celibacy. Would you be celibate still if you found yourself in China ten or twenty years hence? As celibate, I mean, as you are now."

Francis winced at the priest's apparent knowledge of his occasional visits to Flower Houses and replied weakly: "I suppose not. Certainly not if I *were* here ten or twenty years from now. Or, I suppose, even two or three years."

"That principle established, there is no impediment to discussing Dr. Paul's proposal, is there?"

"True Jesuitical reasoning, Father Adam, erecting a sure conclusion upon a frail hypothesis. I should have expected it. Yes, you may talk about it as much as you wish. But remember, I will never agree!"

Peking

"CHING ting wo shuo hua..." Marta Soo was plaintive. "Please listen to me, Aunt Candida. I'm so confused and afraid. Sometimes I think I'd rather enter a convent."

The women's quarters of her father's house were a sanctuary where Marta could let slip the demure calm she displayed in public like all well-bred Chinese maidens. An air of self-effacing obedience she always put on before venturing outside, just as she blackened her eyebrows and rouged her lips. To omit either artifice would be unmaidenly, even unwomanly—and would frighten away the parents of prospective bridegrooms. She was ripe for marriage, perhaps faintly overripe, having passed her seventeenth birthday two months earlier.

"I sympathize with you, my dear, but you know you cannot enter a convent." Candida smiled encouragingly. "Where could you find a Christian convent in China?"

"But you must know how I feel." Marta pleaded with her aunt. "Christianity teaches that women are not chattels. We have souls just like men. Yet it seems your grandfather just wants to give me away...like a jade carving or a celadon bowl....But I'm not..."

"Assuredly not, Marta. You are far more valuable. You're

113

an exquisite work of art, much more beautiful than that silk you're embroidering."

"Aunt Candida, really I'm not a treasured piece of art without a soul. You said so yourself." Marta dropped her voice, looking at her maidservant, who sat in the corner darning a peach-colored undergarment. "Please don't let this happen to me. Please don't let me be given to a man I hardly know just to bind his loyalty to Dr. Paul."

"How many brides really know their grooms, Marta? Just think. How could you choose your own husband? How many maidens have? Anyway, you would unquestionably be the only wife. That's what you've always wanted."

"Of course I cannot arrange my own marriage. And I do want to be the only wife. But there are so many sons of good families...good Christian families. Please don't let them marry me off to a nobody, a barbarian adventurer. I couldn't bear it."

"The Arrowmaker is a major, the Emperor's officer."

"Aunt Candida, you must know that only makes it worse for me. A soldier...almost the lowest of the low." Tears of frustration at her aunt's obduracy clouded Marta's eyes. "Please, Aunt Candida. It would almost be like marrying a beggar."

The bamboo embroidery frame bent double under Marta's anguished grip and cracked, tearing the fragile silk. The maidservant Ying looked up mildly from her darning. Her round face registered no surprise; she knew her mistress's passionate nature—and, in time, all her secrets.

"Liu-mei tao-shu!" Candida quoted the traditional description of a beautiful woman's anger. "The lovely willow-leaf eyebrows are knotted in unbecoming anger."

Marta did not protest that she was stricken not by anger, but by fear. Unable to speak, she bent down to pat the golden *shih-tzu kou* lying beside her lacquered stool. The lion-dog's silver-and-white mate was stretched on the cool red-and-black floor tiles, forelegs and hindlegs extended languorously.

"All else aside—forgetting he's a foreigner—don't you find him attractive?" Candida pursued her implacable argument. "He isn't really hideous in your eyes, is he?"

"How can I forget he's a barbarian? His looks...his manner, they're so strange. They make me shudder, Aunt Candida. And you are talking about marriage—marriage, not flirtation or...or...dalliance."

"Marta, my dear, what do you know about flirtation...or

114

dalliance? I tell you frankly I'd marry him myself in a moment, if I could. He would assuredly *not* be a tyrant in the house. I like his shy manner and his size. I like a big man, and..."

"I believe you, Aunt Candida. It's hard for me to understand but I believe you really feel that way." Despite her distress, Marta's full lips twitched in involuntary amusement; Candida was already twenty-three, well beyond the age when a woman could think such thoughts about any man other than her husband. "But that's not the question. You're talking about my marriage...the husband I will live with all my life."

"Aside from his yellow hair, he could be Chinese," Candida persisted. "His eyes are a lovely warm brown, not cold blue or gray like some of the Fathers. Their eyes always remind me of bits of broken glass or porcelain. Not Francis, though."

"But a nose like a beak and those great hairy hands." Marta colored at the thought of those hands touching her. "Please don't force me. You know the Court would never approve my marriage to an ocean barbarian and..."

"That is by no means true. Do not forget that Grandfather Paul is Minister of Rites. The decision is his. And I've told you he discovered the Founding Emperor specifically authorized marriage to Western barbarians and Mongols."

"But that was centuries ago. We are—we must be—more civilized now. How can he be so cruel...finding a way to make me...with a barbarian..."

"You weren't so cool when we first talked about Francis."

"But I never thought, Aunt Candida. That was only a wild notion, a foolish notion we giggled about like ten-year-olds. Now it is real...and I am afraid. Can't you try to understand that I'm afraid of this marriage?"

"Afraid? No, I really cannot understand, when your elders are deciding what is truly best for you."

"For me or for them, Aunt?" Marta's distress flared for an instant into anger. "You are pressing me to agree, you keep saying, so that I will help spread Christianity in the Empire. But my Christian faith tells me it is not right for me to be married off like a naughty slave girl who..."

"That is why we beg your willing consent, Marta."

"Aunt Candida, it may be childish of me. But I keep remembering that marriage is the most important step in a woman's life....Even a marriage for reasons of state determines a woman's entire future." Marta paused to compose her confused thoughts. "Even marriage to the son of one's parents' oldest friends. That is why the Sage counseled 'A wise bride is always fearful...'"

"'...but a wise bridegroom need only concern himself that his bride is of good character, since he has other opportunities.'" Candida automatically completed the maxim that encapsulated the bitter wisdom of Chinese women.

"Aunt Candida, please listen to me. This marriage... marrying a barbarian... would be like sailing on an outlanders' ship to an unknown country." Marta smiled in entreaty, and her fingers fluttered as if trying to grasp the elusive thought. "I couldn't know its laws beforehand, but I would have to live by them all my life. I would be an exile in my own land! Can't you see it? Really, can't you?"

"Marta, you are too fanciful for my poor brain." Candida's light tone belittled her niece's fears. "But I do know you are a Christian and he is a Christian. Holy Christian matrimony is blessed—and is far less uncertain than other marriages. Besides, your husband would be the exile...dependent on your family. You would hold the whip hand. For an independent young lady like yourself, it sounds ideal."

"I'm sorry if I am unfilial and rebellious. I do not mean to be. But I beg of you to consider another thing. Not only the Arrowmaker and I are involved. What of the children, Aunt Candida?"

"You *are* strange, Marta. One moment you refuse marriage. The next you worry about children not even conceived. But what of the children?"

"They would be neither Chinese nor barbarian. They'd be half-blood outcastes. What would they look like, barbarians or Chinese? What would they be? Please think about it, Aunt Candida."

The circular wooden moon gate to the inner courtyard trembled under gentle rapping, and the round-faced maidservant laid down her darning. When she opened the door a crack, the warm breath of late summer blew into the shaded chamber.

"The majordomo announces that the Lady Candida's noble grandfather has come," the maidservant said. "Minister Hsü wishes to speak with my lady and her aunt."

"We won't be a moment, Ying," Marta replied. "Please see that Dr. Hsü has tea and tangerines."

"They are already provided, My Lady."

The maidservant helped the ladies resume their light pongee overgowns. The small silver-and-white female *shih-tzu kou* cocked her shaggy head, one brown eye peeking inquisitively through the hair that fell like chrysanthemum petals over her face. The golden male stretched luxuriously, bowing on his extended forelegs so that his black beard brushed the red-and-black tiles, then slowly extending his hind legs. His eyes were hidden by a thicket of silken hair.

"Wang looks like a Taoist bonze performing sacred exercises on Mount Omei," Marta observed inconsequentially. "Come, Mu-lan. Come along, Wang. Good children."

His silk robe a splash of scarlet against the yellow-brick walls of the courtyard, Paul Hsü sat in the shade of a standing blue umbrella beside the shallow fishpond. A side table supported a cylindrical teapot, a handleless teacup, and a platter on which golden tangerines and white steamed buns were arrayed. He was rolling pellets of dough from the sweetmeat-stuffed buns and flicking them to the somnolent goldfish that trailed the diaphanous streamers of their fins among the jade-green water lilies.

"Welcome, Dr. Hsü, to our lowly hovel." Marta was excessively formal. "Has the esteemed Minister been given what poor refreshments we can muster?"

"As you see, child," Paul Hsü smiled at her stilted courtesy.

"Grandfather, Marta is worried about her...her unborn children," Candida said without preamble. "She feels that half-bloods would be outcastes."

"Your fears become you, Marta." Paul Hsü magisterially stroked his white goatee, and Marta winced, knowing he was most stubborn when most bland. "It is wise to consider all eventualities before reaching a decision."

"I am honored by Your Excellency's approbation," Marta sought still to fend off the Mandarin with rigid formality.

"Your fears are not wholly unfounded, though greatly exaggerated," Paul Hsü conceded. "The good Fathers teach us that the Lord God loves all His children equally. The Lord sees us not black or yellow, white or tan, but all as His beloved children."

"Grandfather Hsü, that is not what I am trying to say...as best I can." Marta abandoned cool courtesy to plead for the Mandarin's understanding. "Even if I wished—wished with all my heart—to marry the Arrowmaker, I would still be afraid. We would still have to think of practical matters...of the family and the future."

"My dear Marta, you know your father and I have pon-

117

dered long on your future. The family is, naturally, our first concern."

"What of my children, Grandfather Hsü? They wouldn't be Chinese, and they wouldn't be—not even...true ocean barbarians!"

"Count Huang was born a Hun." Distressed by her unhappiness, Paul Hsü soothed Marta in his own terms. "But his son by his Chinese wife rose to be a marquess and prime minister. Like our own, his times were unsettled. A career is always open to the man of talent in unsettled times. The wise ruler chooses his officials for their merit, not their blood."

"Forgive me, Grandfather. You know I honor your profound knowledge of our history.... And love to hear you expound on history. But a historical parallel is not always an answer to such a—forgive me—a personal question. The children, my sons and daughters, would they... *could* they... be happy and whole? I fear they would be split—inside themselves—by their mixed blood."

"Marta, your father wished to *command* you to obey—as any other father would. But I have persuaded him that commanding your obedience cannot ensure your harmonious marriage to the Arrowmaker. You must be convinced that the choice is right."

"I am deeply grateful for your concern," Marta said faintly. "But how can I convince myself? The Lord of Heaven knows how much I...I already feel terribly lonely in my...my stubbornness. I feel isolated, quite alone."

"That feeling tells you that you are wrong. Your conscience is speaking to you. Just think, Marta, what this marriage of yours will mean for the Faith—and for the Empire. We must bind the Arrowmaker to ourselves...by a harmonious marriage, which will make him almost wholly Chinese. His military skills can serve the Empire greatly, and his prowess in the Emperor's service will propagate the Faith. You two can advance God's Word better than a half-dozen celibate priests."

"Grandfather, I, too, love the Faith, and I am, of course, loyal to the Emperor. But my duty is to my future husband, my future Lord, whoever he may be, and to our children."

"*Ni-tze, pieh jang wo...*" Neither Paul Hsü's gentle tone nor his honeyed endearments softened his harsh message. "My dear, do not force us to take actions we would all regret—and no one more than you. Do not force me to send the Arrowmaker back to Macao. Don't compel your father to lock

118

you up for unfilial defiance. You would then never find a good husband. Above all, do not force the Lord God to punish you for disobedience."

"That is my choice, then?" Marta faltered. "No other?"

"Your father will tell you the same. I merely speak on his behalf. For myself, I plead with you not to ruin your life and..."

"Grandfather, I beg you to consider my fears." Her voice was faint, and her eyes were luminous with tears. "I beg you not to..."

"And I plead with you in the name of the Lord to offer up those selfish fears. Only a humble and obedient heart can serve the Lord."

"And that is *all* you have to say to me?" Marta appealed to the man who had always been even more loving and indulgent than her own father. "Nothing more? That is *all?*"

"That *is* all," Paul Hsü replied. "Is it not enough?"

The lion-dogs looked up, frightened by the Mandarin's flinty tone. The white-and-silver female fluttered her feathered tail in anxious innocence. The golden male studied the goldfish, his tense posture belying his air of superior unconcern.

THE reception room of Paul Hsü's mansion was sultry in the early evening of that same day. The split-bamboo blinds that barred the windows to the intrusive sun by day excluded all breezes during the long northern twilight the Chinese called *huang-hwen,* the golden dusk. Entering warily, Francis Arrowsmith missed the welcome the empty room had offered a half-year earlier. The oppressive red walls seemed to close in on him.

Alone with his apprehensions, Francis knew he could not fight the cunning of a man three times his age who stood at the peak of a civilization far more subtle than his own. Cunning was a first principle of Chinese statecraft, and Dr. Paul Hsü had not attained great power in the Empire by Christian virtue alone. The Mandarin who out-maneuvered the wily Court Eunuchs could easily manipulate a European who was dependent on his good will.

At least the interview would be short. He had come to bid Paul Hsü farewell after concluding their discussion of the problems of the Battalion of God. He would have to leave within the hour if he were to reach the camp near the Nankou

Pass that evening. Six troopers waited in the *hutung* outside the mansion. An armed escort was only prudent against the bandits and the rebels who swarmed a few miles from the Northern Capital of the Empire that was still the world's most powerful.

Casual in a lounging robe of cream pongee, Paul Hsü came down the stairs. Francis's unease dissipated like autumn leaves in a breeze when he saw the commonplace figure with the stately paunch and the large, innocent eyes. He felt himself again at home in China.

"I see they've given you tea and salted melon seeds." The Mandarin spoke slowly in courtesy to the foreigner. "This won't take too long. Anxious to get back to the troops, are you?"

"Yes, Sir," Francis replied. "It's a long ride in this heat."

"Still worried about sabotage and spying? You'll be glad to know I've taken some steps since we talked yesterday. I have others in mind."

"I'll be glad of your closer support, Dr. Paul."

"You shall have it. I have been thinking.... You must make it a habit to write Father Adam three times a week. Say on Mondays, Wednesdays, and Saturdays. Write in Portuguese.... No, write in Latin. I've heard that the...ah ...other party has found in the south two or three Portuguese-speaking Chinese."

"My Latin, Sir, is rusty."

"I do not expect eloquence. Father Adam will reply on Tuesdays, Thursdays, and Sundays by the same trusted courier. Any break will signal that something is wrong. How does that strike you?"

"Fine, Sir. I won't feel quite so isolated. But what of Simon Wu, my Adjutant?"

"I could transfer him, of course. But no...the Eunuchs would only plant another spy, one harder to detect. No! No transfer! Instead, we'll use Simon Wu to deceive the Black Premier."

"Father Adam spoke of 'doubled agents.' Will you bribe him or terrify him?"

"Neither! But can you deceive him...make him think the battalion is falling apart?"

"Difficult, Sir. After all, he *is* Chinese. His sources are far better than my own."

"But he knows little of the arquebus. He is hardly an expert on modern tactics, is he?"

"Hardly, Sir." Francis grinned. "He's a quick learner, but he's learned all he knows from me."

"If you complained loudly about Chinese clumsiness...belittled the soldiers' progress...vastly exaggerated the effects of the obstructionism...could you convince him?"

"No need to exaggerate that much. But, no, within limits, Sir, there'd be no difficulty. Quite broad limits."

"Then do so. Above all, the...ah...other party must not know how well you progress. The Black Premier must judge the Battalion of God despicable and therefore not to be feared. We win time that way, you see?"

"Yes, Sir. But the device can only work briefly. Simon Wu is not stupid. I cannot imagine deceiving him when the battalion makes final preparations for battle. No matter what I say, the men will be too obviously skilled and fit."

"How much time can you win?"

"Another month—perhaps two at the utmost."

"Better than nothing. And you must watch this Simon Wu secretly. The slave Joseph King could undertake that surveillance. As I have told you, you may trust him in all matters as you trust me. And Joseph can find others to assist him."

"I'll see to it, Sir." Francis wondered again about his Christian slave; at that moment, his own trust of Paul Hsü was far from perfect.

"By the way, you will have to make more frequent visits to Peking."

"A pleasure," Francis acknowledged. "But why?"

"I shall want to talk with you to supplement the written messages. Besides, if you're constantly dashing off, young Simon Wu will reach certain conclusions. You will appear light-minded, much fonder of the pleasures of the city than your duty—and therefore a bad officer. Since you'll always be running to me for help, he'll be convinced that the...ah ...other party's plots are working well."

"I'll look terribly ineffectual," Francis objected.

"Would you rather be a dead lion or a live lion disguised in a sheepskin?" the Mandarin asked. "Moreover, your visits will serve another purpose."

"Another purpose?" Francis was fascinated by the web of deceit Paul Hsü was weaving.

"Yes, another purpose." Paul Hsü's plot was far more intricate than the young Englishman could imagine. "But I shall have to keep you longer than I'd planned. What better time to talk about your future?"

"I have no particular plans for the future. Only to serve the Faith, the Empire, and yourself—as best I can."

"You must have thought about the matter Father Adam broached on Sunday."

"Of course, though I am still not clear," Francis prevaricated. "You...the Lady Marta...do me too much honor. I am unworthy. But what has that to do with sabotage and spying?"

"Everything, my boy, everything...as you'll see. The plots are directed at you personally as well as at our enterprise. But let's have something to eat. You'll be riding late tonight."

The Mandarin clapped his hands twice. While the second sharp report still reverberated from the red-painted walls, a manservant appeared. He wore a white jacket over black trousers secured by white puttees, and he carried a complete service on an orange-lacquered tray: pickled radish strips, a fish soup, and bamboo sieves of *hsiao-lung pao,* the small pursed dumplings, with a vinegar and ginger sauce. All were delicacies of Paul Hsü's native Shanghai, the trading port on the mud flats of the Yangtze River. A second manservant identically dressed followed with an identical tray.

"Do try these," Paul Hsü urged. "I think you'll find them pleasant. You will need sustenance for your long ride."

When the servants had withdrawn, Francis asked a carefully phrased question: "How can great events of state and my insignificant person be connected, Sir?"

"There's really no reason for your being here in the Empire—that's the line the...ah...other party will take." Paul Hsü spoke through a mouthful of *hsiao-lung pao.* "You are not covered by the agreement giving the Jesuits the right of residence in gratitude for Macao's arms and soldiers. And you are no longer a member of the barbar...ah...foreign military unit."

"That's absurd," Francis protested. "The Court invited us—all of us. And I'm doing more for the defense of the realm than Captain Texeira can sitting in Tengchou."

"Pettifogging or not, that is their position. Their spying is central to their plot to expel you. They will report to the Emperor that your services are obviously not necessary, since you perform them so badly. Then...out you go."

"Then, Sir, with much respect, your plan also appears absurd. The better I succeed in deceiving Simon Wu, the closer

I come to expulsion." Francis had learned that Chinese etiquette permitted pointed observations—as long as they were harmoniously phrased. "And Sir, without me...I say this in all modesty...you cannot train your arquebusiers."

"I am fully aware of that fact. My plan, however, is *not* absurd, because it includes one further element. I call it matrimonial diplomacy."

"Matrimonial diplomacy?" A display of stupidity, Francis felt, was his only recourse against the web of deceit Paul Hsü was spinning around him.

"When you are married to Marta, you will enjoy a different legal status," the Minister explained. "The Eunuchs would not dare exile an innocent Chinese from her Motherland by expelling you. I also propose to adopt you—as the intended husband of my great-grandniece. Adopting a prospective son-in-law is common practice when a good family needs an heir...and a fatherless man needs a good name. You know I have no grandsons of my own name."

"Sir, I'm still puzzled." Francis was touched by the old Mandarin's gesture of affection, calculated though it was, but he could not restrain the question that might reveal him to be less than a fool. "Why, then, not adopt me without this marriage, Sir? And why could our enemies not just kill me, instead of spinning such an elaborate plot?"

"Well asked, Major Arrowmaker!" Paul Hsü twinkled. "I see I shall never be able to deceive you."

"You honor me, Sir." Francis finally filled the vacuum of the Mandarin's beaming silence. "But what of my questions?"

"*Chiu shih che-yang*..." The Minister chose his words with great care. "It's this way. Public killing isn't the Chinese way, not when it can be avoided. They *could* kill you...just as they *could* kill me. But that would be too blatant and would provoke retaliation. Besides, bald killing lacks finesse and brings opprobrium. But your expulsion after what you call an elaborate plot, that is another matter. All Chinese admire such subtle stratagems."

"I understand, Sir. But why could you not adopt me without forcing the Lady Marta to marry an ill-favored, half-civilized lout."

"You are learning, Francis, learning fast...even faster than I had hoped." The Mandarin's pride in his reluctant pupil's use of Chinese self-denigration was already paternal. "But a bald adoption would also lack finesse. And it simply would not be credible. There is no reason for me to adopt you unless a marriage is planned."

"You are saying then, Sir, that I have no alternative? It is either marriage or expulsion?"

"That is *your* conclusion. I am only presenting the alternatives. You must make up your own mind what you wish...and what you do. It lies between you and your conscience."

"You have neatly....That is to say, I'm trapped."

"Not I...as you have just realized. Circumstances have trapped you, if you are trapped. Either you choose to remain in China, serving the Lord greatly, or you choose expulsion, perhaps death. The Lord God has given us free will..."

"Certainly I'm free to choose." Francis did not conceal his bitterness from the old Mandarin to whom, he realized, he was already turning like a true father. "I can force myself on Marta, presumptuously and ignobly. Or I can run away, dishonorably and cravenly. It's not much of a choice."

"Is the lady, then, so unattractive...a harridan or a shrew? Why is this marriage so repugnant, Francis?"

"I did not say that, Sir." Francis nervously flicked his hair off his forehead. "I never meant that."

"Then why such great reluctance? Marta *was* concerned about the difference in race. Do you...No, it's unlikely. But, I must ask: Do you shrink because you consider yourself inferior to a Chinese?"

"By no means." Francis was amused by the inversion of the European assumption of superiority. "That is to say, I am well aware of the honor, but I am not overwhelmed."

"Then why such picturesque dismay?" Paul Hsü demanded.

"You, Sir, you are hurrying me to a monstrously important decision." The Englishman was purposefully pompous. "I must marry for all my mortal life. You ask me to commit my life to a nation assuredly greater in power and more refined in civilization than my own. But it is still *not* my own nation....Nor, I fear, can it ever be."

"It can be your own," the Mandarin interjected. "China is hospitable to men of promise, whatever their origin."

"With great respect, Sir, I have not marked such hospitality to ocean barbarians. I yearn someday to return to England to reclaim my family's small holdings for my own heirs. I cannot believe the Lady Marta would willingly quit your glorious nation, where she enjoys luxury and position. Brisk insecurity and rough hardships are the only certainties for a junior officer in Europe. I could not ask her to ... You, therefore, require me to become a Chinese ... or, at the least, to aspire to that high status."

"I became a Christian, did I not?" Paul Hsü demanded, but amended his heated retort an instant later. "No, that is not the same. I embraced the Truth, but retained my country and my rank. I sacrificed nothing, but gained all, above all, my soul's salvation and ..."

Francis barely heard the Mandarin's soliloquy, and he still did not know that Paul Hsü had repeatedly hazarded both his position and his life to defend his faith. As his mentor wished, the young Englishman was calculating the consequences of expulsion from the Empire.

Whatever he had already built for the future he had built in China, Francis saw starkly. If he were exiled, all his hopes would be shattered. He could no longer even dream of reclaiming the Arrowsmith lands. Marked by the opprobrium of expulsion, he would be virtually penniless, virtually friendless, and, above all, alienated from the Society of Jesus, the only family he had ever known. His intransigence would inflict grave injury on the Mission to China. Adam Schall had pleaded the case for the marriage not only out of simple affection but also, perhaps primarily, because it would serve the Jesuit cause.

In Macao, Francis reflected, he could count on the good will of only Antonio Castro, the Marrano secretary of the Loyal Senate. The vindictive Portuguese would rejoice at his fall. He would, moreover, be twelve thousand miles from Europe—where he could, in any event, look to neither friends nor family.

Was this marriage, after all, so dire and or so confining as he had thought it? Was Marta so repugnant to him?

Her he could make shift to live with, though he might have preferred a more vivacious woman who was more frankly sensuous.

But were there any such Chinese ladies? Francis was revolted when he thought of the cramped horror of her maimed, perhaps rotting feet. But he had heard that Chinese ladies never removed the silken half-stockings that covered their golden lilies in their husbands' sight. Nonetheless, it would be like lying with a cripple.

More important, he asked himself, was either Marta or China so abhorrent that he must renounce position, wealth,

125

and honor because they required him to wed her and to remain in China for some time?

"...and therefore I shall not press you further now. But do remember that her dowry will be lavish and your rank elevated." Paul Hsü concluded his soliloquy, which had been a counterpoint to the young Englishman's troubled calculation, and smiled benignly. "Be that as it may, would you like a few words alone with Marta before you go?"

Alone with Marta! The Minister must wish the marriage desperately, Francis realized, since he was prepared to concede not merely formal etiquette, but a fundamental canon of Chinese morality. A maiden of good family was never allowed a tête-à-tête with an eligible male, but he would have had two such meetings.

Though no more than a pawn in the game of power, Francis saw, he was a pawn in a critical position. Not just one among five European military officers in China, he was the only Chinese-speaking officer. He was not indissolubly attached to those institutions that appeared so much more powerful to the Chinese than they actually were: the Kingdom of Portugal and the Society of Jesus. Once given to China (and to Paul Hsü by marriage to the great-grandniece) his loyalty would be entirely theirs. His skills would be at the disposal of Paul Hsü's party of Ming-loyalist Mandarins, who were striving to reform and to modernize the Empire.

Rejecting the opportunity to see Marta alone would be not only churlish, but ill-advised. He was utterly dependent upon Paul Hsü. Time enough to dare the Mandarin's enmity, if he finally decided he could not possibly enter into the proposed marriage. For the time being, the good will of Minister of Rites Paul Hsü Kwang-chi was the breath of life to Francis Arrowsmith, Major of Imperial Arquebusiers.

Francis did not like the frenzied calculation forced upon him. But, he consoled himself, the treacheries of Europe were watered milk to the heady wine of Chinese intrigue. He assumed that Marta was a filial Chinese daughter who would ultimately yield to her family's wishes. Regardless, he owed it to his honor—and to his security—to learn, if he could, her true feelings before he chose his own course. Did she, he wondered, find the proposed marriage utterly repugnant? If she did, he swore, no threat and no inducement would impel him to force himself upon her.

Marta was not alone when Paul Hsü led Francis through the moon gate into the inner courtyard whose gray bricks were mantled by crimson vines. On a bamboo stool in the far corner, the round-faced maidservant Ying was piecing together a swatch of torn embroidery. The Minister did not, presumably, feel that the maidservant's humble presence made her mistress less alone.

Two blue-glazed porcelain lions glared defiance from the near corner. They were almost life-size, and their disproportionately large heads were covered by tightly braided manes. The female sheltered a cub under her left forepaw, and the male rested his right forepaw upon an orb that symbolized the world. Between the lions Marta sat on a cane chair. Gazing at the empty chair beside her, Francis was startled by Paul Hsü's affectionately clapping him on the back in farewell.

"*Ying-chang, ni hau-ma?*" Marta Soo did not look up. "Good evening, Major. Are you well?"

"*Hen hao. Hsieh-hsieh, Fu-jen,*" Francis replied as formally. "Very well. Thank you, Madam. And yourself?"

"I am quite well." She pleated her pink skirt between her thumb and forefinger. "The evening grows cooler, does it not?"

"Much more comfortable than the daylight hours," he agreed as gravely. "Do your lessons progress well?"

She looked up startled, a half-smile flirting on her lips, and asked: "What do you mean, my lessons?"

"Merely that we sounded like the first lesson you taught me in the Officials' Language." Francis sought to alleviate their mutual embarrassment lest it should grow into mutual enmity. "You know, proper greetings between friends. You do remember?"

"I do remember, of course," she smiled. "I suppose we did sound comical."

"Have they talked with you?" he asked hesitantly. "About the..."

"For hours I've been talked at. It seems for days. And you?"

"The same...from Father Adam and Dr. Paul. I hardly know what I think."

"I am confused, too...terribly confused."

"What did you answer?" Francis summoned his courage. "What did you tell them?"

"That it...it was an...an interesting thought....But, of course, impossible."

"I said much the same." If she refused the marriage, Francis calculated, even Dr. Paul could not force him. "I regret, of course, that it is impossible."

"I am flattered...of course. But I hardly know what to think. Obedience to my elders should...And they say it would be a very good thing for the Faith...for the Dynasty. How can we two be so important? But it is, of course, impossible."

"Utterly impossible." He agreed reluctantly, looking down on the black lashes that veiled her eyes. His breath caught when she glanced up at him, and he sat on the vacant chair beside her. "I hate myself for placing you in this predicament ...though you know that...that I never sought..."

"I know that, Arrowmaker. I must apologize for causing you embarrassment. It is not good to treat a foreigner...a guest...in this manner."

They were, Marta realized, unwillingly coming together in a tacit conspiracy against their elders. Was that Dr. Paul's design, she wondered? Did he plan to force them into a peculiar intimacy through their mutual desire to avoid marriage? However bizarre, a common purpose was a powerful bond.

"Will they," Francis ventured, "let you say no?"

"I do not know," she replied deliberately. "Perhaps not. But, I promise you, I would commit suicide rather than...than embarrass you further."

"That's not very complimentary." Francis smiled at their bizarre conversation. "For myself, I would rather marry than burn for the sin of suicide."

"There is that, too." She spoke as if his banal observation were profound. "There *are* worse things than marriage. Of course, if the man were crippled or deformed or evil, it would be...another matter. But...but there *are* worse things."

"True enough. One might commit suicide before marrying someone who was grossly deformed or evil. But a bride who is beautiful, accomplished, and virtuous is quite another matter."

Did the barbarian, Marta wondered, really want this bizarre marriage? Was he wooing her in his own curious fashion—directly without the intercession of a go-between? It was wrong—unfair of him to trifle with her. Yet her parents, the Minister of Rites himself, Father Adam Schall, all were pressing her. Could she in conscience resist their counsel? Could a Chinese maiden possibly reject a marriage her elders so strongly wished?

The barbarian was ingratiating. But he was still grotesque and ill-mannered. No gentleman, as his behavior proved. Marriage to the Arrowmaker could lead only to disaster.

"We must then resist . . . as long and as strongly as we can." Marta steeled herself against the temptation of the easy— the filial—yielding to his unseemly wooing. "You must agree?"

"We must resist. We have no choice."

Francis agreed reluctantly. Despite his resolution not to commit himself to both Marta and China for a lifetime, he suddenly yearned toward Marta. Her distress touched him deeply, attracting him when it should have repelled. But he would still avoid this forced marriage—if he possibly could.

"Then we, at least, are agreed," she said slowly. "Something could still occur to change . . . their minds."

"You believe Dr. Paul might change his mind if we resist long enough?"

"Perhaps, he might. But, no . . . he's immovable . . . like the Great Wall . . . when once he has decided. We can only hope and pray."

"I shall pray hard for deliverance, Marta. But, I must admit, with some regret."

Marta lifted her hand in tentative dismissal. She was shocked when Francis took it between his own and held it for a moment.

"Then there is no more to say, is there?" she asked hastily. "I see you're dressed for riding."

"I return to camp tonight. It's a long ride through the night."

"Then I suppose, that is all. There is nothing more to say, is there?"

"No. Nothing at all."

Francis strode through the outer courtyard to the street gate, where his impatient escort waited. During the long ride along the winding road, he weighed every word and every gesture of their first unrestrained conversation. He was, somewhat incongruously, dismayed by her stern resolve to refuse the marriage. But he hardened his own resolve.

Just before night became day at the Double Hour of the Hare, the horsemen saw the fires of the Battalion of God in the valley beside the stream. The triangular banner above the main gate was teased by a light breeze. The double-barred white Cross of St. Omer glowed pink on its dark-green field in the flickering light of the sentries' torches.

The Camp near the Nankou Pass

MONDAY, SEPTEMBER 24, 1630–SUNDAY,
OCTOBER 14, 1630

A TENTATIVE glowworm winked in the darkness where by day the maples spread the crimson glory of their autumn foliage. The Valley of the Tombs was a black pool amid the surrounding hills. When the wind swept away the clouds, monumental arches shone amber under the frail crescent moon. Bobbing in the hands of retired sergeants-major of the Imperial Guard, two lanterns traced a pale circle around the mausoleums. The watchmen moved in opposing arcs from the Dragon-Phoenix Arch astride the broad Triumphal Way, where gigantic marble warriors guarded the former Emperors' eternal sleep.

The mortal guardians were superfluous. Despite the Ming Dynasty's decay, awe still deterred even the boldest thieves from rifling the treasures of the Imperial Tombs. Besides, each tumulus concealed a subterranean maze only the most astute—and most fortunate—intruder could traverse. He would then be barred from the chamber of the tomb by marble doors locked for eternity. Marble pawls had dropped into place inside as the last mourners pulled the ponderous doors closed.

It was, nonetheless, prudent to post living guards. Brigands were blasphemously bold since the accession of the weak Chung Chen Emperor two years earlier. Even those desperadoes were terrified of the luminous circles drawn by the floating ghost lanterns. No mortal, they knew, would dare walk alone among the deified spirits of the former Emperors and their fierce attendant specters.

Superstitious dread preserved only the Valley of the Tombs inviolate. The surrounding hills, where the glowworm flickered, were no longer sacrosanct. Eager eyes watched the lime-green glimmer descend westward toward the camp of the Battalion of God. The movement of the wingless beetle was preternatural; equally preternatural was its regularity. The light flashed briefly three times, then once long. After a minute of darkness, the cycle was repeated.

Peering through the flap of the tent he shared with Francis Arrowsmith, the slave called Joseph King watched the recurring pattern until he was convinced that no beetle ever flashed its signal of passion so precisely. His felt-soled boots soughed across the close-woven Samarkand carpet that covered the plank floor. Groping toward the heaped cushions where Francis breathed rhythmically, the Christian slave placed his palm over his master's mouth. His lean fingers gently pulled an earlobe, persisting until he felt the lips move against his palm.

"*Silêncio*," he hissed in Portuguese.

"Oh, it's you, Joseph." Francis whispered drowsily. "I feared for an instant...an assassin."

"*Na yeh keh-neng, Ying-chang...*" Joseph King reverted to heavily accented Officials' Chinese. "That is also possible, Major. But not while I keep watch."

"And you have seen?"

"Again, Your Excellency, the same flashes, clumsily imitating a glowworm."

"You're certain, Joseph?"

"Of course, Major. The green is also too deep. It flashes too regularly, and it is alone."

"A glowworm alone? Impossible!"

"Precisely, Major. And alone the other times I've seen it."

"In the hollow, you think? In the hollow among the pines beside the Vermilion Arch?"

"They've met there in the past. But we must hurry to be there before their rendezvous."

"Are you sure of a rendezvous this night?"

"If they follow their normal practice."

Joseph King shrugged his shoulders. In the moonlight, his narrow Cantonese face with its snub nose and deep-set eyes was a mask of ignorance. Francis had learned that Joseph would not speak unless he was certain, though he spoke freely. If his judgment and his services as a confidential secretary had not already proved invaluable, the Englishman might have been irritated by his invariable assurance.

"He is a slave through no fault of his own, but because of his father's misplaced zeal for an autonomous South China," Paul Hsü had advised when he gave Joseph King to Francis. "Though I should like to, I cannot free him, since his father was executed as a traitor. He is loyal, intelligent, an excellent scholar...and a devout Christian. Joseph King should be your other self, your Chinese self."

That recommendation had soothed the Englishman's qualms at owning a fellow Christian as his slave. Joseph King was himself as well placed as he could be as long as he remained a slave, far better off as the alter ego of a Christian officer than he would be as a scribe to an arrogant Mandarin. A committed Ming loyalist despite his degradation, he also spoke freely of his resentment at his status. He had, after all, qualified for a Mandarin's appointment by his demonstrated knowledge of the Classics in the First Civil Service Examination before he was enslaved by the harsh law that punished not only a traitor, but also the traitor's entire family. Yet Joseph King was not resentful of his new master, whom he treated with slightly irreverent and humorous regard from the eminence of his seniority of some fifteen years. Having discussed Joseph's predicament at length, master and slave were at ease with each other.

Musing on the injustice his secretary had suffered, Francis tucked his gray trousers into his boot tops and tied a sash around his heavy tunic. After checking his pistolet's load, he thrust the weapon into his sash. Joseph handed him a short sword blackened with soot before smearing soot on their hands and faces. When the pacing sentry's footfalls dwindled into the distance, the two Christians slipped through the tentflap, clambered over the twelve-foot brick wall, and dropped into the dry moat.

An alert observer might have glimpsed them moving through the gullies in the powdery soil, though they lay face down when the wind whisked the veil of clouds from the sickle moon. But the only eyes watching the hills were intent on the flashing glowworm. Crawling where there was no cover, stooping among the high grass, and finally standing among the pines, the English Major and his slave moved through the night toward the Vermilion Arch.

The green glimmer floated down the ridge, hanging motionless each time it signaled: three short flashes, a long flash, and a minute of darkness. The Court Eunuch of the Fifth Grade who flipped the lantern's shutter shivered, though the night was warm. He detested the stumbling among the dark hills his rank would normally have excused him from. But he had been assigned directly by his commander, the spymaster called the Black Premier, because the mission was too sensitive for rapscallion civilian agents. The Eunuch swore in an undertone at the clumsiness of his escort of a lieutenant and three sergeants of the Flamboyant Cloaks.

The five special agents had descended to the plain when Francis Arrowsmith sensed the loom of the Vermilion Arch through the black night. Joseph King led him through the head-high grass to the blind he had prepared on the edge of the clearing. Four minutes later they heard twigs crackle and the grass rustle under the feet of the special agents. Shining in stripes through the black grass spears, the green lantern glowed for forty heartbeats, went dark for twice that time, and glowed again for forty beats. Then the hollow was dark and silent within its ring of pines.

In the camp of the Battalion of God, where sleepy sentries paced the footpath on top of the brick wall, Adjutant Simon Wu had cursorily checked the changing of the guard at midnight, half past the Double Hour of the Horse. His ears had been tuned to the voices of the night: the high bark of a fox, the lowing of a restive bullock, the whinnying of a frightened colt. His eyes had been intent on the lime-green glimmer moving fitfully down the hillside to expire in the hollow beside the Vermilion Arch after two half-minute flashes.

The sentries who had finished their tours were hurrying to their tents, swearing good-humoredly at each other. The Sergeant of the Guard lingered in obedience to Simon Wu's nod.

"I heard something out there near the Tombs," the Adjutant told the Lieutenant of the Guard. "No idea what it was, but we'll investigate."

The Adjutant and the Sergeant of the Guard strode through the main gate, where torches burned beneath the green flag flaunting the double-barred Cross of St. Omer. Believing themselves unsuspected, they disdained stealth.

They were secure in the hauteur of agents of the Special Service, which lay over the Empire like an unbreakable net so fine it was virtually invisible, but so close-meshed no one escaped its coils. When darkness swallowed them, they broke into a dogtrot.

Hearing the patter of felt-soled boots, Francis Arrowsmith and Joseph King held their breath. Footsteps rustled through the long grass two yards from their covert. Though the heavy breathing of the two agents was loud in the silent night, the sky was so black they saw no movement.

The Court Eunuch and Simon Wu appeared between the vertical bars of grass when the Eunuch unshuttered the glowworm lantern. Lit from below, his pendulous cheeks were a sickly green mask stippled with black shadows, and his eyes were dark cavities. Simon Wu's flat-planed face glowed the creamy olive of Sung Dynasty celadon, but red spots blotched his broad cheekbones. His eyes were hidden by the reflection off his heavy spectacles.

The glare burned away all subtlety, and Francis saw that Simon Wu wore the face of fanatical ambition, at once obsequious and arrogant. Tension clenched the Adjutant's heavy jawbones and wrinkled his forehead, which was thrust forward like a shining shield against the arrows of the world. His mouth gleamed cherry-red, wide but thin-lipped in a square face almost as broad at the chin as the temples.

The Adjutant's face vanished when the Eunuch closed the lantern's shutter, and Francis heard their conversation like a blind man at a playhouse. The Eunuch's treble voice, speaking the thick-tongued Peking argot, was readily distinguishable from his agent's baritone, which slurred the sibilants of Shanghai.

"*Kua tien...*" Simon Wu offered the password. "Do not stoop in the melon patch."

"*Li hsia!*" the Eunuch responded. "Or linger under the plum tree."

"Lest you provoke suspicion," Simon Wu completed the formula.

"What news have you brought to justify my tripping blindly about these accursed hills at this unearthly hour?" The Eunuch's petulant tone altered when he glanced at the ghost-lanterns bobbing in the Valley of the Tombs. "May the Heavenly Gods protect us from the vengeful spirits of the Sacred Ancestors of the Emperor if we intrude upon their rest!"

"The peace of Christ be with you!" The Adjutant returned a Christian prayer for a pagan invocation. In the Empire of the Ming different sects lived together tolerantly. Their harmony was, however, occasionally shattered by persecutions mounted by the dominant Confucians. Those agnostics worshiped only the power of the state.

"For that, much thanks." The Eunuch's gratitude was unfeigned. "You must tell me more about your creed. Is it true, as men say, that in your single Heaven Eunuchs enjoy a special.... But first your report."

"Undoubtedly, Your Honor!" Simon Wu replied. "Just as Eunuchs are rewarded with honor and power on earth because of their deprivation, in Heaven they will.... But you require my report?"

"Yes, of course," the Eunuch conceded reluctantly. "First your report."

"All goes according to plan. The battalion is in confusion. The barbarian constantly confides to me, his Christian brother, that he is close to despair."

"Constantly? Why should he be so confiding? Is it that he seeks to deceive you for some devious reason of his own?"

"The Arrowmaker? The straightforward Arrowmaker? Hardly! Now, if he were Chinese..."

"He is in touch with Minister Paul Hsü, is he not?"

"Constantly, of course."

"Could not Minister Hsü prompt him..."

"The ocean devil is too simple. Even monkey-clever Paul Hsü couldn't teach him cunning. Besides, my own eyes confirm his fears. Your Honor, he cannot possibly be misleading me."

"I suppose you're right. The game is too complex...and he is *not* Chinese. Subtlety is as unknown to barbarians as table manners to sows."

Francis started indignantly, and Joseph laid a restraining hand on his arm. The pines creaking in the rising wind covered the brief rustling of their movements amid the grass.

"*Pang-ting-che pu huei ting hau-hwa!*" Joseph King quoted wryly. "The eavesdropper rarely hears good of himself! Did you expect them to praise you, Major?"

"*Pieh-nao...,*" Francis answered testily. "Be quiet and attend to their talk."

"...certainly not subtle. The Arrowmaker complains that the men damage weapons and waste gunpowder by careless-

135

ness," Simon Wu was explaining. "I have arranged a few accidents myself..."

"We know that. But what exactly does the barbarian say? Can he make the battalion a fighting unit? How soon?"

"He says after a few cups of wine he'd rather command the wild, pig-headed peasants of *Wah-leh-ssu,* wherever that barbarous place may be. He says hard driving may make the men fit to take the field against a troupe of singsong girls. But even that will take six months...perhaps longer."

"I commend you, Captain Wu, for your cunning. What else does the red-haired devil confide?"

"He's had a bellyful of this rough life...didn't come to China to live in a tent far from the sweet cities. He may simply give up...leave the Empire. After more wine, he calls himself *hu-sün wang,* the king of the monkeys, because he's trying in vain to teach his hobbledehoys discipline and skill."

"I do not like his calling Chinese soldiers monkeys. But we've contrived to make them look like monkeys, so I suppose.... What further?"

"If he could lay his hands on enough gold, he'd resign and return to Europe.... For two pennies, he says, he'd leave."

"We might manage ten pennies...even more. The barbarian's mood fits the new instructions I bring you, Captain Wu. You must draw him into our web."

"Easily done, Your Honor. But what of the commitment to me? Do you have word for me?"

"I came tonight to tell you your terms were accepted. When the Arrowmaker leaves the Empire—on his own feet or in a shroud—you will be designated commander of all arquebusiers. A colonel with special allowances of five hundred gold taels—as well as normal salary and allowances."

"That's fine. I am Your Honor's humble servant and the abject slave of Senior Court Eunuch Tsao."

"Act as you speak, and the prize is yours. Now I must be gone before some prowling soldier stumbles on us."

The rising wind had rent the veil of clouds, and the figures in the hollow were black silhouettes against the sickle moon. After saluting the Eunuch, Simon Wu and his sergeant were entering the shadows of the thick feathered pines.

"A moment, Captain!" The Eunuch's voice piped high. "We have arranged a diversion for your ocean devil. You'll be informed of your own role. Now be gone."

The Eunuch turned his plump face south, wearily contemplating the four-mile walk to the deserted post station where their horses waited, guarded by five Flamboyant Cloaks. Their gaudy uniforms flaunted the immense power of the Special Service, which was normally concealed. Their rust-yellow capes frightened off both honest men and brigands. No honest man willingly approached that despised uniform, and the brigands preferred easier prey than the horsemen of the Flamboyant Cloaks. *Snakes, wolves, and rats* (the proverb counseled) *do not fight to the death against their own kind!*

"I agree with the simpleminded barbarian Major." The Eunuch's querulous voice floated in the well of light as his dark shape blended into the darker pines. "I know better ways to pass time than stumbling among these hills...thick with malevolent ghosts, no doubt, at this hour."

"Cochon...chu-tou... swine...*porco!"* Francis mixed his languages in his anger. "So I'm a witless fool...a simpleminded barbarian!"

"I told you the eavesdropper never hears good of himself." Joseph King's eyes were slitted, and his cheeks were flushed by laughter.

"It is not funny, Joseph!" Francis's voice crackled from anger to laughter. "At least, not *that* funny."

"Did you think, Sir, they came together secretly in order to...to..." Renewed laughter drowned the slave's words. "Did you think they met to compose odes in your honor? Perhaps to hold a literary competition? Three taels for the best verses praising Major Arrowmaker? Did you, Sir?"

"Not really," Francis grinned. "But are all Chinese always so contemptuous of all foreigners?"

"Not usually...by no means," Joseph replied. "You got off lightly. They still respect your military skill. You cannot imagine what the pagans say about some of the Fathers."

"This diversion the Eunuch spoke of. What could it be?"

"I know only that it will not be too strong."

"How can you be so sure?"

"It's obvious, Major. You have gained your first objective. The other party already underestimates you greatly. A fairly simple diversion, whatever that means, will confound you, they must believe. Besides, they want the battalion for themselves—don't want to destroy it. It's quite simple."

"I have found," Francis replied with ponderous humor, "that quite simple to a slow-witted Chinese means devilishly complex to the canniest foreigner."

"That's true, of course, Sir. But a little foresight...some stealthy preparation....We'll manage quite handily. Neither

137

the Eunuch nor Captain Simon Wu is half as wily as he—or you—thinks."

FRANCIS ARROWSMITH shared his breakfast with Simon Wu on the next Saturday. The Adjutant wore the mask of amiability his commanding officer had seen removed in the hollow among the pines. His flat cheekbones were not blotched, and his narrow eyes were bland behind his black-rimmed spectacles. The breast of his padded blue jacket displayed a captain's lynx insignia, while his gray-canvas trousers were tucked into black field boots. But spectacles beneath the red helmet struck Francis as wildly incongruous.

A European general might slip on spectacles to study a map, but his junior officers shunned them as unmartial and expensive. Junior Chinese officers, however, unashamedly wore spectacles, which were readily available and inexpensive. The Jesuits had introduced the European invention to the Empire, and intelligent Chinese craftsmen had improved their models. Deficient vision was, moreover, a mark of caste. All gentlemen, even military officers, wished to have it thought their eyesight was impaired by diligent study of the Sacred Classics.

Sipping tea after breakfast, the Major and the Captain tamped tobacco into the brass-thimble bowls of their two-foot bamboo pipes. When the white smoke drifted in the autumn sunlight, Simon Wu turned from pleasantries to the affairs of the Battalion of God.

"Major Arrowmaker, I'm worried," he confided, sitting erect in his canvas field chair. "The men are complaining about the food."

"What's the trouble?" Francis was cheered by the distant barking of drill sergeants.

"Putting Southerners and Northerners in the same company, even the same squads."

"You agreed when Minister Paul Hsü decided to try it. If we enlisted only Southerners or only Northerners, we wouldn't have a truly national battalion."

"You can't mix Southern oyster sauce and Northern sesame oil, Southern rice and Northern wheat."

"What changes could we make, Adjutant?"

"Food first, as I said. The Northerners complain about too much rice...not enough steamed bread and noodles. The Southerners say the rice is second-rate."

"Then order better rice and serve more bread and noodles."

"Food's only the tip of the dragon's tail. Last night there were three fights between Northerners and Southerners...one almost a riot. Fortunately, Lieutenant Wang was quick to quash it."

"I'll commend him." Francis did not confide that Joseph King had already told him all three quarrels were instigated by Shanghai men, Simon Wu's fellow townsmen.

"Commendations won't solve the problem, Major. Not just North–South antagonism, but provincial antagonism. The Shanghai-landers can't abide the Cantonese. Swear they smell of the dogs they eat. The Shantung men hate the Shansi men. Call them thieving mule traders. Separate messes might relieve some friction."

"Separate messes are out, Adjutant. Paul Hsü stipulated from the beginning...no separate messes. Said you might as well disband the Battalion."

"It may come to that," Simon Wu said mournfully.

"I know it may." Francis decided to alter his confident tone. "But what can I do? I'd happily walk away from this mess if I had the cash. But I don't. So I have to put up with it...and explain any failure as best I can."

"Failure, Major Arrowmaker, cannot be explained to His Imperial Majesty. If the Battalion must be disbanded, you ...we...will face severe punishment, perhaps execution."

"Do you mean there is *no* way out for us?" Francis demanded.

"There *is* a way out, Major."

"Not the way you've been talking. No gold, no escape."

Francis paraded his venality to emphasize his despair. In response to his Latin dispatch of Tuesday reporting that Simon Wu would attempt to compromise him, Paul Hsü had instructed him by Wednesday's courier to fall in with whatever scheme the Adjutant proposed.

"With great respect, Major, you do not wholly understand how matters are arranged in the Empire. Gold is the key. With enough gold we could buy not only immunity, but also promotion when the Battalion collapses."

"But, Captain, you've told me you're strapped for funds. And I have no gold...none at all."

"We can get all the gold we need. The Battalion could be a goldmine, if worked the Chinese way."

"The Chinese way?"

"A Mandarin always pays lavishly for a good post. Then

he owes it to his family to enrich himself. That's the custom, and no one suffers."

"Only the poor commoners he fleeces." Francis knew that expressing concern for the common people would mark him as a fool. "Anyway, we've got no commoners to fleece. I can't fine my privates and sergeants or sell them promotions."

"That would be a start, Major. As well, we could discharge a third of our men but report a third more enlisted. All the additional gold for rations, pay, clothing, and ammunition, we could split between us."

"Two parts for me and one for you." Francis trailed the cloak of his venality. "But let's not cut our numbers at all."

"Why not, Major? If we don't, profits would be too small....And I couldn't see your getting twice my share."

"My plan will gain us not just two-thirds more, but twice as much. We'll double our reported strength, but keep the number the same."

Francis calculated rapidly. If he pocketed two-thirds of the battalion's monthly budget, some three hundred gold taels, a year would make him independent of both Paul Hsü's threats and Simon Wu's traps—all their convoluted Chinese plots. The Minister had instructed him to fall in with the Adjutant's schemes but had said nothing of returning the gold that came to him. China had taught him that his first duty was to himself.

"That would, obviously, be preferable," the Adjutant agreed. "We would kill two birds with one stone...also keep the Battalion intact on the off chance of making it a real fighting unit."

Simon Wu was delighted with a scheme that promised him not only more gold, but a full-strength battalion as well. It would make him more valuable to the Black Premier—and less vulnerable to that Eunuch's treachery. Suspicion of Francis's sudden shrewdness flickered in Simon Wu's eyes, but was suppressed by his own good sense. Any Chinese could outmaneuver any barbarian—and Simon knew himself for a highly intelligent Chinese.

Besides, the scheme was neither as shrewd nor as daring as the barbarian thought it. No military unit in the Ming Empire failed to falsify its strength reports, and the deception was normally on a far grander scale than the Arrowmaker had proposed. The rolls listed forty thousand soldiers in the Peking garrison, but everyone knew the actual number was no more than fifteen thousand. The true strength of the Imperial Armies was irretrievably lost in the bureaucratic maze of the Ministry of War. Almost three million soldiers were officially enrolled, while the actual number did not exceed a million—including the lame, the halt, and the blind. The dull-witted barbarian was a small boy telling his first stumbling lie beside the audacious duplicity of senior Chinese officers.

CAPTAIN Simon Wu was not only shrewd, but already adept in chicanery before he was commissioned. He had matured into a master of fraud since becoming a thread in the Divine Skein. The great strategist Sün Tze's term for an intelligence service now described the Black Premier's vast network of espionage, intimidation, and extortion. To survive as a special agent Simon Wu had to be adroitly deceitful.

The Adjutant reported some ten to fifteen phantom recruits a day and ensured verisimilitude by also reporting a lesser number of deaths, transfers, and desertions. It would take about two months to enroll enough paper soldiers to double the Battalion's strength—and its budget. If the incorruptible Minister of Rites Paul Hsü inspected the unit, he could obviously count no more than five hundred soldiers. The Arrowmaker would tell the Minister the remainder were in the field.

The Adjutant ensured that the childish ideograms of the barbarian Major's signature verified every report. His own signature was either omitted or merely attested to his having seen the report, not to its validity. More than a thousand documents flowed to and from the Ministry of War each month. Obfuscating his own role in the swindle was, therefore, easy. The more paper, the greater the confusion.

Francis Arrowsmith passed all those documents to Joseph King, who skillfully amended them to heap responsibility on the Adjutant. During the following months, Simon Wu was to puzzle over references by the Ministry of War to matters of which he had no knowledge. But he concluded that those discrepancies were connected with the grand peculation the Minister and his Mandarins were practicing in turn.

Except for the common soldiers, who did not matter, the entire Battalion was delighted. Receiving a generous fortieth of the embezzled funds, Joseph King decided to hedge his own secret reports to Paul Hsü. His master could inform the Minister of the full extent of the fraud—if he wished to. A twentieth rewarded the Battalion's ten lieutenants and twenty-eight sergeants for their essential cooperation—supplementing their independent extortions from the common soldiers.

Francis Arrowsmith convinced himself that the Battalion's efficiency was only marginally impaired by the web of corruption. Not only his professional pride was engaged. He knew that he must give Paul Hsü the most effective fighting unit in the Empire—or suffer the Minister's wrath. He wondered only occasionally when Dr. Paul would renew the pressure to marry Marta Soo. When he thought of Marta, he was surprised by the tenderness he felt—and the muted passion. But he still had not made up his mind whether it would be wise to marry her. Part of him wanted her, but another part was appalled by the lifelong commitment he would have to make to a young woman he hardly knew—and to China. Absorbed by the grand fraud, he tried not to think about the inevitable confrontation with Dr. Paul over the proposed marriage.

THE profitable enterprise was still burgeoning on October 14, 1630, at the beginning of the Double Hour of the Ox, one o'clock on a stormswept morning. Whipped by high winds, rain streamed under the sentries' helmets to cascade down their collars. Their waxed-canvas ponchos leaked profusely, soaking their padded jackets and their cotton trousers. The horizontal rain swamped the watchfires and the torches normally protected by miniature roofs. Since stormclouds blanketed the half moon, the camp was feebly lit by oil lamps in the officers' tents. The emergency oil lanterns hanging on the wall outlined the huddled sentries in a yellow nimbus, but cast no light beyond the wall.

The main gate and the watchtowers at the four corners were initially secure, because their broad foundations were planted deep. But the northeast tower trembled as the floodwaters rose inside the camp and wavelets rippled into tents set on wooden platforms. The wall suffered most severely, since its bricks had been dried in the summer sun for only a week when the camp was constructed in haste. The downpour dissolved the mortar and crumbled the edges of the bricks. Having withstood the torrents for three hours, a seven-foot stretch of the north wall collapsed at two in the morning.

A sentry tumbled into the moat, where the water was

already a foot deep. He twisted his ankle, but the chief injury was to his dignity. An herbal doctor's stubby-fingered hands bound the ankle firmly.

Francis withdrew his sentries to the shelter of the watchtowers and the main gate and also turned out Lieutenant Wang's alert platoon, fifty-two men trained without Simon Wu's knowledge. They were to patrol the inner face of the wall and to repair any breach with timbers and stones heaped against such emergencies. From the watchtowers the sentries searched the surrounding plain for movement—when they could see through the blackness.

Having taken all possible precautions against an unlikely attack through the storm, Francis retired to his tent. He tried to sleep, knowing his lieutenants could find him immediately. Halfway through the Double Hour of the Tiger, at four in the morning, he was awakened by a reed pipe keening an alarm. A second pipe shrilled, then a third. A single shot cracked above the drumming rain and the wailing wind.

Francis hurtled from his tent. His sword was in his hand, and his pistolet was free in his sash. He could see neither friend nor foe in the black opacity, though he heard swords clashing and men shouting. The cacophony of battle mounted, exasperatingly invisible. A dark form flung itself at his chest, blocking his sword arm, and he leveled his pistolet.

"Arrowmaker, it's me...Lieutenant Wang," the man gasped.

"What is it, Wang?" Francis shouted. "Are we attacked? Where?"

"Can't say exactly, Major. But at the main gate.... You can hear the swordplay...and the far wall...the west wall."

"I'll take the gate," Francis commanded. "Get to the west wall to lead the resistance."

Kettledrums rumbled a bass retort to the growling rain, and brazen handbells clamored. Swearing and stumbling, the Battalion turned out to assist the hard-pressed alert platoon.

The clouds shifted, and moonlight trickled down their sable flanks to light the camp. As Francis climbed the ladder to the tower above the main gate, the wind whipped the clouds away from the half moon. In the renewed light he finally saw the enemy. Six men wearing tattered gray cloaks and white headbands swung broadswords at his soldiers. Four arquebusiers were trying to fire on the attackers who swung a massive log against the planks of the main gate.

"Cover your flash pans," Francis roared, "and shield your matches."

The butt of his own wheel-lock pistolet was damp, but the covered flash pan had kept the priming dry. He sighted on the foremost man on the battering ram, a heavy figure with drenched black hair lying on his shoulders. Francis pulled the trigger, and the man sprawled in the mud. The ram's rhythmic thudding against the main gate faltered, and the arquebusiers' fuse matches glowed one by one like awakening fireflies.

Two shots cracked simultaneously, then three more followed. The crew of the battering ram apprehensively turned mud-spattered faces upward. When two more fell, the remainder abandoned the log and fled.

Several hundred assailants were streaming across the plain. Their shouts shrilled above the pelting rain: "*Sha! Sha! Sha wang-pa-tan yang-kuei! Sha!* . . . Kill! Kill! Kill the son of a turtle-bitch foreign devil! Kill!"

The wave drew closer, feet churning foam from the waterlogged ground. A sergeant pointed at a triangular battle flag inscribed with two red ideograms.

"*Chuang Wang!*" he shouted. "The Dashing King! It's One-Eyed Li . . . the brigand One-Eyed Li!"

"Hold your tongue!" Francis commanded. "Order your men to load and then hold their fire!"

A mud-smeared figure slithered over the wooden parapet like a water snake, and a stiletto gleamed in the moonlight. As the blade darted at Francis, the sergeant thrust his pikehead into the brigand's stomach. Bright arterial blood spurted, staining the yellow fat that bulged from the jagged wound. The sergeant twisted the pike and drew out coils of pallid-pink intestines splotched black with half-digested food. The pikehead ripped the delicate tissue, and a fecal stench fouled the sodden air. The sergeant thrust again, and the brigand toppled backward over the parapet.

"*Sha! Sha wang-pa-tan!*" The shrill war cry rose again from the brigands in the mud below. "Kill! Kill the son of a turtle-bitch. Kill! Kill the foreign devil!"

"*Teng ta-men* . . ." Francis ordered. "Wait till they're closer. . . . Now! Now! Shoot! All shoot!"

Twelve arquebuses fired. When the wind shredded the black-powder fumes, Francis saw the enemy running toward the shelter of the pines. The moon lit five squat shapes on the edge of the grove. Their waving arms commanded the

144

brigands to attack again, but the fleeing men streamed around them. When the five turned to flee, moonlight shimmered on the rust-yellow capes worn only by the Flamboyant Cloaks.

"We've thrown them back from the west wall." Joseph King spoke at his elbow. "Lieutenant Wang did well. But the attack was half-hearted. After twenty-four hours in the moat, what else could they expect?"

"Twenty-four hours in the moat?"

"The first dashing lads lay concealed in the moat since last night. Otherwise they'd never've found the walls in the darkness."

"We must teach the sentries to be more alert," Francis remarked. "Perhaps a touch of the lash."

"Thirteen on the west wall won't need teaching. They're dead. And some forty wounded."

"And our fine adjutant, Captain Simon Wu, how is he?"

Francis spoke lightly, determined not to yield to the depression that suddenly settled upon him. He had learned the meaning and the lonely responsibility of command when men died under his orders.

"You know, Major," Joseph King replied. "I haven't seen him all night."

Peking

MONDAY, OCTOBER 22, 1630

DR. PAUL HSÜ'S mood was portentous, his manner didactic. Whenever he was troubled the Mandarin retired into the stronghold of China's sacred Classics, which was buttressed by two millennia of learned commentaries. He ignored the tumult in the courtyards of his mansion on the Plumtree *hutung* near the Hsüan Wu Gate. Barricaded in his study behind high shelves crammed with paperbound volumes in silk-covered cases, he was considering the wisdom of the strategist Sün Tze.

"We must turn to Sün Tze. His precepts are directly applicable to our problems." The Mandarin addressed Francis Arrowsmith with the wry precision of a tutor toward a promising but ignorant student. "You should memorize his every word."

Francis nodded mechanical acquiescence. He was drowsy after the flowing rice wine and the abundant food Paul Hsü had offered his guests to celebrate *Chung-chiu Chieh,* the Midautumn Feast, the Empire's harvest festival. A banquet of thirty-two courses was no fitting finale to a twenty-five-mile ride through the harsh and bandit-ridden North China countryside. Despite his fatigue, the Englishman was tense.

Having thus far avoided Marta, he looked toward their inescapable meeting with unease.

"...only the enlightened sovereign, who can intelligently utilize highly intelligent agents, is certain to achieve great results." Paul Hsü repeated the closing words of Sün Tze's counsel on the Divine Skein. "Yet clandestine operations are the most essential element of warfare. The army that is successful diligently studies its intelligence reports before making any move."

"I can hardly disagree, Dr. Paul," Francis conceded. "China has taught me intelligence is fundamental. But I do object to being surrounded by spies of my own side."

"Your own side? Have you not also learned that there are many sides within the Empire?"

"So many I can't count them. And each with its own spies?"

"You must assume so. One commentator summed up Sün Tze's counsel on espionage with a homely analogy: *An army without spies is like a man without eyes or ears.* Where were your eyes and ears that night?"

"Dr. Paul, I am only a simple English soldier. My eyes and ears are no more than Joseph King and Lieutenant Wang. But we did catch Simon Wu and the Eunuch plotting. We *were* forewarned!"

"Barely, Francis, barely. You did not know precisely what your enemies planned. Now, my own eyes and ears have been busy since the assault..."

"You did not warn us, Sir." Attacking, Francis knew, was the best defense against a censorious Paul Hsü.

"It was a tactical matter," the Minister equivocated. "I assumed you would ensure that you knew exactly what the enemy..."

"We did the best we could." Francis was hurt, having expected praise for repelling the brigands. "The center of the conspiracy is here in Peking, and I have no way of..."

"*Ni yo tao-li.*" The Mandarin repressed his irritation with the young barbarian, who was not an ideal instrument of his will but was the best instrument available. "You have a point. My own eyes and ears will be more alert in the future. They have already....But where was Simon Wu during the assault?"

"I did establish that. Lieutenant Wang found the red lantern Simon used to signal the attackers still hanging from the east wall. When the attack came, Simon fled to his tent."

"What action have you taken?"

"I have only sworn Wang to secrecy. It is not a military matter, but a political matter for your decision. What action shall I take?"

"None! Do nothing at all!"

"Nothing? Leave the traitor unpunished?"

"Precisely!" Paul Hsü savored Francis's mystification. "Do nothing!"

"But your original plan is undone. You surely cannot expect to deceive the Divine Skein still. How could they judge the Battalion of God ineffective...about to collapse...after we repelled the attack handily?"

"Ah, but they still do." It was hard work, Paul Hsü mused, instructing the green youth in the complexities of the human soul, but it was necessary. "Another piece of mooncake, Francis? Nothing can match a Shanghai cook's light hand with pastry."

Francis took a large wedge. When the sweet-bean filling dissolved against his tongue, he reached for another piece.

"I'm glad you enjoy them, Francis. Do you know their story?"

His mouth full, Francis nodded vigorously to discourage Paul Hsü's didacticism. While they still exchanged language lessons under Candida's gaze, Marta had told him the story. Round as the full moon they celebrated, those cakes were an ancient dish sacred to the Great Ming Dynasty. The revolt against the Mongols that set the Ming on the Dragon Throne had been commanded by Chu Yüan-chang, a former carpenter and monk who later reigned as Hung Wu, the Founding Emperor. Messages hidden in mooncakes for the Midautumn Festival had conveyed the final orders for that rising.

"The Black Premier is no fool." Francis ran the tip of his tongue around his teeth to catch the remaining crumbs. "How could he still believe my battalion a paper tiger?"

"Because he wants to," the Mandarin replied. "He who constantly practices deceit is himself most easily deceived, since he cannot imagine others' telling the unvarnished truth. You must not punish Simon Wu—or show by the slightest gesture that you know of his treachery."

"Let him go scot-free?" Francis exploded. "A fine way to maintain discipline!"

"Just ignore the incident...as if you assumed he had done his duty. And, Francis, henceforth tell Simon Wu that the Battalion makes excellent progress...will soon be the best in the Empire. Also, give up your talk of leaving. Tell him that you are now well content."

"Tell him the truth? But you want the Black Premier to believe the Battalion is collapsing and I am planning to desert."

"I do. And he will. He will henceforth believe anything but the truth from your lips."

"I see your point. But I'll never understand the mazes you Chinese construct, never."

"Do not try too hard," Paul Hsü advised gently. "But you should know what happened that night. My eyes and ears tell me the brigands were astonished by your resistance. The Special Service had assured them the Battalion would collapse and they could easily seize the fire-spitting weapons."

"You mean the attack was not meant to destroy the Battalion?"

"*Tuei-la*...correct. The brigands had no stomach for a pitched battle. The Special Service wanted to savage the Battalion, not destroy it...not yet."

"Is nothing in the Empire ever straightforward, not even treachery?"

"Sometimes, but rarely." Paul Hsü judged with pleasure that Francis would soon comprehend the rudiments of Chinese politics. "The Eunuchs expected One-Eyed Li's brigands to be thrown back with severe losses. But not so quickly, only after they had savaged your men."

"And my new line with Simon?"

"When you confide that you have changed your mind about leaving, he will believe his golden arrows have hit the mark." Despite his fondness for Francis, the Mandarin wondered why the Lord God afflicted him with the instruction of a youth still so naïve he did not realize his peculation was known to the last farthing. "I believe you will soon be offered employment as an agent of the Divine Skein. You have proved yourself greedy and venal..."

"And then, Sir?" Francis winced when Paul Hsü's arrow also hit the mark. "What are my orders?"

"Accept! By all means accept! You cannot have too many strings to your bow."

"And my duty to you...to the Fathers...to Holy Church?"

"Most doubled agents are bribed or intimidated, as you know. Do you possess the strength and the faith to choose that hazardous calling?"

149

Warming again to the Minister, Francis was tempted to ask permission to keep the gold secured by embezzlement and espionage. No, silence was wiser, though Paul Hsü himself had certainly gained far more than his meager salary from the offices he had held.

"I believe I possess the faith." Francis formulated a reply that implicitly assigned responsibility to the Minister. "And I shall follow your instructions in all things."

The evening was warm and the split-bamboo blinds were rolled up to admit air. The wooden cylinders of the scrolls clattered against the blue walls when the breeze caught them. The cries of children pierced the hush of the study. They were pleading for more mooncakes and racing around the courtyard waving lighted lanterns shaped like animals. Hundreds of colored lanterns hung from the eaves above the courtyard. Reflecting the splendor of the orange moon, they also recalled the battle lanterns that had signaled the Chinese rebels to march against the Mongols.

The lanterns' rays animated the scroll paintings. A tiger crouching on a cliff glowed successively violet, red, and green—and appeared to move as the light touched its striped flanks. The rays alternately lit and obscured the objects tumbled on Dr. Paul's redwood desk.

Between his cupped hands lay a protractor, a two-legged compass, and a Latin treatise on artillery translated from the Arabic of al-Ras'is Ibrahim. The Minister of Rites, guardian of the nation's doctrinal and liturgical orthodoxy, was an ardent student of trigonometry and, of course, ballistics.

Dr. Paul's left hand stroked a stack of printed pamphlets. The square ideograms on the cover identified a monograph on the telescope "Composed by the Calendrical Bureau of the Department of Astronomy, Edited by Hsü Kuang-chi." The manual of optics was Paul Hsü's most recent work. Most Mandarins composed epigrammatic verse, but the Minister of Rites uniquely translated treatises to instruct his countrymen in European science.

The enigmatic Minister was erect in a clean-lined Peking chair of shimmering *huang-hua-li,* the Chinese rosewood whose golden sheen is lighter than English rosewood. His large eyes glittered when he talked of his hopes for the future, but glowed softly when he recalled the glories of China's past.

"You think me peculiar at times, do you not?" The abrupt question startled Francis. "A Christian who loves devious stratagems. A Christian who plots against the neighbor he should love—and does not always disdain illicit gain.

"*Autres pays, autres moeurs!*" Francis too could retreat behind aphorisms. "Different places, different customs! As the Spanish say: 'The rabbit does not presume to judge the elephant!'"

"An elephant, am I, and you a rabbit?" Paul laughed. "You must understand that only *Chinese* ways can repel the Tartar threat and win China to the True Faith. I despise the deviousness of my people and the venality of the Court Eunuchs. But I must be even more devious and equally venal to realize my vision of a secure Christian China."

"But European science...the learning you disseminate ...it can only be practiced in a straightforward manner."

"I do not see the necessity. Science cannot be used straightforwardly by men who live deviously. Even science must adapt to Chinese ways. Just so did the holy Father Matthew Ricci adapt the forms of Christian worship to Chinese ways...losing not a drop of their essence."

"I honor your purpose, Sir," Francis answered neutrally.

"Still noncommittal, my boy? You *are* learning Chinese ways. And still noncommittal on the other matter—your marriage to Marta? You have already had several months. Time is growing short...if you are to save yourself."

"Months usurped by other concerns, as you know, Sir." Francis fended off the Minister's renewed threat. "But I am thinking hard."

Francis rose, although he was not unreservedly eager to join the revelers in the courtyard. Powerful Mandarins were engaged in a competition better suited to strolling troubadors than officers of state—or a fighting officer. Composing extemporaneous verses in praise of the full moon was beyond him in English, much less Chinese. Besides, the ladies had been invited by Paul Hsü's indulgent laxity to join the celebration, and he wondered whether he wished to encounter Marta. But he longed to escape the Minister's inquisition.

"A moment, Francis," Dr. Paul commanded. "We're not quite finished, are we?"

"I can hardly say more at this moment, Sir, bedevil me as you may."

"Do you really expect me to accept that evasion?"

"Well, not quite." The Minister's patience could erupt in anger. Dr. Paul, Francis realized, could be revenged for prolonged opposition to his will, as well as the insult to his family and his race. Well aware of the Chinese passion for "settling accounts," Francis knew he must honor his heavy moral debt to the Minister.

"The match is not abhorrent to me, Sir." Francis mingled truth and pretexts. "I entertain the most profound admiration for the Lady Marta. But I must be certain that I am doing injustice to neither her nor myself. Can she be reconciled to a foreign—I'll not mince words—a barbarian as a husband?"

"That is my affair, not yours." Paul Hsü glared across his desk. "I shall decide what is meet for her, not you—or she. I cannot be patient much longer. You must choose soon . . . very soon. Will it be marriage or exile? Far worse than exile if I take my hand away and leave you to the Black Premier's gentle mercy."

"I'm sorry, Sir, deeply sorry." Francis realized he could no longer temporize with the Mandarin. "I shall make my choice very soon."

"Within the week, Major, no longer. Now, be off with you!"

When the young Englishman had left, Paul Hsü opened his treatise on the telescope with anticipatory pleasure. But he gazed unseeing at the symmetrical ideograms. Since the marriage was necessary, he had alternately cajoled and threatened. If Francis and Marta would not come together of their own free will, they would come together to oppose his will. Though united against himself, they would still be united.

Why, he wondered, had the Lord of Heaven chosen to disturb his old age, which should be serene, not only with the Tartars but also with willful children? His lips moved in silence as he prayed for guidance—and for patience. Then he smiled. He was warmed by his paternal affection for the stubborn young outlander.

THE inner courtyard was a cauldron of shifting light, bubbling laughter, and shimmering color. Boys dressed like miniature adults darted about fiercely, and grave Mandarins displayed histrionic terror of paper lanterns with candles glowing in their gaudy fish, dragon, and tiger bellies. Girls were as brilliantly adorned as grown-up ladies—and as quiescent, since their feet were already compressed by broad bandages. The females sat together on porcelain stools in the corner of the courtyard.

Francis waved to Father Adam Schall, who was seated

regally in a cane chair between the glowering porcelain lions. One hand held a cloisonné cup which the manservants replenished from blue-and-white wine pots. His other hand offered sweetmeats wrapped in red paper to a semicircle of enraptured boys. The Jesuit smiled and told an endless German fairy tale. When he paused, the boys demanded more, calling him *Shen-fu Po-po*...Uncle Spiritual Father.

A servant handed Francis a cup of warmed rice wine, and Adam Schall lifted his cup in salutation. The Englishman drained the yellow wine and held his cup upside down over his head to show that it was *kan-pei*, a dry cup. The priest pointed his bearded chin at the corner of the courtyard, where the women sat, their eyes modestly cast down on the crochetwork growing under their flying fingers.

Francis obeyed the unmistakable command he could not pretend to misunderstand. He wove through the throng, nodding greetings to the Christian Mandarins he had met. When he approached the seated women, Candida rose from her green-glazed porcelain stool, which was set beside Marta's, and mimed an invitation to take her place.

"I must hurry the lazy servants," she said. "Will you sit with Marta for a moment?"

The blatant invitation was observed by every adult in the courtyard. Candida's unconventional behavior left Francis little choice. If he rejected it, he would appear churlish and would render a grave discourtesy to Marta. Accepting could precipitate the decision he had avoided for several months. Resignedly, he seated himself on the porcelain stool.

"Are they," he asked abruptly, "still pressing you?"

"Worse than ever." Marta's whisper accentuated the intimacy implicit in his bald question and her direct reply. "And yourself?"

"Dr. Paul is threatening me even more strongly," Francis confided to the only person who could understand his predicament. "Now he's set a time limit—a week from today. I don't know what we're to do. I can't see any way out."

"Of course, he *might* not carry out his threats." Marta wondered resentfully why Paul Hsü's Christian God had chosen her for this bloodless martyrdom. "He might just be trying to force us together. He is not usually vindictive."

"Do you really think so?" Francis grasped at the slim hope offered by her far greater knowledge of Chinese ways. "Will he accept our refusal?"

"He usually *does* carry out his threats," Marta mused. "No,

153

I'm afraid he won't relent. He hasn't given an inch to all our resistance these past months."

"Then what do we do? What can we do?"

"Well, as far as I.... I'm prepared to.... But of course..."

"Of course *what?*" Francis recognized in his impatience with Marta the fierce irritation aroused only by those for whom he felt strong affection. "You're prepared to *what?*"

"Major, don't snap at me. I am not yet your..." Marta paused, dismayed by her slip of the tongue.

"Nor likely to be my wife, you would say? But we cannot avoid it, can we?"

"You can, quite simply," Marta flared. "He cannot force you, but can only exile you. If you simply choose exile, the problem is solved."

"Your problem, not mine. Exile...and I'm finished. There would be no future for me anywhere. And I would betray the Lord's Manifest Will that I serve the Faith in China."

"Then you condemn me never to marry," Marta pleaded, her chin trembling. "My father is under Dr. Paul's thumb. And Dr. Paul would condemn me to eternal spinsterhood."

"You can always marry me and solve your problem." Francis brushed the wings of hair off his forehead in perplexity; at that moment he wanted this woman more than he feared marriage to such an alien being. "At least you'd be married.... And that's what you want."

"Yes, I desire marriage, but *not* to you, Major Arrowmaker." If she had not rejected the three suitors her father offered, Marta realized, she would not be trapped by this barbarian.

"Then the matter is closed, is it?"

"Again, so simply, Major? I said I did not want to marry you, not that I would not if I had no other choice."

"It's nice to be a last resort. You flatter me, Madam."

"I hadn't meant to flatter you," Marta smiled despite her anger.

They sat silent amid the tumult that imperfectly masked the intimacy implicit in their silence—and Francis examined his dilemma for the hundredth time.

His cooperation with Paul Hsü had entangled him deeply in the fierce intrigues of the Ming. He would be inextricably entangled if he were offered—and accepted—profitable employment by the Divine Skein. The alternative was leaving the Empire, voluntarily or involuntarily. Outside China, his prospects were at best negligible, at worst, fearful.

He could not, Francis saw clearly, remain in the Empire, where riches awaited him, unless he enjoyed the protection marriage to Marta and adoption by Paul Hsü would bring him. Of themselves alone, his military skills, however highly valued, could not protect him against the enemies he had already made and the enemies he would make. Yet an irrevocable Catholic marriage would virtually commit him to a lifetime in China. He wished for an instant that his devoutly Catholic father had apostatized. The new Church of England not only permitted divorce, but apparently encouraged divorce.

Still, annulment was by no means impossible for a faithful servant of Holy Church—though he wondered if he would wish to be parted from Marta. The rub was not committing himself to Marta, but committing himself to China. Nonetheless, coercion was certain grounds for annulment—and he was unquestionably coerced.

"It seems the only way." He broke their silence at last. "I can think of no way out. Can you possibly bring yourself to consent?"

"Candida says it won't be so bad...not desperately bad." Marta expressed her own deepest concerns. "I wouldn't be like Wang Chiang, the Han Dynasty lady the Emperor forced to marry a Hun chieftain and live among the Huns. I would remain in China with a...a barbarian who know our ways a little. And..."

"And...," he prompted after waiting half a minute for her to overcome her shyness.

"...and...and if there were children, they wouldn't ...not necessarily..."

"Not necessarily what?" Her hesitation again irritated him as if they were already married.

"They wouldn't necessarily be barbarians." The words tumbled from Marta's lips with mock bravado. "Brought up as Chinese...in Chinese culture...they would be Chinese."

"Is that your chief worry?" he asked, incredulous.

"Of course." Marta was, in turn, astonished by his question. "Everything else is small beside that question. Your wishes...my wishes...they don't matter so much, after all. But the children."

"Something else is just as important," Francis explained

155

patiently. "Could we bear to live together? Could we be happy? Could you live with an outlander who is often away soldiering?"

"I suppose...if there is really no alternative..." she mused aloud. "We could learn to live together. Chinese have done so for many centuries."

Pleased despite her grudging assent, Francis brooded on Marta's curious mentality. One minute hotly opposed, the next she spoke calmly of their living together like any other husband and wife.

Watching the play of thought on his barbarically expressive features, Marta marveled at Francis's concern for something he called happiness, which really did not enter the question yet. Happiness, whatever that was, would take care of itself in time. If it did not, she would have her household and he his battalion.

Observing the decorum Confucian etiquette enjoined between husband and wife would avoid unseemly strife. It would go smoothly enough—if only he were not so blatantly frank and so emotional. Still, there was virtue in filial submission—and he could learn civilized behavior.

"What else can we do?" Marta added. "This seems to be our fate."

"It appears that we must." Expressing his resignation, Francis startled himself by blurting: "And I know we will be happy."

"I do hope so...very much," Marta smiled. "I shall pray for happiness."

She had taken the irrevocable decision, the decision she had almost known from the beginning was inescapable. Fearful one moment, eager the next, she wondered what it would be like, his lovemaking. Subtlety she could not expect from a heavy-handed outlander, though she could in time guide him. But he was big and powerful, this strangely passionate being to whom she was committing her life. She felt perverse excitement well within her.

"At least," Marta said slowly, "it will be different."

Peking

MONDAY, FEBRUARY 25, 1631

THE golden cloak of twilight draped the gray roofs of the Northern Capital. Though sooty dusk was staining the bright haze, yellow motes still danced in the retreating sunlight. It was the middle of the Double Hour of the Monkey on the eighth day of the first month of the fourth year of the reign of the Chung Chen Emperor of the Great Ming Dynasty.

Under the yellow tiles of the Palace of Absolute Purity, His Imperial Majesty had been dithering for twenty minutes. He was torn between the skills of the Lotus Concubine, his latest favorite, and the mysteries of his newest plaything, a baroque clock, an orrery that displayed not only the time but also the phases of the moon and the movements of the constellations. The Emperor finally delivered himself of a Solomonic decision. He commanded a Eunuch to bring the Lotus Concubine to the chamber where the orrery stood in blue-and-gold enameled dignity. It would be amusing to make love to the sonorous ticking of that tribute from the reigning Prince of Bavaria.

In the red-walled reception chamber of Minister Paul Hsü on the Plumtree *hutung*, Father Adam Schall glanced indulgently at the austerely elegant clock he had presented to the household. It showed thirty-three minutes past four on the afternoon of Monday, the twenty-fifth day of February in the Year of Our Lord 1631, less than six minutes since Francis Arrowsmith had for the third time nervously asked whether the clock was not running fast. The priest knew it was correct to a sixth of a minute, having that morning set it by the master clock of the Bureau of the Calendar, which was calibrated against the movement of the planets.

The household of Mandarin of the Third Grade James Soo still reckoned time by the notches on a slow-burning vermilion candle. Though ingenious, like most things Chinese, a time-candle could err by as much as an hour. The wedding procession should have left James Soo's mansion three hours earlier, more than time to have reached the Plumtree *hutung* even at the stately pace tradition required. However, the procession, like most things Chinese, had probably started late.

Adam Schall assured himself that a punctual departure was as unlikely as James Soo's changing his mind. However his daughter Marta might feel, the Mandarin could not allow her to withdraw. Too much time had passed since the exchange of contracts while the astrologers determined the auspicious wedding day by casting horoscopes and studying *feng-shui*, the portents of the winds and the waters. If he gave in to his daughter, James Soo would be publicly dishonored. Nonetheless the Jesuit had learned how inconstant women were since coming to China and, for the first time in his adult life, talking with many women.

Adam Schall suppressed his misgivings to soothe Francis Arrowsmith. The bridegroom was pacing the red-walled reception chamber like a tiger in a pit. On each outward journey Francis feared that Marta had undergone a change of heart; on each return journey he wondered whether he could still change his own mind. Where in the Devil's name, the priest wondered, could the procession have got to?

THE declining sun painted the red-lacquered pig with a patina of tarnished gold. The roast boar was borne shoulder-high by two coolies in ostentatiously new white trousers and blue jackets. The crimson sashes draped diagonally over their shoulders and knotted over their hips were inscribed in gold with double-joy ideograms, the symbol of married bliss.

Twenty-four plump piglets followed two abreast, displaying their scarlet glory on trays balanced on coolies' heads.

Behind marched forty-eight coolies with bamboo poles slung between their shoulders. Yellow dragons cavorted on the ten-gallon wine jars hanging from those poles, every jar boldly labeled *chia-fan*. No spectator could be unaware that the Mandarin James Soo had provided the choicest rice wine of Shaohsing for his daughter's wedding—as he had lavished the richest silks, the finest furniture, and the costliest jewelry on her dowry.

Six crimson umbrellas followed, the silk tassels on their four tiers dancing in the winter wind. Three umbrellas of three tiers were the normal number, and some well-to-do Mandarins happily made do with two umbrellas of two tiers. But James Soo had spurned such economies, determined to mount a display that would not have dishonored the bride of an Imperial Prince.

Horrified at the thought of his favorite daughter's marrying an ocean barbarian, James Soo had rejected Paul Hsü's first approach. Finally persuaded by the strong-willed Minister, he was comforted by Francis Arrowsmith's new status. After his adoption by Paul Hsü, the bridegroom was no longer an unknown barbarian, but in every significant respect the son of one of the most powerful men in the Empire. He was now known as Hsü Shih-jen, Hsü the Arrowmaker.

Still uneasy, James Soo had resolved to offer a spectacle the Northern Capital would recall over its teacups for decades. His lavishness would prove that the alliance was a great honor for his family, rather than the somehow disreputable affair Peking's gossipmongers had gleefully denigrated. The splendor of the wedding procession further declared that his daughter came to the nuptial bed with her honor unstained.

Laden as heavily with those emotional burdens as it was with material wealth, the procession moved with majestic slowness. The crowds its splendor attracted further impeded its progress. The venerable matchmaker who had negotiated the contract was relegated from his traditional position at its head to safety behind the umbrellas. The company of the Battalion of God detailed as a guard of honor was struggling to clear a way through the throng. When the double-barred white cross on their green banner halted, their lieutenant ordered his men to level the bamboo poles that symbolized the Mandarin James Soo's judicial powers.

"A prince and a princess you'd think they were," shrilled
159

a wizened bondservant, her tongue's razor-edge blunted by the lavish display. "It's a grand match."

"Is it true this ocean barbarian, the Arrowmaker, is seven feet tall?" asked a peddler of dried fruit. "I hear he goes into battle alone except for a few coolies to carry ammunition for his thunder cannon."

"Absolutely true!" replied a streetsweeper. "Many times I've seen him ride from the house of his father, the Honorable Minister. He carries an eight-hundredweight cannon over his shoulder as you or I would a fly whisk—and his horse is as big as an elephant."

"Ah, the poor, poor dear!" The mood of the harridan bondservant altered abruptly. "A good Chinese maiden sacrificed to a baby-eating ocean barbarian. Just listen to the song they're playing."

The sixty-four-piece band shuffling behind the aged matchmaker was so tightly packed that its glittering brass long-horns prodded the umbrella bearers. A knot of flautists intertwined with drummers and cymbalists around four *suona,* short horns with flaring bells and ebony shafts.

Flustered by the throng, the bandleader had lifted his trumpet and blared the preliminary trills of the melody that moved the old bondservant to tears. Dour Peking humor overcoming discretion, the musicians played the "Lament of Wang Chiang." All the spectators knew the folksong of the Latter Han Dynasty, some fifteen centuries past, which bemoaned the sorrow of the Court Lady the Emperor had forced to marry a Hun chieftain.

James Soo fumed impatiently, but the throng held his horse fast and its music drowned his shouted commands to halt the scandalous song.

The poignant melody was muffled by the crimson curtains of the bride's flower-palanquin. Only Marta Soo, isolated by the felt curtains, did not shiver when the north wind whistled through the *hutungs* and lanced the avenues with sleet that heralded a blizzard. When she recognized the swelling tune, Marta was overcome. Had Candida not assured her that, unlike Wang Chiang, she would not be a pitiful exile among uncouth barbarians?

All brides were carried to their weddings in a turmoil of regret for girlhood irrecoverably lost and for families irrevocably abandoned. All brides came to their grooms in terror of the new families to which they were inextricably committed—even after death, when their names were carved on their husband's ancestral tablets rather than their own. Worse, she was marrying a barbarian. Through her anguish, the crowd's good-humored chaffing sounded like the growls of wild beasts. The tragic "Lament of Wang Chiang" crushed the little self-possession she had retained.

Feeling a tear trickle through the powder on her cheeks, Marta gulped back the sobs trembling in her throat and blotted her eyes with her gorgeous sleeves. Her elaborate makeup could not be repaired in her tiny cell, and it would be disgraceful to stand before the altar with teartracks seaming her face.

She should have persisted in her refusal; far better to have remained a spinster. If only she had not yielded! If only she could have become a nun!

Marta longed to escape from the prison of her wedding palanquin. Her thighs trembled beneath her gold-encrusted gown when she imagined the barbarian's embraces, and she clasped her arms over her breasts to contain her revulsion. She must not think of violation by his distended red stalk—so titillating in the gaily colored drawings of a bride's pillow book but so repulsive when imminent. Whatever the humiliation, she longed to flee her moving cell, which was dyed sickly red by the light filtered through the curtains.

The palanquin no longer swayed on the shoulders of twelve sturdy coolies, and the faint "Lament of Wang Chiang" stopped abruptly. When the procession halted, the band embarked upon "A Visit to Fairyland," just composed by the Emperor for his subjects, who idolized composers and performers of popular songs. The uninspired melody dulled Marta's agitation but did not cheer her. She sank again into the morass of her misery.

The splendor of the flower-palanquin mocked its passenger's grief. Silk garlands adorned the carrying poles; the crimson-lacquered panels were emblazoned with golden double-joy ideograms invoking wedded bliss; and a rosette like an enormous peony crowned the peaked roof. But the bright tassels on the palanquin's eaves swinging in the rising wind warned of the approaching storm. Clumps of snow already clung to the red-felt roof, and sleet pelted the lacquered sides.

His anger cooled by the band's changing its tune, James Soo looked at the procession that stretched two thousand yards. His five sons rode with him, while his wife and three daughters were carried in sedan chairs flaunting scarlet streamers. Massed lanterns behind them glowed against the

161

sky. Those hundreds of fantastic shapes were dominated by two birds towering sixteen feet above the throng. Iridescent feathers glittered on the scarlet bodies and the golden wings of the male *feng* and the female *huang* phoenixes, the pair symbolizing joyous wedlock. Each was illuminated by five candles, two in each outspread wing and two in each great body. The largest candles, in the silver heads, shone yellow beams through the golden beaks. Coolies prudently carried water buckets behind.

Twenty musicians mounted on white horses with crimson saddle-cloths followed the lanterns. Gongs, cymbals, and clapping boards like great flat castanets hammered out the beat, while the melody swelled from flutes, miniature trumpets, and cloud gongs, ten metal plates suspended in a gilded bamboo frame. Atoning for the indiscretion of their fellows, the mounted band played the lilting tune "The Wild Geese Alight on the Shore," a favorite of the Emperor.

The swirling snow obscured the tail of the six-thousand-strong procession. The display had cost James Soo a tenth of the wealth he had wrung from Kwangtung Province in his six years as vice-governor, when his annual salary was no more than three hundred taels. Two years' salary would not pay for the fireworks that painted glowing pictures in the darkening sky and frightened off malevolent spirits with their fusillades.

The Jesuit Fathers, James Soo had heard, exhorted European officials to keep neither bribes nor presents. But the intelligent Fathers made no such demands upon Christian Mandarins. Parsimonious Peking expected its officials to live off the people, since they could not live on their minute salaries. The Mandarins could take as much as they pleased—as long, in theory, as their extortions did not arouse public disorder, which in reality they did. The Mandarins' primary duty was collecting taxes to support the corrupt luxury of an Imperial Court of lechers, sadists, and drunkards, many of whom were, like their Emperor, also homosexuals and opium-smokers.

James Soo knew why rebellions tormented the Empire, but he could do little to alter the pernicious system. Paul Hsü was, at least, trying, but.... The Mandarin shivered and pulled the collar of his red-fox coat around his ears. The rising wind was hurling pellets of hail and clumps of snow at his head.

So much gold spent, James Soo sighed to himself, and the

spectators could only glimpse the costly splendor of the procession through the storm: the ancestral tablets, refurbished with gold, flanking the gold-inlaid plaque bestowed by the Emperor upon his retirement as vice-governor of Kwangtung; food enough for fifty banquets, so abundantly diverse that twenty-five suckling pigs were a meager introduction; twenty-four dragon heads draped with silk; two hundred banners, flags, and pennants emblazoned with invocations of good fortune. The climax was Marta's trousseau, each costly garment and piece of linen ostentatiously displayed on a platform held high on poles.

Toward the end of the procession, the greatest treasures were guarded by forty arquebusiers of the Battalion of God. The first was banal but awe-inspiring: twenty gold bars, each weighing twenty taels, some twenty-five ounces. The second was extraordinary and even more valuable than the first: a cross three feet high carved from pale-green jade.

The very end of the procession like the fox's brush tipping a dragon's tail was a gaudy marching band. Some of its members played the *sheng,* seventeen purple bamboo tubes in a bowl-like gourd; others trilled silver flutes; and the rest beat snare drums with padded sticks.

James Soo lamented the snow flurries and the encroaching darkness, which obscured his purposeful extravagance. Knowing himself unobserved, he drank from the flask of fiery *mao-tai* spirits he had slipped into his long sleeve before setting out. The *mao-tai* restored his normal ebullience, and he concluded that the expenditure was well worth while. Next to official corruption, the chief occupation of Peking was gossip. All households from princes' to coolies' would recall his lavishness for a generation, their normal exaggeration compounded because the spectators had only glimpsed the treasures through the veils of snow and dusk.

The people of Peking would praise him extravagantly, and their praise was the essential political capital of an ambitious Mandarin. Even foolish Emperors who disdained the commonalty were served by Ministers who were, at least, clever enough to listen to the voices of the mob. The most splendid wedding procession the Northern Capital had seen in a decade would, moreover, light the life of his beloved daughter. Marta would enjoy an aura of good fortune and great wealth a princess of the Blood Imperial would not scorn.

Hidden by whirlwinds of snow, James Soo drank another deep draft from his flask. What, he wondered, was holding them up? The soldiers should already have unraveled the knots of spectators who impeded their progress. He sighed in renewed irritation, stoppered his flask, and touched his horse's flank with his heel.

The horse pushed past the flower-palanquin toward the vanguard, where the coolies bearing the roast pigs huddled against the sleet. James Soo heard shrieks over the wind keening through the *hutungs*. Through the rippling snow, he saw the soldiers flailing the unmoving crowd with bamboo poles. His anger rising, the Mandarin watched a wiry youth in a tattered tan tunic dart under the poles to swing a wooden cudgel at a soldier's stomach. The arquebusier collapsed retching, and the youth slipped back into the crowd, which welcomed him with a triumphant shout.

"Destroy the infidels!" The high-pitched cries were tossed by the wind. "Down with the ocean-devil god! Expel the barbarians!"

A black object flashed past the Mandarin's head, and a shower of stones rained on the soldiers' helmets. A brick crashed against a horse's flank. The animal reared, and its flailing forefeet smashed a coolie's chest. The coolie toppled, scarlet gouts spurting from his mouth. The roast piglet he carried on a tray rolled on the snow-covered pavement. Its red-sauce coating left crimson smears on the whiteness beside the fan of scarlet arterial blood.

Felled by the stones, three soldiers lay in the snow. When the lieutenant bellowed an order, his men dropped their poles and drew hooked scimitars. They formed into a wedge, scimitars whirling above their heads. The crowd slowly gave way before the flashing steel blades.

"Expel the barbarian idolators!" The shout was less strident, dwindling in midcry. "Down...with...the...foreign-devil...god!"

The crowd fell back, parted slowly, and disintegrated like a dam crumbling under a flash flood. The soldiers surged forward as the fleeing agitators emitted one last defiant cry from the mouth of a *hutung*: "Expel...all...barbarians!"

The procession moved forward again, its dignity marred by its haste. All the spectators had scuttled to shelter. In appalled silence, the wedding party traversed the final hundred yards along a deserted avenue to the Plumtree *hutung*.

Knowing the Divine Skein, James Soo assumed the demonstration had been incited by a few provocateurs among the volatile rabble. The Black Premier, he feared, had himself ordered the outrage. Who else would dare interfere in the affairs of Minister of Rites Paul Hsü?

James Soo shuddered at the evil omen. His daughter's married life was beginning with strife in a blizzard, rather than the sunshine the astrologers had promised would ensure her happiness.

Marta's father regained his composure when the procession crept through the narrow Plumtree *hutung* to the gate of Dr. Paul Hsü's mansion. Coolies would trudge between the high walls late into the night to deposit their burdens of food, wine, wedding gifts, and trousseau. Despite the Black Premier's interference, the flower-palanquin had come safely to its destination. The Lord God, James Soo recalled a sermon of Father Adam Schall, imposed trials upon his children to temper their spirits and test their faith.

When he dismounted, the Mandarin had convinced himself that the omen was actually good. The ease with which the demonstrators had been dispersed portended his daughter's triumph over the perils that beset all humans in all ages—but particularly in the reign of the Chung Chen Emperor of the Great Ming Dynasty.

The distant scuffle Marta had heard within her palanquin hardly impinged on her gray misery. She was numb when she reluctantly stepped into the snow flurries. Feeling neither joy nor sorrow, she tottered across the outer courtyard on the arm of her maidservant Ying. No emotion disturbed her white-powder mask when she entered the reception hall, which was banked with chrysanthemums.

Marta felt no more than would a life-size Szechwan puppet manipulated by steel rods, and she was painted like a puppet. Her caked face-powder was so thick it would split if she smiled; her brows and lashes were beaded with kohl, and rouge heavily encarmined her cheeks and lips. She was also attired like a puppet in a historical play-with-music.

Her headdress of peacock feathers above a gold-filigree diadem was studded with emeralds, pearls, and sapphires. Her wedding gown resembled the court costume worn by Empresses of the Tang Dynasty a thousand years earlier. Tied with a fringed crimson sash, her gown was cut from brocaded blue tribute-silk embroidered with hundreds of many-colored phoenixes, each regarding an astonishing world through a single eye carved from a tiny emerald. The gown's broad crimson border, which swept the checkerboard tile floor, was embroidered in gold thread with rampant dragons, as were the six-inch lapels crossed over her breasts and the cuffs of her sleeves. Those sleeves were so long she kept them from trailing on the floor by holding her hands rigidly clasped before her bosom.

Though a supple seventeen-year-old, Marta moved as stiffly as a rod puppet within the weighty carapace. She could not have moved at all if she had not been supported by her maidservant. She could not turn her head more than an inch without dislodging the gold-wire pendants hanging over her ears.

The bride slowly rotated her entire body to look across the reception chamber at the bridegroom. Her kohl-rimmed eyes were liquid with the tears she had not dared shed. Marta's eyes appeared her only living part to Francis. He was half-stupefied by the fumes of charcoal braziers and by the miasma of heat and perfume rising from some three hundred guests crammed shoulder to shoulder.

The scent of incense and the fragrance of flowers were overpowering. Coming from the northern winter outside, he was stunned by the brilliance of those unseasonable blossoms. Orange and crimson, yellow and white, bronze and heliotrope, thousands of chrysanthemums wired to tall bamboo frames dominated the hothouse lilies, roses, and peonies in glowing porcelain jars. The display diminished the Lunar New Year's plants: pink-flowered peach trees and miniature orange trees in scarlet jardinieres. An artificial spring had supplanted the world of sleet and snow outside the red-painted walls.

Francis Arrowsmith recoiled from the inhuman apparition that was his bride. The sensation of unreality that had haunted him all that day overwhelmed him. He felt detached from the fairyland spectacle, no longer a chief player but a bemused spectator.

Why, he wondered, was a blond Englishman dressed in the formal robe of a Military Mandarin of the Sixth Grade of the Great Ming Dynasty? To what purpose did a German priest wearing a black horsehair hat stand, overtopping the surrounding Chinese, before the massed chrysanthemums? Why was the priest wearing a green-embroidered chasuble over his white surplice?

The bridegroom was recalled to bizarre reality by Dr. Paul Hsü's hand on his arm.

"Are you ready, Francis?" the Minister asked. "It is time."

The lilting Officials' Language scourged the bridegroom's nerves. He was, he realized, by no means ready for the irrevocable marriage—and he would never be ready.

A painted puppet, a product of Chinese artifice, tottered interminably toward him through the chattering throng. He was to pledge himself to a creature of silk and metal and paint, not a living woman of blood and flesh and feeling.

Her gait revolted him. How could a Christian European live among a people who distorted God's handiwork by twisting their women's feet into hard little hoofs? How could he bind himself inalienably to a woman who had submitted to that torture? The ironically named golden lilies were but a token of the perversity of the Chinese. The bitter bile of revulsion clogged his throat.

When Dr. Paul propelled him forward, Francis reminded himself that the destruction of all his hopes—and, perhaps, violent death—was the alternative to this marriage. He gingerly took the pale, clawed hand that peeped from Marta's dragon-embroidered cuff. He saw with disgust that she still braced her arms to keep her extravagantly pendant sleeves from brushing the floor. A single saving thought preoccupied him: marriage contracted under duress was not true marriage.

That realization sustained Francis. Marta was beyond rational thought or coherent emotion. She longed only to escape to the flower-palanquin like a she-bear retreating to hibernate in a sunless cave.

Neither looking at the other, bride and bridegroom advanced to the crimson-and-gold altar. Square red candles burned in carved wooden candleholders stained the repellent maroon of dried blood; incense sticks smoldered in squat maroon burners encrusted with cobwebs of faded gilt. Between them stood the black tablets with rows of golden ideograms listing the sacred ancestors of Minister Paul Hsü. Already Francis's ancestors by adoption, they would soon be Marta's ancestors by marriage.

The two gorgeously clad automata fell to their knees. They genuflected thrice, each time touching their foreheads to the cold floor tiles thrice in the kowtow the Chinese rendered only to the Emperor and their ancestors.

Mere mummery, Francis consoled his conscience, a meaningless act. Ancestor worship, so called by Europeans, was not actually worship, Father Adam Schall had rationalized. The ceremonial Chinese honored their ancestors by their obeisances but did not worship them as deities. The First Commandment thus remained inviolate, since adoration was reserved for the One True God.

Marta was fully aware while they awaited the next stage of the ritual. She had never before that moment kowtowed to any ancestral tablets other than her father's. She knew she would not be truly married until she was united in the Sacrament of Holy Matrimony by the Priest of the Lord of Heaven. Nonetheless, obeisance to Paul Hsü's ancestors had snapped her ties to her own family. She was already a different being, no longer the daughter of James, but the wife of Francis and the daughter-in-law of Paul, his adoptive father. That revelation passed, she relapsed into gray ination.

Moving in unison, though their hearts were far apart, the bride and bridegroom took the eggshell-jade cups the stout marriage broker offered on a red-lacquered tray. They raised their cups to each other and sipped the yellow Shaohsing wine. They raised their cups to the widower Paul Hsü and to Marta's parents, and sipped again. They saluted the altar with its ancestral tablets, sipping once more before exchanging cups to drink the last drops of each other's wine.

They thus became man and wife by the traditional Chinese rites. Marta was bound to Francis for all her mortal life; he was legally bound to her only until it pleased him to send her back to her parents. But the Christian couple still awaited the rites that would unite them perpetually in Holy Matrimony.

Father Adam Schall stood before the altar, which had been covered with white silk embroidered with gold crosses. A choir of boy sopranos sang as Marta teetered down the lane between the guests on her father's arm. Imprisoned within her despair, she saw the brilliant colors of the massed chrysanthemums through a mist. His face set, Francis waited beside the white-silk cushions laid before the altar. He took her hand, and they kneeled together.

Adam Schall's normally saturnine features were lit by grave joy as he intoned: "In the name of the Father, the Son, and the Holy Ghost..."

Marta and Francis kneeled and rose in response to the Priest's gestures.

"Marriage is a sacred institution." Father Adam Schall addressed himself to the congregation as well as the bride and the bridegroom. "God Himself it was who established it

168

when he placed our First Parents in paradise. It became more sacred still when Our Lord Jesus Christ made the marriage of Christians a sacrament symbolizing the union between Him and His Bride, the Church."

The brief sermon that followed Francis understood imperfectly. Its sentiments were so elevated as to be incomprehensible, its language so refined as to be unintelligible. Marta was roused to silent dissent by the few phrases that penetrated her torpor: "Shining exemplar of the joining of two great civilizations...in their persons....The Universal Holy Catholic Church blesses....This happy pair embodies the harmony..." She smiled bitterly, careless of her makeup, despising her entire family—above all, herself—for submitting to that alien mummery.

Francis responded mechanically when the priest asked: "Francis Shih-jen, do you freely and willingly take Marta Mei-lo, here present, as your lawful wife according to the laws of God and Holy Church?"

"I do," fell dully from Marta's lips in her turn, but she clutched Francis's hand fiercely when the priest instructed: "Join your right hands." Her voice was vibrant when she repeated "I, Marta Mei-lo, take you, Francis Shih-jen, for my lawful husband to have and to hold from this day forward, for better for worse, for richer for poorer, in sickness and in health, until death do us part."

Her hand tightened convulsively when Father Adam Schall declared: "I join you in Holy Matrimony....What God hath joined together, let no man put asunder."

Marta glanced at her bridegroom, who was looking down at her. This marriage, she realized, was as great an ordeal for him as for herself. He was an outlander in a society that must make him feel greatly inferior. She was Chinese, and she would remain at home in the splendor of the Great Ming Empire.

Somewhat consoled by that realization, Marta acknowledged the reality of her marriage. She would, she resolved, extract every pleasure she could from the grotesque union forced upon her. She perceived the nuptial bed not as an altar upon which she would lie inert like a sacrifice, but a battlefield where she and the Arrowmaker would meet naked in equal combat. She would take all possible pleasure there. For the rest, no injunction of either the Sage Confucius or Holy Church demanded that wife and husband love each other obsessively. They were chiefly required to behave decorously in the public eye.

Overwhelming knowledge of her own power suffused Marta. He looked so pathetic, so woebegone, her dashing officer—and he would suffer more, much more. She might, in time, take pity on his suffering.

Francis felt Marta's grip relax and her hand slide into his. He knew he was truly and irrevocably married—whatever canon lawyers might prate of coercion. Truly, no man could put them asunder. Not knowing whether he rejoiced or grieved, he sighed with relief that the deed was done.

Tengchou, Shantung Province

JULY 5, 1631–SEPTEMBER 8, 1631

"YOU'RE very quiet, Francis. Daydreaming?" Marta's voice drifted from the shadow of the standing umbrella that shielded her fair skin from the sunrays dancing off the Straits of Pohai. "Is there anything you need?"

"No, Marta, nothing," Francis replied from his perch on the low stone wall surrounding the terrace of the villa General Ignatius Sün had allotted them in Tengchou, some 350 miles from Peking. "I'm fine. Just thinking."

"Pleasant thoughts, I hope?" Marta shifted lazily on her cane chaise longue. "Are you thinking of me?"

"Among other things," he answered truthfully. "You know I'm always thinking about you—even when I'm thinking of something else."

"You're worse than the Jesuits for twisting words, Francis. But what were you thinking?"

"Just thinking how strange it is. Less than five months ago, we almost hated each other because Paul Hsü was forcing us together."

"It *is* only five months, isn't it? It's hard to believe July's just begun. Sometimes it seems a lifetime."

"Or only a day or two. And I'd bless Paul Hsü for forcing us to..."

171

"But not for letting us be sent here, Francis."

"Yes, it's hard to be charitable. But we wouldn't be married without him, Marta."

"Mostly, I bless Dr. Paul. Anyway, he probably couldn't help your transfer. And it won't last forever. Mandarins always get some bad assignments, but good ones follow."

"If only I could get the Battalion back, I could forgive Paul almost anything. But I never will."

"Can't you forget the Battalion for a while, Francis? Think about us for a change. Doesn't that help?"

"I'm always thinking about us. It helps tremendously...almost entirely."

Francis Arrowsmith felt with some justice that he had been badly treated. He had undertaken the journey to Tengchou with bad grace. It was a mean fortress town despite its commanding position on the straits leading to the Gulf of Pohai, which separated Shantung Province from the Tartar-held Liaotung Peninsula. Nor was his assignment to a provincial backwater redeemed by the eminence of its governor, General Ignatius Sün Yüan-hua, who used the green-bronze cannon with striking success against the Tartars.

Even a less passionate man than Francis would have felt it no honor, but ill-camouflaged disgrace to have been relieved of command of the Battalion of God in order to serve under General Ignatius Sün. Though he retained his rank as a major, his meager pay had been reduced by half because he commanded no troops. Though his stipend from the secret service called the Divine Skein compensated him threefold for his reduced pay, he had been deprived of the Battalion's abundant graft—and he was always aware that he still had his fortune to make. It was only small consolation that he served again with the Macao Expeditionary Force and its veteran commander, Captain-Sergeant Miguel Gonsalves Texeira Correa. Besides, the Portuguese were also disgruntled in virtual idleness.

Francis's pride had been lacerated by the ceremonial tattoo in which he relinquished his battalion. His former Adjutant, Captain Simon Wu, would lead into battle the soldiers Francis had trained. He had nodded morosely when his slave Joseph King praised his Christian forbearance, remarking that a Chinese similarly humiliated might well have resorted to craven suicide to reclaim his lost face—which meant, of course, his honor.

The intense pleasure he and Marta had discovered in their

nuptial bed after a fumbling beginning had, however, brightened the past few months. He had forgotten his professional humiliation for many hours in that joy. No bawd of the camp, no lady of skill in a Peking Flower House had led him to such transports of sensuality.

The late-afternoon sun gilded the ruffled waters and lit the miniature grotto under Marta's sun-umbrella. In the dark cavern beneath her chaise longue, the two small lion-dogs stirred and looked up. Before turning on her back to sleep again, the silver-and-white female rumbled in her throat like a pigeon cooing hoarsely. The golden male stared haughtily from obsidian black eyes.

In the late-summer heat, Marta wore only a light pongee dressing gown over the tissue-thin shift that just covered her hips. She yawned and stretched languorously, delighting in the caress of the evening breeze. The movement strained her loosely knotted sash, and the dressing gown fell away from her body.

Distracted by Marta's yawn, Francis looked up from the whitecaps on the sapphire water. Her sheer shift had lifted to expose the delta between her thighs, the Jade Terrace hymned by Chinese erotic poets. Intercepting his gaze, Marta blushed and drew the skirts of her dressing gown together. Disarmed by his smile, her hands fell nerveless to the ground.

Francis rose and walked barefoot toward her umbrella. His light robe clung to his sweat-damp skin, and a half-smile lingered on his lips. Wang, the male lion-dog, keened a shrill greeting. Mu-lan, the female, chuckled companionably deep in her throat.

"I'm not having them," Francis picked up Wang and stroked him. "Those beasts can just stay outside."

"You want to go inside?" Marta's smile challenged him. "Is there any particular reason?"

"We might think of a reason ... if we tried hard."

"I can't think of any reason to go inside. The sun's too nice."

"In Peking," Francis mused provokingly, "there'd be so many diversions: jugglers and acrobats, plays-with-music, conjurers.... And I could always visit a Flower House on a dull afternoon."

"Francis, don't you dare ... even think about Flower Houses." Marta had learned to respond to his banter, but she recoiled from that jest. "I won't have it."

"What else is there to do in this dull, Godforgotten place?

173

If only...anywhere else..." Francis probed again the pain of his betrayal by Paul Hsü as a tongue tests a hollow tooth.

"I won't allow you to talk that way. Perhaps we'd better go inside right now." Marta stretched sensuously again. Yielding to the thrust of her breasts, her dressing-gown again slipped from its loosely tied sash. "Yes, I think we'd better."

"Just because there's nothing else to do in Tengchou?" he laughed. "Perhaps we could try the Winding Dragon?"

"Too strenuous for a hot summer afternoon." With an effort, Marta recaptured the light manner that pleased him. "But, if you insist..."

Tantalizingly slowly, Marta rose from the chaise longue and turned her back to Francis. Her loose sash opened and the dressing gown slipped off her shoulders. The light fabric slithered down her back to crumple around her ankles. Wearing only the gauzy shift that barely covered her rounded buttocks, she teetered toward the open door of their bedchamber.

Francis gazed at her retreating back, at once aroused and repelled by her awkward gait. He wondered again at the bizarre torture that had shaped her golden lilies, which were tiny in embroidered scarlet slippers. Scarlet ribbons tied around her ankles secured the slippers, which were like minute skiffs with high sterns. Since she put her weight on her crippled heels, Marta shuffled. But the gait that had originally reminded him of a waddling duck was now lubriciously exciting. Her buttocks did not rotate like a wanton European woman's but shifted against each other. The twin dimples at the base of her honey-pale spine shimmered violet through her diaphanous shift.

Francis threw off his robe and followed Marta into the cool bedchamber. Half-ashamed, he marveled that the barbarically distorted gait should arouse him just as it did jaded middle-aged Chinese men.

He knocked away the bamboo props, and the rush-mat shutters barred the door to the lion-dogs. The male yelped in falsetto indignation and the female scratched vigorously at the matting.

"*Pu-hsing, Mu-lan, Wang!*" Marta called, "No, Mu-lan, Wang!" Their protests dwindled to whimpers.

Despite her crippled feet, Marta stepped lithely from a stool onto the *kang,* the brick platform on which their bedclothes were spread. The *kang* was cool, for the fire that burned in its hollow interior during the bitter winter had

174

been long unlit. Bending from the waist to stretch her slender fingers along her white-silk ankle-stockings, Marta untied the scarlet ribbons of her slippers. She dropped them to the wood-plank floor, where they lay like gaily painted flowerboats stranded by the outgoing tide.

Marta propped herself on her right elbow in the posture of the nude ivory statuettes on which modest ladies pointed out their symptoms to herbal doctors. Her lolling breasts were somewhat full for a Chinese, though pertly firm. Her small, heliotrope nipples pressed against the gossamer silk of her shift, which was rucked around the delicate incurve of her waist.

Francis leaned over the *kang,* resting his palms on the perfumed bedclothes. When her hand reached out to stroke him, he marveled again at the smoothness of her pale-gold skin, and he was aroused by her perfect nakedness. The delta between her thighs was covered by almost invisible down. That hairlessness had at first repelled him, as if he lay with a child, but he was now excited by her own visible excitement. A hairy European woman would offend the fastidiousness he had learned from her immaculate delicacy.

"I see," Marta smiled, "the Jasper Stalk is already eager to invade the White Tiger Grotto."

Bending toward her lips, he felt Marta recoil fleetingly before her mouth opened under his. He had taught her to kiss as Europeans did, but she did not enjoy that mingling of tenderness and desire. They had not talked of that feeling, though she avidly discussed every other aspect of their lovemaking with an anatomical explicitness that still shocked him. But she could not share his pleasure in the play of their lips and tongues.

Otherwise Marta was skillfully wanton, utterly different from the frightened virgin who had come to their bridal bed. The Chinese called the wedding night, *yü shan chih hsi,* the "evening to drop the fan" behind which the timid bride had previously hidden her blushing face. Once married, that maxim implied, a bride must put aside all hesitance and all concealment to join her lord in ingenious intertwinings and interpenetrations of all members and all orifices. It had taken several months, but, guided by the erotic classics, they had attained a sexual Nirvana of utter abandon.

Aside from minor variations, the delicately tinted sketches in the brides' pillow books portrayed thirty-two positions in minutely realistic detail. China's erotic poets had also written

175

a lexicon of sensuality. Francis and Marta spoke of their sexual organs as the Jade Terrace, the Jasper Stalk, the White Tiger Grotto, the Fabulous Pagoda, and the Twin Lotus Peaks. The postures of love they called Silk Reeling, the Sea Goddess Aroused, the Winding Dragon, the Pair-Eyed Fish, the Red-Horned Unicorn, and the Green Dragon.

Francis had at first been faintly repelled by Marta's insistence on keeping her handbook of venery open beside their pillows. But he was entranced by the exquisite pleasure its counsel yielded. He had become captive to joys he would six months earlier have thought perverse—if he could have imagined them.

This once disdaining athletic gyrations, Francis slipped the gossamer shift over Marta's head and caressed her gently. Careless of subtlety, she quickly attained the arousal her pillow book called "emerging from the gray clouds into the sunlight on the mountain peak." All artifice forgotten, she cried her need aloud in a crescendo of trilled syllables.

"Ai...ai...Wo ai...Wo ai ni....Hau...hau...hen hau! Oh...oh... I love...I love you....Good...good...so good!"

When her fingernails raked his back, he did not hear her satiated gasps: *"Tai...hao....Tai...hao...la!* Too...good. ...Much...too...good!" Nor did he hear his own hoarse shout of triumph. He did hear a clear voice within his head: "This is why you remained in China. This is all the reason you need...this Marta!"

In the next instant, exaltation dissolved into farce. The matting covering the door quivered under the assault of the lion-dogs. Alarmed by the human cries, the animals clawed at the screen that kept them from their mistress. The male's shrill keening and the female's high-pitched barking were a distorted echo of their own exultant cries. The screen banged repeatedly against the doorframe, and the matting bulged inward.

"Do let them in before they tear the screen." Though Marta laughed at the discordant anticlimax, a note of reproach crept into her voice. "They'll be good. They're always good. I don't see why you locked them out."

THE lion-dogs were more often with Marta and Francis during their protracted lovemaking, while maidservants giggled and menservants leered at the frequency with which the door to the bedchamber was barred. Mu-lan and Wang lay motionless on the cool floor, their dark eyes peering through thickets of hair to assure themselves that the new master did not hurt their mistress. When Marta or Francis cried out, the shaggy heads lifted from outstretched forepaws to watch the humans' antics with grave attention. Normally the dogs slept, exhausted by their romping among the azaleas and rhododendrons in the garden, which was deliciously wide after the narrow courtyards of Peking.

The long days were golden with unbroken sunlight. The nights were silver with starlight, and moonbeams gleamed from burnished skies. Francis was later to remember the summer of 1631 as the season of constant light, which suffused the first protracted joy he had ever known. Other men were to recall that glorious summer as the last moments of untroubled ease the Great Ming Dynasty ever knew. Shimmering on the sapphire sea and the topaz sands, the brilliant light enveloped Tengchou with a gold-and-silver radiance.

Throughout that glorious summer, Marta glowed with the realization of the joys her pillow book promised. Though she sometimes shuddered inwardly at Francis's bizarre appearance, he was the instrument of her pleasure and, therefore, hallowed in her eyes. Because he was bigger and stronger than most Chinese men, her surrender was the more thrilling. Her victories, when she dominated him with her slight body, were exultant.

The posting to Tengchou had at first dismayed her with the knowledge that she was married not only to a Western ocean barbarian, but also to a Military Mandarin in disgrace. Yet all Mandarins were regularly transferred between provinces. Having grown up expecting such a shifting existence, she could not wholly share her husband's indignation. Habituated to injustice, she smiled at his oscillation from despair to confidence that justice must soon be done because Paul Hsü must soon discover that Francis Arrowsmith was indispensable to the creation of a modern Chinese army.

Marta was immersed in her new joy. Events that did not impinge on her sensual delights were not quite real, but amorphous shapes on the periphery of her vision.

How right, she reflected, her mother had been to assure her with the timeworm cliché, whose truth only experience could prove, that "real courtship comes after marriage, not before." When he was downcast, she almost liked Francis, which was quite different from delighting in using his body. He was almost attractive when his normal arrogance was tempered by misfortune, as he was not when he rode the crest of the wave, insensitive to everything except his own ambition. Her husband was a peculiar creature who could not simultaneously pursue his public life and his domestic life with equal vigor. Marta was secretly pleased by his disappointment, which turned all his attention to herself.

Besotted by the ecstasies she evoked, Francis was bemused by affection for Marta. His tenderness grew with his realization that she had irrevocably committed her life and her happiness into his hands. Her high spirits and her stubborn will endeared her to him. Her assertiveness, which often brooked his will, made it plain she was not the painted rod-puppet he had thought her on their wedding day. Marta was a vibrant human being who demanded her due rights in their marriage.

His physical repletion spiced by that awareness, Francis nonetheless felt he should not be quite so happy. His nightly prayers reproached his excessive delight in carnal love, though it was sanctioned by the Holy Sacrament of Matrimony. He pledged to moderate his mindless transports and to reduce their shameful frequency. But his resolution was swept aside by his transcendent pleasure in their increasingly sophisticated coupling. Drifting on the gold-and-silver sea of sensuality, he could forget that he was a half-pay officer whose future was as clouded as the summer was brilliant. He could almost forget that his career had been blighted by circumstances as far beyond his control as the revolutions of the sun and the moon.

TENGCHOU was worse than a backwater. It was a rubbish heap for all the outlanders who had come to China to fight the Tartars. Tengchou was also a dungheap for those Christian Chinese who had proved the lethal power of the green-bronze cannon against the Tartars. Chief among those Christians were General Ignatius Sün and his civilian deputy Ambassador Michael Chang, who had accompanied the Macao Expeditionary Force north.

Captain-Sergeant Miguel Gonsalves Texeira Correa and his hundred-odd surviving men had been bundled off to Tengchou a year earlier because the Court was alarmed by

the threat they could pose to the old order. With Francis
Arrowsmith separated from the formidable Battalion of God,
the Grand Eunuch and his henchmen could again sleep
soundly. No longer did the Christians and the reformers command formidable military units near the Northern Capital.
No longer did they possess the armed power to purge the
corrupt Court and force the sweeping social changes that
alone could enable the Ming to resist both Tartars and rebels.

Having overawed the Tartars, the outlanders had been
relegated to a remote quarter of the Empire. If they insisted,
they could still fight the Tartars who swarmed in the Liaotung Peninsula, only thirty-two miles north of Tengchou
across the Pohai Straits.

Most galling to Francis's pride was the memory of his
constant obedience to Paul Hsü, who had withdrawn his protection shortly after the marriage that was his wish alone.
Francis cursed the naïve loyalty that had made him a doubled
agent. He had reported secretly to both sides, and he had
obeyed both sides. As a result, he no longer knew which side
in the convoluted power struggle he truly served—or which
of his actions benefited the forces of evil and which benefited
the forces of good. He finally wondered whether good was
distinguishable from evil in the murky half-world of Chinese
espionage. Having become a familiar of the Devil, he doubted
the existence of the Devil. He prayed that he might not soon
doubt the existence of the Lord God Himself.

Aside from Paul Hsü's obvious clambering toward the
power of a Grand Secretary, Francis could not comprehend
his purposes. Eager for Francis to become an agent of the
Divine Skein, the Minister had shortly thereafter grown cool
toward his protégé. Perhaps he resented Francis's gold, which
was stored in four crimson-and-gilt leather trunks in Father
Adam Schall's strongroom: four thousand taels, enough to
purchase manors in England. But Paul Hsü had never even
asked about that hoard.

Francis did know that he had been inexcusably naïve in
believing that either the Divine Skein or the Minister of Rites
would permit an outlander to command a Chinese battalion
in action. If the Battalion of God should acquit itself well
under his command, it would become a greater threat to the
status quo. If the Battalion should break, its sponsor, Dr.
Paul Hsü, would be punished for allowing an inexperienced
barbarian to command a unit of the Imperial Guard. The

Minister must have known from the beginning that he could not thus risk demotion or execution.

Like all Chinese a gambler, Dr. Paul knew that the wheel of fortune spun wildly. He had staked Francis's life on his visceral conviction that fate would, somehow, halt the wheel where he wished.

THE pink ball soared out of the knot of Portuguese soldiers, who wore only cotton-duck breeches tucked into leather boots in the heat of early September. The wind carried the ball toward the wall separating the villa of General Ignatius Sün from the parade ground. A stick-thin Angolan slave, his torso shining blue-black above his white loincloth, hurtled upward. Bounding ten feet high, he engulfed the inflated pig's bladder with one enormous hand.

Some thirty Portuguese, Francis saw, were playing against blacks and Indians, who rushed to screen their teammate. A stocky Portuguese corporal slithered under their churning feet to hurl the Angolan onto the brown grass with a one-handed tackle. An Indian trailing a white dhoti scooped up the ball that squirted from the Angolan's hand and looked around for protection. Finding himself alone, he prudently grounded the ball but was nonetheless submerged under a mound of kicking Portuguese.

When the scrimmage disentangled itself, the Indian gingerly shook his head. Wiping blood from his nose, he screamed imprecations in singsong pidgin Portuguese. The Angolan patted the Indian on the shoulder and took the pig's bladder.

When the teams lined up in half-circles, Francis saw that five Chinese soldiers stripped to baggy undershorts were playing for each side. Surprised by their participation, he watched the ball arc high from the Angolan's unshod foot.

Though the ball bounced outside the parade ground, rebounding from the wall of the General's villa, a Portuguese caught it and ran. Trapped by his opponents, he lobbed the ball to a Chinese sergeant. The Chinese swiveled and twisted toward the straw butt at the far end of the parade ground. He slithered through clutching hands until he faced only the goalkeeper. But a pack of Indians and Africans brought him down five yards short of the goal.

His features working in anger, the Angolan snatched the ball and shouted at the Chinese sergeant. The stocky Chinese, flushed with exertion and indignation, swore in his thick Manchurian dialect at the African, who stood two heads taller.

Francis strode toward the knot of quarreling players that formed around that pair. Their rudimentary rules put both sides in the wrong: the Portuguese should not have played the ball that bounced out of bounds; their opponents should not have tackled the ball-carrier within the five-yard free zone before the butt.

When fists were raised, Francis quickened his pace. Since all the troops were tense, a fight on the playing field could spark a riot between sword-wielding outlanders and halberd-armed Chinese.

"*Atencāo!*" a Portuguese sergeant shouted as the officer approached. The men struggling on the ground stopped thrashing, while those standing stiffened.

"Play it again!" Francis directed, first in Chinese, then in Portuguese. "Both sides were in violation."

The Englishman stiffened in astonishment when the meaning of the sight he had just seen registered in his mind. Two of the six pairs wrestling on the ground had been Chinese against Chinese; rather than arraying themselves against the outlanders, the Chinese had supported their teammates against their own countrymen.

Francis was thoughtful as he hurried to his appointment with the General. Only Ignatius Sün's enlightened discipline, he realized, had prevented an outbreak erupting from the squabble—as it had previously prevented other quarrels turning into riots.

At fifty, General Ignatius Sün was a victim of his own reputation as a beloved commander and a brilliant strategist. Having studied mathematics and ballistics with the Jesuits, he had, as early as 1622, urged in a Memorial to the Throne that foreign green-bronze cannon be deployed against the Tartars. Supported by General Ignatius, the Field Marshal who commanded the Ming's frontier forces had driven the Tartars from all the territories south of the Great Wall and from large areas north of the Wall. When the Field Marshal was beaten to death by Flamboyant Cloaks in a Peking marketplace in 1630 on the Emperor's direct order, General Ignatius Sün was appointed governor of Shantung Province. That banishment was called promotion, since the Court might need him again. Meanwhile, he could do the conservative faction no harm from Tengchou.

The General was an unmartial figure, plump and short with delicate hands and small feet. In his scarlet tunic with the stylized lion of his rank on its breast, he looked like an actor thrust into an incongruous role by a desperate stage manager. His fair skin was lightly scarred by smallpox, while his beard and mustaches were foppishly curled with wax.

But General Ignatius Sün's troops were devoted to him because he was devoted to their welfare. Almost unique among Ming generals, he strove to keep his casualties to a minimum. He was enamored of the green-bronze cannon not only because of their frightful power, but also because they expended shot and powder on the battlefield, conserving his soldiers' flesh and blood.

Though the Christian General commanded a motley garrison in Tengchou, harmony prevailed because of his intelligent lenience. Moreover, Francis had reported to both Paul Hsü and the Divine Skein that there was *no* embezzlement in Tengchou—because Ignatius Sün was astonishingly honest and because there was so little gold to divert. The Ministry of War was niggardly with supplies and miserly with soldiers' pay. The General had almost emptied his private purse to feed a force made up of Shantung regulars, units from southerly Kwangtung Province, and Manchurian levies drawn from both ethnic Han Chinese and nomad tribesmen hostile to the Tartars.

The malign Ministry of War had believed the Portuguese unit would be the spark that set off the mixed powder of that garrison. Billeting some eighty Portuguese artillerymen, Indian bondservants, and black slaves with mutually antagonistic Chinese units was intended to produce friction. Though the Ministry did not actually wish to lose Tengchou, the vindictive bureaucrats were eager to make mischief for the Christian General because he was too successful against Tartars and rebels.

Both Captain-Sergeant Miguel Gonsalves Texeira Correa and Major Francis Arrowsmith that afternoon reported to the little General that the troops from Macao were no more than restive. Still happy to amuse themselves with the Flower Girls of the port, the foreigners were, however, surfeited with uneventful garrison duty. They were also indignant at reductions in pay and rations forced by the parsimonious Ministry of War.

"There's only one way to keep my lads from becoming as rotten as the Ming soldiers," Miguel Texeira mused that evening after dining with Francis Arrowsmith. "They desperately need a good fight."

"Little prospect of that, Miguel, just now," Francis replied.

"Well, they'd better get active service soon." The Captain-Sergeant's swarthy-gray forehead wrinkled, and the flat planes of his cheeks twisted in a grimace. "Otherwise, I won't be answerable."

"Somehow, Miguel," Francis smiled, "I don't think the Emperor will invade Tartary just to oblige you."

"If the Chinese prefer a mutiny, they'll get it. Especially if my men aren't paid in full soon. The Flower Houses are demanding their money. Cut off my lad's entertainment...and God knows what..."

"I'll have a word with the General. He can probably arrange extended credit by threatening to close the Flower Houses down."

"Thanks, Francis. I didn't like asking him. But the lads still need combat."

"You could always join the Tartars," Francis laughed. "They'd pay a stupendous price for two batteries of cannon."

"Would they, indeed?" Texeira mused. "How do you know?"

"Just hearsay," Francis parried. "The talk of the bazaars. But it stands to reason."

"Only hearsay! Is that so?"

"Really, it's only hearsay!" Francis saw no need to confide that he had been approached through his secretary Joseph King to join the Tartars as an extravagantly paid colonel of artillery and master cannon-founder. "But it's logical. The green-bronze cannon are the Ming's master weapon. Without them the Chinese would still be running....They'd probably've reached Nanking or Shanghai by now. So, the Tartars *must* get their own cannon—and the men to use those cannon."

"That makes us very valuable, doesn't it? Worth a hundred times what the Chinese pay so grudgingly."

"Just two of us, but we could decide the fate of the Empire—and make ourselves very, very rich." Though lured by the thought of much gold, Francis remained realistic: "It's nice to think about, Miguel, but only to think about."

"It scorches my soul. Just think of all that beautiful gold. If only..."

"If only the Fathers wouldn't excommunicate us for joining the Anti-Christ. But the Jesuits didn't bring us into the Empire to make our fortunes. They brought us to propagate the Faith. They certainly didn't bring us to back the Tartars against their Chinese protégés."

"By God, it's tempting. Even the Tartars would make better Christians than these Chinese. A herd of Iberian hogs would make better Christians...except for a few good men like Dr. Paul, General Ignatius, and Ambassador Michael."

"What do you know of the Tartars, Miguel? Besides, of course, that they run like gazelles from unshotted cannon."

"That was a fine device, wasn't it?" Texeira chuckled reminiscently. "But I know a lot more about the Tartars than you think."

"How's that, Miguel?"

"Francis, for your ears only? You'll keep it close?"

"Who would I tell, Miguel? Be reasonable."

"Your hand and your honor on your pledge of secrecy?"

"Of course, Miguel!" Francis offered his right hand, marveling at the passion for ceremony that overcame all Iberians from time to time. Texeira and he were the only senior European officers in Godforgotten Tengchou. Yet Texeira demanded a formal pledge of secrecy. "Now, what is it?"

"A week ago, that Colonel Gong...Goong...Gang... or whatever. How do you say his heathen name?"

"You mean Lieutenant Colonel Keng?"

"That's right, Gong, the one the troops call the Halfwit. He sidled up to me the other day. You know I've picked up a little of their heathen chatter. I can get the gist."

"And the gist was?"

"He just wanted to warn me against the Tartars. He'd heard...wouldn't say how, of course...they'd pay a fortune, an Emperor's ransom, for my unit."

"What did you tell him?"

"Oh, I lost my temper." Texeira laughed. "Told him I'd report him for spreading sedition if he didn't stop right there."

"You had to tell him off...otherwise you could end on the headsman's block. Yet, he could just've been spreading dissension....Not necessarily treason, just mischief-making."

"So I reckoned, Francis. But I'm convinced he was really trying to recruit my artillerymen for the Tartars. I don't like that Halfwit. His head would look grand on a pike. But if only the Fathers were more reasonable..."

"If they were they wouldn't be Jesuits, Miguel. The gold's tempting, very tempting. But this isn't Europe. Once read

184

out with bell, book, and candle, you'd find no priest to church you again. It's a great pity."

"A pity indeed," Texeira agreed. "But you won't forget my lads and the Flower Houses? Otherwise they might go over to the Tartars on their own."

"Losing us the profit?" Francis laughed. "Never! I'll see the General in the morning."

Francis pondered those confidences after they said their goodnights. General Ignatius Sün's two chief subordinates were Manchurian Chinese who jibed at his orders and fanned their soldiers' smoldering dissatisfaction. The senior was Kung Yu-teh, whose given name meant Virtuous. The junior was Keng Chung-ming, whose given name meant Half-Bright, which the soldiers had inevitably transformed into Halfwit. The two lieutenant colonels had been comrades-in-arms since they began their careers as demibrigands in their native Manchuria. They had, he knew, flirted with the Tartars before offering their swords to Ignatius Sün in 1630.

DESPITE the odd tasks he did for the General, Francis chafed for lack of full employment. Since he could not spend all his free time making love, he began his first serious study of Chinese literature. His tutor was Joseph King, who had passed high in the First Civil Service Examination. He had been a member of the ruling class of scholar-officials before his father's purported treason condemned him to slavery.

Francis wanted to read the Five Classics, the Sacred Canons that were the Chinese equivalent of the Holy Bible. Joseph King insisted that they begin with the Four Books, the equivalent of the writings of the Fathers of the Church. The Five Classics, Joseph said, were written in a grossly archaic style. The Four Books were easier. None had been written more than six centuries before the Miraculous Birth of Jesus Christ.

"*The Dialogues of Kung Fu-tze*, which the Jesuits call the *Analects of Confucius,* are most useful for a foreigner," the secretary explained. "Though ancient, the style is easier because the Master's disciples wanted to disseminate his doctrines widely. *Everything* in China derives from the Master: family life, government, philosophy, morality, even table manners and cuisine. Even when we rebel or dissent, we rebel

185

against a Confucian ruler or dissent from Confucian orthodoxy."

"I know the Jesuits take great pains to reconcile Holy Doctrine and Confucius." Francis was happy to sit again at the feet of a learned master, as he had in the College of St. Omer before he was expelled to live by the sword, the arquebus, and the green-bronze cannon.

"The Fathers are wise not to challenge the Master's teachings," Joseph King replied.

"This is damnably difficult." Francis riffled the paperbound booklet. "You said it was easy, but I recognize only one ideogram in five."

"*Wo shuo-la keng-jung-yi...,*" his secretary answered. "I said easier or easiest. I didn't say easy. True knowledge is never easy, certainly not the Master's."

Chastened, Francis bent his blond head over the black ideograms that marched down the pages unimpeded by punctuation. It was certainly not easy when he could not tell one sentence from another.

"It's not as bad as it looks," Joseph King reassured him. "Take the chief Confucian virtue, *hsiao*, filial piety. Here it says: *Tze Yu asked about filial piety, and...*"

"You're not looking at the book," Francis objected.

"Of course not." Joseph was startled. "If I didn't know the *Analects* by heart, I'd be a sorry scholar. Every schoolboy can recite the *Analects* with his back turned to the book. But I'll give you the passage in our spoken tongue first."

"As long as I don't have to memorize it."

"*When Tze Yu asked about filial piety, the Master replied: Present-day filial piety seems to mean no more than feeding one's parents adequately, as one feeds a horse or a dog. Unless there is reverence for parents, the action is meaningless.*"

"He didn't mince words, did he?"

"No, Major. You must understand the Master's concept of filial piety, since the entire Confucian Empire rests on it. The Emperor is the Son of Heaven, to which he renders reverent obedience. The Emperor is also the father of his people, who obey him. Filial piety binds China together."

"If you insist."

"Take this passage: *The Duke of Sheh proudly told the Master: My people are totally honest. If a man steals a sheep, his own son will bear witness against him. The Master replied: Honest people in my native land are different. A son will con-*

ceal his father's wrongdoing, and a father will conceal his son's. That is filial piety, the highest honesty."

"I see, then: Whatever a man does is right, as long as he does it for his family." Francis was as exhilarated as a school-boy by his insight. "It is the *highest honesty* to take...to steal, we'd say...even from the nation in order to give to one's family."

"You begin to comprehend China, Major."

EXCITED by his first systematic penetration of the orthodox Chinese mind, Francis paraded his new knowledge for Marta at dinner that evening. She had, he knew, been given a re-spectable classical education by her indulgent father.

Since the evenings were chilly in early September, they were dining in the reception room. Despite the glow of the charcoal braziers, Marta was huddled in a padded green-silk gown whose heavy folds made her look like a stuffed toy. She showed scant interest in the food and less in Francis's rev-elation of mysteries that were commonplaces to her. To her husband's irritation, she was withdrawn in self-contempla-tion, her frequent mood during the past month. Beyond self-obsession, she seemed enraptured by self-adoration like Nar-cissus, who worshiped his own reflection.

"I know the passage." Marta languidly caressed her left hand, admiring her pink-nailed fingers. "Of course a son owes *all* loyalty to his parents. Even a daughter does, until she marries and obeys a new lord."

"That's why I sometimes can't understand you Chinese. Europeans believe in absolute right or wrong—even if we don't always..."

"You believe...you really believe a son should betray his father for the sake of outsiders?" Marta was shocked.

"My schoolmasters used to say a lie serves the Devil, but truth serves God. A son betrays God if he lies...even for his father's sake."

"*Kuo-la ban-nien yi-hou...*" Marta's lips curved in a pus-sycat smile, and she stroked her cheek lovingly. "You may feel differently in half a year's time."

"Why ever should I, Marta?"

She rose and bowed low, her hands clasped within her sleeves, while Francis stared in astonishment.

"You will understand filial piety because you will be a father. Your son will be born then."

"My son? You never told me! A son? How can you know?"

Francis took Marta in his arms. The news was splendid, and he was overjoyed. The news was also shattering: another responsibility, another bond to China. But he thought of a son of his own, and he laughed with delight. No, a son for Marta and himself and a grandson for the amiable Mandarin James Soo, whom he liked greatly. Also a grandson for his own parents, who would look down from Heaven and rejoice. A pledge to God and the future, a pledge of joy.

"I couldn't tell you till I was sure, Francis. But Ying can tell. She knows the baby'll be a boy.... He's so high in my womb."

"And I never noticed."

"It's not your part to notice. This is women's business, not men's business."

"But it will be mine, too...my son." His exhilaration mingled with possessive concern. "You must look after yourself well...very well.... Women's business it may be, but you couldn't have done it without me."

"You are quite right, My Lord." Marta bowed again to conceal her laughter. "I most certainly could not have done it without you."

Tengchou, Shantung Province

SEPTEMBER 30, 1631–JANUARY 16, 1632

THE last three weeks of September 1631 were a penance for the glorious summer just past. Cold fogs froze old men's bones with a sepulchral chill. Sullen boys played *shao-chi,* Chinese martial chess, in cramped rooms, and resentful girls performed their household chores. Unhappy indoors, the people of Tengchou were miserable out of doors.

The days were sodden with rain falling from rumpled gray clouds. The sooty nights were feebly lit when a star glimmered through the overcast or yellow rays streamed from the bobbing oil lanterns of men on urgent errands. A pall lay on the spirits of soldiers confined within damp, drafty hutments, which reverberated with harsh quarrels. Daggers flashed in the gloom when jaded tempers transformed trivial slights into mortal insults.

The unending downpour pelted the red-brick houses of Tengchou, falling as thick as the blue lines that depict rain on a Japanese print. Cloudbursts transformed lanes into marshes laced with filth-gray streams. Under oiled-paper umbrellas, which tossed like overturned coracles in the gusts, peddlers, workmen, and servants waded barefoot through the sucking mire. Gelatinous mud clung to their legs beneath high-rolled trousers, soiling the kitchen hearths where they dried themselves. Women despaired of preserving any island of cleanliness in fug-filled rooms.

The smoke from soft-coal fires billowed over corrugated roof tiles, and acrid fumes seeped through oiled-paper windows to coat walls. Soot drifted into the officers' villas far from the dwellings of the worthy poor, and the parade ground became a swamp. Iridescent ducks paddled among clumps of grass where His Imperial Majesty's troops had drilled a few weeks earlier.

Marta's lion-dogs pawed the Turkestan carpets to protest their confinement. Wang, the golden male, stared in aggrieved silence. Mu-lan, the silver-and-white female, scratched at the oiled-paper door to the terrace.

"Mu-lan, behave yourself. It's just as bad for us locked up here." When Marta spoke sharply, Mu-lan scrambled up the *kang,* slipping down just short of the top.

Marta was cocooned in perfumed quilts on the *kang,* her head on Francis's arm. The fire crackling inside the brick platform made her pleasantly drowsy after their lunch of shrimp and noodles.

"It's not really as bad for us, you know." Francis stroked her breast. "We have our diversions. But why not let the dogs out?"

"And have them drenched? You know it takes their maid-servant hours to comb them."

Startled by her vehemence, Francis withdrew his hand.

"Don't stop now," she commanded. "You woke me just when I was half asleep!"

"Is that better?" He moved his hand exploratorily. "Or do you want to sleep?"

"How can I sleep now? That's much better....Just a little harder. Don't be afraid you'll hurt me."

"But the child. We must be careful."

"My Lord, it's still another four months before the little lord appears. You won't hurt me or the baby."

Francis wondered how to convince Marta she must be more careful of the infant. Her ardor, which should have been cooling, had actually grown hotter. She took her slow thickening as a challenge to her ingenuity—and his agility. Her sensuality, previously somewhat restrained by fear of pregnancy, had been heightened by the reality of pregnancy. The indispensable pillow book, which provided for all eventualities, was constantly consulted for suitable postures.

More demanding in bed, Marta was otherwise lost in herself. During her hour-long silences she ignored him. Always slightly withdrawn, she now seemed transported to another plane far beyond her husband.

"Is that what you want?" Francis gripped her buttocks, kissed her lips roughly, and thrust his tongue into her mouth.

"Yes...harder, a little harder," she gasped. "But, Francis ...look! Just look!"

"Look at what?" He was hurt when she pushed him away and sat up.

"Just look at the door, that bright glow through the paper. It's the sun...really the sun. The first time in three weeks I've seen the sun."

The sun's reappearance on the afternoon of September thirtieth heralded a splendid summer-after-summer, the renewed warmth of autumn the Chinese called *hsiao-yang chün*, the "spring of the small sun," and the Portuguese *verão de São Martinho*, "Saint Martin's summer." Under whatever name, the next five weeks were a glorious interval between sodden September and the fierce North China winter. The townspeople laid out bedding and clothing to air, and women's gowns shimmered bright when they put off their dark coats. The soldiers' spirits rebounded, and their officers resumed training with springtime vigor.

On the morning of October fifth, the sentinels atop the West Gate spied a plume of tawny dust on the road from Peking. In the van, a yellow pennant bearing the scarlet ideogram *ling*, obey, signaled that the approaching party traveled under the Emperor's own orders. When the scale armor of a cavalry escort flashed in the morning sun beneath the scarlet banner of a Mandarin of the Second Grade, the lieutenant of the guard turned out his men.

Major Francis Arrowsmith joined the junior officers drawn to the West Gate by the signal drum. As senior officer, he acknowledged the halberd-pounding salutes of the guards on the inner doors of the square gate tower. The officers sauntered through the gloom of the sixty-foot-long tunnel under the tower, blinking in the sunlight when they emerged into a vast courtyard enclosed by a semicircular curtain wall. They stood within the enclosure of the barbican that clung like an enormous blister to the main city wall. A guard of honor was drawn up in that courtyard, which was dominated by two four-story towers, one over the West Gate, the other over the gate in the curtain wall.

Perhaps, Francis mused, the General's confidence in those

191

massive walls was justified. Perhaps Miguel Texeira and he were excessively cautious. Girt by walls, towers, and moats, Tengchou epitomized the siege mentality of the Ming. The west barbican of that provincial stronghold was stronger than the main walls of European capitals. Since the guard towers were virtually impregnable, an enemy who broke through the curtain wall would be trapped under a cataract of arrows, spears, arquebus balls, and fuse bombs within the semicircular courtyard of the barbican. Tengchou was invulnerable to frontal assault—if the defenders stood fast.

Alerted by flourishes of trumpets, the lieutenant of the guard sent a detachment through the barbican gate and across the drawbridge. Five minutes later, hooves sounded on the stone blocks that paved the gate tunnel. Standard-bearers, trumpeters, and troopers trotted out of the tunnel and formed up in the courtyard.

Slow-padding hooves echoed from the tunnel before a horseborne litter emerged. A standardbearer riding behind the litter flaunted a gold cross on a vermilion field. *In Hoc Signo* was embroidered on the crossbar and beneath it *AMDG* for the motto of the Society of Jesus: *Ad Maiorem Dei Gloriam*. Chinese ideograms repeated those invocations: *By This Sign* and *For the Greater Glory of God*.

A narrow face stippled with the liver marks of age appeared between the litter's curtains, and two blue eyes peered from wrinkled mulberry lids. A lean hand beckoned, and a reedy voice pierced the skirling of pipes and the ruffle of drums to call out "Francis!"

Though almost seventy, Father Juan Rodriguez appeared more vigorous than he had when they parted eighteen months earlier. But he was no less testy than he had been when he left Peking to bully the Loyal Senate of the City of the Name of God into sending a Second Expeditionary Force of musketeers and artillery north to fight the Tartars.

"Francis, come here!" the priest called in Portuguese. "And tell your popinjays to stop their caterwauling. I want to talk to you, and I'm tired."

"You've rarely looked better, Father Juan."

Francis performed the deep bow due the Jesuit's honorary rank as a Mandarin of the Second Grade, obviously bestowed by the Emperor to ensure his smooth journey. Juan Rodriguez required that rank for no other reason. Whatever his purpose in Tengchou, his imperious personality would ensure that his words were heard and that his advice was weighed.

"I've rarely felt sillier, Francis. All this parading for an old priest.... But, my boy, you've grown... filled out. By Our Lord, it's good to see you."

"My new family responsibilities, Father Juan. I need broad shoulders to carry them." Francis responded to the priest's frank affection. "Do you come alone?"

"Alone except for these thundering nuisances in uniforms gaudy as court fools. Escort of honor, they call it. Escort of nonsense is more like it."

When Francis rested his hand on the litter's pole, he remembered his talks with the Jesuit on the road from Chochow to Peking almost two years earlier. He had not even then glimpsed the women and men who now dominated his life: Marta and Candida, Minister Paul Hsü and Father Adam Schall, the slave Joseph King and General Ignatius Sün.

"Why alone, Father? I thought you..."

"...would return in triumph with the Second Expeditionary Force, didn't you, Francis? So did I...for a while. But I've learned."

"Learned what, Father Juan? Where is the Second Expedition? Following you?"

"I've learned.... At my advanced age, I've finally learned never to trust a prince or a minister, particularly not if they're Chinese. My hotheaded, treacherous Japanese were honorable, straightforward men by comparison with these cool, devious Chinese."

"Father, where *is* the Second Expedition? There's never been a better time to crush the Tartars. A few hundred men...and the Empire can be saved...all China opened to the Faith."

"The Second Expedition is stranded in Nanchang, a thousand miles to the south—and likely to remain there. Worse, the Chinese are demanding vast sums for food and transport. There's still a chance, of course, but..."

"Why do you come here, then?"

"You know, I'm not quite sure myself. Perhaps because I came north with the men of the First Expedition. Adam Schall insisted they needed their chaplain here in Tengchou. And the Chinese were eager to get me away. Said the Portuguese here needed an interpreter. That's nonsense, from what I've heard about your progress with the language. I suspect the Chinese think it's tidier to tuck all the foreign devils away in the same place. As for myself, I suppose I just felt I belonged here with Texeira and his men."

"And Paul Hsü? What did he say?"

"Little, except for urging me not to be difficult."

"That was all?"

"No, not quite. He insisted that neither Christian priests nor Christian laymen should make themselves obtrusive just now. And he expects a major promotion soon."

"There's only the Grand Secretaryship left."

"Then China may have a Christian Chancellor."

"Perhaps!" Francis still nursed his resentment of Paul Hsü. "But you must come home with me...a hot bath and a good meal. I'll make your excuses to General Ignatius. Texeira can join us, if you wish."

"I came to see the old campaigner, not just you. How is he?"

"Lean and restless, but not yet poxed."

"I'm delighted by the last...and not surprised by the first. But how did he come to lose weight?"

"He'll eat only as much as his men. Slim rations, but a feast compared to the Chinese troops."

"Starvation? In Tengchou, the bastion of Shantung?"

"No, Father, not starvation. Not by a long way. But very short commons."

CAPTAIN-SERGEANT Miguel Gonsalves Texeira Correa was indeed lean. His gray face was seamed; his orange-velvet doublet hung loose; and his blue-silk stockings sagged on his shrunken calves. Father Juan Rodriguez was a black shadow. His cassock with its flapping Chinese sleeves was austere beside Texeira's splendor and the blue-silk tunic with the lynx insignia Francis wore above gray-canvas field trousers tucked into black-felt boots.

"It's hard, Father, damnably hard." The Captain-Sergeant sipped the red wine of Oporto, Juan Rodriguez's precious gift. "General Ignatius is the best they've got. He's good, very good, but even the best Chinese general is no Portuguese. As for the troops...you can no more expect them to fight like Portuguese musketeers than watery Chinese grape-wine to taste like full-bodied Oporto."

"It *can* be done, Miguel," Francis interjected. "My arquebusiers were coming along well...very well. If they'd only left me with them..."

194

"Precisely, Francis. The Chinese generals took them away from you, didn't they?"

"Not precisely the generals, but let it pass. What of the Second Expedition, Father Juan? We've been boring you...telling you what you already know instead of hearing your news."

"The Second Expedition may have returned to Macao by now, for all I know," the Jesuit replied. "Canton put the spoke in our wheel again. Above all else, the Cantonese Mandarins and merchants fear direct communication between Macao and Peking. They're afraid of losing their profits...and their extortions."

"What have profits got to do with the Second Expedition?" Texeira demanded. "And why are merchants involved in a military affair? Who's foolish enough to listen to their ignorant gabble?"

"Only the Court, Miguel, only the Emperor ultimately," Juan Rodriguez patiently replied to Texeira's naïve indignation. "Their arguments were very persuasive—as were their bribes. They strove like fiends to retain their monopoly on foreign trade."

"I can see that, Father," Texeira persisted. "But what could the Cantonese *do?* Surely the Ministry of War..."

"It's nothing to do with the Ministry." Impatience elided the Jesuit's explanation. "Memorials went to the Emperor...and lavish bribes to the Court Eunuchs. Pressed by the Eunuchs, the Emperor ordered the Second Expedition to return to Macao. He praised Paul Hsü and lauded Portuguese valor but declared there was no need for further outside troops."

"So that's that," Texeira observed gloomily. "When do *we* return to Macao? Peking seems to think the war's over, the Tartars defeated."

"Not all Peking," the priest said. "Not Paul Hsü and his allies."

"What of the Fathers?" Francis asked. "Are they permitted to stay and preach the Faith? What about myself? I'm still in the Chinese service, you know."

"I don't really know. But there are no orders to recall the First Expedition, Miguel. And no orders for you, Francis. Adam Schall...all the Peking missioners...remain confident. They've faced worse, they say, and ridden it out."

"So we rot here in inaction?" Texeira refilled his winecup. "So much for dreams of glory and gold."

"I repeat, Miguel, I don't know," Juan Rodriguez answered. "As far as I can see, no one wants to take a decision. As long as you don't make trouble, the Court is content to let you remain. You may be needed urgently some day...even your scant force. For the rest, Dr. Paul counsels patience."

PATIENCE was essential in Tengchou, where the only change in the next five weeks was the weather. Saint Martin's Summer ended just before that saint's feast day as abruptly as it had begun.

November 9, 1631, was as warm as mid-August, and the townspeople grumbled that the cold would never come. Some housewives bemoaned unnecessary expenses incurred for winter clothing, for fuel, and for pickled vegetables; others worried about their half-smoked hams, normally preserved in cold-safes outdoors. Glum merchants took inventory of excess stocks of winter goods, and gloomy farmers feared the winter wheat would sprout puny before the snows fell. The sacred progression of the seasons, they said, was disrupted by Heaven's displeasure with the profligate Ming Dynasty. A group of Tengchou men joined the delegations from all North China that implored the Emperor to conduct sacrifices at the Temple of Heaven to make the seasons march harmoniously again.

On November tenth, Saint Martin's Eve, snowclouds gathered over Tai Shan, the sacred mountain, where the Master Confucius was buried. The winds rose through the day, tossing the clouds like gray dandelion heads. Shortly before dusk at four in the afternoon, black clouds enveloped Tai Shan and the cities of the plains. Baleful bolts of lightning split the skies and raked the valleys with taloned fingers. Snow falling in feathered clumps as big as men's heads gleamed in the lamplight glimmering through the windows of Tengchou.

The blizzard lasted four days, and snowdrifts rose to the gray-tiled roofs. Householders cut channels with axes for the smoke from chimneys choked by five-foot snowbanks on roofs. Otherwise, their families would either have asphyxiated amid coal fumes or frozen in unheated houses.

On the fifth day, the blizzard abated. But fifteen days of constant gentle snowfall heaped streets and roofs six feet higher. If intermittent gales had not scattered the drifts, the entire city would have been buried under a frozen tumulus.

Screaming with delight, children slid along the tunnels carved through snowbanks to privies. But even the children rejoiced on the sixteenth day when, clambering up the vertical ventilation shafts driven into the snowbanks, they saw that the snowfall had stopped.

During the following week, snow fell only a few hours each day, adding only a foot to the white drifts. From the patrol paths on top of the city walls, the sentinels saw that the Pohai Straits had frozen solid. A perfect white mantle, wind-rucked into fantastic shapes, stretched thirty-two miles northward, and the point of the Liaotung Peninsula reared in the pellucid air like an immense snowdune.

Just before dusk on December eighth, two couriers led their horses by their ice-rimed bridles across the Pohai Straits. General Ignatius Sün summoned his senior officers to a council of war the next morning. Captain-Sergeant Miguel Gonsalves Texeira Correa, who commanded the garrison's most formidable unit, was invited as a matter of course. Father Juan Rodriguez and Major Francis Arrowsmith were invited as a matter of courtesy.

Francis was delighted to escape from the snowbound villa in which he had been confined with a testy Juan Rodriguez and a withdrawn Marta. The days had dragged their sluggish length through rooms begrimed by oil lamps, and the ingenuity of the Shantung chef had been taxed by the lack of ingredients. Not even *pai-tsai*, the ubiquitous long white cabbage, was available, and dried or pickled vegetables grew tedious. The troops' spirits, Francis knew, were sinking again. Spare before the blizzard, their diet afterward lacked the ducks, chickens, eggs, and pork provided by the penned animals his servants hand-fed with precious grain.

Francis ate too much highly seasoned food. Like his body, his mind grew flabby for lack of exercise. His study of the Classics had lost its savor, and Marta sulkily dismissed his new insights into China.

Despite the hope he drew from Dr. Paul Hsü's hints, Juan Rodriguez feared his life's work was ending in drab failure. Deprived of contact with the princes and the ministers who moved the world, the old priest was unhappy and short-tempered. The linguistic facility that earned him the nickname The Interpreter had for decades endowed him with influence over men in power. That influence was an essential stimulant to the Jesuit, and he declined visibly in his deprivation.

Preoccupied by her resentment of the new life growing in

her womb, Marta was unhappy and short-tempered. Moreover, her usually supreme vanity was being eroded by her increasing ungainliness. When Francis moved from their nuptial bed because of his concern for the child, she was convinced that she had become hideously unattractive. Though her pillow book also advised abstinence, she yearned for the sensual delights that had previously reconciled her to her unwanted marriage. In her deepest depression, she loathed her unborn child.

Marta had grown up amid the unflagging admiration of a large family, which courted her smiles and feared her rages. Her chief interest in other human beings was in their sustaining praise. Bereft of that adulation, she retreated into sullen silence, from which she could be drawn only by her maidservant Ying's outrageous flattery. Francis, whom Marta blamed for all her deprivations, felt himself favored if she addressed a single sentence to him in an entire day.

"Just think how it will be when the baby comes." He had attempted to cheer her. "You and I together again...and a beautiful child, too."

"Beautiful? I doubt that very much."

"Why not? We're neither of us ill-favored. It'll be a beautiful baby."

"It won't be a baby, My Lord. It'll be a monster."

"A monster? I'm shocked, Marta."

"Not as shocked as you'll be after it's born."

"How can you say that, Marta? It's blasphemous."

"Blasphemous or not, it'll be a monster, a horrible mixed-blood monster."

Deeply offended, Francis could only reply with silence to his wife's perverseness.

"Look what you've done to me," Marta raged. "I've become a hideous swollen balloon. And for what? To produce a half-barbarian child. It can't be anything but a monster."

Recalling that ghastly scene, Francis welcomed the summons to the General's conference, which he was sure portended active service in the field.

The couriers had brought General Ignatius Sün a desperate entreaty from his cousin, the governor of the Taling Region, which lay across the Gulf of Pohai west of the Liaotung Peninsula. Though some distance north of the Great Wall, the Taling River Basin was still occupied by Chinese farmer-soldiers—and the Tartar resurgence mortally threatened their settlements. Since the General viewed the assault as the precursor of a renewed attack on China proper, he was determined to assist the embattled governor.

The staff conference was protracted and contentious. Captain Miguel Texeira argued that his cannon would slaughter the Tartars, terrifying them into a general retreat. Ignatius Sün was coldly decisive, though his obligation to his cousin strained his judgment. Always happier as a field general than as a fortress commander, he assessed the situation and his own resources with remorseless logic. Despite his slight stature and his dandified mustaches, he was no less imposing than the silver lion of his rank with the ideogram *wang,* king, on its forehead, that declared it the monarch of the beasts. The General refused Texeira permission to lead his artillerymen to the rescue of the hard-pressed Taling garrison.

"The only possible route is almost forty miles over the frozen Pohai Straits and thence several hundred miles on the snowbound trails of the Liaotung Peninsula," General Ignatius Sün said. "Even if they didn't break through the ice, your heavy gun drays would never come through the Peninsula. I'd rather keep you here against need than make a present of your guns to the Tartars."

Ambassador Michael Chang, the General's deputy, supported Francis's request to lead two field pieces and a company of Chinese arquebusiers on the relief expedition.

"The same objection to even one field piece," the General pronounced. "Besides, the arquebusiers couldn't keep up with the light cavalry. No, Arrowmaker, I want you here."

The Ming officers stared in wonder when the outlanders pleaded for active service. Having assessed the expedition's grim prospects, no Chinese officer volunteered. The commander finally chosen, Lieutenant Colonel Keng Chung-ming, whom the soldiers called the Halfwit, was not elated by the honor.

"Light cavalry are the only hope," General Ignatius Sün finally decided. "Lieutenant Colonel Keng, since you know the terrain intimately, your cavalry can fall on the Tartar's rear. Once driven from their prepared positions, the Tartar siege machines and their cumbersome infantry will be locked in winter's grip."

The following day, Lieutenant Colonel Keng Chung-ming took formal leave of his blood-brother, Lieutenant Colonel Kung Yu-teh, who was called the Virtuous. Halfwit Keng commended his family to the Virtuous Kung's care, sealing that responsibility with the gift of the sword his father had carried during forty years of alternately fighting the Tartars and intriguing with them against the Ming. Knowing his blood-brother's character, Keng told only his weeping wife where he had hidden his hoard of gold on a desolate island off the Korean coast. Having ensured his family's future as best he could, he led his eight hundred light cavalrymen down the ice-rimmed beaches to the snow-covered Pohai Straits.

Except for the doggedly optimistic General Ignatius Sün, Tengchou thereupon forgot the foolhardy expedition. The townspeople were happy that fewer "useless mouths" would consume the fortress's foodstocks. Convinced the cavalrymen had vanished as if the ice had opened to swallow their comrades, the soldiers remembered the light cavalrymen only when they gave thanks that they had not been ordered to join the doomed expedition.

"Did you really want to ride with the Halfwit, Master?" Curiosity overcame Joseph King's discretion a week after the cavalry's departure. "Or is it European etiquette to plead for the honor of certain death?"

"Of course I wanted to go, Joseph." Francis was disarmed by the ingenuous question. "Soldiering is my trade, and the expedition will be very interesting."

"*Too* interesting for me. But I'm only a humble slave. My highest wish is not death, but freedom some day."

"I offered, but you..."

"Yes, Major, I refused. Free me now, and there's no place I can go...no niche in all China into which I'd fit. I'm just talking...wishing aloud."

"But, some day, you think?"

"Some day, perhaps yes, perhaps not. Better to remain a slave and use your generous gifts to buy young slaves to look after my old age. If, of course, we survive this winter."

"Why shouldn't we?"

"Master, you know the common soldiers talk frankly with me?" Joseph King riffled the paperbound *Analects of Confucius* to belittle his question.

"So I've gathered."

"Being Chinese, they're convinced I can't possibly be loyal to an outlander...not even a fellow Christian. So they speak very frankly. Most are convinced that Tengchou is doomed— and we with it."

"Why, Joseph? You know the fortress is impregnable. Besides, the Tartars can't attack in force in this bitter winter weather."

"The soldiers say there won't be enough food. Anyway, their mood could produce the disaster they foresee. The men haven't been paid for six months, but they constantly receive letters pleading for cash. Their families could die of starvation while they sit on their bony backsides in Tengchou."

"Really that bad? I must talk with the General."

"Don't bother, Major. The General knows, but he's powerless. His private purse is empty and so is the Tengchou treasury. But Peking won't pay the soldiers because the Court Eunuchs are determined to destroy Ignatius Sün."

"Even at the risk of a mutiny...losing Tengchou?"

"*Because* of the risk of a mutiny, Major. Mutiny will destroy the General. He's too successful...and too reform-minded...for the conservatives."

"Precisely what do you fear, Joseph?"

"Mutiny first. The troops will mutiny, seize what valuables remain, and scatter to their homes. That's already open talk in the barracks."

"But the Flamboyant Cloaks would hunt them down. Not one man in ten would escape. And their families would be cruelly punished for their treason."

"*We* know they couldn't escape. But *they* don't. They're desperate...and desperate men don't think clearly. Particularly if they've never had to use their brains before."

"Of course, they could find an alternative," Francis mused. "For mutineers only one course would be open. They could only..."

"...desert to the Tartars," the secretary completed his master's thought. "The land is so overrun with brigands they couldn't take to the marshes and the hills as freebooters. That occupation's already overcrowded."

"How many realize they'd be forced to join the Tartars?"

"Very few, just yet, Major. As I told you, their brains are no more use than cold rice gruel. But some others have already drawn the same conclusion."

"And who are those others?"

"The Tartars' agents—in the garrison and outside. They promise fabulous bounties to deserters for 'rallying to righteousness.' They've approached me again to ask..."

"No, Joseph, I can't. Even if I wanted to, I couldn't. Excommunication...my wife...it's impossible."

"I told them so, but they insisted I ask. I'm only asking, not urging. I don't really fancy sleeping in smoky, lice-ridden yurts cobbled out of half-cured hides and living on half-raw flesh washed down with sour milk. I'd rather take my chances."

THE transition from December 1631 to January 1632 was marked by the dispirited Portuguese with a feeble toast to the New Year. Christmas had passed dismally, while the forced gaiety and the fireworks of the lunar New Year were more than a month away. Isolated in an endless white landscape, Tengchou was suspended in time as well.

General Ignatius Sün and his deputy, Ambassador Michael Chang, still hoped despite constant disappointments that the malicious Ministry of War would pay their rebellious troops before the eastern keystone of the Empire's defenses crumbled. Almost despairing, the General listened to the elliptical urging of his most senior officer, Lieutenant Colonel Kung Yu-teh the Virtuous, that he save himself by joining the Tartars. But he concluded that he could only wait for a miraculous change of heart in Peking or a more likely disaster in Tengchou. General Ignatius Sün was irrevocably bound by his loyalty to the Ming Dynasty, though he knew the Court would lightmindedly betray him.

Amid the gloom, Marta bore her unwanted burden with ill grace. She had taken to her bed after the dismal Christmas season, refusing to see either her husband or her spiritual counselor, Father Juan Rodriguez. Only the round-faced handmaiden Ying was admitted to her presence. Even Ying, who was callous after years of friction, chafed at returning menial service and outrageous flattery for the diatribes her mistress screamed at her.

Ying nonetheless clenched her lips and fed Marta nourishing broths steeped with the herb called *tang-kwei*, a panacea for all the ills of female flesh—and the specific for an easy delivery. Affection for her self-willed mistress moved Ying to such abnegation, but, even more than affection, her utter dependence upon Marta. If her mistress were displeased, Ying could be sent to labor twelve hours a day on the Soo family estates near Peking. If her mistress were well pleased, Ying might someday be released from service with a generous bounty, which would ensure her marriage to a worthy artisan.

Aside from continually demanding Ying's assurances that the infant would be male, Marta was little concerned with

202

her unborn child. Instead, she worried that her body would be thick and lumpy after the birth. She reproached Ying for "fawning insincerity" when her handmaiden reminded her that hundreds of thousands of young wives gave birth each year without turning into haggard crones. She spent hours examining her teeth in a circular hand mirror—repeatedly testing each tooth between her thumb and forefinger. "You'll lose two teeth for each child," her grandmother had warned, and Marta distrusted Ying's promise that the powdered eggshell in her broth would prevent that loss.

On the sixteenth of January at a quarter past the Double Hour of the Tiger, which was 3:30 A.M. by European reckoning, Major Francis Arrowsmith and Father Juan Rodriguez were awakened by the lion-dogs' bounding into the reception chamber where they slept. Between the dogs' high-pitched barks of alarm, they heard moans from Marta's bedroom. Mulan and Wang darted back into the corridor, whimpering shrilly and looking over their shoulders to be certain the men were following.

The dogs scratched frantically on the sliding door of the bedchamber, which opened slightly to display a red-faced, exasperated Ying. Her arms were heaped with towels, and a small oil lamp dangled from her fingertips.

"Bad dogs! Go away immediately!" She blocked the doorway with a slippered foot. "You're not wanted here. We've got more important things to worry about."

"What...what...is it?" Francis stammered. "Is she...now, is she? Is all well?"

"All will be well if the esteemed master will just take these noisy beasts away," Ying shouted over the dogs' barking, while Marta groaned.

"Has it come?" The agitated Francis spoke in English and then repeated in Chinese. *"Ying-erh yi-ching lay-la ma?"*

"Tsen-ma yi-hwer shih ne?" Ying's astonishment dissolved into laughter. "How could it possibly be? She's just begun. She'll be hours yet. Please send to fetch the midwife, and for Kwan Yin's sake, put these beastly dogs out before they drive us all mad."

When the maidservant of the Christian household invoked Kwan Yin, the Buddhist Goddess of Mercy who was the patron of women, Francis was startled into frenzied activity. He thrust the lion-dogs into the garden and instructed the majordomo to fetch two midwives—as well as an herbal doctor for good measure. After sending three maids carrying towels and hot water to assist Ying, Francis sat on an octagonal stool and stretched out a shaking hand for the cup of wine the majordomo offered.

"I blame myself, Father." His voice trembled. "If it weren't for me, she would never...she wouldn't be suffering."

"Self-evidently, my son." The priest's faded blue eyes almost vanished amid the wrinkles on his long eyelids, and his age-bleached lips smiled. "However, the good Lord arranged it so."

Francis sat in the reception chamber with Juan Rodriguez and the herbal doctor, whom the scandalized Ying would not allow into the bedchamber. Later, Miguel Texeira joined them, as did a Chinese lieutenant sent to inquire by General Ignatius Sün. The five men sipped yellow rice wine and munched boiled peanuts. Their long silences were broken by Francis's self-reproaches, by the Jesuit's murmured consolation, and by Miguel Texeira's loud reassurances.

"Don't worry, my boy," the Portuguese captain brayed. "She's a healthy wench. She'll whelp as easy as a good collie bitch. Now, sometimes it's not so easy...not if the mother's not healthy. I remember once in Flanders, a sickly camp follower...took two days to get it out. You never saw such a sight. Blood, piss, and shit everywhere."

Taking pity on Francis's green face and quivering hands, Juan Rodriguez motioned Texeira to silence, but his frail shoulders shook with suppressed laughter as he murmured "*Inter urinam et faeces nascitur!*"

Though the Jesuit sought to divert him with interminable tales of his days in Japan, the shrieks from the bedchamber transfixed Francis. He mechanically refilled his cup and mechanically drank the wine. He was ruddy-cheeked and mock-jolly when Ying slid open the door of the reception chamber at three-quarters past the Double-Hour of the Dragon, eight-thirty in the morning by European reckoning.

"It's a girl, a fine healthy girl!" Ying's tone was belligerent. She had heard that Christians did not bemoan the birth of a worthless girl, but was nonetheless poised to defend her mistress's lapse. "My Lady sleeps...finally."

Ying did not tell them that Marta had pulled a pillow over her face when told the infant was female. She knew the Mistress would make her own life a perpetual torment because she had erred in promising a boy. But those reproaches would be a summer zephyr beside the gales of disappointed fury that raged about the Master's head.

After his first happiness that both Marta and their child were well, Francis was cast down for an instant because he, too, had counted on a boy. But what difference did it really make? A girl could be an even greater joy than a boy to a father. With God's Grace, there would be other children later, since Marta would surely forget her sulky rages when she saw her daughter. United by their love for their daughter, his wife and he would rebuild the affection that had bound them before her pregnancy.

Francis realized that he was delighted. He would strive to prove himself worthy of the blessing his God and his wife had bestowed upon him.

In his elation, the Englishman embraced Miguel Texeira and clapped Father Juan Rodriguez on the back. He called for more wine and, half-fuddled, proposed a toast to his daughter. They must, he shouted, all see the infant immediately. But Ying forbade even his entry, saying that both mother and daughter slept.

Marta awoke late in the afternoon to demand of the exhausted Ying whether the baby was "in foul truth" a girl. Then she sullenly nodded permission for Francis and Juan Rodriguez to enter her bedchamber.

Ying stood beside the *kang*, holding the infant encased in swaddling clothes. Marta neither asked to hold the infant nor even glanced at her daughter. She stared at Francis in baleful silence; she ignored Ying's praise of the baby's beauty; and she replied with an exasperated sigh to the Jesuit's plans for a gala baptism.

"Where are they?" Marta interrupted the priest's murmurs. "Where are they? Bring them immediately. I must see my darling dogs, my beautiful Mu-lan and Wang!"

The majordomo returned ten minutes later. His hands were empty, and his tongue was busy with apologies: "The honorable beasts are nowhere to be seen, Master. Perhaps the noble, high-born lion-dogs have run away."

"*Never* before!" Francis snapped. "They *never* run away. For God's sake...for Kwan Yin's sake...find them. The Mistress will be frantic. And I'll not be very happy either."

While the servants ran through the icy lanes calling for the lion-dogs, Francis confided to Juan Rodriguez: "She's half-moon-mad about them. But I'm fond of them too."

By nightfall, the dogs had still not been found. Though Francis insisted that the search continue by lanternlight, he was half-convinced by the fearful cook's report: "Master, I saw three soldiers of the Canton detachment skulking near the garden gate. And, Master, you know...you know how the dirty Cantonese like a fat dog in the winter cold—especially when they're very hungry."

Tengchou, Shantung Province

JANUARY 18, 1632–FEBRUARY 22, 1632

"SHE shall be called after Our Lady," Father Juan Rodriguez insisted. "The first Christian child born in the Empire with the blood of Europe in her veins. Maria she must be."

Francis already wished to name his daughter for his mother, Marie Dulonge Arrowsmith. Marta said shortly that they could call the child whatever they wished—as long as they didn't involve her. It therefore fell to Joseph King to choose a Chinese name, and he searched through the dictionaries, the encyclopedias, and the chrestomathies that were the greater part of his possessions.

"We could call her Mai-lo," he finally suggested. "*Lo* means joy, as in her loving mother's name, Mei-lo, Roseate Joy."

Francis glanced sharply at his slave, but could detect no mockery on the dark Cantonese features.

"*Mai* means distant or surpassing." Joseph King slipped unaware into the didactic half-chant of classical recitation. "Mai-lo, thus, means Surpassing Joy, which is appropriate and auspicious. Her father came from a great distance, while surpassing joy is to be wished for all."

"And bestowed by the Grace of Our Lady and Her Son," the priest added. "But Maria Mai-lo...a fine name."

Her father marveled at the red-faced scrap of humanity that lay in a scarlet-lacquered cradle covered by the mantle of red-fox fur that was the gift of General Ignatius Sün. Maria's mere existence was a miracle to him, and he was delighted by the promise of the great beauty the maidservant Ying praised. Maria's minute hands and feet, with their tiny nails, were the white-gold of fresh cream, while her perfect features were dominated by a finely arched nose. When her eyes were not slitted against the glare of daylight, they were wide, almost round. Above all, the curious servants exclaimed at the aureole of fair hair that flared around her high forehead.

Ying assured her mistress that many Chinese children were born with fair—or even red—hair, which gradually turned a civilized black. But the barbaric yellow of her daughter's hair was an indelible disfigurement in Marta's eyes. Since all efforts failed to find a willing wetnurse in the malnourished city, Marta herself suckled her daughter. But she sighed with relief when Ying took the baby—and resumed her anxious examination of her face and her teeth in her round mirror.

Maria Hsü Mai-lo was baptized late in the afternoon of the nineteenth of January 1632, three days after her birth. Aside from the household, the hurried ceremony was attended by General Ignatius Sün, Ambassador Michael Chang, and three Portuguese officers headed by Captain-Sergeant Miguel Gonsalves Texeira Correa. Though Father Juan Rodriguez had planned a splendid ceremony followed by a feast, the exigencies of war intervened.

Tengchou had awakened to its normal hungry unease that morning. But the sentinels watching the Pohai Straits sighted a column of cavalry riding without banners at half past the Double Hour of the Snake, which was ten o'clock. At three-quarters past that double hour, the General ordered the gates closed and the walls manned against the unknown threat. A few minutes before the Double Hour of the Horse began at 11 A.M., the Captain of the north gate recognized in the van of the cavalry the lean figure and the sharp features of Lieutenant Colonel Keng Chung-ming—Halfwit Keng, as the soldiers called him.

The Captain rejected a Lieutenant's offer to open the north gate and sent a messenger to inform the General. An officer, the Captain had learned, was rarely punished for following orders, even if his literal-minded obedience should appear ludicrous to his subordinates.

The silver-fox cloak draping by Halfwit Keng was worn and weathered. His narrow face was pinched by cold and hunger, the greasy yellow skin blotched by windburn. His steel helmet was dented, and his scale armor was rusty. But the ranks of his troopers had not appreciably diminished during their month's absence.

Halfwit Keng rode up the snowdrift that covered the frozen moat. Almost level with the battlements of the north gate, he raised his voice only slightly.

"Open up, Captain!" he demanded. "Open immediately! My men are tired, cold, and hungry."

"Just awaiting orders, Sir," the Captain replied. "It's only a formality, but the General ordered all gates closed."

"It won't do, Captain," Keng blustered. "Keeping your superior officer and these stout-hearted troopers freezing in the snow. It won't do at all! When I come in, you'll..."

"We'll get you, too, you stuffed popinjay!" A trooper's bellow broke into the Lieutenant Colonel's threats. "All officers are turtleshit, but you'll be the first to dance on our pikeheads."

The astonished Captain waited for the Lieutenant Colonel to order the trooper's arrest. Knowing Halfwit Keng's reputation as a martinet, he was sure the offense would be brutally requited. Impaled on a sharpened bamboo stake, the loudmouthed trooper would die with cruel slowness. The captain was doubly astonished when the Lieutenant Colonel turned in his saddle and spoke softly to the trooper with placating gestures.

"Open now!.... Open now!.... Open now!" The cavalrymen chorused, and the foul-mouthed trooper, who was apparently their spokesman, shouted: "...or we come over the wall—and slit you from your bollocks to your beard."

Scarlet with fury, the Captain ordered his men to cock their crossbows. While they still cranked the springs of those cumbersome weapons, arrows feathered with goose pinions soared from the cavalrymen's short hornbows.

"If it's a fight you want..." The Captain's shout was half-strangled by his rage. "We'll give it to you. Bowmen: shoot!"

Compressed steel springs hurled the heavy quarrels from the crossbows. At that short distance, some pierced the shields of the front rank to strike down men in the second rank. Screaming imprecations, the cavalry scattered out of range.

Seven troopers flopped on the snowbank like landed fish, their blood seeping crimson into the sunlit silver crust. Three horses screamed into the white silence, their hind legs kicking at the barbed quarrels imbedded in their withers. Two of the wounded men rose and tottered toward safety. A third wrenched a quarrel from his belly and dragged himself across the slick snow. He left crimson handprints each time he scrabbled for a hold.

"Kill them! Kill them! Kill the traitors!" the Captain raged.

The crossbowmen's hands hesitated on their crank handles and their belated second volley flew wild. Calmed by his men's reluctance, the Captain ordered them to cease shooting and sent a second messenger to the General.

General Ignatius Sün climbed to the battlements twenty minutes later. His personal banner danced on a long staff, and his trumpeter sounded a fanfare as he stepped onto the parapet.

"Come forward, Lieutenant Colonel Keng," the little General shouted. "Come forward and explain this insanity. You will not be harmed."

Knowing the General's absolute honesty, Halfwit Keng unhesitatingly exposed himself to the crossbows. He cantered his horse up the snowdune, followed by a trooper swinging a flag of truce.

"I apologize for this unfortunate incident, Sir," he said calmly. "My men were somewhat hasty."

"Hasty? Somewhat hasty, you say?" The silver lion insignia on the little General's chest quivered with his indignation. "If that was somewhat hasty, how do they behave in anger? Explain this madness!"

"Not madness, General! We offer you life and riches—or death. Just as you choose. We got halfway to the Taling Region. Men and horses were dying in the frozen wastes. Finally, my troopers persuaded me to turn back."

"Persuaded? Mutinied, you mean, don't you?"

"I myself would not use such a harsh word. But we'll fight no more for a Dynasty that has lost...fumbled away... the Mandate of Heaven. We'll carve out our own kingdom and live in luxury like Court Eunuchs. We'll take what we want, not wait for miserly pay that never comes. I invite you

210

to lead us, General. Under your command, we'll be invincible."

The Christian General stood silent for almost a minute, the ermine tails that trimmed his sealskin cloak fluttering in the wind. One small hand tugged his pointed black goatee, which had been flecked with gray by the hard months just passed.

"You've been much tried, Lieutenant Colonel Keng...you and your men," the General finally said. "Lay down your arms and come into the city. We'll make you welcome...as your suffering deserves. We still have food to fill your bellies and coal to warm you. I promise pardon to all. Only come into the city unarmed— and all will be well."

Lieutenant Colonel Halfwit Keng's head drooped until his chin rested on his breastplate and only his beaky nose was visible beneath his helmet's rim. Silent and still, he bestrode his horse like a funerary statuette of a warrior.

"I'll amnesty all of you...to return to the service of His Imperial Majesty." Encouraged by his opponent's silence, the little General called out. "This temporary madness will not count against you."

After the flagbearer leaned across to whisper into his ear, Keng finally spoke: "No amnesty. Matters have gone too far. Shake off the tyranny of the Ming Dynasty, General Sün, and lead us. Otherwise, face slow starvation. No man or woman, no child or beast shall enter or leave Tengchou, no food and no drink, not a lump of coal or a twig of firewood. Think hard on my offer, General."

"I'll return whenever you're ready to talk sensibly." The little General's voice was gentle. "At any time of the day or night. You must abandon your treason and return with honor to our ranks."

The Christian General set his foot on the ramp leading down to the city, and the rainbow cloaks of his staff officers swirled behind him. But he spoke over his shoulder to the Captain of the north gate: "We won't attack them, not just yet. Only keep them away from the walls. And call me any time they want to talk, night or day."

FIVE times during the three weeks that followed the hurried baptism of Maria, the little General returned to parley with the rebels. And five times he parleyed in vain. Lieutenant

211

Colonel Keng Chung-ming would not—or could not—accept the offered amnesty. General Ignatius Sün could not turn against his decadent Emperor and carve out his own principality, despite the urging of his senior troop commander Lieutenant Colonel Virtuous Kung. Instead, the Christian General slipped a dozen messengers over the city walls on successive nights to carry his appeal for assistance to the garrison of Tientsin, 260 miles away.

The ranks of the besiegers swelled as the brigands of the countryside swarmed to join Halfwit Keng. They delighted in blockade duty, stripping every smuggler and refugee they caught of his coins and his clothing before they cut his throat. By the first week of February, the rebel force was fourteen hundred strong.

General Ignatius Sün still commanded some three thousand fighting men behind the walls of Tengchou. As hunger gripped the garrison, his staff urged him to sally against the rebels, but the General rejected their advice.

"I will not," he reiterated, "have it said in Peking that I was forced to slaughter my own cavalrymen in order to crush their rebellion. Those fellows will come around, I promise you."

On February 9, 1632, at the close of the third week since the mutineers rode out of the white waste of the Pohai Straits, the General acknowledged that the balance was tilting against him. The rebels were still increasing in numbers and vigor; his own force was dwindling as the sick and the weak died of hunger.

The General therefore decided to order his remaining cavalry to sally from the west gate of the city. Circling behind the rebels, the loyal cavalrymen were to harry them toward the north wall. The General also shifted a company of Chinese arquebusiers and the six remaining Portuguese field pieces to the north wall. Their combined fire would rake the rebels driven before the loyal cavalry.

"I'd prefer to bring them to their senses by reason," the General explained. "But I have no alternative. If we don't crush them they will starve us into submission."

The General's senior troop-commander, Lieutenant Colonel Kung Yu-teh, called the Virtuous Kung, stared unspeaking at the battle map on the wall. The Manchurian Lieutenant Colonel was a heavyset man with a broad, flat face. Unlike his rebel blood-brother Halfwit Keng, Lieutenant Colonel Kung was courtly in manner and punctilious in consideration of others. But, this once, he sat in stolid silence.

"Lieutenant Colonel Kung, you fully understand your role, do you not?" the General prodded.

"Not quite, Sir," Kung finally replied. "Frankly, I'm not certain of my troopers' temper. Their bodies are weakened by hunger...their spirits sapped by the rebels' honeyed promises and sour threats. Many...most...might refuse to attack. Better not to try the troops' temper than tempt them to turn against us."

"Arrest him!" the General barked in anger, and two lieutenants laid their hands on the Virtuous Kung's shoulders. Before they could lead him out, the General countermanded: "No, leave him for the moment. Leave him alone with me."

When the staff officers had filed out, shaking their heads in bewilderment, General Ignatius Sün spoke softly: "Now, Lieutenant Colonel Kung, what does this mean?"

"General Sün, it's too late. My men will *not* fight. But you can still join the rebels...take up my blood-brother's offer to give you command. At the worst, we could serve the Tartars. They will in time assuredly conquer *Tien Hsia*, All that Lies Under the Heavens....And we would be rewarded with high offices and much treasure."

"Are you demanding that I surrender or join the Tartars? Must I relieve you?"

"No, General, merely advising... and informing you of realities. But I stand, as always, at your command. Order me to lead the sally, and I shall do so."

"No, Colonel, it is too late. Return to your command. We can now only wait for spring and succor from Tientsin."

"One of your messengers should have gotten through, General."

"Perhaps, but I doubt it. The Will of Heaven, it appears, does not favor us. Yet we can but stand."

DEEPLY troubled, Francis Arrowsmith told his secretary Joseph King of the Virtuous Kung's refusing orders and the General's failing to punish him.

"Our little General is a good man, honest and merciful, a good Christian gentleman," Joseph King observed. "A brilliant commander, too, but now too lenient."

213

"Mercifulness has become irresolution, Joseph. The General is no coward. He fights like a lion against the Tartars. But he has no stomach for disciplining his own men."

"He's called Sün, like the strategist Sün Tze," Joseph mused. "But he has forgotten his great ancestor's counsel: *If troops are loyal, but punishments are not enforced, it is impossible to employ them.* General Sün is destroying us with his accursed lenience."

THE rebels swarmed over the west wall of Tengchou just before dawn on February 11, 1632, brushing aside the token pike thrusts leveled by the troops of Lieutenant Colonel Kung the Virtuous. Like the rebels, those men were Manchurian Chinese, and they were not prepared to die for the Great Ming Dynasty. Comrades and kinsmen met again on the wall to toast each other in foul-smelling *pai-kar*. They roistered for almost two hours before swooping down into the city across the roofs of the shanties that leaned against the inner face of the wall.

That respite allowed the few loyal troops to withdraw into the massive four-storied tower that crowned the north gate. Several hundred Cantonese infantrymen remained true to General Ignatius Sün because the Northern rebels scorned all Southerners. The Portuguese unit, less than a hundred strong, of necessity remained true to its Christian commander, and Father Juan Rodriguez accompanied his flock to the citadel. Francis Arrowsmith shepherded his wife Marta, her handmaiden Ying, and their three-week-old daughter Maria to safety.

But the foreign artillerymen were virtually disarmed. Though two light culverins were already emplaced in the tower, Miguel Texeira's four beloved cannon remained outside, their muzzles pointing impotently north across the Pohai Straits.

Too late, General Ignatius Sün regretted his excessive mercy. Had he attacked when his officers urged him to, he could have crushed the rebels. Trapped in the gate tower, he could now only wait and hope that one of the messengers who had slipped out of Tengchou during the long nights had reached Tientsin. He could only wait and hope that the Court would repent of its self-destructive spite when it learned that the eastern cornerstone of the Empire's defenses was crumbling. He could only wait and hope that the cumbersome Ministry of War would assemble a relief expedition in time to save his besieged loyalist force.

The General's hopes were not high, since it was most unlikely that all three essential conditions could be met. He could, however, hold out for several months, since the north gate tower was adequately provisioned and virtually impregnable.

Prayer, he concluded, was the most effective course open to him. General Ignatius Sün prayed hard and long for grace in Peking. He prayed on his knees for two hours each day, and he prayed for ten days.

The Virtuous Kung and his ally Halfwit Keng had more pressing matters in hand. After burning incense before the shrine of Kwan Ti, the God of War, to celebrate the victory that had cost them not a single casualty, the rebel leaders reorganized their four thousand fighting men. The Virtuous Kung Yu-teh took the rank of brigadier and promoted Halfwit Keng Chung-ming to full colonel. Under their new commander's vigorous direction, the Virtuous Kung's soldiers cut wide swaths in the surrounding pine forests. With that abundant timber, the carpenters, metalworkers, and tanners of Tengchou were compelled to build siege engines to assault the Christian General's citadel.

While that construction progressed, the rebels turned the four cannon on the north wall against the citadel at point-blank range. But their crews were cut down by Cantonese crossbowmen and Portuguese musketeers from the gate tower's embrasures. Brigadier Kung ordered the cannon abandoned. Even without the guns, he was confident he could wear down the citadel's defenses within a few weeks.

In the dark tower, Francis Arrowsmith and Miguel Texeira exulted at that first small victory. They watched contemptuously as the rebels drew out of range inside the city to construct mantlets. Those horizontal shields large enough for twenty men were made of heavy timbers faced with rawhide. At dawn the first mantlet trundled across the plaza that separated the red-brick houses of Tengchou from the tower.

Francis commanded one culverin, Texeira the other. Furious at the treachery of the Chinese, the Portuguese gunners shouted in glee as their culverins raked the mantlets. Solid shot, exploding bombs, and grapeshot plowed through the timbers to scythe the rebels with iron balls, dismember them with explosions, and impale them with massive flying splinters. A red gruel of shattered bodies covered the plaza, and the rebels fled to the shelter of the brick houses. The culverins' fire pursued them until Francis and Texeira ordered the crews to conserve powder.

Unmoved by that carnage, Colonel Halfwit Keng ordered his men to build mantlets three times thicker and faced with six layers of bullocks' hide. But Brigadier Virtuous Kung was sickened by the spectacle of two heavy-bodied North China sheepdogs tossing a thick-bearded head in their blood-rimed jaws.

"Leave off making mantlets," the rebel commander ordered. "If strong enough for protection, they're too heavy to move. Leave off! And, for Kwan Yin's sake, kill those filthy beasts."

The culverins, Brigadier Virtuous Kung knew, outranged all his catapults, which hurled enormous boulders and fuse bombs, while at short range, the match-fused grenades of the Portuguese wrought savage execution. Even if some of his men could storm through cannon fire, musket balls, and crossbow quarrels to the foot of the tower, a torrent of grenades would slaughter them long before battering rams could burst open the spike-studded, iron-banded seven-ply doors of the citadel.

Perhaps, the rebel commander brooded, human sea tactics. If thousands of his men hurled themselves at the tower, the survivors might swarm up scaling ladders to overwhelm the defense. But the defenders could cut down most of the assault force before it reached the tower. Even if the human sea swamped the defenses, the toll would be too high. He wanted live warriors to follow him, not dead fools he must bury.

The citadel would fall, Brigadier Virtuous Kung concluded, only if he laboriously undermined its foundations—and the spirit of its small garrison. But he was pressed for time, since many of his freebooters would desert during a protracted siege. Yet one plan could both win time and placate his men. He called his strategy: *The tortoise catches the hare and becomes a dragon*.

Brigadier Virtuous Kung advanced across the shambles of the battlefield beneath a flag of truce. The snow crackled under his bootsoles, and his armor creaked in the cold.

"I shall give you precisely five minutes." The Christian

216

General spoke from the embrasure that shielded him from rebel archers. "But talking is vain—unless you've come to surrender."

"I could offer you surrender and safe conduct." The Virtuous Kung's flat features were expressionless. "But I know you won't surrender. I honor your courage... and deplore your judgment. What I have to say won't take five minutes."

"Say it then and be done!" the little General exploded.

"I do not make war upon venerable age nor upon women and children. On the contrary, I am anxious to relieve their suffering. If I were as cruel and ruthless as you think, I would leave the aged, the women, and the children to consume your small substance. But..."

"Did you come to trade jests with me?" the General interrupted. "You know how well my citadel is provisioned. We can hold out for many, many months... a year if necessary. Long before then, Peking will have sent an overwhelming force to scourge your rebels."

"That, General, is as it may be. But I haven't come to discuss your housekeeping. I am prepared to give safe conduct to all females as well as to all males under twelve and over sixty."

"Why so benevolent?" General Ignatius Sün taunted. "And what guarantee you won't kill my people or hold them hostage?"

"*Ni chueh-teh ni-men Tien-chu-tu pao-pan jen-ching ho po-ai ma?*" The Virtuous Kung's indignation was sincere. "Do you think you Christians have a monopoly on humanity and benevolence?"

"By no means," the little General's fairmindedness compelled him to admit. "Even rebels may be humane."

"I am a good Buddhist," the Virtuous Kung said. "Though you're a Christian, General, you must know the practice we Buddhists call *Fang Sheng Teh Eng*— Releasing Living Things to Gain Merit. I propose to release not animals, but humans."

"And what guarantee of your sincerity?" the General asked again.

"The guarantee is implicit. If I slay good men who have given me their trust... if I hold all hostage, your garrison will resist more fiercely." The rebel commander used a somewhat unusual term for good men; *hao-Han* meant literally "good [men of] Han," China's first long-lived dynasty.

217

"I'm not fool enough to provoke my enemies to greater ferocity."

"*Ni-de chien-yi yu tao-li...*," the Christian General conceded. "Your suggestion makes sense. I'll consider it."

Major Francis Arrowsmith and Father Juan Rodriguez disagreed on that offer. The English soldier advocated acceptance, the Portuguese priest rejection.

The priest instinctively distrusted the Virtuous Kung's oath upon the sacred Buddhist practice. Nor was he impressed by the rebel leader's contention that he could not break his promise for fear of goading his enemies to fiercer resistance. The Jesuit had learned during four decades in the Extreme East that Orientals—no more than Europeans—would normally heed the counsel of self-interest to self-restraint when base passions inflamed them.

Though he was not usually cautious, Francis was overwhelmed by relief. The rebels' offer could ensure the safety of his wife and his daughter—and honorably rid him of Marta, who was an unbearable distraction while they were fighting for their lives. Her sullen silence had given way to shrill complaints in the dark tower. Irrationally and unfairly, as he believed, she blamed Francis for their predicament—and assiduously reminded him of his guilt. If he had not offended Minister Paul Hsü, Marta insisted, they would not have been posted to Godforgotten Tengchou. If he had been more adroit in the intrigues of Peking, they would not have been besieged by paltry rebels in the gloomy citadel where excrement and blood stank nauseatingly despite the bitter cold.

"I've had a bellyful of the Chinese—*all* Chinese," Francis confided in Portuguese to Juan Rodriguez and Miguel Texeira. "I'm stuffed with their villainy... their intrigues and their treachery. They are born to endless, smiling deceit."

"Even your own wife and daughter?" Texeira asked curiously.

"Of course not," Francis replied hotly. "Well, I suppose not.... Anyway the baby, Maria, isn't really Chinese."

"You consider *all* Chinese betrayers. Yet you'd entrust Maria... and Marta... to them?" Juan Rodriguez ignored Francis's implicit repudiation of his wife. "The rebels, too, are Chinese!"

"Look here, Father Juan," Francis replied. "In this tower, Maria will certainly die... and Marta probably. They're too delicate to endure months of siege. Marta's milk already runs

218

thin and soon will run dry. And there's no wetnurse among the rabble in this tower."

"Since you've made up your mind, I must go with them," Father Rodriguez said gently. "Even my feeble protection is better than none at all."

General Ignatius Sün accepted the rebels' offer two days later. Six women, thirteen children, and seven old men waited in the dank corridor for the seven-ply oaken doors to open. After removing the barricades, ten men leaned their weight on the ponderous doors. Beside double-shotted culverins on the battlements, arquebusiers and crossbowmen with weapons cocked scanned the empty courtyard of the north barbican. The General had insisted that no rebels stand ready to rush the open gate.

Four Cantonese soldiers parted from their tearful Northern paramours with loud promises of perpetual devotion. Soldiers bidding farewell to aged comrades knuckled their wet eyes with callused hands. Miguel Texeira, that granite-faced veteran of many wars, embraced Father Juan Rodriguez. Kneeling for the Jesuit's blessing, Francis was overcome by memories of his last day at St. Omer's College. He felt a chill presentiment that the farewells in the stone tunnel were another such final parting at the end of an era in his life.

Marta neither spoke nor reached out to touch his extended hand. Dry-eyed and self-possessed, she teetered toward the open door. Francis ignored her hauteur to lean over his infant daughter, who lay swathed in her red-fox cloak in the arms of the maidservant Ying. His grimy fingertips caressed Maria's pale cheek, and he wondered when he would see her again. When he kissed her forehead, her skin was warm and soft against his chapped lips.

"*Pax vobiscum!*" Francis called.

Pausing at the open door, his wife turned and said lightly: "*Tsai-chien tsai Peiching* . . . I'll see you in Peking."

Her slender form, draped in a glossy stone-marten coat, vanished into the square of light. The Jesuit's black caracul cloak hung on his spare frame. Finally the green padded-cotton mantle of the handmaiden Ying was swallowed by the dazzling glare off the snow.

Francis raced up the steep steps to the second story to watch the foreshortened figures trudge in single file across the snow-blanketed courtyard. Already diminished by the tower's height, the figures dwindled into tiny manikins as

219

they approached the barbican gate. When they disappeared into the dark mouth of that tunnel, Francis feared they were vanishing forever from his sight. Tears prickled against his closed eyelids.

Waiting at the far end of the tunnel, the Virtuous Kung smiled and said: "The tortoise has caught the hare. Next, the tortoise becomes a dragon."

TWO days passed without incident, while the besiegers remained invisible. No rebels moved in the courtyard of the barbican north of the citadel. Only scavenging dogs scampered across the battlefield to the south, which was ramparted by derelict red-brick houses and strewn with putrefying corpses. From the top of the tower, the sentinels saw only sporadic movement in the rebels' camp, which was an efflorescence of circular gray-and-brown tents half-covered with snow.

At the Double Hour of the Dragon, seven in the morning of the third day after the departure of the noncombatants, February 17, 1632, a flag of truce appeared in the mouth of the barbican gate. Behind the flagbearer walked Halfwit Keng, his bell-shaped helmet flaunting a red fox's tail from its spire. The fishscale plates of his armor shimmered in the watery sunlight, and his deep-crimson cloak rippled like coagulating blood.

"I'll talk to him," General Ignatius Sün decided. "It serves to pass the time."

Halfwit Keng prudently halted some fifty feet from the tower, just beyond the range of the devilish match-fused grenades of the Portuguese.

"Get General Sün," he damanded. "I must speak with the General."

"You have my ear," the Christian General replied. "What is it now?"

"My blood-brother Virtuous Kung has sent me in his stead," the Halfwit called. "He is ashamed to confront you. But he prays you to remember that he said *hao-Han,* good Chinese. For the rest, he is powerless."

"What new deviltry is this?" The little General waited for Halfwit Keng to confirm what he already sensed.

"My blood-brother and I are powerless. Our men hold the

220

foreign-devil monk and the half-devil infant. But we've offered the mother safe conduct north."

"And your demands?" The General's voice was laden with an ancient weariness.

"The two barbarian officers must surrender themselves. We will release them, having no use for them. But they must surrender themselves—or the infant and the priest die in torment."

"Rejected!"

Backing out of the embrasure, the General stumbled. That brief exchange had exhausted him more than the perils and hardships of the preceding months.

"We give you seven days to decide." Harsh and thin, the rebel officer's voice pierced the embrasure. "The Virtuous Kung wrung that concession from his men. On the morning of the eighth day, however, you will see the devil-people tortured. My blood-brother and I cannot prevent it. Heaven itself cannot prevent it. You may pray to your Christian God, but He is a long way from His own lands."

At ease in his commodious tent, the Virtuous Kung gazed at a haughtily silent Marta across a table heaped with preserved delicacies. His broad features were bland, and he spoke indifferently, neither inviting nor rejecting a reply: "Time has stopped. The tortoise will soon burst from the earth. And, shortly thereafter, the tortoise will become a dragon."

In a dark cell on the third story of the tower, Major Francis Arrowsmith pleaded with General Ignatius Sün while Captain-Sergeant Miguel Gonsalves Texeira Correa listened uncomprehending.

"Let me go, General. I'm useless here. You can spare me easily. Texeira will remain, and he's a far better artillerist. Let me go and save them from torture. I beg of you in the name of Christ."

"Please inform him, Francis, that I am opposed," the Portuguese instructed. "Our honor demands that we remain with our troops and our commander."

"*Ni pu pi fan-yi, Ying-chang* ..." The General was beyond emotion. "You needn't translate, Major. Whether he supports your pleas or, as I suspect, demands to stay, it is unimportant. I have made up my mind, and I will not waver."

"Then you permit me, General? To go to my child... and...my wife?"

"You may not! You will remain with us! May God forgive

221

me, but I will not surrender the two pillars of my citadel. I would sooner blow up our gunpowder than release you."

"You will...will not reconsider, General? I beseech you."

"I will not reconsider, Major. Now be gone. And pray for me, if you can."

THE earth parted on the third day after the rebels' demand that Francis and Texeira surrender themselves. A wide pit opened in the semicircular courtyard of the north barbican. The earth parted and spewed out torrents of russet soil.

Cannonballs sailed over the pit, for the culverins could not be depressed low enough to bring them to bear. Arquebusiers and crossbowmen shot in vain, for they could see no living targets amid the flying clods. Within a day, a mound of tawny earth rose twelve feet above the white courtyard.

Impotent and swearing, Francis and Texeira watched a curious structure grow behind the shelter of the mound. Brick walls supported a peaked roof composed of three layers: first bricks, rubble, and stone set in mortar; next raw bullock hides twelve deep; and, finally, water-drenched pine branches.

"Francis, Francis, they build a *testudina*, a tortoise," Texeira shouted. "I never thought to see it in this day and age...a Roman tortoise. First a mine, a tunnel under the courtyard, then the tortoise. Brilliant!"

"I'm glad you find it interesting," Francis said sourly.

"Look there! Pine branches thick with needles to absorb missiles, the hides against fire, and the solid inner shell—all sloping from the rooftree to cast off our shot. Absolutely brilliant!"

"Miguel, leave off your professional raptures. What can we do about it?"

"Do? I hadn't thought, but give me a few minutes."

"Only a few minutes to conceive a brilliant master stroke?"

"If I can't think of something in a few minutes, Francis, I never will."

Francis leaned against the sloping wall of the embrasure, his eyes drawn alternately to the silent Texeira and the advancing tortoise. After ten minutes he opened his mouth to recall the Captain-Sergeant to the world. But Texeira forestalled him.

"I have it; a *ballista*," he exclaimed. "If they can return

222

to antiquity, so can I. A catapult can hurl grenades as easily as stones."

The Portuguese soldiers took only an hour to build their small catapult. Far removed from the classic symmetry of a Roman *ballista,* it was essentially a wooden beam with a crude metal bowl fixed to one end and a counterweight of cannonballs secured in a net to the other end. Though it looked like a children's seesaw, the device worked. The counterweight on the high end snapped the bowl upward when the string securing the low end was slashed. The grenade then soared from the bowl with a velocity far greater than any human arm could impart, flying far and striking hard.

The creeping tortoise was well within the catapult's range, as was the excavation. Indeed, the catapult was initially too powerful. Sheltered by the overhanging eaves of the tower's second story, Texeira experimented with different weights, removing and adding cannonballs until, finally, a stone the size and weight of a grenade dropped square on the roof of the tortoise.

"Now for the grenades," Texeira commanded. "The Romans didn't have to contend with explosives when they used their tortoises. We'll blow up that ancient monster."

A stream of grenades soared across the courtyard, their match fuses limning golden arcs against the sky. Some overreached, and some fell short. But many landed on the peaked roof where the tangled pine boughs trapped the exploding grenades. As their water-heavy needles dried, tongues of flame licked the boughs.

"Francis, look now! A good fire already burns. With persistence, we'll destroy the beast."

"With persistence, yes. But how long? Maria and Rodriguez are tortured in two days' time."

"I cannot help that. You cannot help that. We can only keep the devil's spawn of mutineers from taking our tower—and our heads."

"They will. If not this day by this device, then another day by another device. I'm weary, Miguel...and sick at heart for Maria and Juan Rodriguez...Marta, too."

"Be weary another day. Not today. The best cure for heartsickness is work."

"Work won't cure my heartsickness, Miguel. I am pierced by grief...impaled by sorrow."

"Look you, Francis, a little less poetic, if you please.

223

Enough of your English emotion. You must be as practical as a Portuguese. First, we must preserve ourselves...destroy the tortoise. Afterward, when they bring the hostages into the courtyard, then a quick sally to rescue them."

"We'd be slaughtered by the rebel archers, Miguel."

"Our good Spanish plate, Toledo armor tempered in fire and water, will mock their puny arrows."

Captain-Sergeant Miguel Gonsalves Texeira Correa leaned out through the slit of the embrasure to watch the flight of a grenade. The trail of fire the burning fuse traced against the ashen dusk culminated in the black-veined flare of an orange explosion among the flames devouring the pine boughs.

"A brilliant shot," the Captain-Sergeant cried. "Shoot just there again and again, and..."

Miguel Texeira broke off his ebullient instructions, apparently struck by inspiration for a new stratagem. Francis saw only the back of Texeira's voluminous padded-cotton breeches and his heavy canvas doublet, both smeared with the filth of battle. The Captain-Sergeant stood silent and rigid, his shoulders jammed into the sloping embrasure, his head craning out through its slit.

"Well, Miguel, what of it? What new deviltry are you pondering?"

Texeira neither moved nor replied, and Francis saw with horror a scarlet rivulet trickling through the black-powder stains on the Portuguese officer's doublet. He hooked his hands under Texeira's armpits and tugged hard. When the Captain-Sergeant remained still unmoving, Francis braced his feet on the paving stones and pulled with all his strength. The crack of a breaking twig reverberated in the narrow embrasure, and the Portuguese tumbled to the granite-block floor.

Blood and mucus seeped around the broken arrow shaft that protruded from the Captain-Sergeant's left eye. Texeira had died the instant the iron arrowhead pierced his brain. His mouth was still open to shout orders to the crew of the catapult. His red lips gaped like a wound, transforming his neat features and flat swarthy-gray cheeks into the mask of a fiend, a creature from the Inferno.

Salt tears running down his cheeks, Francis crossed the Captain-Sergeant's arms on the greasy canvas doublet. For the first time since childhood he allowed his tears to flow. He

224

could not force himself to pluck out the broken arrow so that he could close Texeira's eyes in decent repose.

Dusk was retreating before the black cavalry of the night, but there was still light to aim grenades. Francis watched their fall through the slip in the embrasure, his helmeted head protected by the granite. When fire flared higher among the pine boughs, he altered the aim for greater effect.

The flames flared high before sputtering lower, then soared against the sooty sky. A few minutes later, the fire shot out red sparks and died. The pine boughs were entirely consumed. By the halfmoon's light, Francis saw that the rawhides beneath the bough had, as the tortoise's builders intended, served as a fireproof barrier. Miguel Texeira was dead, and his catapult was a fiasco.

All that night the tortoise crept closer to the citadel through the pallid moonlight. The rebels methodically laid brick walls and roofed them, sheltered by mantlets from arquebuses and crossbows. The grenades still tracing their fiery parabolas against the dark sky could not halt the implacable advance. No longer fearing the heavy missiles the resilient pine boughs were intended to repel, the rebels left off that layer, which had retained the grenades. The grenades slid off the bullock hides to explode impotently in the snow.

Just before morning, Francis watched the tortoise halt some ten feet from the citadel and abruptly change its shape. A square of brick walls began to rise at the foot of the citadel, and the defenders were helpless to halt its growth. Two men sprang from the mouth of the impregnable tortoise to replace each man who fell to a musket ball or a crossbow quarrel. The rebels worked under the protection of a square roof, assembled during the night from sections carried through the tunnel and the tortoise. That roof rested on thick tree trunks standing free of the walls. Each time a row of bricks was mortared into place, the roof was lifted above it by linked pulleys, levers, and screws.

Fortunately, the cumbersome siege tower's growth was slow, unlike the terrifyingly swift advance of the tortoise. Consulting with General Ignatius Sün, Francis calculated that it would be three days before the siege tower rose level with the first story of the citadel. The defenders, the General decided, would then sally across the four-foot chasm between their own citadel tower and the rebels' siege tower. Anticipating the rebel assault, they would slaughter their assailants.

That confident projection left Francis anguished and disconsolate. After two days, the rebels would torture Juan Rodriguez and his helpless month-old daughter Maria—watched with unavailing rage by the loyalists in the citadel.

The mutineers' leaders stood outside their tents, savoring the bright winter dawn. The Virtuous Kung remarked to his blood-brother, Halfwit Keng, with satisfaction: "The tortoise has become a dragon, and the dragon is growing large!"

Throughout the day, the defenders hurled missiles onto the roof of the siege tower: grenades and bombs, great boulders and flaming torches. The rawhide charred but did not burn, and the tower rose six inches every hour.

The Christian General drew strength from their acute peril, though he might have despaired. Death had deprived him of the warcraft of Captain-Sergeant Miguel Gonsalves Texeira Correa; Major Francis Arrowsmith's limited experience of war could conceive of no strategy to halt the siege tower's inexorable growth. But General Ignatius Sün rubbed his small hands in anticipation.

"Tomorrow I'll drill the first assault team," he told Francis and his deputy, Ambassador Michael Chang. "In two days' time, we'll brush the rebels off the siege tower like buzzing flies. Hand-to-hand, we'll destroy them."

An hour before midnight, in the middle of the Double Hour of the Rat, the Chinese General and his English second-in-command wrapped themselves in their cloaks and knelt to pray beside their pallets of piled furs. The General slept in his cell on the second story, Francis on the third.

While the two Christians murmured prayers of entreaty, the ranks of their Cantonese soldiers clanged with angry talk. The Southerners' will had been broken by the twofold disaster: Texeira's death and the rising siege tower. The sentinels on the battlements exchanged dire predictions of new disasters, each wondering if he might survive. At 3 A.M., the beginning of the Double Hour of the Tiger, a group of Cantonese descended stealthily to the corridor leading to the ponderous ironbound door.

The din from the basement did not reach the third-story cell where Francis slept, but died in the citadel's narrow, winding stairways. General Ignatius Sün himself awakened his second-in-command. The General's cloak was torn, and his right arm was slashed by a long, shallow wound. Blood dripped from his hands onto the carved Christ figure that arched in agony on the persimmon-wood crucifix he clutched.

"Wake up, Francis! Wake up!" The Christian General's face was haggard in the gray half-light beneath the grime that bent his juanty mustaches. "The Cantonese have opened the doors to the rebels. We are fated to die in Tengchou. The ways of the Lord are mysterious beyond all comprehension. We must fight awhile—and then compose our souls for death."

The Wrath of Heaven

July 1632–June 1644

Mukden, Peking, Mukden

JULY 23, 1632–JANUARY 7, 1634

THE gray mastiff cocked its ears when it felt the tremors the pony's pounding hooves sent through the ground. It rose slowly, stretched its shaggy legs, and yawned contemptuously. The mastiff was as big as a Shetland pony, and none of the dozen curs lying around it in the deep grass was smaller than a full-grown German shepherd. When the mastiff stirred, all the dogs snuffed the breeze sweeping off fields bright with the blue and yellow wildflowers of the high summer of the year 1632. Slipping out of the dappled shade between the hemispherical rawhide yurts, the pack loped toward the dirt road from the center of Mukden, the Tartar capital.

Careless of the growling watchdogs, Francis Arrowsmith slid from the piebald pony's back and strode toward the nearest yurt. The cracked and torn hide covering offered little protection from either the rain flurries or the dust storms of Manchuria and no protection from the baking heat. Nonetheless, their Tartar masters considered it almost demoralizingly luxurious for the two Christian slaves presented to the Emperor Abahai by the Virtuous Kung a few days earlier. Scratching his licebites, Joseph King had disagreed vehemently. The only amenity that kept their hovel from perfectly resembling a small mansion in Hell, he had insisted, was the skimming of the swallows over the board slung from the ridgepole to invite them to nest.

Francis's fascinated contemplation of the swallows darting through the smoke hole in the top of the yurt was shattered when the mastiff sprang. Seizing the six-inch spikes hedging the beast's collar, he hurled it away, fell to his knees, and whipped a cudgel from his belt. Crouching, he whirled the cudgel around his head to keep the growling dogs at bay.

Jaws gaping, the curs circled him. A pair darted under the swinging cudgel to clamp their teeth in the skirts of his coarse robe. While he teetered off balance, the mastiff hurled its weight at his chest. The Englishman shouted as the gleaming fangs lunged for his throat and rolled away as the jaws snapped shut.

Drawn by the tumult, a small girl scurried from the neighboring yurt and shouted shrilly at the dogs. She strode into the pack, seized the mastiff's collar, and pulled it off the Englishman. Though it was four times the child's weight and overtopped her height of two feet, the animal yielded docilely. Driving the pack before her with a twig, the girl smiled at Francis and chattered unintelligibly. Whatever their past condition, all were equal in the hovels that housed the slaves of the Tartars.

The Englishman rose gingerly and dusted himself with quick flicking motions. He smiled in self-derision at having forgotten the pack of curs that guarded the slaves' settlement, but was in the next moment overcome again by the joy of simply being alive. When he gazed at the green meadows strewn with glowing flowers, his heart sang. He glanced at the distant mountains looming in the east before staring with renewed wonder at the grasslands rippling to the far horizon. Awed by the vast, empty land, he waved at Joseph King, who stood in the opening of the dilapidated yurt laughing at his master's discomfiture.

"Joseph," Francis shouted, "good news...at last. We move out of this stinking hovel tomorrow."

"The Lord be praised," Joseph replied fervently. "But where are we bound? The iron mines or straight to prison?"

"Neither, Joseph, you'll be pleased to hear." Francis's half-grown yellow beard bobbed as he spoke. "We are to be honored guests of the Tartar Emperor Abahai in the Imperial Hostel."

"I *am* delighted.... But your head, Arrowmaker." Joseph's bronze features wrinkled like an amiable pug dog, and his

232

incisors gleamed wetly when he grinned. "I see they've made a Tartar out of you."

"It will come to you, too, my friend." Francis rubbed his palm over his shaven head, which shone slick white above his tanned forehead. Only a patch at the back had been spared the barber's razor, and that long sun-bleached hair was plaited into a thick braid.

"Better lose my hair than my head." Joseph clapped his master on the shoulder, and the exuberant Francis threw his arm around his secretary's shoulders.

"And by that sacrifice we buy not only our lives. We are, it appears, to become men of substance among the Tartars."

"A few days ago, I would have given you long odds that we were to become coolies in their quarries. What has changed our fortunes so radically? And you return without your guards?"

"Joseph, there's no place to run. We're prisoners twice over ... prisoners of the Tartars and prisoners of the endless grasslands."

"It's good to know the happy ending before the tale begins. But don't keep me waiting forever."

"I won't, I promise you. Just let me get my pipe going. They've given us tobacco, the first, they say, of many gifts."

Francis squatted on the straw bale covered with a tattered blanket and slipped his bamboo pipe from his leather boot, the only item of their original clothing their captors had left them. Squinting in the pungent smoke of the dried-dung fire, his eyes smarted. At least, the fumes kept off the fierce Manchurian mosquitoes, which were as big as musket balls. Tamping down the tobacco in the small porcelain bowl, he studied the miniature of his mother that was propped on the battered leather trunk against the side of the yurt.

What if she should see me now, he thought, *my loving mother? Not a priest as she wished, but a rough soldier and, by the ways of Europe, a prisoner of war among half-civilized nomads. But actually a slave of the barbarians. Nonetheless, it is the Lord's Will. By His Grace, I may yet be of as much service to Him here as a priest. But, by Our Lady, I wish I had paid more attention to my mother's wishes.*

Francis lifted a glowing fragment from the fire with the bronze chopsticks he took from his belt. When his pipe was drawing well, he still remained silent. With unwonted patience, Joseph King waited for his master to speak. He sensed that Francis was brooding on the events that had brought them to captivity among the Tartars—for the first time since the fall of the citadel at Tengchou they were no longer standing in the shadow of imminent death.

THE Cantonese traitors, Francis recalled, had admitted the mutineers to the citadel in the early morning of the twenty-second of February, 1632. The clash of swords that awakened the Christian General endured less than an hour before the mutineers streamed into the basement to bear down the few loyal soldiers who still resisted.

Nonetheless, the struggle continued on the winding stairs to the upper stories of the tower. After slaughtering some fifty Portuguese, Indians, and Africans, the mutineers made prisoners of General Ignatius Sün, Ambassador Michael Chang, and Major Francis Arrowsmith, as well as the fourteen surviving Portuguese. They were manacled and brought before the rebel leader, the Virtuous Kung.

The Englishman was astonished to discover that the rebel commander actually practiced the Buddhist mercy he had promised to blunt his enemies' will. Having expected quick death, the prisoners rejoiced when they found that the Virtuous Kung was truly eager to Acquire Merit by Releasing Living Things.

Only General Ignatius Sün grumbled. "It is demeaning to receive the same mercy accorded to fish, larks, and pangolins."

When his own men cheered the Christian General, the Virtuous Kung had no choice but to exercise clemency. Since they loved General Ignatius Sün for his generosity and his warcraft, the mutineers might have risen against their new leader if he had executed the little General. After the General again refused to join the rebels, the Virtuous Kung bundled him off to Peking. He was accompanied by Ambassador Michael Chang and three loyal Chinese subalterns, Marta with her infant daughter Maria and her maidservant Ying, Father Juan Rodriguez, and the surviving Portuguese artillerymen. Kung detained only Francis Arrowsmith and his slave Joseph King.

Marta did not plead for her husband's freedom; she was apparently too glad to receive her own. It was beneath her dignity to weep at the feet of the Virtuous Kung, though he might well have yielded to her tears. Her classic example of

234

Confucian virtue might have moved him to display his own Confucian virtue. But Marta retained her dignity, and Francis remained a captive.

The Englishman was bitterly aware that the mutineers were avidly watching his parting from his wife. He was determined to give them no opportunity to scoff at an outlander's unseemly display of emotion. Marta herself concealed whatever emotion she felt so adroitly that even Francis could not tell whether she grieved or rejoiced at their parting.

Marta stood alone in the sunlight, waving away her maidservant's supporting hand, though her minute golden lilies sank into the soft snow. No expression marred the enameled pink-gold perfection of her features. Stiff within her lustrous stone-marten coat, Marta bowed profoundly to her husband as Confucian etiquette required. She murmured a ritual farewell and stepped into her waiting litter. Before Ying drew the curtains, Marta sat quite still, neither turning her head nor fluttering her hand. After the curtains closed, she did not look out.

Francis stood stunned for an instant before turning away. Marta, he finally told himself, had done no more than maintain the serenity before gaping strangers he was also determined to preserve. Despite his sorrow at their parting, he was proud of her dignity. Joseph King, who observed the byplay with astonishment, did not tell his master that true Confucian virtue would have required his mistress to share her husband's captivity rather than depart with dignity. Consoled by his ignorance, Francis stoically turned his back. He did not watch the small procession depart, but chatted negligently with the Virtuous Kung.

The rebel leader remarked casually that he had never intended to torture either Juan Rodriguez or the infant Maria. He had, Francis reflected, not intended to torture them—except as a last resort.

But Kung insisted that he had threatened the hostages only to lull the citadel's defenders. He had wished them to believe he would not attack before February the twenty-fourth, the date set for the torture.

"Under that cloak of deception," the Virtuous Kung boasted, "I pursued my twofold strategy. I extended the armored tortoise until it became the dragon of a siege tower. And, at the same time, I searched out traitors among the Cantonese. Thus I took the citadel with little cost of my men's lives."

"It was a cunning plot," Francis agreed, since Kung was so manifestly proud of his wiliness.

So many Chinese glory in double-dealing, the Englishman mused bitterly to himself, and they boast of their duplicity. But most Europeans who are equally sly veil their deceit with decent hypocrisy.

"I AM thinking, Joseph, of Virtuous Kung." Francis was recalled from his brooding by his slave's irritable cough. "It was truly artful the way he deceived us as to his true intentions regarding Juan Rodriguez and Maria, was it not?"

"If he was telling the truth that second time, Arrowmaker. But who knows?"

"Who, indeed?" Francis slapped at the mosquitoes buzzing around his bare shoulders. "But he was certainly merciful when he presented us to the Tartar Emperor rather than slaying us. He could have cut off our heads when he found our knowledge of ordnance useless to a rebel band that moved too fast for the green-bronze cannon."

"Arrowmaker, was it not more artful of the Virtuous Kung to give us as slaves to the Tartars? He has won the Tartar Emperor's good will by that gift at least as much as he might by offering a blood horse or a silver-inlaid fowling piece. But I am content with his choice."

"We can hardly complain now that the Tartars have given us our lives."

"For another reason, as well. I derive some sour satisfaction, I must admit, from now being the slave of the slave of an Emperor. My master will undoubtedly soon exercise greater power than any major of the Ming forces—and probably possess greater wealth."

"I hadn't thought of it that way, Joseph. But it's galling to have my crown shaved and my hair braided. English sailors, you know, call that plait a pigtail."

"You must know, Arrowmaker, that all the Tartars wear that style. To display their subservience, so do all outsiders in the Tartar service...whether they're Chinese or Central Asian...whether they're nobles, Mandarins, or generals."

"I know that, Joseph, but it still galls. By the way, I've been told they don't like to be called *Ta-ta*, Tartar, but prefer Manchu. As Manchus, they say, their ancestors ruled all

North China and called their Imperial House the Chin or Gold Dynasty."

"So they say, Arrowmaker. But who can blame them? *Ta-ta* is derogatory. You know we Chinese say barbarians can't speak properly, but can only stutter *ta-ta, ta-ta*."

"Just like the ancient Greeks. The word *barbarian* is the same. The Hellenes thought all outlanders could only stutter incomprehensibly *bar-bar, bar-bar*."

"Interesting, Arrowmaker. We shall, I suppose, have to call them Manchus. But my patience is wearing thin. I implore you to tell me what transpired today between yourself and these...Manchus."

"My reception was astonishing, Joseph. You remember how the two Tartar—that is to say, Manchu—soldiers awakened us this morning, of course?"

THE soldiers had allowed Francis only a cup of the mixture of tea, salt, and meal kept warm all night over the fire. Since they spoke no Chinese, they had gestured to him to mount the pony they led. But the young officer who received the Englishman at a side gate of the complex of low stone-and-wood structures that were the Imperial Palaces spoke rapidly in the Officials' Language of the Empire. Though his accent was barbaric and his grammar chopped, his meaning was clear.

"You are the ocean barbarian called the Arrowmaker, are you not?" the officer demanded.

"I am the Arrowmaker." Despite his fear at lying utterly in the power of the Manchus, Francis barely suppressed a laugh. Just how many yellow-haired European slaves did the barbarians possess, he wondered, that they required him to identify himself so formally?

"You are, Outlander, to be admitted to the presence of the second most important man in our realm." The young officer had learned Confucian punctilio from the Manchus' Chinese advisers, but slipped into the straightforward manner more natural to his people. "Prince Dorgon is Commander-in-Chief of our forces. Perhaps you know that our forces are divided into eight great armies, each called for the color of the banner it follows."

"I know of your Eight Banners," Francis acknowledged.

"Prince Dorgon commands two Banners directly—and all

the Banners at the Emperor's pleasure. He could, men say, have been Emperor himself. He is, after all, the fourteenth son of the Founding Emperor Nurhaci, who made us a nation. But he has given his total loyalty to the Emperor Abahai, who is his half-brother, the son of the Founding Emperor by a previous wife."

"Why do you tell me all this?" Francis was encouraged to put that bold question by the officer's candor.

"So that you will know with whom you deal, Arrowmaker. You must come into Prince Dorgon's presence deeply humble before his great worth."

"And who is this Prince Dorgon, beyond being your commander-in-chief?"

"Some men say the Founding Emperor designated Dorgon his successor. They whisper that the present Emperor Abahai destroyed their father's testament and put to death the Chinese scribes who took it down. All that is nonsense, of course. No more true than the rumors that the Emperor Abahai forced Dorgon's mother, the Dowager Empress, to commit suicide lest she unite her sons against him."

"I see," Francis responded noncommittally.

"Actually, Prince Dorgon looks on the Emperor as his father. They are as close as the lips are to the teeth. And the Emperor depends utterly on Dorgon's warcraft, though the Prince has not yet completed his twentieth year."

"So young and so brave and so wise!" Francis offered the appropriate—and politic—response.

"You do understand, then, Arrowmaker. You may call Dorgon Your Highness as befits a Prince of the Blood Imperial. But he prefers *Mergen Daising*, which means Wise Warrior. The Emperor gave Dorgon that title after he crushed rebellious Mongols when he was only sixteen. He is the bravest and the best of us all, though he suffers an affliction of the lungs."

Walking through rough-plastered corridors as they talked, they came to a door guarded by two archers wearing buff surtouts under short black tunics trimmed with red braid. The workmanship of the heraldic devices of beaten brass set into the wooden door was crude, as was the joinery. The officer closed the door behind Francis, but himself remained in the corridor.

The chamber was austerely furnished except for the bright Samarkand carpet on the pressed-earth floor. The young Manchu seated in an ebony armchair beside a low briarwood table was lean and taut. Beneath the upturned brim of his black-cloth hat, whose rounded crown was topped by a ruby, his slender face was drawn. Thick mustaches sprouted beneath his small nose to frame his narrow mouth, and his pointed chin was adorned by a wispy goatee. His eyes were wide, but strangely shadowed because, Francis surmised, he suffered continual physical pain, as the young officer had hinted. A string of jade beads interspersed at intervals with larger amber beads hung around Dorgon's neck, cascading down the breast of his violet tunic. Fastening in front rather than on the side in the Chinese manner, the Prince's tunic displayed the five-clawed dragons of the Imperial House coiled in tight circles.

"Sit down, Arrowmaker." Speaking in slow Chinese, the Prince waved at the low stool beside the table. "Since I know who you are, we need waste no time in preliminaries. Presumably, you know who I am."

"I do, Your Imperial Highness, very well indeed." Though he warmed to the young Prince's direct manner, Francis knew that ornate Chinese flattery would hardly be resented. "All men know the fame of the Wise Warrior Prince Dorgon."

"Be that as it may, I have work for you, Arrowmaker."

"I am at your command, Wise Warrior." Resenting the arrogant Manchu's power over his life, the Englishman added rashly: "How could it be otherwise? I am, after all, only a miserable slave, no more than dust beneath your feet."

"Do not make so much of it, Arrowmaker," the Prince smiled. "We all know the fortunes of war. If we were in Peking, I could be sitting in your place."

"That is most unlikely, Wise Warrior. Your Imperial Highness would never be so foolish as to allow himself to be captured."

"Perhaps not," Dorgon smiled again. "But, within very broad limits, I intend to reconcile you to your circumstances."

"I am honored, Your Highness. May I ask why?"

"Because I have need of you. What better reason to treat you well?"

"And how can I be of service, Your Highness?"

"I should.... Yes, I shall leave you free to work as you please," the Prince mused. "You will be provided with ample materials and with all the skilled metalworkers I can muster. In return, you will cast the cannon I require to defend the Emperor's realms against the aggressive Ming."

"I stand as I said, at Your Highness's command." Although

239

he was helpless, Francis could not lightly relinquish his loyalty to the hard-pressed Ming Dynasty, which the Manchu Prince castigated as aggressive. "I cannot do otherwise."

"That is absolutely true, is it not? You cannot do otherwise." When Dorgon laughed, Francis felt the cruel authority beneath his mask of youthful suffering. "You will therefore cast cannon and train my men in their use. Also in the use of the arquebus. We have a fair store of those small arms."

"*Pu kan-tang! Kuo chiang!*" Francis took refuge in the stylized self-abnegation of the Officials' Language of China. "I am unworthy! You honor me too highly!"

"You will not be compelled. You must understand that." Prince Dorgon was almost placating. "We know that an unwilling servant will not serve the Emperor well. You will, therefore, be allowed ample time, though you must not delay inordinately. I have great need of cannon. And you will be given rich rewards."

"Rewards, Your Highness, to a slave? That is not the normal practice in the Ming Empire."

"It is not Chinese, perhaps, but it is our way to ensure loyalty. You will be permitted to trade on your own account. Manchuria is rich in white ginseng, the miraculous herb. It is a curative and..."

"...and aphrodisiac like the herb we Europeans call mandrake, Your Highness?"

"Reputedly, though I have never had occasion to test that property."

"Nor I, Your Highness," Francis responded in kind to that youthful bravado. "Though, perhaps, when we are older, we may be thankful..."

"Perhaps, Arrowmaker. But, regardless, the ginseng, the furs, and the gold of Manchuria are much prized elsewhere. You may ship them to your Christian merchants in Macao. The profits will be great."

"*Kuo chiang!*" Francis exclaimed again. "You honor me too highly!"

"We shall see about that. Meanwhile I can assure you that you will be happy among us."

Such silken consideration, sustained by golden persuasion, was overwhelming to a captive who had only two days earlier completed an exhausting ride of several hundred miles over summer-dusty roads to Mukden. One moment, he and Joseph King had been prisoners guarded by twenty of the Virtuous Kung's cavalrymen. The next moment he was an honored guest, received, in truth, like the ambassador of a powerful ally.

Why, Francis wondered, did Prince Dorgon strive to ingratiate himself with a powerless prisoner? Why such lavish inducements when the Manchu could snuff out his slave's life between his thumb and forefinger like a manservant pinching out a candle flame?

Prince Dorgon did not discuss technical matters when he finished congratulating Francis on his good fortune in being a slave. Instead, he led the Englishman through dim corridors bustling with preoccupied officials. One in three was an obvious Chinese who did not walk with the Manchu horsemen's bandy-legged swagger. The knot of courtiers in front of a plank door studded with copper nailheads parted before Prince Dorgon.

They entered a chamber remarkable only for the dais that supported an enormous black-lacquered armchair inlaid with mother-of-pearl. The stocky Manchu of some forty years seated on that demi-throne wore a robe of golden yellow, the Imperial color. The cut and the fabric were, however, plain compared to the elaborately brocaded robes of the Ming Emperor with their hectic parade of dragons, phoenixes, and cocks. A strip of simple scrolled embroidery adorned the hem, and a single high lapel fastened on the right shoulder. The Emperor's thumb was tucked casually into a blue-leather belt clasped with a round buckle of green jade.

Courtiers clustered around the heavy-faced figure with the thick pointed mustaches. Set in a gold diadem, his green-velvet crown was topped by a miniature spire of five graduated gold balls. The Emperor's eyes glittered through openings that were hardly more than slits in fleshy lids. They differed further from wider Chinese eyes in being set straight, rather than obliquely, in his weather-reddened cheeks.

Francis dropped to his knees to perform the ceremonial kowtow, the "bending of the head" three times three times. He had touched his forehead to the ground only once when he felt Prince Dorgon's hand on his shoulder.

"You need not kneel," the Prince said. "A simple bow will do. This is not a state reception."

Astonished by such informality, Francis rose and, resting his hands on his knees, inclined his body until it was parallel with the orange-and-red Turkestan carpet. It would have been inconceivable for an ocean-barbarian slave to enter the presence of the Ming Emperor, whom his ministers saw only

241

four or five times a year. Excusing that slave the demeaning kowtow would have been sacrilegious.

But rough manners more suited to the camp than the court prevailed even in the Imperial Palaces. Princes and ministers spoke of the Manchu Emperor as Abahai, which was the personal name of the eighth son of the Founding Emperor Nurhaci. Moreover, they saw the Emperor whenever necessary and without obsequious formality.

"*Ah, Ying-chang, ting-shuo ni huei chih-tsao Hung Yi Pao...*" The Emperor Abahai's small mouth smiled, and his plump chin bobbed when he spoke in laborious Chinese. "Well, Major, I've heard you can cast Red Jacket Cannon. Is that so?"

"That is correct, Your Majesty."

Hearing the words *Hung Yi Pao* from a Manchu mouth, Francis was struck again by the curious Chinese name for the green-bronze cannon that could, he was convinced, dominate the battlefields of Asia as overwhelmingly as the English longbow had once dominated the battlefields of Europe. Because of the ambiguity of Classical Chinese, *Hung Yi Pao* could also mean either Gory Extermination Cannon or Red Barbarian Cannon. But the term was commonly written with ideograms meaning Red Jacket Cannon because of the scarlet fabric that clothed the guns in order to terrify enemies with a portent of the blood they would shed. That honor neither Chinese nor Manchus rendered their own feeble iron cannon.

The Emperor coughed peremptorily, recalling Francis from his brief revery.

"Yes, Your Majesty," he repeated. "I can make cannon...given proper materials and skilled metalworkers."

"That is Dorgon's concern," the Emperor said. "But tell me, how far can your Red Jacket Cannon throw a ball?"

"That depends on their size, Your Majesty, but perhaps two *li*." Francis would not promise more than he could easily perform; two *li* was less than a mile, though a range of almost two miles was possible. "I'd start with culverins, light field pieces."

"How big would they be? What weight? What length? How transported?"

The Emperor questioned Francis for half a double hour, revealing a searching curiosity, a lively intelligence—and a profound ignorance of ordnance. When he glanced at a sheaf of papers offered by a Chinese secretary, the Englishman understood the signal for his departure and bowed deeply. As he shuffled backward from the room, the Emperor looked up.

"We are renowned for Our generosity to those who serve Us well," he said softly. "But We cannot keep a useless slave by Us."

Perhaps perversely, Francis felt more confidence in the Emperor's word after that plain threat, which was subsequently reinforced by Prince Dorgon.

"Abahai is lavish with servants who please him, so lavish his ministers sometimes protest against his excessive generosity," the Prince said. "The slaves he discards are sent to the mines, where they may live for a year...two at most. Slaves who displease Abahai are sent immediately to the executioner. You may go now—unguarded. Tomorrow I shall find you better quarters in the Imperial Hostel."

Francis was already half-convinced that he could rely upon the Emperor Abahai's word. The Manchu's promises and his threats were explicit, quite unlike the silken deviousness of the Chinese. The Manchus were obviously heavy-handed in both their kindness and their punishments. Were they, he wondered, also even-handed?

Riding alone through the Manchu capital, Francis pondered his reception—and his future—in the city he was to come to know very well, perhaps too well.

Unlike age-old Peking, unlike even provincial Tengchou, Mukden was an open city without walls. It was essentially an encampment on the wide plains, rather than a citadel erected against hostile nature and hostile men. The walls around the Imperial Palaces were low and narrow, offering a passing obeisance to the convention of fortification, but making no true fortress.

The country town was dominated by the endless grasslands that rose in the east to the inhospitable Long White Mountains where, legend related, the Manchus had originated. Not even in the Imperial Palaces was Francis ever to feel sheltered by the works of man. Nowhere was he to feel comfortably enclosed by great buildings, brick-hedged avenues, and soaring monuments. The secure ambience of civilization, he realized, could be created only by tens of generations living, breeding, and dying in an environment made by man.

Moreover, the Manchurian climate was severe, baking in summer and freezing in winter, with spring and autumn only fleeting respites. The unpaved streets, which were wastes of dust in the dry summer, were transformed into quagmires by the rains of autumn. During the long bitter winter, those streets were glistening rivers of ice between heaped snow cliffs. The late spring thaw transformed them again into quagmires.

The few buildings fronting on the mean square of the Imperial Palaces were ephemeral. Covered with crude dun tiles, their projecting eaves swept high in front and low in back. Those structures were patterned on the tents of state that sheltered Manchu princes in their nomadic encampments. If their gray-stuccoed façades were knocked away, their roofs would still stand on stout pillars, which were like tentpoles set inside the walls.

Even more disconcertingly, no fixed boundary separated the town from the countryside, since innumerable domed yurts and highswept tents spilled into Mukden itself. That confusion pleased the Manchu warriors, who hated the confinement of a walled city.

The Manchus, Francis was to learn, were far graver than the Chinese. Given to neither light amusements nor idle laughter, they were as dour as Scots. Crude in intellect and rough in manners, the single-minded Manchus were more forceful than the people of the Ming. They left delicate arts like painting and sculpture to the Chinese, whom they despised for light-mindedness. But they delighted in verse epics that recalled their past glories. Though envying the wealth of their more civilized neighbors, the Manchus, like the Scots, despised the people of the South as profligate triflers who would, given time enough, compound their own destruction. Thereupon the virtuous Manchus would undoubtedly triumph—and rule their dissolute Chinese subjects wisely though sternly.

The character of its masters shaped Mukden, Francis saw even on that first day when he rode back alone to his tumbledown yurt through seething streets. The Manchu capital lacked not only the monumental grandeur of Peking, but the ordered gaiety of the Northern Capital. It lacked even the solid self-assurance of provincial Tengchou because the Manchus, unlike the Chinese, were not bound by mystical ties to the acres where lay the sacred bones of their ancestors.

Mukden, however, possessed an assertive vitality that had flickered low in the cities of China. It was quite obviously the center of an empire in the making, an empire that already extended for thousands of miles across the steppes. The mean streets flowed with the peoples and the tribes who acknowledged the Emperor Abahai as their overlord.

Francis prudently pulled his pony aside to make way for a band of Mongols, whose fur-trimmed robes were thrown back from their shoulders to expose hard-muscled brown torsos. The chains of silver coins hanging from their headdresses clanked before flat faces flushed with alcohol. Some rode astride, flourishing lances that trailed multicolored streamers. Others, further gone in drunkenness, squatted on their wooden saddles, rising occasionally to their feet to shout barbaric war cries. Still others hung by a single stirrup alongside their mounts, their heads popping up behind the horses' necks to shout incomprehensible jests that roused their companions to raucous laughter.

Turning his pony back into the street, Francis was startled by the haughty camel that emerged from the clouds of dust trailed by the boisterous Mongols. A caravan of more than a hundred swaying Bactrians choked the narrow street. Their panniers were heaped with raw wool and with carpets, while their leading-reins were held by hook-nosed Turkyi traders from Inner Asia.

Knowing them for Moslems, infidels far more pernicious than simple pagans, Francis crossed himself. He was astonished when one Turkyi trader also crossed himself and waved amiably. That man, he surmised, must be a Nestorian Christian who was still true to the Faith that had been planted in the depths of Inner Asia by fearless missionaries a thousand years earlier.

Seeing that he must push his way through the throngs or lurk indefinitely beneath the eaves projecting over the street, Francis twitched his pony's reins. He was gratified when a group of dignified Koreans edged away to let him pass.

Their high-cheekboned faces with slit eyes were grave beneath the faintly ludicrous miniature top hats fixed to their high-piled hair with jeweled bodkins. Among the mounted Koreans, who wore gorgeously brocaded plum-colored robes, swayed a gold-and-red lacquered palanquin as gorgeous as any Ming prince's. A triangular banner borne before the litter displayed not only the ubiquitous dragon of the Extreme East, but, in scarlet Chinese ideograms, the legend: *Embassy of the Stalwart King of Korea to the Emperor Abahai.*

Francis was astonished by the profusion of monks and priests who walked and rode through the streets of Mukden: traditional Buddhists in saffron vestments, Shamans in gaudy tunics adorned with skull-and-crossbones designs, and heavily bearded Moslem imams whose green turbans proclaimed that they had made the pilgrimage to Mecca.

He saw Tibetans twirling prayer wheels set with turquoise and coral, their faces broad-boned and their noses higharched. All the lamas let their blanketlike robes hang to expose their right shoulders. Seeing that some wore red vestments and others yellow, Francis assumed the colors declared their ecclesiastical rank. As the Tibetans passed, he recoiled from the stench of rancid butter and sour sweat.

Most astonishingly, women and girls walked purposefully through the streets, while other females rode astride beside their men. In their short boleros and flowing skirts, the Manchu ladies were as self-assured as the armed warriors who accepted their company as natural. The retiring modesty of Chinese ladies was obviously unknown to those forward women. Some lifted silver flasks to their mouths, drinking deep while their ponies trotted.

Dazed by the tumult of Mukden, Francis rode soberly back to the yurt in the slave settlement where Joseph King waited. The vigor of the Manchus and their vassals had aroused in him not only astonishment but also fear. He also felt a wholly Chinese contempt for peoples so indecorously undignified.

The Manchus, he knew, had been trying in vain to cast green-bronze cannon for some years. The Emperor had therefore welcomed him like a noble hostage rather than the slave he was. But he swore not to be taken in by the Manchus' courtesy. He had, after all, been received by the Chinese most demonstratively, only to be discarded like a worn-out coat a few years later.

LATE into the night Francis Arrowsmith and Joseph King discussed the Manchus' intentions toward them. They squinted in the feeble light of the wick coiled in the rancid oil of an earthenware lamp like a water snake at the bottom of a fetid pond. Rank fumes rose in broken spirals toward the smoke hole in the roof, and the lamplight flickered in the breeze that swept under the open sides of the yurt.

"Why should Prince Dorgon be so effusive if his promises are sincere?" Joseph asked. "Our good fortune could better have been allowed to become obvious to us by deeds, rather than words."

"Any Ming minister who woos a helpless captive's cooperation so sweetly," Francis agreed bitterly, "would unquestionably be spinning a plot that must end with the captive's destruction."

The excessive subtlety learned from the Ming misled both Francis and Joseph. Slow-witted beside the sophisticated Chinese the Manchus undoubtedly were. But, the two Christians discovered, they were also straightforward, rarely lying—unless, of course, for a good reason.

Delighted by his freedom to work unhampered, Francis did not yearn for the civilized pleasures of China—which had, he felt, treated him shabbily. Nor was his conscience greatly troubled by his serving the enemies of the Ming Dynasty, to which he had sworn an oath of allegiance. He was, after all, a slave at the mercy of his captors. He was also a mercenary—a soldier of fortune, as he more delicately put it—and his mercenary's honor compelled him to return faithful service for generous wages and respectful treatment.

Vastly distant Europe was rarely in the Englishman's thoughts. No purpose was served by longing for the lands of his ancestors. Besides, he knew the Lord's Design required his presence in the Extreme East.

Francis endured his separation from his infant daughter with the same stoicism. He yearned for Maria and bitterly regretted his inability to watch her grow from a helpless infant into a lively small girl. When his mind lowered its defenses, he looked longingly at the small children who played around the Imperial Hostel where he and Joseph King occupied a pleasant apartment. Though he subdued his waking fantasies of dandling his daughter on his knee, he could not control his dreams.

Francis was, however, profoundly puzzled and deeply hurt by his wife's rejection. How, he wondered, could a lady like Marta offer him her soul so confidingly and her body so wantonly if she did not truly love him? How could she have changed so totally?

He finally rationalized Marta's coldness. The aberrant behavior brought on by pregnancy had, he assured himself, lingered briefly afterward. If they were still together, he was certain, they would already have rediscovered the perfect bliss of the first year of their marriage.

When he longed for his infant daughter and the perfect wife enshrined in his imagination, Francis ached to return to the Great Empire. His itch to leave was aggravated by the small discomforts of Mukden. He could not refuse the Manchus' generous hospitality, but he gagged on the half-raw meat they devoured and choked on the fermented mare's milk, the *koumiss* that was their favorite drink. Bravado moved him to match his hard-drinking hosts cup for cup of *arak*, the spirits distilled from *koumiss*, though he invariably regretted his folly the next morning.

Francis deplored the bodily itch that drove him to the Chinese and Korean courtesans of the Spring Flower House. There were no Manchu ladies of skill, since the women of the tribes were free persons, unlike their more civilized sisters. Some of the courtesans were beautiful; many were brilliant conversationalists or inspired musicians; all were skilled in the arts of love. Except with Marta, whom he loved, he had never experienced such sensual ecstasies. But he invariably felt revulsion from his lustful weakness and remorse for betraying his wife when he left the next morning.

Nonetheless, he consoled himself, he was a sinful soldier and still youthfully lusty, not a holy, self-sacrificing priest. He was, further, reconciled to both his misdeeds and his nominal slavery by the profits of his trade with Macao. He shipped gold, furs, and white ginseng in small coasting junks too ramshackle to attract the pirates who terrorized the China Seas. His first partner in the Portuguese settlement was Father Giulio di Giaccomo, whose visit to St. Omer's College had originally drawn an English youth to fabled China. Treasurer of the Society of Jesus in the Extreme East, the Italian was delighted to earn funds to support the Holy Mission. Later Francis consigned some cargoes to the Marrano Antonio Castro, secretary of the Loyal Senate. In time, he accumulated a substantial hoard of gold in Macao.

The Englishman prudently concentrated his energies on casting cannon and training officers. Prince Dorgon would be generous as long as he forged those vital parts of the war machine with which the Manchu Emperor was determined to conquer the Ming Empire.

The Manchus had abandoned the earlier pretext that they fought only to defend their own territory against Ming incursions. On the advice of his Chinese counselors, the Emperor Abahai had required the Ming to acknowledge the Manchu Empire as the equal of the Ming Empire. That demand created the pretext Abahai needed to attack China.

"Abahai, of course, knows that his demand cannot be met," Francis wrote to Giulio di Giaccomo. "As you know, the

Chinese maintain that their Emperor has received the *Tien Ming,* the Mandate of Heaven that gives him dominion over *Tien Hsia,* All That Lies Under Heaven. The Chinese Court can no more receive Manchu envoys as the ambassadors of a monarch of equal standing than they can fly over mountains or sail under the sea.

"Only armed might can commamd respect for the Manchus from the Chinese. By armed might, I am constantly reminded here in Mukden, the Manchus' cousins, the Mongols of the Yüan Dynasty, and the Manchus' ancestors, the Juched of the Gold Dynasty, conquered China. The Emperor Abahai is determined to command equal respect—and he is preparing for a war of total conquest."

Father Giulio di Giaccomo's replies gave Francis news not only of Macao, but of Peking. The Italian priest's reports finally convinced the English slave that the Ming could offer no effective resistance when the Manchus' Eight Banners finally marched. The Ming was apparently set on destroying itself. One of Giulio di Giaccomo's reports distressed Francis. He felt deep anguish because the writing was so vivid that he could virtually see the terrible scenes the Italian described.

THE candle clocks of Peking had just burned down to the Double Hour of the Boar on an early autumn evening in the sixth year of the reign of the Chung Chen Emperor of the Great Ming Dynasty. The long northern twilight lingered over the throngs strolling in the mild warmth at nine in the evening on September the seventh, 1632. But the stone floor of the dank vestibule was cold when Father Johann Adam Schall von Bell crept past guards in the gaudy uniform of the Flamboyant Cloaks into the Eastern Hall.

For the first time, an outlander voluntarily penetrated the inner circle of the invisible web that bound the Empire to the Court Eunuchs' will. Despite the silent prayers that held his terror at bay, Father Adam shivered as he entered the Eastern Hall. That nondescript building near the city wall was the nerve center of the Divine Skein, the plexus where all the tangled threads of the Secret Police met. Few of the prisoners confined in the Eastern Hall emerged alive, and those few were broken in body and mind.

The Jesuit crawled up the stone steps to the tower cells. His cramped muscles stabbed by pain, he took his weight alternately on his knees and his palms. A picul of coal, a Chinese hundredweight of one hundred thirty-three European pounds, hung on his back in an elongated basket secured around his shoulders and his forehead by broad cloth bands.

Only disguised as a coal vendor could Adam Schall enter the place he called the Unholy of Unholies, the cells where the Eunuchs conducted their "examination of prisoners" by excruciating torture. Coal dust obscured his bold features, and his sooty eyelids were lowered over his blue eyes. A grimy scarf hid his long blond hair, which was streaked with white in his forty-first year. The abject posture forced by the load of fuel for the inquisitors' stoves concealed his height and his breadth of shoulder, which would have betrayed him had he walked erect.

Although the guards had been liberally bribed, Adam Schall feared treachery in that evil atmosphere. Pausing with his forehead resting on the gritty steps, he surreptitiously crossed himself. He detested the subterfuge necessary to visit the two hapless Christian gentlemen who were tormented by the executioners of the Flamboyant Cloaks. But he could not come into the Eastern Hall in his own character.

The prisoners had been denied the Holy Sacraments by a vindictive court-martial. Only the venality of the Flamboyant Cloaks permitted Father Adam Schall to offer consolation to the condemned men, General Ignatius Sün and Ambassador Michael Chang. Even lavish bribes would not have availed without the influence of Dr. Paul Hsü, who had a few months earlier been elevated to Grand Secretary. The Christian Chancellor could not save them from the executioner's two-handed scimitar. The young Emperor required their deaths to atone for the loss of vital Tengchou.

Chained to the rough stone wall, General Ignatius Sün and Ambassador Michael Chang sat on the damp floor. Their bodies were barely covered by torn garments of white sack-cloth stained with excrement and blood. Their bare feet were swollen twice normal size, and their soles were lacerated with bloody welts. Every one of their toes was broken, hardly distinguishable as separate members amid the mass of purulent flesh.

When they extended their hands in welcome, Adam Schall shuddered with uncontrollable revulsion. The ends of their fingers, where nails had once grown, dripped green pus from mangled black-and-carmine pads. Shattered bone and torn tendons gleamed iridescent white amid the rotting flesh of their palms. The stench of corruption hung so thick in the cell that the priest gagged and tasted copper bile in the back of his mouth. The two Christians' wounds were a devil's parody of the agonies inflicted upon Our Lord.

The little General waved his maimed hand to invite the Jesuit to take the bamboo stool that normally served his torturers. His grotesquely courtly gesture strained the chain that bound him to the wall, and he gasped with pain.

The infinitely greater pain endured during the weeks past had melted the flesh from General Ignatius Sün's face. His skin sagged limp and gray over his delicate cheekbones. His long mustaches, once waxed into martial ferocity, hung limp beside lips raw with the festering wounds his own teeth had inflicted in his agony. But his eyes, enormous in his shrunken features, looked at the Jesuit with serene certainty.

Ambassador Michael Chang slumped beside the ravaged figure who had been the most brilliant strategist and the most gallant field general of the Great Ming Dynasty. His broad frame had collapsed upon itself, and his big bones pressed against his fleshless skin. One side of his bushy mustache had been plucked out hair by hair, and one eyelid was crumpled over an empty socket that oozed green pus. His other eye stared in frightful perplexity at the priest who wore the grimy rags of a coal vendor.

The Mandarin who had so eloquently represented the Ming Dynasty as its first ambassador to a foreign nation could speak only in broken phrases. His body was broken, and his pride was extinguished. But, at the end, his faith was unmarred.

Neither General Ignatius Sün nor Ambassador Michael Chang spoke of his grievous injuries, and Father Adam Schall did not press them. They said only that they had been most severely tortured *after* the court-martial condemned them to death. Their tormentors had then relentlessly pressed them to confess that they had deliberately betrayed Tengchou to the mutineers. The Eunuchs were determined that the two Christian gentlemen must admit that they had from the beginning plotted with the two traitor Lieutenant Colonels to proclaim General Ignatius Sün emperor of a new dynasty.

All else the condemned men had confessed in their agony: disloyal communication with the rebels and massive theft, even unjustly executing loyal soldiers, though their true crime had been excessive lenience. But treason they would not admit. Instead, both Ignatius and Michael had repeatedly

251

asked the same question: Why should they have returned voluntarily to Peking to submit themselves to the Emperor's will if they had actually plotted against the Ming Dynasty?

Their vicious inquisitors had finally despaired of extracting a confession of treason. The Eunuchs had finally relented in superstitious awe of their prisoners' faith.

In their anguish, the doomed men had continually recited the *Pater Noster*. That simple prayer had comforted them greatly, they said, even in the most excruciating pain. Speaking to their Father in Heaven, they realized that they had been chosen to endure martyrdom for His sake.

"Only once did I despair," the little General said haltingly. "Only once was I sorely tempted to apostasy and a false confession. Not torture itself, but words brought me to that extremity. I despaired momentarily when the Eunuchs threatened to postpone our execution. *We will keep you alive indefinitely,* they said, *examining you constantly—until you confess! . . ."*

What else passed between himself and the prisoners in the foul cell Father Adam Schall would never afterward say. He would not reveal the discussion that occupied them through the night of September the seventh until six the next morning, the middle of the Double Hour of the Horse. Then, the Eunuchs' varlets carried General Ignatius Sün and Ambassador Michael Chang to the execution place in the courtyard of the Eastern Hall.

"All the martyrs said was under the seal of Holy Confession," Father Adam Schall later declared. "I can only say further that, after the executioner's assistant flipped their long hair over their faces to bare their necks to the scimitar, our brothers Ignatius and Michael died in the bosom of Christ. They serenely accepted the martyrdom that was the Divine Will of the Lord of Heaven."

WHEN Francis Arrowsmith had served in Mukden for almost a year, Prince Dorgon, Commander-in-Chief of the Manchu armies, reported to the Emperor Abahai that the European was executing with great vigor his twofold task—casting cannon and training officers. Although the lack of skilled artisans and the inadequacy of improvised foundries was imposing long delays, the English slave was absolutely invaluable to the Manchu armed forces. Four field pieces with highly competent crews had already joined the Red Banner. Nonetheless, the conquest of China would have to be postponed for some time.

The Emperor Abahai ratified Prince Dorgon's two further proposals. Some Banners were to be kept in trim by "pacifying" recalcitrant tribes along the distant Amur, which the Chinese called Heilungchiang, the Black Dragon River; others would assert Manchu authority in the troublesome Korean Peninsula. The Manchu Emperor was determined that his rear areas would be secure when he marched against Ming China. As methodically, the Emperor Abahai gave orders to bind to closer loyalty the European whose martial skills could be as vital as a secure base to his Grand Enterprise.

Francis was summoned to a private audience in the Secondary Throne Room on a gray afternoon late in November 1632. As a particular mark of favor, he was attended by his slave Joseph King. Like the Chinese, the Manchus felt that a man of standing should not come alone into the Imperial Presence. The Emperor Abahai was attended by a single Chinese secretary, and Prince Dorgon sat on a stool beside the dais.

"We have summoned you, Arrowmaker," the Manchu Emperor said in his slow Chinese, "to express Our commendation for your arduous endeavors."

"Your Imperial Majesty!" Francis acknowledged the Imperial praise with a low bow; behind him, Joseph King bowed as low to the barbarian monarch he considered a presumptuous would-be usurper.

The Emperor gestured, and the Chinese secretary handed Francis a pouch of soft-tanned calfskin closed with silver drawstrings.

"As a mark of Our commendation, We present you with ten gold taels," the Emperor said. "Nine for you and one for your slave... if you so choose."

Contrasting the niggardly ways of the Ming Emperor with the largesse of the Manchu Emperor, that Chinese patriot Joseph King felt higher regard for the barbarian monarch. When his master bowed again, the secretary-slave bowed even lower.

"We have also commanded that you marry the maiden Babutai, daughter of Our faithful Baron Obotu." The Emperor beamed benevolence. "She is already sixteen and most beautiful, as well as dutiful and skilled in housewifery."

"I am deeply honored by Your Majesty's intentions." Francis spoke after a respectful pause. "However, I am constrained to point out with the greatest humility that I am already married to a lady of China."

"That is no hindrance, Arrowmaker," the Emperor declared. "You live here under Our rule."

"But my religion, Your Imperial Majesty, forbids..."

"We are not concerned with your religion, Arrowmaker. Nor may you be. In the realms of the Manchus Our word is the creed of all men."

"Why am I to be so greatly honored, Your Majesty?" Francis pleaded. "I have done nothing to deserve such great favor at Your Majesty's hands."

"That is for Us to judge... not you." The Emperor frowned, and Francis felt Joseph tug his sleeve in warning. "But your loyal service does merit an explanation."

"After your marriage, Arrowmaker, your interests will be identical with the interests of our own Manchu nobility." Prince Dorgon spoke earnestly when the Emperor nodded. "To be quite candid, His Imperial Majesty finds your services valuable and wishes to bind you closer to our cause."

"I could not possibly serve Your Majesty more devotedly than I do now." Despite his resentment at the Manchus' compulsion, Francis was amused that the straightforward Emperor Abahai should have chosen the same device as the subtle Dr. Paul Hsü to ensure his loyalty. "Your Majesty does his slave too much honor."

"That is for us to judge, Arrowmaker," Dorgon snapped. "You must understand that this marriage will make you virtually a Manchu. You, too, may look forward not only to being released from slavery but to the high titles and the vast estates His Majesty will distribute among his followers after the Ming falls to the Eight Banners."

"But I am not a Manchu, Wise Warrior Dorgon. How could I aspire to such rank and riches?"

"We make no distinction among Our loyal subjects by race, Arrowmaker," the Emperor condescended to explain. "Chinese, Mongols, Turkyi... men of whatever nation... are equal in Our eyes if they serve Us well."

"Your Majesty, I hear and obey."

Francis uttered the conventional formula of compliance because he had no choice. A slave did not defy an Emperor and keep his head on his shoulders—no matter how valuable he might be to the Emperor.

254

When they had withdrawn from the Imperial Presence, Francis Arrowsmith justified his decision to Joseph King: "I could not do otherwise. You see that, don't you?"

"I suppose so, Arrowmaker, though I hardly think the Manchu Emperor would punish you severely for resisting. After all, he wishes to bind you closer, not to indulge your physical needs. Abahai is not fool enough to execute the man whose services he requires merely because that man rejects a marriage intended to ensure his loyal service."

"It is not so simple, Joseph," Francis argued. "The Emperor cannot brook disobedience. Besides, this will be no true marriage, since I am already married irrevocably to Marta."

"Irrevocably?" Joseph smiled "Are you quite sure of that in your own heart?"

"Well, perhaps not. After all, I did marry Marta under compulsion. That union could, perhaps, be annulled—if I wished it."

"But you do not."

"Never, Joseph, never! Nonetheless, if my marriage to Marta is flawed, as you suggest, I shall not be committing adultery with this...this Babutai. Concubinage is a lesser sin."

"A pity you didn't become a Jesuit, Arrowmaker. You possess their tortuous habit of mind.... And as a priest you could not be forced to take this Manchu woman."

"Could I not, Joseph? Do you think Abahai would respect a priest's vows any more than a husband's vows?"

"Perhaps not, Arrowmaker. For that matter, this marriage will assure that both our heads remain on our shoulders. You will also please a generous Emperor by drawing closer to the Manchus."

"I had not overlooked that, Joseph. But you overlook a much greater boon."

"And that is, Arrowmaker?"

"I believe with all humility, Joseph, that the Lord has chosen me...us, in truth...to bring the True Word to these tribesmen. I can best serve the Lord by making myself one with the Manchus as the Jesuits have made themselves one with the Chinese. The Manchus are tolerant of all religions. Since they possess no true creed of their own, they are more open to our Holy Message."

"I take your point, Arrowmaker," Joseph laughed. "And I cannot dispute it. But I never thought to be a missionary to wild barbarians."

"God disposes, Joseph. Besides, I grow sick of the lust that drives me to the Spring Flower House. As Saint Paul wrote, 'It is better to marry than to burn'—with unsated carnal lust in this world or because of unsanctified sated lust in the hereafter. I shall submit with good grace to the pagan ceremony. The Lord God will know that it was not my own choice."

Joseph was tactfully silent. It was not for him to point out that his master would have married twice—while pleading each time that he had been coerced.

THE maiden Babutai first saw the yellow-haired outlander called the Arrowmaker when he was drilling a group of young officers with a light field piece. Though her eldest brother was one of those officers, she neither called out nor waved when she swept toward the snow-covered parade ground in a group of young noblewomen on heavy-bodied ponies with short, sturdy legs. Her mauve redingote swirled among other bright colors, and she was no more obviously flirtatious than any other maiden when they walked their ponies past the tyro gun crew.

But Babutai stared hard at the tall foreigner, and she trailed her violet scarf a moment longer than did her companions in response to the officers' shouts. The Arrowmaker, she saw, looked up for only a moment when the young ladies called to their kinsmen. But that was as well. He was clearly no avid womanizer, always alert for the rustle of a new skirt or the smile of unknown eyes, this man from a land so far away not even the oldest shaman or the most learned Chinese scribe could tell where it lay. His grave demeanor and his unbroken attention to duty were pleasing to the daughter of a hundred generations of warriors. And if he was, for the moment, a slave, he was the Emperor's slave—a far more important personage than any free archer, or many senior officers.

Even at a distance, Babutai was drawn by the Arrowmaker's air of authority and, she acknowledged shyly to herself, his height. Among the shorter Manchus, even her own favorite brother, he towered like a spruce golden above dark pines. The beard that framed his long face was as bright and soft as the morning sunlight, and his shoulders were broad under his green tunic trimmed with red. Beneath the upturned brim of his domed hat, his features were strong, perhaps a trifle stern with the nose arched like an eagle's beak. But, when he smiled briefly at the maidens' shouts, his face glowed like the sun at high noon.

Babutai, daughter of the Lord Baron Obotu, rode pensively away from the parade ground, hardly hearing her companions' excited chatter. She knew that the man chosen for her by the Emperor himself was the proper choice. She already knew that she would be happy to live with that golden man for all her days. Somehow, she also knew beyond doubt that she would live with him all his days in great happiness.

"Well, my daughter," her mother asked when she returned, "you have seen this outlander?"

"Yes, Mother," Babutai replied softly, "I have."

"And does he please you?"

"How can I tell, Mother? I have seen him only once and then at a distance. But if it is your wish...and Father's ...and the Emperor's...how can I possibly..."

"He does please you then, Babutai?" her mother pressed.

"Yes, Mother, he does," she acknowledged. "He pleases me...greatly."

Babutai came not merely submissively but willingly, even eagerly, to her marriage to the outlander who could speak only a few words of her language. Unlike a Chinese maiden, she had not been brought up expecting her parents to select her husband without regard to her own wishes. The Manchus allowed their women much freedom in the choice of a husband, as in many other matters. Although she had always known that, as the daughter of a baron, she could be married for reasons of state, she also knew her father would not force her into a marriage she abhorred—even if he had to defy the Emperor Abahai himself. Her own wishes were important, if not necessarily decisive.

Her parents, therefore, contrived several occasions for Babutai to see her prospective bridegroom without his knowledge. She was gratified—and fixed in her preference—by those opportunities.

Giving a reception for the officers of his *niru,* approximately a regiment, the Lord Baron knew that the Arrowmaker could not refuse his invitation. While the men ceremonially exchanged pinches of snuff from minuscule bottles of painted glass, Babutai studied the foreigner. Despite his height and his breadth of shoulder, he moved with an easy air that made the Manchu horsemen appear clumsy. When he bowed over her extended hand, not knowing who she was, her breath caught, and she stared at the Kashgar carpet spread on the earthen floor of the tent.

He murmured a courteous greeting, perhaps by rote, and she gave an equally formal reply. But she offered him a candid smile, and she was delighted when she saw that his eyes still searched her out after he fell into conversation with her father's Chinese secretary.

Those light-brown eyes under brows darker than his sunlit hair evoked a melting exhilaration in Babutai, and she felt her knees tremble. Though untutored in the refinements of lovemaking, she was no more than most Manchu maidens prudish. At that moment, she longed for the preliminaries to be done so that she could lie with that glowing man on a palliasse of furs, her legs gripping him fiercely.

Francis was given opportunities to see his intended bride by the magnanimity of the Manchu Emperor, though he believed she had not been told of their proposed marriage. Convinced that he could not refuse Babutai, he was pleased by her appearance and her manner. Despite his residual guilt at the unsanctified liaison, he grudgingly acknowledged that her simplicity might well be a pleasant change from Marta's complexity.

Babutai was of medium height for a Manchu woman, some five feet three inches. She was strong-boned and supple rather than reed-slender. Since all young Manchu noblewomen played at sports, particularly at competing with kicks to keep a feathered shuttlecock in the air, she moved with lithe grace that was the antithesis of Marta's swaying shuffle. Her feet were long, for the Manchus detested the Chinese practice of foot-binding, and her step was springy with exuberant youth.

Her eyes, Francis saw, were straight and large and green-flecked, their hazel as light as his own beneath broad temples. Her nose was straight and small with delicately flared nostrils, while their carved bone structure made the contours of her face appear more slender than they actually were. Her blue-black hair, parted in the center, hung over her shoulders in a dark curtain that rippled to reveal her finely whorled ears. Essentially artless, she used only a touch of rouge to accentuate her generous mouth and to brighten her cream-gold cheeks.

Though Babutai was the daughter of a wealthy baron who could count thousands of sheep, horses, and bullocks among his possessions, the pattern of her clothes was no different from those of a daughter of an archer in the ranks. The artificial Chinese modes impeded movement, while the Manchu women's simpler costume was well suited to their active life. During the hot summer, Babutai wore a short jacket that hung an inch or two below her waist. She owned several dozen such jackets and as many thigh-length tunics for the winter, as the daughter of an archer did not. They ranged from cherry-red damask through orange satin to royal-blue silk, but her favorite color was a glowing emerald green. The jackets she wore for holidays were thickly embroidered and edged with strips of exquisite petit-point flowers and butterflies.

Her ankle-length skirts, usually light in color, were so voluminous as not to impede her in any way. Tucking those skirts about her, she rode astride, the high-pointed tips of her flat-heeled shoes set firmly in the stirrups. But the fashion was already changing to quite different skirts for evening or formal wear. Cut comparatively narrow, those skirts were as gorgeously embroidered as her jackets. They were slit to her knees to reveal straight back trousers in winter and diaphanous pantaloons in summer.

For all the adornment her father lavished on her, Babutai was, above all, perfectly natural. Like a sleek young vixen, she appeared to Francis to have been shaped by nature alone, marked by none of the self-conscious artifice that had molded Marta. Babutai was, he felt, as simply attuned to the Lord God's original creation as any wild creature of the great grasslands. Robust and uncomplicated, she was tinged with a vixen's spontaneous viciousness. But there was no wilful malice in her.

After they had met perhaps a dozen times, the last three or four as avowed betrothed, Babutai gave her love to the Englishman as wholly as if she had chosen him herself. Indeed, she mused, she had virtually chosen him herself, since her father would not force the marriage upon her. She longed for her bridal night, and in her fantasies she already saw the beautiful children she would bear the Arrowmaker.

Francis, for his part, felt Babutai would suit him well. Her candid carnality was intensely exciting to a man deprived of lovemaking leavened with affection for more than a year. He could not respond to her profoundly, but he liked her well— as he would any lively and accommodating young female animal. The light affection aroused in him by Babutai's sprightly manner and sensual promise might in time deepen, he felt.

The Manchu girl could, of course, never threaten—much

less usurp—his devotion to Marta. So Francis reassured his tender conscience. But the great love he insisted to himself he still bore for his wife was marred by sour memories of their two partings. Each could have been—indeed was—final, as far as Marta could tell. Neither when she left him in the citadel nor when she set out for Peking, leaving him a captive, had Marta displayed any grief. She had not even offered him a smile as a token of her love. The exigencies of war had parted them, and the exigencies of war might bring them together again. Meanwhile, his image of Marta was tarnished, despite himself.

NEITHER Francis nor even Babutai ever remembered clearly the week of ceremonies that made them man and wife in the eyes of the Manchus; they were too sozzled by drink. As well as the portentous ostentation of Chinese weddings, the Manchus indulged in madcap mummery fired by constant consumption of *koumiss,* their fermented mare's milk. The increasingly drunken gaiety inflamed the spectators with mirth and exhausted the bride and groom.

Francis later recalled long rides across the plains ending with theatrical assaults on the tent of state of the Lord Baron Obotu, Babutai's father. Standing before that cloth pavilion, Babutai's brothers denied entry to Francis and his groomsmen. Only after prolonged mock wrestling and fencing with cudgels was he allowed to lay at the Baron's feet the bride-price of several hundred gold taels advanced by the Emperor Abahai's magnanimity. Though fuddled, he saw that the contestants took the greatest care not to spill a drop from the skins of *arak,* the distilled spirits of *koumiss* that were an essential component of the bride-price.

After the ceremonial acceptance of Francis's suit, Babutai set out at three in the morning for the tent Prince Dorgon had given him. That precise time, the astrologers had declared, was the propitious instant for her to start her journey to her new life. But she rode less than a hundred feet in the streamer-hung bridal cart before dismounting to spend the remainder of the night in the tent of an uncle. At the more convenient hour of nine in the morning, the bridal procession resumed its progress. The token departure six hours earlier had satisfied the soothsayers' requirements.

When they finally lay together on heaped furs in Francis's

tent, both bride and groom were totally exhausted. They barely embraced before turning their backs to sleep. His head whirling, Francis was still sensible enough to avoid the fumbling that could only end in a cursory joining together or, worse, in a failure of his manhood. Having drunk almost as much, Babutai was no more eager to force the pace of their lovemaking. Her natural ardor was banked, and she was instinctively obedient to Francis's obvious disinclination.

The next morning they came together in an explosion both would remember all their lives. In contrast to Marta's awkward timidity on that other bridal night, Babutai opened herself fully to Francis. She was untutored in the arts of love. But she was naturally desirous, and her spontaneous passion was not marred by the self-centeredness that inhibited Marta. Babutai was as eager to please Francis as she was to please herself. Though her lovemaking lacked ingenuity, she pleased them both greatly.

Inspired by his surprised delight at their physical joy, Francis later reached out toward Babutai's mind and her spirit. The Manchu bride was puzzled by his clumsy overtures—and not only because they lacked any satisfactory common language. Her foreign husband, she sensed, wished more of her than would a Manchu husband, but she could not divine exactly what he wished. Anxious to please him in all things, she was pained by her inability to comprehend his curious desire to communicate regarding matters she had never before considered.

In the beginning, they could not really talk with each other. Babutai spoke no Chinese, while the few hundred Manchu words Francis had learned were chiefly useful for military discussions. After a time, they communicated in a mixture of those two tongues. Since the grammatical structure of Manchu was hideously complex for Francis, they laid Manchu words upon the simple frame of Chinese syntax. Since they invented new devices when necessary, their private tongue was quite flexible and expressive. Having originally spoken half with gestures, they later held long conversations with only slight awkwardness.

Babutai taught Francis Manchu customs and beliefs in response to his questions but was incurious regarding the strange lands he had seen. It was, for some reason, important for her to know where he had come from, but she was content once she learned the meaningless label: Europe. She did not question him regarding neighboring China.

Francis, even more than Babutai, was frustrated because they could not progress beyond a certain point in mutual understanding. Their invented language was, of course, deficient in nuance, but that was not the chief barrier to their communication. Even when he learned to speak adequate Manchu, Francis could not reach beyond an obdurate obstacle in Babutai's mind— perhaps because little lay behind it. Babutai could no more cast her thoughts beyond her native grasslands than she could fly to the wondrous cities of China, India, and Europe Francis ached to tell her about.

"Barbara, how do your people know that the Long White Mountains gave birth to the first men of your race?" Francis asked once. "Why is a man's origin so important to your people?"

"It has always been so," she replied patiently. "I do not ask further."

Francis called her Barbara because that English name, so close to her Manchu name, seemed to draw her closer to himself.

"Why do you call me Barbara?" she finally asked one day toward the end of their first month together. "What is Barbara?"

Francis was delighted by her inquiring about an abstraction. Her interest was normally confined to the persons and the animals, to the objects and the deeds that touched her daily life directly. Yet she was not really concerned with an abstraction, but with a matter that touched her intimately. A woman's name is an integral part of herself. What could be more personal than a name?

Francis told her the story of Saint Barbara: how that maiden's pagan father tortured her to recant her Christian faith; how she, remaining stalwart, was beheaded; and, finally, how lightning from a cloudless sky struck down her tormentor.

"That is why the great guns are called Saint Barbara's lightning," he concluded. "Why I call you by the name of the patron saint of artillerymen."

Moved by the tale of a girl who might have been herself, Barbara for the first time asked Francis about his faith. Again, her interest was direct, since the daily life of the Manchus was governed by the complex mythology interpreted by their shamans, who were priests, soothsayers, and physicians in one. Realizing that his spiritual exercises were the core of Francis's life, she asked him to instruct her in the

Faith. At length, she demanded that he baptize her, since a wife should share her husband's creed.

Francis should, of course, have baptized Barbara, assuming that the Holy Truth had been revealed to her by Divine Grace. But he withheld that Sacrament. Having been instructed and baptized, she would, he knew, demand a Christian marriage—and he was already married to Marta. But Barbara was as cunning as a vixen regarding her own interests.

"Why will you not baptize me?" she asked. "Even without a priest, why can we not pledge ourselves in Christian marriage?"

"I am already married," he explained, "and my Church prohibits a second marriage."

"That is no real difficulty," she rejoined. "I am content to be your first concubine. This creature Marta can remain *taitai*, the first wife."

Francis dared not tell Barbara that Holy Church also forbade concubinage. She could only have concluded that he was lying to avoid marrying her by the rites of his own God. She could simply not have believed that his people were so perverse as to require monogamy and prohibit concubinage. Knowing that he was separated indefinitely from his wife, Barbara would have logically concluded that singular and exclusive marriage flouted nature. Francis therefore allowed her to believe that she was his lawful concubine by Christian practice— though they had taken no Christian vows.

SHORTLY before his Manchu marriage in November 1632, Francis Arrowsmith had been deeply distressed to learn of the execution of General Ignatius Sün and Ambassador Michael Chang on false charges of treachery at Tengchou. He was stricken when another letter from Father Giulio di Giacomo in Macao reported a death that was a far more severe blow to both the True Faith and the Great Ming Dynasty:

As you know, Francis, Dr. Paul Hsü was in March of 1632 raised to the dignity of Grand Secretary, the equivalent—and perhaps more than the equivalent—of the Chancellor or Prime Minister of a European Kingdom [the Italian Jesuit wrote]. China thus possessed a Christian Chancellor who was second in formal power only to the Ming Emperor and second in real power only to the Court Eunuch men call the Black Premier, the master of the Secret Police and the Flamboyant Cloaks.

Although he could not prevent the foul judicial murder of the two martyrs of Tengchou, Dr. Paul strove even more mightily afterward for the welfare of the Faith and the Empire. We all rejoiced, having seen the realization of our prayers that a Christian statesman should govern China. But death has intervened. The Good Lord has taken Dr. Paul Hsü unto Himself.

As much as Father Matthew Ricci, Francis was reminded by his secretary-slave Joseph King, Dr. Paul Hsü had been responsible for planting Christianity in China. After Father Matthew's death in 1610, Dr. Paul's indefatigable endeavors ensured that the Jesuits remained to preach the One True Doctrine. Despite persecution, despite the carping Dominicans and Franciscans, despite the foolishness of some Jesuits, the Faith had flourished bright as a field of lilies. That flowering was primarily due to the devotion of the sublimely gifted Mandarin Dr. Paul Hsü.

Dr. Paul had not only kept the Jesuits in China, Joseph King contended, but had prevented the collapse of the tottering Ming Dynasty by assuring that European astronomy and ordnance were used in China. By correcting the calendar according to European reckoning, Dr. Paul had maintained a degree of civil order among the superstitious Chinese. The green-bronze cannon the great Mandarin brought to China still intimidated the Tartars after the last European artilleryman had been harried from the Empire by the Court Eunuchs.

"Beyond those vital accomplishments," Joseph King added, "Dr. Paul fostered agriculture, trigonometry, theology, and hydraulics, though the slothful self-satisfaction of most of us Chinese had forgotten our own ancestors' great accomplishments in those fields."

Falling ill of a "consuming fever" at the age of seventy-one on September 11, 1633, the Grand Secretary Dr. Paul Hsü had not halted his endeavors for his people and his Faith, Giulio di Giaccomo wrote. On October 31 he petitioned the Ming Emperor to reward the diligence of the Jesuit scientists in the Bureau of the Calendar and to continue the Bureau's invaluable work under another Christian Mandarin. Dr. Paul Hsü thus strove to ensure the continued life of the True Faith after his own passing by ensuring that the scientists who were its priests would continue to serve the welfare of the Empire.

The Ming Emperor sent his own physician to the sickbed and Dr. Paul Hsü also benefited from Father Adam Schall's medical skill. Nonetheless, he died on November 8, 1633, after confessing three times to his Jesuit friends and receiving first *Viaticum*, the Last Communion for the dying, and then Extreme Unction.

Francis Arrowsmith wept when he translated Giulio di Giacomo's letter to Joseph King. The English soldier wept for his adoptive father even more bitterly than he had for his comrade-in-arms Miguel Texeira. He was not ashamed to let his Manchu wife see his tears when he sat down to reply with profound feeling to the Italian Jesuit's letter.

"Above all I regret, Giulio, that I parted in anger from Dr. Paul," Francis wrote. "I regret equally that I never told him of my profound gratitude for his making me his son. At the time I did not truly appreciate the immense honor he paid me, but thought my adoption merely a matter of policy. Nor did I ever express to Dr. Paul the profound affection I felt for him."

Francis realized that Barbara was staring at his tears in astonishment. He realized also that he was, unaware, composing a eulogy for a man who had been truly his father in his formative years, the man to whom he owed at least as much love and devotion as he did to the father of his body, whom he had never seen. He took up his pen again and wrote with all the eloquence he could command:

"No more than any other mortal was Dr. Paul Hsü Kwangchi perfect. He was compelled by the age and the land in which he lived to the deceit, the fraud, and the expediency practiced by all who exercise power during the decadence of the Ming Dynasty. However, he benefited little personally from those excesses, for he strove always to serve the True Faith and the Great Dynasty, rather than to enrich himself. Dr. Paul was closest to sanctity of all the Lord's devoted servants I have been blessed to encounter. Would that Holy Church were moved by my relatively valueless observations, as by the wise testimony of the good Fathers of the Society of Jesus, to examine Paul Hsü's life and works to ascertain whether he was truly a saint in China— as I am convinced he was."

In reply to that passionate epistle, Francis received another doleful letter from Giulio di Giaccomo. The Jesuit, who was still a superstitious Italian, observed that the inevitable cycle of three catastrophes that began with the execution of the two martyrs of Tengchou and continued with the death of Dr. Paul Hsü had concluded with the death of Father Juan Rodriguez, who was called the Interpreter.

After leaving Tengchou, the Interpreter had lingered in Peking through 1632, seeking a renewed invitation to Macao's Second Expeditionary Force to return to fight the Tartars. He had also occupied himself writing an account of the heroism of Captain-Sergeant Miguel Gonsalves Texeira Correa, who had been granted a posthumous title by the Ming Emperor. That *Small Record of Gonsalves's Achievements and Fealty* enjoyed wide circulation among the literate classes, proving again the Jesuits' conviction that the Faith could be effectively propagated in popular works, the wide publicization many men called propaganda.

Father Juan Rodriguez respectfully declined the personal honors the Emperor offered him. Instead, he submitted a humble memorial describing the services rendered the Great Ming Dynasty by Portuguese soldiers. The Emperor responded by sending an embassy to Macao to express sympathy for the slain. He also issued an Imperial Rescript praising Portuguese achievements and singling out Juan Rodriguez for particular commendation.

Father Rodriguez was not happy at having been requited with words rather than an invitation to the Second Expeditionary Force to return to China. Since he could do no more in Peking, he left for Macao early in 1633 after parting forever in this world from Dr. Paul Hsü.

Not long thereafter the death of Juan Rodriguez at the age of seventy-two ended the chapter in the annals of the Holy Catholic Mission to China whose climax had been the Tengchou Mutiny. With him expired all hopes of effective Portuguese military assistance to the Ming Dynasty. Dr. Paul Hsü, Father Juan Rodriguez, Captain-Sergeant Miguel Gonsalves Texeira Correa, General Ignatius Sün, and Ambassador Michael Chang—the men who had fostered and commanded the Expeditionary Forces—all died within fifteen months.

The Portuguese had never been defeated by the Manchus, but had prevailed whenever they met on the battlefield. They had been betrayed by the machinations of the Court Eunuchs, and their prowess was afterward never given an opportunity to prove its full effectiveness. The great advocates of Portuguese intervention all died when the Manchus were expanding both their territory and their armed might.

FRANCIS ARROWSMITH, who had come to the Extreme East to fight for the Ming, participated in one of the thrusts the Manchu Emperor launched to subdue his lesser neighbors before he marched against China. As an Imperial slave, the Englishman would have been compelled to join the punitive expedition the Emperor Abahai sent against Korea in early 1634 regardless of his own wishes. But Francis requested the assignment—in part to free himself for a time from the dilemma that had troubled him since his concubine Barbara first demanded that he baptize her in Holy Church and marry her by its rites.

That dilemma had confounded Francis for some time. As a faithful son of the Church he should have welcomed her conversion; as a weak human being, he would not encourage devotion that could force him into bigamy. They did not constantly discuss his refusal either to baptize her or to marry her. It was not in Barbara's nature to remain preoccupied with abstract concerns. Her extended periods of disinterest allowed him to prolong their muted quarrel—and to evade the issue.

But Barbara became more pressing immediately after the birth of their child on December 26, 1633. Her persistence was hardly blunted by her absorption with the boy, whom she called Babaoge, which his father transformed into Robert. Francis baptized Robert in secret to avoid inflaming Barbara's grievance at his refusal to baptize her. Barbara was doubly delighted with the son in whom she saw not only a replica of his father but also a tie binding her restless husband to herself. Francis was simply delighted to have a son, even a son who could never be his true heir.

Robert would not be burdened by any bias against mixed blood, Francis reflected, as would his half-Chinese daughter Maria, whom he had not seen since she was six weeks old. At the time of Robert's birth, the Manchus were still as tolerant as their Juched ancestors and their Mongol cousins. Themselves the products of innumerable crossmarriages over the centuries, the Manchus were obsessively concerned with genealogy, but not with pure bloodlines. Rather, they valued men for their accomplishments and for their loyalty to the Emperor Abahai.

I feel more for my son than for my daughter [the Englishman wrote to Giulio di Giacomo before setting out for Korea]. He is, after all, my *son*, although he can never follow me into my own world of Europe. Perhaps the knowledge that I shall some day be forced to abandon him to his mother's sole care makes me dote upon him.

I shall provide for Robert as best I can, laying aside substantial quantities of gold for his use when he comes of age. I know his grandfather the Lord Baron will bring him up as a Manchu warrior, but I hope he will remember his European father with some affection.

However, paternal love has already induced me to write overlong of Robert. To anyone else, he is, I know, an infant who is of no more interest than any other infant. That is to say he is of hardly any interest at all.

Northern Korea, Mukden, Peking

MARCH 16, 1634–JULY 21, 1636

SPRING came early to northern Korea in March of 1634. Aiguillettes of yellow forsythia festooned the mountains' robes of dark pines, while the snow that clothed the summits still trailed its white ribbons down the gullies scouring the slopes. A hawk drifted on outstretched wings among the rocky peaks.

Francis Arrowsmith and Joseph King rode a little apart from the artillery train. The Englishman did not command the field pieces of the Manchu Emperor's punitive expedition against Korea but was a "special adviser," ranking as a colonel. The Manchus would not yet trust the European with operational command, though the general and his deputy were both Chinese who had joined the Manchus a year after Francis Arrowsmith.

The Emperor Abahai had readily granted Francis's request to accompany the force and observe the use of his Red Jacket Cannon. The Emperor, Francis believed, had heard of his differences with Barbara and did not wish the union intended to bind him closer to the Manchus to divide him from them. The expeditionary force was led by his former comrades-in-arms and later captors at Tengchou, the Virtuous Kung and Halfwit Keng. Kung was already a lieutenant general and Keng a major general. They were gracious

269

to Francis, only in part because they had been brother officers in Tengchou. Having already campaigned with foreign ordnance, both regarded the Red Jacket Cannon highly and both were determined to learn all the Englishman knew.

Francis reproached himself for failing in Christian charity. But he could not forgive the mutineers who had made him a slave and brought about the execution of General Ignatius Sün. He had, however, learned to swallow his bitterness, as the Chinese said, though he was determined to revenge himself in good time.

"Watching us smile at each other, an ignorant observer would think us great friends," he said venomously to Joseph King. "We bow low and mouth courtesies like boyhood companions who have been joyously reunited. But my time will come."

There were many stealthy observers among the Manchu army. There were many more among the phantom enemies, who vanished into the jagged mountains overlooking the Yalu and Tumen rivers when challenged. Some of those observers knew Francis's predicament—and his vulnerability.

"*Tuan-chang, wo*..." Joseph King instinctively dropped his voice despite the overwhelming clatter of the artillery's wheels. "Colonel, they've been at me again, the Ming agents."

"What do they want, Joseph?"

"Our souls ultimately, I suspect. They are as persistent as a Jesuit who sniffs a convert." Joseph's prominent teeth shone like yellowed ivory in his dark face. "For the moment, though, information will satisfy the Divine Skein."

"And why should they think that we.... The Chinese abandoned us and the Divine Skein executed our comrades. How can they think we will..."

"They don't just think, Colonel. They *know!*"

"They *know* we will do their bidding? Betray Abahai? He's treated us far better than the Ming ever did."

"They know, Colonel, because their persuasion is irresistible. If we do not obey, the Lady Marta will be exiled to wild Yunnan as the wife of a traitor.... And your daughter, the small Maria, will be sold to a Flower House to be trained as a courtesan."

"The latter threat touches me more closely than the former!" Francis answered coldly, for the first time suspicious of the one Chinese he had always trusted. "And what, Joseph, did they offer you?"

"Manumission of the slavery I suffer for my father's deeds,"

Joseph King confessed freely. "A new life as a free man and appointment as a Mandarin when they finally command us to return to China."

"And when would that be?" Francis moved to reclaim his secretary's wavering loyalty by recalling him to reality. "If we do well, supplying much intelligence, the Black Premier will keep us here. If we serve him ill, what reason for such splendid gratitude?"

"I didn't say I trusted the Divine Skein, Colonel. I'm merely relaying their message."

"They want only intelligence, you say? The Banners' weapons and strength...rivalries among commanders...the Emperor's changing favorites. That sort of thing?"

"So they say, Colonel."

"We wouldn't have to tell the Divine Skein everything we know," Francis pondered. "But we would have to tell them something."

"My feeling exactly, Colonel. China is too much to us both. We can't defy the Black Premier—even in exile. But we must also be wary of the Manchus."

"The Manchus, Joseph? The Manchus aren't subtle like..."

"More subtle than you know, Colonel. Remember how Abahai's doubled agents destroyed the Field Marshal in 1630...tricked the Ming Emperor into executing his best field commander."

"I hadn't heard."

"Court Eunuchs in the Manchus' pay dripped poisoned words into the Ming Emperor's ears. The Field Marshal, they said, had sold himself to the Manchus—and had, therefore, neither warned of the Manchu attack nor resisted it, but fled. Always suspicious, the Ming Emperor believed them."

"Well, we must be very wary."

"What am I to tell the agents?" Joseph asked.

"Tell them we'll cooperate fully...that our hearts remain always with China. Later, we'll work out just how little we can tell them—and how to avoid alarming the Manchus."

Whenever the Manchu force drew close, the King of Korea disappeared into the mountains or the forests. The punitive expedition took his capital of Seoul easily, since no city in Korea could withstand the green-bronze field pieces. But the King was long gone. The invaders chased him into the Sambok mountain range in the southwest, toiling through crags and valleys so convoluted they swallowed the entire army.

Finally withdrawing, they were harried by Koreans who ambushed them in mountain defiles and vanished when pursued.

Lieutenant General Kung returned to Mukden in late 1634 to report his failure to capture the Korean King and his loss of some three thousand men, a fifth of his command. To his astonishment, the Emperor Abahai professed himself well pleased.

He had, he told the Virtuous Kung, neither expected nor wished to conquer Korea. Too many soldiers would be required to hold its stubborn people in subjugation. He had sought only to savage the Koreans. The havoc wreaked by the punitive expedition, the Emperor Abahai was certain, would keep his rear unharried by Korean raids when he marched against China.

Since they had attained his true goal, Abahai did not punish the first Chinese to whom he had entrusted an independent command. Instead, he promoted the Virtuous Kung to field marshal and Halfwit Keng to full general. He also made Francis Arrowsmith an acting brigadier in recognition of the service the green-bronze field pieces had rendered.

Francis swore never again to underestimate the Manchu Emperor, who was all cunning beneath his straightforward manner. For the first time, Francis seriously considered the Manchus capable of conquering the Ming Empire, a feat he had previously thought impossible.

"WELL, Joseph, we took up the Devil's work again in Korea," Francis remarked to Joseph King. "And we must continue."

"That's true, Arrowmaker." In their new intimacy, Joseph had given up calling his master by his rank. "The Black Premier won't hesitate to abduct Maria and sell her into prostitution if we defy them. And there's no longer Dr. Paul to protect her."

"But exactly how we serve him is up to us. We could, of course, greatly exaggerate the Manchus' numbers and the deadliness of their weapons."

"To what end, Arrowmaker?"

"We might thus gain two ends. If he is frightened by Manchu strength, the Black Premier might permit the upright Mandarins to reinforce the Imperial armies effectively. Besides, when we finally return to China we will be rewarded for sounding the warning that awakened the Ming Dynasty to its mortal peril."

"Do you really think so?" Joseph asked. "I've found that the bearer of evil tidings is never rewarded...particularly if his news is true. But the bearer of good tidings, he is usually rewarded...even if his reports prove false."

"You have a point, Joseph. Besides, those great affairs of state are too uncertain for us to influence decisively."

"We must, then, look to our own interests, must we not?"

"Yes, Joseph, by greatly understating the Manchus' power. We will bear good tidings, even though they are false."

"And thus hope for rewards. Besides, the Manchus may well learn of our spying. And they will be pleased to allow us to reinforce Ming complacency."

During the remaining year and a half Francis Arrowsmith spent among the Manchus, their strength increased so greatly it was difficult for him to report credibly on their feebleness. That strength was forged by the ambitious Commander-in-Chief, Prince Dorgon. Though Dorgon was tall, his body was frail and his heart's beat sometimes faltered. He was, nonetheless, a dashing cavalryman—brilliant in horsemanship, tireless on campaign, skilled with weapons, and unsurpassed in courage. He was wise in statecraft as well as warcraft, almost as cunning as his half-brother the Emperor Abahai.

Under Dorgon's generalship, the Eight Banners crushed all opposition and enforced Manchu rule on all territory north of the Great Wall. But he left a few Ming enclaves untouched to avoid provoking the Chinese into desperate counterstrokes. The Manchu Emperor still feared a massive Ming attack like that the unjustly executed Field Marshal had successfully mounted in the late 1620s.

The ruse worked well. Although the swift rise of Manchu power was glaringly obvious, the inquiries the bemused spymasters of Peking sent Francis Arrowsmith remained smug.

"When will the Manchu league collapse?" asked one smuggled despatch on tissue-thin rice paper early in 1636. "When will the loose union of the barbarian tribesmen dissolve? When will they begin killing each other again?"

Joseph King wept for his people after receiving that haughty inquiry. He was finally convinced that an Empire feebly ruled by those fatuous semiliterates, the Court Eunuchs, could not endure. Francis was virtually certain that

273

the Manchus not only could but would conquer the Ming Empire—unless Divine Providence intervened.

"You recognize the hand, of course?" Joseph was still studying the message from Peking.

"I'm afraid not, Joseph."

"No, I suppose you wouldn't. It is disguised, though feebly. I'm certain Simon Wu wrote this message. I of all people know his hand."

"You mean my old Adjutant?" Francis asked incredulously.

"Who else? With respect, Arrowmaker, I know no other Simon Wu. And who better to direct our spying than the man who recruited us into the Divine Skein?"

"Why should he allow us to learn he's still directing us? Earlier messages weren't in his hand, were they?"

"No, certainly not. Now, he clearly wants us to know he pulls our strings."

"Whatever else, Simon was never a fool. I wonder, Joseph, if he believes the Manchus are as weak as we paint them."

"If he wishes to, certainly. But, whatever he believes, he is playing our game."

THE shallow pool in the courtyard of the mansion of the Mandarin James Soo reflected the clear sky over Peking in early May 1636. Half-hidden among green fronds, the goldfish delighted in the spring warmth of their pool. The ancients floated unmoving, the orange streamers of their fins rippling. The younger fish played among the forest of stems, darting upward to suck insects from the surface and to nibble on the broad lotus pads.

Marta sat beside the pool in a cane chair, cracking dried melon seeds between her small front teeth. Over the objections of her father, who sat beside her gazing into the pool, she had sent her half-barbarian daughter Maria inside with her maidservant Ying.

Marta stared defiantly at her father, who had just returned from his office at the Ministry of Works. He was still in his formal scarlet robe, which bore the peacock of a Mandarin of the Third Grade. She wore a shantung lounging robe in the long, warm twilight before night draped the Northern Capital with its spangled cape.

"No, Father, I cannot, much as I'd like to follow your guidance." Marta spat out the husk she had sucked empty. "It must be done now."

"I've been too indulgent with you, Marta," James Soo mused. "Your mother always said I coddled you."

"Well, Father, that's all past now, isn't it?" Marta replied levelly. "It's too late to do much about my character. You should, at least, be glad I'm not coddling Maria."

"But it's barbaric at her age. You could certainly wait another half-year or so...at least until she's five."

"No, I can't...and I won't. Father, I'm deeply grateful to you for taking me in, even though I do pay my way with the gold..."

"The gold the Arrowmaker provided for you."

"As he should. And, as a married woman, I'm not subject to your commands, but my husband's."

"Surely Francis wouldn't wish to subject Maria so young..."

"Ah, Francis..." Marta's voice crackled with cool disgust. "Regardless of yourself and...Francis...I must do what I think right. You may consider me unfilial, but, I assure you, Father, I am profoundly filial. Above all, Maria must be Chinese. I can't darken her hair, that awful yellow-white hair, but I can..."

"Perhaps her hair will darken of itself. I've seen red-haired babies turn a decent black. But you're too hard on the child."

A small girl's piping protests drifted through the open moon door of the garden pavilion James Soo had given his daughter. The maidservant Ying murmured reassuring endearments, and Maria was quiet. James Soo opened his mouth to press his protest, but a shrill scream cut him off. He listened in silent anguish to the regular screams piercing the twilight. Marta cracked another melon seed between her front teeth.

James Soo could not expel one vivid image from his mind. He remembered too well the conventional torture he had spared his own daughter until she was six, the torture she now insisted upon inflicting upon his granddaughter almost a year before the normal age.

The child's screams rose louder. Dropping briefly to soft blubbering, they shrilled again so high the Mandarin winced and covered his ears with his palms.

James Soo could see his granddaughter's agony as if he were inside the pavilion. Two maidservants held the child immobile, and a third clutched her chubby leg with both hands. Ying was tightening broad cotton bandages around

Maria's foot, murmuring consolation through her own tears for the pain she was forced to inflict. Round and round those heavy bandages coiled, forcing Maria's pliable big toe up and over her other toes, which were wrenched under the ball of her soft foot. Maria would bear that implacable pressure for years—until her feet finally became numb under thick-horn calluses.

James Soo wondered why his daughter Marta required that Ying begin the binding of her daughter's feet. The childless maidservant loved the small girl, indeed doted on Maria. Her sturdy affection was the chief constant in the child's life.

Had his daughter Marta, the Mandarin wondered, insisted that Ying must herself wind the first bandages because she was jealous of the love between her daughter and her maidservant? He had seen that Marta offered Maria only perfunctory affection.

Whatever the reasons for Marta's insistence that the deed must be done prematurely and be done by Ying, Maria would never again run to him to claim the crystallized fruit he carried for her. She would never again toddle like a healthy four-year-old.

James Soo regretted the necessity for binding his granddaughter's feet. It was, of course, necessary, but it could have been postponed.

Maria's screams were subsiding. Low sobbing drifted through the moon door, mingling with Ying's broken-voiced endearments.

Father and daughter sat silent for almost ten minutes, immured in their own thoughts. James Soo concluded wearily that it was far too late to risk a breach with his self-willed daughter by asserting the authority he should have impressed upon her twenty years earlier. Marta wondered briefly if she had really been hasty. But, she told herself, the deed had to be done—and the sooner it was done, the better.

James Soo looked up from the ruffled pool when the moon door opened wide. Supported by two maidservants, Maria tottered into the courtyard. Ying encouraged her from within, crooning half-choked meaningless syllables. Tearmarks stained the child's narrow face beneath delicate cheekbones like her mother's. Her plump fist knuckled the tears seeping from light-brown eyes, which were large and barely slanted. Her fine light-blond hair ruffled around her high forehead.

Maria smiled sunnily at her grandfather, but tottered determinedly toward her mother. Clutching her mother's knees, she looked up proudly and asked, "*Ma-ma, wo shih ta-jen?*...Mama, am I grown-up, a grown-up lady?"

A manservant wearing a black jacket and white trousers secured with ankle bindings sighed into the courtyard on felt soles.

"*Hsien-sheng, Wu Tuan-chang lay-le.*" He spoke formally. "Sir, Colonel Wu is here."

"Show him in," Marta directed. "No, ask him to wait a few minutes. I'll send to fetch him."

Oblivious of her father's disapproval, Marta motioned the maidservants to take her daughter inside. She studied her face in a circular hand mirror before calling "Ying, bring me a comb and brush—and my small cosmetics tray."

While his daughter repaired flaws in her appearance that were invisible to himself, James Soo's patience dwindled. Finally he rose and stood before her, tensely annoyed.

"Must we have that man here again? He is always here."

"My dear Father, you know we must keep in with both sides. Simon Wu is an influential man, I can't offend him by turning him away."

"Why, Marta, the elaborate concern with your makeup? He is not a suitor, and you are not..."

"You always like me to look my best, Father, don't you?" she replied lightly. "If you don't wish to see Simon, you needn't, you know."

"I certainly do not."

James Soo stalked toward the moon door of the garden pavilion, his heels slapping angrily on the brick courtyard. He reached into his pocket and found the candied ginger for his granddaughter.

Simon Wu's domed helmet was tucked under his arm, its red-fox streamer hanging limp from its central spike. The breast of his scarlet robe was faced with a crouched leopard, and the hilt of his dress sword flaunted its colored ribbons at his side. Though his square face was sunburned, two hectic red spots flared on his flat cheekbones.

"You are well, Marta?" he inquired conventionally. "But it is superfluous to inquire. I have rarely seen you more beautiful."

"Simon, you should really not talk so." Marta lowered her eyes. "What if my husband were here?"

"You mean I should not tell you the clear truth?" Simon's voice was silky. "In any event, the Arrowmaker is not

277

here...not within a thousand *li* of Peking. Nor is he likely to be for some time to come."

"I had not really thought otherwise." Marta dismissed her long-absent husband, but her voice softened when she asked: "And why do you come to this house today, Simon?"

"As always, Marta, to give myself the pleasure of seeing you. I thought, also, you might wish to know that the Arrowmaker is well...in Mukden, of course."

"You have had word again? However, it is of no great moment, is it? He is well, you say, and...in Mukden."

"And he is likely to remain there for some time."

"I shall not grieve." Marta paused. "And his Manchu doxy, she is still..."

"I have not heard of any change. He keeps his barbarian concubine."

"Well, in that case..."

"Marta, I shall beg of you again. It could be useful if you sent him a brief note. Could you not?"

"I am grateful for your concern, Simon. You are a true gentleman, a true Christian gentleman to offer. But I have nothing to say to him. Has he, I ask you, sent any word for me?"

"No, I'm afraid not. I've offered to pass on messages many times, but he ignores my offers."

"That, then, is how he feels. Why should I feel otherwise? But, I suppose, those are barbarian manners."

"If that is what your heart tells you, I suppose..."

"That is. Let us talk of pleasanter things."

Marta Hsü and Simon Wu sat with their heads close together while purple dusk obscured the tarnished gold of twilight. They sat together while the black cape of night fell over Peking. Their figures were silhouetted by the glow of oil lamps through the windows, and the breeze carried the tang of pines through the courtyard.

Despite her bravado, Marta was momentarily troubled. Should I, she wondered, be sitting here alone with a man, even a distant cousin? But times have changed, she reassured herself, and the servants are all around, watching our every move. Surely, there can be no thought of impropriety. Besides, I'm a grown woman, a grown-up lady as Maria would say. If my husband deserts me, what can he expect?

* * *

"SOMEDAY, I trust, we will learn precisely what game Simon Wu is now playing." Joseph King looked up quizzically from the latest message from Peking. "If the Lord chooses, we may discover why Simon compounds our deception regarding Manchu weakness."

"Simon plays such a deep game he himself may not know." Francis smiled over the ledger of their trade his secretary had given him to check; then his expression darkened. "But why has he sent no word about Maria or Marta? Christian compassion alone, you'd think, would..."

"We cannot ask, Arrowmaker," Joseph reminded his master anxiously.

"I know that, Joseph. We can't even acknowledge that we know he directs us. As for asking for news of my family, that would be demeaning."

"Not only demeaning, but worse...dangerous. Very dangerous if your request were seen by anyone else in the Divine Skein."

"Well, there's nothing for it but to go on. To twist the Skein as we do...to serve the Manchus as we do."

"Both against our will...and our consciences."

"Yes, Joseph, but the Good Lord, I know, planned this captivity for us for His own purpose. At least, you're not summoned to watch the Bannermen play polo this afternoon."

"But I like watching their polo, Arrowmaker, I like their animal earnestness. And I can laugh as uproariously as the Manchus themselves when a man falls and is trampled under the hooves of his own team. I like seeing Manchus die."

"In India, I'm told, they play with a ball and mallets rather than the carcass of a sheep."

"For a humble Chinese, it's a much greater pleasure to watch them snatch the carcass from each other and try to carry it over the goal line. I like those polo matches. I've never seen one end without four or five players dead and a score injured."

Unlike his Chinese secretary, Francis did not gloat over the Manchus' self-destructiveness. He knew the Emperor Abahai encouraged polo because it developed horsemanship as well as the martial spirit. The Emperor counted the loss of a few warriors a small price for keeping his troops always tempered for war. Besides, the Englishman considered the Manchus' great hunts even less sporting—and more barbaric—than their polo. The hunt was the favorite diversion of princes and generals too valuable to risk on the polo field.

A European monarch's stag coursing, Francis reflected, was to a Manchu hunt as a dozen punts to the Great Armada Philip of Spain sent against England in 1588. Two months before an Imperial Hunt, brigades of beaters encircled an area of several hundred square miles. No animal, however small, could break through that cordon, which constantly contracted to trap tens of thousands within some ten square miles. Then the slaughter began.

To open the Great Imperial Hunt that celebrated his second enthronement in May 1636, the Emperor Abahai urged his favorite roan up a hillock that overlooked the trapped game.

"No use for your big guns here, Arrowmaker," the Emperor laughed. "But you'll see how we Manchus deal with our enemies—all our enemies."

His square face beaming with pride, the Emperor looked down on the thousands of bears and tigers, ibexes, wolves and stags, as well as tens of thousands of smaller animals, milling within the impenetrable hedge formed by the spearheads of his Bannermen. The blood lust of his nomadic ancestors glowed red in Abahai's slit eyes as he chose his target. He did not hurry, but allowed his leisurely gaze to sweep over the terrified beasts, apparently impervious to the din that made Francis's nerves scream in sympathy.

The pandemonium was clearly heard in Mukden more than fifty miles away. Wolves howled and stags belled, tigers roared and ibexes bleated. In their common fear the carnivorous beasts momentarily ignored their normal prey. A tidal wave of sound crashed around the hunters on the hill, making conversation impossible. Frantic with greater terror, the carnivores shook off their trance of terror and turned on the smaller animals. A stoat screamed as a wolf snapped it up, and Francis imagined he heard field mice squealing as stoats ripped out their throats.

The clouds of yellow dust rising from the valley of the slaughter soon made it impossible to distinguish any but the larger beasts. Under those clouds stripes, spots, and shiny pelts rolled back and forth like a sea whipped by a storm in an enclosed bay. Overhead the wild geese cawed, and sleek pigeons cooed in instinctive sympathy with their wingless fellows. An overpowering stench rolled around the hunters, rank and feral.

The Emperor finally chose the largest tiger, a magnificent beast twelve feet from muzzle to tail. Standing in his stirrups,

Abahai drew arrows from his triangular silken quiver and fitted them to his double-curved horn bow so rapidly eyes could not follow his hands. A torrent of thick-feathered arrows streamed through the dust cloud toward the tiger.

Its yellow-and-black hide bristling with arrows like a porcupine, the tiger twisted and arched in agony. Striking out frenziedly with scythelike claws, it hewed a path through the massed beasts to the first line of beaters. Despite the spear buried in its breast, the tiger broke through that line, leaving two beaters dead behind it, and sprang wildly toward the beaters halfway up the Emperor's hillock.

Princes and generals glanced slyly at each other. Some smiled, not bothering to conceal their grim amusement at Abahai's discomfiture. To the Manchus even the Emperor was, at that moment, only another hunter-warrior, first certainly among them, but by no means a divine being above their criticism.

Abahai sat unmoving in his saddle, smiling beneath his bristling mustaches. Only when the maddened tiger sprang at the final line of beaters did he draw back his bowstring. His arrow pierced the tiger's eye, and it died before it completed its leap. Abahai could not speak above the din, but gestured expansively to invite his chief subjects to choose their prey.

The slaughter continued for four days, not even halting by night when the archers and pikemen in the ranks slaughtered the game under the full moon. Remorselessly the cordon drew inward over bloody carcasses, compressing mutilated animals within an unbreakable hedge of spearheads.

When the hunt drew to its close on the fifth day, no one could count the carcasses. Innumerable bears and tigers, wolves and foxes, sables and ermines, badgers and deer, yaks and stags, ibexes and wild cattle, even hares, minks, weasels, and stoats transformed four square miles of Manchurian grassland into one vast abattoir.

Many men died as well, even nobles and senior officers. Raging with the pain of their wounds and the stench of their fellows' blood, the maddened beasts hurled themselves repeatedly at the encircling cordon. Not one broke through.

Any man who allowed an animal to escape would be scorned as no better than a woman or a eunuch. If his cowardice was obvious, the Emperor would order him executed. All the hunters preferred death beneath claws and fangs to retreat.

"The Emperor counts these gargantuan hunts well worth while—and not only for the wholesome exercise they give him," Prince Dorgon remarked to the Englishman upon whose technical skill he counted to slaughter human game. "Organizing tens of thousands of warriors for the hunt is not much different from commanding on the battlefield. Besides, our hunts winnow out the few weaklings and cowards among us."

Francis nodded respectfully and spoke a few sentences extolling Manchu valor. There was, he reflected, nothing remotely subtle about their polo or their hunts, for the Manchus were not subtle. Nonetheless, they were striving to alter themselves in vital matters, relying upon the advice of the many Chinese they bought with munificent rewards. If subtlety could be learned by passionate intent and honest sweat, the Manchus would learn subtlety. Since it could not, they learned instead organization, administration, and discipline.

The Manchus were a nation in the making. Each year the structure of the Manchu state grew more like its Chinese model. Flexibility, which the Chinese had bred out of themselves, the Manchus still possessed. It was, however, impossible to wholly subordinate the arrogant independence of Manchu nobles to the Chinese ideal of perfect obedience to superiors. Nonetheless, a modern state was being created in the grasslands. Its raw material was men whose grandfathers—indeed, fathers—were fierce tribesmen who obeyed only the chieftains of their small clans—and those chieftains only when they chose.

The Great Imperial Hunt, Francis concluded, demonstrated how close the Manchus had moved toward their twin goals. The first was, of course, a nation in arms, wholly responsive to the Emperor's single will. The second, for which the first was designed, was the conquest of the Great Ming Empire.

ON the morning of May 16, 1632, Joseph King stood behind his master, Acting Brigadier Francis Arrowsmith, among the multitudes assembled to behold the second coronation of the Emperor Abahai. Wearing a gold diadem studded with jade and pearls, Babutai, whom Francis called Barbara, sat among the women of her father's clan. The hectic colors of their garments shone like inharmoniously massed blossoms. The spring sunshine glowed on the yellow-and-black stripes of the fresh tiger skin draped on the dais below the ebony throne inlaid with mother-of-pearl.

Joseph King marveled at the verbal legerdemain behind this reenthronement of the Manchu Emperor, who had first assumed the Imperial Crown nine years earlier. The canny Chinese slave marveled at—and was grudgingly impressed by—the elaborate play on words that would hasten the Manchu conquest of the Ming Dynasty.

The Manchus had called their Imperial House *Hou Chin Chao,* meaning the Second Gold Dynasty, since its proclamation nineteen years earlier. Harking back to the Gold Dynasty under which their ancestors once ruled North China, that name had outlived its usefulness. Worse, it had become a handicap. The dynastic name Ming stood for bright fire, which would melt gold.

Having learned Chinese symbolism—and its power over Chinese minds—the Manchus were changing their dynastic title to Ching, meaning pure. That name not only rang more authentically in Chinese ears than did the barbaric gold, but the ideogram for pure also embodied the sign for water. The soothsayers therefore predicted confidently that the Manchu torrents would extinguish the Ming flames.

Eminently practical, Joseph was even more deeply impressed by the display of Manchu power. The thousand princes and generals who paid homage to the Manchu Emperor commanded more than a million men in arms. Chief among them were Prince Dorgon, Commander-in-Chief of the Grand Army, and Field Marshal the Virtuous Kung Yu-teh, who represented the Manchu Emperor's growing dominion over the Chinese.

Across the parade ground were drawn up major detachments from the Eight Banners under their distinctive flags. Solid red, blue, yellow, and white for the senior Banners, the same colors fringed with tassels for the junior Banners. The eight Banner Princes who bowed in submission to Abahai were virtual kings in their own right, each ruling a semiautonomous nation in arms. All the peoples of the steppes—and even the Manchus' Chinese subjects—had been integrated into the Banners. Francis Arrowsmith's expanding corps of artillery was aligned under the Yellow Banner.

Surrounded by his senior princes in armor, by his ministers and his Mandarins in splendid Chinese robes, and by lamas and shamans in gaudy vestments, the Emperor Abahai

283

spoke to his people. He wore the Imperial yellow robe and the gold-encrusted crown of a Chinese Emperor, and he sat with his heavy fists clenched on his thighs.

"In the past, We repeatedly rejected our followers' pleas that We assume a new title of honor," Abahai declared, and Joseph King was struck by his perfect Confucian piety. "We felt that the Will of Heaven above was not yet fixed, while We did not yet possess the total confidence of the people below. We have now yielded to the universal desire, mindful that We must tirelessly exert all Our strength for the welfare of our subjects."

Abahai then mounted a golden throne set on the broad steps leading to the granite Throne Hall of Mukden. The eight Banner Princes presented him with eight seals of state so massive the warrior-princes strained to lift them with both hands.

Joseph King approved, despite himself, of that characteristically Chinese harmonization of humble words and ostentatious display. But he shuddered at the barbarically Manchu excess of the next stage of the ritual. Except for the single symbolic sacrifice the Ming Emperor offered at the Temple of Heaven each year, the Chinese had many centuries earlier given up offering live animals to the gods. But not the wild nomads who aspired to rule the world's greatest civilization.

Four hundred black horses and four hundred black bulls were pawing at the spring-green turf, their eyes rolling in dumb apprehension at the throngs of humans that surrounded them. A thousand warriors took station amid the animals, flourishing two-handed scimitars. The sun glinting off the broad blades in a blaze of pure light dazzled the humans and terrified the beasts.

A hundred clarions pealed; five hundred conch horns wailed; a thousand kettledrums rumbled. The scimitars flashed against the sky, their razor-honed edges descending on the animals' necks. A few died immediately, scarlet arterial blood spurting from their headless necks in pulsating sprays. Some of the butchers were less powerful or less skillful. Drenched by the red mist, they hacked repeatedly at the screaming, bellowing animals whose urine steamed in the clear air. Trailing excrement down their broad hindquarters, a hundred bulls and horses broke away and stampeded toward the spectators. Blinded by the blood streaming into their eyes, they hurtled into each other and struck out wildly with their hooves.

After half an hour, the last sacrificial animal died. Striding among the carcasses, shamans in gaudy masks sprinkled libations on the killing ground. The sour odor of the *koumiss* puddling on the earth amid the blood, the excrement, and the urine assailed Joseph's nostrils like the mephitic reek of the Inferno. He turned away, his palm clapped over his nose and his eyes watering.

But, Joseph saw, the ritual had reverted to Confucian propriety seasoned with Confucian hypocrisy. Files of officers were laying the insignia, the sacred tablets, and the bright banners of the Imperial Guard at the feet of the Emperor. When these gaudy symbols were heaped before the throne, the Emperor spoke again.

"Splendid insignia and tablets of honor are no more than a stage setting that charms the eye," the Emperor declaimed. "They are only empty symbols of glory—but no practical use to the nation. All Our decisions will be based on the knowledge that symbols are trumpery, while devoted service to the people is all."

Truly Imperial assertion lay behind the obligatory protestations of humility, Joseph knew. Abahai's second coronation had explicitly asserted his claim to rule the Great Ming Empire—expressly reaffirmed his determination to conquer all China. The reign-name he chose had sealed that irresistible claim and that implacable intent. The decadent Ming Emperor ruled under the reign-name Chung Chen, meaning Exalted in Good Fortune. Abahai's reign was called Chung Teh, meaning Exalted in Virtue. Since virtue was the supreme Confucian attribute, the springtime virtue of the Manchu Emperor would inevitably prevail over the autumnal opportuneness of the Ming Emperor.

HIS second coronation clothed the Emperor Abahai with the mystical authority essential for dominion over the Great Empire. Its aftermath precipitated a crisis in the life of his slave, Acting Brigadier Francis Arrowsmith.

Barbara as well as Francis had been obliged to drink great quantities of *koumiss, arak,* and *pai-kar,* the reeking white spirits made from sorghum, at the banquet that followed the coronation. Manchu liberality required noblewomen to join their men in striving toward total drunkenness. The next morning, Barbara suffered as acutely as Francis from a splitting head, an inordinate thirst, trembling hands, and a morbid sensitivity to noise. Both eagerly took the only possible remedy, measured quantities of the same liquors.

"A wonderful banquet, wasn't it, Francis?" Barbara lolled on the pillows laid over the furs piled on the earthen floor of their tent in her father's encampment. "I've never known better. But my head, it aches as if a horse kicked me."

"For all we know, ten horses could've kicked us." Francis gingerly raised his fourth cup to his lips with both hands. "It was practically impossible to tell the guests from the beasts."

"What do you mean by that?" Barbara flared. "I've never seen a better banquet. Everyone, even the Emperor, was roaring drunk only halfway through. A great beginning for a great campaign."

"As for that, time will tell," Francis answered shortly. "The Chinese still have a few soldiers left."

"Do you think the Chinese could possibly..."

A small form wearing an archer's buff tunic over blue trousers hurtled through the flap of the tent, cutting off Barbara's objections. Their son's tiny horn bow was drawn taut, the arrow aimed at his father. Without pausing in his stride, Robert released the bowstring. The sharp arrow transfixed the fabric six inches from his father's head.

Roaring in rage, Francis sprang to his feet and snatched at his small son. But the miniature archer darted behind his mother, clasping her around the waist with both hands.

"Let me have the brat," Francis demanded. "He could have killed me. It's time to teach him manners."

"Francis, he's only two and a half," Barbara soothed. "Time to teach him manners later. Let him run free now, as a child should."

"You really think there's nothing wrong with his manners?"

"No, not really. For his age, he has good manners."

"Good Manchu manners you mean, the little devil."

"What do you mean by good Manchu manners? What's wrong with Manchu manners?"

"What's wrong? What isn't wrong? Letting children run wild till they're nine or ten.... The entire nobility getting drunk as fiddlers and glorying...glorying...in their own vomit. Women as free and insolent as court fools. Eating flesh coated with grease and boiled just enough to make it stringy,

286

but still raw. Manners? A fiddler's bitch has better manners than a Manchu prince."

"I'm sorry, Francis, if you're displeased." Barbara was instantaneously conciliatory. "I never thought you were unhappy."

"Well, I have been happier. It's not you, primarily, Barbara. . . . Not you at all." Though inflamed by anger and alcohol, Francis instinctively avoided offering her greater provocation. "I'm just a little tired of this life. But I'll be all right."

"No, you won't, Francis. You need a change . . . a big change. Why don't you apply for duty with the new expedition to Korea—or the armies Abahai is sending to China soon. My father always says a man needs to spend half the year in the field. You've been trapped in Mukden too long."

"Not Korea again. I couldn't bear another game of blindman's buff. And China. . . . No, Abahai would never trust me in China. But, still . . ."

Although he had choked back his spontaneous complaint, Francis was mortally tired of Barbara herself. He found her simplicity as irritating as her constant attempts to bend to his moods.

Even now she sat biting her knuckles to hold back the tears she knew displeased him. Her eyes implored his forgiveness for whatever offense she had committed. But she clearly did not know how she had offended him, and the bovine submissiveness of her love was itself infuriating. She would, he knew, alter herself in any way she could in order to please him. But he could not tell her how to change—and she could not really change herself, even if he could have told her.

Besides, Barbara's renewed pleas for baptism and a Christian marriage scourged his conscience, while her hearty kinsmen aroused him to contemptuous disgust. It was, he concluded, sipping his fifth cup of *pai-kar,* well past time for a change—and he suddenly knew exactly the change he wanted.

The next morning, Francis Arrowsmith requested an audience with the Wise Warrior Prince Dorgon, Commander-in-Chief of the Grand Army. Larding his rough Manchu with Chinese formality, he told Dorgon he could no longer train artillery officers properly or cast the large cannon the Emperor was demanding. He profusely regretted that he had reached the limits of his skill. Unless he could refresh his knowledge of musketry and ordnance by studying the latest European developments in Macao, he declared, he could no longer render the exemplary service the Emperor demanded—and merited—from all his obedient subjects.

Those protestations were chiefly nonsense, Francis knew, but not entirely. The sciences of musketry and artillery did not move so fast, and Macao was hardly a center of scientific information. But he was determined to leave Manchuria, though not for the uncertain perils of China. He respected the Manchus as he could not respect the Chinese, but he could not live among the Manchus as he could among the Chinese. He knew that he had, as Joseph King said, eaten too much half-raw meat and drunk too much half-fermented mare's milk. He yearned for more civilized fare for his mind and his spirit as well as his stomach.

Nonetheless, Francis consoled his conscience, his self-serving self-abnegation was sincere in one respect. He could not cast larger cannon until he had enlarged his knowledge in the foundries of Macao, which could also provide essential machinery and skilled workmen.

"When the Emperor himself summoned me," Francis wrote to advise Giulio di Giaccomo of his imminent arrival, "I told him that only the justifiably famous Manuel Tavares Bocarro, the master cannon-founder of Macao, could provide the knowledge, the machines, and the artisans the enterprise required. I also suggested that I could buy cannon in Macao for shipment to Mukden. The Emperor Abahai thereupon shrewdly gave me leave to sail on one of my coastwise junks. He commanded me to return when I had supplied my deficiencies."

Francis did not confide to either of the royal half-brothers that he also feared the consequence to himself of the Manchus' projected raids in force on the Empire. All Mukden knew that Abahai was planning to send two large armies into North China to sack many cities and to terrorize the people by pillage, rapine, slaughter, and fire. Those assaults, Francis felt, must demonstrate the reality of Manchu power so forcefully that even the Ming Court, cloistered in its self-indulgent complacence, could no longer ignore the overwhelming menace posed by the Northern barbarians.

Finally awakened, Francis feared, the vindictive Black Premier would punish him severely for his systematic understating of Manchu might. Ineffectual in defense of the Empire, the Divine Skein was as relentless as imps out of Hell in pursuing revenge. Above all, he feared he would be abducted and taken to the Eastern Hall to be tortured like

General Ignatius Sün. Even abduction from the Manchu capital was well within the power of the Divine Skein. But not abduction from Macao, where he would be surrounded by fellow Europeans—and constantly alert against assassins.

Macao, Hongkong, Macao

SEPTEMBER 6, 1640–JULY 21, 1642

FRANCIS ARROWSMITH woke to the sound of guns soon after seven. Fusillades shook the small house on the Rua do Chunambeiro, and the mottled glass rattled in his bedroom window, which was latched open to catch whatever breeze might pierce the sodden heat of Macao on the sixth day of September in the year 1640. The damp linen sheet chafed his bare skin when he stretched, and he heard contralto church bells above the bass roar of the cannon.

Francis felt older than his thirty-three years each time he awoke to the debilitating humidity of the hot season. Many Europeans died before the age of thirty in Macao, either quickly of endemic fevers or slowly of "wasting bloody fluxes," as leeches called the diseases they could not understand. Most Europeans died before the age of forty-five, leaving the alien land in possession of native Chinese, Negro and Indian slaves, Japanese *ronin*, and Eurasians. Those races were, somehow, inured to the pestilential climate.

He was nonetheless glad he had fled Mukden for Macao. He enjoyed the wealth accumulated by his trade in Manchu goods—and its increase in trade with both Japan and China. In those enterprises, Antonio Castro, secretary to the Loyal Senate, was his staunch partner. That new Christian was far more intelligent than the old Christians who despised him because his Jewish grandfathers had chosen baptism over exile. The man the established families called Marrano, meaning swine, was also more straightforward than the established Portuguese merchants. The two aliens, Francis Arrowsmith and Antonio Castro, had formed both a profitable partnership and a firm friendship during the past four years.

Knowing he could not sleep again, Francis swept the crumpled sheet onto the blue-and-yellow tiles of the floor. When it exuded the mingled fragrances of sandalwood and musk, he smiled with reminiscent pleasure. Recalling the *muitsai* who had slipped from his bed shortly after midnight so that her body heat would not disturb his sleep, he glanced critically down at himself.

Aside from the sword scars on his forearms and the black powder embedded in his hands, his body was unmarked by his strenuous life. His stomach was still flat, unburdened by the vast paunch that was the normal accoutrement of Europeans who drank hard, ate full, and moved lethargically in the enervating Orient. The skin clothing the taut muscles of his legs was covered with a fine pelt of yellow hair.

His face, he knew, was only faintly lined, but had filled out. He was today a man of substance, far removed from the half-fledged youth who had come to Macao in callow excitement more than twelve years earlier. His features had firmed with good living, and his arched nose complemented the aggressive chin revealed again when he shaved off his Manchu beard.

The general impression was pleasing, he was told by the Portuguese ladies with whom he flirted discreetly. The Japanese geishas and the successive Chinese bondservants called *muitsai* who slaked his physical needs were also flattering. They particularly admired the contrast between his tanned face and his long thick hair, bleached flaxen-white by the subtropical sun.

The melody of the bells lilted above the familiar chorus of the guns. Francis's artilleryman's ear told him that Macao was not repelling a surprise attack, but firing black powder from unshotted cannon and pealing churchbells—presumably in jubilation. Habituated to the din of the foundry four doors away, he was disturbed because he did not hear the pounding of hammers, the squealing of pulleys, and the sighing of air through enormous bellows.

Francis grunted in response to his majordomo's tapping

291

on the door. In deference to Chinese prudery, he pulled the rumpled sheet over his nakedness when the wizened man-servant presented a silver beaker on a silver salver. He drank off half the cup in one long draft and was invigorated by the customary mixture: sweet sack from Jerez mixed with clear water from a hill stream.

"*Djou-shang, Ah Sim. Mat-yeh* . . ." Adulterated not by the breathy fricatives of Portuguese but the soft sibilants of the Officials' Language of North China, Francis's Cantonese amused the southern Chinese. "Good morning, Ah Sim. What's that infernal din?"

"*Ngow mgn jee-do, Seen-sang,*" the body-servant replied. "I don't know, Sir. But Master Castro is waiting with news. He's most impatient. Hungry, too, he says."

"Tell him I'll be right down."

Francis relieved himself in the narrow closet adjoining the bedroom, exhaling in satisfaction as the pale stream poured into the Chinese-porcelain chamber pot. In the adjoining bath-chamber, which drained onto the road, he sluiced himself perfunctorily from a four-foot earthenware jar that had once held yellow rice wine.

Toweling himself, he grinned at the horror his domestic arrangements would awaken in the ladies of England or Portugal. Bathing once a day in the cold season would appear a barbarous indulgence. His four daily baths in the hot season would appear as effete—and as unhealthful—as placing both a closet and a bath-chamber adjacent to every bedroom. Modern Europeans knew the Romans had sapped their vitality by their prolonged baths. The Mandarin class's habit of also using bathhouses as clubs like the Romans would appall seventeenth-century Europe.

Already dewed again with sweat, he decided not to shave and stepped into a tube of dark-blue fabric which he knotted at his waist. The sarong of the Indies was a gentleman's most comfortable lounging garment in the damp heat, while the ladies had adopted the light cotton *yukata* from Japan.

Antonio Castro was also in dishabille. A porous cotton shirt hung outside his white-duck trousers, and he wore plaited-leather sandals on his bare, narrow feet. Dominated by hooded black eyes and a long, aquiline nose, his lean face was almost forbiddingly imposing. He lacked only a laurel wreath around his baldness to complete his resemblance to a shrewd senator of the Roman Republic.

"Join me at your own table, Francis," Castro invited in precise Portuguese. "And fortify yourself against my news."

"With what little food you're leaving me, Antonio."

The Marrano resumed his attack on Francis's morning repast. His long fingers were stripping a braised pigeon, and the gnawed drumstick of a roast capon lay beside his plate. He had taken only a spoonful of the salted codfish in green sauce, the *bacalhau* that was as indispensable to the Portuguese diet as the crusty loaf on the polished black table. He had not yet touched the fried rice dotted with tiny pink shrimp, the platter of mixed *chorico* sausages, or the thin-sliced Chinese pork marinated in honey and soy sauce before it was roasted over charcoal.

Cracking the pigeon's legbone between his stained teeth to bare the marrow, Castro did not reply to Francis's gibe. He wiped his greasy mouth and fingers with a square of toweling dampened with rosewater. Still ignoring Francis's impatience, he considered both blue-glass pitchers before pouring the heavy red claret rather than the light white Canary wine.

"Come on, man," Francis exclaimed. "Leave off devouring my substance and tell me your news. Why the salutes and the pealing?"

"It's the way of Macao." Castro's dark lips twisted in a slow smile. "We Portuguese are *aficionados* of tragedy. We *always* celebrate our disasters."

"What new disaster?"

"The priests celebrate a martyrdom...a mass martyrdom. They rejoice with solemn masses that an earthly mission has ended with a message flown straight to heaven."

"Not the Embassy to Japan?"

"You have it, my friend. You may forget all your investments in the Japan trade. It is finished...for all time, I fear."

"So it's come?" Francis realized that the high-handed Japanese had impoverished him. "The last act of the Christian persecutions?"

"And nothing can be done...no hope at all." Antonio Castro prided himself on his realism, but his saturnine composure was forced. "All four ambassadors...with fifty-three officers, sailors, and soldiers...have attained holy martyrdom. The Bishop has ordained a day of rejoicing."

"Fifty-seven dead...and Macao rejoices! They order things differently in England. I'll never understand you Portuguese. Even the Chinese are easier to read."

"I'm only a *Novo Christão*...a Marrano, a swine as my countrymen charmingly call those whose fathers and grandfathers placed devotion to King and Church before our ancient Judaism," Antonio Castro replied bitterly. "I am the last to criticize. As a foreigner, a suspect Englishman, you too had better hold your tongue."

"The servants hardly know enough Portuguese to..."

"Are you quite sure, Francis?"

"For that matter, no, I'm not. Yet they'd carry tales to the Mandarins or the Divine Skein—not the Bishop. But, for the Lord's sake, tell me whence came this news."

"A common sailor who was spared to bring Macao the tidings came ashore from a trading junk last night. He spilled out the gory tale. Our ambassadors and their entourage landed at Nagasaki early in July...and were immediately imprisoned for violating the ban on trade between Japan and Macao."

"But they carried no cargo. They weren't traders...only emissaries to conciliate the Japanese."

"So *they* pleaded. But the Shogun's decree came from Edo within two weeks: All were to be decapitated! On August third the sentence was carried out. They were, at least, spared the crucifixion and boiling in acid native Christians have suffered."

"So the trade's dead? And our gold gone with it?"

"As dead as the ambassadors...and with no more hope of resurrection before Judgment Day. No more Chinese silk sold to Japan at a profit of a hundred to a hundred fifty percent. Since the Chinese still won't trade directly with the Japanese, the Dutch will take over the trade. We must set our minds to recouping, my friend."

"We must look to China—above all to Manchuria," Francis said.

"Do you know, Francis, some men call you the Manchu Ambassador? They believe you're obsessed with the wild tribesmen."

"The Manchus are the men of the future, Antonio. Nothing can keep them from conquering China. I would be with them—and I would have you with me. Meanwhile, Manchuria's furs, gold, and ginseng will keep us in tolerable comfort."

"A people...barely a people...living in rawhide yurts and maddened by fermented mare's milk. How can their trade ever amount to a ten-thousandth of China's or Japan's? How can they threaten the Ming? Spare me your mad conviction that the Manchus can conquer the Great Empire."

"Antonio, all Manchu warriors are valorous to death, and their leaders are wily. The Chinese are unwarlike and decadent. How can you believe the Manchus will *not* conquer China?"

"*Bastante, Francisco! Bastante!*" Laughing, Antonio Castro threw up his palms. "Enough, Francis! Enough! We argue about events that have not happened ... that will never happen. We should be considering how to recoup our fortunes. That's enough to busy our brains."

"I *must* say it again, Antonio," Francis persisted. "The Manchurian trade can keep us until the Manchus conquer the Empire. Then the new China trade will make us as rich as a Grand Eunuch."

"Recoup our vast losses in the Japan bubble?" Antonio Castro remained skeptical. "Perhaps, Francis, perhaps. When the lion and the lamb play together ... and our Ethiopian slaves turn white as milk!"

THE vast losses Antonio Castro mourned were as amorphous to Francis Arrowsmith as their earlier inordinate profits. He had been unable to visualize the fifteen thousand gold taels standing to his credit when he returned from Mukden in 1636. He could no more envision his thirty-five thousand taels invested in the Nagasaki trade when the execution of the ambassadors severed Macao's relations with Japan. He never saw that wealth, only neat entries in Castro's ledgers.

A tael or *liang,* a Chinese ounce, was roughly one and one-third English ounces. Ten taels of silver was a lavish bounty to a bond-servant, whose indentures could be purchased for twenty to thirty taels. The Jesuits gave converts three taels to welcome them into Holy Church, and that was extremely generous. But his mind could no more encompass thirty-five thousand taels than his eyes could behold the Heavenly Host of cherubim and seraphim. He knew he had lost a fortune sufficient to keep a hundred Chinese families in ease for two generations. But the loss disturbed him less than would a broken swordblade or a cracked culverin.

Besides, the trade the excessively hard-headed Antonio Castro derided supplied Francis's modest needs. Voyages between Macao and Manchuria were beset by swarms of pirates and the few patrol vessels maintained by conscientious local Mandarins. Since the Imperial Ming navy, the most powerful in the fifteenth-century world, had decayed into impotence, most of his coasting junks won through. The regular gains those voyages yielded were more real to Francis than the enormous profits of the Japan trade, which he had never grasped with either his hands or his mind, but like the angels, only by faith.

A junkload of matchlock arquebuses, graced by the personal gift to the Emperor Abahai of a half-dozen new wheellock muskets, would earn perhaps a hundred taels of Manchurian gold. The small junks could carry only the field pieces. Larger, more stable junks were required by a single cannon, its four tons concentrated in a length of eighteen feet. He had shipped some thirty field pieces and a dozen cannon during the four years since his return to Macao.

That trade reconciled Francis's conscience to his dishonoring his pledge to return to Mukden promptly. He had won the Emperor Abahai's permission for a longer stay by pleading that he still had much to learn and shortly thereafter had recruited twenty Chinese workmen under a proficient Eurasian foreman. They were released, albeit reluctantly, by the master founder Manuel Tavares Bocarro to cast field pieces in Mukden.

"We shall permit Our servant, the Arrowmaker, to remain in the Portuguese city—as long as is necessary to perfect his skills and to supply weapons for Our forces," Abahai then wrote Francis. "When he returns, we have reserved for him a command of ordnance in Our armies."

The arms trade made it convenient for Francis to live on the Rua do Chunambeiro near the foundry of Manuel Tavares Bocarro, who embodied the skill of three generations of master founders. Only thirty-five years old in 1640, Bocarro had been invited by the Loyal Senate to establish a foundry in the late 1620s. He had subsequently so greatly excelled his father and his grandfather, the master founders of Goa, that his guns were treasured not only in that Portuguese enclave on the west coast of India and by the Spanish in Manila, but in Lisbon and Madrid as well.

The world's premier cannon-founder was as spritely, as vigorous, and as high-spirited as a youth. Slightly below medium stature, he was heavily muscled by his arduous trade. His fair skin, burned ruddy by the subtropical sun, contrasted with his curled black beard and mustaches. When he laughed, his dark-brown eyes crinkled and his snub nose wrinkled like a statue of the Great God Pan. Even when he spoke of the cannon he almost worshiped, his manner was free.

"Chinese labor makes the difference," Bocarro told Francis soon after they met. "Not cheaper than India or the Philippines, of course, though cheaper than Portugal. Above all, the Chinese are diligent and intelligent! Monkey-clever they may be, but, by Our Lord's Wounds, they are very clever. That's why some men say my little foundry makes the best cannon on earth."

Manuel Tavares Bocarro was totally open, perhaps because Francis could not threaten his preeminence. He revealed the exact quantities of Philippine copper and Indies tin that made his bronze. Nor did he conceal the laborious yet precise processes that shaped the most devasting modern weapons: leavening the alloy with traces of zinc; breaking the set casting loose; scouring the bore with abrasive sand; and, finally, rasping fine the coats of arms, the inscriptions, and the dolphin-shaped lifting hooks on the exterior. Francis ruefully realized how crude had been the techniques he had used in Mukden.

ENLIVENED by that learning, as well as by his *muitsai* and geishas, Francis's first two years in Macao had passed pleasantly. But the third year dragged. He was confined to the narrow valleys and the narrower foreshore of Macao, which covered only two and a half square miles in all. As the agent of the enemies of the Ming, the Manchus, he dared not venture to Canton when the Mandarins allowed foreign merchants to visit that metropolis of the South twice each year. Antonio Castro argued that the Southern Mandarins were not interested in remote barbarians, but only in the overt taxes and the covert squeeze they levied on the partnership's transactions in Canton. But the Marrano conceded that Francis had reason to fear the vengeance of the Divine Skein for his betrayal, and, therefore, to avoid Canton.

During his fourth year in Macao, Francis chafed at the restrictions on his freedom. He missed not only the interplay of great historical forces he had known in Peking, Tengchou, and Mukden, but also the frequent sharp bouts with danger.

He finally found a diversion. Accompanied by Joseph King, he embarked on a swift forty-foot junk to explore the tangle of islands fringing the muddy estuary of the Pearl River. Though his two skilled boatmen knew the waters well, sailing the uncharted South China Sea was never uneventful. Unpredictable storms and marauding pirates often struck vessels on the approaches to Macao, providing a welcome frisson of danger.

Manuel Tavares Bocarro and Antonio Castro warned Francis not to taunt fate. Refusing to give up his excursions, he mounted a four-hundred-pound gun called a serpentine on the foredeck and another on the aft deck, increased his crew to four, and conducted regular cannon drill. Nonetheless, his friends prudently declined his invitation to sail with him.

"All Englishmen are mad," Bocarro admonished. "How else could they defeat Philip's Great Armada? If you want danger, seek it in the salons of Macao. I shall introduce you to my cousin Teresa Dolores Angela do Amaral. She is dangerous enough for even a mad Englishman."

"I have not been honored by the lady's acquaintance. Who, may I ask, is she?"

"Only the third greatest heiress in the Holy City," Bocarro replied. "And still unmarried at nineteen. Many gallants pursue her, but her quick tongue and her father's jealousy repel them. Only great valor can woo my cousin Dolores."

"A quick tongue and a jealous father are not great inducements—whatever her wealth," Francis replied lightly. "Besides, I'm a married man...too much married. I already bear scars enough from women's tongues to last my lifetime."

"Just meet her, my friend," Bocarro advised. "You may think differently. Or is the peril too great?"

"Far too great, Manuel!" Francis evaded the invitation. "The perils of your salons are infinite. At sea, I can measure the peril."

The braggadocio bred by boredom was nurtured by his friends' counsel to caution. Knowing he was safest when least conspicuous, he perversely flaunted a great ensign on the mizzenmast of his junk, which bore in gold lettering on its high counter the name *Maria*. When the ensign streamed in the gusts of the South China Sea, its green folds opened to reveal the white double-barred Cross of St. Omer.

Early in March 1641, Francis's restlessness took him some fifty miles northwest. He made for a mountainous island group picketed by brilliant green islets and sheltered from the great winds the Cantonese called *daifoong* and the Europeans typhoons. Their deep harbors attracted the pirates, rebels, and smugglers who swarmed in South China like maggots in the Ming's decay. The outlaws called their haven Heunggong, Fragrant Harbor, which became Hongkong on the Europeans' clumsy tongues. The prosaic Portuguese, recoiling from such lyricism, called the islands Os Ladrones, The Thieves.

No other vessel roiled the white-flecked sea as *Maria* was borne steadily northwest by a strong beam wind. The junk's prow plowed between a dumbbell-shaped islet and the yellow-sand beach of a larger island that rose to folded peaks as if terraced by a giant hand. The subtropical sun glowed on groves of deep-green pines and lit their fringes of scarlet hibiscus.

"The boatswain says he knows these waters well, Joseph." Possessing not even a rudimentary chart, Francis exulted in exploring the unknown. "So give over your worries."

"If he does," Joesph King observed dolefully, "he must have been a pirate."

"Cheer up, Joseph. He could have been the fisherman he says he was."

"Not without the pirates' permission," the secretary insisted. "At best, he's in league with the pirates."

"Regardless, he says he knows where we can find giant lobsters and crabs. These waters aren't fished out. Not like Macao."

Joseph King was not persuaded. He sat primly disapproving when *Maria* entered a broad channel and heeled over to port. Plunged into the jade waves, the prow trailed crystal droplets. The boatswain gave the name Lama to the rocky island to starboard, whose narrow bays lay between high cliffs. The inlet to port he called Heunggong Dzai, meaning Little Hongkong.

Russet sails veined by bamboo battens swung like enormous autumn leaves, and *Maria* entered the narrow inlet. The gray-rock cliffs to starboard were pierced at the water line by the dark mouths of caves. Ahead the silver thread of a waterfall fell to the stony foreshore near thatched bamboo huts. Eight deep-sea junks were beached like sabots discarded by Titans while bonfires burned off barnacles and sea grasses.

"No unpeopled Eden, is it?" Joseph King asked with melancholy satisfaction.

Francis's eyes were fixed on the glimmer of movement in the black cave mouths. The limpid water was churned to white froth when ten sampans darted out of the caves. Propelled by twelve-foot-long stern oars, they bore down on *Maria*.

Francis trained the foredeck gun on the sampans while his boatswain lit a match fuse from the fire under the tea kettle. Before the serpentine bore, a puff of black-powder smoke rose from the foremost sampan, and he heard the unmistakable bark of an arquebus. Clutching his right shoulder, the boatswain fell and Francis snatched the burning match. An explosion rocked *Maria*, and the narrow hull gyrated crazily from the recoil of the aft-deck serpentine.

Joseph King's shot struck true. A sampan spun broadside, splinters flying from its frail hull. Slowly, its teak timbers opened like enormous tan petals. But the nine remaining sampans surged through the maelstrom.

"Fool's work this day!" Joseph King screamed from the afterdeck. "I knew it! I knew it!"

Francis sighted along his serpentine's barrel. When the junk rose on its roll, he plunged the match fuse into the touch hole. The serpentine reared in its rope harness, and its recoil flung him to the deck. When the cannonball soared over the sampans, he knew he had fired too late. He saw the waterspout when the ball plunged into the sea, but not the rearmost sampan floundering in the turbulence. Two pirates wrestled with their sculling oar, and the long shaft snapped.

The eight remaining sampans came on relentlessly while *Maria*'s crew awkwardly reloaded the serpentines. Sprawled on the slippery decks to evade the arquebuses' fire, they slithered back and forth as the junk rolled and pitched.

Francis calculated that the pirates must have at least thirty arquebuses to maintain such constant fire. That many arquebuses represented not only a large expenditure, but a grievous loss of weapons from someone's cherished arsenal as well.

The after serpentine coughed harshly. The cannonball skipped across the whitecaps, and Francis cursed Joseph's impatience. But an erratic wave tossed the ball into the air. It skittered against a sampan's prow, forcing a timber-rending collision.

Though two more sampans were temporarily eliminated, the odds were impossible. Francis Arrowsmith felt mortal fear clutch his throat for the first time since the fall of Tengchou.

His eyes streaming from powder fumes, Francis saw Joseph defiantly hoist the green ensign on the mizzenmast. It was fitting, he reflected coolly, that they should go to certain death under the Holy Cross of St. Omer.

He put the glowing match to his gun's touch hole and watched the flight of the cannonball, which plowed the length of the nearest sampan. He felt neither the serpentine's recoil nor the arquebus ball that smashed his thigh.

Francis toppled, unaware that his leg no longer supported him and wondering at the blood oozing across the oiled-teak planks. The first numbing shock passed, and torrents of pain engulfed him. On the verge of consciousness, Francis watched Joseph and the three unwounded sailors try to fire their arquebuses. Seawater leaping over *Maria*'s sides drenched their matches.

"Cease fire! Cease fire!" Francis shouted. "Use your steel! Repel boarders!"

His crew could not hear him. Just before losing consciousness, he was shouting in silence.

Francis did not see the hundred-eighty-foot junk gay with pennants beneath the flag of a Mandarin of the First Grade. He did not hear the thunder of a gun far bigger than his puny serpentines, a green-bronze cannon clothed in red silk. Nor could he rejoice when the sampans drew back and the war junk hoisted a scarlet banner emblazoned with a golden cross. Joseph King raised his eyes from the tourniquet he was tightening around his master's thigh to see a skiff dancing across the whitecaps toward *Maria*. An elderly gentleman clambered aboard. He wore a wispy white beard and was simply but richly dressed, more like a retired Mandarin than a sea brigand. His distinctive crimson-leather satchel identified him as an herbal doctor.

Joseph King bowed. He cleared his shot-deafened ears with his thumbs when the venerable herbal doctor spoke.

"Do not fear! The Admiral of the Coastal Seas gives you your lives." The voice was reedy, but the accent was pure Peking. "He bids me welcome his fellow Christians. And he commands me to attend to your wounds."

Crouched protectively over his unconscious master, Joseph King raised his clasped hands before his chest in formal greeting. The elderly doctor ignored his stammered thanks to examine Francis's wound.

Joseph King closed his eyes and addressed a prayer of thanksgiving to the Lord of Heaven. Francis Arrowsmith's vainglorious ensign had saved them from his folly; St. Omer's Cross had preserved them from violent death. But who, Joseph wondered, was the Admiral of the Coastal Seas, a Mandarin of the First Grade—and a Christian as well? He had never heard that title, though he thought he knew every exalted rank in the Ming Empire.

"MY son is at the Imperial Court. Highly favored by the Son of Heaven, he is already a licentiate—and only seventeen years old."

"He must possess great merit, Admiral." Joseph King winced, for it had taken him fifteen years of study before he passed the First Civil Service Examination and became a licentiate qualified for official appointment. His tone was obsequious, since they were still locked in their savior's crushing embrace.

"Men *do* say he's brilliant." The complacent father beamed. "I am filled with humble awe when I reflect that such a paragon sprang from my own unworthy loins. A rough seaman, no more am I. But his mother is a noble lady of the great Tagawa family of Hirado."

"All men know the repute of the Tagawas ... and your own magnificent accomplishments, Admiral."

Joseph King squirmed at fawning on the freebooter who held their lives between his thumb and forefinger. Cheng Chih-lung, his personal name meaning Noble Dragon, was the legitimized overlord of the sea brigands, Joseph had learned. He had been licensed by the Black Premier, with whom he shared his loot in return for his rank as a Mandarin of the First Grade and his grandiloquent title, Admiral of the Coastal Seas. Since his pirates were Japanese as well as Chinese, marriage to a Japanese noblewoman had consolidated the Noble Dragon's sway over his watery realm, which stretched from the Lioatung Peninsula in the north to Hainan Island in the south.

The spacious after-cabin of the war junk was heaped with the Admiral's spoils. Violet tribute silk woven for the Imperial Palace covered the palliasse on which Francis Arrowsmith lay, the wound in his right thigh covered with a drawing poultice spread on the hairy skin of a freshly butchered dog. Ancient statuettes were secured in crimson-and-gilt niches by heavy gold chains. In the central niche, a five-foot image of Tien Hou, Goddess of the Sea, reflected the lantern's light from its shimmering *fei-tsui* jade. Despite its excessively

302

sophisticated (and, therefore, virtually characterless) work-manship, Joseph King estimated its worth at eight thousand taels. The embroidered wall hangings, the gold-and-silver utensils, and the gleaming porcelains ostentatiously displayed were worth twice as much again.

The master of that magnificence was enthroned on an ebony chair inlaid with marble plaques picked with turquoise and coral. His broad face was framed by a bushy beard. Silver thread outlined each feather on the outspread wings of the crane on his scarlet robe of a Mandarin of the First Grade. His dark eyes were large and sharply tilted. They glittered with intelligence—and avarice.

"And who is this young barbarian?" the Admiral of the Coastal Seas asked.

Francis's eyes were open, but his pupils were pinheads. The opium that alleviated his pain had borne him to a distant realm of euphoria.

"The adopted son of the late Grand Secretary Hsü Kwang-chi." Joseph King was determined to impress their captor with Francis's importance. "He is a grandee of Macao as well."

"Ah, Doutor Paulo..." The pirate chieftain paraded his small Portuguese. "The first great Christian Minister, spiritual father to all us Christians. I trust the Young Lord is comfortable."

"He feels nothing, Admiral," the herbal doctor assured his master.

"Good! Good! Then we won't need you."

The Admiral waited until the physician withdrew before speaking again: "We must now discuss assuring your safe return to Macao. I regret your reception, but my followers' ships were beached. They had to defend themselves."

"Of course, Admiral, I wholly understand. As to how..." Joseph King's voice trailed off tantalizingly as they began negotiating the ransom.

"Some recompense, of course, is necessary for my men. Six were killed, and their families must be looked after. I would happily say to you 'Go under the protection of the Lord Jesus Christ.' Unfortunately, I cannot. Justice, simple justice demands..."

"Assuredly, Your Excellency. Please accept as our gift the guns that wreaked the damage."

"Accepted gladly. They are pretty toys, though not really..."

"Assuredly not, Your Eminence." Joseph King wondered

303

just how much flattery the Admiral would lap up without gagging.

"And then...," the Admiral prompted.

"The guns are only a token of our gratitude for your Christian charity. But the Young Lord is also a great cannon-founder, master of many cannon."

"That *is* interesting. How do you propose..."

"Five field pieces, Your Eminence... five field pieces equally lethal on land or sea... would *begin* to express our gratitude."

"That is *truly* interesting. I could buy them from the families of the slain... paying lavishly, of course. Then they'd be provided for. But how could you assure me delivery? The red-haired devils won't venture into these waters unarmed, and I cannot allow them to come armed. Yet I cannot release you till those cannon are delivered... and, perhaps, some other trifling tokens."

"Of course, Your Eminence. Yet, I would propose that you release us first. We would then make delivery ourselves."

"It grieves me deeply, Master King, but my men would never permit that without surety. For me your word as a fellow Christian would be more than enough. But my men, unfortunately..."

"Your Eminence, surety already exists. It will be in the Young Lord's own interest to make delivery of those cannon— and more—after his release. In a sense, our interests are linked.... A veritable fortune lies at our fingertips."

"Tell me more, Master King." The freebooter's dark eyes glittered. "This is *very* interesting."

Joseph King eloquently put forward the proposal that had germinated while he waited for the Admiral of the Coastal Seas to receive them. After two hours of hard bargaining adorned with florid courtesies, the ransom was finally agreed upon. It was, as Joseph had promised, munificent.

Two serpentines and five cannon were the smallest part. Joseph undertook to provide the freebooter with a regular supply of Chinese silks for sale in Japan, the profits to be divided between Francis and the Admiral. The Japanese ban on Portuguese merchants had increased the value of silk five-fold, since the Dutch, who were barred from China, could obtain only small quantities from smugglers. The Admiral could not buy silk directly, despite his friends at Court, since no Chinese was permitted to trade with Japan. Even the

Black Premier could not rescind that prohibition for his protégé.

"I further beseech Your Eminence to provide protection for arms shipped to the Manchus," Joseph added. "Your trouble will be gladly recompensed with a tenth of their value—and the Emperor Abahai's favor."

That outlay, Joseph reckoned, would be more than repaid by the certainty that every coasting junk carrying arms would reach its destination. Cheng the Noble Dragon controlled all the pirates of the China Seas.

Two days later, when Francis Arrowsmith could travel, Joseph King and the Admiral parted amid sincere expressions of mutual respect and mutual satisfaction. Standing at the water's edge as his men pushed the disarmed *Maria* off the beach, the Admiral megaphoned his hands.

"*Viagem con Deos e voce Jesus louvar,*" he called in broken Portuguese, tracing a cross in the air. "Go with God and Jesus protect you."

"How does he speak Portuguese, if you can call it Portuguese?" Francis was propped on pillows, his wounded leg stretched out on *Maria*'s poop.

"That man, Arrowmaker, I'd long wanted to meet," Joseph answered. "Though not to find myself in his power."

"Tell me about my new business partner, now that, thanks to God, we're out of his clutches."

"Every Chinese Christian knows his name, though he wears his faith like a cloak, putting it on and off as he pleases," Joseph replied. "He was born Cheng Yi-kwan in Fukien Province some thirty-seven years ago. When his father sent him to Macao to make his fortune, he was baptized Nicholas Gaspard. He finally settled in Taiwan, apprenticed himself—so to speak—to a pirate chief. Later he was persuaded to submit to the Ming. His rapacity is now officially sanctioned. Set a pirate to control pirates, they say at Court."

"A valuable business partner," Francis said drily. "I admire your choice."

"I had *no* choice," Joseph protested. "Besides, we'll make a fortune...what he doesn't steal."

HAVING learned propaganda from the Jesuits, Joseph King concealed their arrangement with the pirate Admiral under a cloak of flamboyant words. He broadcast through Macao his account of their heroic fight, their capture by overwhelming numbers, their miraculous rescue from death by the Christian Admiral of the Coastal Seas, and their release by God's Grace.

"A small miracle does no harm," Joseph remarked with lighthearted cynicism. "It's remarkable how credulous priests, even Jesuits, can be when they *want* to believe the impossible."

It was neither necessary nor desirable that their competitors should know of their partnership with the predator upon Portuguese shipping. It was desirable that the Macanese should believe God had softened the Noble Dragon's heart— and simultaneously renewed his faith. Joseph's handmade miracle also breached the invisible barrier between Francis and the nervously haughty Portuguese.

The Englishman had been the suspect protégé of the suspect Jesuits, whom laymen respected for their learning— and distrusted for their excessive cleverness. Besides, the Portuguese feared he was an English agent spying out the secrets of their trade in the Extreme East. Aside from the friendship of Antonio Castro and Manuel Tavares Bocarro, Francis had felt himself subtly isolated, an invisibly moated island within the isolated settlement.

Joseph King's miracle ended that isolation. Francis was no longer a demipariah, but a hero. Besieged by visitors, he wanted to shut his door to all but his two friends. He also rejected the barber-surgeons' desire to probe for the arquebus ball as firmly as his friends rejected his desire to lock himself up.

"The town is agog to see the wounded lion," Manuel Bocarro insisted. "You cannot disappoint them. Admiration could quickly sour into anger at such churlishness. Even your Jesuit friends couldn't protect you if certain people demanded your expulsion as an English spy. You must be open to all."

Taking his own counsel, Manuel Bocarro appeared the next morning with his young cousin Teresa Dolores Angela do Amaral. Despite his mild misogyny, Francis was charmed by her direct manner and her sprightly conversation. Senhorina do Amaral, he sensed, disdained feminine pettiness and frippery. She was not coy, but candid; she neither giggled nor simpered. Besides, she discussed politics and Holy Doctrine far more intelligently than most men. Her doting father had given his only child a broad education, which, his cronies felt, would have been excessive for a boy not destined for the priesthood and was virtually indecent for a girl. At nineteen, Dolores do Amaral could dispute as gravely as a doctor of the Church, but she laughed often—and frequently at herself.

Despite his distrust of respectable ladies, Francis had not lost his eye for a good-looking woman. Dolores was trim and well rounded, but flexible and quick in movement. Her short, tapered fingers danced like jeweled butterflies when she talked. Parted across her high forehead and caught in a chignon at the back, the black wings of her hair glinted with blue highlights. Either by artifice or by nature, her dove-gray eyes looked out through lashes that appeared faintly sooty. The determination of her pointed chin was belied by her inconsequential, almost snubbed nose. But her red mouth was full and firm against the olive skin of her oval face.

Manuel Bocarro was abashed by the quick fire that had flashed when he brought the spark to tinder. After accompanying Dolores on her fourth visit in six days, he warned Francis: "I know it's all innocent and proper. After all, I come along like a duenna. But I warn you, my friend, my lady cousin is as devious as any of her sex. Her sharpest wile is appearing to scorn all feminine wiles."

"Nonsense, Manuel," Francis exploded. "I'm not interested in her that way, not as a woman. Dolores might as well be a boy, even a priest, as far as she affects me that way. I'm only interested in her mind. Besides, she makes me laugh."

"On your own head then be it, my friend."

Though he disclaimed responsibility, Manuel Bocarro still chaperoned his cousin's frequent visits. Dolores assured her suspicious father that her heart was in no way engaged by the wounded Englishman. It was merely, she said, that his conversation was so much more stimulating than the vapid murmurings of Macanese gallants.

"His brain attracts me, Father, nothing else," she said. "For all that sort of thing, he might as well be a eunuch or a priest. After all, Father, you taught me the pure pleasure of abstract discussion. The poor lamb is desperately bored lying in bed all day alone."

"As long as she doesn't join him," Senhor Sebastian Lobo do Amaral muttered to himself. But he returned to his counting house mollified—and did not prohibit his daughter's visits.

"To hear her talk you'd think that they did nothing but discuss philosophy and play chess," he nonetheless grumbled to Manuel Bocarro.

They did play chess when they were not trying their mental wings in the first unconstrained discussion Francis had ever enjoyed with a woman and Dolores with any man except her father. Prudent concern for self-preservation had circumscribed all Francis's conversations since his expulsion from the English College of St. Omer at the age of seventeen. He had walked always among foreigners, all potentially hostile. Having learned from his English Jesuit schoolmasters to delight in intellectual disputation, he had thereafter hobbled his tongue.

With Dolores he could be candid and uncalculating, since her opinion of him was ultimately of no consequence. Though valuing his opinion of her more highly, Dolores, too, cast aside constraint. She was happy neither to parade her orthodox propriety nor to simper vapid replies to empty gallantries. She was mortally bored with the suitors who pursued her inheritance. They could only praise her charms and her dress—or offer tidbits of malodorous gossip like a terrier proudly dropping a dead rat before its mistress.

Dolores further diverted Francis from the pain of his wound by inviting personal confidences. He showed her the miniature of his mother. First limpingly, then freely, he told her of his father's death, his mother's devouring grief, her death, his own lonely childhood, and his cloistered youth at St. Omer's. Her gray eyes remained serene whether he spoke of the brutal battles of Spain, condemned the self-absorption of Chinese women, or recalled the barbarous customs of the Manchus. Responding to her gentle probing, he was drawn out of himself—as she intended.

Francis lay listening for Dolores's light footsteps and the rustle of her petticoats on the stairway—followed, as always, by the heavy tread of Manuel Bocarro. The pale-gray folds of her bell-curved skirts exhaled the fragrance of spring flowers when she entered his bedchamber. Her boned bodice of old-rose satin tapered to her eighteen-inch waist. Around her bare shoulders she wore a stole of ivory lace held by a ruby brooch. A strand of graduated pink pearls clasped her throat, lying on her delicate collarbone. Her headscarf was Alençon lace, and two small diamonds dangled like dewdrops from her lime-green jade earrings.

Francis winced when Manuel Bocarro shook his hand heartily, and Dolores's eyes clouded with concern.

"Francis, it is worse, isn't it?" she asked severely. "More pain each day? You grow thin and worn."

"It is not pleasant," he admitted reluctantly.

"Something must be done," she insisted. "And very soon...today."

"I'll have no barber-surgeon clawing at my leg. I've seen more men die of surgeons than of wounds."

"You will die, my friend, if the wound rots much longer. Or lose your leg to a barber-surgeon in the end."

"No surgeon," Francis insisted. "If I must, then....But no!"

"Then...what? There must be a way. You must not give in."

"I won't, Dolores, I promise you I don't mean to die just yet." Francis's forced jest did not cheer her. "Joseph King says he knows an herbal doctor who works miracles. You know the Chinese are..."

"A Chinese?" Her revulsion was spontaneous. "Not a *Chinese!*"

"Since I won't have a dirty-handed, wine-swilling surgeon, it must be the Chinese. Otherwise, I would be giving in."

"A *Chinese!*" Dolores shook her head in baffled dismay. "A *Chinese* doctor! No, Francis, no!"

FRANCIS was incensed by Dolores's feminine unreason, for he had thought her above such pettiness. He would not, he swore, be dictated to by any woman, and he told Joseph King to fetch the herbal doctor the next morning.

The physician was surprisingly young and burly. He scrubbed his hands for three minutes before his blunt fingers gently worked the stained bandage loose. His flat nose crinkled fastidiously at the stench of the running pus. Francis's body arched in agony, and the bamboo bedhead crackled under his grip when a long forefinger probed the channel the ball had carved in his flesh before lodging against his thighbone.

"We'll try drawing poultices and fomentations for five days," the doctor instructed Joseph. "Also a healing soup, two quarts a day. Nothing else except rice gruel with boiled chicken. And no visitors...none at all."

Brewed with snake's gall, tree bark, wild grasses, bat droppings, and pangolin's testicles, the medicinal soup tasted like the sweepings of a Manchu stable steeped in the sewers of

Lisbon. But Francis's fever dropped after the second day and he felt himself stronger, though he slept most of the day.

Joseph could not keep out two visitors who followed each other on the fourth day. Francis agreed that no Chinese Christian, still suspect as a cryptoheathen, could dare turn away those priests.

The first was a Franciscan friar, his features shadowed by the cowl of his coarse brown habit. He introduced himself as Brother Jeronymo, the confessor of Senhorina Teresa Dolores Angela do Amaral. He offered not comfort, but stern advice.

"You must repent of your stubbornness, my son, " he commanded. "Dona Dolores fears this heathen magician will kill you . . . not cure you."

"I'll consider it." The friar's intimidation strengthened Francis's determination.

"Then I may tell the Senhorina my mission has not been in vain?"

"Tell her I'll consider your words carefully," Francis reiterated, then relented. "Also tell her I'll be glad to see her any time after tomorrow."

"I shall do so, my son, most happily." The friar was emboldened by Francis's apparent acquiescence. "Another matter I would discuss with you. You understand it is my own initiative, not the Senhorina's."

"And that is?" Francis asked wearily.

"The matter touches the welfare of her soul, which is in my care. It is not fitting. . . . It imperils her soul to remain unwed at almost twenty."

"I'm a married man, Father," Francis warned. "I did not seek the lady's acquaintance. She graciously bestowed her friendship on me. However, anything beyond friendship is impossible."

"I am by no means convinced, my son. Hear me out. It would be better if her inclination were fixed upon a Portuguese gentleman. But it is fixed upon you. If she persists, it will lead to carnal sin or to barren spinsterhood. She has, you see, no vocation for the religious life."

"I assure you she will not sin with me. Not for a long time . . . you see my condition. Not ever . . . if you could read my heart. I would never use her as a doxy. But I am already married, so the matter is closed."

"Married under duress by your own account to Dona Dolores. That is no true marriage. And to a *Chinese* . . . in part by a heathen rite. How can such a marriage be valid? In

Rome you would receive annulment in an instant. But annulment is unnecessary. I am prepared to marry you to the Senhorina do Amaral...since you are *not* married to that cryptoheathen Chinese woman."

"The Jesuits would say otherwise. A Jesuit Father married me to my Chinese wife."

"The *Jesuits,* pah! The Jesuits are no better than heretics. A Jesuitical wedding...meaningless." The Franciscan's right hand clenched in a fist with his thumb protruding, the ancient pagan sign against the evil eye. "And she is, do not forget, rich in the goods of this world."

"I *am* truly wed. Were I not, I would not now wed...not even the Senhorina do Amaral."

"You must alter your stubbornness. Think upon it, my son."

After the Franciscan's sandals had clattered down the staircase, the bedroom reeked of the sweat-stained habit he wore in the heat of early April.

The second priest was Giulio di Giaccomo. The volatile Italian agreed that a Chinese herbal doctor's treatment offered more hope than the brutal ministrations of a barber-surgeon of the garrison.

"I'm glad you agree, Father Giulio," Francis said. "My last visitor was of another mind."

"Your last visitor? Not the dirty Franciscan I saw striding down the street...all arrogant in his mock humility? He came to visit you?"

"I'm afraid so, Father Giulio. But not on my invitation."

"I should hope not, my son." The Jesuit flung the window open. "His stench still lingers. They are filthy beasts, those Franciscans, worse even than Dominicans."

"He was not overclean."

"They never are. But I have not come to discuss the sad state of certain so-called servants of Holy Church. You know I returned from Peking only two days ago?"

"And how are my friends there, Father Adam and the rest?"

"Very busy is our Father Adam, but distressed by your long absence. He bade me tell you that all Peking misses you, particularly your wife. He wonders when you will return and prays that it will be very soon."

"As you see, Father Giulio, I'm in no state to travel. I won't be able for months, even if the treatment is successful."

"Nonetheless, you must think upon it, Francis. I'd like to

send word to Father Adam that you'll return just as soon as you can."

"I'm afraid not, Father. There are other reasons..."

"The Divine Skein, is it? Father Adam can work out those difficulties—as soon as you promise to return."

"Why is it so urgent? I'm not that important."

"Father Adam needs your assistance. The Emperor demands that he cast cannon. Your presence is also necessary to avert a schism in the Christian community. Your wife Marta..."

"I thought we'd come to Marta before long," Francis interjected sourly. "What is she up to now?"

"She is infuriated by your long absence...close to apostatization in her anger. Her complaints divide the Christian community. Father Adam fears a public scandal, since the Chinese prize harmony above all else...outward harmony. Public disharmony arising from the first Chinese–European marriage could bring the wrath of the Court upon us. Our enemies are strong..."

"Surely the Court would not expel the Jesuits, above all, *not* Father Adam."

"It hasn't come to that yet, my son. Father Adam they need for his knowledge, slim as it is, of ordnance and fortifications. But a prohibition on all public services... proselytizing banned. That has happened before."

"Tell Father Adam I would not come if it were my own free 'choice. But I understand how delicate the matter is...and I will think about it. I cannot, regardless, travel for some months."

"I'll tell him you're considering. I'll advise him to placate the Secret Service by whatever means he plans...and to seek your visa."

"I fear Marta more than the Grand Eunuch." Francis wondered why his wife should suddenly demand his presence when she had not sent him even a single word for nine years. "Marta is a she-devil! I would do almost anything to avoid her."

"She *is* your wife," the Jesuit admonished. "No man can alter that reality, not even the Holy Father in Rome."

EARLY the next day, Joseph King again led the herbal doctor into the bedchamber. The slave who respected neither persons nor position was deferential, calling the doctor *Daifoo,* Master Physician.

The doctor stripped away the poultice. The stench of corruption was less nauseating. The black-and-red swelling had subsided and the leg no longer resembled a monstrously bloated scaly snake.

"*Ho! Ho yeh! Leung-la...,*" the doctor muttered to himself, and Francis's hopes rose. "Good! Very good! The skin is much cooler to the touch, and the fever is down."

"Then it will be all right?" Francis asked in Cantonese.

"Oh, it'll be all right. It'll be all right—after I've removed the ball." The doctor's thick lips twitched in a half-smile at the foreigner's comical accent. "The inflammation is sufficiently reduced so that I can snatch the culprit out. By the way, you won't lose your leg. I had feared..."

That confidence comforted Francis, who had dreaded becoming at the age of thirty-four that most pathetic creature, a useless one-legged veteran of the wars. He chewed the dark-brown opium cake Joseph handed him and did not wince when the doctor inserted two silver needles into the curve of his right jawbone at the neck. Three half-inch gold needles were deftly implanted in a triangular pattern in his left groin.

"Why the needles?" Francis was wide awake but strangely withdrawn from his own body. "There's nothing wrong with my jaw or my bollocks."

"The body's humors flow through fixed canals," the physician explained. "By blocking their flow we insure that you feel little pain."

"Seems to know what he's about," Francis murmured.

"He should, Arrowmaker," Joseph replied. "His family has been treating wounds for six generations. With wars and rebellions they've never lacked for practice, he tells me."

The doctor smiled, guessing their meaning from the few words of the Officials' Language he understood. After washing his hands with perfumed boiled water, he took up a slender rod tipped with a miniature spearhead. Before Francis could tense his muscles, he thrust the rod down the raw channel to lance the abscess that encysted the musket ball.

Francis felt a pinprick, then searing pain when the spearhead was withdrawn. Yellow-green pus spurted from the wound. Its stench was foul, and sour vomit welled in his throat. He spat bile onto the yellow-and-blue tiles of the floor.

The physician cleaned the wound with a white-silk swab soaked in a solution of sorghum spirits and cat's urine. From

313

his red-leather bag he extracted a seven-inch steel forceps like a stork's bill.

Though dazed by the opium and the acupuncture, Francis felt a minute vibration within his thigh. He clenched his teeth when the ball grated harshly against the bone, but the sensation was remote. The flattened arquebus ball clanked on the tiles when the stork's bill opened.

The physician wiped his face with the damp cloth Joseph offered and washed his hands again before packing the wound with silk gauze soaked in the solution of spirits and urine. He studied his patient's pale face, noting with approval that Francis's eyelids were closed.

"I'll be back this evening," he told Joseph. "He should sleep now for some ten hours."

"My humble gratitude, Master Physician!" Joseph said. "No other physician in South China could have done half as well."

"Only South China, Master King? Why so niggardly? No other in all China. I am grateful for your generous fee.... And it is interesting to see that the barbarians are made no differently from us."

"All will be well now?" Joseph asked.

"All will be well—if the gods so choose. As long as the fire element does not again become dominant, all will be well. It will be some months before he can walk without pain, and almost a year before he walks easily. He will always limp and feel pain in rainy weather. But he is very lucky. You saw my sketch. If the ball had entered two inches to the front, he would never have walked again."

Some time later, Joseph showed Francis the doctor's sketch. Ten muscles were stippled in pink within an irregular oblong around a white bone lying toward the front. Blood vessels were indicated by vermilion circles. Francis was fascinated by the transverse section through a thigh, having seen only the crude, highly colored, and grandly inaccurate anatomical sketches of European barber-surgeons.

"The ball entered here, the Master Physician told me." Joseph pointed to the small gap between the heavy muscles at the back. "Slipped between these muscles, tearing them and ripping the blood vessels. If you hadn't been kneeling side on to load the gun, it would have entered at the front and shattered the bone. And you would never have walked again...probably have lost your leg."

"I thank God...and your Master Physician. How does he

314

have such knowledge of muscles? The sketch looks as if drawn from a leg sliced clean through."

"It was," Joseph answered. "For six generations his family has dissected corpses."

"But dissection is forbidden by Confucian law...as by Holy Church."

"Nonetheless they have. Would you have him find his way blindly through your flesh—like a barber-surgeon?"

FROM the citadel of convalescence Francis Arrowsmith fought a delaying action through the long steamy summer and the brief glorious autumn well into the damp winter of the year 1641. Malingering was his best defense against the three importunate women each of whom, quite inexplicably, wanted him for herself. As long as he could not walk normally, much less travel, he could resist the pressure of the powerful men through whom those ladies worked.

From Mukden, the Manchu Commander-in-Chief, Prince Dorgon, sent orders to return immediately to command the Emperor Abahai's artillery. Francis surmised that Barbara's father, the Lord Baron, had instigated that command on his daughter's urging. Shortly thereafter he received a letter written by a Chinese scribe for his Manchu concubine. Barbara pleaded with him to come back to her and his son Babaoge, whom he called Robert. To Francis's plea that he was more useful to the Manchus in Macao overseeing the shipment of arms, Prince Dorgon replied shortly: "Bocarro can carry on the traffic. His Imperial Majesty has need of you here. You are required to return."

From Peking Adam Schall sent frequent letters with trusted travelers to Canton or Macao. Jesuit influence extended throughout the Empire, and native Christians appeared to have developed a passion for the pleasures of Canton. Though Adam Schall's letters varied in wording, their import was constant: "You must return immediately to your wife and daughter. Marta is making my life a misery, and I refuse to be either her surrogate husband or her scapegoat. (The Fathers of the Church were profoundly wise when they decreed that priests might not marry; celibacy, I have learned, is not a deprivation but a blessing.) Your wife is creating a scandal that divides the Christian community. I too require your presence, though not for your charm or your conversation. You are the only skilled artilleryman and cannon-founder who both speaks Chinese and is—now again by my efforts—acceptable to the Chinese authorities."

In the Portuguese settlement, the pressure was more subtle—and quite inescapable. Teresa Dolores Angela do Amaral resumed her visits, and Francis found them pleasant. Too clever to woo him directly, Dolores enlisted her cousin Manuel Bocarro. Greatly embarrassed, Bocarro confided in late November that Dolores's father, the powerful merchant Dom Sebastian Lobo do Amaral, was urging him to repudiate his partnership with the Englishman. Early in December, while Francis still lay abed, though he could hobble when he tried, Manuel Bocarro spoke bluntly.

"I cannot carry on our arrangement beyond the spring," he said. "Dom Sebastian threatens to recall his loans. Besides, the Loyal Senate will declare you *persona non grata* if you persist in the Manchu trade. Dom Sebastian has convinced the senators that tolerating that trade alienates the Mandarins of Canton. That is *not* true. He further warns that all provisions and trade goods for Macao will be embargoed by order of Peking. That *could* be true, though it is unlikely. Dom Sebastian is so enraged he is striving to make it true. Meanwhile, half Macao believes it true."

Antonio Castro did not evade the issue when Francis questioned him.

"I wouldn't put it quite so strongly, Francis," he said. "But there's much truth in what Manuel says. Dom Sebastian has now enlisted the Jesuits. Since they want you to return to Peking, they are happy to join Dom Sebastian, who wants your marriage to Dolores, in making your position here impossible."

"The Jesuits, of course, assume that I must go home to my lawful wife, do they? How do they know I won't marry bigamously if the pressure becomes irresistible?"

"Aren't they right, Francis? Dom Sebastian is being used by the Jesuits, not using them as he believes. China could be your only resort."

"Antonio, I won't go back to Marta. She freezes my blood. Even my savage Barbara is better, though I'm sick of Manchu barbarism."

"Your sins are finding you out, Francis. You never could resist a woman who threw herself at your head. You always flee till you catch her. Now you're caught. The Loyal Senate

316

will not allow you to sail for Mukden. They fear Chinese reprisals."

"Then China it must be?"

"It appears so. But your weakness can certainly persist a few more months."

ON June 21, 1642, Francis Arrowsmith yielded. He could no longer play the charade of slow recovery, though he limped heavily. Since he could not remain in Macao by marrying Dolores bigamously, he dolefully left amid public rejoicing. Fetes, plays, concerts, parades, and masses attended his departure, and he remarked to Father Giulio di Giaccomo: "They seem very happy. All Macao is celebrating our going."

Midsummer's Day 1642 was the twentieth anniversary of the Portuguese settlement's victory over the landing force commanded by Admiral Cornelius Reyersen, which had preserved the Extreme East from Dutch domination. But Macao had even greater reason for rejoicing. A former Captain-General had landed from the Dutch frigate *Capella* with tidings that had taken more than two years to come from Lisbon.

Portugal and the Netherlands were no longer at war. Dom John, Duke of Braganza, had been set upon the Portuguese throne by a patriotic coup in December 1640, ending the Spanish domination called the "sixty years' captivity." The Dutch would no longer attack Macao or Portuguese shipping because they were at war with Spain.

Macao was convulsed by patriotic frenzies. In the square before the Loyal Senate building, the Governor swore "fealty and homage on the oath of the Holy Evangelists, to . . . His Majesty the King Dom John, the fourth of this name, whom God preserve." The students of the Jesuit Seminary presented a pageant of loyalty and homage to the House of Braganza. The seagulls mewing overhead were scattered by musket salutes.

Macao was *en fête* for weeks. Buildings draped with bunting were illuminated by lanterns at night. All the churches of the settlement held repeated services of thanksgiving. Parading in gaudy uniforms, the Chinese militia proved its marksmanship by killing hundreds of gulls and pigeons. A torchlight procession of the Japanese community displayed splendid costumes envied by the Portuguese ladies. The African slaves donned gaudy yellow and crimson to march singing hymns and screaming war chants.

To prove their patriotism, the suspect Jesuits sang repeated masses. They also permitted the garrison to fire salutes inside the Church of St. Paul, regardless of the damage to hangings and carvings. For once, the Black Priests were in complete harmony with the laymen of Macao.

Father Giulio di Giaccomo and Francis Arrowsmith were isolated amid the merrymakers by their dejection at leaving. As always, the bull-baiting at the foot of Mount Guia enchanted Joseph King, who was delighted to be returning to China.

"The poor bull hasn't got a chance against fifty men," Francis commented sourly. "Typical Portuguese hypocrisy ... to pretend bull-baiting on foot is kinder than the mounted Spanish style. The bull is tortured and, finally, dead for all that."

"Only an Englishman would worry about a savage beast—but happily eat its flesh," Joseph King retorted. "The coup de grâce is swift and merciful."

"I wish," Francis replied, "someone would render the coup de grâce to your blessed Ming Dynasty. We are leaving celebrations over the peaceful restoration of a dynasty after foreign oppression. And where are we going? To the bloody overthrow of another dynasty by barbarians."

Hangchow, Kaifeng, Peking

JULY 18, 1642–OCTOBER 9, 1642

FRAMED by pink peach boughs, the shrine's scarlet pillars gleamed through the morning mist. Creamy clematis entwined the mauve wisteria clinging to the stone walls, and orange azaleas lit the foreshore. Their fragrance floated like incense above the altar to the deified Sung Dynasty Mandarin who had created the otherworldly beauty of Hangchow. The causeway that Mandarin had built into the West Lake in the eleventh century was aflame with vermilion rhododendron blossoms amid emerald foilage. The placid lake was cupped by hills, their purple peaks hazy in the golden dawn.

The cavalry escort's banners hung limp, and the morning calm was hardly disturbed by the creaking of their saddles or the jingling of their bridles. The three travelers astride heavy-bodied ponies halted where the road south to the Chientang River mounted the shallow pass between hillocks overshadowed by Mount Phoenix to the east. Silent, they gazed back on the loveliest city in China.

The three Christians had broken their journey at Hangchow four weeks earlier. They were departing reluctantly, finally deprived of any pretext to linger. Amid the glory of Hangchow in late summer, Francis Arrowsmith had fallen again under the enchantment of ancient China, the spell of peace that flowed unbroken from the primeval past into the eternal future. The realism acquired from those supreme realists, the Chinese, told him that Hangchow's serenity was a preposterous illusion. But he cherished that illusion.

The opulent playhouses, eating-houses, and inns were, Joseph King reminded his companions, gilded relics of an age that was rapidly passing. Besides, they had seen only the fairest aspects of the city the Chinese called Heaven Below. They were received with extraordinary courtesy by the Municipal Mandarins because they traveled under the seal of the Ministry of War. Francis again wore the blue robe and the lynx insignia of a Military Mandarin of the Sixth Grade, a major. The black robes of the Jesuit Giulio de Giaccomo were cut like a senior Mandarin's, and he wore a Mandarin's square black hat of stiff horsehair. Though still a slave, Joseph King wore the green robe and the rhinoceros of a lieutenant.

The Minister of War's patronage had admitted them not only to the most luxurious official guesthouse, but also to the most opulent houses of pleasure in the city renowned for the beauty, the talent, and the ingenuity of its ladies of skill. Their preeminence challenged only by the master chefs whose wizardry excited palates jaded by decades of indulgence, those courtesans were the glory of Hangchow. "Like goddesses of music," as one poet rhapsodized, the ladies of skill played zithers or lyres, sang ancient ballads or popular tunes, and performed classical ballet or folk dances.

When the evenings wore on to the Double Hour of the Snake and the candles began to gutter, Francis and Joseph enjoyed the scented pleasures of the bath and, later, the raptures between silken sheets where the ladies exercised their highest skills. More tolerant, perhaps, than he should have been, Giulio de Giaccomo heard their confessions and shrived them. In Hangchow, Francis Arrowsmith submerged himself in more intense and more subtle sensual delights than he had ever known or was ever to know again. Departing, he ached with deprivation.

"If you had to be ill, Francis, I'm glad it was in Hangchow." Father Giulio de Giaccomo twitched the reins and clucked to his horse. "You couldn't have picked better than the city Marco Polo ruled for the Mongols."

"If the story's true," Joseph King muttered.

"Why should not Kublai Khan make a brilliant Italian a governor?" the Italian Jesuit flared. "The present Emperor has virtually given a brilliant German, our own Father Adam, the Bureau of the Calendar."

"Peace, Father Giulio, peace!" Francis laughed. "Joseph meant no offense to Italy."

"At any rate, Father," Joseph added, "the tale's no more embroidered than my master's playing up his symptoms to keep us in Hangchow."

"*I* exaggerate, Joseph? Impossible," Francis leniently reproved his secretary. "Anyway, the fever was no ruse."

"Certainly not, Major," Joseph replied. "But were you really so ill that we were compelled to remain so long?"

"Well, as for that, I'm in no hurry to reach Peking."

"Nor I, though Father Adam may be displeased," Giulio di Giaccomo agreed. "And you're determined to come to Kaifeng with me?"

"I would not miss your Israelites," Francis answered. "Even a soldier can wonder how the lost tribes came to China—and what remains of them."

"The diversion will take a month or more," Joseph pointed out.

"I hadn't overlooked that point," Francis said. "Nor that traveling by barge on the Grand Canal will add several additional weeks. My convalescence obviously demands that comfort."

Walking sedately, their horses brought them to the Chientang River, whose banks had been buttressed with hewnstone walls against floods. The quays that stretched for two miles along the west bank swarmed with men and animals loading the great cargo junks tied alongside prow to stern.

The docks were white with powder shaken from hundreds of thousands of rice sacks. The fragrance of incense and anise mingled with the prickly odor of peppercorns and the sweetbitter scents of cinnamon, cardamom, and coriander. Bright tribute silk was piled in thick bolts beside pale-brown bales of tobacco and thousands of crates cradling eggshell porcelains. Ten-gallon wine-jars from nearby Shaohsing stood beside baskets of tropical fruit from distant Hainan Island; chests of Japanese silver bars crowded jute-bagged hard coal from Shansi. All the bountiful produce of the Empire—and its few imports—were tumbled in profligate abundance on the stone wharves.

"The great interchange." Joseph King's normal irreverence was subdued by the countless wealth. "Everything comes here from everywhere in the Empire."

"For once you understate, Joseph," Giulio de Giaccomo said. "This is the greatest interchange of goods in the world."

Having bypassed Hangchow on his first journey northward thirteen years earlier, Francis Arrowsmith was awed by the enormous quantities of goods regularly shipped throughout the immense Empire. The Imperial Grand Canal wound a thousand miles from its beginning at Hangchow to its northern terminus near Peking. It linked the Empire's two great rivers, the Yangtze Chiang, which the Chinese called the Long River, and the Huang Ho, the turbulent Yellow River. Linked inland waterways reached a thousand miles southwest from Hangchow through the gorges of the Yangtze to Chungking in the Great Szechwan Plain, the richest agricultural basin in the world—and almost as far from Tsinan in Shantung Province to Hsian in the northwest.

"And do you still think the Manchus will conquer this Empire?" Father Giulio di Giaccomo twitted Francis. "Greater wealth is piled here on this one day than all Manchuria produces in a score of years."

"Wealth, perhaps, but not power," Francis countered weakly. "This wealth is only a lure to the Manchus... unless it feeds the armies that defend the Empire."

"We shall see," the Italian replied. "But where is our vessel?"

"They'll come to us, Father," Joseph assured him. "The crowd parts before our escort like wheat under the scythe. They'll find us easily."

FRANCIS was astonished again by their reception on the flagship of a flotilla of some four hundred junks. The admiral of the fleet was a youthful Mandarin of the Second Grade with a dense black beard and flowing hair. On his insignia-square a pheasant soared, its golden hue repeated in the filigree insets on his black horsehair hat. He clasped his hands before his chest to greet Francis and Joseph, but dropped to his knees before the Jesuit.

"*Shen-fu, wo bi-hsing...*," the Mandarin said. "Father, I am called Ignatius Chin. I ask your blessing."

When the priest had blessed him, the Mandarin added: "All is prepared for Holy Mass."

Admiral Ignatius Chin himself served Father Giulio di Giaccomo's Mass on the capacious poop of the flagship. Afterward, the priest blessed the fleet's banners of yellow silk emblazoned with red crosses. The flotilla slipped the hempen snares that had bound it to the wharves of Hangchow, sped by farewells in every dialect of China. At nightfall, it was bearing northeast on favorable winds toward Suchow some one hundred thirty miles away, where it would load cargo from Shanghai.

The pace was stately, for the Grand Canal tortuously followed existing rivers linked by manmade channels before entering the great lakes of the Yangtze Delta. When the wind failed, the ponderous craft were towed by mules and oxen whipped by foul-mouthed drovers. Having left Suchow behind, the fleet was approaching Chinchiang, where it would cross the Yangtze. It had, Giulio di Giaccomo calculated, taken nearly eight days to cover two hundred sixty miles, a speed of less than a mile and a half an hour.

In the early afternoon of the eighth day, August 23, 1642, the flotilla left Chinchiang to move under bellying sails into the muddy stream of the Yangtze. The golden late-summer sun had just dispelled a squall, and the gulls diving for refuse mewed raucously. The breeze whipped the banners of the Holy Cross, and the elongated sails strained at their rope tethers.

"The Emperor himself couldn't travel more comfortably." Joseph King looked up from his book. "If this is decadence, then I like decadence."

"I, too. The most luxurious travel the world affords... and it rests my wound. Pity we can't forever..." Struck by Father Giulio di Giaccomo's attitude, Francis broke off his idle remarks.

One hand grasping the red-painted poop rail, the other pointing rigidly north, the Jesuit stood immobile. His long sleeves streamed like somber pennants, and tears trickled down his plump cheeks. His teeth flashed within the thicket of his brown beard in a rictus of joyous astonishment.

"Look! Look! To the north!" he shouted. "Look, Francis, Joseph! As far as the eye can see—and beyond! A veritable miracle!"

A squadron of sleek war junks, escorting several hundred deep-bellied cargo junks, was debouching from the northern branch of the Grand Canal onto the wide Yangtze. Francis saw sails too numerous to count. Remarkable, truly, that multitude, but what had moved Giulio di Giaccomo to tears?

Then he saw. Every junk carried a square yellow foresail under its bowsprit. Distended by the wind, every foresail displayed an immense scarlet cross. Speechless, Francis blessed himself. Drawn by the Jesuit's shout, Admiral Ignatius Chin joined them at the rail.

"*Ni kan! Ching kan-yi-kan! Chiu shih chi-chi!*" Francis finally formulated his thoughts in Chinese. "Look! Look there! It's a miracle!"

"*Yi-ting pu-shih. Chiu shih wo po-po...*" The Admiral was matter-of-fact. "Definitely no miracle. Only my uncle, General Lucas Chin. He sails south to crush rebellion in Kwangsi Province with more than five hundred vessels and one hundred thousand troops."

"It *is* a miracle! A sign of the Lord's Grace!" Father Giulio insisted. "Who could ever imagine...here in the heart of pagan China...two great fleets meeting thus? Both commanded by Christian gentlemen. Both displaying the cross of the Crucified Christ."

"It is *somewhat* unusual," the Admiral conceded. "Not something you'd see every day."

"But with God's Grace, someday such a sight will be commonplace," the Jesuit declared. "It portends the victory of the True Faith, the Gentle Nazarene's conquest of the pagan hearts of China."

Joseph King kept his own counsel. Why, he wondered, was the Jesuit blind to the deeper meaning of the meeting of the fleets? To satisfy the rapacious Imperial Court the northbound fleet bore riches scourged from a resentful people. The southbound fleet carried many regiments to suppress the rebellion provoked by that merciless stripping of the rich land. It would be far better, Joseph felt, if neither fleet had ever sailed. If the Court did not suck the wealth of the Empire, there would be no need to spend vast sums on pacification.

The Jesuits were often subtle. They were, however, naïve in their passion for portents; childishly naïve in their overleaping optimism, which hailed the faintest portent as a guarantee of the success of their Mission; and doubly naïve in their belief that they could alter the fundamental nature of China by conforming to Chinese customs.

On the third day after the meeting of the fleets, Admiral Ignatius Chin finally reclaimed his crews from the Flower Houses of Yangchow and the flotilla cast off from China's second city of pleasure. The trembling of the tall sails in the vagrant breezes mocked the shaking hands of the crewmen after their carousing.

The late-August sun transformed the poop of the flagship

into a warm terrace. Joseph King was patiently instructing his master in the mysteries of calligraphy. Disgusted by the contrast between Joseph's flowing ideograms and his own smudged scrawls, Francis flung down his brush and vowed for the hundredth time to leave Chinese calligraphy to those who had been born to its mysteries.

"Did you perhaps, Major, notice something amiss in the meeting of the fleets the other day?" Joseph was incapable of concealing his misgivings indefinitely. "Something beyond the blessed portent Father Giulio saw?"

"You mean *why* those great fleets ply the Grand Canal?" Francis was continually amused by Joseph's tendency to look upon him as an intelligent but untutored child. "Yes, it would be better if both stayed home. But not a word to Father Giulio. In his heart he too knows that portents can be read in different ways."

During the next two weeks of their slow progress through the ancient land heavy with the ripeness of the harvest, Joseph King pointed out the pagodas, temples, and commemorative arches that rose amid the autumnal fire of yellow and crimson leaves. For every such memorial to the human spirit he recalled tales of war and treachery, of rebellion and suppression, of outrages and revenge. The chronicles of the districts through which they sailed reeked of blood.

Depressed by his secretary's unremitting account of the suffering that had scourged the land for millennia, Francis gazed suspiciously from the cushioned security of the flagship at every town they passed. What inhuman deeds, he wondered, had been committed behind its sunlit walls? Having found idyllic harmony with China in serene Hangchow, he felt an interloper in North China. The junk's heavy timbers and the military patrols along the Grand Canal sealed him from the life of the human beings all around him.

Disembarking at Chining thirteen days after the meeting of the fleets, Father Giulio di Giaccomo eagerly anticipated the overland journey to Kaifeng. Anxious to see the Lost Tribes of Israel, he had sought that goal for seven years. Only four months earlier had he obtained the essential sanction of the Ministry of Rites.

Next to his breviary the Jesuit cherished his stiff-paper passport. A yard square, it was covered with the red seals and the flowing endorsements of two ministries, four boards, six bureaus, nine departments, and ten sections of the swollen Ming bureaucracy. Those symbols conjured up the military escort, the accommodations, and the provisions essential for their journey. Only with that magical document, to which village headman kowtowed as if to the Emperor himself, could the foreigners penetrate to the metropolis that had been the capital of the Northern Sung Dynasty six centuries earlier.

The journey of three hundred miles along the secondary Post Road was slow. They made regular stops to rest their horses, since deserted post stations could not provide fresh mounts. The insouciant Lieutenant who commanded their escort wanted to press on. But Francis feared being marooned in the inhospitable countryside by foundered horses. Besides, twenty-odd miles a day was strain enough on his leg.

Joseph had warned that the countryside was devastated beyond strips ten to twenty miles wide along the Grand Canal. Francis and Giulio were initially surprised by the brisk life in the green fields they rode past. But on the fifth day after leaving Chining they entered Honan Province, where rebellion had been endemic for decades—and the face of the land altered.

They passed through nameless villages where mangy dogs with protruding rib cages scavenged among deserted huts, their ratlike tails tucked between their ulcerated haunches. In some villages, seamed crones and stooped dotards contended with the dogs for the few scraps the successive depredations of brigands and Imperial Braves had left them. The travelers saw a number of young cripples, the debris of civil war attended by faithful women. They saw few children.

Afterward they rode for four days across a region of total devastation. Almost all dwellings had been burned to the ground, while those still standing lacked roofs. Mutilated corpses with protruding iridescent bones stared from eye-sockets plucked empty by the crows and ravens. Some intact corpses were black with corruption and monstrously bloated by the gases fermenting inside. A maimed body dangled in a noose from every second tree palisading a three-mile stretch of the pitted road. Even the dogs had fled the blasted land, abandoning the struggle with vultures and wolves for the spoiled human meat.

"These villages were burned...totally razed, you see, and the people hanged." The Lieutenant might have been checking his squadron's stores for all the feeling in his voice. "Served them right, too. They were rebel filth."

"We journey through Purgatory." The emotional Italian

priest shuddered and crossed himself. "What fiends out of Hell did this?"

"They were rebels, the people were." The Lieutenant was shocked by the priest's vehemence. "Deserved what they got from the Flamboyant Cloaks. Mind you, it's not soldiers' work. But someone had to teach them a lesson, so the Flamboyant Cloaks..."

They came to Kaifeng, where Father Matthew Ricci had discovered the Hebrew community, on the fourteenth day after leaving prosperous Chining on the Grand Canal. The ancient fortress-city was an island of Imperial authority amid the sea of devastation. A few miles from the city walls they passed the debris of a departed army and the deserted barracks that had housed the besieging host. Drawing nearer, they saw that a long stretch of the city wall was stripped of its facing stones and that its inner core crumbled dust.

"We've returned to the land of the living." Francis Arrowsmith expressed their common relief when they entered Kaifeng, though only a trickle of townspeople flowed over the cobblestones, while boarded windows and gaping doors declared more than half the houses deserted.

"More like a city of living ghosts... uneasy spirits from the grave," Joseph King said somberly.

Father Giulio di Giaccomo did not reprove the Chinese convert for expressing the old superstitions. He stared straight ahead, willing himself not to see the emaciated men and women who tottered through the narrow streets. His lips moved in silent prayer.

"IT began in earnest for us in Honan Province in the sixth year of the current reign, some nine years ago."

The aged Mandarin who was the Vice-Governor of the blighted province read from the scroll of his memory. Dynastic law prohibited a Mandarin's serving too long in a single province lest he grow too attached to its people—or too bloated with their bribes. Dynastic law also prohibited a Mandarin's serving in his native province. Though both prohibitions were flouted in the Ming's decline, it was extraordinary for the Vice-Governor to have served more than two decades in his native province.

"Just nine years ago, Li Tzu-cheng, the One-Eyed Li who calls himself the Dashing King, first entered this fertile and peaceful province," the Vice-Governor continued. "As you know, Honan means South of the River, the great Yellow River which nourished the Chinese race in its cradle many millennia ago. Until that thrice-cursed year, the Yellow River still fed a happy Honan."

The Governor had received the three Christian travelers with the formal courtesy due their exalted patronage. But his manner had been cold and his welcome hollow. Angered by outsiders intruding into his gutted domain, he had instructed his deputy to see to them. He had then withdrawn, pleading urgent business.

The Vice-Governor was a frail manikin hardly five feet four inches tall. His dark skin was seamed with wrinkles, and his lank gray mustaches seemed pasted above his bloodless lips. He spoke of Honan's suffering after offering his guests a dinner that was meager compared to the extravagance of Hangchow but indecently lavish amid the desolation of Honan.

A fourth Christian dined with the Vice-Governor, the Jesuit Rodrigo de Figueredo. Giulio di Giaccomo had made straight for the Mission House after entering the city the previous day. The forty-seven-year-old missionary, who had lived in Kaifeng for a decade, was bone-thin. His long brown hair was laced with white, and his pale blue eyes were red-rimmed with weariness. He spoke his native Portuguese haltingly, not having used that tongue for several years. To Father Giulio di Giaccomo's anguished questions regarding the devastation they had seen, he replied: "Be patient, my friends. Others can tell that tale far better than I."

Rodrigo de Figueredo had, however, gladly led them to the Hebrew quarter. Giulio di Giaccomo's first disappointment was the appearance of those presumed Israelites when he met the elders of their thirteen families—all that remained of a community of several hundred Father Matthew Ricci had visited more than forty years earlier. They were virtually indistinguishable from other Chinese in their dress and their features. Their beards were, perhaps, heavier and their noses more prominent than their neighbors', but the more numerous Moslems were as heavily bearded and their features more aquiline. Like the Moslems, the Hebrews spoke only Chinese; like the Moslems, they were known to their ethnic Han Chinese neighbors as "sinew cutters" because they removed all veins and tendons from their meat; like the Moslems, they would eat no pork. That abstinence—and admitting boys

328

to the dignity of adulthood at thirteen—were the two traditional observances the Jews of Kaifeng still practiced.

"The chief difference between the Jews and the Chinese is the Jews' stubbornness," Father Rodrigo de Figueredo said bitterly. "I have made many Han Chinese converts and a few among the Moslems. To have brought even one member of the ancient Hebrew race to acknowledge the Messiah would have been a wondrous accomplishment. But not a single Jew has accepted the True Faith. They are a stiff-necked people."

Though they shook their heads sheepishly when Giulio di Giaccomo wrote a few Hebrew letters, the elders produced with pride an antique scroll-book of great size protected by an embroidered red-velvet cover worn tissue-thin by age. They called their Scroll of the Law *taw-lah*, which the priest equated with the Hebrew word *Torah*. The elders acknowledged that the script of their *taw-lah* was like that the Italian had written, but admitted shamefacedly that none of them could read it. They were, Giulio di Giaccomo saw with distress, far prouder of the Imperial Tablets presented to those Jews who had won official rank than they were of their Scroll of the Law. Some of those Jewish Mandarins, the elders said, could with difficulty read Hebrew, but they were serving "far away."

Crestfallen, the Italian Jesuit had agreed with his Portuguese colleague that the depleted Jewish community was of little interest to either scholars or missionaries. He had with little reluctance put aside his researches for the obligatory honor of dining with the Vice-Governor.

"Driven out of Shansi Province, One-Eyed Li descended upon my unlucky Honan to transform it into the waste you have seen," that aged Mandarin continued his tragic account. "And all this destruction in the name of the people... for the people's welfare, he says. But really for revenge.

"One-Eyed Li, his followers claim, was driven into brigandry. He was the hereditary headman of his native village in Shensi Province before he fled to the hills because he could not, he said, meet the tax collectors' extortionate demands. The number of his followers grew rapidly—other refugees, landless men, and many soldiers discharged into penury. Waxing powerful, he summoned a formal conference of thirteen brigand chiefs who commanded many tens of thousands. They met in Honan in the first month of the eighth year of the reign of the present Emperor."

Joseph King, seated beside the three Europeans, leaned across to whisper, "That would be February 1635."

"The thirteen brigand kings proposed no less than to divide the Ming Empire among themselves," the Vice-Governor continued. "The Mandate of Heaven, One-Eyed Li insisted, had passed into their hands.... They would soon rule the entire Empire under his suzerainty.

"Those vicious rebels took strange titles: the King Who Alters the World, the Nine-Striped Dragon, the Scourge of the Universe. Sadly, they today command many hundreds of thousands who prey on the people."

Unable to contain himself, Joseph King whispered in Portuguese: "Insatiable tax collectors and avaricious Mandarins force honest men to become rebels. Also the ferocity of the Imperial troops, particularly the bloodthirsty Flamboyant Cloaks. You've seen their handiwork."

"Measures to suppress rebellion have not always been wise." The Vice-Governor's candor startled Francis, who had forgotten during his protracted absence from China how outspoken and daring the few upright Mandarins could be. "Moreover, many Mandarins have unjustly exploited the *lao pai-hsing,* the common people. The Emperor is, of course, generous and just. But he is isolated—and sometimes deceived by his wicked advisers."

"Even so, Sir, support for the rebels is widespread," Father Figueredo interrupted. "Why do so many flock to the banner of One-Eyed Li?"

"It is as you say, Spiritual Father," the Vice-Governor conceded. "It came about by a perverted miracle. One-Eyed Li's head is extremely large, and his cheekbones are extremely high, while both his owl-like eyes—before he lost one—were extremely deep-set. You all know those signs of ferocity. His nose is scorpion-shaped and his voice like a wolf's baying. His nature is suspicious and cruel. He formerly delighted in hewing off feet and ripping out beating hearts. Because of his cruelty, the common people did not go over to him, but defended their villages desperately."

"And how, Sir, did that change?" Francis was fascinated, though he suspected that the Vice-Governor's account was weighted in the Dynasty's favor, despite the old man's apparent fair-mindedness.

"Because of a certain Mandarin, Dr. Li of Honan, who is not related to One-Eyed Li of Shensi. A loyal subject of the Great Ming, Dr. Li gave food, clothing, and medicines to innocent victims of strife. The people praised him, saying: 'Only young Master Li keeps us alive!'"

"Tell them about the Red Lady, Governor," Father Figueredo urged.

"I was just coming to her. A famous tightrope-walker was called Hung Niang-tze, the Red Lady. When her circus closed because of general poverty, she led a rising in Dr. Li's native county. Infatuated with that young Mandarin, she abducted him and won his love. When he escaped, the authorities jailed him as a rebel. The common people rose in sympathy when the Red Lady attacked the jail to rescue her lover.

"With the Red Lady, Dr. Li then joined One-Eyed Li. The rebel leader greatly respected the learning of the first Mandarin to join him. When a soothsayer prophesied that One-Eyed Li would be the next emperor, young Dr. Li counseled: 'To conquer the Empire you must first conquer the hearts of the common people by refraining from indiscriminate slaughter.' Then, One-Eyed Li not only stopped wanton killing, but fed and clothed the suffering *lao pai-hsing*.

"The simple folk made no distinction between Dr. Li and One-Eyed Li and shouted again: 'Young Master Li keeps us alive!' And Dr. Li's verses became One-Eyed Li's marching song: 'Welcome the Dashing King, and escape all taxing! Support his valorous band, and own your own land!' Tens of thousands of the dispossessed flocked to the banner of One-Eyed Li."

"Why, Sir, do you still denounce him as ferocious," Father Giulio di Giaccomo asked imprudently, "if he has abandoned his evil ways?"

"His nature has not changed," the Vice-Governor answered. "Just last year, One-Eyed Li captured the Imperial Prince of Fu, an uncle of the present Emperor who owned tens of thousands of acres. His palace was so vast it burned for three days. The rebels slew the corpulent Prince Fu and mixed his blood with minced venison. They called the potion *fu lu chiu,* meaning either 'wine by the grace of Prince Fu' or 'lucky victory wine.'

"One-Eyed Li next turned on Kaifeng. But our Red Jacket Cannon slaughtered thousands of rebels, and an arrow pierced their leader's eye. That is why he is now called One-Eyed Li.

"But the cunning rogue turned misfortune to advantage. We Chinese have a prophecy for every occasion, and one pre-

331

dicts the Ming will fall to a one-eyed hero. One-Eyed Li now proclaims himself that hero."

"Yet the siege of Kaifeng is hardly at an end, is it?" Father Rodrigo de Figueredo asked rhetorically.

"Hardly, Father, as you know well," the Mandarin replied. "But my old voice is tired. Will you tell the rest of the tale?"

"Gladly, though the end remains unknown," the Portuguese Jesuit agreed. "One-Eyed Li reverted to his old ways after his first retreat from Kaifeng, wantonly killing, pillaging, raping, and burning. He defeated several Imperial armies and sacked a dozen counties. He cannily slaked his troops' blood lust while sparing the common people. He slew the men of letters he captured, whether licentiates, Mandarins, or only candidates for the Civil Service Examinations. In just one county, some two hundred men of letters died after he cut off their noses and their feet."

"I must admit his tactics are effective," the Vice-Governor interjected. "One-Eyed Li has divided the common people from their natural protectors, making the *lao pai-hsing* hate all Mandarins and gentry."

"When One-Eyed Li besieged Kaifeng again," Father de Figueredo resumed, "he did not use ladders and battering rams but his great superiority in numbers. He commanded his men to pry out the great stones that clad the earthen core of the city wall. They obeyed, fearing One-Eyed Li's executioners more than our Imperial Braves. They tunneled into the core of the wall. And, finally, a great section groaned and collapsed."

"Yet we sit here in Kaifeng this minute," Giulio di Giaccomo objected.

"That we do," the Portuguese Jesuit answered. "But for how long? Apropos of that question, I firmly urge you..."

"Could you finish your tale first, Father?" Francis's professional curiosity was aroused.

"As you wish. Buttressed on the inner side, the wall was so strong that it still stood. The Governor sank countermines above the rebels' excavations and poured down flaming oil, pitch, and acids. One-Eyed Li then used gunpowder explosions to gnaw away the wall. In March of this Year of Our Lord 1642, he ordered the final assault."

"The walls," Francis mused, "are thrice the thickness of the strongest I ever saw in Europe."

"Kaifeng was twice the capital of the Empire," the Vice-

Governor recalled. "We Chinese have always built massive walls around our capitals against barbarians and rebels."

"The assault was an anticlimax," Father de Figueredo resumed. "We stood behind the parapets, awaiting the onslaught...and my legs trembled. One-Eyed Li's mines exploded with a roar like a thousand siege guns, and innumerable squadrons of armored cavalry charged into the breach. But the wall still stood. When our archers and cannon slew tens of thousands, One-Eyed Li rode south to seek easier prey. I sang a Mass of Thanksgiving, which our host attended—though he is, more's the pity, not yet a Christian."

"Father de Figueredo, what was the other matter you raised?" asked Joseph King, uneasily shifting on his low stool. "To me this city smells not of victory but of impending defeat."

"You are perhaps right, my son," the Portuguese Jesuit answered. "The matter in my mind is this: You must be gone at daybreak tomorrow. Scouts report that One-Eyed Li is at this moment advancing in great force to besiege Kaifeng again."

"Why not remain?" Francis asked. "I'd like to see this army of One-Eyed Li's."

"Because our duty takes us north to Peking," Giulio di Giaccomo answered.

"You must not be delayed by a siege that could last months," Rodrigo de Figueredo added.

"Then, Father, you will come with us?" Francis asked. "You must not perish here."

"I have business here, the Lord's business," the Portuguese replied. "Kaifeng is my home, and I cannot desert my flock. Do not fear for my life. The Governor has pierced the dikes holding the Yellow River a few miles away. If need demands, half a day's work will complete the breakthrough—and the rebels will drown."

"I should remain," Francis insisted. "Joining this defense is the best service I can render the Empire."

"Major, you are here under my jurisdiction—and I command you to depart." The Vice-Governor spoke with austere authority. "We cannot feed a single extra mouth!"

ONLY Francis Arrowsmith was reluctant when the three Christians rode out of Kaifeng the next morning. Joseph King was in a fever to leave the city he swore was doomed. Father Giulio di Giaccomo was also eager. He feared the rough tongue of Adam Schall if Francis Arrowsmith's arrival in Peking were long delayed. Most joyous were several hundred civilians who rode under the protection of their cavalry escort.

Haste dominated the travelers from Macao, and they did not return to the Grand Canal, but took the Post Roads. Finally they came to Chochow, where the Manchus had fled the unloaded cannon of Captain-Sergeant Miguel Gonsalves Texeira Correa almost thirteen years earlier. On October 9, 1642, they rode into Peking through the Fucheng Gate.

Father Adam Schall welcomed them brusquely, saying to Francis: "I see the Lord's Grace has finally brought you back! You took long enough! I need your help in casting cannon and building fortifications. The Emperor has loaded me with that responsibility as well."

"What news of Marta, Father Adam?" Francis asked reluctantly.

"She's still a nuisance, so I'm doubly glad you've come. Now, perhaps she'll give me some peace."

"Adam, what other news?" Giulio di Giaccomo asked.

"Much news...and all bad. Last summer the Manchus took cities only a few score miles east of Peking and held them as long as they pleased. They have now retired...to prepare a new assault, I fear. We must work fast to prepare this unready capital for a siege."

"Is there, Father, any news of Kaifeng?" Joseph King asked. "When we left, it, too, was preparing for a new siege."

"Haven't you heard, then?" Adam Schall replied. "You heard nothing on your way north? No, I see not. Apparently bad news travels faster than good Christians."

"What is the news of Kaifeng, Father Adam?" Francis demanded. "Can you leave off abusing us long enough to tell us?"

"I'll try, Francis." Adam Schall's slow smile apologized for his hectoring. "A week ago, a courier arrived from the Governor. As he feared, One-Eyed Li besieged Kaifeng in overwhelming strength. Since provisions were short, the Governor ordered the dikes of the Yellow River breached. Thinking like the Governor, One-Eyed Li had cut the dikes elsewhere. Floods swept away the rebel host, as the Governor had planned. But the north gate collapsed under the torrents. A river flowed through the city, sweeping away buildings and killing thousands."

"Then Kaifeng is still in Imperial hands?" Francis asked.

"For what it's worth. Most sadly, our brother in Christ

334

Rodrigo de Figueredo was among those drowned. Pray for his soul, as I do."

"And the rebels," Francis persisted. "What of One-Eyed Li?"

"Fled south again to recruit and reorganize. But he will return to Kaifeng—just as surely as the Manchus will return to Peking!"

Peking

OCTOBER 12, 1642–JUNE 14, 1643

"DID you *really* think I had nothing else in the world to do except wait for you? Did you *ever* think for an instant of Maria...my poor half-barbarian daughter...growing up without a father? Did you *ever* think of anyone besides yourself?"

Not quite making out her words, an eavesdropper outside the garden pavilion the Mandarin James Soo had given his daughter would have judged from Marta's conversational tone that she was chatting about the departed guests. Her pink-nailed hands were steady as she creamed the heavy makeup she had worn for the banquet her father had insisted must celebrate Francis Arrowsmith's return after a decade. Her manner displayed no stronger emotion than relief at laying aside her formal gown and removing her formal makeup with unguents from the enamel boxes on her black-lacquered vanity chest.

Marta's calmness was itself belligerent. Aside from her words, her profound resentment was apparent in her breathy emphasis on some syllables and her stressing their musical tones.

"But, Marta, I have come back." Francis Arrowsmith evaded his wife's accusing stare, which was reflected threefold by her folding mirror. "You know I was a prisoner in Mukden. Believe me, I would have flown like an arrow back to you if I could."

"Were you also a prisoner in Macao?" Marta swiveled on her barrel-stool.

"No, not formally, that is." Francis's glance dropped to the cream-and-blue Tientsin carpet spread on the floor tiles against the mid-October chill. "I wasn't a prisoner, but there were obstacles."

"Obstacles, you say? Obstacles! For four years you were a prisoner of the northern barbarians. Perhaps you couldn't escape, though I wonder how hard you tried. You were free in Macao for six years...while I withered alone in Peking and your daughter cried for her father."

"Maria seemed jolly enough when she went to bed tonight." Regretting his defensive levity, Francis wondered why Marta pressed the quarrel so relentlessly. Withdrawn hauteur or screaming rage had in the past been more her style than this cold anger. "But it didn't matter whether I wished to return. I tell you again, I...could...not."

"Could not or *would* not?" Marta's features tightened, momentarily losing the slight fullness that had made her more attractive during the ten lost years; her rounded chin appeared pointed and her delicately arched nose predatory. "Were you too busy with those Portuguese ladies...with their fishbelly-white skin and their radish-colored hair? Did you teach them from *my* pillow book?"

"I hardly touched a Portuguese lady. And then no more than shook a hand." Francis suppressed his smile. "Most, by the way, are darker than you...almost swarthy beside your luster, like an oystershell beside a pearl."

"You really expect me to believe you never made love to one of those...those gray-skinned bitches?"

"Believe what you will, it won't change the truth. I never did." Francis was honestly indignant, since he had, in truth, not slept with a single Portuguese woman. Other women were another matter, as were the six years of celibacy his denial implied. "And I could not return any time I wished."

"Why not?" she challenged. "You were free there...even if you were the fugitive slave of the northern barbarian Emperor."

"And you the wife of a slave, a slave who resisted marriage to the daughter...the very attractive daughter...of a Baron
337

because he thought only of you?" He rose to her taunts. "You do not know the practices of your own country. No man may come into the Empire unless specifically invited. I was *not* invited until a few months ago."

"That's nonsense... utter nonsense." Marta would not be diverted. "Father Adam sent word to you years ago."

"I... was... not formally invited... until seven months ago. And... I could *not*... enter... the Empire." Francis had virtually convinced himself that the disingenuously literal truth he told Marta was the entire truth. "And those last few months together in Tengchou... your ice-cold departure.... I could hardly believe you wanted me back so desperately."

"*Shih, shih, shih nien!*" The tears that trickled down Marta's cheeks left no trace on the film of face cream. "Ten, ten, ten long years! An eternity! That was long ago, the foolishness of a girl of nineteen, lonely and carrying her first child. I was utterly alone. No other woman except my bond-servant Ying.... And... and I was afraid."

"Nonetheless, you did..."

"Nonetheless, it *was* ten years ago," she interrupted. "And I have repented of my foolishness bitterly, which is more than you..."

"I said I regretted... deeply regretted... being away so long. What more can I..."

"Regretted? Regretted? Do you know... do you have the *faintest* idea... what it means to be a deserted wife in China? I was a widow who wasn't really a widow, and our child was fatherless." Marta's calm dissolved. "I was afraid I'd never see you again. Now you act as if I should embrace you... *must* embrace you, forgiving all, forgiving your desertion. Just forgetting those long, lonely years."

Francis was astonished by her passion. How could she be the same woman who had two days earlier greeted him with a profoundly distant bow? He could still hear her fluting words: "My Lord has deigned to return! My Lord is ten thousand times welcome!" He could not understand the reversion to petulance by the tactful woman who had pleaded female indisposition and slept in their daughter Maria's room the last two nights.

Their parting had been so cold that he shrank from forcing any communication on her during their long separation. She had certainly not tried with any conviction to send word to him—though she certainly could have.

"But, Francis," Marta added softly, "I do want you back ... very much."

Francis reflected guiltily that he had had much experience of women since they parted, too much experience of too many women. But he had, at thirty-five, gained some understanding of women. He knew Marta was not flaunting a false passion but expressing her deepest feelings.

He lifted his eyes from the blue Buddhist symbols woven into the cream carpet and looked into his wife's eyes. Sighing in resignation, Francis felt the manacles of domesticity close on his wrists. He had come home to another captivity.

While her husband surrendered himself in an instant to the renewed bonds of marriage, Marta's tragic expression masked her swift calculation. Above all, she warned herself, you mustn't overdo it. If you either forgive too easily or cling too avidly to your grievances, you will arouse his suspicion. For a barbarian he's no fool, and he's grown shrewder these ten years past. Above all, don't overdo it. Get it just right.

Marta had, in truth, desperately wanted Francis to return to Peking, but not because of affection. That was almost comical. Why should she miss him after enjoying a decade of almost perfect freedom? Nor was she overly concerned about her daughter's fatherless state. Maria could manage quite happily without the parent she had never known. The child was neither particularly unpleasant nor particularly appealing—if one overlooked her somewhat barbaric appearance. In any event, Maria had Ying to look after her—cloyingly dote upon her.

No, Marta reflected, she had wanted Francis for other reasons. She had actually told him one reason. A widow had no standing in Chinese society unless she was the aged matriarch of a large family. A deserted wife had no standing whatsoever. Humiliated by the assumption that she had lost her husband because of her own faults, she was not pitied but quietly despised.

Generally indifferent to the feelings of others, Marta was acutely sensitive to those opinions that touched her. She required her husband's nominal presence to testify to her successful married state, though she owed no fealty to the marriage she had resisted. She was confident that Francis's military duties would take him away from Peking for extended periods. Respected because of her husband's occasional appearances, she could pursue her own happiness in his absence.

339

"There was another reason I couldn't come back till now." Moved by her sincere affection, Francis sought to placate Marta with truth. "Another matter we'd better not discuss after tonight. You didn't know that I..."

"You mean the vengeance of the Black Premier...the anger of the Divine Skein?" Marta immediately regretted revealing her knowledge of his connections with the Secret Police. She had never intended to tell him.

"How did you know?" Francis demanded. "I never told you...nor did Paul Hsü, I swear. Father Adam?"

"Perhaps." Marta smiled defensively. "Perhaps it was Father Adam."

"I'll ask him tomorrow. I can't really believe he..."

"No, Francis, don't bother asking him....It wasn't...wasn't Father Adam."

"Then how in the name of God did you know? That secret...I swear not more than five men in Peking knew."

"You know how people gossip, Francis."

"This was no matter for idle gossip. How *did* you know?"

"You remember Simon Wu, Francis." Marta was compelled to brazen candor. "He is a distant cousin, and he comes here occasionally. Cousin Simon told..."

"Cousin Simon, is it?" Francis's guilty resignation was swept aside by a torrent of anger. "Cousin Simon, by God! Yes, I do know Simon Wu. My former Adjutant, the most courteous blackguard who ever stole a man's battalion. The biggest blackmailer in a nation of blackguards and blackmailers. The smiling tool of the Black Premier. He's loathsome."

"He is not loathsome....And he could not help the role he played with you."

"Forced, was he, by God? Is that what he told you? You've been awfully close...you, my wife, and that nancy-boy...that plaything of the Court Eunuchs."

"He's a better man than you. He wouldn't skulk in hiding for years." Marta's rage erupted. "A *far* better man than you...in *all* ways."

"And what, my lady, does that mean? Exactly what?"

"Just what I said. No more. But no less, either."

"I've had enough of your perfidy!" Francis exploded.

He stormed out of the bedroom, hurling the door shut behind him. He slammed open the wooden moon gate to the inner courtyard. Moonbeams trickled across the brick walks, lighting the hoarfrost with a pale glow. In the shallow pool the goldfish swirled their gossamer fins among the lacy ferns. When the fresh air cooled his anger, Francis wondered why he had instinctively denounced her perfidy. Was Marta's association with Simon Wu perhaps not mere heedlessness, a lapse of discrimination and discretion? Did their apparent intimacy signify much more?

Francis paced the courtyard for almost an hour. The lamp in Marta's room winked out, and he knew she had retired alone to the red-and-gold marriage bed where he himself had slept alone the past two nights. Drowsiness smoothed his roiled emotions. Yielding to sleep, he snored gently in a cane long-chair beside the goldfish pool. His wife Marta lay under the high canopy of their marriage bed listening to the sighing of the night wind.

THE tentative morning sun warmed the yellow-tiled roofs of the massive Tiencheng Men, the Gate of Heaven's Sanction.* The four red-brick stories were still shadowed, as were the crimson walls stretching on either side. When the sun's spears transfixed the Imperial City, the clouds genuflected like white-robed penitents against the cornflower-blue sky.

It was just past six on the morning of October 14, 1642, the middle of the Double Hour of the Horse, and the Emperor of the Great Ming Dynasty still slept in the Hall of Absolute Purity. He dreamed of an Empire untroubled by rebels or Manchus, an Empire whose treasury overflowed with the willing tribute of grateful subjects. The Empire had never known those blessings during all his thirty-one years.

In his own princely apartments, the Senior Court Eunuch Tsao Chun-hua had been awake for two hours. He was dispassionately assessing his interests, which did not invariably coincide with his Imperial master's. The interests of the two most powerful men of the virtually bankrupt dynasty were diverging. The Black Premier scanned the reports of his secret agents among the Manchus and moved closer to a treasonous decision.

The castrato was the effective ruler of the fifteen thousand Court Eunuchs and five thousand Palace Women who served the Imperial Court. That community was protected not only by the city walls of Peking, but also by its own two concentric

---

* Later called Tienan Men, the Gate of Heavenly Peace.

walls. The inner walls enclosed the Emperor's private domain, two hundred fifty acres barred to all but those he summoned, known as the Purple Forbidden City. Surrounding the Imperial City, the outer walls were pierced by four gates, the Gate of Heaven's Sanction the chief among them. That outer sanctum was barred to all but those whose service to the Dynasty required their admission.

The three horsemen who approached the Gate of Heaven's Sanction from the south along a narrow avenue palisaded by the Imperial Ministries were authorized to enter the Imperial City. The Captain of the Guard saluted the lynx insignia of a major Francis Arrowsmith wore on his blue tunic. His white-canvas trousers bloused over black boots, Francis was dressed for work, not ceremony. Joseph King wore the same uniform with a lieutenant's rhinoceros insignia. When they emerged from the dark tunnel under the gate, the Sergeant of the Imperial Guard who had escorted them from James Soo's mansion on the Silver Fox *hutung* saluted perfunctorily and rode off.

The grassy meadow that lay before them was withered by the flames spouting from ten furnaces like enormous beehives. Francis heard the pounding of hammers, the rasping of files, and the roaring of gigantic bellows, all the familiar uproar of an ordnance works. The fifty-odd Court Eunuchs who worked those furnaces had doffed their bright robes, but not their black-horsehair caps of office.

Many more Eunuchs lounged on the grass. Dedication to hard work by Northern Chinese was not among the miracles Paul Hsü had once enumerated to prove the Lord of Heaven's love for the Ming Dynasty. Whatever Emperors ruled the Empire in the decades and the centuries to come, none would be able to compel the men of North China to toil diligently.

A tall man with a spatulate nose and silver-gilt hair greeted them, wiping his forehead with a green kerchief. The skirts of his black cassock were tucked into his belt to free his hairy shanks and his sandaled feet. Father Adam Schall's movements were vigorous, though he had passed his fiftieth birthday a half year earlier. But his thinning hair had been leached gray by the labors he had performed and the hardships he had borne since entering the Empire nineteen years earlier. His duties as a Chinese subject in the service of the Emperor were as arduous as his duties as a missionary priest.

"Welcome! Welcome to the bridegroom!" the Jesuit called

out with Germanic jocularity. "And how go the renewed joys of matrimony?"

"I have much to thank you for, Father Adam," Francis replied. "Much, indeed!"

"As I told you the other day, your assistance is essential." The priest ignored his protégé's sarcasm. "You know we have not yet cast a usable gun. And we began this devil's work last July."

"At least you're trying hard, Father Adam."

"I must work hard, Francis. Like my patron Adam, I must earn my bread by the sweat of my brow. If I depended on the remittances or the Emperor's generosity, the entire Mission would starve."

"Is it that bad, Father?" Francis had thought the China Mission wealthy. "Surely you still receive large sums from Macao. And the Emperor has honored you time after time."

"Since the Japan trade ended, Francis, we get only a pittance from Macao. The Emperor is free with honors but mean with cash. Without my pay for this work, all the Fathers would be begging in the streets like Buddhist bonzes."

"But the Emperor has honored you greatly," Francis persisted.

"Honored? Indeed yes. Three years ago he presented me with a tablet emblazoned with gold. I would have preferred cash. *Chin Pao Tien Hsüeh,* it read, Imperially Approved Astronomy. A procession followed the Vice-Minister of Rites to our door—junior Mandarins, secretaries, musicians, lictors, hangers-on, and servants...more than a hundred. We had to feed them all...after kowtowing to the tablet. More such honors and we'll all starve."

"How goes the work, then?"

"Francis, I've already told you it's not going well. I wish I were back at the Bureau of the Calendar. Nice clean work, not like this sweaty labor. But you're just in time for a pour. We'll try again, though I have little hope for success."

A portrait of the Lord Jesus was propped on an altar-table covered with white silk embroidered with green crosses. Behind it stood the paraphernalia of the foundry. Stacked ingots of copper and tin surrounded two furnaces on a brick platform. A giant leather bellows pumped by two patient donkeys turning a wheel forced air to the fires.

A long wooden box was propped diagonally beneath the furnaces. The shape of a small cannon was impressed upon

343

sand mixed with clay inside that mold-box. Molten alloy would flow into that hollow space to form the cannon.

"Think backward, always backward, my fine English gentleman," Manuel Tavares Bocarro had repeatedly admonished. "Where the sand is, the metal won't be. Where the sand is not, the metal will be. The air now within the mold-box is your future cannon. Where the separate solid core now hangs will be the gun's hollow bore!"

Assessing the Jesuit's primitive arrangements, Francis advised: "The mold-box must be absolutely vertical. Otherwise the pour won't..."

"Later, my son, later," Adam Schall interrupted. "The most important task comes first."

"And that is?"

"A Dedicatory Mass, of course. I cannot prevent the pagans' sacrificing to their god of fire." The priest pointed to the roasted chickens and ducks heaped before a red-and-gilt shrine. "But I can dedicate the gun to the service of the One True God."

"Don't the pagans object?"

"The Emperor himself gave me permission. When our Christian guns drive back the Manchus and the rebels, who will not wish to be a Christian? This falconet is dedicated to Ursula, the patron saint of my native Cologne. If the good Joseph King will consent to serve..."

Assisted by the slave in his incongruous lieutenant's uniform, the priest shook out the skirts of his black cassock. He drew a white surplice over it and put on a tall black hat like a cardinal's biretta.

Murmuring the responses, Francis Arrowsmith and Joseph King were surprised when several Court Eunuchs joined them. Father Adam Schall's pale-blue eyes shone with tears when he placed the Host on the tongues of five kneeling Eunuchs. Afterward he prayed fervently for assistance in casting a perfect cannon—"a Christian cannon to serve Your Divine Purpose of bringing all the men and women of China into the True Faith."

He then briskly put off his vestments and girded up his cassock.

"We have now rendered unto God, and it is time to work for the Emperor," he said. "What was your suggestion?"

"Set the mold-box straight, and half your problems will disappear."

"That is not so easy, my young friend. We should have to

344

put the furnaces on a higher platform. Then, how to lift the heavy ingots and coal?"

Engaged by the technical problem, Francis neglected his normal tact toward the Jesuit. "Several small furnaces would distribute the weight more evenly. And there's no need for a higher platform. Just build a spiral ramp to the platform."

The Jesuit clambered onto the platform where the furnaces roared. Taking up a long pine bough, he stirred the molten mixture of nine parts copper, one part tin, and one-quarter part of zinc. That "greenstick" mixed the molten alloy evenly and, transformed into carbon, leached out impurities. In the theoretical aspects of cannon-casting, what could be learned from books, Francis could not fault the Jesuit.

Adam Schall's workmen tilted a crucible, and glowing metal poured hissing into the mold-box. After a pause, a second crucible voided into the box. Francis knew a flaw in the finished gun would mark that interval, while the bore would be awry because the core did not hang absolutely vertical. Unless, of course, the divine intercession invoked by the Jesuit's prayers remedied the inherent faults in the process.

A cannon boomed, and Francis started. Black smoke was drifting from a small gun at the end of the meadow.

"They've done it again," Adam Schall exploded. "I'll have to explain once more to the Emperor that we haven't had an accident, but only a miscalculation."

"What was the purpose of that exercise?" Francis asked. "Are you using a new technique...shaping the bore with round shot?"

"This isn't the first time. They will thrust a ball down a bore that hasn't been scoured properly, a rough bore probably far off true. Then the only way to clear the gun is by firing it."

"The Lord *is* watching over you. It's a miracle the gun didn't blow up. You could have had a few injured, perhaps a few dead."

"Oh, we have. The first time, there was a full charge in the chamber. Bronze flew all around. Two dead and a half dozen badly hurt."

Adam Schall beckoned to a young man. Though he wore a workman's rough clothing, his assured manner suggested a higher status, while his slim mustache demonstrated that he was no Eunuch.

"Ching chieh-shao...." Adam Schall rolled the Officials'

Language off his tongue. "I'd like to introduce Master Cheng Cheng-kung. You already know his esteemed father, Admiral of the Coastal Seas, Cheng Chih-lung, the Noble Dragon. This is the renowned Arrowmaker."

The youth bowed to Francis and awaited instructions.

"Go tell those fools they'll be severely punished if this happens again," Adam Schall directed. "And send a messenger to the Grand Eunuch so that he can reassure the Emperor."

"*Shen-fu, wo kan-pu-kan...*" The youth was deferential. "Father, dare I make a suggestion? Cut off the head of the one who put the match to the fuse...and flog the others. Then it certainly won't happen again."

"*Tai li-hai...,*" the priest responded. "Too fierce, much too fierce. Just reprove them. But tell everyone the next time it happens, there will be beheadings and floggings."

When the youth had set out, Adam Schall said to Francis: "My good right hand, that lad. Eager to learn and straight as a die—even if his father is the biggest pirate unhanged in the Orient."

"I do not remember his father with affection," Francis said.

"You should. He set you free."

"Only after Joseph bribed him royally...but that is another story. Do you have much pilfering?"

"Pilfering? I call two tons of copper and a half-ton of tin more than pilfering. They'd steal the sugar out of my tea if they used sugar in tea. But theft's not as bad as stupidity. Why the Emperor...he wanted monstrous cannon that would fire balls weighing ninety pounds. After we persuaded him that was folly, he wanted little cannon...no more than sixty pounds so two men could carry one easily. I almost wrote the Emperor that Chinese troops scurrying in retreat—at which they're best—would hardly carry sixty-pound guns on their backs, but would throw them away."

"Father Adam, do you ever despair?" Francis was disturbed by a Christian priest's casting cannon for a pagan Emperor in the capital of an Empire sealed against all other outlanders.

"I've come close, I must admit," Adam Schall replied. "But with your help, we'll soon be turning out reasonable guns."

"I didn't mean despair only...just of this project, Father. Do you ever despair of the entire enterprise? God's Grace will someday bring the Chinese to the True Faith, but in our time?"

346

"I do not permit myself to despair." The Jesuit was severe. "And you *may* not. Despair is a sin. We must serve the Lord with total faith and total dedication."

"Though it's often almost impossible to get through to the Chinese . . . to make them see that the only way to salvation . . . the only way to cast cannon . . . is our way?"

"Father Matthew Ricci was by no means certain that our way . . . the European way . . . was always best. Consider instead the wonder of our enjoying any communion at all with the Chinese, the miracle of our being in China at all—as Dr. Paul Hsü was wont to point out."

"Really now, what miracle, Father Adam? Learning Chinese and adopting Chinese ways is no miracle. You've done it brilliantly and even I, though feebly."

"Francis, we stand with our feet in China but our hearts halfway between China and Europe. Our ways of thought are still separated from theirs by thousands of leagues. It is a miracle that we communicate at all."

"Father Adam, we are in China, so we speak Chinese."

"Francis, you are shaped not only by your own experience. You are yourself because of the experience and the learning of all your ancestors. Otherwise you would be a heretic, for one thing."

"What has that to do with the Chinese, Father?" Francis had grown unaccustomed to discussing abstractions. "What I am has nothing to do with what *they* are."

"What *they* are has everything to do with what their ancestors were and how those ancestors lived and thought. Francis, you and I talk to the Chinese—except for a glorious exception like Dr. Paul—across a gulf almost as wide as the gulf that divided their ancestors from ours."

"Perhaps. Even with Dr. Paul, I often couldn't fathom his purposes."

"Though all the children of God, we are different from the Chinese." The Jesuit's delight in disputation was aroused. "Our essential natures are different. It is a miracle that we understand each other as well as we do."

"In all respects, Father Adam?"

"No. The Universal Truth can sometimes bridge the chasm. I am convinced by faith that all Chinese will some day, at the Lord's pleasure, acknowledge the Only True Doctrine. I am also convinced that they will some day, again at the Lord's pleasure, adopt our scientific knowledge in root as well as branch—and excel us in its practice."

"Father Adam, do you believe both propositions equally?" Francis's smile drew the sting from his question. "Do you believe with the same certainty in the salvation of the Chinese and their mastering European science?"

"Not quite, Francis, though I try." Adam Schall laughed. "It required no effort whatsoever to believe... to know... the Chinese will be converted. Else why were we here? But it requires a great effort... sometimes a stupendous effort... to believe they will master our science. However, I do so believe."

"I shall make the effort, Father," Francis promised.

"You'd better, if you're to be any use to me. Now let's go back to work."

THE principles of casting cannon, Francis soon concluded, could be described succinctly. A few pages would suffice for the lay reader interested in the mechanical arts, while the apprentice would require a fuller account. Nonetheless, the entire body of knowledge could be compressed into a short work like the *Huo-kung Chieh-yao*, literally, *A Summary of Fire Attack*.

That treatise on manufacturing cannon and using them in battle was published in Peking early in 1643. The booklet bore the impress of three hands: Francis Arrowsmith's for his command of technique, Adam Schall's for his command of expository writing, and Joseph King's for his command of the elided written language. As custom dictated, the treatise was attributed to but one author, Tang Jo-wang, which was Adam Schall's Chinese name.

The actual casting, which was both protracted and laborious, was to demand most of Francis's energy through the remainder of 1642 and the following year. For the rest, he was to train artillerymen, often close to despair despite his promise to the Jesuit. By the beginning of 1644, when even the Court Eunuchs recognized One-Eyed Li's rebellion as a threat to Peking itself, the Christians were to have produced some sixty guns, which saw hard service in the last campaigns of the Ming Dynasty. They were to use new techniques and to train artisans to replace the indolent, troublemaking Eunuchs. The only aspects that were not to alter were Father Adam Schall's Mass before each pour and the dedication of each gun to a Christian saint.

When a weapon was ready for the field, a small host of

Buddhist and Taoist monks offered sacrifices, burned incense, and intoned incantations. The barrel was then encased in red silk. Finally, Father Adam Schall blessed the gun again.

After commissioning a fourteen-hundred-pound saker (which the Portuguese called *sagre*, meaning holy), Francis questioned the Jesuit regarding the first of two matters over which he had long puzzled.

"Father Adam, how could you possibly reconcile the Divine Skein to my return? And how have you kept them from stabbing me in the back once I was here?"

"*Ja, Franz, die Vergeltungslust* war *ungeheuer gross, aber...*," Joyful at commissioning the saker and flushed with rice wine, Adam Schall replied in German. He continued in Portuguese when he saw the blank look on the Englishman's face.

"Yes, Francis, their desire for revenge *was* overwhelming. But I told the Emperor and the Black Premier I could not make cannon without your aid. We Jesuits, I told them, are amateurs. There is only one expert who speaks Chinese, only one professional artilleryman and cannon-founder who will come to Peking. I also told the Black Premier only a princely wage would draw you. He is content, since he receives half your twenty golden taels each month—the half you never see."

"Never see, Father? I didn't even know I was getting twenty gold taels." Francis gasped at the sum. "But I still don't see why the spymasters have accepted me...left me unharassed. My reports of Manchu weakness were treasonous."

"Treasonous? What is the meaning of treason in this devil's labyrinth of treachery? Nearly half the Court Eunuchs must be in the Manchus' pay."

"Half, Father Adam? So many?"

"Well, at least a quarter." The Jesuit grinned. "And more joining every day...those who are not wagering on One-Eyed Li's victory."

With that explanation Francis was for the moment content, though he suspected Adam Schall neither knew all the ramifications nor had confided all he did know. No matter was ever resolved in the Empire so simply and straightforwardly, particularly no matter involving the extravagantly devious Divine Skein. The second matter, which touched his soul's welfare as closely as the first did his physical safety, Francis reserved for another occasion.

THE field test of the first ten cannon produced by the Imperial Ordnance Works took place in mid-June 1643 between the Nankou Pass and the Ming Dynasty's Imperial Tombs. On that same parade ground, the newly commissioned Major Francis Arrowsmith had in 1630 trained China's first arquebusiers, the Battalion of God. The same Francis Arrowsmith—thirteen years older, though no higher in rank—had no time to indulge his nostalgia. Assisted by Joseph King and Adam Schall's protégé Cheng Cheng-kung, he organized the movement of several hundred workmen, half as many Court Eunuchs, and some sixty Mandarin observers. Harried by constant requests for instructions, he spared only a single glance for the tumbledown stockade where he had beaten off the attack of the brigand-rebels of One-Eyed Li, who called himself *Chuang Wang,* the Dashing King.

Adam Schall was in a high holiday mood, still chuckling at his latest victory over the Court Eunuchs. Having requested fifty thousand pounds of copper and five thousand pounds of tin, he had learned from young Cheng Cheng-kung that the Quartermaster Eunuch had requisitioned five hundred thousand pounds of copper and four hundred thousand pounds of tin in his name. Raging when he read Adam Schall's report, the Emperor had ordered the Quartermaster Eunuch beheaded and his accomplices banished to arid Kansu Province between the Northern Steppes and the ice mountains of Tibet.

After a bad beginning, the spectacular success of the gun trials further inflated Adam Schall's high spirits. The Mandarin observers stood a quarter of a mile from the gunstand, since the Eunuchs had warned the guns would surely burst. The Eunuchs' fury at Schall's quashing their embezzlement was inflamed by their envy of the Imperial favor he enjoyed and their fear that he was undercutting their own influence.

The Eunuchs reported that the first cannonball fell far short of their position. But young Cheng Cheng-kung rode with two military Mandarins to prove that the ball had actually soared far over the Eunuchs' heads. A volley from ten guns, all exceeding the expected distance, completely discredited the Eunuchs. Knowing the Emperor would be well pleased and expecting a generous Imperial contribution to the Jesuits, the priest chortled with malicious, childlike glee suitable to neither his official dignity nor his years.

"Francis, my lad, it's spectacular...fantastic. Did you see the faces of those Eunuchs? We have today proved beyond all doubts the enormous superiority of our Christian manufacturing—and our Christian guns."

"*Christian* guns, Father Adam?" Francis asked.

He was pleased by their success, but a maggot of doubt had been gnawing at his faith. He was also disconcerted by the other side of Father Johann Adam Schall von Bell, the detached, sardonic observer transformed into a roistering partisan. Nonetheless, he raised the second question that troubled him deeply.

"Father Adam, you rejoice at forging deadly weapons," Francis said. "I cannot rejoice when I think of the death these weapons will deal out. Yet I'm a soldier, and these are my tools. How can a priest of the Prince of Peace rejoice at having made those weapons?"

"Francis, sometimes I think *you* should have been the priest...or even a sober-sided Puritan preacher. You know you're a terrible killjoy, don't you?" The Jesuit's deep-set blue eyes sparkled with resentment. "Do you really think I want to do this devil's work?"

"Perhaps I am a killjoy," Francis replied stiffly. "But you seem to enjoy it thoroughly."

"Well, I do not," Adam Schall snapped. "I would rather be ten thousand miles away drinking good Rhine wine in Cologne. My proper instrument is the pen, not the cannon. I shall rejoice when I can return to the pen. But, for the moment, I have no choice."

"God granted us free will, Father." Francis's temper rose. "You are not compelled on pain of death to make cannon."

"Am I not, then? Could I just say to the Emperor: 'No thank you, Your Majesty, I have other things to do. I won't make your cannon.'? Duty commands free will."

"Duty, Father? Forgive me, but your duty is to God."

"I serve God by carrying out the duties He has assigned me...through His Own Holy Church and the Father General of the Society. I am commanded to serve the Emperor as a faithful subject—in order to propagate the True Faith in China. My duty to God and my duty to the Emperor run parallel. Christianity can take root in this highly cultured realm. Christianity can bring tens of millions of souls to salvation—and simultaneously restore the Empire's earthly glory. Do you think the Faith would fare better under rebels or barbarians?"

351

"No, Father, but..."

"But me no buts, Francis, but let me finish. By providing modern weapons, I...we...actually reduce the killing. Better a quick decisive battle than protracted agonies—the pillaging, the murder, and the rapine of One-Eyed Li and the so-called Emperor Abahai. Besides, if we didn't make the Emperor's guns, he would call in Dutch artillerymen and cannon-founders. If I refused, we...the Society of Jesus... would be expelled from the Empire for insubordination, for lèse majesté. What then of the glorious prospect of a Christian China, a Catholic China?"

"I can understand your position, Father. But I still..."

"Let me finish, Francis. I *must* carry out my task—my inescapable duty. Whether I personally—I, Johann Adam Schall von Bell of Cologne—like it or not. I, a priest of the One True God, and I, an obedient member of the Society of Jesus, *must* make guns for a pagan Emperor."

Peking

JUNE 22, 1643–DECEMBER 25, 1643

FRANCIS ARROWSMITH loathed the straw mat hanging in the reception room of the garden pavilion. Irritated rather than elevated by the Mass just concluded, he would have been delighted if the straw had caught fire from the candles still flickering in the breeze of that Sunday, June 22, 1643. The mat had been the chief prop in a farce played first by his wife Marta, then by her Aunt Candida Soo with Father Giulio di Giaccomo.

If a Jesuit and a Christian lady were left alone, scandal-mongers would draw an obvious conclusion. But the Holy Sacrament of Confession required that priest and penitent be alone, though separated by a screen, which notionally preserved their mutual anonymity. The Chinese mat replaced the European screen. Hanging in an open room rather than an enclosed confessional, it maintained the conventional fiction of anonymity. As master of the household, Francis stood at the far end of the reception chamber. Unable to hear the whispers passing through the mat, he had seen that no scandalous deed occurred.

The Jesuits found such expedients constantly necessary to preach the True Doctrine. Sometimes, Francis felt, they were too eager for the conversion of the Chinese. Was the prize they sought, he wondered, worth the sacrifices they made? If Universal Catholic Doctrine were cut to each nation's taste as a tailor fits a doublet, it would be neither universal nor catholic. Not only the Dominicans and Franciscans in the Extreme Orient but also cardinals in Rome were already muttering that the Society of Jesus had compromised far too freely in China.

Francis was host to the ill-matched guests gathered by Marta's Aunt Candida, the granddaughter of the great Dr. Paul Hsü. Candida Soo was still domineering. Her will had been unchecked since her grandfather and her husband died ten years earlier, and her eight children diverted only a portion of her energy. Nor was her officious piety sated by the hundred chapels, schools, and orphanages she supported around her native Shanghai.

Candida had decreed that groups of Christians should, regardless of their social position, meet "as brothers and sisters" every Sunday. Three women and two men of middle years sat stiffly over tea and date cakes. Though the women wore gowns as rich as any Mandarin's lady's, they obviously came from well-to-do merchant families. The men's robes were cut from beige stuff, rather than vermilion or aquamarine silk. Francis never learned their names and never expected to see them again.

Marta glowed with the ripeness of her thirty years. Her matte skin had been marked neither by her endemic discontent nor her periodic quarrels with her husband. Her dark eyes were untroubled, and no wrinkles marred the skin around them. Recalling their furious rows and their passionate reconciliations, Francis was again irritated by the passion for self-beautification that dominated his wife almost to the exclusion of all other concerns.

Seated between her mother and her great-aunt Candida, Francis's eleven-year-old daughter Maria wore their Sunday finery in miniature. High-heeled slippers peeped beneath her lime-green skirt. The red silk concealed the bandages that had compressed her feet since the age of four. Her overtunic was lustrous peach silk, and her hairpins were green-white jade. Maria's amber eyes glanced bashfully at her father, who was too often away from home. She adored the tall man with the light eyes and the high-bridged nose, and she wondered how she could draw all his love to herself. Since his return eight months earlier, she no longer hid her yellow-white hair beneath a scarf. In her world only two persons had hair so gloriously distinctive: herself and the man she called *Diehdieh,* Papa.

Francis's fond glance altered to quizzical amusement when he looked at Candida Soo. Next to Marta and Maria, she was closest to him among all Chinese and, perhaps, all mankind. His aunt by marriage, she was also his niece because of his adoption by her grandfather. Punctilious as well as possessive, Candida called him uncle, though she was his own age. She felt their twofold relationship required her to guide him through the labyrinths of Chinese society.

Candida's faith was written on her face. Her high forehead was unlined, and her large eyes were serene. Though time had sharpened her long nose and pouched the sallow skin beneath her pointed chin, her piety did not disdain rouging her cheeks and lips. Swatches bought from peasant women filled out her thinning locks in a fashionably rolled and knotted coiffure.

"*Shu-shu, ching chin...*" Senior to Marta in the family hierarchy, Canadida spoke as the hostess. "Uncle, this Sunday please read from your Holy Bible to welcome our new friends."

Francis opened the leather-bound Vulgate. Peking Christians envied his Latin Bible, since they possessed no full Chinese translation. Before reading Saint Paul's Epistle to the Galatians, Francis eyed his former adjutant, Simon Wu. He was forced to tolerate the stocky man wearing the scarlet robe and the crouched leopard of a full colonel who, he suspected, had been his wife's lover.

His hair graying, Simon Wu was more formidable than he had been a decade earlier. His manner was wholly assured; his narrow eyes cool behind his tortoiseshell spectacles; while the red patches flaring on his cheekbones revealed his autocratic temper. As the chief liaison officer between the Secret Police and the military, he held great power. One did not trifle with him, Candida had warned. He could not be excluded simply because he had betrayed his host to the Divine Skein ten years earlier.

"There is neither Jew nor Greek, and there is neither slave nor free!" Francis freely rendered Saint Paul's Epistle into Chinese. "Nor is there either male or female. For you are all one in Christ Jesus.... Amen. That is the word of the Lord."

"Thanks be to God!" The congregation's response made Francis feel he had usurped a priest's prerogatives.

"I remember when my grandfather came across that passage. He didn't completely agree about females." Though her hands were decorously clasped in her blue-silk lap, Candida laughed. "In the name of the Lord and in memory of the revered Dr. Paul Hsü, I bid you all welcome. We are all children of the Lord God and we are all one in Christ Jesus—whether we be great ministers or humble artisans."

"You are too gracious, Lady Candida." The stout man of some fifty years wearing the cotton gown of a respectable shopkeeper spoke as if by right for all the guests. "You entertain us unworthy humble folk too lavishly. But the Lord will bless you for it. We *are* all his children, all equal, whether high or low."

Francis was amused by the reply that blended conventional Chinese humility and new Christian individualism. A social inferior had pleaded his unworthiness in one breath and asserted his equality in the next. Christianity, it appeared, had already changed China—or some Chinese—more than he realized.

Behind his mildly comical manner, the snubnosed commoner was entirely self-possessed. The brushmaker John Yao, who had moved his business from Nanking to Peking a decade earlier, was highly respected by lay Christians, but he was sometimes a trial to their priests. Both his courage and his faith were beyond question, but not his prudence. He had, Francis knew, years ago twice demanded martyrdom from a Vice-Minister of Rites who viciously persecuted Christians.

John Yao's courage had passed into the folklore of the Christian community. The pale artisan of twenty-three was highly regarded in the year 1616. Because he made writing brushes for the scholar-officials—as had his ancestors for generations—he was touched with the Mandarins' prestige. His fervor was regarded even by his pagan neighbors as a sign of Divine Grace.

When the Jesuit Fathers warned the Christians of Nanking to brace themselves for persecution, John Yao believed they exhorted to righteous strife rather than spiritual preparation. He accordingly made four large banners inscribed with the bold declaration: "I am John of the Yao family, the brushmakers who came originally from Wusih. The True Word of the Crucified God has been revealed to me. I am ready to die for the Only True Faith."

Putting on his best robe, John Yao marched to the office

of the Vice-Minister of Rites. Each time that champion of Confucian orthodoxy slid open his oiled-paper window, he saw the rotund figure beneath the yellow banners—and heard John Yao demand punishment for his Faith, which he would never renounce.

"A somewhat excessive zeal for martyrdom," commented John Yao's Jesuit pastor, smiling in spite of himself. He sent a message instructing his parishioner to return home.

"The inception of a Christian rebellion, but let him be," the Vice-Minister observed to his amanuensis. "Add to my dispatch the intelligence that the rebels are now marching through the streets of Nanking beneath their own banner, preaching their seditious doctrines to all, and inciting revolt."

Since all Chinese loved a spectacle, a crowd gathered. Besides, the Vice-Minister was not beloved; many men were delighted to see John Yao taunt his guards. Goaded by his audience, the would-be martyr shouted louder. He planted two banners beside the brass-studded doors of the Vice-Minister's office and twirled two more in the air like a juggler. The yellow banners gyrated wildly, one moment attacking each other, the next embracing tenderly.

"Go it!" the crowd shouted. "Go it hard! A place in your Hell for the Vice-Minister."

"Look at the banners now!" an idler cried. "They're making love. What a lusty God is John Yao's!"

John Yao leveled his banners like spears and charged the sentries, lifting his knees in the martial prancing of a warrior in a play-with-music. Finally, an angry officer of the guard arrested him, but an amused magistrate told him to return home and tend to his brush making.

"Add to my dispatch," the Vice-Minister of Rites ordered, "that the magistrates were compelled to detain a rebel who created an intolerable breach of public order. So bold have the Christians already grown!"

Later that day, the police reluctantly carried out the Vice-Minister's orders to arrest the two Jesuit Fathers remaining in Nanking. A crowd gathered to shout good-humored taunts.

"Does it take ten of you to arrest two bonzes? A hundred, no doubt, to guard a fierce fishwife."

"You . . . you Spiritual Fathers, why don't you use your secret weapons?"

"They're not allowed to," piped a young maidservant. "Not

even with me. Their God doesn't permit the Spiritual Fathers to use their weapons."

"Maybe that's why they're secret," laughed an older woman.

The priests' half-smiles froze when they saw John Yao's yellow banners leading a procession. The Christians chanted in time to the waving banners: "Release our priests! Condemn the Vice-Minister!"

"Exactly what do you want?" a police officer demanded.

"To die a Christian, shedding my blood for Christ," John Yao replied.

The exasperated police bound the brushmaker's hands and threw a noose around his neck. But his passion for martyrdom was again frustrated. Determined to avoid further provocation, a magistrate let him off with a lecture. Though never again so dramatically, the brushmaker had staunchly maintained the morale of the Christian community since that day.

The minutely snubbed nose of the young woman seated beside John Yao twenty-seven years later proclaimed their relationship as unmistakably as did her round face with prominent cheekbones like twin hearts. Mildly comical in John Yao, those features were delightful in his daughter.

The mauve sash that secured her tunic of russet cotton over a long tan skirt was the only silk she wore. Her slippers of scarlet cotton were markedly larger than Marta's or Candida's. Those ladies had whispered in horror that the girl called Yao Mei-ling, who was already eighteen, would never possess the tiny golden lilies that were the caste mark of upper-class femininity. Her fainthearted father had not permitted her mother to bind her feet until she was ten.

The Yaos were, after all, yeomen rather than grandees like Francis's Chinese family. They were the same breed as his English family—the salt of the earth and the pillars of Holy Church.

Francis had felt instinctive kinship with the Yaos even before he met them, when Marta sniffed: "And then there'll be the Yaos. John Yao you know of...the so-called hero of Nanking. His daughter is called Mei-ling. It's a common name....Beautiful Tinkling, indeed. The priests call her Margaret."

"It's a solid name," Francis had answered. "Maggie's a good country name."

"Call her what you will," Marta had replied. "She's really of no consequence, you'll find."

358

Francis had thereupon resolved to like both Yaos greatly. His resolution was reinforced by Maggie's unassuming manner and her unclouded gaiety. He liked her father's straightforwardness, so different from the deviousness of the Mandarin class. He particularly liked Maggie's piquant demeanor, even when her eyes laughed at his solemn reading from Saint Paul.

"We should have our own Chinese Bible to read whenever we wish." The brushmaker was eloquent in his excitement. "Especially because there are so few priests."

"Even in Europe, Master John Yao, few Christians have their own Bibles," Francis interjected. "Most depend on their priests."

"Quite properly, too," Candida insisted. "We are not qualified to understand the Lord's Wisdom directly. We need the priests to teach us the One Truth!"

"*Soo Fu-jen, ni chih-tao.*" John Yao would not yield. "Do you know, Madame Soo, that some priests disagree with other priests?"

"Impossible," Candida said complacently. "How could they?"

"Francis, what do you say to that?" Marta was almost submissive when she appealed to her husband; a European *must* understand religious questions. "Is it true?"

"I'm afraid it is true." Francis was torn between his duty to the Mission and his duty to the truth that might scandalize the Chinese converts. "Priests are only men, you know, and all men are fallible. They sometimes disagree."

"See there!" John Yao exclaimed. "In Nanking years ago I met some priests who were not Jesuits. They called themselves after Saint Francis of the Animals. And they disagreed with the Jesuits on many things."

"How so?" Simon Wu pounced. "Can you tell us exactly?"

"For one thing, over what name to call the Supreme Being in Chinese." Having defied ministers and magistrates, John Yao was not intimidated by a colonel. "Some wish to call Him *Shang-ti,* the Emperor Above, while others favor *Tien-chu,* the Lord of Heaven, as did Father Matthew Ricci. Still others prefer *Dei-yah-sze,* the Latin name for the Supreme Being."

"How can priests disagree and quarrel...just like Mandarins or Court Eunuchs?" Candida shook her head in bewilderment. "Then Europeans, even priests, are not better than we are, but..."

"Do you know the biggest question raised by those priests

of Saint Francis of the Animals?" John Yao interrupted. "The biggest question of all for Chinese Christians?"

"And what may that be, Master Yao?" Colonel Simon Wu was relentlessly inquisitorial and remorselessly patronizing.

"Whether we commit sacrilege when we burn incense and bow before our ancestral tablets. Also, whether a Christian Mandarin may properly pay homage to Confucius."

"If he didn't," Simon Wu observed dryly, "he wouldn't be a Mandarin for long."

"That's the dilemma, isn't it, Major Arrowmaker?" John Yao asked.

"That question is already called the Rites Controversy." Francis was reluctantly drawn into the prickly discussion. "The Franciscans object, but..."

"And what do *you* say, Arrowmaker?" Simon Wu asked.

"It is not for me to say, but for you. Do you worship your ancestors and Confucius...adore them as divinities?"

"Well, I...you, too, Arrowmaker...*must* pay homage to Confucius as well as our ancestors," Simon Wu pondered. "The Dynasty requires us to if we hold office. But I do not, I think, worship my ancestors and Confucius...or adore them, as I do the Lord of Heaven. It's quite different."

"What, Francis, do the other priests say about the Jesuits?" Candida was fascinated by the human interplay. "What is all the trouble about?"

"It's just human, Candida," Francis replied. "The Franciscans and the Dominicans are jealous of the Jesuits. They want to come to China in their coarse habits...with shaven heads and smooth chins like bonzes. They want to preach directly to the common people, ignoring the Mandarins. Yet they hardly speak—much less read—Chinese. They denounce the Jesuits for adopting Chinese manners and dress...for studying the Officals' Language and the Confucian Classics."

"What else could the Jesuits do?" Candida was perplexed. "If they weren't as cultivated...as learned...as Mandarins, they would not be allowed to live in the Empire. Besides, how many Chinese would become Christians if they could not pay homage to their ancestors and Confucius?"

"Candida is right." Marta had made up her mind. "The Franciscans act as if Christ's religion were European first and Christian second. Why should we do all things as Europeans do them?"

"*Fu-jen-men, wo kan-pu-kan...*" Speaking for the first time, Maggie Yao modestly addressed herself to the women.

"Ladies, may I humbly suggest we Chinese should change a little? Otherwise, a Christian wouldn't be different from a pagan."

"A little, of course." Candida was impatient. "But not by becoming un-Chinese. We must be *Chinese* Christians...not mock-Europeans."

"All this has wandered far from my point about priests disagreeing." John Yao asserted his authority. "But, Major Arrowmaker, what else do those jealous priests say about our Jesuits? We must be wary of their errors."

"Must I say, then?" Francis asked of them all, but mostly of himself. "Well, the Fathers in Europe are accused of being more Jesuit than Catholic, in China more Chinese than Christian, Mandarins rather than priests. Their critics charge that the Jesuits are seduced by worldly honors and by worldly power. Finally, the critics denounce the Jesuits' devotion to worldly science...from astronomy to ordnance. The Franciscans demand the Jesuits only preach...say they need less learning and more faith, less subtlety and more devotion."

"Those other priests sound like barbarians who hate learning," John Yao mused. "Major Arrowmaker, could you condescend to visit me? I should like to talk further, but would not impose on your hospitality."

"We are always pleased to see you here, Master John Yao, but I should like to visit you."

Francis Arrowsmith received a less welcome invitation as his visitors departed.

"I think, Arrowmaker, it would be well if you called upon me," Simon Wu said. "We have things to discuss...practical matters, not theological persiflage."

ON the afternoon of the third day after Holy Mass in the garden pavilion, Francis Arrowsmith dismissed his litter-bearers and set out on foot to find the shop-house of John Yao on the Street of Literary Implements. Even in his thoughts, the constant dialogue between his outward self and his inner self, he called the day *hsing-chi san,* the third of the week, rather than Wednesday or *Quarta-feira.* Rather than the English of his schooldays or the Portuguese of his young manhood, he used Chinese almost exclusively. Like the Jesuits, he had become habituated to the Chinese tongue as well as to Chinese customs.

But the Franciscans and Dominicans apparently assumed

that all heathens must understand Portuguese or Spanish spoken slowly and distinctly. Laughing aloud at the thought of brown-cowled Franciscan friars preaching eloquently in Spanish or Portuguese to mystified Chinese, Francis dodged a woven-cane litter carried between two horses.

Why was it necessary on the paved streets of the Northern Capital, he wondered, to use two horses and two drovers to transport one man? Surely a one-horse cart seating four would be more sensible.

If he asked, he knew, he would be told: "We've always done it that way. Why change?" He had once suggested to a wheelwright that the cumbersome carts of the countryside might roll more smoothly and more rapidly if their flat beds were mounted on leather springs. "What does it matter?" the craftsman had replied. "After all, only peasants and pigs rid in those carts. The gentry have their fine litters."

The first landmark John Yao had described was a thatched roof with a long pole flying red-white-and-green streamers. That wine flag was the sign of a tavern. Although it was not quite four in the afternoon, every bench was full beside the tables that protruded into the street under a matting canopy. The bearded proprietor sat behind a counter, complacently raking in the coppers flung down by sweating waiters.

Francis was startled by his excitement when he saw the square street-gate beside the tavern. Pink-flowered clematis clinging to its weathered red bricks, the old gate was charming but hardly so memorable as to evoke such poignant delight. Nonetheless, passing through the gate, he thrilled to the wonder of discovery he had constantly felt when he first came to Peking. The noisy alley crammed with pedestrians was much like any other alley in the city, but his pulse leaped.

Anticipation was succeeded by a sense of homecoming when he found John Yao's house by the ebony cross above the open shopfront. Clerks attended customers at counters set in the alley to display writing brushes, inksticks, and inkstones. John Yao sat on a stool inside the shop fitting sable bristles to a bamboo shaft. Beside him, Margaret Yao frowned in concentration over the same task.

"Ni tze-chi hui kan...," John Yao said expansively. "You see male and female are equal here—as Saint Paul preached. Welcome to my poor hovel, Major Arrowmaker."

Francis could not afterward remember what they discussed that first day, beyond the brushmaker's explicit questions regarding Holy Church. Nor could he, a month later, completely understand why he kept returning to the modest dwelling on the Street of Literary Implements. It must be, he felt, his feeling of belonging, associating with his own kind of people, simple, direct, and devout. He never felt totally at home with the worldly Mandarin class, not even his own family. With the Yaos he had no need for either self-serving pretense or self-protective caution.

Francis was genially avuncular with Maggie Yao, the only child of an indulgent father who had not remarried after her mother's death four years earlier. Unlike the febrile daughters of the rich, she reminded Francis of an impulsive and candid European eighteen-year-old. Her spontaneous humor and her good-mannered freeness accorded with Francis's conception of a well-bred English girl. Chaperoned by her maid, Maggie shopped in open markets and watched strolling players on the streets. When he accompanied them, he saw that her movements were little hampered by her late-bound feet. But he felt protective when she took his arm.

Francis was soon an intimate of the Yao household. Both father and daughter called him simply Arrowmaker, and he relaxed with them as he could with no one else. Even John Yao's fervently fundamentalist Catholicism was a relief from the sophistical complexities of converts of the Mandarin class. Blessedly, Marta did not object to his finding relief from the growing tensions of Peking with the Yaos, though Maria complained of his frequent absence.

FRANCIS ignored Colonel Simon Wu's invitation. If the Colonel was merely toying with him, it would soon be forgotten. Otherwise it would be peremptorily renewed. By mid-August, he believed his former adjutant had forgotten his whim.

But he returned from the Imperial Ordnance Works late in the afternoon of Thursday, August 16, 1643 to find a foot-square red card propped on the low table in the reception chamber.

"What's this?" he asked unnecessarily of Marta, who was sipping green tea and cracking melon seeds between her front teeth. They had not had a serious disagreement for three weeks and had even made love most satisfactorily the preceding night. The physical passion that had once bound them occasionally overcame the guarded distaste they still felt for each other.

363

"See for yourself," she replied perfunctorily. "Surely a Mandarin doesn't need a woman to read for him."

"Do stop baiting me," he replied without heat. "I only asked out of common politeness."

"Out of common politeness, I'll tell you." Marta wore a withdrawn expression, the closed face that was her response to external irritation. "Simon Wu wants you to dine with him tonight. It must be a large party. The invitation comes from the Hall of Distant Harmony."

"What is the Hall of Distant Harmony?" Francis was accustomed to last-minute summonses to all-male dinners at pretentious restaurants that obliged their patrons by sending their own printed invitation cards. "I've never heard of it."

"A most superior Flower House," Marta said primly. "I'm surprised you've never heard of it."

"Now, Marta, you know very well that I don't...unlike a Chinese husband, even some Christian Chinese husbands."

"I suppose that's true. I should, I suppose, be grateful. But I want you to start tonight."

"I assure you I won't." Francis wondered whether his wife was most trying when she stormed at him like a camel-driver's woman or when she was ostentatiously docile. "For that matter, I won't go."

"You must go. Candida and I are agreed. Better not offend Simon Wu. He has a violent temper—and he carries a grudge for years. Besides, it's a semiofficial invitation. That Hall of Distant Harmony is a government Flower House."

"And you really expect me to go?"

"I'm convinced you must go. We can't snub Simon Wu." Marta was insistent. "The Hall of Distant Harmony is top-class, even a bit above Simon's rank. It must be important, his big dinner."

"I could do without his company, but, if I must..."

"You're obliged to go. But, you know, you're not obliged to sleep with a Flower Girl."

"I won't. You know that."

"Do I indeed? But I'll have the maids draw your bath. You'll have to hurry."

THE fading orange paint was blistered and peeling, while the hinges were rust-encrusted on the gate before which Francis Arrowsmith's litterbearers set him down in the lingering summer dusk. The walls surrounding the Hall of Distant Harmony were dilapidated even for drab Peking, where the propertied shunned the outward display that attracted those twin pests, thieves and tax collectors. Unpainted for a generation, the bricks were rent with fissures and splattered with filth.

A doddering watchman creaked to his feet. Limping in ragged straw sandals, he grudgingly opened the warped doors to admit the guest.

Francis entered an enchantment of vermilion-pillared pavilions floating in a sea of crimson peonies, yellow roses, and orange azaleas. Somewhere among the gold-and-green-tiled façades an unseen musician strummed "The Ballad of the Forgotten Soldier" on an antique lute. From a distance, a lonely flautist piped a soprano reply to the deep lament. The instruments spoke to each other in a melody now broken and hesitant, then swift and passionate.

A humpbacked vermilion bridge arched the manmade brook that moated the pleasure garden. Later, winecups would float on the water in paper boats lit by small candles as patrons and ladies of skill entertained themselves with refined diversions. After competitions in playing the zither and composing verses, the vanquished would drink from those cups. At the moment, the clear surface mirrored a thicket of stunted forest-green firs, their reflection black against the pink glow of twilight.

The young woman standing on the bridge bowed deep. Her face was painted like a marionette's and a flower-brocade robe encased her from her nape to her tiny pink-satin slippers. It resembled the kimono worn by geishas in Macao, except that a pink sash replaced the wide *obi* that compressed the geishas' breasts and hips. She carried a rhinoceros-horn wine cup and a bronze wine pot with a crooked spout.

"*Huan-ying Ko-hsia lai fang-wen...*" The flower-girl's voice rose in the chant of formal speech. "Welcome, Your Excellency. You honor our poor hovel with your radiance. Will you condescend to come with me after you have sullied your lips with our bitter brew?"

Francis took the cup she offered between cupped palms. Faintly yellow-tinged, the wine dissolved softly on his tongue.

Following the courtesan along a twisting corridor lined by sliding doors, he heard the tinkling of bells, the bass reverberation of men's voices, and the contralto chimes of women's laughter. Occasionally the passage broke free of the buildings to wind under a peaked wooden roof through groves of blue-white hydrangeas hemmed by red-feathered dahlias. The courtesan halted in front of a door covered with gold paper over a diamond lattice. She slipped to her knees and slid the door open.

The room was so sparsely furnished that Francis felt he had stepped out of the gaudy Ming era. A scroll depicting an ethereal dancer in the simple costume of the Han Dynasty hung in a niche lined with lustrous ivory paper embossed with silver arabesques. The eighteen-hundred-year-old dancer whirled above a translucent bowl of the Sung Dynasty, only half a millennium past. A single purple aster floated on the clear water.

Only a ceiling lamp glowed in the pink-gold twilight filtering through the latticed-paper window. In the circle of light stood a circular table of polished briarwood, whose swirling black-and-brown grain reflected a pewter wine pot.

Simon Wu sat beside the table on a rosewood stool. Moistened with wine, the stubby forefinger of his right hand traced an aimless pattern on the shining wood, and his left hand held the bamboo stem of a tobacco pipe. His light summer robe of beige pongee was, like Francis's own, devoid of ornamentation except for the black-silk sash that matched its shawl collar.

"Welcome, Arrowmaker," Simon Wu said casually. "Welcome to the Tang Dynasty. How do you like going back a millennium?"

"I trust you are well, Simon. But I don't take your meaning."

"You don't? Just look at the ladies' gowns...straight out of the Tang. And also the furnishing. You never see anything so simple nowadays. Not outside the Hall of Distant Harmony."

Francis had not noticed the second courtesan, who stood beside the table. Her dress looked more European than Chinese, albeit of a mode centuries old. Her kaftan of sheer amethyst silk hung from a wide pleated yoke, which left her neck and collarbones bare. Its shimmering folds fell to the scarlet-silk slippers that encased her golden lilies, and her triangular sleeves hung to her knees. A wimple of the same color fell from her pillbox hat to cover her hair.

"I see what you mean, Simon." Francis seated himself on the single vacant stool. "But why so eager to escape from the present?"

"Wouldn't you? Wouldn't we all? My glasses and your cannon are the only modern things I'd miss if I could go back to the Tang. And, of course, my pipe. We can, at least, smoke again."

One of the stranger phenomena of Peking was the ban on smoking tobacco the Emperor had imposed a year earlier—and as arbitrarily lifted ten months later. The Emperor had prohibited tobacco neither because of its costliness nor because it was debilitating like the opium he enjoyed—as had his father and his grandfather. He had, rather, dreamed that Peking was ablaze and had awakened to command that none of his subjects might enjoy *hsiang-yen*, fragrant smoke. Yenching, meaning the Capital of Yen, was an alternate name for Peking, originally the chief city of the feudal state of Yen. *Shao yen*, burning tobacco, therefore, sounded like *shao yen*, burning Peking, and the Emperor feared that omen.

"That was pure superstition, prohibiting tobacco." Francis tossed out the provocative remark while stuffing his own pipe with golden leaf. "Rankest superstition!"

"You could say that," his host agreed amiably. "Rank superstition."

Francis knew then his former Adjutant felt himself invulnerable because he was upon the business of the Divine Skein. He would otherwise not have permitted an observation verging upon lèse majesté to pass without a refutation that would, as surely as Francis's words, be reported to the Secret Police by the attendant Flower Girls.

"We are agreed on that, at least. But why have you brought me here?" Francis retained the initiative. "I had the impression it was to be a large party. Quite plainly, it is not."

"No, just you and me, Arrowmaker. More companionable that way."

"Why this sudden fondness for my company, Simon?"

"Just for old time's sake. It has been a long time, hasn't it?"

"We can agree on that, too. But do tell me why you crave my company."

"Can't we leave it till later, Arrowmaker? After we've enjoyed the food and the wine...after the ladies of skill have entertained us with their singing and their dancing. There's no hurry. We have all night...till tomorrow morning, if you choose."

"I'd rather not, Simon. I'd much rather we got through with business right now. I couldn't enjoy myself otherwise."

"Well, if you insist..." The Colonel was startled by the barbarian's bald approach. He waggled his fingers to command the Flower Girls to withdraw.

"Now, Arrowmaker, we can talk freely," Simon Wu said when the young women had shut the sliding door behind them. "It's about you and the...ah...Skein, the Divine Skein. You must pardon my abruptness, but I understand you barbar...ah...you esteemed Western ocean people prefer directness."

"We do, though not invariably. But in this case, certainly." Francis puffed out smoke to hide his smile at Simon Wu's clumsy retreat from the word *barbarian*. "But what is on your mind?"

"Bringing you back to the Skein. We miss your special knowledge."

"You're joking, of course," Francis replied. "The Black Premier likes me not at all. He certainly didn't like my reports from Mukden, did he?"

"Perhaps...but things change. We have need of your talents now."

"And all is forgiven? My deceiving you regarding Manchu power? That's hard to believe."

"As I said, things change. Perhaps there is nothing to forgive. What might have been bad seven years ago can be seen in an entirely different light today. It might even be good today."

"What *are* you saying, Simon? I lack your Chinese subtlety, you know."

"I shall be as obvious as black ideograms on white paper. We are, above all, interested in four things: Manchus, Jesuits, cannon, and rebels. Only with the last can you not help us. As for the other three, you know as much as anyone under Heaven...and can learn even more. We need you—and will pay well."

"You can be direct, can't you, Simon?" Francis sparred.

"As you wished, Arrowmaker!" Simon Wu replied. "Do have some more wine."

"Are you betting on a Manchu victory?" Francis thrust out the question. "How else excuse my reports from Mukden?"

Simon Wu removed his tortoiseshell spectacles and held them at arm's length. With a silk kerchief he deliberately wiped away the mist the warm wine and the humidity had deposited on his thick lenses.

"Well, Simon, what of it?" Francis prodded. "One *could*

say...ah...not wholly accurate reports of their weakness helped the Manchus. Are you wagering on their victory?"

Simon Wu smiled, but the pink splotches on his cheek-bones flared crimson. He expelled blue smoke before replying with calculated candor: "We don't entirely rule it out, I must admit. Let's say that we take all possibilities into account.... And that is a definite possibility."

"How much?" Francis asked brusquely. "Exactly what am I worth to you?"

"Well...let me think," the spymaster drawled. "For a good doubled agent, twenty taels would be high but not excessive. For a tripled agent like yourself, say thirty taels every month. What do you say to thirty taels?"

"I'm afraid I can't decide without knowing what you expect of me."

"We'll get to that later. But take the rest of the evening to make up your mind—even if you're not spending the night."

"That won't be long enough. I'll need a week...at least a week."

"I don't see why. But all right, as long as you come back to me. I won't send any more invitations..."

"That's understood, Simon."

"And do remember, Arrowmaker!" The Secret Service Colonel relished his melodramatic warning. "Some others are not as well disposed to you as I am."

COLONEL SIMON WU neither sent any more invitations nor appeared in the garden pavilion, though four weeks trickled through the greedy fingers of time like glass beads. The gentle warmth of August gave way to the crisp chill of September, and Francis Arrowsmith had still not made up his mind whether he wished—or was compelled—to join the Divine Skein again. Against his revulsion from espionage he weighed prudence—and the lavish reward.

Since he owed true allegiance to neither the Ming nor the Manchus, he was free to choose the most advantageous course. Nor did his affection for the people of Peking deter him from a free choice. Having virtually despaired of the reigning Dynasty, most Mandarins of the Northern Capital were considering their personal interests. The foreign new-comer was hardly different in his opportunism from men whose families had for centuries faithfully served the Ming Dynasty.

A countercurrent did flow, but weakly. Detached because he gave no hostages to fortune, Adam Schall pointed out that a surprising number of Mandarins were committed—even to the death—to the Dynasty. They were not the sycophants who had enriched themselves by toadying to the Emperor, but the persistent critics who had suffered Imperial disfavor and severe punishment for their frankness.

"The question is which will perish first, those loyalists or their Dynasty," the Jesuit had added. "However, most Mandarins...and almost all Eunuchs...are behaving normally. They are concerned solely with their own survival and their own enrichment. Most Chinese are now deciding whom they will betray—and for what price. A pity we cannot do the same!"

Unlike the Jesuits, Francis was bound by no inviolable vows. He refused to make up his mind because, he finally realized, he preferred not to choose between odious alternatives. Having for more than a decade been tossed by forces beyond his control, he preferred to abandon himself to fate rather than make a fatal choice. Moreover, Joseph King, who usually advocated decisive action, was little help, having reverted to the fatalism of his ancestors.

"The only possible course is Taoist *wu-wei*," Joseph King observed. "*Wu-wei* means inaction, deliberate inaction, not flabbiness of will. No man can see through the veil of the future. Only the Lord God Himself knows whether the Manchus or One-Eyed Li will triumph—or, against all likelihood, the Ming will survive. The only thing to do is to do nothing."

"Watchful waiting, in short," Francis summed up.

"If you like. But I prefer determined inaction."

Supine submissiveness, as it would appear to a European, was thus elevated to bold policy by Chinese philosophy. Francis was half-convinced by Joseph King's equivocal counsel that he had actually made a choice rather than rejected any choice.

By surrendering his will to fate, Francis attained a paradoxical peace. The darts Marta hurled at his self-esteem no longer struck home. Even she was less aggressive. Astonished by his early return from the Hall of Distant Harmony, she accepted the compromises necessary to live together—since it was necessary that they live together. Admitted for once to his thoughts, she had agreed that *wu-wei*, deliberate inaction, was the only possible action.

Like their neighbors, Francis and Marta grasped avidly at pleasure. All Peking knew it might soon be deprived of all pleasure. The wealthy and powerful lived as if trapped on the slopes of a smoking volcano by a flood on the plains below. They could not avert nemesis, but they could enjoy themselves in the time that remained to them.

Perhaps because it had less to lose, one group strove to preserve both its lives and its property. Merchants and artisans sold off not only their stocks, but their ancestral treasures. Curio shops and pawnbrokers overflowed with the jades, porcelains, bronzes, scroll paintings, and jewelry hoarded by successive prudent generations. Their owners were turning their heirlooms into portable wealth—gold, silver, and gems to carry on their inevitable flight.

Francis was moved by the city's reckless mood to a passion for the ceramic funerary statuettes of the Tang Dynasty, particularly its exquisite figures of horses, elephants, and camels. He spent his taels freely, returning with new acquisitions almost every day.

Marta derided his premonition of disaster. It was still intellectually inconceivable to her—and to almost the entire Mandarin class—that the Ming stood in mortal peril. Some Mandarins felt an era that had endured three centuries was coming to its end, but they ignored their instincts. Marta and her Aunt Candida grudgingly acknowledged that Francis's forebodings might be valid. The worst that could happen, they nonetheless maintained, was the Ming's replacement by another Chinese dynasty that would soon restore order. That possible dynasty must employ the indispensable Mandarins. The Manchus the ladies dismissed as a congeries of dull barbarian tribes who could never conquer the Empire. In the thrice-unlikely event of the Manchus' prevailing, they, too, would require the Mandarinate to administer a Confucian state.

Marta disdained to join Francis in "looting the treasures of the past." But she neither restrained his acquisitive passion nor objected to Maggie Yao's accompanying him to the curio shops. Sensibly, she made light of his adolescent infatuation with "that pleasant though common child." She was confident that the brushmaker's daughter threatened neither her preeminent place in Francis's household nor whatever place she occupied in his heart. In the old days, her husband might, at the worst, have made the Yao girl his concubine. As a Christian, he could of course take no concubines.

"Perhaps a pity," Candida observed enigmatically. "She might quell the beast in his heart."

With Marta's implicit consent, Francis set out with Maggie Yao and her maid on the early afternoon of Wednesday, September 10, 1643, for the avenue in the Southwestern District called Liu-li Chang, the Porcelain Works. The Imperial Tile Factory on that avenue had made roof tiles for the Forbidden City when the Ming moved the capital to Peking in the fifteenth century. Liu-li Chang had subsequently become a thoroughfare of bookstores and curio shops. Francis had heard that a Tang statuette of an Imperial elephant was available at a shop called the Old Treasury on the Street of the Temple of Extreme Longevity off Liu-li Chang. When he set out for the Yaos', his conscience was easy. Marta had emphatically refused to join him "hunting elephants in the Southwestern District."

Even if his luck were out, he should at least find the trappings of a live Imperial elephant, the hammered brass rings and plaques set with semiprecious stones. The Court Eunuchs had become extremely bold—perhaps desperate. They were selling off minor objets d'art that were unmistakably the property of the Reigning House.

Maggie Yao and her maidservant rode in a rented litter with its orange curtains drawn. The bearers hooted shrill warnings before swinging sharply left off Liu-li Chang into the Street of the Temple of Extreme Longevity. Two years earlier, excavation for a new sewer had uncovered a tablet bearing the inscription *Ta Chin Yen Shou Sze*—the Temple of Extreme Longevity of the Great Gold Dynasty. Under that dynastic title, the Manchus' ancestors had ruled North China in the twelfth century.

Temple Street was crammed with commoners in holiday dress, while bands of Taoist and Buddhist bonzes clashed cymbals and intoned passages from their sacred books. Before plunging into the human maelstrom, Francis signaled the litterbearers to halt and lifted the side curtain to let Maggie Yao see the scene.

"What is the occasion?" He was convinced that Maggie, who was Peking-reared, must know every mood of the city.

"Only some pagan festival...nothing to us." Maggie's devout Christianity had bred scorn for the older religions. "Nothing to bother us...And I do want to see your elephant."

"I'm not sure it's quite safe." Distrusting the Peking mob, Francis was dubious.

"Of course it is safe, Arrowmaker," Maggie replied impatiently. "There's nothing to worry about."

The bearers lifted the litter again. Hooting their demands for a clear path, they thrust into the tide of holidaymakers.

The crowd was good-natured, though slow to make way. Men and boys shouted ribald speculation on the identity—and the purposes—of the ladies in the litter. Their wit drew appreciative titters from servant-girls and bondmaids in sleazy cotton skirts dyed blush-pink and bottle-green. Cheap perfumes mingled with sour sweat and camphor fumes from infrequently worn finery. The sunlight glistened on the pates of Taoist monks, transforming into black pits the twelve ritual scars burned into every bald skull. The sweat trickling from Buddhist monks beating drums and shaking tambourines left damp patches on their saffron robes.

Halfway down a tortuous *hutung* off Temple Street, the Old Treasury's signboard displayed a bold black *shang* ideogram, the symbol of the pawnbroker, who was often a curio dealer and a banker as well. The three strokes clustered at the top of that ideogram fascinated Francis, recalling the three golden globes of Lombard pawnbroker-bankers. The lower part of the *shang* ideogram was a mouth within a square open at the bottom.

"First the pawnbrokers invite you to enter through the open door," Peking's wits joked. "Then the mouth devours you."

Unable to penetrate the *hutung*, the bearers set the women down. Francis glanced uneasily at the crowd pressing around the fragile woven-straw litter and said, "Too many people here. Shouldn't we go back?"

"Arrowmaker, you are edgy today," Maggie laughed. "Of course there's no danger."

Francis sheepishly decided not to oppose his alien apprehensions to the certainty of a native. After elbowing through the throng toward the hanging sign, he was startled to find heavy boards covering the windows and an enormous padlock in the cast-iron hasp that secured the door. Despite his disappointment, he congratulated himself on his insight. Since shops normally closed only for the Lunar New Year celebration, an extraordinary holiday must have induced the Old Treasury to shut its doors to business.

Hundreds of voices began chanting rhythmically, that incantation presumably the climax of the ritual. He stiffened when he understood their words.

"*Ta-tao Chi-tu Tien-chu!*" the chant swelled louder. "Overthrow the Christian Lord of Heaven! Destroy the false God Above! Expel the ocean devils!"

Francis flattened himself against the padlocked door of the Old Treasury. He felt isolated and vulnerable among millions of enemies in an alien continent. He was defenseless against the mob's malice. He would be borne down in an instant if the orchestrated hatred welling around turned into violence.

He stood frozen for some forty seconds before remembering Maggie Yao in the frail litter amid the throng fifty yards away. His fear transformed into anger, he thrust into the crowd. To his astonishment, it parted before him. Two burly coolies wearing black trousers beneath white tunics lowered their bamboo carrying-poles and stepped aside.

"*Ta-sha yang-kueirh!*" They bobbed quick bows of respect while shouting: "Kill the ocean devils!"

Francis's heart beat wildly against its imprisoning ribs, and his throat closed. He had never been in greater peril on any battlefield, but his will drove him through the throng.

"*Pieh ta yang-kueirh!*" A voice rose over the mass chant. "Do not beat the foreign devil! Do not attack him!"

Francis saw the mob on the corner boiling around the straw litter. Coolies' carrying-poles rose and fell like flails above bobbing heads. He thrust aside two sweating Buddhist monks whose writhing lips were shouting shrilly.

"*Ta-ta Han-chien!*" the mob was crying with terrible insistence. "Beat the traitors. Beat dead the ocean devil's paramour! Kill the Christian whores!"

The crowd began to disperse. When he reached the corner seconds later, the *hutung* and Temple Street were deserted. The litterbearers having fled, Maggie's maid leaned dazed against a gray-brick wall. The afternoon sun lit the empty thoroughfare like the remorseless light of conscience.

Shredded yellow straw, all that remained of the litter, was sprinkled like macabre confetti on the cobblestones. Maggie Yao lay amid the chaff, her right arm wrenched at an impossible angle behind her head. Her tan-pongee overtunic and her cream-silk shift had been torn, baring her small breasts. A shallow wound across her rib cage dripped blood. Her skirts were flung back to reveal her slender legs in pitiful nakedness. One pink-satin slipper lay away on the gritty cobblestones, but the white-silk half-stocking concealing her maimed foot was unstained. Sunlight gilded her mute mouth and her closed eyelids.

Francis gazed unspeaking at the squad of constables who appeared at the junction of Temple Street and Liu-li Chang. Formidable in blue tunics and white-cotton trousers tucked into black-leather boots, they flourished their useless long-swords.

"FIVE days have passed....And she's no better." Francis clutched Marta's hand. "Her arm is broken...and six ribs. They'll heal, the doctors say. But they fear she'll never speak again...nor understand a single word."

"You can only pray." Marta stared into the goldfish pool in the inner courtyard, her hand limp in his. "Pray for a miracle."

"And who will hear my prayers, Marta? I am unworthy to pray. God has turned His face away from me."

"You can only pray," she repeated flatly. "Only a miracle can cure her."

"It was miracle enough that she lived...though so desperately hurt."

"I can do nothing more than advise you to pray." Marta could not offer him the babble of consolation he sought. She could abide Francis stricken and mild better than Francis triumphant and domineering. But it was his own fault, the mock-comic tragedy.

"It was my fault...my fault alone!" Unaware of her coldness, Francis spoke Marta's thought. "I ignored Simon Wu's warning...his obvious threat. I stood paralyzed with fear for God knows how long, cowering in the doorway. If I'd come back to her a minute earlier, all might have been different."

"God moves in mysterious ways, Francis."

"To punish an innocent girl for my...my sins!"

"It cannot be helped now!" Marta finally comforted him abstractedly. "All you can do is pray."

For a week, while he could still hope Maggie Yao would recover, Francis was bowed by grief. When all hope was gone, he appeared to others to cast off that burden. But he still condemned himself in silence and refused the comfort of Confession. He endured the castigation of his conscience as if to atone by that suffering for his negligence and his cow-

375

ardice. His only respite from self-reproach came when he reproached himself to Marta.

Francis knew he could do nothing for the eighteen-year-old girl he had destroyed. His guilt was intensified when Simon Wu drew him aside after Holy Mass two weeks later.

"Arrowmaker, I did warn you," the secret police Colonel chided. "It was not my doing...this pointless violence. But I did warn you that you had many enemies. You *must* join us now so that I can protect you...and your family...from your enemies within the Divine Skein as well as outside it."

His self-confidence shattered, Francis saw no alternative. If he did not rejoin the Secret Service, the next attack could strike Marta or his daughter Maria. Despite his revulsion from the lewd game of espionage, he awaited Simon Wu's instructions.

Only later could Francis reconstruct the sequence of events dispassionately. Only later did he wonder how Simon Wu, who must have instigated the attack, had known where he would be that September afternoon. No one but Marta had known he was going to the Old Treasury. No watching spy could have reported their destination in time for Simon Wu to stage-manage the mass demonstration. Only his wife had known his destination well ahead of time.

Communication between Francis and Marta was, as ever, strained. Simon Wu had consistently lied to Marta about offering Francis opportunities to send her word from Mukden. Wounded pride had prevented their discussing why not writing had become the fixed habit of them both after his escape to Macao. Nor had he ever charged her with his suspicion of her relations with Simon Wu.

Francis could not ask Marta whether she had betrayed him again. The accusation was too monstrous. He never put the question—and never gave her the opportunity to refute his suspicions.

Peking

THE FIRST DAY OF THE SEVENTEENTH YEAR OF THE CHUNG CHEN EMPEROR
FEBRUARY 14, 1644

"I'VE been looking around and thinking." Joseph King was heavily casual.

"When did you ever stop looking around and thinking?" Francis Arrowsmith's hand nervously stroked the crimson tassels of his sword hilt, but his manner was jocular. "What now? A catastrophe or only a disaster?"

"Neither...just yet." The secretary lowered his voice, though the throngs were intent on their own enjoyment. On Lunar New Year's Day even his tall, yellow-haired master attracted no stares. "But, tell me, do you believe in curses?"

"Curses? Yes, of course, though I've never seen a curse work. But so many men have it's impossible not to believe them!"

"I didn't till recently, though there are innumerable tales of Chinese families being cursed." Joseph King's high, narrow forehead wrinkled in unaccustomed perplexity, and his lean hand stroked his long upper lip. "But I felt that had nothing to do with us. Our Christian God, I thought, had done away with curses."

"Moses was cursed after striking the stone that gave water.

For his lack of faith, the Lord cursed Moses... and he never entered the Promised Land."

"I am thinking of a stronger curse—the Children of Israel condemned to wander forty years in the desert for sacrilege. Punishment inflicted on an entire people, not just their leaders, for gross transgressions."

"You're not talking about the Mandate of Heaven, by any chance?"

"I suppose, Arrowmaker, I am talking about the Mandate of Heaven." Joseph smiled tensely, and his crinkled cheeks accentuated his resemblance to an intelligent Pekingese. "It's a heathen concept, but nonetheless, I..."

"I don't see any real difference, Joseph." Francis was amused that his secretary, like his wife, should consider him a font of theological wisdom because he happened to be a European Christian who had had his schooling from the Jesuits. "The Dynasty and the people cursed for their sins. The Mandate of Heaven... the Lord's favor... withdrawn so that the rulers perish and the people suffer greatly. It is possible, but what..."

A small boy collided with Francis, and he clutched Joseph's shoulder. The tide of spectators was flowing through the narrow avenue between the Imperial Ministries toward the Gate of Heaven's Sanction, that massive red-brick edifice crowned by a three-tiered gold-tiled roof. His head well above the throng, Francis could see the four shining arches and the cavalrymen in silver armor before that splendid portico of the Imperial City. Their helmets a string of scarlet beads, infantrymen in blue tunics with green facings leveled a fence of pikes around the Gate.

Though the piled clouds were black-fringed in the north, the air was still crisp. The month of February was notorious in Peking for fitful sunshine followed by storms, but the extreme cold was constant. At the beginning of the Double Hour of the Snake, nine in the morning by European reckoning, this winter's day was no exception. The wind howling south from the Gate of Heaven's Sanction carried the threat of hail in its teeth on February 14, 1644, the first day of the first month of the seventeenth year of the reign of the Chung Chen Emperor of the Great Ming Dynasty.

Beneath his formal blue robe, Francis was protected by a long-gown padded with raw silk. Joseph might see an evil omen in his wearing for the first time on such a day the insignia of a lieutenant colonel, a snarling bear, which had

378

replaced the lynx of a major. But he could not reject his promotion, though it was, he assumed, contrived by Simon Wu. Joseph was obviously ill at ease in the green robe of a lieutenant with a rhinoceros recumbent in its square of rank.

The Imperial Court had summoned Lieutenant Colonel Hsü Shih-jen, the Arrowmaker, and his secretary, Lieutenant King Chou-sze, to the mass audience within the Purple Forbidden City that would simultaneously welcome the Lunar New Year and celebrate the Emperor's birthday a few days earlier. Once each year the Emperor summoned his Ministers and his Senior Mandarins to the Forbidden City, where he lived amid Court Eunuchs and Palace Women. An invitation to a middle-ranking military Mandarin was not merely an overwhelming honor, but an inexorable command. Some Mandarins of the First Grade passed a lifetime of service unrequited by an audience with the Emperor.

Francis surmised that he had been summoned to call attention to the powerful weapons the Great Ming Dynasty was acquiring by employing European servants. Perhaps those green-bronze cannon in their red-silk jackets could restore the resolution of the dispirited regime. Rulers as well as subjects had finally become aware that the Manchus hovered in the north like hawks, while in the west the rebel One-Eyed Li rolled up a string of victories ever closer to the Northern Capital.

Whatever hopes were placed in the cannonmakers, the Court Eunuchs' Office of Palace Protocol had not overlooked the ocean barbarian's low status. No more than an artisan who held rank as a Mandarin at the convenience of the Monarch, he was commanded to approach on foot "owing to the press of the palanquins of Mandarins of Exalted Standing." No greater number had ever attended an Imperial Audience during the present reign than were summoned to the formal celebration of the Sacred Birthday. It was the Emperor's thirty-third by European reckoning, but his thirty-fifth by Chinese reckoning, since he was accounted a year old at his birth on February 6, 1611, and two years old on the following Lunar New Year's Day.

"You spoke of curses and the Mandate of Heaven, Joseph," Francis reminded his secretary when the vermilion seal on their invitation had passed them through the infantrymen into the square before the Gate of Heaven's Sanction. "What in particular is troubling you?"

"So I was," Joseph King recollected. "Was the pestilence

379

that struck the Eunuchs' rival Imperial Cannon Foundry a curse...a judgment of the Lord God?"

"Perhaps, Joseph, though Father Adam forbade such talk."

"And none survived, though Father Adam tended them lovingly. Was that not God's judgment on the half-men for usurping the task of making cannon God has laid upon the Society of Jesus and ourselves?"

"It could well be. But it was a small matter, hardly withdrawal of the Mandate of Heaven."

"Of course, there are greater signs—like widespread natural catastrophes: floods and pestilences scourging entire provinces. And constant defeats by the Manchus and the rebels. But I have seen an unmistakable sign that the Dynasty's folly has lost it the Mandate of Heaven. The Ming is cursed...irrevocably doomed."

Francis curbed a caustic retort to the melodramatic expression of a judgment he had reached a year earlier. Joseph King was not merely indulging in histrionics. Despite his family's disgrace, he was a loyal subject of the Dynasty, and he reported with anguish his loss of all hope for the Ming.

"Arrowmaker, the Ming seeks its own destruction." Joseph's whisper was portentous. "The Court is so foolish and avaricious that it flung away its best hope of defeating the Manchus."

"We all know that, my dear Joseph. Only it's hard for you to accept."

"Arrowmaker, I'm not talking generally, but of one specific act. After the Manchus seized twenty-six cities in one day a year and a half ago, you'll remember, the Emperor...even the Court Eunuchs...were truly alarmed. The Council of Ministers planned a devastating counterattack. Since we still possess the finest shipyards and the best seamen in the world, the Ministers proposed to attack the Manchu stronghold in Liaotung from the sea. Herdsmen and cavalrymen cannot oppose us on the water."

"A brilliant conception, Joseph. Given enough cannon, it could still crush the Manchus. What has happened?"

"The proposal was specific: Build some three thousand oceangoing warships armed with bombards, culverins, falconets, and flamethrowers. And then..."

"The entire Empire does not possess enough green-bronze cannon to equip one hundred ships," Francis objected. "As for casting them..."

"At sea, at close quarters, iron cannon would do, as they

would for bombarding shore targets. For only six million silver taels the fleet could have been launched, armed, and manned. Striking across the Pohai Straits, the Grand Fleet could have landed an overwhelming force in the Manchu heartland."

"Where would the artillerymen have come from, Joseph? With all our efforts, Schall and I have trained only a few hundred—and cast less than one hundred cannon."

"By concentrating *all* our resources, Arrowmaker. You still do not appreciate the immensity and the power of this Empire. We could have done it...and afterward dealt with the rebels at our leisure."

"What became of this brilliant plan?"

"What else?" The secretary's shrug caricatured his own despair. "As you know, the Grand Fleet was never launched."

"Just so?" Francis asked. "Simply didn't work out?"

"Not simply. Failure was, as always complicated. After the Emperor approved the plan, the Ministers could not find a paltry six million silver taels. The Imperial Treasury could have supplied the sum fifty times over, but the Emperor declared he would not fritter away the patrimony of his Sacred Ancestors. Fritter away! He ordered the Ministers to raise the money by taxes and loans. But no one could collect new taxes. The people were already groaning..."

"And loans?"

"The honor of offering a loan was assigned to the rice and textile merchants of South China. But the southern merchants stalled, knowing there was no hope in this world...or the next...of ever getting their money back. They finally subscribed a token fifty thousand taels."

"Then, no money and no ships, I suppose." Francis wanted the tale finished before they passed through the Gate of Heaven's Sanction.

"Nonetheless, the Ministers persisted...assigned a master shipbuilder. Knowing he'd lose his head if he failed, the shipbuilder sought material and carpenters in Kwangtung and Fukien provinces in the south."

"And then?"

"Naturally, the Southerners again refused. They hardly felt touched—much less threatened—by troubles in the north."

"So the Ministers gave it up?"

"Not quite. One brilliant Mandarin asked: Why not convert some of our tens of thousands of river and canal boats

381

into blue-water warships? The shipbuilder argued the only similarity between oceangoing and rivergoing craft was they both floated on water. Everything else was different from masts to keels, from rigging to rudders. I still believe he was inventing difficulties to save his neck."

"That was the end of the Grand Fleet, was it?" Francis pressed, since a cavalry lieutenant stood among the crush of Mandarins, examining their vermilion-stamped invitations.

"Not quite, Arrowmaker. The Grand Fleet was officially scuttled without ever being launched. The Mandarins of South China presented a Humble Memorial to the Dragon Throne, declaring: 'The Manchus have now withdrawn from North China. The seas are calm, and all disturbances under Heaven have been brought into order. There is, therefore, no need to build the Grand Fleet.'"

"And that was that?"

"The Emperor took up his writing brush, dipped it in vermilion ink, and on the memorial wrote the single ideogram: *Shih...* Approved."

"So simply?" Francis asked.

"Rather than persist against difficulties, with nine brush-strokes the Emperor destroyed all hope of saving the Dynasty. And we must now render homage to that Emperor. It is not easy to display reverent loyalty when the Mandate of Heaven has been withdrawn."

The cavalry lieutenant who kept the Gate of Heaven's Sanction glanced at the tall Englishman and waved them through. Sometimes it was an advantage to be conspicuous.

An avenue a quarter-mile long ran from the Gate of Heaven's Sanction to the Meridian Gate of the Forbidden City. A hundred yards wide, its oblong paving blocks were hidden by the scarlet, blue, and green robes of civil and military Mandarins. Francis looked over their heads at the Imperial Ordnance Works where eight sakers swathed in red silk were attended by a guard of honor from the Battalion of God. The furnaces were sheltered by mat-shed structures thrown together when the autumn rains began. The Court Eunuchs' Office of Palace Works had rejected Father Adam Schall's plea for a permanent structure with the curt notation: *It will be necessary to maintain the factory for the manufacture of Red Jacket Cannon for only the brief time until the Manchus and the rebels have been crushed.*

The Imperial Elephant Herd was housed in stone-built stables, though attempts to use them in battle had failed spectacularly two centuries earlier. The ponderous beasts displayed the might and the wealth of the Great Ming Dynasty. The power of the guns was, however, only evident on the battlefield. Francis considered the twelve elephants an expensive indulgence, their drain on the dwindling resources greater because their Eunuch keepers drew funds sufficient to feed a hundred pachyderms.

Nonetheless, the elephants lined up beside the broad avenue were an imposing spectacle. The bridles of gilded leather under their corrugated trunks were secured around their domed heads by massive bronze clasps studded with semi-precious stones. Their foreheads and their trunks were painted with silver-and-green arabesques, while their long-lashed eyes were outlined with white. They were caparisoned in ground-sweeping coats striped in the Buddhist colors: yellow, blue, orange, white, and green.

Like the Great Bright Dynasty, Francis concluded sourly, the elephants were magnificent but useless. They were all show and no performance. Above all, their time had passed.

A curtain of orange light shimmered before the vermilion façade of the Meridian Gate, and a monotonous chant rose from hundreds of monks in saffron and yellow robes. While they intoned the sinified Sanskrit of the sacred Buddhist Sutras, blue tails drifted from the incense sticks in their hands into the clear air beneath the dappled clouds. Their wooden clappers clacked like old bones rattling.

All the Mandarins halted, their gaudy robes shining like the chips of a broken kaleidoscope. Peering over their black-horsehair caps, Francis saw the monks form an orange semicircle like a fan opening around the Meridian Gate. A pyre of logs soaked with pitch and oil was heaped in the center of that semicircle.

A pale young monk sat on the pyre, his eyes closed in contemplation. Despite the cold, he had shrugged his robe off his shoulders, and the saffron folds hung from the rope tied around his waist. His bloodless-white torso was so emaciated that his ribs stood out like an iron cage covered with hoarfrost. His head was an elongated skull covered with almost transparent parchment. His square jaw and flat cheekbones framed slablike teeth bared in a grin of agony. His shaved scalp was pitted with the twelve sacred brands, and his purple lips twitched as they recited the mantra: "*Pradjna Paramita Dharani!*"

"So it's going forward, after all." Joseph King surrepti-

383

tiously crossed himself. "I hoped someone would think better of it."

"Why not?" Francis replied. "The poor damned heathen believes he'll instantly become a Boddhisattva in Nirvana."

"No saint enters Paradise so easily, Arrowmaker. Nor, certainly, by self-destruction."

"Does he really want to die, Joseph? Or is he drugged?"

"No need for drugs. He is drunk on anticipation. By cremating himself to celebrate the Emperor's birthday, he believes he will ensure great good fortune for the Empire. And, as you say, he attains Nirvana in a single jump, rather than enduring untold millennia of painful reincarnations."

"He'll more likely ensure damnation for a nation that rejoices in suicide," Francis objected. "Did I tell you who carried the Emperor's gift to the Lungfu Monastery to recompense the sacrifice?"

"No, though I can guess."

"You'd guess right, my friend." Francis lowered his voice, though no Mandarin present could understand his Portuguese. "My esteemed superior, the Senior Court Eunuch Tsao Chun-hua...the Black Premier. Though he commands the Divine Skein and its Flamboyant Cloaks, he was not too grand to personally draw three thousand taels from the Imperial Treasury for the Abbot of Lungfu."

"Arrowmaker, the Abbot received just one thousand taels. The rest, obviously, stuck to the palm of the Black Premier. The Abbot's receipt naturally read three thousand taels. He is not so foolish as to risk the wrath of the Flamboyant Cloaks. Anyway, he'll take a hundred thousand taels in donations after this *auto da fé*."

A single sigh rose from some hundred motionless Mandarins, an unaware inhalation through lips stilled by awe. At first only a ghostly flicker of heat, yellow-and-scarlet flames leaped seconds later. After half a minute, a ring of fire soared from the heaped faggots. The Mandarins watched entranced.

The emaciated monk still sat unmoving. Only the writhing of his lips showed that life remained within his chalky body. The fire-tongues lapped at the saffron robes that flared around his hips and legs like an inverted hibiscus, and the ice-white figure quivered. An instant later the robe was ablaze.

The young monk rose, frantically flapping his hands against his tortured body. The chanting of three hundred monks swelled higher, and three hundred wooden clappers

384

clacked incessantly. But still the spectators heard the inhumanly shrill screams from the martyr's purple lips. The tongue protruding between his square teeth was a deeper crimson in the crimson cavern of his mouth, a bloody wound splitting his parchment face.

The spectators stood unmoving around the pyre for three minutes so protracted the sun might have risen and set twice in that time. The gorgeous throng of middle-aged men was motionless except for the unaware grimaces that distorted features plump with self-indulgence. Incredulous horror twisted some faces. On others, lewd fascination rose to lascivious delight.

Shriller and shriller, the monk's shrieks of agony pierced the chanting and the clacking to lance taut eardrums with pain. The flames from his robe licked the martyr's protruding ribs, and his chalky skin glowed rose red. He stooped and scrabbled frantically among the burning faggots with hands that were charred black as they groped toward impossible escape. For half a minute the monk writhed among the greedy flames. Then he collapsed into the fire and lay still.

A canopy of silence covered the broad avenue, its invisible bulk muffling the monks' chanting. Finally a portly Mandarin wearing the white crane of the First Grade asked of the empty air: "Is that all?"

Smoke billowed black and greasy from the flames, and a new odor overbore the musty staleness of winter robes. Prevailing even over the dry sweetness of incense, the smell of roasting flesh tickled the spectators' nostrils. The Senior Mandarin's tongue stealthily licked his lips, and Francis's mouth watered. The oily pall exuded the succulent odor of suckling pig turning over glowing coals.

"He was only eighteen, this monk," Joseph King said tonelessly. "They always tell the martyr they've left an escape hatch at his feet, in case he decides not to die. They always tell him that, but they never do."

"It is said to bring great good fortune, this blasphemy?" Francis asked dully.

"So it is said. But to me it seems... I think it brings damnation."

A bell tolled on the Meridian Gate, and several hundred dignified Mandarins scurried like tardy schoolboys through the postern doors flanking the main entrance. Francis Arrowsmith and Joseph King passed through last. Behind them, twelve elephants trumpeted on command, and the pair before the Meridian Gate crossed their trunks to bar late arrivals.

A feathery drizzle obscured the clarity that separated the earth from the clouds, and the morning was gunmetal gray. The Mandarins crossed the moat called the Golden Stream on five white-marble footbridges symbolizing the five cardinal Confucian virtues. The white foam on the water was flecked with black soot from the pyre, and the luster of the Imperial-yellow tiles on the surrounding palaces was dulled. Its splendor dimmed by the grimy overcast, the Forbidden City admitted the apprehensive Mandarins.

Officers of the Imperial Guard in silver armor draped with rainbow cloaks flanked two broad flights of marble steps. Still as mist-wreathed statues, they presented ceremonial pikes chased with gold. Behind that elite bodyguard, whom the Emperor did not fully trust, stood four rows of standard-bearers, their array tarnished by the mist twining their banners.

Sooty droplets trickled down the scarlet flagpoles. On blue-bordered pennants Imperial Dragons clutched at clouds with five-clawed feet, while tigers were rampant in fields of flowers on red-bordered pennants. Yaks' tails were suspended beneath miniature green canopies on poles surmounted by golden dragons' heads, and spear-tipped poles flaunted leopards' tails.

The array was barbaric to a European eye. The banners exhibited no coats of arms, only the animals that symbolized the innumerable aspects of the Emperor's universal power. In the Empire where resided all the Englishman's hopes of earthly happiness—and almost all his hopes of salvation thereafter—no feudal lords held virtual sovereignty over broad estates. No bishops ruled their own temporal fiefs.

In China, there was only the Monarch. All power, all mercy, all justice, and all favor flowed only from him. The Emperor, who was also the Supreme Pontiff, stood alone, ruling all men's lives. The Empire was a vast tent supported by a single great pole from which all the subsidiary poles and guys depended. When that central pole trembled, the tremendous fabric shook violently; should it break, the entire Empire would collapse.

If the Emperor was wise, industrious, and benevolent, all men were secure and happy. If the Emperor was foolish, indolent, or vicious, all men were threatened by misery. Since the Chung Chen Emperor was weak, corrupt, and avaricious, all China was desolate.

Francis took his place among the military Mandarins. Only Joseph King was below him among the field marshals, the generals, and the brigadiers summoned to the Imperial Audience. The civil Mandarins occupied the place of honor opposite the marble stairs. Between a red-lacquered railing and five gold-encrusted filigree panels, the gilded Imperial Throne stood at the head of the stairs under a frieze of dragons carved on upcurved marble eaves.

A Court Eunuch wearing a scarlet robe stalked self-importantly out of the shadows behind the Dragon Throne into the watery light under the marble eaves. His plump, beardless face was blandly superior, and his dimpled hands clutched a thirteen-foot whip of braided yellow silk. He raised the red-lacquered staff topped by a golden dragon's head and cracked the whip three times with contemptuous ease. Letting its serpentine length trail down the marble steps, the Eunuch uttered a falsetto bellow: "His Imperial Majesty has arrived!"

The Chung Chen Emperor stepped from a golden-curtained palanquin borne by twelve Eunuchs. Sixteen Mandarins flanked by Senior Eunuchs walked backward before him, bowing at each step. Muttering irritably to himself, the Emperor ascended to the Golden Throne and seated himself behind a low desk draped with yellow silk embossed with dragons. His crown was two dragons so cunningly intertwined that the shining flaps extending from his temples were their wings. His stiff yellow-silk robe was embroidered with two larger dragons in the same attitude. The golden glow from his throne and his garments lit the air around the Emperor.

Within that aura, his face appeared haggard and pallid. His thin-lipped mouth was set petulantly above his sparse beard, and deep lines engrossed his sallow cheeks. His mustaches hung lank below his hooked nose, and his bloodshot eyes roved suspiciously over the faces of his Ministers and his Senior Mandarins.

The Emperors who were his ancestors had held audience attended by nine Eunuchs. Five had held four-tiered yellow-silk umbrellas aloft on long staffs. The remaining four had wielded round yellow-silk fans three feet in diameter.

Because of his unremitting suspicion, only three Eunuchs attended the Chung Chen Emperor. A single umbrella protected him from the mist, while the two fans crossed behind him concealed steel shields in their heads and swords in their staffs. Terror of assassination rarely left the Emperor's thoughts, and he did not completely trust even the three Eunuchs he had known from boyhood. But he had to trust someone, since his constant fear was not relieved by the humiliating knowledge that the Dynasty's enemies preferred to keep his ineptitude alive.

The Grand Eunuch stepped from the darkness behind the Dragon Throne to declaim: "Let all his officials now pay homage to His Imperial Majesty!"

Several hundred middle-aged Mandarins fell to their knees. "Bow heads!" the Grand Eunuch commanded, and they touched their foreheads to the marble flagstones. "Raise heads!" he shouted, and the Mandarins straightened their backs but remained on their knees. Responding to the Grand Eunuch's commands, they twice again touched their foreheads to the flagstones in self-abnegation.

Francis Arrowsmith rose to his feet when the Grand Eunuch called out: "All stand!" He knew he must repeat the humiliating obeisance twice again before he had rendered full homage to the godling on the Dragon Throne. When he rose the third time at the Grand Eunuch's command, he was sweating with suppressed anger.

His anger flared high when a gorgeously attired Eunuch kneeled before the Throne to read the Address of Loyal Reverence and Profound Congratulation on the Imperial Birthday. He was lean for a castrato, and his voice was a light baritone, rather than half-falsetto. Rage rose red behind Francis's eyeballs, and a chill of revulsion shook him.

The Mandarins gazed at the flagstones rather than look at the kneeling Eunuch. Staring straight ahead, Francis saw the stealthy sidewise glances of detestation they cast at the kneeling figure. All normal men hated and feared Tsao Chunhua, the Black Premier, the master of the Secret Police and the Flamboyant Cloaks.

All heads turned as the Black Premier completed his florid address. A distant drum rumbled. The tumult outside the walls impiously intruded upon the respectful silence within the Forbidden City.

"What is that filthy row?" The Emperor looked up querulously from the scroll listing the Mandarins summoned to the Audience. "Did We not order the petitioners from Shantung Province dispersed? Did We not command you to placate

388

them and send them away? Let the responsible Minister advance and explain himself!"

The elderly Minister of Finance fell prone before the Dragon Throne. When he raised his hand to speak, his winged horsehair hat tumbled from his bald head.

"Your Imperial Majesty, I most abjectly beg forgiveness." The Minister's voice quavered. "I ordered the delegations dispersed. I promised them succor in the Imperial Name. But they have lingered. Now, I surmise, they beat the Drum of Appeal to the Emperor's Justice—as is their right. I have erred grievously. I have failed in my office, and I request that His Imperial Majesty punish me as I deserve."

"Nonsense, Minister!" the Emperor replied. "This once, you have not erred. The people are Our children, and We are ever sensitive to their needs, as the Sages advise. We know that Shantung had been struck by famine and plagues of locusts, as well as the depredations of the Manchus and sundry malignant rebels, now all supressed, thanks to Heaven's Benevolence..."

"... and Your Majesty's wise and puissant leadership." The Minister interjected the expected flattery.

"We have not always met the superlative standards of Our Imperial Ancestors. Our performance is deficient in many respects, just as We Ourself are deficient in virtue." The Emperor responded with the fulsome self-deprecation Confucian etiquette demanded even of him. "But We have not been wholly deficient toward the suffering of Our loyal subjects in Shantung. Have not they been told that all taxes will be remitted for a period of three years, as We directed?"

"They have, Your Imperial Majesty. But they still cry out, pleading that the Imperial Purse be opened to relieve their suffering."

"Then they are unreasonable, unworthy—and disloyal in their importuning. Drive them from the gates with whips and clubs, lest their excessive lamentations mar this auspicious occasion, blessed by the supreme sacrifice of Our devoted subject, the monk of the Lungfu Monastery." The Emperor's petulant irritation mocked the sonorous formulas of the Language of Ceremony required by an Imperial Audience. "However, it is not meet to reimpose the taxes. We never forswear our promises, though only Heaven Above knows where We are to obtain the funds necessary for the defense of Our Realm."

A Eunuch of the Third Grade and a Brigadier of Infantry

slipped away to carry the Emperor's command to the guards outside the Imperial City. His subjects would be scourged from the gates where they pleaded for His Imperial Majesty's help. The Emperor's decision to relieve them of taxes for three years was a very small mercy. Entire counties had been so stripped by tax collectors, brigands, Manchus, and natural disasters that they could not pay their taxes if they wished to. Besides, no man in North China could say with confidence that he—or the Emperor—would be alive three years thence.

"Where, oh where, are We to obtain the funds to make Our Empire, the Sacred Realm of Our Ancestors, secure against the depredations of the evil rebels and the impious barbarians?" To the Mandarins the orotund Language of Ceremony endowed the Emperor's lament with splendid poignancy. To Francis Arrowsmith, who understood only one word in three, it was the windy rhetoric of a hack actor mumming a king in a provincial playhouse. "Cannot one among Our Loyal Ministers tell Us where the essential treasure can be found?"

"Your Imperial Majesty, may I make a humble suggestion?" The Minister of Finance, still prone before the Dragon Throne, offered desperate counsel. "The people of the Northern Capital are fervently loyal to Your Imperial Majesty. Let each householder and each place of business pay now a tax of a year's rent in advance. Whether merchants or artisans, theaters or houses of pleasure, shops or factories, let everyone pay. Later, they can be rewarded by remission of other taxes."

The Emperor listened intently to the Minister's improvisation. Initially hopeful, then briefly downcast at the banal advice, he was finally avid for the new revenue. He spoke a single syllable: "*Shih!* . . . Approved!"

The assembled Mandarins knew their master had already plucked Peking's citizens to the skin. They knew the common people could give little more and the rich would give no more. But the bland respect on their faces honored the Imperial Birthday Audience—and frustrated the agents of the Secret Police, who, even within the Forbidden City, watched avidly for the faint play of expression to reveal treacherous thoughts.

The Senior Mandarins of the Great Ming Dynasty wondered if the Emperor actually believed he could avert catastrophe by screwing a few silver taels from a master carpenter or a brothel mistress and a handful of coppers from his journeyman or her ladies of skill. But the Emperor revealed his true mind to no one, not to his trusted Eunuchs—not even, perhaps, to himself. His policies altered so rapidly that no Minister, however astute, could discern any constant purpose.

The Mandarins were forbidden to compose "impious writings" or to think "disloyal thoughts," forbidden the slightest implication that the Emperor might not be all-wise and all-virtuous. Nonetheless, the Mandarins, like the commonalty, gossiped behind doors locked against the swarm of spies deployed by the Senior Court Eunuch Tsao Chun-hua, the Black Premier.

In the hive of rumor that was Peking all men from Mandarins to streetsweepers knew the Emperor had recently suffered three great financial setbacks. The first was the matter of the Imperial Princes. The second was the defiance of the Marquess of Wuching. The third was the compliance of the Earl of Chaiting.

The Founding Emperor had three hundred years earlier commanded that neither a prime minister nor feudal lords might infringe his absolute power. His successor tolerated not only the Court Eunuchs' Black Government, but also regional magnates who exercised great power without responsibility. Successive Emperors had enfeoffed their brothers in the provinces in order to remove them from the Capital. Those princes had passed their titles and their wealth to their descendants. Scores of Imperial Princes lived in royal state throughout the Empire, holding extensive lands and receiving lavish subventions from the National Treasury. The corpulent Prince of Fu, slain by One-Eyed Li near Kaifeng in 1642, was one of those princely parasites.

When bankruptcy pressed, the Emperor had appealed to the Imperial Princes, who were his brothers, his uncles, and his cousins, to assist the Dynasty. If a dozen had opened their purses, the Grand Fleet would already have sailed to victory and the Imperial armies would have been paid for several years.

No Imperial Prince had responded with a substantial donation, though many offered impractical advice and magical amulets. The infuriated Emperor dared not press them further for fear of weakening the amity of the Imperial Family, which was the chief pillar of the Empire.

Determined to preserve the Imperial Treasures intact, he had looked closer to home. The Imperial Relations, the connections by marriage of the ruling Chu family, were also exceedingly wealthy. The wealthiest was the Marquess of Wuching, brother to the Dowager Empress, who was the widow of the grandfather of the Reigning Emperor. So rich he casually diverted a river to his private park, the Marquess owned manors around Peking and drew enormous profits from his commercial establishments in Tientsin, Shanghai, and Canton.

The Emperor sent a Court Eunuch to ask his great-uncle to donate half a million taels. The Marquess was shocked and ungiving. Bribing the Eunuch to put the Emperor off, he assembled the Imperial Relations in a united front. They were accustomed to receiving from the Emperor, not to contributing to the nation. The Eunuch went back and forth between the Forbidden City and the Marquess's palace, each time collecting further bribes.

Placards called *ta-tze pao,* big-ideogram posters, appeared on the walls of Peking. Since he paid for them, most endorsed the Marquess's "principled stand." Only a few supported the Emperor.

Still the Eunuch plied between the Forbidden City and the Marquess's palace, relaying the Emperor's increasingly urgent demands and his great-uncle's ingenious prevarications. The Eunuch collected thirty thousand silver taels for his private purse, but not a copper penny for the Ministry of War.

Finally, the Marquess displayed his belongings in the street before his palace. Placards declared that a poor nobleman had been forced to auction his heirlooms to satisfy extortionate Imperial demands. The exasperated Emperor ordered his great-uncle imprisoned, and the Marquess took the only course that could preserve his property for his heirs. His suicide was the ultimate reproach a subject could make to an unjust sovereign.

The Imperial Relations wept for the Marquess of Wuching—and rejoiced at his courage. After his great-uncle's suicide, the Emperor could not demand contributions from them without losing all dignity. But the wily Earl of Chaiting, who held the courtesy title Prince Kuei and was the father of the Reigning Empress, voluntarily sent ten thousand taels to the Forbidden City.

His father-in-law's token compliance was more bitter to the Emperor than the willful incomprehension of the Imperial Princes or the defiance of the Marquess. Behind the decorous expressions they showed the Secret Police, the citizens of Peking laughed at an Emperor who had set out to collect more than one hundred million taels—and had, in the end, collected ten thousand.

Recalling the Emperor's travails, some Senior Mandarins chuckled to themselves. Others would have wept if they could. None risked the wrath lowering behind their master's rote humility by pointing out that the common people of Peking would be enraged by new taxes when the wealthiest refused to contribute a copper penny—and were not pressed.

"Is there any other matter requiring Our attention? Would anyone else speak?" Expecting no answer, the Emperor offered the obligatory invitation to his Mandarins. "In that case..."

In the rear rank of military Mandarins, Francis Arrowsmith felt himself at a Last Judgment where the damned sat upon the Throne. When a thin, gray-haired Mandarin wearing the peacock of the Third Grade stepped from among the Civil Mandarins, he nudged his secretary inquiringly.

"Yeh Ho-li...a Junior Censor...once a student of Father Matthew Ricci," Joseph King whispered through unmoving lips, as he had learned in prison. "Almost baptized a Christian, too. But wouldn't put aside his beloved concubine. He is low in rank for a brilliant scholar of almost seventy because he's always been too outspoken."

The Mandarin Yen Ho-li prostrated himself before the Emperor, then kneeled to speak. It was his unpleasant duty as a Censor, the Chinese equivalent of a Roman Tribune of the People, to inform the Emperor of the malfeasances and mistakes of other Mandarins. It was his perilous duty as a Censor to give the Emperor an honest appraisal of the Imperial deeds.

"Your Imperial Majesty, I would make a most humble submission." The Mandarins strained to hear the old man's faint voice, hoping he would say what they dared not say. "New taxes levied upon the patient people of Peking will drive them to sullen disobedience or, worse, open resistance. With rebels and Manchus approaching the Northern Capital, it is not wise to tear out the hearts of its citizens. If the people are further oppressed, they will count one ruler as good—or as bad—as another. Scourged by new taxes, the people will see no difference between the rule of the Sacred Dynasty under the Mandate of Heaven and the sacrilegious rebels— or, even, the northern barbarians. I beg Your Imperial Majesty to rescind that command."

"You fool!" The Emperor's sallow cheeks flushed; his

sparse black beard jutted in anger; and he forgot the courtesies of the Language of Ceremony. "Explain just one thing: Where is the money to come from? Money to pay the troops, money to build new ships, and money to cast new cannon? With willing troops, a fleet of warships, and more cannon, We will prevail. But *where* is the money to come from, *where?*"

The aged Censor paled beneath the febrile fury he had provoked. Embarrassed by his Emperor's loss of self-control, he lowered his head to the paving.

"Your Imperial Majesty has, as always, unerringly touched the heart of the matter." Yen Ho-li paid out the worn coin of flattery to buy time while he sought a solution that would also placate the Emperor. "Foolish and cowardly, I had not intended to come to the crux of the matter so soon. Your Imperial Majesty has incisively cut through useless ceremony. I pray the indulgence of Your Imperial Majesty for..."

"Answer us! Immediately!" the Emperor raged, and Francis Arrowsmith heard the Lord's Prayer sigh from Joseph King's unmoving lips: *"Pater noster, qui es in caelo..."*

"So be it!" The Censor placed his head in the balance, hazarding his own life for the Dynasty's life. "Your Imperial Majesty, there is only one possible source of the vast sums the Sacred Dynasty requires. Drawing upon that ready source will, moreover, unite the common people around the Dragon Throne. I speak not only of the Imperial Princes, against whose excessive wealth I have memorialized in the past, but of the Imperial Relations as well. And they are but the beginning."

A frown knotted the Emperor's forehead, and his hands twitched on the arms of the throne. But the Censor Yen Ho-li continued.

"Tens of thousands of great landholders are in league with corrupt Mandarins to evade all taxes. Only make all those parasites pay their just taxes, Your Imperial Majesty. The bloated rich, who will not contribute voluntarily in this hour of extreme peril, must repay the wealth they have stolen from the people and from Your Imperial Majesty himself."

The Censor prostrated himself to speak his final words: "Then there will be treasure enough for all needs. Then the people, seeing justice done, will once more flock to the defense of the Empire, knowing the Emperor to be wise and just. If my words displease Your Imperial Majesty, deal with me as you wish."

The Emperor sat husbanding his rage for some time after the Censor Yen Ho-li had concluded his audacious proposal with the obligatory formula of abject subordination. The drizzle had become a steady rain. The downpour washed soot from roof tiles and soaked the Mandarins' robes. Gray drops dripped from embroidered sleeves, and felt shoes became sodden pulp. The stiff silk banners wilted, and red dye ran from the yaks' tails. But still the Emperor brooded under the marble eaves.

"And how are We to accomplish that end?" His voice was soft in perplexity. "It is improper for Us to press the Imperial Princes and the Imperial Relations as far as We have. Our Sacred Ancestors already look down in wrath at Our impious behavior toward the Imperial Family that is the state. Tell Us this, Censor!"

"Your Imperial Majesty, the people are the state—the people and the Emperor. All the rest are meaningless."

"Blasphemy! Rank blasphemy!" The Emperor's shriek released his pent rage. "Your advice is designed to destroy the Sacred Dynasty. You would bring the wrath of Heaven and Our Imperial Ancestors down upon Our head. Your advice is treachery, sheer treachery. Withdraw immediately and await Our Judgment."

The Censor Yen Ho-li sighed and abandoned hope for the Ming Dynasty, as he had already abandoned himself to his own fate. Bowing at every third step, he walked backward between the soaked ranks of civil Mandarins and military Mandarins.

"Hear me, oh Lord God," Joseph King murmured. "I beseech You to preserve the life of the virtuous Junior Censor Yen Ho-li!"

"Hold a minute!" The Emperor's shrill command halted the slight figure in the scarlet robe alone on the rain-washed marble flagstones between the bedraggled officers of the Imperial Guard and the drooping banners. "How dare you come here and slander the greatest in the Empire?"

"Your Imperial Majesty, I am not a slanderer, but a loyal subject. I am true to the responsibilities of my office as Junior Censor." The words of the Mandarin Yen Ho-li rang in the rainswept morning. "I have nothing to gain and very little to lose at my age. Accordingly, I speak the truth. I can say no more. I await whatever punishment Your Imperial Will decrees."

"This scoundrel defies the Will of Heaven by his gross

insubordination," the Emperor shrieked. "Flog him. Flog the blasphemous traitor."

Two guards dragged the Censor, his heels thumping on the flagstones, toward the Meridian Gate. The Emperor stalked to his palanquin, not waiting for the profound mass kowtow to conclude the ritual. A Senior Eunuch hastily intoned: "The Imperial Audience is at an end!"

"I'VE seen floggings before," Francis Arrowsmith brusquely told Joseph King. "We must return to our duties."

The Englishman did not dare add—even in Portuguese—that he had never seen a private soldier or a black slave flogged for so little cause. Frank devotion was obviously more pernicious than fawning treachery in the eyes of the Emperor.

Francis ratified his own emotional decision with cool logic: better the Manchus than the corrupt Ming or the vicious rebel One-Eyed Li. While the weak, sadistic Chung Chen Emperor sat on the Dragon Throne, Francis Arrowsmith could neither serve God in China nor consolidate his own fortunes. He would, therefore, look to his own welfare by rendering all possible assistance to the Manchus—through the treacherous Divine Skein. Since the Emperor had created a climate in which treason flourished, his reluctant subject Lieutenant Colonel Hsü Shih-jen, who was called the Arrowmaker, would not jibe at treason.

As Joseph and he walked through the postern door of the Meridian Gate, Francis's thoughts were fixed on the Imperial Ordnance Works a quarter of a mile distant, where stood the silent batteries whose thunders had been intended to climax the Imperial Audience. But his eyes were drawn to the preparations for the public flogging of the aged Junior Censor Yen Ho-li.

The Emperor's vengeance first deprived his victims of all dignity. The Censor lay spreadeagled face down in the mud before the west wing of the Meridian Gate, his robe slit to bare his withered buttocks and bony back. He could move only his head, since ropes tied to his ankles and wrists were pulled taut by four powerful privates of the Flamboyant Cloaks in embroidered red tunics and black trousers. Four officers and fifty soldiers wearing the same uniform encircled the wizened elder, who had been stripped for chastisement like a naughty child.

The Censor Yen Ho-li was already tormented by the affront to his physical modesty and by a Court Eunuch's presiding over his humiliation. The Black Premier Tsao Chunhua exhorted his soldiers to strike hard to prove their loyalty to the Emperor. The tableau epitomized the self-destructive madness of the Great Ming Dynasty. The half-man, whom Francis knew to be a traitor, licked his lips with salacious delight over the courageous Censor, who had proved his devotion by inviting punishment.

A heavy-bodied private lifted a red-lacquered bamboo pole and laid its butt on the Censor's pallid back. The Black Premier spoke, and an officer bellowed the command to begin the flogging. Fifty shouting soldiers echoed his words. The private raised the bamboo pole high above his head and brought it whistling down on the Censor's flabby buttocks. The spreadeagled figure twitched, and a broad crimson welt sprang up on the meager flesh. The soldier brought down the red pole each time the Black Premier's low command, relayed by an officer, was repeated by his men. After the fifth stroke, a fresh soldier took the rod to ensure that the torturer's weariness did not alleviate the victim's torment.

"You won't believe it, Arrowmaker," Joseph King said softly. "But they're actually holding back. At his age, ten good strokes would bring unconsciousness...and twenty, probably, death. That would end the entertainment too soon."

"Whatever, Joseph, I can bear no more. Let us go."

Behind him, Francis heard the soldiers' roar that signaled each stroke an instant before the bamboo's whistling descent. The heavy thud that followed sounded like a cook pounding a pork loin into tenderness. The Censor did not begin screaming until the twelfth stroke, and his cries ceased after the eighteenth.

"Passed out," Joseph King commented, his detached tone belied by the pain on his dark features. "They'll revive him and go on."

Thunder rumbled in the east, and jagged lightning split the sky over the Imperial City. The downpour from ruffled clouds became a torrent from black thunderheads. The watery light gave way to dusk at eleven in the morning, the beginning of the Double Hour of the Horse. Above the thunder, Francis heard the Censor's screams renewed as the count mounted to thirty strokes. Before the mat-shed Imperial Ordnance Works, red dye streamed from the scarlet jackets of the eight silent cannon.

THE Lord of All Under Heaven paced the bedchamber of the Palace of Absolute Purity at nine-fifteen that evening, shortly after the beginning of the Double Hour of the Dog. He wore a bed-gown of orange tribute-silk and felt slippers on his crabbed feet. Between two immense crimson pillars the scarlet curtains of the Imperial Bridal Couch were open to display a violet coverlet. The Emperor ignored the Court Eunuchs who knelt at his feet to present an open green-silk casket. He shivered despite the heat waves dancing above the charcoal braziers. Neither sleep nor the pleasure the Eunuch offered attracted the sovereign of the world's richest Empire.

Despondent and aimless, he walked down a corridor and opened the door to the Throne Room. Alone for an instant, the Emperor gazed at four blue-enameled cranes holding white tapers in their upturned beaks. Their light played feebly on the Golden Throne, and, above it, the great black plaque emblazoned with gold ideograms: CHENG TA KUANG MING: TRULY JUST AND ENLIGHTENED.

Behind that plaque, earlier emperors had placed envelopes with parchment slips sealed inside bearing the name of the heir-designate—in hope of ensuring an orderly succession unmarred by dynastic strife. When, the Emperor wondered, would it be necessary for him to choose the heir from among his three sons and to confide his choice to the Plaque of Justice and Enlightenment? Not for some time, he assured himself, since he was young and vigorous, despite occasional headaches. TRULY JUST AND ENLIGHTENED! The Emperor pondered the exhortation. *Are We truly just and enlightened? Should We have condemned the Censor Yen Ho-li to the flogging that killed him? Was it just? More important, was it wise...enlightened?*

The answer emerged, slowly at first, then, as certitude grew, decisively from his thoughts writhing like Imperial Dragons: *We were, of course, just. How could We maintain the dignity of the Throne, which is the foundation of the Sacred Empire, if We allowed subjects to berate Us as he did? And enlightened? Yes, enlightened as well. The Censor is ...was...no aged dotard. He knew the danger he ran. He was impious. He plotted to commit suicide in order to reproach Us...as did the cunning Marquess of Wuching. No. We had*

398

no other course . . . in justice or enlightenment. But where will We find the funds we need?

Believing himself content with that answer, the Emperor closed the door of the Throne Room and walked slowly toward the Bridal Chamber. Yet he was not content. The Memorials he had read that day reported new calamities in the provinces. The rebels were storming out of the west, and the Manchus were poised in the north. The Imperial Princes and the great landowners, who were the pillars of the Empire, were cracking, while Ministers and Mandarins mocked the Emperor to his face. Only the Court Eunuchs were loyal. Without their devoted services, he would be helpless. Without the Eunuchs, the Great Ming Dynasty would be doomed.

The Emperor smiled at the Eunuch messenger who knelt in the Bridal Chamber, his rain-cloak dripping on the boldly patterned Samarkand rugs that covered the cold flagstones. He ignored the Eunuch still kneeling with the green-silk casket balanced on his outstretched palms. The messenger presented a scroll so weatherbeaten it was unfit for the Imperial touch. Frowning his displeasure, the Emperor reached out his hand. The cringing messenger presented the unworthy object with both hands, then touched his forehead to the flagstones.

Relays of cavalrymen wearing rust-yellow cloaks had ridden through snow and sleet, crossing frozen rivers and ice-choked passes to carry the scroll sent by a spy from the headquarters of One-Eyed Li in Sian, six hundred miles to the southwest. The Black Premier had debated with himself, finally concluding that the risk of suppressing the message was greater than the risk of transmitting it. But he would not carry it to the Emperor himself.

Sian, 15th day of twelfth month of sixteenth year of Chung Chen, the Emperor read. *Rebel Li Tze-cheng, called One-Eyed, saturated with evil, will on first day of first month of seventeenth year proclaim himself the Yung Chang [Eternal Splendor] Emperor of Ta Shun Chao [Great Heaven-Fearing Dynasty], claiming dominion over all China—then march on Northern Capital.*

The Emperor flung down the tattered scroll. Clutching his head, he seated himself on the perfumed Bridal Bed. The iron bells on the palace eaves pealed in the wind, and his throbbing veins warned that a headache was tightening a steel band around his temples. The Emperor glanced listlessly at the two kneeling Eunuchs. One still presented the green-silk casket, which displayed rows of ivory slips, each inscribed with the name of an Imperial Concubine. The Eunuch's gaze implored the Son of Heaven to condescend to select a slip so that the ten-times fortunate lady he chose could prepare herself for his favors.

"Get out!" the Emperor muttered hoarsely. "Be gone, both of you! I want nothing tonight but quiet!"

The Eunuchs bowed from the Bridal Chamber, delighted at escaping without punishment. As the door closed, a high voice pierced the drumming of the rain and the pealing of the iron bells. The Emperor strained to understand the words through the rolling of distant thunder. Heaven, he knew, sometimes manifested its will to a worthy emperor through an otherworldly messenger.

"The Empire...is...at...peace! The Empire...is...at ...peace!" Incredulous, the Emperor made out the faint syllables and feared that Heaven mocked him. "The Empire...is...at...peace! The Empire...is...at...peace!"

A woman spoke, a human female, not a heavenly messenger. The Emperor bitterly recalled that one punishment imposed by the School for Court Ladies required the miscreant to pace from gate to gate of the Forbidden City, tolling a bell and crying out: "The Empire is at peace!"

The Emperor struck a brass gong to summon a Eunuch to silence the girl. He waited while the reverberation of the gong died in tinny dissonance. The unearthly voice intruded again into the Bridal Chamber of the Palace of Absolute Purity, and a handbell tolled a dirge.

"The Empire...is...at...peace!" The assurance rose over the drumming rain. "The Empire...is...at...peace! The Empire...is...at...peace!"

Mukden

ON that Lunar New Year's Day, February 14, 1644, three Emperors claimed to rule all the Great Empire. The Chung Chen Emperor of the Ming gave his ill-omened Audience in Peking. In Sian, One-Eyed Li was proclaimed the Yung Chang Emperor of the *Ta Shun Chao*—the Eternal Splendor of the Great Heaven-Fearing Dynasty. In Mukden, a child accepted the homage of the Manchus.

His reign-name was Shun Chih, meaning Heaven-Fearing Government, and he was not to attain his sixth birthday for another month. His Audience was shadowed by mourning for his father, the Emperor Abahai, who had died four months earlier. Yet Heaven had not only given the Manchus a new Emperor without fratricidal strife but was opening the road to Peking before them.

The Shun Chih Emperor sat erect on the Ebony Throne inlaid with mother-of-pearl, though the upturned tips of his felt boots dangled above the rungs of the Throne. But his eyes were bright within his plump golden face, and he keenly observed the Princes, Ministers, and Generals who pledged their loyalty. A miniature green velvet crown with a finial of five golden balls sat on his shaven head, and his short queue hung down the back of his miniature Imperial robe. He was a prodigy, extraordinarily advanced for his age.

The child-Emperor gravely acknowledged the homage rendered by the threefold genuflection and the ninefold touching of seamed foreheads to the Kashgar carpet before the Throne. One Prince was awkward, scrabbling to his feet without grace and pausing before bowing his head.

"Where does this man come from?" the Emperor piped to the Master of Protocol, who hovered behind the throne, fearful of childish errors in the Imperial etiquette. "He is very clumsy."

"He is of the Kalka tribe, Your Imperial Majesty," the Master of Protocol whispered into the delicate ear beneath the golden diadem. "His people only recently made submission, and he is not accustomed to the manners of the Court."

"Reward him particularly," the child-Emperor commanded. "He tries hard to do it properly. He must be a faithful subject already."

A buzz of approbation swept the Throne Hall. Princes and Ministers whispered to each in delight, sincere or affected.

"He is already a true Emperor...so young," the Chinese Grand Secretary observed to Prince Dorgon, the general who had employed Francis Arrowsmith. He was not only Commander-in-Chief of the Eight Banners, but the actual ruler as Senior Prince-Regent for his nephew. "We may expect great achievements of one who is already so sagacious so young."

"Truly he is," the Prince-Regent replied. "My duties will therefore be lighter until the blessed day when he takes the rule of the realm into his own hands."

The Grand Secretary blandly regarded the Prince-Regent, the man whose reputation for vaulting ambition was already firmly fixed. The Grand Secretary watched Dorgon under lowered eyelids as the prolonged ceremony proceeded with perfect Confucian propriety. Just before the child-Emperor was to depart, Dorgon rose from his chair at the foot of the throne.

"May I humbly beg of His Imperial Majesty," the Prince-Regent asked with ostentatious humility, "leave to discuss a matter touching the welfare of the realm?"

"You may, Prince Dorgon!" the Emperor replied without prompting from the Master of Protocol. "We are eager to hear your wisdom."

"I have a matter of some importance to put before this distinguished assembly. The King of Korea, the vassal of his Imperial Majesty, has for several years sent me presents richer than those he gives to other Princes." The Prince-Regent stood lean and hollow-cheeked before the assembly of his peers, obviously first among those nominal equals. "He wishes, he explains, to requite my clemency in sparing his consort and his children when I captured them."

The great men of the Manchus looked covertly at each other. What new assertion of Dorgon's pride, they wondered, was to be paraded before them?

"As I was bound by duty to do, I reported those gifts to his Former Imperial Majesty," Dorgon resumed. "When His Majesty ordered me to accept them, I did so. However, the realm is now under a regency until His Imperial Majesty comes of age. A Regent may permit himself no private dealings that might influence his public deeds. I therefore propose to return those gifts to the King of Korea."

The assembly sighed in relief at Dorgon's self-abnegation.

"If I were to accept such rich gifts, all our vassals would vie to please with treasures not only my humble self but the other Princes," Dorgon continued. "Since that would be pernicious, I propose that personal gifts be prohibited to all here assembled for all time."

"Wise! Wise!" The Manchu dignitaries chorused the conventional approbation. "Hear the words of the Wise Warrior the Prince-Regent!"

Dorgon sat down, smiling with ostentatious benevolence. He had, he reflected, trapped his peers, who thought he wanted more riches and more power. But he had proved that he did not—any more, they would now think, than he really wanted to be Emperor.

The Grand Secretary smiled with satisfaction. Dorgon is cunning, he reflected, more cunning than I thought. His good example will bring harmony among the Princes, rather than strife.

A bitter quarrel had erupted after the death of the Emperor Abahai. The Council of Princes had been unprepared, thinking itself years removed from a divisive debate over the succession when Abahai passed from vigorous life to death at the age of fity-two on September 21, 1643. They had wrangled for seventeen days before choosing Abahai's ninth son, the five-year-old Prince Fu Lin, who could not for some time threaten their prerogatives.

He would, they proclaimed, have been Abahai's choice—
and he was already hallowed by legend. During her pregnancy, the Empress had often been clothed by a red radiance,
which glowed "like the shadows of dragons," a Court Lady
remembered—when prompted. Just before the child's birth
on March 15, 1638, the Empress had dreamed of an apparition
that declared, "Here is the Lord who will unite the entire
world under his scepter!"

The Emperor Abahai had greeted that revelation with joy.
He had marked with equal joy the bristling tufts "quite unlike the hair of ordinary mortals" on his newborn son's head;
he had marveled at the red glow that lit the Imperial Palace
and the "wonderfully sweet fragrance that perfumed the Empress's apartments." Abahai's belief that his ninth son was
marked for a great career had subsequently been confirmed
by the child's precocity.

The Senior Princes chose the Shun Chih Emperor for his
obvious weakness rather than his potential strength. The
nomad chieftains preferred a child-Emperor and a protracted
regency to the bloody strife that could follow selection of one
of themselves. The inescapable choice as Senior Prince-Regent was Dorgon, the thirty-one-year-old half-brother of the
Emperor Abahai, who had proved himself their greatest military commander. Since Dorgon had learned to subordinate
his ambition to Abahai, the Princes hoped he would be an
even-handed Regent.

Dorgon was apparently satisfied to possess Imperial power
without the Imperial title. Under his wise leadership the
grand design of the Manchus was already unfolding. Abahai
had allowed the great fortress city of Ningyüan in Manchuria
to remain in the hands of the Ming. Dorgon was, however,
moved by bitter memories of the stronghold that had broken
his father's heart. The Founding Emperor had died late in
1627 after the Banners were thrown back from Ningyüan by
the Red Jacket Cannon of the Ming Field Marshal. Dorgon's
first major decision as Regent was to launch the Grand Army
against Ningyüan, which lay seventy-five miles northwest
of the Shan-hai Kwan, the Pass between the Mountains and
the Sea, which led through the Great Wall into China.

Dorgon first rolled up the chain of Ming-held towns that
linked Ningyüan to the Pass. During the first two weeks of
November 1643 three walled towns and, finally, Ningyüan
fell to the Manchus. The Grand Army captured seventy-four
hundred Ming soldiers and "incalculable quantities of fire-

arms, as well as cannon, horses, camels, cattle, silver, and gold."

Everywhere victorious, the Manchus slew three generals, thirty colonels, fifty junior officers, and eighty-five hundred common soldiers.

Ming power was thus swept from all Manchuria after three centuries of military occupation, Dorgon reflected with immense satisfaction on that New Year's Day. The road to Peking was open to the Eight Banners, but the Prince-Regent could wait a little while before stretching out his hand to seize the Great Empire of the Ming.

Peking

APRIL 8, 1644–MAY 8, 1644

APRIL goaded North China from its sour winter torpor. Spring freshets swelled the meandering Yellow River, and the ocher-silted waters spilled over the dikes. The golden banners of forsythia on the hills heralded the earth's reawakening. Purple crocuses put out the flag of life around the tombs of the sacred ancestors. The sun flaunted his new robe of Imperial yellow, and the spear-straight poplars unfolded their pale leaves.

When a nightingale sang again in North China, the tainted hopes of men quickened. Ministers and princes rewove their plots; generals and troopers refurbished their armor; priests and bonzes reprised their prayers. Some were as eager as youths in the first tide of manhood. Others were as weary as dotard time itself, having seen too many bleak winters and too many false springs.

Pouring out of mountain-girt Shansi Province, the Land within the Passes, the hosts of the rebel-Emperor men called One-Eyed Li were on the march to the Northern Capital of the Great Ming Dynasty. A million men followed the former post-courier who called himself Yung Chang, Eternal Splendor. Though they lacked modern firearms, his tautly disciplined troops were the most formidable in all China.

One-Eyed Li's host had crossed the Yellow River and struck northeast at the beginning of March. Pausing neither to rest nor to loot, the exultant rebels engulfed the countryside and stormed Taiyüan, the capital of Shansi Province. The old society crumbled at their touch like an oak honeycombed by termites.

In mid-March, flying columns feinted east into the Metropolitan Province of Chihli through the defile called the Ancient Pass. The rebel-Emperor led his main force north about to overwhelm the Mark of Tai, which had been a border fief protecting the capital for almost two thousand years. Hardly breaking stride to slay the Imperial Prince of Tai, the host swept south through the Great Wall to the Nankou Pass and the Valley of the Tombs, where Francis Arrowsmith had trained the Battalion of God. On April 19, 1644, the thirteenth day of the third month of the seventeenth year of the Chung Chen Emperor of the Ming, One-Eyed Li razed Changping, just eighteen miles northwest of Peking.

"THE people are calling him *wu-ge shao-ping Huang-ti,* the five-bun Emperor." Father Adam Schall disgustedly crumbled the circular breadroll topped with sesame seeds. "Our brilliant...our inspired...Emperor finally rewarded his loyal troops...hoping to keep them loyal. He could spare only twelve farthings a man. Just enough, the soldiers say, to buy five buns."

"That's not right." Marta was hotly serious. "Sesame buns are no more than two farthings, even today. Each soldier could buy six...maybe seven."

"That makes all the difference, doesn't it, my dear?" Francis chuckled at the housewifely meticulousness of the lady who might enter her own kitchen twice a month. "One more bun for each soldier...and we can hold Peking forever."

"It always comes down to money," Adam Schall ruminated. "Judas sold Our Lord for thirty pieces of silver. The Emperor bids twelve copper bits to preserve the Dynasty. And both prices somewhat low."

"Father Adam, you blaspheme!" Marta traced the sign of the cross, hoping Adam Schall's levity would not spoil what might be the last breakfast he would eat with them. "Surely, the Emperor has much more. What has become of the Imperial Treasury?"

"Still locked up in the Forbidden City," Francis answered.

"God alone knows what our fine Emperor's saving it for...perhaps his funeral."

"Dieh-dieh, ni yi-ting hui..." Maria laid down her chopsticks to speak with twelve-year-old gravity. "Papa, you can surely save Peking. You and Father Adam can destroy Bandit One-Eyed Li with your Red Jacket Cannon, can't you?"

"Mei pan-fa, hsiao-ling..." Francis replied as he would to an adult. "There's no way, my dear. If the soldiers won't fight, all the cannon in the world are useless."

"But, Papa, you can go up on the walls and shoot the cannon, can't you?" Maria's absolute faith rejected the thought that even her father might be powerless. "The way you did at Tengchou just after I was born. Ying told me how..."

"But we lost at Tengchou, Maria."

"Ying didn't tell me that...just how brave and strong you were....and you never had time to tell me." Maria shook her head in bewilderment, and her fair hair shimmered. "But, Papa, you and Father Adam *must* be able to do something."

"Oh, we can do a great deal, Maria," the Jesuit replied. "We can inspect. We can encourage and instruct. We can promise them the world. But we cannot make men fight when they don't want to fight. We must all pray. You, too, Maria."

"Meanwhile we'd better hurry, Father Adam," Francis interposed. "Let's get on with our inspection while there's something left to inspect. But it's hopeless...totally hopeless."

"My son, sometimes you're too pessimistic. The will of God will prevail!"

"Father Adam, sometimes you're a bit hypocritical," Francis riposted. "You know as well as I do...the people are resigned to Li's victory. They are apprehensive, naturally, but also relieved that the farce is finally coming to an end. The troops are on the verge of mutiny. Eunuchs and Flamboyant Cloaks guard the city walls...reinforced by those City Police who can be spared from keeping order in the streets. When the Emperor appealed to all able-bodied men to man the battlements, how many responded? A scant thousand or two."

"We can pray, Francis. Remember Dr. Paul's miracles and pray."

"I do pray, constantly. Particularly when I remember the defense is commanded by Tsao Chun-hua, the Black Premier. Perhaps the Lord God knows where his loyalty lies, but I do not. Yet you say I'm pessimistic. If I were realistic, I'd have fled with Marta and Maria."

"*Can* we leave, Francis?" Hope quickened Marta's voice. "Where can we go? When?"

"Into chaos, Marta," Francis replied. "I'm sorry...didn't mean to awaken false hope. You know there's no place to go. The entire countryside is aflame with rebellion, and in the north the Manchus..."

"We are all rushing to climb rainbows as if they were bridges to paradise, aren't we?" The Jesuit wryly recalled the traditional Chinese metaphor for desperation. "Though we're not fleeing from butterflies, but from men with bloody hands."

"Right now," Francis rejoined, "I'm afraid of even butterflies!"

"God won't let anything terrible happen to us, will He?" Maria demanded reassurance. "He couldn't.... He only punishes the wicked....And we're not wicked, are we?"

"Of course not, my dear." Marta wished she had not allowed Maria to breakfast with them. "We are not wicked, and God will not let anything terrible happen to us. Francis, Father...you're frightening the child. But I am not afraid, Maria, not really."

"Truly, your faith is great," the Jesuit said.

Adam Schall no longer jested. He would remain in Peking although all his colleagues, even the ebullient Giulio di Giaccomo, had already fled southward on the instructions of the Vice-Provincial. Adam Schall could not desert his flock. He feared the women would incur damnation by committing suicide to avoid dishonor if he were not present to dissuade them. He did not seek martyrdom, but he had forgotten how to be afraid.

"I'm delighted that you're not afraid, Marta." Francis was surprised and delighted by his wife's steadfastness. "But how can you be so sure?"

"God will look after us, as Father Adam says. Even if the rebels take Peking, it won't be so bad. They won't destroy the city or harm the people. They want to found a new dynasty, so they need the Capital. And they need the Mandarins to administer the Empire."

"Papa, I think this time you may be wrong," Maria reflected judiciously. "This time, I think, Mama is right—and you are wrong."

"We can only hope and pray, Maria." Adam Schall reserved a particular gravity for children, all of whom deserved serious consideration—as most adults did not. "Many Christians have in the past waited like us for the fury of the barbarians

409

to overwhelm them. We must pray to the Lord to turn the rebels back ... or to temper their fury."

THE Grand Army of the Manchus, the Eight Banners that were the spearhead of a people in arms, waited north of the Great Wall. Warriors sharpened their swords and drilled with their few arquebuses and cannon. Holding all the Northern Steppes in thrall, Prince-Regent Dorgon chose to remain aloof from the civil war in the Empire—and to allow the Chinese rebel hounds to pull down the faltering Ming Dynasty.

While the hosts of One-Eyed Li closed on Peking, the Prince-Regent massed his forces just north of the Shan-hai Kwan, the Pass between the Mountains and the Sea, which barred the high road to China. He saw no need to attack the heavily defended pass, which he could open by other means. The last effective Ming army, some one hundred thousand cavalry and infantry under Lieutenant General the Earl of the Pacified West Wu San-kuei, held the Shan-hai Kwan.

The Earl was a forceful field commander whom Francis Arrowsmith had met at a drinking-party in the mansion of the Ming Emperor's father-in-law, Prince Kuei. The Englishman had seen instant attraction flare between the Earl and the prima donna called Lady Chen when she sang for the nobleman's guests. Prizing the good will of the most powerful general in the Empire, Prince Kuei had bought Lady Chen's contract for ten thousand taels, the same amount he had contributed to the defense of the Empire, and presented her to the Earl of the Pacified West.

Since the Earl did not consider One-Eyed Li's rabble a serious threat, he believed Lady Chen quite safe in his father's house in Peking while he himself guarded the frontier. Pondering the personal opportunities the disorder offered, the Earl tarried when the Emperor ordered him to march to the relief of Peking. In his professional judgment, he declared, he could best serve the Ming Dynasty by holding the Pass between the Mountains and the Sea against the Manchus.

THE sun gilded the square tower over the Changyi Men, the Gate of Manifest Virtue, at seven in the morning of April 24, 1644, the beginning of the Double Hour of the Dragon. The robes of the different grades of the Eunuch officers glowed like sapphires, emeralds, and rubies in the lambent light. Cold fire touched the rust-yellow mantles of the Flamboyant Cloaks, and the dew glistened on the crimson jackets of cannon pointing west into the retreating darkness. Cheerful breakfast fires dispelled the mist and painted the troopers' faces with rosy flushes.

Lieutenant Colonel Francis Arrowsmith and Father Adam Schall paused on the ramp leading to the battlements, struck by the troopers' tensely dramatic postures. The illusion was perfect. The curtain had just risen on the first scene of a martial play—and victory would inevitably reward those watchful troops.

"You'd almost believe it..." Adam Schall spoke softly in Portuguese. "It's almost impossible to believe it's all empty show!"

"Perhaps, Father Adam, we are both too pessimistic. Even the Black Premier must realize he will lose everything if One-Eyed Li takes Peking."

"Gentlemen, you still do not completely understand China." A low voice spoke in slow Portuguese beside them. "But, I admit, even I would almost think the Eunuch Tsao Chunhua meant to fight."

"And does he not, Joseph?" Francis asked his privileged slave. "If he does not he will lose everything...his life, too."

"He does not think so, Colonel. He thinks he can deal with One-Eyed Li...thinks he'll be indispensable to the new Emperor."

"How are you so sure, my son?" Adam Schall asked. "Even I am half convinced he'll fight....and I have no high opinion of Eunuchs as a tribe nor this particular specimen. But he would be foolish otherwise, and he is canny. It looks as if he must fight. How can you know?"

"Not a chance in Heaven or Hell he'll fight, Father. With respect, I know because I know my own people. You did post me here to observe, didn't you?"

"Yes, Joseph," Francis acknowledged. "Let's have it."

"All yesterday, strange folk scurried out the postern gates....And the sentries turned a blind eye. They were One-Eyed Li's spies returning to their master. For months he's been sending agents into Peking disguised as merchants or peasants selling their produce. And he has informers in every Ministry. Not only the Emperor has flooded the administration and the army with secret agents..."

411

"What else happened yesterday, Joseph?" Francis brought him up sharply. "Don't tell us what we already know."

"Our own scouts...sent to Changping to count the rebels' strength...never returned. If I'd been one, I'd have gone over to One-Eyed Li, too."

"And the Emperor?" Adam Schall pressed. "What news of the Emperor? What action has he taken?"

"None of any moment, Father. Late last night he summoned the Senior Mandarins: Grand Secretaries, Ministers, and Censors. When he appealed for counsel, no one answered, though some wept. Since the Emperor had nothing to say, they dispersed. That was just after the rebels invested all nine city gates—and three regiments outside the walls went over to them. What advice can anyone give?"

"I see why the Black Premier won't fight." Francis told himself again that the last agonies of the Ming Dynasty were no longer his concern. "We're wasting our time here. We should assemble the Christians in the Mission Compound and barricade it against killing and looting."

"I tried, Francis, as you know," Adam Schall said. "But my flock call me an alarmist. Later, they say, if necessary. But later will be too late."

"Always too late in China, isn't it, Father Adam?"

"This time certainly, Francis. To think you and I could have made Peking impregnable with half the present garrison...if only the soldiers would fight."

"Leave off, Father Adam, leave off. We could do nothing, since they would do nothing. And we can now do..."

"Colonel," Joseph King interrupted. "The Eunuch Tsao Chun-hua requires your presence. I am sorry. I was to tell you as soon as you came."

"Little lost, Joseph. I am not panting to see His Black Excellency. But I'd best go...or he'll turn his wrath on you."

The Senior Eunuch was ringed by aides awaiting his orders. His lean face was framed by the upturned collar of the sable cloak he wore against the morning chill. Beneath his furs, his tribute-silk robe of office billowed in stiff scarlet folds. He smiled thinly when he saw his European subordinate and beckoned with a hand glittering with gems.

"Ah, Arrowmaker...delighted to see you." The incongruously deep voice was satin-smooth. "I may have need of you. But, first, do I recall correctly? You *are* a friend of the Earl of the Pacified West, the General Wu San-kuei, are you not?"

412

"Hardly a friend...an acquaintance, no more."

"That is good enough, Arrowmaker. I've been thinking..."

A single trumpet blared through the mist, and the clatter of hooves resounded from the cobblestones. The hoofbeats drew nearer, insistent beneath the tinkling of silver bridlebells. The Black Premier glanced at his aides, and two detached themselves to peer over the inner rampart.

"The Emperor comes!" A shout-from the battlement reported. "The Emperor himself rides through the Northern Capital!"

The Black Premier turned and strode down the ramp leading to the city. Leaning over the rampart, the two Europeans watched his scarlet-and-black form descend in haste to wait in mock humility before the inner gate.

Two armored horsemen emerged from a narrow lane like silver projectiles, their steel helmets flashing when the sun touched them. One flourishing a triangular dragon-banner, the other a brazen trumpet, they cantered into the square before the inner doors of the Gate of Manifest Virtue. Behind the heralds, thirteen junior officers of the Imperial Guard debouched from the dark mouth of the lane. In their midst the Emperor bestrode a black charger with white fetlocks. The hammered-gold plate covering the horse's forehead flaunted a vee of striped pheasant pinions.

Himself stiff with shock, Francis knew how profoundly that apparition must astonish the Chinese. No sovereign had shown himself in the Northern Capital since the Wan Li Emperor chose a half-century earlier to conceal himself in curtained palanquins because his corpulence made dignity impossible—and because he feared assassination. An Emperor on horseback on the public streets must, Francis realized, confound the superstitious Eunuchs and Flamboyant Cloaks as the Devil in red velvet would a European court. Moreover, the Emperor was attended by not a single Court Eunuch, but by junior officers of the Imperial Guard, whom he had so obviously distrusted at his New Year's Audience two months earlier.

The Black Premier appeared unmoved. His clasped hands concealed in his scarlet sleeves, the Eunuch Tsao Chun-hua bowed so low before his sovereign that his square black hat tumbled to the cobblestones. The Emperor looked down from his saddle, and molten sunlight spattered on his golden armor. Over his mail he wore a surtout embroidered with golden dragons, and the golden finial of his steel helmet flaunted a red yak's tail surmounted by two white egret plumes. Beneath the gold-filigree coronet encircling his helmet, the Emperor's bearded features radiated Imperial dignity. He was no longer the petulant trifler Francis had despised at the New Year's Audience. Confronting the recalcitrant Eunuch, the Ming Emperor was truly majestic.

"Your Imperial Majesty, I am, as ever, humbly obedient." The Black Premier's words rang clear to the spectators on the Gate of Manifest Virtue forty feet above the square. "What is Your Imperial Will?"

"Open the gates, Tsao," the Emperor commanded. "We have sent back the treacherous Eunuch Tu Hsün...your former protégé, we recollect. We have sent him back to tell his master, the Brigand One-Eyed Li, that We will never surrender. Now, We go into battle Ourself—to prevail or to perish."

"I regret, Your Imperial Majesty, that is inadvisable." The Senior Eunuch's tone revealed neither pity nor gloating at the plight of the man he had corrupted, the monarch whose whims had for almost two decades alternately enriched him and terrified him. "The enemy is almost at the Gate."

"Nonetheless, We will ride out to battle." The Emperor spoke the elevated Language of Ceremony. "If Heaven so wills, We will rally our loyal subjects in the south and return in triumph to the Northern Capital. We should have gone south when Our devoted Ministers so counseled—had not the Court Eunuchs deceived Us into remaining....If Heaven wills otherwise, We will die. Who follows Us into battle?"

The thirteen junior officers of the Imperial Guard drew their sabers and cheered raggedly as the Emperor's single dragon-banner dipped in salute and the Emperor's single trumpet blared. On the ramparts of the Gate of Manifest Virtue, the troopers of the Flamboyant Cloaks clutched their sword hilts. But their Eunuch officers frowned in warning, and no other voice answered the Emperor's plea. The sun glinted on the thirteen sabers drawn to support the Monarch who had once commanded three million swords.

"Tsao, think hard before you defy your Sovereign Lord." The Emperor's tone was calm, almost negligent, the voice of a Sovereign who knew he would be obeyed because he had never been disobeyed. "The Sacred Ming Dynasty still rules, and you are still its unworthy servant."

"So be it, Your Imperial Majesty," the Black Premier responded unperturbed. "But I cannot permit my Emperor to sacrifice his life. To do so would be truly unworthy."

"Then step out of Our way. Our loyal subjects will open the gate at Our command."

"So be it, Your Imperial Majesty. With Your Majesty's permission, I shall withdraw."

The Black Premier placed one black boot behind another, withdrawing backward from the Imperial Presence. When he came to the ramp, he turned and strode briskly upward.

His chin sunk on his chest, the Emperor sat on his ebony charger ringed by Guards officers and fingered the jade pendants on its bridle. The Imperial dignity that had fleetingly clothed him had flown, and he appeared no more than a play-actor attired in the stage-mail of a mock monarch. Finally lifting his chin, he twitched his horse into a walk. The two heralds slunk back into the darkness of the lane. The thirteen Guards officers rode with their Emperor toward the inner gate, which remained barred.

"Ready your pieces!" The Black Premier's baritone commanded, and thirty-two arquebusiers blew on their match fuses. The crews of two inward-pointing culverins strained against the gun carriage, and the muzzles gaped at the fourteen horsemen moving slowly toward the ironbound inner doors of the Gate of Manifest Virtue.

"My...our...cannon," Adam Schall whispered to Francis Arrowsmith.

"...and my arquebusiers," the Englishman replied. "We have done great services to the Ming Dynasty, have we not?"

"Fire.... Fire...your pieces!"

The Black Premier's voice broke on the sacrilegious command, and no trooper obeyed. Moved by the same awe that gripped the troopers on the ramparts, the Flamboyant Cloaks guarding the doors put their hands on the beams that locked them. The Emperor and his junior officers rode forward unperturbed.

"Fire your pieces! Fire upon command! Now!" The Black Premier's voice cracked. When no hand moved, he bellowed: "Would you be racked and beheaded for insubordination? Fire! Now! Fire!"

One shot sounded, its echoes reverberating from the buildings enclosing the square. The recoil wrenched the arquebus from the trooper's hands, and the ball flew wild. He looked in astonishment at his smoking weapon, not believing that he had fired upon his Emperor. Another shot cracked across the flat echoes of the first. Then all the arquebusiers fired a volley. The awe that had bound them shattered, the gunners

415

thrust their burning matches into the culverins' touch holes. The salvo smote Francis Arrowsmith's battle-thickened eardrums, and the Flamboyant Cloaks cowered.

"They'll never learn to shoot," Francis said inanely. "Too much powder, as always . . . and, as always, ill-aimed."

"Hush, Francis!" Adam Schall swept his hand down commandingly. "Be quiet now!"

The Emperor's pale face displayed neither surprise nor fear. His mouth set, his eyes fixed on his goal, he led the thirteen Guards officers toward the barred doors. Almost upon them, he twitched the reins, and his black charger swung in a stately parade-ground turn. Disdaining haste, the Guards officers turned their mounts behind the Emperor. The cavalcade rode across the square to the slow drumbeat of a recessional heard only within the riders' heads. Four minutes passed before the last swaying tail vanished into the dark lane.

Francis shuddered, feeling cold tentacles coil around his chest. Tears glistened on the arquebusiers' wind-chapped cheeks, and their weapons dropped.

The clatter of butts on the flagstones wrenched the Eunuch Tsao Chun-hua from the spell that had gripped even him. He gestured imperiously. Avoiding each other's eyes, the Flamboyant Cloaks grounded their arquebuses. None spoke.

"Father Adam! Colonel Arrowmaker!" Joseph King whispered hoarsely. "You and I today . . . we have seen the death of a dynasty."

THE Ming Dynasty's effective life ended after almost three centuries when the Flamboyant Cloaks—the troops he trusted most, though not entirely—fired on the pathologically suspicious Emperor of the Ming. A single volley dealt the mortal wound, a single volley from the arquebuses provided by European Christians, whose assistance may have prolonged the Dynasty's existence briefly, but could not preserve the Ming. That volley was not a coup de grâce. The heart of the Great Ming Dynasty did not stop beating for another day, and its death throes were agonizing.

Finally resigned to fate, the Emperor looked squarely upon reality for the first time in his thirty-three years. Though tears blurred his vision, he saw clearly that both he and his Imperial House were inescapably doomed. Half-demented by grief, he nonetheless acted with resolution bred of despair.

The Emperor might, perhaps, have saved the Dynasty if he had—a decade earlier—abandoned his capricious cruelty, purged himself of avarice, curbed the power of the Eunuchs, and disciplined the parasitic nobility. Had he been capable of such transcendent alteration, the excesses of his immediate predecessors might still have weighed too heavy in the balance of history for any action of his own to preserve the Great Ming Dynasty even a few years longer.

At the end, the Emperor's course was clear. He could only die and sustain some hope for the Dynasty by saving his three sons.

Shortly after dusk on April 24, 1644, the loyal Eunuch Wang Cheng-eng brought the Emperor the intelligence he feared. The Black Premier Tsao Chun-hua had opened the Gate of Manifest Virtue to the self-proclaimed Emperor, One-Eyed Li. The rebels were swarming into Peking.

The Emperor was half-incredulous. Even overpowering shock could not dispel the delusions of three decades in a day. He climbed the five-peaked hillock north of the Forbidden City called Coal Hill with only the loyal Eunuch Wang Cheng-eng in attendance, and he looked down on his capital. Though all the lamps of the city were extinguished, the night sky glowed with an unearthly red light. Conflagrations blazed everywhere, and the torches of the victorious rebels glittered like the scales of serpents coiling around every quarter of the Northern Capital.

"Heaven pity my people!" the Emperor implored the north wind and slowly descended Coal Hill.

His faltering steps took him to the Throne Hall of his favorite dwelling, the Palace of Absolute Purity. For some twenty minutes he stood before the Golden Throne, his eyes fixed on the black signboard with the gilt ideograms reading CHENG TA KUANG MING: TRULY JUST AND ENLIGHTENED.

There was no need to seal the name of the heir-designate in an envelope placed behind that plaque. Reconciled to pitiless reality, the Emperor bowed deep before the Dragon Throne of his Sacred Ancestors. Afterward, he returned to the Nuptial Chamber, where the Bridal Bed spread its perfumed quilts between vermilion pillars. Only the faithful Eunuch Wang Cheng-eng followed the Emperor down the corridor that had yesterday rung with the footsteps of hundreds of Court Eunuchs and Palace Women.

Wang Cheng-eng summoned the remaining officers of the Imperial Guard, and the Emperor gave his last orders. Dressed as commoners, the Crown Prince and his two brothers were to be taken to their grandfather, Prince Kuei, the Empress's father. The Empress and their two daughters, the Emperor knew, awaited in the Hall of Prolonged Tranquility. After belting on a curved saber, he picked his way down the the steps from the Palace of Absolute Purity, which were unlighted for the first time in two centuries. He walked slowly between the pair of golden lions, four times life-size, that guarded the Palace Gates, and turned right onto the path leading to the Empress's quarters.

The ladies of the Imperial Family were sobbing as they sifted aimlessly through their jewelry boxes. When the Emperor entered, his eldest daughter fell to her knees and clutched his robe. He looked at her with detached sadness, recalling that she was past sixteen, quite old enough for marriage. Although she was betrothed to a young nobleman, their wedding had been repeatedly postponed because of civil disorder. Tears welled again in the Emperor's red-rimmed eyes when he remembered her tantrums over those postponements. The Princess who had never been denied any indulgence in her life could not understand why the indulgence she most desired was denied her.

"Heaven help you, Our Child!" the Emperor murmured softly, almost meditatively, in the Language of Ceremony that was his birthright. "Heaven help you that were born into the House of the Ming!"

Unhurriedly gentle as he had been when he held her as an infant, he loosened the Princess's clawed hands from his robe. She sank down upon the floor. The Emperor drew his saber and swung two-handed at his daughter's bowed head. Warned by the rush of air, the Princess twisted aside, and the curved blade slashed her left shoulder to the bone. The Empress screamed in terror, but the Emperor did not hear.

Still unhurried, he turned to his wife and his younger daughter. The Empress thrust the Princess behind her as the saber descended. Dripping with their elder daughter's blood, the saber whistled harmlessly through the air.

When the Empress screamed again, the Emperor looked uncomprehending at the stained blade and laid it gently on the flagstones. He gazed at his Consort for a moment before turning his back.

"Do what you will with her," he said dully. "But you ... you know what you must do ... you and your ladies. We shall not see each other again, you and I."

Offering no other farewell, the Emperor left the Hall of

Prolonged Tranquility and returned to the Palace of Absolute Purity. Early next morning, when the loyal Eunuch Wang Cheng-eng brought him the news he awaited, he rose from his sleepless bed and washed his hands and face. The Empress and a half-dozen of her Ladies in Waiting had hanged themselves in the Hall of Prolonged Tranquility, as he had commanded.

After putting on full Court Regalia with the faithful Eunuch's assistance, the Emperor left his palace and walked slowly south into the sooty darkness that preceded the dawn. No guards lined the avenue from the Palace of Heavenly Purity to the Meridian Gate, the focal point of the Ming Empire. Not a single Eunuch or Court Lady moved on the avenue at the heart of the conquered Capital. Even the shaggy lion-dogs and the popeyed Pekingese had vanished from the Purple Forbidden City.

The Imperial Elephants that still kept vigil outside the Meridian Gate curled their trunks to blare a salute, and the Emperor saw tears rolling down their gray cheeks. All was not lost then, he concluded irrationally, and pulled the rope that sounded the Audience Bell on the Meridian Gate. The liquid peal rolled over the Imperial City, calling the Grand Secretaries, the Ministers, and the Senior Mandarins of the Great Ming Dynasty to council with their sovereign.

No Mandarin responded to that summons. Unperturbed, the Emperor waited ten minutes before tolling the bell again. His head was bowed as if meditating on the vagaries of fate. He was actually wondering what would become of his collection of European clocks, music boxes, and mechanical toys. When, after another ten minutes, the courtyard remained empty, the Emperor nodded cursorily as if a trivial premonition had been confirmed by his Mandarins' failure to answer his last appeal. He turned north again.

The Ming Emperor strolled through the Forbidden City that spring morning, bidding farewell to the enclosure in which he had spent his entire life, a prisoner of his own pomp as much as his own weakness. Turning right before the marble entrance steps, he meandered along the eastern wall of the Palace of Absolute Purity. Aimlessly he counted the workshops, the kitchens, and the offices where tens of thousands of Court Eunuchs had labored for his comfort, while enriching themselves inordinately. He thought fleetingly of the Imperial Treasures he had hoarded as if the Empire—and even the Emperor—existed to keep intact that vast accumulation, rather than the Treasures to serve the Empire and the Emperor. He was approaching the northern boundary of the Forbidden City, the narrow enclosure that had bounded his movements for all his years. Unaware, he shortened his pace to prolong those final moments.

The cherry trees clustered pink and white beside the darker plum trees in the radiant dawn. The Emperor paused to admire the symmetry of the Yü-hua Yüan, the Sovereign's Own Garden. Behind the Gate of Truth-Seeking in the north wall of that garden towered the Gate of Divine Prowess. Its crimson wings were still dark against the blush of the morning sky when the Emperor passed under the Imperial-yellow eaves for the last time. Leaving the Forbidden City behind him, he wearily began to climb Coal Hill. The scarlet-robbed Eunuch Wang Cheng-eng reverently followed six paces behind his Sovereign's golden back.

The fires of dawn flamed above the eastern plains while the Emperor ascended Coal Hill, where earlier dynasties had stored fuel against sieges. Neither hurrying nor tarrying, he climbed through the disciplined profusion of foliage toward the Small Pavilion, which commanded a panorama of the Northern Capital. From that pavilion, the Emperor remembered, he had gazed down into the southeastern quarter of the Imperial City to watch Court Eunuchs fire the Red Jacket Cannon cast by the ocean barbarians. Fearing a gun might explode, the Eunuchs would not let him approach closer. Above all, the Emperor must keep himself safe so that the Empire would prosper and endure.

Well, all safety was gone. Both Empire and Emperor were perishing.

The Emperor seated himself on an unpainted wooden stool before a rustic plant table. It had amused his Consort and his children to play at simplicity in the Small Pavilion on Coal Hill. He removed the Imperial Crown, and his fingertips traced the network of braided gold studded with jewels. He did not see the sunburst bird-of-paradise plumes crumple when they touched the ground—or the mud that smeared the five-clawed Imperial Dragons embroidered on the Crown in gold thread. Kneeling at his master's feet, the Eunuch Wang Cheng-eng pulled off the Emperor's felt boots.

The Emperor took a bamboo writing brush from the loyal Eunuch. He moistened the sable-hair tip in the black ink the Eunuch had prepared by grinding an inkstick in water, and he began to write. He should, he felt, compose his farewell rescript before offering the ultimate reproach to his quarrelsome people, to his traitorous Eunuchs, to his ineffectual Mandarins—and to capricious Heaven itself.

ONE-EYED Li's soldiers found the Chung Chen Emperor of the Great Ming Dynasty dangling from a beam of the Small Pavilion when their search finally reached Coal Hill. His corpse was slight within the stiff Imperial Robes, and his blood-engorged features were veiled by his long hair. Beside him hung the Eunuch Wang Cheng-eng, the last loyal servant of the last true Sovereign of the Ming.

The soldiers paused in involuntary awe. When they cut the bodies down with rough reverence, a sergeant saw the slip of ricepaper pinned to the lapel of the Imperial Robe. He handed the flimsy sheet to his captain, who had studied for the Mandarinate before joining the brigands after strangling in drunken rage his rival for the easy affections of a Flower Girl in a Sian winehouse.

Only Our own deficiencies are responsible for Our grievous disappointment at the hands of our Ministers, the Captain read aloud, pausing to explain the elided classical phrases to his illiterate soldiers. *Our own insufficient virtue and Our own wretched nature have caused Us to sin against Heaven Above. We die knowing that We are wholly unworthy to stand before Our Sacred Ancestors. We have Ourself put off the Imperial Crown and covered Our countenance with Our hair. Let the rebels tear Our miserable body to pieces. But, let them touch not a single hair on the head of the least of Our subjects.*

Peking, Shan-hai Kwan

MAY 12, 1644–MAY 27, 1644

THE caravan appeared among the afternoon shadows striping the tawny stones of the Great Wall. Each time the camels daintily lifted their shaggy hooves, their twin humps swayed. Their knobby heads cocked high and their dun coats molting, they reminded Francis Arrowsmith of aging singsong girls in motheaten finery. The beasts peered arrogantly through rheumy eyes, condescendingly tolerating their tattered drovers.

Hardly more than the camels, Francis reflected, did those men know their importance to the world's greatest empire, just battered by the collapse of a great dynasty. As long as caravans bore goods along the roads of the north, the Chinese people could rebuild their shattered lives. As long as cumbersome cargo junks plied the waterways of the south, the people could hope for better days.

North China lived in unremitting fear. Each morning, farmers scanned the horizon for brigands. In Peking, where the rebel-Emperor was bemused by his immense spoils, men awoke to terror. They had survived the end of the world as they had known it. But the people of both the countryside and the Capital knew that the tragic drama had not ended with the Black Premier's tawdry treachery and the Emperor's forlorn suicide.

They waited tensely for the last act and doggedly went about the daily business of living. The unthinkable of yesterday had become the commonplace of today.

Francis Arrowsmith gaped at the caravan in the loom of the Great Wall, affronted by its prosaic intrusion into the most extraordinary mission of his life. Why should men and animals plod unconcerned on their habitual rounds when the world had just crashed?

Five days after leaving Peking, Francis was still a day's ride from the Shan-hai Kwan, the Pass between the Mountains and the Sea. On May 12, 1644, only two and a half weeks had passed since One-Eyed Li rode into the Northern Capital through the Gate of Manifest Virtue. The Englishman was physically exhausted and emotionally depleted by the frenzies of that protracted fortnight.

After the first pillaging, the rebels had been restrained by their officers' savage discipline. Nonetheless, Francis Arrowsmith and Jospeh King had stood watch on the compound of the Mandarin James Soo, backed by manservants and a few old soldiers of the Battalion of God. For almost a week, no man of substance—and certainly no woman—had dared venture out for fear of being stripped clean and strangled.

Confined as they had once been in Tengchou, Francis and Marta had affirmed their new understanding. Passion was spent, and love there had never been. But they felt a tolerant affection for each other. Knowing himself bound to Marta for a lifetime, Francis was sustained on the hard ride from Peking to the Gulf of Pohai by his knowledge that they would, at least, no longer gratuitously inflict pain on each other.

"How ridiculous they are!" Rocking with laughter in his saddle, Francis pointed at the mangy camels and their grimy attendants. "You'd think nothing had happened. You'd think this was an ordinary day in an ordinary year."

The young cavalrymen turned in their saddles to confirm their suspicion that all foreigners were mad. The Black Premier, who had dispatched the mission, and Colonel Simon Wu, who commanded it, had prudently detailed regular soldiers as their escort, rather than the detested Flamboyant Cloaks. Most of the elite troops of the Secret Police had already burned their rust-yellow mantles and embroidered uniforms—and donned workmen's clothing to evade the vengeance of the people.

Joseph King studied his master, his eyes troubled and his mouth pursed. He knew he himself had been toughened by the twelve tumultuous years since the siege at Tengchou. At the age of fifty-three, Joseph's body had become more wiry and his pugnacious features leaner. Although the skin over his snubbed nose and his flat cheekbones was creased by fine lines, he had not altered materially.

A schoolmate had once chortled that he had the face of a Pekingese dog whittled from a smooth, straw-colored hazelnut. He knew he now resembled a Pekingese whittled from a tan, seamed walnut, and he was resigned to resembling in his old age a Pekingese whittled from a dark-brown, gnarled lichee. But he knew he would endure many years.

The Arrowmaker was another matter. At thirty-seven, his finely carved features were overlaid not only by the exhaustion of the last strenuous years, but by the strain of living so long among an alien people.

When he met Francis Arrowsmith in 1630, Joseph King had been reminded of the miniature of the Archangel Michael Father Adam Schall treasured. The Englishman's shining thick yellow hair and the clear gaze of his light-brown eyes were just like the warrior angel. Once accustomed to his bizarre features, one could see the vigor expressed by his arched nose and the determination manifested by his firm chin. Though coarse-pored beside a Chinese, his taut skin was astonishingly white where the sun had not touched it. His face glowed ruddy, frightening children who knew that devils had red faces.

The years had blurred the Arrowmaker's likeness to the Archangel—as if a turpentine-soaked rag had scrubbed the portrait. A few white strands tarnished the faded yellow of his hair, which was at that moment filmed by ocher dust; his light-brown irises were dull in bloodshot eyes, and a gray tone underlay his weathered skin, which was puffy beneath his eyes and his jawbone.

Joseph King knew his master's muscles were still hard beneath fat built up by the food and drink he consumed to allay tension as more civilized Chinese officers smoked a few pipes of opium. Appraising the Arrowmaker, Joseph King revised his analogy. Not a turpentine-soaked rag that spoiled the portrait irreparably, but a waterladen sponge that soaked the colors. Carefully dried, the portrait would be almost pristine. Not quite, but almost.

When, Joseph King wondered, would he and his master

be allowed to rest? Certainly not soon. Although an honorable death had closed the Ming Emperor's unworthy life, the Empire was still in turmoil. Besides, the Divine Skein had embroiled them in a mission whose perils were as multifarious as its purposes.

The Englishman had commended his wife and his daughter to the protection of Father Adam Schall. His father-in-law, the Mandarin James Soo, was a broken man after the disintegration of the Dynasty he had served all his life. They had then ridden eastward out of the Chaoyang Men, the Gate of the Morning Sun, as reluctant envoys of the rebel-Emperor.

THE brigand-generalissimo One-Eyed Li, who called himself the Yung Chang Emperor, had entered the Imperial City in state on the twenty-sixth of April, the morning after the Ming Emperor's suicide. Soaked by rain, One-Eyed Li's light-blue robe clung to his skin. His predatory face was concealed by a rainhat, and his triumphant words were drowned by the rumble of thunder. When his piebald mount approached the Gate of Heaven's Sanction he rose in his stirrups and drew his short cavalry bow. He promised the arrow would impale the ideogram *tien*, meaning heaven, to prove that he now ruled *Tien Hsia*, All Under Heaven. But the bow was wet, and the arrow glanced off the red brick.

Laughing to conceal his dismay, the brigand-Emperor cantered through the Meridian Gate into the Forbidden City. The wet flagstones were slippery under his bootsoles when he dismounted, but he briskly climbed the marble stairs to the Golden Throne of Audience. Disdaining ceremony, he briskly seated himself behind the small desk covered with Imperial-yellow silk embroidered with Imperial five-clawed dragons. Disregarding the rivulets falling from the dragon-carved marble eaves, he announced his appointments to the chief offices of the Empire, then briskly but mercifully dealt with the remnants of the Imperial Family.

The three princes had been brought from the mansion of their grandfather, Prince Kuei, to the Forbidden City. The rebel-Emperor bestowed the title Prince of Sung on the Ming Crown Prince and summoned the Imperial Physicians to attend the wounded Princess. He also ordered the manacled officers of the Imperial Guard released from both their chains and their confinement in the Ministry of Justice.

His troops, however, mocked the Senior Mandarins who

came to pay homage to the new Emperor. Elderly Ministers sputtered in outrage but did not dare protest when common soldiers knocked off their horsehair hats of office. Stout officials gasped when the soldiers prodded them with spears but kowtowed humbly to the wild figure on the throne. Still not quite forty years old, One-Eyed Li looked like the brigand he had been half his life rather than the Emperor he had proclaimed himself two months earlier. His wet mustaches hung around his slit mouth, and droplets glistened on the sharp tip of his hooked nose. The blue dye running from his robe puddled around his feet and stained the yellow silk on his desk.

The rebel-Emperor had already learned to delegate to subordinates the gory enforcement of his will, but he had not learned to curb his rapacity. The next day, a thousand noblemen, Mandarins, and magnates were brought before his chief inquisitor. The officer, known even by the rebels as the Cruel General, asked the captives only one question: "Where have you hidden your valuables?"

The fainthearted were totally intimidated by the bearded executioners standing around the Cruel General, their torsos bared to reveal heavily muscled arms and chests. Even the stouthearted were intimidated by the executioners' tools: broadaxes and many-thonged whips, sledgehammers and sharp bamboo stakes, racks to tear men apart and gridirons above coal fires. Most of the terrified dignitaries of the former Dynasty gave up their treasures before the executioners touched them.

Disdaining subtlety, the Cruel General broke the shinbones of stubborn captives with a single blow from a sledgehammer. Thus encouraged, most of the recalcitrant yielded. Some wealthy Mandarins who still clung to their treasures were stretched on the gridirons while their torturers blew on the coal fires with bellows.

The father of the Ming Empress, Prince Kuei, gave up after three minutes' scourging with bamboo poles all the wealth he had deviously safeguarded from his son-in-law. He disgorged twenty million taels, having put the Ming Emperor off with ten thousand taels to pay the troops who should have defeated the rebels.

Marta's father, the Mandarin James Soo, was less pliable. Humiliated when the executioners ripped off his scarlet robe, leaving him in his baggy underdrawers, he found new strength when whips cut his back and chest. Although he himself had no reason to live after the Ming's demise, he was determined to preserve his children's patrimony. The blood seeping across his round paunch to mingle with his sweat was washed away by the rain. He glared defiantly when the whiplashes curled around his soft shoulders.

An executioner grasped James Soo's wrist and laid his hand on an iron anvil. When a sledgehammer smashed bones and flesh into gritty red jelly, tears ran down his plump cheeks.

"I'll tell," James Soo gasped when the executioner again raised the sledgehammer. "Under the...the threshing ground of my estate...near Nankou. My gold and my son-in-law's. I'll take you there."

Thus stripped of his wealth, Francis Arrowsmith was, aside from Adam Schall, the only European in Peking. Having chosen not to flee, they knew their peril. The forebodings were somewhat allayed when three "rebel thieves," as Schall contemptuously described them, took from the Jesuit House only a Khotan rug. They were puzzled when a notice stamped with the Cruel General's seal was posted on Schall's gatepost to command all rebels to leave the Europeans in peace. They were summoned to the Forbidden City on the third day after the Ming Emperor's suicide, the twenty-eighth of April, 1644.

Maliciously delighted that the Europeans were to share their tortures, the captive Mandarins clapped their hands mockingly and shouted viciously: "Hail the Teacher of the Law! Hail the Master of Ordnance!" Their meaning was clear: the Europeans had also been great officers of the Ming and had also amassed great fortunes. Perversely piqued that the Europeans should take precedence into the torture chamber, the waiting Mandarins eagerly awaited their gory exit.

Seated behind a desk beside the Baffo harpsichord in the music room of the Palace of Absolute Purity, the Cruel General marked with his forefinger his place on the list of Mandarins summoned to his presence before looking up. He stared in rude curiosity for a half a minute before reluctantly commanding, "Pass them through to the Emperor."

Attired in an Imperial-yellow robe embroidered with Imperial dragons, the brigand-Emperor sat on the Golden Throne beneath the black plaque that exhorted in gold TRULY JUST AND ENLIGHTENED. The Black Premier of the Ming bent obsequiously over his new master, his scarlet robe shimmering in the light of the candles in the beaks of the blue-enameled cranes. The wicked, Francis reflected impiously, always flourish.

"Some call you Spiritual Father." The brigand-Emperor's remaining eye glared at them under his heavy brows, and his voice rasped. "We shall not, since you are no father of Ours, but an official of the former dynasty. Tell Us, Former Official, are you prepared to serve Us?"

"In any way that does not interfere with my duties to the Lord of Heaven and my flock, " Adam Schall replied.

"*Hau! Hau!*" the brigand-Emperor barked. "Good! Good! We can make use of your knowledge of cannonmaking . . . and your wisdom regarding the stars. You can read the Will of Heaven, We are told."

The Jesuit did not protest to the superstitious rebel-Emperor that he did not read auguries from the heavenly bodies, but merely charted their movements. When he bowed in silence, One-Eyed Li turned his gaze on the English soldier.

"And you, Lieutenant Colonel of Ordnance, can also serve Us." The patch that covered the dead eye, Francis saw with astonishment, was of Imperial-yellow silk. "You can serve Us in Our armies. We must pacify the Empire, which is troubled by brigands and rebels. But, first, We have a special mission for you."

"*Pu kan-tang . . .*" Francis instinctively offered the ritual phrases of self-abasement. "I am unworthy. . . . I do not dare."

"Dare you will . . . or perish," One-Eyed Li retorted.

"Your choice is simple, Arrowmaker." The Black Premier spoke for the first time. "Honors and riches . . . or a slow, painful death for yourself and your family. Your wealth restored . . . or your life forfeit."

"I shall endeavor to overcome my unworthiness," Francis replied, and the Jesuit pressed his lips together to suppress a smile.

"That is well, then," the brigand-Emperor declared, but did not smile.

"You are, I understand," the Eunuch said, "a close friend of the Earl of the Pacified West, Wu San-kuei. I am . . ."

"No friend, but merely an acquaintance," Francis protested.

"He had better be your friend," the Eunuch replied shortly. "If he is not, you will need other friends badly . . . very badly. I want you to go to him as a friend and . . ."

"I suppose," Francis said slowly, "you could call him a kind of friend."

"I am pleased to hear that, Colonel Arrowmaker." The rebel-Emperor smiled for the first time. "And do remind him that We hold Lady Chen—unharmed for the moment."

THE Earl of the Pacified West, Lieutenant General Wu San-kuei, had ignored the Ming Emperor's appeal to march to the rescue of the Northern Capital. His eighty thousand battle-tempered veterans included four battalions of arquebusiers and six batteries of Red Jacket Cannon. Holding the Pass between the Mountains and the Sea against the Manchus, the last intact Ming army also held the balance of power.

Colonel Simon Wu and Lieutenant Colonel Francis Arrowsmith rode on a virtual embassy to a virtually independent prince. The message they carried from the rebel-Emperor appealed to the Earl as a Chinese patriot. If he swore fealty to the new Dynasty, he would be rewarded with high office, a dukedom, and many bars of gold. United, the Chinese forces would hurl back the Manchus and ensure that Chinese continued to rule All Under Heaven.

As the Black Premier's military alter ego, Simon Wu headed the mission to the most powerful surviving Ming general. Francis Arrowsmith rode with him not only because of his presumed friendship with the Earl, but also because his fame as a master of ordnance would win him a hearing. Besides, One-Eyed Li wanted the Englishman to command his artillery when he fought his inevitable battle against the Manchus.

The Black Premier had, however, deputed Francis Arrowsmith because he feared the Chinese armies would *not* unite against the Manchus. If the Earl rejected the rebel-Emperor's invitation or joined the Manchus, the Eunuch wanted a friend at the Manchu Court. Most of the clandestine reports the Divine Skein had sent to Mukden during the past two years had purportedly come from the Arrowmaker, as many had in truth. The Eunuch, therefore, believed the Englishman enjoyed the affection and the trust of Prince-Regent Dorgon, whom he had also served as artillery adviser in Mukden and purchasing agent in Macao.

Francis Arrowsmith was charged to deliver a second message if the Earl refused to join the new dynasty. The Black Premier trusted no man more than he himself could be trusted. His baritone purr had reminded Francis that Marta, Maria, and Candida were surety for his obedience. If he failed

429

to sway the Manchus, not only their heads, but Adam Schall's as well, would be forfeit. Francis was to pledge the Black Premier's loyalty to the Manchus and convey his promise to serve them, as he had already served One-Eyed Li, by opening the gates of Peking.

"MY esteemed father has already written urging me to join the new dynasty." Lieutenant General the Earl of the Pacified West Wu San-kuei felt the usurper might have chosen emissaries less notorious for their connections with the Divine Skein. "But I am compelled to disobey his command...even to act unfilially. I know he wrote under duress. My duty to the Ming requires me to disregard my father's words."

The Earl stared into the teacup encircled by his fingers. They had come to his field headquarters to talk, these two ill-chosen ambassadors. Then let them talk!

He had received them because he was eager for news from Peking, but he had received them in the cramped anteroom where his guards normally waited. The table and stools had been knocked together from unplaned timber, and obscene scrawls defaced the poster tacked to the wall with rusty nails. On the poster, a gaudily painted lady of skill, her lips parted in lewd invitation, advertised a winehouse in Tientsin.

"You could never act unfilially or ignobly, Lord," Colonel Simon Wu cajoled. "We have not come to press you, but to explain the new situation in the Northern Capital. You will, of course, act as your own wisdom counsels."

"If that is the case, Colonel, why waste your breath?"

"Lord, it behooves all Chinese to join together, lest the northern barbarians overwhelm the Empire. Only by joining together can we Chinese..."

"You are not wholly mistaken, Colonel. Why, then, did you bring a western ocean barbarian with you?"

"He is a harmless barbarian, a helpful barbarian, Lord Earl. His is the power of the guns, the Red Jacket Cannon that could disperse the Manchus if they were a thousand times stronger than they are. But I was discussing..."

Francis Arrowsmith was bored by the arguments Simon Wu had repeatedly rehearsed on their six-day ride to the Earl's camp some fifty miles southwest of the Pass between the Mountains and the Sea. He picked at the sunflower seeds, the dried beef, and the pickled radish the Earl had offered them as token repast. He had not omitted ritual Chinese etiquette, but had brutally foreshortened it, so that the insult stung worse. Sipping green tea, Francis studied their reluctant host under lowered eyelids.

The Earl looked soft, deceptively soft for a general of thirty-two who had commanded the rear-guard brilliantly when the Ming withdrew from all Manchuria over his own protests the preceding autumn. Like many Chinese officers, his face was plump with good living. Francis would have recognized him as a lover of the most refined ladies of skill and the finest dishes of the most accomplished chefs even if he had not known the Earl's reputation and roistered with him at Prince Kuei's drinking party. Francis would not, however, have thought the Earl capable of the single-minded passion he felt for Lady Chen. Yet that passion dominated him, the gossip of Peking reported—and grew with each day of his separation from her.

Beneath the cultivated, self-indulgent patina, Francis glimpsed ruthless ambition. The Earl had recently been promoted to lieutenant general over the heads of scores of seniors. His climb had been hastened by the influence of his father, a full general and lately commander of the Peking garrison. But the Earl's appointment to command the last effective Ming army owed less to nepotism than it did to his own hard competence and to his having been in the right place at the time that was wrong for all other senior officers.

Behind opaque eyes half-hidden by the abundant flesh of a head the size of a small watermelon, the Earl assessed his visitors and pondered his future. Simon Wu he dismissed with a symbolic wave of a hand as big as a fan. The sooner that lickspittle of the Divine Skein was gone, the easier he would feel. He did not want the spy Colonel intriguing with the remaining agents among his own troops.

The Earl rose, overtopping Francis by two inches, and wiped sweat from his columnar neck with a green-silk kerchief. The Englishman would make a useful ally when the commanding general of the last Ming army could aspire to any position—even the Dragon Throne. He was dissatisfied with his artillerymen's performance, and his arquebusiers' volleys were ragged. While Simon Wu droned on ingratiatingly, the Earl made up his mind to act as he had already decided to act.

"We do not, Colonel, have at our disposal all the eons since the Great Yü dammed the floods in antiquity." The Earl assumed the elevated language and the swinging cadence of

431

formal speech. "I appreciate your lucid explanation, but I am puzzled by its purpose. Do you truly believe I would do for you what I could not do for my own father? I am loyal to the Great Ming Dynasty, and I cannot make common cause with rebels."

The Earl seated himself and drained his teacup to signal the end of the discussion. Outrightly rude, he set the teacup upside down on the plant table. That gesture declared that neither Simon Wu nor, of course, the barbarian was sufficiently well bred to understand the dismissal implicit in their host's finishing his tea.

Simon Wu could not conceal his discomfiture. He rose and bowed, his square face flushed and his flat cheekbones stained by angry blood.

"Since you have said all you have to say to me, Colonel, I shall not detain you further." The Earl's voice dripped honey and acid. "I shall not offer you a night's rest, since I would not inflict upon you the pain of being forced to the discourtesy of refusing my invitation. I know how anxious you are to report to your principals."

The envoys of One-Eyed Li turned to leave the spartan anteroom. Simon Wu could not force the rote courtesies of farewell past his compressed lips to screen his withdrawal, and Francis did not care.

"Arrowmaker," the Earl invited, "will you stay a moment?"

The Englishman was warmed by the smile on the Earl's big face. A huge hand waved him to his seat before pounding on the table to summon a servant.

"Food," the Earl commanded. "Food and drink... immediately."

"I am honored, Your Excellency," Francis said. "But what of Colonel Wu? He, too, might welcome... and my secretary?"

"We'll see to your secretary. The informer I want out of my camp immediately," the Earl responded. "But you, Arrowmaker, I'm delighted to see you again."

"I am twice honored, Your Excellency." Francis withdrew behind the palisade of conventional etiquette. "You do my worthlessness far too much honor."

"Forget the *Excellency*. I'm just damned glad to see you again. That was quite a party at old Prince Kuei's. How is he, by the way?"

"Stripped naked as the day he was born... his treasures all seized by One-Eyed Li and the Cruel General. Kuei hasn't a copper farthing to buy a bandage for his broken ribs. And he badly needs salves for his wounds...opium, too, to help him forget how they tortured him."

"That bad, eh? And the others? All my friends and colleagues, how are they?"

"Much the same as Kuei. Peking's not a happy city today."

"But you serve this brigand, this one-eyed rebel, do you not?"

"Not by choice, I assure you. When a man's family is held hostage, what can..."

"Suppose I keep you here by force...arrest you for, say, insolence? Then let the informer carry the tale back to Peking? How would that suit?"

"For a time, General, it would suit. My family would not suffer.... As long as Peking thinks me unable to leave...as long as the rebels think they can use my women to blackmail me."

"Whatever happens will happen quickly. So time is no problem. My artillerymen, my arquebusiers need shaking up. You're just the man, I think."

"As you wish, General."

"Well, then, that's settled. But tell me more of Peking. My father is well, is he? I haven't heard for a week."

"Yes, he's fine. Naturally, since One-Eyed Li thinks he can use your esteemed father to win you over."

"We'll see about that. But, I tell you, Arrowmaker, it's damnably hard having to put the old gentleman's head in peril."

Francis nodded discreet agreement rather than risk comment. His quirky sense of humor cherished the ingenious pretexts by which the Chinese circumvented the absolute imperative of filial obedience when policy—or convenience—required otherwise.

"And, by the way, another thing." The Earl was ponderously offhand. "Do you happen to know about Lady Chen? Still safe with my father...safe under his protection, isn't she?"

"Well, let me think what I've heard," Francis prevaricated, wondering if he dared either plead ignorance or sweeten the truth.

"Speak out, man, speak out!" the Earl commanded. "Don't spare me with sly words. She's not hurt, is she? The sons of turtle-bitches haven't been at her, have they?"

"No, General, not that." Francis concluded abruptly that

the Black Premier could no longer harm him if One-Eyed Li fell. "Not that, General. But she's been given to One-Eyed Li's inquisitor, the one they call the Cruel General."

"And they dared send envoys to treat with me!" The Earl flushed crimson with rage, and his huge hands trembled. "They dared, did they?"

"Your Excellency," Francis murmured, fearing the Earl would remember that he was one of those envoys.

"Oh, you're all right, man. Don't worry about yourself. I'm not fool enough to punish you for an honest report." The Earl regained the icy self-control that made him formidable. "So they've given her to the Cruel General. Well...not for long!"

"Another matter may interest you, General." Francis prodded the Earl toward the decision that would complete the destruction of One-Eyed Li and the Black Premier. "I carry another message, but not to you."

"To whom, then? And what is it?"

"To the Manchu Prince-Regent Dorgon from the Eunuch Tsao Chun-hua, who offers to deliver Peking to the Manchus."

"Well, you'll not deliver that message, will you, now?" the Earl pondered. "But not only he can play at that game."

FRANCIS ARROWSMITH was virtually forgotten a half hour later when Simon Wu and his cavalrymen dejectedly turned their horses' heads toward Peking. The Earl ordered his Adjutant to place his artillery and his arquebusiers under the temporary command of the foreign Lieutenant Colonel for training. Then the Earl locked himself in his reception chamber with his senior commanders. After two hours of discussion, those brigadiers and colonels emerged elated. Their commander remained at his desk with his secretary beside him, summoning other advisers from time to time.

The Earl emerged two days later and ordered his army to march to the Shan-hai Kwan, the Pass between the Mountains and the Sea. He sent ahead the Colonel who was his chief of operations and the Major who was his aide to deliver a letter to the Manchu Prince-Regent Dorgon:

Since the deceased Emperor made him General of Liaotung, San-kuei [referring to its author in the third person, the formal epistle read in part] has striven with his heavy duties, though his ability is no more weighty than a mosquito. He had long

434

admired Prince Dorgon, but has not presumed to pay his respects in person....

The rebel riffraff have defied the Will of Heaven and taken the Forbidden City after traitors opened the gates to them.... The sacrilegious rabble now rape and plunder. They are detested by Heaven and despised by mankind. May their downfall be speedy!

Volunteer units are already forming, inspired by love for the Ming Dynasty.... San-kuei will soon march on the Capital to wreak revenge on the rebels. However, he begs assistance, since his strength is insufficient.

Prince Dorgon, who surpasses all in heroic courage, can earn great merit by overthrowing an evil usurper. The opportunity will not come again!

The desolate servant of an ill-fated Dynasty abjectly requests a few elite units to support his forces.... Together, we will drive the rabble from the Forbidden City.

Since he does not know the correct forms of address, San-kuei implores the Prince Dorgon to convey this message to His Majesty, the Emperor of the Worthy Ruling House of the Manchus.

Since Prince-Regent Dorgon's Eight Banners could seize the Great Empire when he pleased, the Earl was truly the humble suppliant he called himself. The Prince laughed at the Earl's assertion that the Ming Dynasty still existed and smiled at his request to transmit his epistle to the child-Emperor. Dorgon smiled and did not reply for three days to impress upon the Earl his total dependence upon Manchu good will.

"When I heard that the rabble had taken the Capital and brought the Ruler of the Ming to a frightful end, my hair stood on end," Dorgon wrote on May 21, 1644. "I immediately resolved to lead the Grand Army into China to destroy the rebels and rescue the Chinese people."

Elated because the Earl's request provided the long-awaited opportunity to conquer the Empire at small cost, Dorgon was magnanimous. If the Earl made submission to the Manchus, acknowledging that the Ming Dynasty had perished, he would receive great estates and the title of Prince.

"It is given to you to revenge the fallen Dynasty!" Dorgon stressed. "You can also establish your own house so solidly

435

that successive generations will enjoy riches and honors as eternal as the mountains and the rivers."

From the Earl's headquarters at the Shan-hai Kwan, his reply reached Dorgon's camp northeast of the Pass on May 25, 1644. After a flowery salutation, the Earl dealt briskly with strategy. More than two hundred thousand rebels led by One-Eyed Li himself were "swarming like ants" only fifteen miles southwest of the Pass. If the Prince would order his elite Tiger Battalions to march, the rebels would be trapped in a pincers. After their defeat, a joint proclamation would calm the people and reestablish order. The Earl, somewhat ambiguously, further "prayed that the Grand Army of the Manchus be instructed not to overstep the limits."

The Earl thus mutedly asserted Chinese independence in his invitation to his "good neighbors" to help him put down disorder within the Empire. He ignored Dorgon's invitation to become a vassal of the Manchus and receive the title of Prince. Knowing, however, how negligible was any hope of restoring the Ming, the Earl implied the Manchu domination he could not yet bring himself to state explicitly: "After our victory, the hearts of the people will yield, while the land and its treasures will submit—and nothing will be impossible."

ON May 27, 1644, the twenty-second day of the fourth month of the first year of the Manchu Shun Chih Emperor, the commander of the last Ming army met the commander of the Eight Banners at the Pass between the Mountains and the Sea. Both were confident of victory, since the rebels had been put to flight in every preliminary skirmish.

Heaven beamed auspiciously. The sky was bright, and the morning clouds were high. To the southeast, where the Great Wall met the Gulf of Pohai, black thunderheads over choppy green waters portended the rebels' doom.

The Great Wall ran south from the mountains to the sea, and the yellow-brick Gate of the Pass faced due east. Under a two-tiered roof covered with green tiles hung a plaque reading TIEN HSIA TI-YI KUAN—THE PRIME PASS UNDER HEAVEN. That tower was protected by a barbican facing the barbarian steppes. On the Chinese side, two concentric walls were pierced by two ceremonial gates.

Francis Arrowsmith rode into the inner enclosure among the Chinese staff officers behind the Earl of the Pacified West. Passing through the ceremonial gate, he marveled again at the Chinese passion for creating walled fastnesses within walled fastnesses like the Forbidden City within the Imperial City, which in turn lay within the city walls of Peking. Ironically, those enclosures were here appended to the Great Wall, which itself deluded the Chinese with the illusion of security from the terrors of the northern grasslands.

Though neither so precipitous nor so narrow as Francis envisioned Thermopylae from reading Herodotus, the Pass between the Mountains and the Sea could obviously be defended by a single regiment. The fortifications were, however, useless if their garrison was not resolute—as the Manchus had repeatedly proved. They were children of the steppes, born to the saddle and to cavalry warfare as the Chinese were born to fortifications and to siege warfare.

The embodiments of those two opposed habits of mind met within the innermost enclosure beside a small Confucian temple with peeling vermilion pillars. When they dismounted, the Earl's silver helmet overtopped Dorgon's golden helmet by only a few inches. The Manchu Prince was tall, though slight.

The two generals burned incense before the shabby altar of the Confucian temple and addressed their separate prayers for victory to the nebulous deity both called Heaven. When the rites were completed, they conferred again briefly before remounting.

Prince Dorgon's restless eye alighted on the English Lieutenant Colonel. He reined in his horse and beckoned to Francis.

"It is you, Arrowmaker, I see," Dorgon said in slow Manchu. "It has taken you some time to return to my command, has it not? Eight years I make it. Somewhat long for a slave who swore to return whenever I summoned him. But we are all friends and allies now—as long as you command the Earl's artillery."

The Manchu Prince then called to the Chinese Earl: "Return to your troops now and tell them to tie white scarves around their arms. Since they are Chinese like the rebels, my men couldn't tell them apart otherwise. A pity if we killed your men by mistake."

Neither elated by securing Manchu assistance nor exultant at the coming victory, the Earl of the Pacified West was preoccupied with forebodings as he rejoined his battle-ready troops. Dorgon had sharply demonstrated that their nominal alliance required him to obey Manchu orders peppered with

Manchu arrogance. He would, the Earl concluded bleakly, have to live with barbarian incivility—and accept with a smile humiliation like Dorgon's offhand assumption that Manchus would always prevail over Chinese.

He had invited the Eight Banners to enter China. Neither cunning nor force, the Earl realized, could compel the Manchus to withdraw after they had lent their indispensable weight to crushing One-Eyed Li. He could neither restore the Ming Dynasty nor seat himself on the Dragon Throne. Unquestionably the most powerful force in Asia, the Manchu Banners were backed by a civil administration that had been shaped by Chinese advisers into the most efficient on the continent. Prince-Regent Dorgon would impose Manchu rule on the former Ming Empire—and the Chinese would be a subject race.

But it was too late for reservations. One-Eyed Li had mustered two hundred thousand men west of the Shan-hai Kwan, almost twice the number of his own and the Manchu forces. He did not believe the reports of the rabble's iron discipline, and he knew they lacked modern firearms. The sweepings of a half-dozen provinces could outmaneuver neither his own veterans nor the Manchu cavalry. The Earl feared only their overwhelming numbers. But he would turn that apparent advantage against the tatterdemalion horde, which was already exhausted by its two-hundred-fifty-mile forced march from Peking.

One-Eyed Li stood on a hill that gave him a commanding view of the battlefield. He knew his men's magnificent discipline, and he could see their overwhelming numbers, but he nervously pulled his beard. His army had never fought a major set-piece battle. Fearing that its size would make it cumbersome, he sent repeated orders to his rigid formations not to yield an inch of ground. The enemy must be compelled to batter himself to death against the rebels' rocklike line of battle.

The rebel-Emperor was heartened by his own Imperial dignity. Golden scale armor clothed his arms, and Imperial dragons writhed on his blue-checked surtout fringed with scarlet and gold. His charger's forehead was protected by the plate of beaten gold topped with the vee of striped pheasant pinions the Ming Emperors had worn. His domed steel helmet was chased with gold arabesques, and its finial flaunted a yak's tail beneath a golden ball crowned by egret plumes.

Uneasily, One-Eyed Li reassured himself that the guards

were watchful over his two hostages, the Ming Crown Prince and General Wu Hsiang, the Earl's father. He then studied again the many-colored banners that marked his front, extending some five miles from the Great Wall to the Gulf of Pohai. Surely their tremendous number would prevail! Surely Heaven had given him the Great Empire to rule.

The brigand-Emperor's single eye appraised the eighty thousand men of the last Ming army drawn up in compact phalanxes. Defying frontal assault, the formation invited the encirclement One-Eyed Li did not dare order because he feared his men could not execute it. On the Earl's right flank, some twenty thousand cavalrymen of Dorgon's Tiger Battalions were poised for attack. The Earl's twenty-four cannon, gaudy in their red-silk jackets, were the hinge between his main force and the Manchus.

Commanding those guns, Lieutenant Colonel Francis Arrowsmith drew tensely on his tobacco pipe. His rank and his reputation as the Empire's best artilleryman had effectively displaced the middle-aged Major who nominally commanded the ordnance. The battery commanders instinctively looked for orders to the Englishman who had trained them. Arquebusiers of the former Battalion of God protected the cannon.

In his hilltop command post, One-Eyed Li chafed because he could not trust his own men to take advantage of his enemies' tardy arrival on the battlefield. He could not initiate the action, but could only wait to be attacked. It was 11 A.M. before the Manchu and Ming dispositions were complete. The rebel-Emperor held his five-mile line abreast, its tension revealed by the rippling of banners as the standardbearers nervously shifted their feet.

The sky was still bright, and visibility was excellent. The brigand-Emperor looked down on the two great armies aligned as if for a training exercise, as if waiting for the signal to begin a mock battle. The wind, he saw, was rising in the east, and black thunderheads were storming from the Gulf of Pohai toward the Great Wall.

Just before noon, the Red Jacket Cannon thundered. Two regiments of Ming cavalry charged the gap the salvo tore in the rebel formation. The rebel line opened, twisting in disarray. When the cannon fired again, the Earl of the Pacified West rejoiced at the easy victory that lay within his grasp. Perhaps he had not needed the Manchus after all.

While the Earl exulted, the rebel line reknit itself, closing the gap and enfolding the Ming cavalrymen. The artillery could not fire into the melee without killing its own men.

The Earl committed his cavalry regiments two by two until twenty thousand Chinese were struggling amid the rebel mass. The cavalrymen could neither advance nor fall back. They could only endure the thrusting pikes, the slashing swords, and the falling arrows.

The Earl saw with alarm that he had gravely underestimated the rebels' tenacity. They were fighting as well as veteran regulars. Where, the Earl wondered, were the Manchus when he needed them?

A hundred kettledrums rumbled, a hundred conch horns wailed, and a hundred trumpets pealed. The Eight Banners streamed red, yellow, blue, and white in the rising wind as ten thousand Manchu cavalrymen hurled themselves at the rebel center. The rolling thunder of their hooves drowned the clash of swords and the shrieks of the wounded. The rebel line bent like a bow on the point of cracking. In his eyrie, One-Eyed Li pulled his beard in impotent rage.

While the rebel-Emperor despaired, his rebels engulfed the Manchu cavalry. Though thousands had already fallen, neither the number of the rebels nor their courage was appreciably diminished. The valor of their desperation was heightened by their lust for spoils. They would either die in defeat or seize the booty of an Empire in victory. And there were so many more rebels than allies.

The Red Jacket Cannon roared intermittently. Francis Arrowsmith no longer ordered salvos but commanded his men to shoot only when certain of their targets. The gunners swiveled their weapons, but the battle ranged so wide the intervals between their shots grew longer and longer.

When the black-powder smoke was blown away by the rising wind, Francis saw that the melee had rolled away from his front.

"Hold your fire!" he screamed. "Hold your fire and double-load grapeshot for a salvo!"

Minutes passed before twenty-four gun captains reported: "Ready to shoot!"

"Fire now!" Francis screamed. "Fire now!"

Thousands of balls cut down the rebels. Despite the rolling gray smoke, Francis for the first time saw daylight through the enemy line. Coughing from the fumes, his eyes streaming, he saw a faint glow that vanished when the desperate rebels closed ranks again.

The sun was obscured by black thunderheads, and the early afternoon was suddenly dark. A storm was breaking, thunder rolling over the reverberations of the salvo. The east wind hurled torrents of rain laden with sand into the rebels' faces.

On his hilltop, One-Eyed Li groaned aloud and ordered "Kill Wu Hsiang! Kill the Earl's father . . . now!"

Through breaks in the storm the rebel-Emperor saw his line bend inward half a mile before breaking under fresh cavalry charges. The Ming infantry was advancing stolidly, its banners whipped by the wind, its tarnished silver swords flailing in the downpour. The allied line rolled forward when Dorgon and the Earl committed their reserves. The rebels began throwing away their weapons. The Red Jacket Cannon roared again, and the rebel host turned to flee.

Mounting his horse, One-Eyed Li saw his troops streaming westward in full retreat. His lips working above his torn beard, he galloped southwest toward Peking, followed by the men guarding the Crown Prince of the Ming. Riding for his life, the rebel-Emperor left behind the ten-mile-long mob of his fleeing infantrymen.

Astonished and awed, Francis Arrowsmith walked among his cooling guns. He was delighted that his gunners had suffered not a single casualty, though the battlefield was strewn with gaudy corpses. Gazing sadly at the wounded staggering among discarded swords and spears, he winced each time a disemboweled horse screamed like a woman in labor. His powder-grimed hands trembled as he filled the porcelain bowl of his pipe.

The Manchu Prince and the Chinese Earl were also astonished. They had expected a rebel defeat, but not a rout. Fearful of a ruse, they recalled their pursuing cavalry and re-formed their ranks.

When no rebel counterattack materialized, Prince-Regent Dorgon commanded a ceremony of thanksgiving late in the afternoon. He gave precedence to the Chinese commander and his senior officers, Francis Arrowsmith among them. Lieutenant General the Earl of the Pacified West Wu San-kuei was raised to the state of Prince of the Pacified West under the seal of the Shun Chih Emperor of the Manchus. He swore fealty to the Manchus because he had no alternative. Dorgon further rewarded him with the lavish gifts one prince gives another: a belt of shining *fei-tsui* jade, an enveloping sable cloak, a coat of blue tribute silk embroidered

441

with rampant gold dragons, and a stallion wearing a saddle studded with amethysts, topazes, turquoise, and red coral.

The Prince-Regent then ordered the visible mark of their submission set upon the new prince and his officers. Manchu barbers shaved their crowns and braided the long hair remaining into queues like those Dorgon and all his soldiers wore. In high good humor because that symbolic act proclaimed Manchu rule over the entire Empire, the Prince-Regent walked among the Chinese officers.

"Don't worry if the braid is a little short just now. That one knows it will grow long." Dorgon grinned and jerked his chin at Francis Arrowsmith.

"As soon as your men are rested, you will ride west, with ten thousand of my men." Dorgon spoke to the new Prince. "All under your command, since you are now a Prince and a General of the Manchu Dynasty. You will pursue One-Eyed Li, who slew your father. You will bring his head back to me—even if it takes months, even a year."

The Prince of the Pacified West bowed to the Prince-Regent. Bowing behind him, Francis read disappointment and fury from his rigid back. The Chinese commander longed to ride to Peking to find his woman and save her from the indiscriminate slaughter that would attend the rebels' withdrawal from the Capital. Like himself, the new Prince was compelled to pursue the defeated rebel-Emperor, tormented by fear for Lady Chen as he would be tormented by fear for his family.

Peking

MAY 30, 1644–JUNE 6, 1644

JOHANN Adam Schall von Bell, nobleman of Cologne in the Rhineland, priest of the Holy Apostolic Catholic Church, and acting superior of the Mission of the Society of Jesus in Peking, had celebrated his fifty-second birthday quietly on May 1, 1644. Since that day he had been gathering his flock together in the Mission House against the rising storm. Their only remaining pastor, he was also the chief protector of the Christians of Peking during the interregnum of One-Eyed Li. The Jesuit's purported astrological wizardry, which he did not deny, had made an even greater impression than his scientific knowledge. The brigand-Emperor had, therefore, granted the Christians some immunity from his troops' outrages. But Adam Schall knew a hurricane of murder, rapine, arson, and pillage would break over the Northern Capital when the rebel dynasty disintegrated.

The priest's resolution was not tarnished by his fear that only a miracle could preserve his flock from that fury. Miracles were, in a manner of speaking, his business. Unlike some ardent Latin priests, he did not seek martyrdom, but he was prepared to endure martyrdom. Confronting the marauders, he did not fear for himself, but he feared greatly for his converts.

443

When news of the brigand-Emperor's overwhelming defeat came to Peking in the last days of May, Adam Schall's courage was severely tried. Knowing their lives virtually forfeit, rebel looters searched for treasures with which to buy new lives in anonymity elsewhere. They piled hoards of silk, inlaid furniture, and bulky objets d'art as well as gold and silver on stolen carts. Released from fear of the constabulary, the rabble of Peking gleefully joined the looting—and rumor reported uncountable treasure behind the walls of the Jesuit compound.

Only fear of the Christian God and His warlike priest preserved the Mission House from mass attacks. Backed by servants wielding cudgels and spears, Adam Schall took regular turns of guard duty on the main gate. In its silver-chased scabbard at his belt hung the great Japanese saber Father Juan Rodriguez had given him a decade earlier.

Adam Schall wished that the Society of Jesus had not concentrated its proselytizing on the scholar-officials of the Empire. Many Mandarins were proving broken reeds. They were aghast because neither the spiritual force of their adopted creed nor the martial crafts of its priests had prevented the destruction of their world. Their authority and wealth already vanished, they were terrified for their lives.

The less numerous artisans and merchants were better accustomed to adversity. The continuity of the Empire had never guaranteed the continuity of their fortunes. Less cast down than the gentry, the lower classes were the mainstay of the Christian community in that extreme crisis.

John Yao the Brushmaker organized the artisans to patrol the walls of the compound that sheltered his invalid daughter. Some sons of Mandarin families joined the impromptu militia that stood between the marauders in the streets and more than one hundred women, children, and older men assembled under the protection of the foreign priest and his foreign God. The pillar of the defense was, however, Francis Arrowsmith's former adjutant Simon Wu.

In mid-May, the Colonel of Secret Police had returned in humiliation from his mission to the Earl of the Pacified West. Simon Wu was determined to strive to preserve the rebel dynasty. But his mentor, the Court Eunuch Tsao Chun-hua, the Black Premier, was already fading from the favor of the brigand-Emperor. The Earl's refusal to join the rebel dynasty transmuted One-Eyed Li's wary toleration into contempt for a traitor, and the Black Premier vanished from the Forbidden City. He had, gossip reported, fled into the countryside wearing tattered clothing and carrying the pack of a peddler.

Utterly disillusioned with, first, the Great Ming Dynasty and then by the Ming's short-lived successor, Simon Wu's tormented spirit had reverted to its two primary loyalties: the Christian community, the only group that still welcomed him; and Marta Hsü, who had commanded his devotion since their first meeting.

She had great need of his support. Two days after Simon Wu's return, Marta's father James Soo had surrendered to the despair that racked his soul. The Dynasty he had served all his life—and his family for nine generations—had crumbled like a rotten log. Although his new creed prohibited self-destruction, he obeyed the ancient creed that had governed his ancestors' lives.

His tremulous movements betraying mortal sickness of the spirit, James Soo stepped onto a stool in his garden pavilion. Fumbling with his maimed hand, he looped a silken cord around a beam and slipped the noose around his neck. Reciting the *Pater Noster,* he kicked away the stool to follow his Emperor into death. The goldfish in the pool outside did not pause in their stalking of waterbugs.

Though the streets of Peking were as dangerous as a battlefield, Father Adam Schall had responded to Marta's appeal. She pleaded that her father had been deranged by his misfortunes and, therefore, merited burial in consecrated ground despite his suicide. Regardless, the priest could only pray over the coffin of tamarisk wood that lay in a storeroom awaiting the end of disorder to permit its burial. But he added his counsel to Simon Wu's pleas that Candida, Marta, and the maidservant Ying take refuge in the Mission Compound. Escorted by six Christian former musketeers of the Battalion of God, two plain litters had carried the ladies to the provisional safety of the Jesuit House.

ON May 31, 1644, One-Eyed Li returned to the Northern Capital. He had not made directly for his stronghold in the west, as Prince-Regent Dorgon anticipated, because he had not completed his business in Peking. Having killed three horses in his headlong flight, he was saddlesore. He was also sunk in despair, though he still commanded many tens of thousands of desperate soldiers. The city had fallen to him

445

a month earlier because its garrison lacked the will to defend its virtually impregnable walls. His own resolution shattered by his decisive defeat, the brigand-Emperor knew his dispirited soldiers could not hold those walls against Red Jacket Cannon.

Although the Eternal Splendor of his reign-name was glimmering, the Yung Chang Emperor was determined to write that name indelibly on the annals of China. Besides, his defeat at the Pass between the Mountains and the Sea might yet prove no more than another temporary setback. Having ordered his bodyguards to melt the silver and gold vessels of the Imperial Treasure into bars, he hastily prepared for his coronation.

Before the debacle, One-Eyed Li had sat on the Dragon Throne in the Palace of Absolute Purity to receive homage. He had, however, postponed his coronation by the full Confucian rites until he seduced—or defeated—the Earl of the Pacified West. He had not wished his coronation to be followed by even a minor reversal that might shadow his reign. There had been no need for haste, since his dynasty would endure not merely years or decades but centuries. Besides, the astrologers had not yet selected an auspicious day.

None of those considerations any longer mattered. His rout at the Shan-hai Kwan had for the moment freed the brigand-Emperor from his obsessive concern with auguries—good or bad.

Since what he most feared had already occurred, One-Eyed Li was prepared to brave the terrors he had already experienced. Each time he sat on the Dragon Throne, he had been stricken with blinding headaches, and a giant white-robed apparition had threatened him with an enormous saber. "In terror, the brigand-Emperor sprang from the Throne and squatted on the floor gibbering like an ape," Adam Schall noted in his journal. "That base throne was just right for such a mini-Caesar [*diesem Augustulus*]."

On June 3, 1644, the twenty-ninth day of the fourth month of the first year of his reign, the Yung Chang Emperor of the Great Heaven-Fearing Dynasty was solemnly crowned. Seated on the Great Dragon Throne in the Hall of Martial Heroes, he received the secular sacraments of enthronement and heard the Court Heralds raise seven generations of his ancestors to the rank of Emperor. Guarded by thousands of rebel soldiers, the Imperial Procession then rode to the Temple of

446

Heaven in the Southeastern District to report the Accession to the Powers Above.

That evening, the newly crowned Emperor ordered the Forbidden City and the Imperial City put to the torch, and also the nine gate towers on the city walls. The next morning he withdrew from the Capital he could not hold.

In his train trudged thousands of mules carrying tens of thousands of bars of silver and gold. Though no more than a portion of the Imperial Treasures, that wealth would have launched and manned three or four Grand Fleets to crush the Manchus. Yet it was not half the treasure the fleeing rebels carried from the burning Northern Capital. Their trail southwestward to Sian was marked for hundreds of miles by discarded robes of state and bolts of tribute silk, by inlaid tables, chairs, and beds, by household altars and red-leather jewelry boxes, by scrolls of calligraphy and painting, by votary and table vessels of gold, silver, jade, and rhinoceros horn.

One-Eyed Li knew in his heart that he would never return to Peking, and he was determined that no one else would possess its splendors. Besides, he could not resist the ecstasy of destruction in which he had delighted during the decade and a half of his rebellion. The charred and gutted ruins of Peking were to be his monument.

Some three thousand rebels had been methodically burning the largely wooden city since the brigand-Emperor's return from the Shan-hai Kwan. In stone buildings the vandals exploded casks of gunpowder from the Imperial Ordnance Works. When their commander complained that no one had ever undertaken to raze a city of such size, One-Eyed Li assigned three thousand additional men to Peking's destruction. After his withdrawal, that rear guard still labored with diabolical energy. Flames stained the long twilights and early dawns of June with the red glare of the Inferno.

Burning buildings ringed the Jesuit Mission with fire, and the leaves of the trees in the courtyards curled lifeless in the searing heat. Though the tiled roofs of the Mission House resisted the flames, their wooden eaves were scorched. The Christian community's prayers sustained the vigilance of men posted on the roofs with water buckets, and the yellow tentacles that curled suddenly under the tiles were doused time after time.

Elsewhere the conflagrations leaped the narrow *hutungs* like fire-breathing dragons, but the Mission House remained an island in a sea of fire. Though flames blistered the walls and painted the faces of the Christian guards red, the buildings were only charred. Even the adjoining house, where Adam Schall kept his library and his printing plates, was saved from the tongues of fire that licked its thatched roof.

In the octagonal brick chapel the Christian ladies offered thanks to the Lord of Heaven for His miracles, which preserved them. Father Adam Schall dourly observed that he saw no phenomenon inexplicable by human knowledge. Their salvation was the result of constant vigilance and courage. But they could thank the Lord of Heaven for inspiring His children to such supreme efforts.

Adam Schall's professional skepticism did concede the possibility of a miracle when a squad of rebels defied Simon Wu's arquebusiers to lever an oil-soaked bale of rice straw weighing several hundred pounds against the main gate. A whirlwind rose from the encircling firestorm to lift the blazing mass. The gust deposited the bale on the roof of a Taoist temple fifty yards away, and a geyser of flame erupted.

The Christian refuge was in the next instant assailed by some thirty robbers, who broke down the weakened main gate. His face and arms covered with soot, his gray beard and black cassock spotted with burns, Father Adam flourished his two-handed Japanese saber. The flames danced crimson on the striated steel blade.

Adam Schall growled a guttural war cry ending in a great shout: *"Gott mit uns!"* Forgetting prayer in his rage for battle, he swung the saber, and the razor-edged blade flashed silver amid the flames. The saber slashed an assailant's shoulder to the bone and almost beheaded two others before the vandals fled.

But thirty more marauders burst through the side doors and clambered over the walls while the Jesuit was repelling the frontal attack. The battle at the rear of the compound was neither so directly met nor so quickly decided, since the Christian guards were engaged on the walls. Their clothes soaked with water, damp cloths tied over their mouths and nostrils, several robbers groped through the rolling smoke. While the guards defended the beleaguered walls, the marauders broke down the doors to the chapel, where the women and children huddled. Seizing five terrified women, they retreated through the smoke. They escaped into the *hutung* outside the compound as three militiamen led by Simon Wu and John Yao rushed through the shattered doorway.

"Thank God, Simon, it's you!" Marta Hsü shrieked at her protector. "They've taken Maria... Maria and Candida both."

A mine exploded outside, drowning Simon Wu's reply from the inner door of the chapel. Urged and supported by her maidservant Ying, Marta tottered through the outer door into the flames. Panting in the scorching heat, Simon Wu and John Yao followed. They saw Marta and Ying receding into the deserted *hutung*. The other Christian women and their abductors had vanished into the pall of smoke.

"I see them!" Ying cried. "Somebody moving... over there... behind the Taoist temple! Quick, Mistress!"

Marta hobbled on her crippled feet toward the tower of flame that was the Taoist temple, leaning on the arm of the maidservant, who wept for her foster-child Maria. Simon Wu and John Yao again followed, though they could see no movement through the murk.

A beam blazing like an immense fire-arrow impaled itself in the earth behind Marta. She and Ying moved unaware into the conflagration. Horrified, the men saw the flaming beam topple. Falling ever faster, the column of fire bore the women down. Marta screamed shrilly again and again, but Ying was already silent.

The Colonel and the Brushmaker shielded their faces with their long sleeves and fought through the cataract of flame to Marta's side. When they bent to pull her free, her screams stopped.

The two Christians kneeled amid the cracking of shattered beams, the thunder of toppling walls, and the roaring of the conflagration. Blinded and deafened, paralyzed by horror, they did not move for some twenty seconds. They could not move when the roof of the Taoist temple rumbled as its supporting posts snapped, rumbled hoarsely again, and then collapsed.

Marta Hsü and Ying, Simon Wu and John Yao were consumed by the firestorm. The flames of their pyre leaped above the clouds of smoke, twisting orange, gold, and crimson in sinuous beauty.

ON the afternoon of the sixth day of June in the Year of Our Lord 1644, the first year of the Shun Chih Emperor, whose reign-name meant God-Fearing Rule, Prince-Regent Dorgon entered Peking. He led his troops past the blackened remains of the Imperial ministries toward the Imperial City to proclaim the Manchu child-Emperor the successor of the extinct Ming Dynasty.

"*Huang-ti wan-sui! Wan-sui! Wan-wan-sui!*" the Chinese lining the streets cried. "May the Emperor live ten thousand years! Ten thousand years! Ten thousand times ten thousand years!"

Heartsick of strife, revolted by slaughter, and exhausted by terror, the people of the Northern Capital welcomed the Manchus with the salutation reserved for the legitimate Emperor. Stunned by the ignoble demise of the Ming and numbed by the brutal interregnum of One-Eyed Li, Peking hailed the barbarian princeling as its true sovereign. The Mandate of Heaven thus passed to the Manchus, and a new era began in the unending chronicles of China.

The Mandate of Heaven

January 1645–September 1652

The Mandate of Heaven

... of Province, Peking
January ... - December 1979

Shensi Province, Peking

JANUARY 15, 1645–JUNE 6, 1648

GLOWING with victory, they had ridden across the broad North China plain while the bearded wheat and the smooth-cheeked millet danced with the capricious wind. All their lives—indeed, their world itself—appeared totally altered by the decisive victory at the Pass between the Mountains and the Sea. Overcivilized and infinitely corrupt, stinking in affront to Heaven like the crammed hold of a fishing junk kept from port for weeks by contrary winds, the Chinese Ming Dynasty had given way to the half-civilized Manchus, who were vigorous and sound though crude. By that decisive transfer of the Mandate of Heaven the lives of all men under Heaven had been decisively transformed.

So, at least, it had appeared to Lieutenant Colonel Francis Arrowsmith during the glorious summer and the glowing autumn of the year 1644. He was elated with hopes for a future kinder and more settled than the cruel and turbulent past. That part of mankind with whom his fate was cast appeared to have undergone a rebirth as benign as the annual miracle of spring that renews the earth. Not merely the over-lordship of an empire, but the destiny of a civilization had, it appeared, been decided by the encounter of three hundred thousand men in arms.

Like all the victors, the Englishman looked to the future with exultant optimism—before the maggots of doubt, the little white worms of disbelief, began to gnaw at his heart. With the coming of the brutal North China winter, his mood altered and his hopes declined.

The campfires of the army of the Prince of the Pacified West were red flares in the night shrouding mountainous Shensi Province, some five hundred miles southwest of Peking. The General Francis Arrowsmith had known as the Earl of the Pacified West before the Manchus made him a prince was warmed by the charcoal braziers of his tent of state. His Chinese and Manchu troops huddled over their campfires in the bitter cold of mid-January, 1645. They could not pitch tents, since they would mount at first light to continue their interminable pursuit of the brigand called One-Eyed Li, who had briefly sat on the Dragon Throne in the Northern Capital.

Even field-grade officers of the vanguard were denied the luxury of tents. Francis Arrowsmith shivered in his red-fox mantle, and his thoughts were cold and sour.

"I am not, I believe, inordinately sensitive." He spoke meditatively to his secretary Joseph King. "Nor am I lightly drawn from duty by domestic concerns, would you say?"

"By no means, Arrowmaker," Joseph answered. "If you err, you err in the opposite direction."

Francis ignored that sharp reply to brood again on his continuing inability to discover what had become of his family in the sack of Peking. He yearned for his wife Marta, even for her sharp tongue, as strongly as he did for his loving daughter Maria.

"I am not much given to imagining, am I, Joseph?" he asked again rhetorically. "It is not my way to attribute misfortunes to scheming enemies, is it?"

"Arrowmaker, you live among a race of conspirators," Joseph answered drowsily. "It is not phantoms, but humans who move us like chessmen."

Since Joseph so obviously wanted sleep, Francis closed his own eyes. But his restless mind recalled the constant frustration of his efforts to obtain any news of his family since Prince-Regent Dorgon had orderd them to ride after One-Eyed Li without stopping in Peking. He had tried to get to Peking whenever the army halted to rest men and horses. But he had always been thwarted. The Prince of the Pacified West would give him leave, but each time an emergency requiring his attention would arise. Once, too, the Prince revoked his leave without explanation.

The Prince, Francis reflected bitterly, knew that his in-amorata, Lady Chen, had survived the sack of the Capital, cared for by loyal servants when One-Eyed Li ordered her released—presumably to placate her lover. He had visited her several times, but he had invariably pleaded ignorance of the fate of Francis's women because of continuing confusion in the Capital.

Francis tried to quell his unruly thoughts, which denied him the rest he needed. But sleep eluded him, driven off by his fears that either the Prince or some greater personage felt mortal enmity toward him. Not one courier from Peking had brought him a message from Marta or from Father Adam, and all the couriers evaded his questions. The Jesuit, they said, was flourishing under the patronage of the Manchus, but none would admit to knowledge of the Arrowmaker's family.

Perhaps, he pondered, Prince-Regent Dorgon was quashing his leaves and intercepting all news from Peking. The spite Dorgon had casually expressed when they met at the Pass between the Mountains and the Sea must be virulent. His misdemeanor in failing to return to Mukden from Macao must have grown in Dorgon's mind into a grave crime.

"Who else but Dorgon could it be?" Francis mused aloud. "If he did not feel my skills could still serve him, he might execute me, Joseph."

But his secretary was snoring beside the fire, and the camp was silent.

NOT only the Englishman, but other officers were beginning to feel that their world had not been altered as totally as they had originally thought by the Battle at the Pass, which Francis had hailed as a "momentous victory, ranking with the Athenians' defeat of Xerxes at Marathon or Alexander's humbling of Darius at Arbela." Disillusionment stalked the army in its apparently endless pursuit of One-Eyed Li. Little, it began to seem, had actually changed, though the Northern Capital of the Great Empire was held by the Manchus.

The child Shun Chih Emperor had entered Peking in October 1644 and proclaimed his sovereignty over all the lands and the peoples formerly ruled by the Ming. The Manchus' Eight Banners could penetrate anywhere in China. But they could no more hold their conquests than they had been able to occupy the Empire a decade earlier. The Manchus were in possession of the Northern Capital. Their possession of the Great Empire was disputed by rival Ming claimants, since One-Eyed Li had broken the chain of direct inheritance by murdering the Crown Prince and his brothers.

The Manchus were not even done with that usurper. Still commanding half a million men, One-Eyed Li asserted that he, a Chinese patriot, had been granted the Mandate of Heaven, rather than the northern barbarians.

The pursuit continued into the autumn of 1645. One-Eyed Li was vicious in flight, slaughtering not only hapless civilians but his own soldiers and officers. Routed when he turned at bay in October 1644, he had revenged himself on his counselor, the "young Dr. Li" who first advised him to restrain his brutality in order to win over the people. When Dr. Li committed suicide, the last restraint upon his master's viciousness vanished.

Terrified of the copper swords of the brigand-Emperor's executioners, his troops confronted their Manchu pursuers bravely. Only repeated major engagements during the following year finally wore them down. In October 1645, eighteen months after the Battle at the Pass, One-Eyed Li was trapped in Chikungshan, the Seven-Castled Mountains between Hupeh and Hunan provinces.

Francis Arrowsmith was still recovering from the violent fever the Chinese call *chang-ping,* the miasma disease, and Europeans *mal aria,* evil air. But the Prince sent him to investigate an incident deep in the mountains because he knew the features of One-Eyed Li.

"Your Excellency, twenty rebel foragers led by a single officer were ambushed in a defile by farmers angry at their depredations," Francis wrote in his report. "Several hundred countrymen wielding pitchforks, mattocks, and sickles killed them all. When they stripped the officer's corpse, they found an Imperial Dragon Robe under his cloak and a golden Seal of State in his saddlebag. The body, it was further reported, lacked an eye.

"But the body was too decomposed for identification when I finally saw it. It was also terribly mutilated, so that I cannot say whether the missing eye was an old wound or a new wound. Your Excellency, I do not believe the rebel leader was killed by the peasants he had alternately patronized and tormented. The Seal of State has vanished, and the presumed

Imperial Robe is of poor stuff, the dragons embroidered in yellow cotton rather than true gold. Above all, why should the commander of several hundred thousands have led a petty foraging expedition?

"I believe, Your Excellency, the man slain in the defile was not One-Eyed Li, but one of the nephews he had created Imperial Princes. We must, I submit, consider seriously the folk report that the usurper has found refuge in a Buddhist cloister, taking vows as a monk."

Eager to end the tedious pursuit, the Prince suppressed Francis's report, informed the Prince-Regent that the usurper was dead, and led his army back to Peking. Ironically, the remnants of the Ming Dynasty One-Eyed Li had destroyed took in the remnants of his forces, honoring them with the name Loyal and True Battalions. The brigand's widow was given the title Faithful and Righteous Lady, while his heir was ennobled as Marquess Hsingkuo, Restorer of the Nation.

FRANCIS ARROWSMITH and Joseph King returned to Peking just before Christmas 1645, twenty months after they had departed on the mission they thought might take a few weeks. Prince-Regent Dorgon's direct orders, as the Prince of the Pacified West finally acknowledged, had further delayed their homecoming by pointlessly dispatching them to determine what firearms could be salvaged from the rebels' meager arsenal. But they finally rode through the Fucheng Men, the Hill Gate, on December 23, 1645.

A bandage of snow concealed both the savage wounds inflicted on the Northern Capital by One-Eyed Li and the scar tissue of reconstruction. Drifts covered the tiled roofs, and rivulets dripping from eaves froze into glittering ice-monsters. They rode past the Jesuit House, which stood alone in a bare white expanse. The skeletons of the new buildings rising around the Christian compound were wreathed with white clumps like the fleece sheep leave on fences.

Since the fresh-fallen snow had not yet been packed into ice by hurrying feet, they galloped without fearing their horses' hooves would slip. The gray afternoon was tenanted only by an occasional passer-by. Huddled in layers of coats, they were rotund balloons balanced on twin sticks and crowned by smaller balloons. The fragrance of oil and spices drifted through the Silver Fox *hutung* leading to the mansion of the Mandarin James Soo. Lanterns cast a yellow glow on the white-carpeted ground each time a gate opened in the gray-brick walls that hedged the lane.

Though continual delay had made every second precious that brought them closer to the garden pavilion, they might have been gone only a few weeks. Neither the appearance nor the smells of the quarter had changed. When they approached the last turning of the lane between blank walls, Francis's spirits soared in expectation. Although thirty-nine, he was, he felt, coming home, perhaps for the first time. His eyes searched for the familiar gate, and his nostrils sniffed the smoky wood fires that were somehow unique among all the fires of Peking. The servants would be swearing and joking as they prepared the Christmas feast.

Francis Arrowsmith and Joseph King turned the bend and entered desolation. Their horses walked unchecked across the white-blanketed waste where once had stood the mansion of the Mandarin James Soo. It might have been a park untenanted since the city's birth two millennia earlier.

"The house...it's gone, Colonel," Joseph King said gently. "But that means little....Doesn't mean the family is dispersed. We must ask the neighbors."

"Don't be a fool, Joseph. There are *no* neighbors. All are gone...swept away."

"The chestnut-vendor on the corner. He's been there forever. He'll know."

The seamed, windburned face of the old chestnut-vendor peered from the tepee of quilted coats within which he had cocooned both himself and his charcoal brazier. His eyes blinked in watery concentration like an ancient tortoise, and Francis wondered inconsequentially what patrons he hoped to attract that freezing afternoon.

"*Ai-yah...chiu shih ninrh, Tuan-chang?*" the chestnut-vendor asked in a furry Peking brogue. "Colonel, it's you, is it? The Arrowmaker? Been away, have you?"

"That's right." Francis brushed aside the invitation to chat. "I must ask you...the house of my father-in-law, it's gone. And the family...where are they? Are they well?"

"That's hard to say, Colonel. Now the old man, I know what happened to him. Hanged himself just before the bandits left...strung himself up like the old Emperor. When the mansion burned, he went up in smoke too, him in his fine coffin."

"Old fellow, speak up!" Joseph King threatened. "Answer
458

the Colonel's questions properly or I'll clean your dirty ears with my dagger."

"As you command, Lieutenant. The family went away the day after the old Mandarin hanged himself. The two ladies, the little girl, and her nursemaid, they all went with the foreign priest. That's all I know, honestly."

They rode frantically back to the Jesuit House through the sooty twilight, the cheery squeaking of the fresh snow under their horses' hooves deriding their fears. As if awaiting their arrival, Adam Schall greeted them a half-minute after Francis pounded on the gate with his sword hilt.

"I rejoice to see you both safe. Francis, Joseph." The Jesuit's manner was professionally calm, but his lips did not smile above his gray beard. "Have you just returned?"

"No, Father Adam," Joseph answered. "We've already been to the Silver Fox *hutung*."

"Then you will have seen." The priest led them across the courtyard on the path his feet had trampled through the snow. "A tragic sight, yet not as bad as it appears. But I wrote you all this."

"We never received a word," Francis erupted. "For sweet Jesus' sake, don't soothe us with priest's chatter. Where are Marta and Maria? What's become of them? Why aren't they here to greet us?"

"Francis, I can tell you with much joy that Maria and her Aunt Candida are alive.... That is, they were to my certain knowledge alive on..."

"And Marta, Father? What of my wife?"

"I don't really know, Francis. Of course, Maria and Candida being alive, there is hope for Marta...hope even for Simon Wu and John Yao. But I cannot..."

"Father Adam," Francis interrupted, shedding his cloak in the coal-fogged reception room, "I suppose you'd better tell me the story in your own way."

"...so you see, I cannot be sure," the Jesuit concluded his account of the great conflagration when the marauders invaded the Mission House, and Marta, followed by Simon Wu and John Yao, pursued those who had abducted Candida and Maria. "We never found a scrap of their clothing. Nor any...anything at all we could say was theirs. Many men and women perished in the streets that terrible week. There were many.... But you understand. I said a Requiem Mass, and I remember them in my daily prayers. However, there is no certainty that..."

"But little hope...is there, Adam?" Francis's voice quavered. "Thank God Maria lives. But what of her and Candida? You said they..."

"Yes, Francis, in God's truth, little hope for Marta. But this past summer, Maria and Candida were alive in the South...as I wrote you repeatedly."

"Never a word did I receive, Adam. And my letters, did you?"

"Nothing at all. If I had not had other reports, I would have thought both you and Joseph perished."

"That was devil's work....But what of Maria? She is well? And Candida, too?"

"They were both well in Nanking on June first. More I do not know. They have vanished once more into the turmoil."

"God be praised for His mercy." Francis distractedly brushed the thick wings of hair from his forehead. "But nothing of them since, Father, nothing these six months? And how did they come to Nanking?"

"After giving up hope of ransom, the robbers abandoned the ladies a few miles south of the city. Some loyal Mandarins fleeing the Manchus recognized the grandaughters of Grand Secretary Paul Hsü, whom they revered. They took both ladies to Nanking, where the Imperial Prince of Fu was established."

"Son of the sow-fat Prince of Fu whom One-Eyed Li slew? We had only confused reports. Perhaps you'd tell me that tale too, Adam. How did you first hear Maria was alive?"

"I received a letter from Candida when the young Prince of Fu sent an embassy to Prince-Regent Dorgon. You'll understand if I tell you what happened elsewhere while you pursued One-Eyed Li."

"But, you've had no word...no inkling at all...regarding Maria since June?" Francis pressed.

"You'll see why when you hear my tale. And you'll understand why I serve the Manchus *ad maiorem Dei gloriam,* for the greater glory of God, rather than the Ming remnants. When they heard in Nanking, the Southern Capital, that the Emperor was dead, they behaved as one would expect. Conflict divided the partisans of the young Prince of Fu, the Wan Li Emperor's grandson, and the partisans of the Emperor's nephew. The nephew was capable and upright, the grandson a dissolute drunkard and womanizer. Naturally, the wastrel was proclaimed Emperor of the Southern Ming. Wits called him the Frog Emperor because he loved to watch

460

frogs at play. His Grand Secretary they called the Cricket Premier since he loved cricket fights and..."

"What had this mad Chinese fairy tale to do with my daughter, Adam?" Francis knew he was testy in his impatience, but he was consumed by fear for his daughter.

"A great deal, as you'll see. The summer of last year, the Frog Emperor sent an embassy to commend his 'loyal Manchu vassal Dorgon' for driving out One-Eyed Li. The embassy offered to cede the Manchus all territory north of the Great Wall if Dorgon withdrew from Peking after swearing allegiance to the new Ming Emperor. One ambassador brought me Candida's first letter. She said they were both well, though concerned for you, Francis."

"But you've heard further?" the Englishman asked eagerly.

"As shall emerge, since it's all of a piece. Dorgon in turn offered to leave the so-called Ming Emperor unmolested if he acknowledged Manchu overlordship. The Southern Ming Court haughtily refused and again fell to squabbling. The Cricket Premier neglected Nanking's defenses, even when the Manchus descended on beautiful Yangchow in mid-April. They sacked that city for ten days—killing, pillaging, and raping. But the other face of the Manchus is not unfamiliar to you, is it?"

"Not really, Adam." Francis strove for equanimity. "When they spared Peking, I thought.... But why should they behave better than a Christian army? Yet you were saying?"

"Nanking fell a month later. The farce of the Frog Emperor ended when the Manchus captured him in late June."

"And Maria...and Candida?"

"I answered Candida's letter...urged her to bring Maria back to Peking. But she would not live under the Manchus. On June first of this year, her last letter said she was fleeing with the Frog Emperor. Since his capture, there has been no word of your ladies. They must be living somewhere among the rival Southern Ming claimants. I should have heard if they had come to harm."

"You've written to the Jesuit Provincial in Macao?"

"Yes, Francis. And to my brothers in Christ in the south. We must hear soon."

Francis Arrowsmith swore he would find his fair-haired daughter, and Joseph King promised to make inquiries through his kinsmen in the south. Neither Candida, the eldest granddaughter of Dr. Paul Hsü, nor Maria, his youngest

461

granddaughter, was an insignificant person who could remain unnoticed. Joseph also promised to inquire through the remnants of the Divine Skein, though he would not acknowledge before Adam Schall his ties with the militant secret societies that had sworn solemn blood oaths to drive out the Manchus.

Knowing himself helpless, Francis could nonetheless hope that Maria would soon be restored to him. He simply refused to believe that Marta was lost to him forever. He no longer remembered their bitter quarrels, but only their sweet reconciliations. For him, she embodied all the affection and the happiness he had ever known. Marta could not, his faith insisted, have died so soon after they had built the emotional foundation for a new life together.

There was, however, nothing more to say. At dinner they discussed Adam Schall's optimistic view of the Mission's future under the Manchus. Afterward he offered his guests beds, saying he must go to the chapel to pray again that Maria and Candida—as well as Marta—be restored to them. At the door, the priest paused.

"Francis, there is another matter," he said softly. "I have been giving instruction in doctrine, as well as Portuguese and mathematics, to a young Manchu lad. The boy is twelve. He is quick in thought and devoted to study. Though he is named Babaoge, he insists that I call him Robert. Robert, he says, is his father's name for him. And he boasts that his father is the greatest Master of Ordnance in the Empire."

FOR more than a year and a half, Francis Arrowsmith had anguished over the fate of Marta and Maria. He had rarely recalled his Manchu concubine Barbara or their son Robert, who had grown dim in his memory after almost a decade. Separation had brightened his mental image of Marta and Maria; longer separation had smudged his image of Barbara and Robert. But Adam Schall had just reminded him that he was responsible not merely for the one family so tragically dispersed, but also for another, which he heartily wished had vanished.

Francis slipped shivering under the quilts. His exhaustion excluded all feeling except the pleasant realization that Adam Schall's servants had warmed the bedding with glowing coals in a brass pan.

When he closed his eyes, full awareness struck him. He

sat up abruptly to throw a cold weight off his chest. He doubled over gasping, and he knew he would never see his wife again. He retched, and bile filled his throat. His hands clawed at his chest, and he feared he would never see his daughter Maria again.

Spiritual anguish and physical agony flung him back on his pillow, but he drank the poisoned chalice of knowledge. The family for which he yearned was lost to him, while the family he had never wanted claimed his duty. God had thus punished him for having lived in sinful concubinage with Barbara.

Francis never knew whether he slept that first night in Peking after twenty months. His wakeful agonies and his torpid visions were too intimately interwined.

The next morning he was tormented by the fevers and chills of malaria, which the Chinese called the miasma disease. Alternately sweating in streams and freezing despite the quilts heaped on him, he shook so violently the low bed quivered. Obediently, he drank the bitter infusion of cinchona bark from the cup Adam Schall held to his trembling lips. When he vomited it out, Schall brewed a fresh infusion. For four days, Joseph King sat beside the bed, changing the sweat-soaked bedding and heating the cloth-wrapped stones that warmed his master. When Francis's teeth chattered uncontrollably and chills tossed him like a puppet, Joseph held his hand firmly.

During his convalescence, Francis lapsed into a state Adam Schall, as always saturninely precise, called "willful inanition." The New Year passed, and Francis did not leave his bed. He lay reading cheaply printed Chinese folk novels and Latin texts from the Jesuit's library, comprehending the words of both but the meaning of neither. If he did not occupy his mind, he knew, despair would drown him. When the print danced before his eyes, he sipped sweet Chinese brandy and inhaled the acrid-sweet smoke of opium.

Otherwise, he prayed—as Adam Schall urged. For three weeks he lay in bed, looking occasionally into the gray eyes that regarded him from the miniature of his mother propped on the side table. But neither his prayers nor his mother's serene gaze comforted the Englishman.

When his son Robert's treble voice reciting his lessons drifted down the corridor, Francis pulled the covers over his head. Robert did not know his father had returned, Adam Schall said, though Barbara, of course, did. Devotion the Jesuit could command for his servants, but not discretion. Their gossip reported not only Francis's return, but the violent recurrence of his malaria—and his subsequent withdrawal to his bedroom.

Fully recovered, Francis was grateful to Barbara for not summoning him. As his lawful concubine, she could expect his attention. As the daughter of a nobleman of the conquerers, she could command his presence.

Gratitude at last combined with duty to drive Francis to Barbara. Though Adam Schall did not try to persuade him, his own guilt read reproach in the priest's casual glance. Francis finally sent Joseph King to ask Barbara when it would be convenient for her to receive him.

Joseph King returned smiling with her answer: "It is not for his dutiful concubine to say when her Lord may call upon her. She lives in his house by his grace. She will be waiting whenever it pleases her Lord to honor her with the radiance of his countenance. She would abjectly pray only for an hour's notice so that she may prepare herself properly."

Francis accused Joseph of embellishing Barbara's unvarnished Manchu reply with Chinese elaboration.

"By no means, Colonel," Joseph replied indignantly. "The Lady has naturally changed in ten years. The words fell from her own lips in the presence of her maids and her majordomo."

Barbara's mansion, Joseph added, required a large staff, and the reception room displayed scroll paintings and statuettes revealing a connoisseur's taste. Francis asked why Barbara had said she lived in his house, since he owned no house in Peking or anywhere else.

"The Lady," Joseph King suggested slyly, "can explicate that mystery better than can my ignorance!"

Francis sent his secretary to tell his concubine he would call at half past the Double Hour of the Monkey, four in the afternoon of January 28, 1646, the eleventh month of the second year of the Manchu Shun Chih Emperor. He wished to arrive neither so early that he must linger long nor so late that she would expect him to stay the night.

Nonetheless, he asked the servants to smooth with charcoal irons his blue robe with the silver-bear insignia of a lieutenant colonel on its breast. Then he went off to a bathhouse to soak in steaming water before submitting to the kneading fingers and the pounding fists of a stout masseur. His layer of fat had been rendered by hard campaigning. His body was again firm, and the muscles swelled on his yellow-haired arms and his flat stomach. His face, too, had been honed of its puffiness, and the taut skin covering his arched nose and sculpted cheeks was ruddy.

Twinkling scissors trimmed the beard and mustaches he had grown in the field. The obsequious barber murmured that the fashion had changed. Perhaps the Gallant Colonel would prefer to go clean-shaven like so many fine gentlemen nowadays. The Prince-Regent Dorgon, he insinuated, wore no beard. Francis bit back his reply that, to his sorrow, he already knew the Prince-Regent's ways too well and would never ape them. The barber did not speak when he shaved Francis's crown and oiled his queue, which hung below his shoulderblades. No more than a western ocean barbarian did a Chinese barber wish to praise the Manchu hair style both wore to declare their submission to the new Dynasty.

"You are cleansed and anointed and polished more thoroughly than you have been for years," Adam Schall remarked as Francis reluctantly entered a public sedan chair.

When the bearers had trotted a quarter of a mile through the gritty slush, the Englishman ordered them to turn back. He had forgotten the present originally intended for someone else. The tiara of shining *fei-tsui* jade lozenges mounted in ruddy gold and set off by pearls as big as grapes he had taken from a dead rebel.

Francis asked a servant to polish the tiara with lamb's wool. If he were truly the master of Barbara's house, he would arrive when he pleased. Let her prove the submissiveness she avowed by waiting patiently. It was well past the beginning of the Double Hour of the Snake, long after five in the afternoon, before he entered the sedan chair again. The bearers, who had been waiting in the sleet, lifted the staffs and bore him swaying through the twilight.

Huddled in his red-fox mantle against the cold, Francis was surprised by his heart's pounding. Fear it was not, and reluctance never quickened a heart's beat.

When the bearers set the chair down, the evening was already black. Neither moon nor stars shone through the cloud canopy over the Northern Capital. The only light in the *hutung* was the candles flickering in the globular lanterns on the shafts of the sedan chair.

Francis raised the collar of his mantle against the sleet and let his sleeve fall back so that his ungloved hand could grasp the brass bell chain. The gray plank door swung inward before he touched the chain. A stocky Manchu soldier carrying a lantern bowed and said in awkward Chinese: "*Hwan-ying Chu-jen!*...Welcome to the Master! Please come with this unworthy servant."

Holding an oiled-paper umbrella against the sleet, the soldier led Francis across the slippery flagstones of the courtyard and knocked on a green door. A female voice called "*Ching chin-lai....* Please enter."

Candles in wall sconces and standing candelabra made the reception chamber brilliant, but no one moved among the lacquer furniture that crammed the vividly carpeted floor at the foot of three low steps. Scrolls hanging side by side were palisaded with ebony stands displaying brightly glazed Tang funerary statuettes, luminescent Sung celadon bowls, and blue-and-white Ming jars. Charcoal braziers warmed the shuttered chamber, and Francis's fur cloak was oppressively warm.

The chamber was itself oppressive, he realized. Ornaments and furniture were bedizened in the florid manner of the Ming's decadence. Their excessive numbers aggravated the excess of taste. The multitude of gaudy objects had appealed to Joseph King's Cantonese insensitivity. To Francis it appeared the householder had attempted to be perfectly Chinese—and had succeeded in being more tastelessly Chinese than the Chinese themselves.

"*Hwan-ying Chu-jen!*" Barbara's voice was unmistakable, even speaking accented Chinese. "Welcome to the Master of the House!"

Orange silk rippled at the foot of the steps almost beneath Francis's feet. Barbara looked up at him between pendant emerald-and-jade earrings before her forehead again touched the gaudy carpet in a profound kowtow. She had been so still he had thought her bowed back another piece of the furniture that crammed the chamber.

"Barbara, do not kowtow to me. It is wrong...unseemly."

Francis lifted his concubine to her feet, feeling her arms smooth beneath her brocade sleeves. She broke away to bow profoundly, but did not kneel again.

"*Shih fei-chang cheng-chüeh...*" Her fluent Chinese startled Francis. "It is absolutely proper. It is simple courtesy to welcome my Lord by kowtowing."

Francis was astonished by her Confucian decorum. The young Manchu woman had been transformed into the semblance of a cultivated Chinese lady. Nonplussed, he searched for the appropriate words. He had to tell Barbara that their former relationship could never be resumed, though he would naturally be responsible for supporting herself and their son. Studying her, he knew a twinge of regret—and a rush of the light tenderness he had felt for her after their Manchu marriage.

She wore a formal Manchu costume greatly elaborated by Chinese artifice. Despite the weight of her hip-length tunic of brocaded orange tribute silk, she still moved with supple grace. Her narrow skirt of the same fabric, bordered by broad silver-and-gold embroidery, did not impede her. Nor was she impeded by the heavy metallic embroidery on the cuffs of her full sleeves and the single lapel that fastened on her right shoulder.

The collarless yoke bared her neck, which was full and round, though her face was refined by the maturity of her twenty-seven years. But the familiar green-flecked hazel eyes disturbingly returned Francis's scrutiny between lids painted with blue pigment and outlined with kohl. The white powder that misted her provocatively hollowed cheeks and her narrow forehead contrasted with the bold carmine of her lips. No longer hanging loose in the casual mode of her youth, her blue-black hair was twisted into a bouffant double knot impaled by hairpins encrusted with chip diamonds and seed pearls.

The same excess that burdened her reception chamber touched Barbara herself. There was too much artifice too readily apparent in her ensemble. A skillful confection, she was nonetheless an obvious confection—but, withal, a most attractive woman.

"Your Chinese..." Francis said vapidly. "It has improved beyond belief."

"Thank you, Francis," Barbara replied. "I have been very industrious. We all knew we would be coming to Peking some day. The Chinese... we couldn't expect them to learn proper Manchu. And I knew I would come to Peking as mistress of your house. So I was doubly industrious."

"*My* house, you say." Francis recalled his secretary's report. "Why did you tell Joseph this was *my* house?"

"Because it is. It is registered in your name in the Groundbook. Robert will, of course, inherit. His gold bought this house.... The gold you'd laid up for him."

"His gold? Laid up for him? Of course... I forgot." Francis remembered the hoard he had left for his son.

"You forgot many things, did you not, Francis?" She chided

467

him like a free-spoken Manchu, for no Chinese lady would speak so brusquely to the man she called her Lord.

"What else have I forgotten, Barbara?" Her spirit touched Francis. "What else by your reckoning?"

"You forgot to come back to me," she replied equably. "That was the most important thing. You also forgot to keep your promise to Prince Dorgon.... That was almost as important. Because of that he deliberately prevented our meeting until now."

"It *was* Dorgon, then? So implacable over a small failing?"

"Breaking a promise to the Prince-Regent is no small matter. Manchu officers have died for less. But my father saved you... because of me." Barbara strove to impress her love on Francis, her Manchu devotion stronger than any Christian vows. "Even he at first demanded that I cast you off for a Manchu gentleman. But I finally won them around, first Father, then the Prince-Regent. So you have come back to me.... Though hardly too soon."

"Your wishes... your father's wishes... Dorgon's wishes. But my wishes, they don't matter!" Despite himself, Francis was moved by her devotion, but he did not like her reminding him of her power as a noblewoman of the conquering race. "Did anyone consider *my* wishes?"

"I, always, Francis. And you think always about your own wishes. But your duty?"

"My duty? To whom?"

"If to no other, to your son. Your duty to your son... whom you deserted when you did not return from Macao as ordered."

"As for that, Mar... Barbara... I had little choice."

A dolorous echo of another such conversation resounded in Francis Arrowsmith's mind when he realized that he had almost called her Marta. He swore his actions would never again force him to defend his conduct to a woman with half-truths.

"Little choice, Francis?" Barbara was unperturbed, her tone mildly interrogative. "Could not the Arrowmaker do as he wished among the Portuguese?"

"They prohibited my returning to Mukden at the end." That truth was only lightly varnished. "Besides, I was rendering great services to your Manchu Prince. Without the guns I shipped, the Eight Banners would have taken several years more to seize Peking."

"So Dorgon granted when I pressed him. Though, he added,

One-Eyed Li helped far more. But have we met again for political disputation?"

"No, Barbara. Certainly I don't want...but you raised my failure to return...my duty...my..."

"Duty does not rule out pleasure."

Barbara glanced at the curved enamel cases that guarded her long fingernails, and Francis felt tautness in his groin respond to the invitation he had sworn to reject. He had not slept with a woman for some months—and with no woman other than tarnished-gilt officers' camp followers for twenty months.

"Pleasure can spice duty, you know," she murmured. "And I do like your beard.... A little darker, but very attractive."

"Be that as it may..."

They had been facing each other like wrestlers looking for an opening. Having forgotten what he intended to say, Francis lowered himself into a rosewood armchair and pulled his long tobacco pipe from his bootleg.

"I have for our pleasure commanded a small repast." Barbara kneeled straight-backed on a gaudy pillow beside a low table. "My attendants will present it on my injunction."

He wondered how Manchu legs accustomed to activity could bear the cramped posture Confucian formality required, and he suppressed a smile at her Chinese, which was excessively formal, indeed stilted. Despite her industrious study, Barbara lacked feeling for the language, which invariably preferred the simpler expression—except when it wished to overawe. The same insensitivity had crammed ornate furniture and objets d'art into the elegant proportions of her reception chamber—and had led her to adopt manners outmoded for a century. His response was to thrust the jeweled tiara at her.

Francis Arrowsmith was himself more Chinese than the Chinese in his condemnation of Barbara's parvenue airs, though he sensed that she had tried to make herself more Chinese to please him. Having accepted Confucian standards while believing himself too enlightened for their strictures, he felt the disdain of an adept convert for an inept convert.

Neither that disdain, which was mingled with pity, nor his new resolution to avoid entrapment kept him from Barbara's bed that night. She was too obviously willing and too attractive—and he had not lain with any woman under even the illusion of mutual affection for too long. He felt still for Barbara, he told himself, the light affection that had previously responded to her profound devotion, though he could not requite that devotion. Besides, their previous relationship, though sinful in the letter, had not been sinful in spirit. They had lived together as if man and wife and had created a child they both cherished.

It came down to this, he rationalized: He had some right to lie with Barbara; she maintained it was his duty—and they were both highly desirous. Their lovemaking, both believed, was no lubricious rubbing together to relieve bodily itches, but a spirited—and, in part, spiritual—congress.

Nontheless, Francis rose early and returned to his solitary quarters in Adam Schall's house. He was determined not to fall again into Barbara's fleshly snares. He was appalled by his weakness in assuaging his grief in her arms only a few weeks after he had learned of the disappearance—perhaps the death—of his consecrated wife.

Francis had already convinced himself that his marriage to Marta had been something it never was: a relationship based upon mutual love and mutual esteem roiled only by amoral differences that were exacerbated by prolonged separations. When he again yielded to Barbara's lure and went to live in her house, as Adam Schall had from the beginning thought inevitable, he still reproached himself. He was again betraying Marta just as he had betrayed her with Barbara in Mukden. The Manchu lady was mystified by his self-flagellation.

"What can possibly be wrong with turning to another woman when your first woman is taken?" she asked when they lay warm in bed on a cold March night. "How can it be evil?"

"It is just not right," Francis replied. "I don't really know Marta is dead.

"Francis, why turn away from natural pleasure?" she asked. "It's only natural for a man to have a living woman. A ghost makes a cold bedmate."

"You don't understand, Barbara. I am bound to Marta until her death is proved. No more than a good Chinese widow remarries should I be living with you."

"That's nonsense, Francis. The Chinese have many good things, but that is nonsense. A woman needs a man, just as a man needs a woman."

"There you're wrong again." Though he half-acknowledged to himself that he found Barbara's sunny simplicity refreshing after Marta's sometimes sullen complexity, Francis refuted her hotly. "For one thing, men's feelings are different from women's feelings."

"I've seen enough to know that a Chinese widow pretends her grief is inconsolable because that's how people ...men mostly...expect her to act." Barbara astonished him with insight, however erroneous, he would never have expected of her. "Actually, women have feelings much like men's."

"If you really believe that, Barbara, you've learned little of civilization—despite your Confucian propriety. You're still a barbarian from the steppes."

"But *your* barbarian, Francis." She laughed, knowing she must not push him too far too fast. "A barbarian who loves you."

Never wholly at ease with any woman but never able to resist any determined woman, Francis laughed in response, and they twined their legs together under the musk-scented quilt. Afterward, Francis again placated his conscience by telling himself that he had again been driven to Barbara's bed by irresistible pressures, not merely by his sensual hunger and her frank delight in her sexuality. Neither could he fail to respond to her unfeigned love, when it was so easy to make her happy. Nonetheless, he sometimes felt like a fly caught in a web woven by many spiders.

For his own Jesuitical reasons, Adam Schall was foremost among Barbara's advocates. Honored by the new Dynasty for succoring the victims of One-Eyed Li's sack of Peking as well as his learning, the priest stood even higher in the Manchus' favor than he had in the Ming's. Having urged Francis to marry Marta in order to gain a European foothold in Chinese society, he now wanted Francis to marry Barbara in order to gain a Christian foothold among the Manchu nobility. The priest therefore pressed upon Francis his duty to cherish Robert, as well as Barbara, under the seal of Holy Matrimony.

Prince-Regent Dorgon allowed them to live together undisturbed, after affirming Francis's rank as a lieutenant colonel. By containing his spite Dorgon pleased his powerful subordinate, the Lord Baron who was Barbara's father, and retained a veteran officer with special skills. Dorgon, nonetheless, believed the Eight Banners could "pacify" the Empire while depending little on the cannon and arquebuses his conservatism distrusted. Like most Chinese and Manchu officers, Dorgon disliked the foreign weapons, though admitting they were sometimes useful. But he prudently kept those weapons available by keeping Francis available.

The Lord Baron, Francis reflected, was the most straightforward. With Marta's presumed death, Barbara had become his chief wife—in law as well as practice. Having given in to his daughter's cajoling, the Baron had committed his honor to their remaining together. Besides, he wished to please his daughter, whom he indulged as no Chinese gentleman would pamper a female.

Francis was wryly amused when his slave Joseph King joined the cabal. Weary of the upheavals of his life in the Englishman's service, Joseph wanted to settle down. Besides, he said, he liked Barbara's Manchu straightforwardness and enjoyed tutoring Robert in the Confucian Classics. Already fifty-five years old in 1646, Joseph King was determined to go no more campaigning.

Barbara's ardor flattered Francis, but also puzzled him. During their long separation, she could have divorced him without odium—and she could have taken a more satisfactory husband. Instead, she had committed herself by waiting—and scheming—for his return. Having been compelled for reasons of state to accept an oddity, Francis mused self-deprecatingly, she had apparently acquired a taste for that oddity. In much the same way, her Manchu kinfolk continued to devour chunks of barely singed flesh, disdaining Chinese dainties.

The culmination of all those pressures was Barbara's again pressing him to marry her in Holy Church. She had already defied Manchu dynastic law by seeking instruction from Adam Schall for both herself and her son Robert and accepting baptism. The Manchus frowned upon their nobles' conversion, though they placed no obstacles in the way of their Chinese subjects. Barbara now knew she would not be truly married until she was married by Christian rites. She opened her campaign for that Holy Sacrament early in 1647.

Barbara sought to persuade Francis by pleading her great devotion, appealing to his love for their son, and warning that they would both burn in Hellfire. When he remained stubborn, she fell back on threats. She swore she would persuade Dorgon to imprison Francis and transfer the ownership of their house, which was his sole possession, to Robert.

Francis knew she could do all she threatened, but did not

believe she would. He was insouciant, since he could not wound her by explaining why he refused.

"If you carry out your threats," he said after dinner one night in November 1647, "you will only accomplish what you least want."

"How is that, Francis?" Barbara asked.

"You cannot keep me by throwing me out," he replied. "If you denounce me to Dorgon, he may imprison me, but he could as well expel me or execute me. Whatever his pleasure, I would be beyond your reach."

"But why, Francis, will you not marry me?" Barbara wept for her rejected love and her lacerated pride. "We live together happily, do we not?"

"Of course we do, Barbara," Francis placated her. "And that must suffice. After all, we are married in the eyes of your people."

"Then why not in your own eyes—and in the eyes of the Lord of Heaven?"

"I simply cannot, Barbara. I have only one wife, and I can have only one wife. Marta was my wife in the eyes of God and..."

"Marta *was,* you said. Then you admit it. She *is* dead...and you can...you must marry me."

"Marta was my wife in the eyes of God and remains so until her death is proved, I was attempting to say. I cannot marry you bigamously."

"Is it better to live in sin? When Father Adam is willing to marry us, how can you say..."

"That is a matter for his conscience...if he is convinced Marta is truly dead. As for myself...my conscience...I believe she may be dead, but I am not convinced. So, I cannot marry you—even if you rope me and force the responses from the throat with a dagger. It would be no true marriage."

"But I *can* be your concubine?"

"That was...is...your choice. But marriage is impossible."

Francis told Barbara *almost* the whole truth, and he trusted Adam Schall not to contradict him explicitly. He was confident that the Jesuit would not tell Barbara that he could be absolved of doubt and enter into a valid marriage. Because Adam Schall was both scrupulous and intelligent, Francis could predict his actions—as he could not predict the actions of one who was neither. The Jesuit would, of course, press him in the Confessional to reveal his reasons for re-

473

fusing to wed Barbara. But he did not go to Confession, since he could neither profess repentance nor promise to sin no more.

The reasons for Francis Arrowsmith's obduracy were actually not complex. He had acknowledged that Marta was lost to him forever on this earth, though he still cherished a spark of hope. Even Marta's memory was not his chief reason.

Having just passed his fortieth birthday, Francis Arrowsmith exhorted himself, he must at last play the man, rather than the manikin moved by circumstances and other men's wills. He would not again marry under compulsion, and he would never again be a puppet manipulated by a woman. While he refused to marry Barbara, he held the upper hand. Yielding would mean submitting to her wishes in every respect, becoming her ungelded eunuch.

He knew, of course, that living in concubinage imperiled his soul, but he was convinced that he could save his soul only by refusing marriage. If Adam Schall should ask Francis in friendship how he could live with Barbara, being unwilling to marry her, his answer would be simple.

"I am not a saint, but a sinful soldier, who feels nonetheless that there is great work to be done for the Lord in China," Francis formulated his reply in his mind. "I can only remain in China by living in sin with Barbara." (That paradox might tickle Schall's Jesuitical risibility.) "Actually, I am very fond of Barbara and would marry her in an instant—*if* I were under no compulsion to do so, and *if* marriage would not make me her virtual slave. Aside from my last glimmering longing for European heirs, I would marry her."

JUST before Christmas of 1647, another event turned Francis's thoughts from his struggle with Barbara. A courier arrived from the Imperial Prince who held his court near Canton as the Yung Li Emperor of the Southern Ming Dynasty. He carried three parcels hidden among the pots and pans that sustained his disguise as an itinerant tinker.

The first was an appeal from the Christian Grand Secretary Thomas Chü of the Southern Ming. He begged Adam Schall not to throw his great weight against the Ming's appeals for assistance to the Catholic Monarchs of Europe.

"I deplore the tragic naïveté of our brother in Christ,

Thomas Chü," the Jesuit told Francis sadly after burning the letter. "Thomas does not know that Christians often war against each other—in Europe, as well as Asia!"

The second parcel was the recently published *Tabulae Rodolphinae* of the great astronomer Johannes Kepler. That volume not only sustained the Jesuit's belief in a heliocentric universe, an issue the Society had gingerly evaded since the Holy Inquisition condemned Galileo. Its logarithmic tables also made more precise the prediction of phenomena like the eclipses the Chinese dreaded.

Adam Schall held the mint copy in his arms, crooning over it like a father with his newborn son. Declaring that he valued Kepler's tables over all the other seven thousand books in the library of the Jesuit House, he gave thanks in his prayers to Father Michal Piotr Boym, the Polish Jesuit who had sent it with the Ming Emperor's courier.

The courier also brought a letter from Candida Soo, her first since June 1645, and another from Francis's daughter Maria. Candida was considering returning to Shanghai because her unsettled life in the train of a fugitive Emperor was becoming too arduous at the age of forty. She hoped Maria would come with her, Candida added, but was not certain the child would. Both ladies were living in the household of Thomas Chü, who also came originally from Shanghai, and the Grand Secretary of the Ming wished Maria to marry his eldest son. The Lord God, Maria averred in her letter, would decide. Meanwhile, they were both well, and Maria sent her "profound love" to her father.

After reading that letter Francis decided to ride south immediately. But Adam Schall dissuaded him.

"If you go south in haste," the Jesuit argued, "you will make the Manchus suspicious of all Christians."

"I do not see that at all, Adam," Francis replied. "A man may see his daughter. It's a simple family matter.... Nothing to do with high policy."

"Francis, if you are seen to desert the Manchus for the Ming, they will believe that all Christians secretly favor that Dynasty. Your Christian duty keeps you here in Peking. You must wait for a time."

Persuaded to remain, Francis chafed. When Candida wrote from Shanghai in the early summer of 1648, he no longer knew where to find his daughter. Maria, Candida reported, was formally betrothed to the eldest son of the Grand Secretary Thomas Chü. The ladies had been separated in the retreat from the glancing defeat by the Manchus that finally convinced Candida to flee to Shanghai. She had last seen Maria well and happy, Candida wrote, but she did not know within five hundred miles where Maria was. Angry at Adam Schall—and at himself for listening to the priest's counsel—Francis could only wait for a fresh report from South China.

Peking

AUGUST 12, 1648–FEBRUARY 14, 1649

"FATHER, which is better, Asia or Europe?" The stocky boy on the piebald pony squinted into the sun sinking behind the Great Wall. "Where would you rather be?"

"I am here in Asia with you, Robert," Francis Arrowsmith laughed. "Isn't that answer enough?"

"No, Father, not really," the boy replied. "Mother sometimes says you would be happier in Europe, though she doesn't know what Europe is. Joseph King sometimes tells me your heart is split. But, of course, you know more about Europe than anyone except the Fathers."

"I should, Robert, shouldn't I?" Francis answered. "After all, no one else has seen Europe."

"But which do you like better, really?" His son persisted, holding his reins with one hand and supporting a hooded falcon on the other.

"It is not a matter of which is better, Robert." Francis's patience would have astonished his secretary. "Each is good in its own way. But why do you worry about the difference? Do you talk about Europe with your cousins?"

"My cousins, Father? Hardly! They don't properly know where Canton lies...or even the size of the Empire. They think the whole world is just like Manchuria and North China."

"Your uncles then, Robert?"

"My uncles are worse. For them the Great Empire is only an enormous hunting ground and battlefield. They conquered the Empire on horseback, Joseph King says, and their minds are still in the saddle."

"What else does Joseph say, Robert?" Francis probed his fourteen-year-old son's quick mind. "And what do you tell him about the Manchus?"

"The Manchus are the greatest warriors in the world. Who can deny that? But I don't argue with Joseph when he says my uncles live in mansions with marble steps, but their thoughts are still imprisoned...as if they were still in the tents they like better. He is right. My uncles only smile when I tell them about Confucius and Jesus."

"So the Manchus are the greatest warriors in the world, Robert? What about Europe? Are there no great warriors there?"

"That's what I want you to tell me, Father," the boy replied reasonably.

"It's been a long time, Robert. I've forgotten much. But you do know that everyone in Europe is Christian and there are many mighty Christian warriors?"

"What's special about being a Christian if everyone is a Christian?"

"Being a Christian is not supposed to be special." Francis decided not to bewilder his son by speaking of the Protestant heretics. "Everyone, even the lowest, is a child of the Lord of Heaven and worships Him with the True Rites."

"As we do, of course." Robert was smug. "But I don't like everyone's being a Christian. Might as well have everyone a nobleman. There's no honor in that."

"They are Christians not for worldly honor, but for God's Grace and their own salvation."

"I don't think much of that. But tell me more about how everyone fights with Red Jacket Cannon and arquebuses in Europe."

Francis sighed in pretended reluctance, but was soon as enthusiastic in recounting the great battles of the past as was his son in his incessant questioning.

The declining sun threw a pink haze over the Great Wall, and a flock of wild ducks darkened the sky. The flapping of their wings was an immense murmur over the hills as they flew north in great vees.

Robert lifted his kestrel's hood, and the bird's predatory eyes glowed. Thrown from the boy's leather-gloved left hand, the kestrel soared high above the ducks' shining iridescence.

Shielding his eyes with his hand, Robert watched the kestrel circle. He held his breath when the falcon folded its wings and plummeted into the swarm. He grinned when the predator dropped out of the swirling flock with a duck clutched in its talons.

The kestrel flew straight to his hand, and Francis wondered again at its splendid training. There was no need to tempt the bird with cries or bait. Robert pried the bloody duck from the talons and rewarded the kestrel with a chunk of raw meat from his saddlebag. He threw the duck into the game bag at his saddle-bow and licked blood from his bare right hand.

Francis Arrowsmith realized then that his son would very soon be a bloodthirsty Manchu cavalryman. But there was far more to the boy than the stolid determination and the brute aggressiveness of his mother's people. His mind was already more supple in its green youth than almost any Manchu's. Even the wily Dorgon was limited intellectually beside the boy, though the Prince-Regent's mind was, of course, more tenacious. Robert, moreover, possessed Chinese sensitivity and European curiosity that were alien to his Manchu relations.

His appearance was just different enough to set him apart. Though giving promise of greater growth, Robert was heavy of body and short of leg like his Manchu forebears. But his long fingers were clever with aiming triangle, compasses, and the mechanism of wheel-lock muskets as well as with sword, spear, and bow. His wide-set eyes and his skin, paler and finer than his cousins', showed that the blood of Europe flowed in his veins. His irises were green-flecked and no darker than Francis's own, but so too were his mother's.

Francis saw himself chiefly in the boy's high forehead and quick gestures, though he wondered if that were an illusion. He looked away when Robert rode ahead and his long braid bounced against his royal-blue tunic. Even more than he detested his own Manchu queue, which had become tawny with age, Francis Arrowsmith hated the long black braid that grew from the back of his son's shaven head.

"I like Asia very much, Robert." Francis resumed the conversation as if there had been no interruption. "And I like hunting with you. But sometimes, I must admit, I would like to see Europe again."

"Will you take me with you, Father?" the boy demanded.

"That would be difficult, very difficult. What would your mother say if I took you away?"

"We could come back, Father, couldn't we? I'd like to see Europe."

"It's a long way, son, a very long way. But so would I."

The boy flew his falcon again and cantered ahead to watch it fall again on the ducks.

Adam Schall, Francis reflected, is not wholly wrong when he says my desires are mixed, very mixed. He is right when he says I sometimes burn to find Maria, but am held back by Robert, who is a son, not a daughter. He is right, too, about my yearning for Europe, which he says he has put behind him. But I cannot believe him right when he says Maria is to me a symbol, my own Holy Grail, because she is an extension of Marta. And he is wrong when he says that the Marta I remember never existed, that I have enshrined a false Marta in my own mind. Of course, he wants me to marry Barbara and bind myself to Peking forever. That I will not do, however much joy I find in Robert.

The next evening, when they returned jubilantly to Peking with scores of ducks bulging their game bags, Barbara listened with delight to Francis's boasting of their son's horsemanship and falconry. But her gaze dropped to her embroidery when Francis praised the boy's searching intellect.

Their Chinese cook served Francis a domestic duck dried in the wind and roasted in a conical oven so that the crisp skin crackled in wheaten-flour pancakes. Robert and Barbara devoured the wild ducks, which the cook had disjointed and left over an open fire for ten minutes. Blood ran down their chins as they gnawed the half-raw meat from the pink bones.

After dinner, Francis watched Barbara at her embroidery and Robert practicing his Chinese calligraphy. His thoughts, however, drifted to his other child. He should, Francis felt, soon ride south to find Maria. He could not leave it too long, though he was, meanwhile, occupied with Robert, the only heir of his body aside from the vanished Maria. A son required a father's attention.

Francis knew he had not previously made as much of either of his children as he should. Being so often and so long absent, he had not watched them grow from babbling infants into human beings. At fourteen, Robert was old enough to engage not only his father's affection, but also his intellect. By Manchu standards, he was almost a full-fledged warrior. He lacked only a year or so of the age at which Genghis, Khan of Khans, whom the Manchus venerated, rode toward mastery of the world.

Robert was no such firebrand—not yet, at least. The scholarly discipline Adam Schall imposed in mathematics and Joseph King in the Confucian Classics had probably retarded his martial prowess, the sole accomplishment valued by Manchus of the old school. But he was an adept and eager pupil when his father detached him from those schoolmasters to instruct him in musketry and ordnance.

Prince-Regent Dorgon had ordered Francis to train picked officers with culverins in order to maintain a cadre of skilled artillerymen. But Robert grasped the essential principles far faster than those officers. Moreover, his son's pride in his father's mastery was a deep and constant joy to Francis.

Robert's mind was quicksilver, wholly European in its flexibility and its logic. On that Adam Schall and Francis agreed, though they agreed on so little else nowadays. Joseph King insisted that the boy's intellect was—by some miracle—Chinese in its subtlety and its retentiveness. Robert's three teachers agreed completely that his brain was *not* Manchu, whatever else it might be.

Francis looked up. The manservant clearing the table had stumbled and jostled his son. Black ink splashed from the ink-stone and puddled on the table, soaking Robert's paper.

"Dolt!" the boy shouted and slammed the hard edge of his palm against the manservant's thigh.

"*Na chiu-shih-la...*" Francis was stern. "That's quite enough, Robert. If I catch you mistreating the servants again, I'll beat you with my sword. Now apologize!"

"It is for me to apologize to the Young Lord." The manservant bowed. "It was entirely my fault. His chastisement is not only just, but lenient."

"Nonetheless, Robert," Francis told his grinning son, "I shall beat you next time I see you strike a servant."

Though it was not the first time he had been reprimanded or, for that matter, beaten for the same offense, Robert looked at his father with astonishment. How, he wondered, do they keep servants in order in Europe if they do not beat them?

Barbara stared, her embroidery forgotten in her lap. She parted her lips, then closed them. It was really no use. This time she would not protest against her husband's browbeating their son for perfectly normal behavior. The servants would run the household if she and Robert coddled them as Francis demanded. No, better to let it go this time. But she would see that the manservant was thoroughly beaten for provoking her Lord to unjustified anger at their son.

His son, Francis recalled in anger, was always aware that he was the grandson of the Lord Baron. Robert's chief failing was arrogance. He demanded—and received—from both servants and playfellows deference that might in Europe be considered somewhat excessive toward a prince of the blood. They lived, Francis reminded himself, in a different world. It would be remarkable if his son lacked the hauteur of a young nobleman of the people who were conquering the world's mightiest empire.

COOLNESS separated Francis Arrowsmith from Father Adam Schall largely because the Englishman would not marry his Christian concubine. Since Father Giulio di Giacomo had not returned to Peking after the collapse of the Ming, Francis felt estranged from the Jesuits, who should have been his companions and his mentors. That distance, he concluded, was part of the price he paid for being his own man. Nonetheless, he regretted their estrangement, and he was overjoyed by Adam Schall's repeated triumphs among the Manchus.

By foretelling the exact instant of the sun's eclipse over every one of the chief cities of the Empire, Adam Schall humbled both Chinese and Moslem astronomers in a repetition of the competitions the Jesuits had regularly endured under the Ming. His rivals' calculations erred gravely, while his own were absolutely precise because of Kepler's tables.

The Manchus were as anxious as the Ming had been to ensure the calendar's perfect accuracy in order to ensure the spiritual and the temporal welfare of the Empire. They did not impose their own religious practices on their Chinese subjects, but strove to prove themselves the legitimate heirs of the Ming by their Confucian orthodoxy in both religion and administration. Just as Barbara eagerly took to Chinese etiquette and Chinese tastes—except, perhaps, in food—the Manchus adopted Chinese ways. The new Dynasty demanded that the Chinese declare their loyalty by wearing the Manchu queue and Manchu garments. Otherwise, the conquerors accommodated themselves to the conquered, particularly with regard to the Sacred Rituals governed by the planets.

Adam Schall was, therefore, appointed director of the Department of Astronomy, ranking as a Mandarin of the Fifth Grade, Upper Section. As Candida and Marta had complacently predicted, the Manchus had taken over the institution of the Mandarinate virtually unchanged.

Determined that the Holy Cross must be his only insignia, the Jesuit rejected the first formal appointment as a Mandarin ever tendered to a European. The duties he would happily discharge, but he would not accept the rank or wear its paired silver pheasants.

The Jesuit's Superior intervened, fearing that his refusal would reawaken the Manchus' suspicion that all Christians secretly wished the restoration of the Ming. The road to salvation for the Chinese people, the Jesuit Superior remained convinced, must lead through the Imperial Court and the Mandarinate of the Northern Capital, regardless of who ruled the Capital.

Ordered to accept a Mandarin's rank and wear a Mandarin's insignia, Adam Schall still refused the regular salary in gold and rice due the director of the Department of Astronomy. Forgetting that he had gladly accepted a salary from the Ming for casting cannon, he insisted that the rule of the Society of Jesus prohibited rewards for secular work. Pressed again, Schall finally agreed to the Palace kitchens' sending him two meals a day from the Emperor's own menu.

No one was unaware of the Jesuit's modesty, and all praised his selflessness. But Peking was aghast when Adam Schall stubbornly challenged Prince-Regent Dorgon, who was becoming a tyrant as the decade drew toward its close.

Dorgon's appetite exceeded even his constant increase in power and pomp. He no longer placated the other Senior Princes, as he had when he rejected the rich gifts sent him by the King of Korea. Instead, he ordered the King to provide the most beautiful princesses of Korea for his harem, though only the Emperor was entitled to make such a demand. Dorgon replaced his co-Regent with his own brother, whom he named deputy-Regent, but continued to rule alone under the title Imperial Father Regent, meaning the Father of the Nation. Almost all the Imperial Princes had been humiliated by the Regent. One, imprisoned without cause, committed suicide in protest.

But Dorgon brilliantly directed the pacification of an Empire still threatened by bandits and rebels, as well as the claims of Ming princes to the Dragon Throne. No one could deny Dorgon's effectiveness, but most men detested him. No one, however, dared object when he built a palace of Imperial grandeur, wore Imperial robes, and issued Rescripts in his own name, rather than the boy-Emperor's. No one could oppose him, though he was obviously determined to prolong his personal rule for many years.

The Prince-Regent also planned a new capital, where the Emperor would live apart from the people, not merely separated from them by high walls and impenetrable customs as he was in Peking. To build that capital Dorgon increased taxes extortionately, seized construction material, commandeered draft animals—and conscripted tens of thousands of free laborers and artisans. He treated them hardly better than the slaves who built the Great Wall for the First Emperor in the third century B.C.—and calcified its mortar with their bones.

Francis Arrowsmith and Adam Schall almost lost their lives to Dorgon's hubris when a major rebellion shook restless Shansi, One-Eyed Li's home province. A group of Manchu princes rode through the city of Tatung en route to Mongolia to bring back a princess for the boy-Emperor's harem. Wild drunk, Manchu-drunk, they raped respectable women, even a bride stolen from her scarlet Flower Palanquin. When the townspeople attacked the princes, the Chinese governor appointed by the Manchus supported them. When those riots turned into revolt, which was joined by Mongols infuriated by Manchu arrogance, the new Dynasty's existence was threatened.

Prince Regent Dorgon summoned the Europeans to his palace. Lolling on a golden throne only slightly smaller than the Dragon Throne itself, Dorgon gazed unspeaking at them for a full minute after they had bowed profoundly. Austere in his black cassock, Adam Schall returned the Prince-Regent's appraisal from his deep-set blue eyes. Tall in his blue-silk robe, Francis Arrowsmith defiantly met the eyes of the master of the Empire. Dorgon's face, he saw, was drawn and lined. The Prince-Regent rubbed his left side as if in pain, but his voice was cool and cutting.

"*Wo chiao-kuo ni-men...*" The Prince-Regent spoke Chinese, since he knew the Jesuit's Manchu was still weak. "Arrowmaker, here is your chance to prove I was right to spare your life and let you keep your rank. I've decided to lead the expedition against the damned rebels myself, and I require your services."

"My Lord, what can the mightiest general in Asia require of us?" Adam Schall hastily forestalled a resentful reply from Francis. "We await your commands!"

"My ordnance has deteriorated because of my subordinates' neglect," Dorgon replied. "I cannot do everything myself. I require at least twenty batteries of Red Jacket Cannon within, say a month. If you and the Arrowmaker execute that commission well, he will command my ordnance. And I'll promote him...give him the leopard of a full colonel."

"My Lord, we can provide you with a good number of cannon. How many, exactly, I can only say when we survey the arsenals. And we will, if necessary, pour new cannon."

"All is well, then." Dorgon did not notice Francis's astonishment at the priest's promise to cast new cannon. "I shall expect your report within three days."

The priest ignored both that dismissal and the instructions of the Society of Jesus that he must never traffic in astrology. Schall gestured Francis to be silent, and he bowed again.

"As Director of the Department of Astronomy, it is my duty to offer Your Highness counsel," the Jesuit said. "I must advise Your Highness that the auguries of the Heavens are not favorable to a punitive expedition. No more are they favorable to the building of a new capital."

"What is it you say, Priest?" Dorgon's haggard face flushed in anger. "How dare you!"

"It is my duty, Your Highness," Schall replied equably. "The message of the stars is plain. If construction of the new capital is not halted immediately...if all the conscript laborers are not freed...I foresee disaster for the Sacred Dynasty."

"Get out!" Dorgon screamed. "Guards, get them out before I split them with my sword! And confine them!"

Adam Schall spent the night in prayer and Francis Arrowsmith in writing letters of farewell to his daughter and his son. When they were summoned to Dorgon's presence the next morning, both were prepared for death.

They were led through corridors adorned with geometrical gilt patterns by a Manchu major who did not meet their eyes. Holding open the door to the Prince-Regent's reception chamber, the officer looked dully at them. His expression was grim, as if he were already ordering the executioner to swing his two-handed scimitar.

"I have considered your warning carefully, Spiritual Father." The Prince-Regent smiled on his golden throne. "I am convinced that you spoke from a sense of duty with no intent to taunt me or to deceive me."

"I am honored, Your Highness," Adam Schall replied, still bent in a profound bow. "I am sure you will not regret your wise decision."

"I shall halt the construction of the new capital and release the conscript laborers, lest Heaven punish the Dynasty for such presumption," Dorgon said. "Of course, I sought only to build a capital fitting for the Emperor."

"*Mergen Daising...*" Francis used the title he knew Dorgon liked best. "Wise Warrior, that decision confirms your immense wisdom."

"We are twice honored by your wisdom!" Schall knew he could not overdo his flattery, and Dorgon was truly wise to allay the discontent that could have led to revolt in the Northern Capital itself.

"You will, therefore, find me the twenty batteries I require," Dorgon commanded. "You, Arrowmaker, will train my artillerymen and command those batteries when we march on Tatung."

"You risked everything, Adam," Francis said when they walked again on the streets of Peking. "I never thought..."

"God's Grace touched him, Francis. But the risk was necessary. Our Holy Mission requires us to succor all in need. Even by making cannon we can help our suffering fellows."

"It was still a great risk, Adam. For you and for me, too. We won't need new cannon, of course, only field carriages."

"As you say, it will be no great feat to find fieldworthy pieces in the gun parks. And you do require active employment."

That same afternoon, the first thousand laborers released from servitude crowded the *hutung* outside the Jesuit House. While they kowtowed their gratitude, a bearded Mandarin read an address of thanks. Adam Schall glowed with delight, and Francis Arrowsmith clapped him on the back in jubilation.

But the Englishman was still not sure precisely how they served Christ in China by again supplying cannon for slaughter. He could not refute Schall's contention that it was essential to provide cannon for Dorgon, since the Holy Mission to China could succeed only if the Jesuits remained on excellent terms with the Manchus. Yet, for once, impeccable

486

Jesuit reasoning was not convincing. If the argument were taken to its logical conclusion, they would be required by their love of Christ to offer their assistance to the Manchus' every cruel act of repression.

Francis's personal decision crystalized during the next two months. He became convinced that the unswerving support of the Manchus practiced by the Jesuits of Peking was not wise. If he were to take to the field again, a prospect that was not unwelcome, he preferred to fight for the Southern Ming's legitimate claims to both the Dragon Throne and the affections of the Chinese people. The Ming princes were, after all, guided by the Christians who were their chief ministers. Despite his own belief that he was largely governed by prosaic self-interest, Francis Arrowsmith remained a romantic idealist.

When the Imperial Father-Regent prepared to lead to Tatung a great army supported by twenty batteries, the Englishman lay on the broad marriage bed in his secluded mansion. Barbara chided him for passing up promotion by his malingering, but he would not alter his decision. Feigning illness was not, perhaps, the noblest way to avoid an immoral assignment, but it would serve.

THE pretense of illness did not long keep Francis confined to his bed. It was not necessary. After a few days he allowed himself to walk about the house, moving creakily so that the servants could not report to Dorgon's spies that he had recovered. The burden of decision that lay on his mind also slowed his steps. His conscience had forced him to reject Dorgon's offer of promotion and field command. That refusal, he saw, had closed off to him all hope of employment or advancement under the Manchus. He had acted more decisively than he realized.

Francis Arrowsmith was only a few days from his forty-second birthday on February 13, 1649, almost an old man who should have been settled in this world and concerned chiefly with his place in the next. He was, however, still vigorous, and he chafed at inaction.

"Francis, it is not vital that you will not march with Dorgon, though we disagree, you and I," Adam Schall had told him forcefully. "Most important, you are weary of doing nothing. You are wasting your worldly talents and your spiritual gifts in idleness."

Although Francis maintained that he was right in refusing to command Dorgon's artillery, he knew the priest was also right. He was truly rusting in disuse. He could look forward to no occupation other than the hunt and the desultory study of the Chinese Classics, that murky, bottomless well of learning into which some scholars sank without a trace for a lifetime.

The Chinese friends who came to cheer him in his illness were astonished at his discontent. Such an existence was the highest joy for which they could hope. But his European temperament chafed at that idyllic life, just as his European conscience forbade him to advance himself by ignobly ingratiating himself with Dorgon.

Having finally if belatedly resolved to act the man, Francis had to be his own man. Having lived three years with Barbara's alternation of apparent submission and attempted domination, he resolved he would no longer be a marionette on strings alternately flung loose and then pulled in tight. Yet he could only leave Barbara by leaving Peking.

Wrapped in his red-fox cloak against the cold, Francis wandered brooding into the courtyard. As he opened the moon door, a babble of juvenile laughter greeted him. Proud as the Emperor himself in an armchair covered with Imperial-yellow brocade, his son Robert was receiving the kowtows of the servants' children and his base-born playmates.

The Englishman gazed at that scene for an instant uncomprehending before rage at his son's arrogance sent the blood racing in his temples. Unthinking, he plucked his son from the armchair and carried him kicking into the bedchamber. His arm rising and falling with metronomic regularity, he beat the youth with a quirt. Even in his anger, Francis knew Robert's screams were half pretense and half wounded pride. Thickly clad for the winter, the youth could hardly feel the blows that raised puffs of dust from his padded tunic.

"This will teach you!... Must teach you!" Francis shouted. "A little humility becomes a Christian. You are not the Emperor, nor ever will be. But go on this way... and you'll end up a petty tyrant in your regiment. You are a human boy... sometimes a very naughty boy... not a godling."

Robert burst into tears only when his mother, attracted by the noise, stormed into the chamber.

"What are you doing to the boy, Francis?" Barbara's eyes flashed green. "I've told you to leave him alone. He is only a child.... And you don't know how to raise a Manchu warrior."

"A child? When he's close to sixteen? Nonsense, Barbara! He'll be more than another witless, *koumiss*-swilling Manchu cavalry officer if I have anything to do with it. He'll be a good Christian soldier.... He'll be a man...a man with a mind that works."

"Must you have something to do with it?" Barbara screamed as loudly. "That isn't necessary. No, it's not..."

"If I can't raise my own son as I see fit, then..."

"Then you'd better leave. You'd better leave, Francis...." Barbara paused, shocked by her own impulsive words, then resumed more quietly. "Yes, you had better leave us. You are doing no good here...for yourself or us."

"I will leave then, Barbara." Francis watched his son slip out of the bedchamber. "It's best for all of us."

"Yes, Francis, I'm afraid it is best." Barbara had known this moment must come ever since Francis made it quite clear he would never join her in Holy Wedlock. "I've lived as your concubine long enough. Father Adam says it is no longer just peril to our souls...but certain damnation if we continue. And you will not marry me."

"I've explained, Barbara, why..."

He did not love her, and he would never love her. Barbara finally accepted the reality she had so long evaded. She reflected in uncharacteristic introspection that she loved their son so greatly because he had so much of Francis in him. It was strange that in defending Robert she should drive away his father.

"I am weary of that nonsense, Francis," she finally said in resignation. "For Robert's sake...for my sake...for your own sake...it is better for you to leave Peking. Perhaps you'll find that mythical daughter of yours somewhere."

Barbara stalked from the bedchamber, her head stiffly erect. The tears that clouded her eyes were no longer tears of rage.

"I'm sorry, Barbara, very sorry," Francis called after her. "I'm desperately sorry, but you're right."

A MINOR squabble had led to a major decision. Having taken that decision, Francis saw no reason to linger. Barbara's tears reproached him as he made his preparations, and they clung together in bed. On the eve of their parting, he almost loved her, and she was desolate. But both knew the decision could not—and should not—be reversed.

Francis parted in strained friendship from Adam Schall. In his fifty-seventh year the Jesuit's beard was frosted white, and his penetrating eyes were sunken. But his strength was unsapped, and his spirit was untarnished by pessimism. He complained of his great age and recalled that his exemplar, Father Matthew Ricci, had gratefully laid himself down to die when only a year older. But that was only priest's talk.

"Adam, why should I await Dorgon's revenge?" Francis asked quietly.

"'You are a stone in Dorgon's rice, a beam in his eye,'" Adam Schall agreed. "I fear that...seeking revenge on you...he will extend that revenge to the Fathers and the Christian community. Since you must go, go quickly. For the Lord's sake...and your own...be gone!"

"Adam, you've never forgiven me for refusing to marry Barbara or to march with Dorgon, have you?" Francis asked, perversely seeking consolation from his old friend, whose counsel he had rejected.

"No, Francis, that's not true," Adam Schall replied thoughtfully. "I should have preferred...for the Holy Mission ...for the peace of your soul. But, since you cannot, it would be far better for you to go quickly."

The Jesuit was disturbed because Barbara's complaints of the Englishman's rejecting her love—and Holy Matrimony—had created a public scandal. No more than those complaints advanced the China Mission did the example of a European Christian living in sin with a Manchu lady. Having hoped to make Francis a bridge into Manchu society, Adam Schall had concluded that he was an obstacle on the road to the conversion of the Empire. Whatever suspicions of Christians' favoring the Ming his departure might provoke, they would be less deleterious than his presence and his continuing feud with the Prince-Regent.

"I give you my blessing with all my heart, Francis," the priest reiterated. "But...for the Lord's sake...be gone!"

That friendly farewell ringing in his ears, Francis Arrowsmith rode south to do the Lord's work and to reknit his own life. He had, he knew, already delayed far too long his search for Maria, who was wandering with the Ming loyalists in South China. His determination to bring his daughter back to Peking was a credible pretext for his departure.

Besides, Robert was awaiting orders to ride south with his

uncle's regiment to serve his sovereign, the Shun Chih Emperor, by suppressing bandits and rebels. Francis knew he would never beat his son again—or instruct him. He could not know whether they might meet on the battlefield. But he knew beyond doubt that his son's childhood was over. As he himself had told Barbara, Robert was almost an adult, an arrogant Manchu warrior. They embraced, but the easy love that had briefly bound father and son was also over.

Francis had not expected Joseph King to accompany him. Somewhat tardily, he had released Joseph from his bondage, and his former slave could prosper under the new Dynasty. Barbara offered a generous pension to honor her son's tutor, who was already fifty-seven years old. But Joseph stood booted and dressed for travel beside their horses that early morning.

"I am accustomed to your foibles, Arrowmaker," he explained. "And I am too old to learn a new way of life."

"I am flattered, Joseph." Francis gripped his secretary's shoulder in powerful affection. "But is that all?"

"No, Arrowmaker, as you surmise," Joseph smiled. "I would serve a Chinese dynasty, not these Manchu usurpers. And I should be very glad to see our little Maria again."

Their total wealth was their clothing and their weapons, their five horses and Joseph's most cherished books, a letter signed by Adam Schall and twenty taels of gold in their saddlebags. Their ultimate goal was the Court of the Yung Li Emperor of the Southern Ming Dynasty. A good man though weak, that Emperor was sustained by three valiant Christians: a Grand Secretary, a General, and a Eunuch. Their immediate objective was the Ming stronghold in Fukien Province opposite the island of Taiwan, which the Portuguese called Ilha Formosa, the Beautiful Isle.

"Whatever their deficiencies," Francis said thoughtfully as they mounted, "the Ming and its Ministers...pagan as well as Christian...are more truly Christian in their steadfastness than the turncoats of Peking Adam Schall cherishes."

Expecting nothing for themselves and prepared, for once, to give everything of themselves, Francis Arrowsmith and Joseph King rode south to do the Lord's work on February 14, 1649.

Chüanchou, Anhai

JULY 23, 1649–OCTOBER 30, 1649

THE ancient land itself altered. The seamed, pitted, and carbuncled face of the earth changed its expression with every ten leagues Francis Arrowsmith and Joseph King left behind their horses' rumps in their flight of sixteen hundred miles through an Empire in turmoil. The faces of men altered, too, becoming darker and more animated as the travelers moved south circuitously to confuse any pursuit.

The name of time itself altered. Men lived in the sixth year of the Shun Chih Emperor of the Manchu Dynasty on the plains of the Metropolitan Province of Chihli and in Honan Province, where the travelers bypassed Kaifeng, whose shattered city walls still commemorated One-Eyed Li's protracted siege. Coming to Kiangsu and Chekiang provinces, they entered the third year of the Yung Li Emperor of the renascent Great Ming Dynasty. That Emperor, whose reign-name meant Eternal Days, ruled the province between the violet hills and the indigo sea called Fukien.

Ardent supporters of the Southern Ming, the men of Fukien were fierce enemies of the Manchu usurpers. Fukien was the northernmost stronghold of the resurgent Chinese Imperial House, which held sway over eight broad provinces of South China. Having suppressed most brigands, Ming troops held the borders against the encroaching Manchus.

The fugitives' long ride ended in the middle of the Double Hour of the Rat, midnight by European clocks, on July 23, 1649, not far from the twin gates of the ancient city of Chüanchou. Their horses had cantered southeast from Anchi for four hours while purple dusk dwindled into black night. Drenched by a rainstorm, their black garments resembled the Jesuits' sinified cassocks. It would have been folly to wear the distinctive uniform of either dynasty through the interwoven battle zones of an Empire wracked by civil war. The ubiquitous Spiritual Fathers were tolerated for their learning or wooed for their cannon by both Ming and Manchu.

Francis Arrowsmith searched for the lights of Chüanchou through the driving rain. The horses' hooves slipped on the slick pavement of the high road in the dark night, since the moon was cloaked by clouds. Gusting from the coast four miles to the east, the wind whipped their soggy robes around the travelers' bodies and clutched at the shapeless hats that concealed their hair. They had shorn their queues upon entering Chekiang, but the stubble on their crowns revealed that they had recently worn the Manchu tonsure.

When the road mounted a rise, Francis glimpsed a glimmer on the coastal plain. Riding abreast, he and Joseph came over the hill crest and saw a yellow circle inscribed on the darkness below. In its center glowed a dome like an enormous helmet, its red-tiled curves alternately lit by glaring torches and obscured by flickering shadows. When gusts hurled the rain in horizontal sheets, the spiked dome vanished.

"Hui-chiao-tang...," Joseph shouted. "The mosque...I told you..."

Squirming in his saddle, Francis felt his robe bunch under his thighs. Anticipating the physical relaxation of Chüanchou, he relaxed his alertness against danger. When the drumming of his horse's hooves slowed, he started in surprise. Having seen the dome of the mosque shining through the rain, the animal should have quickened its pace toward the beacon promising dry stables and fresh fodder.

Francis was still puzzling six seconds later when his horse crashed into the chest-high barrier it had discerned as a more palpable blackness in the black night. He was flung over the horse's head to land on his tender left leg in the mud beside the road. Seconds later, Joseph sprawled beside him, and Francis chuckled despite his pain. Like buffoons clowning for peasants at a fair, they had been tripped by the unseen barrier, probably a massive log.

A pikehead pinned Francis to the ground, its point biting into his chest. An oil lantern held by a disembodied arm dazzled him.

"*Man-yi di chien-tierh...*" a hoarse voice growled in the accents of Peking rather than the unintelligible dialect of Fukien. "Spies of the Manchu barbarians. I told you so."

Hard hands hauled Francis upright. Through a flash of pain-lightning he saw that the man holding the lantern wore a battle tunic. On its green breast a white horse swum amid stylized billows, the insignia of a sublieutenant in the Ming service. The lantern was lifted higher to illuminate the stubble on the Englishman's crown.

"*Mei wen-ti...*" the Sublieutenant growled. "No question about it. Manchu spies, for sure. You'd think they'd wait till their hair grew in, but they're so damned stupid..."

"Look at me, you fool!" Colonel Arrowsmith cuttingly addressed the bumbling subaltern. "Do I look like a Manchu? Have you ever seen a Manchu who looked like me?"

"The hair color *is* odd, Sir," a second voice spoke in the darkness. "And the nose. Never heard of a Manchu with a great beak like that. More like an anteater than a human being."

"It's not a human being," the Sublieutenant insisted. "It's a Manchu devil. They come in all shapes, all uglier than devils. And the other, unquestionably a Cantonese. Clever to send a Cantonese, even if he is one province short of his goal."

"*Ni hwen-tan...*" Francis interrupted his captor's self-congratulation. "You bloody fool, I'm a western ocean man, not a Manchu."

"Clever," the lieutenant said. "Even speaks the Officials' Language.... Clever, these Manchus. But no point in taking them back. Wang, hand me a bowstring.... Strangle 'em here and get it over with."

"Suppose he *is* a western ocean barbarian, Lieutenant?" a third voice asked. "He couldn't be a Manchu spy, then, could he?"

"Why not? The Manchus have ocean barbarians serving with them...a score of gunners, I've heard. Hand me the bowstring."

"As spies? Hardly!" Joseph King taunted the Sublieutenant. "Anyway, your superiors will want to question us."

"Shut your mouth. You can talk all you want when you report to your Manchu Emperor's ancestors in Hell. But shut your mouth now and stretch out your neck."

"To one invincibly armored in stupidity," Joseph quoted, "the swiftest arrows of wit are broken straws."

"You'll die harder for that, lackey."

"*Shao Lin Ssu lao-ko ssu-pu-liao!*" Joseph's words were clear to Francis, even forming a coherent sentence, but it was nonsense: "The elder brothers of the Shao Lin Temple do not die!"

"He knows the words, Lieutenant. Perhaps, they are..."

"A spy *would* know the words, Wang. But...still... perhaps I will send them in for questioning."

"Might as well, Lieutenant. Squeeze 'em first, then strangle 'em."

Between mounted soldiers, the two Christians rode again toward the dome of the mosque shimmering through the rain. Francis was afraid his superiors would prove as dense as the Sublieutenant. He was annoyed by his own clumsiness in falling into the ambush and nagged by curiosity regarding Joseph's cryptic utterance. But he recalled the secret society organized at the Shao Lin Temple to unite all Chinese against the Manchus. Yet how did Joseph know the current password?

His secretary had apparently added one more layer to the systematic deceits that had seen them safely through the chaos of civil war. They had told the Manchu troops they encountered they rode on the service of the Imperial Father-Regent Dorgon himself. Those officers who had not heard of the yellow-haired Arrowmaker all knew the wisdom of Tang Jo-wang *Shen-fu,* otherwise Father Adam Schall. Validated by his personal seal, the priest's letter had served them better than a passport. But Adam Schall's sponsorship would condemn them to Ming loyalists. They, too, knew Schall—as the Jesuit who served the Manchus.

Joseph's connection with the Shao Lin Brotherhood was their best hope. Yet some senior Ming officers despised the plebeian brotherhood. They might dispose of suspected spies— and not thereafter worry overmuch whether they had made a mistake.

Francis decided he would not immediately inquire after the "golden-haired Chinese girl," as he had inquired in vain since entering Ming territory. How would he react if, still in the service of the King of Spain, he met an English officer who claimed that he had deserted the Protestants and that he searched for his half-Spanish daughter? The truth would seem preposterous!

They might face swift execution. It was such a stupid way to die! Yet the truth would not protect them, and he could contrive no plausible falsehood.

Night and his forebodings veiled from Francis the wonders of Chüanchou, over which Joseph King had rhapsodized. Although recently displaced by Canton, the port had for centuries been the chief point of contact between the Chinese and seafaring peoples from the west.

Not only the mosque whose dome floated over the city, but the tombs of two missionaries recalled the first landing of Islam in China. Pious Chinese Moslems had traveled thousands of miles to prostrate themselves before those miracle-working catafalques since the third year of the Mongol Dynasty, the year 1323 of Our Lord. A time-polished stone statue recalled the earlier arrival of the Buddhist missionary from India whom the Chinese called Abbot Chu. Marco Polo had visited Chüanchou in the thirteenth century, long after the settlement by Syrian Christians whose tombs were inscribed in their own language.

Guarded to landward by craggy mountains, the port was accessible from the sea through a narrow inlet that protected it from both typhoons and pirates. Those natural advantages recommended Chüanchou as the eastern base of the resurgent Ming Dynasty, which looked abroad for the assistance essential to reconquering North China.

Waiting in a dank anteroom under guard, Francis held fear at bay by recalling the port's decaying glories. Would "the miracle-working tomb of the yellow-haired Manchu," he wondered, be counted in later years among the sights of Chüanchou?

An inner door opened, and their guards bowed to two senior officers in scarlet robes. The foremost wore the unicorn insignia of a duke. Francis assumed the rank was hereditary, since the officer could hardly have earned his rank by protracted service to the Dynasty. Despite his air of authority, the Duke's smooth cheeks and open features had been marked by the passage of no more than twenty-five years. His companion, who was no older, wore the leopard of a colonel.

"What have we here?" the Duke asked. "Raise your head, fellow, and let me look at you."

Francis saw recognition flare in the Duke's prominent eyes and, at the same moment, remembered the half-Japanese youth who had been Adam Schall's foreman at the Imperial Ordnance Works.

"Arrowmaker!" the young Duke exclaimed. "You are the Arrowmaker, are you not?"

"I am, Noble Duke. I knew you as Cheng Cheng-kung—Lucky Cheng—didn't I?"

"You can call me Cheng-kung. Duke Chu, if you prefer. The Emperor has honored my small merit by bestowing the Imperial Surname upon me."

"*Kuo-hsing-yeh* . . . Koxinga, the Lord of the Imperial Name . . . of course," Francis remembered. "And now you stand in judgment over me."

"As to that, Arrowmaker, at least I know you're not a Portuguese gunner lately in the Manchu service. Why you come is another matter. Why stealthily in the middle of the night?"

"We planned to arrive much earlier . . . but the rain. And the road was longer than I thought. No more than ninety *li* from Anchi, hardly thirty miles, yet . . ."

"In mountain *li*, a hundred twenty, Arrowmaker." Joseph King's didactic instinct was irrepressible. "I told you mountain *li* were shorter than plains *li*, but you just measured the map."

"So clumsy, the renowned Arrowmaker?" the Duke asked. "And so wise, always, his servant? Yes, I remember well."

"I'm an artilleryman, not a cavalryman. And, I suppose, clumsy when my mind is on other matters."

"What other matters are so important you come stealing in like spies?"

"Your Grace," Francis essayed, "Your Most Exalted Excellency, I . . ."

"I told you to call me Cheng-kung—even Old Chu, if you prefer," the Duke interrupted with harsh geniality. "We know each other, Arrowmaker, too long for such formality, you and I."

"Old Chu, then, you must know if you know me that . . ."

"I know you, but I know nothing else, Arrowmaker. I know you were kind to the young son of the Admiral of the Coastal Seas. Many Mandarins despised me for my low birth and my mixed blood. But you were kind."

"In that case . . ."

"That has nothing to do with today . . . this moment in this place. I *know* you. That does not mean I *trust* you. My business is the Emperor's business! How can I know you do not plot against His Majesty? But tell me what you seek."

"If I may speak, Old Chu....I seek to serve the Lord of Heaven and the Yung Li Emperor of the Ming. I also seek my daughter Maria. Have you heard reports of a yellow-haired lady?"

"That, too, is another matter, Arrowmaker. Nothing to do with your secret mission. You served Dorgon well, did you not?"

"Dorgon hates my soul...feels I've betrayed him. Send for news to your spies. Ask what Dorgon thinks of the Arrowmaker."

"I shall, since old friendship forbids my executing you out of hand. But you will wait in prison and..."

The Colonel had stood silent during his superior's hectoring interrogation. When he heard that judgment, he laid his hand on the Duke's arm with easy familiarity, which widened Francis's eyes. Colonels did not deal so casually with generals, let alone with dukes. Even Joseph King would not offend his master's dignity by such a public gesture. But the Duke, the Lord of the Imperial Surname, listened with a smile to the Colonel's murmured advice. The officers conferred in whispers for several minutes. Finally the Duke shrugged and nodded.

"I have not introduced the Emperor's liaison officer," he said. "You'll forgive my oversight, Arrowmaker...and you, Master Joseph King?"

Francis was bemused by the Duke's abrupt transition from genial bullying to silken courtesy. Was he mocking them or was his excessive politesse sincere?

"I present Colonel Chü Wei-man, also called Edmond. The name tells you he is your coreligionist.... Mine, too, I suppose, by my father's rites and my swarm of uncles, aunts, and cousins. All Christians, you know. I honor my father, as the Master Confucius enjoined, as your...our...Lord Jesus commanded. I do *not* honor his choice...his joining the Manchus ...for a mere viscount's rank."

"Colonel Arrowmaker, we welcome you to Chüanchou." Colonel Edmond Chü was respectful. "And we regret your rough treatment."

Perfectly easy courtesy was perfectly natural to the descendant of five generations of senior Mandarins, as it was not to the mixed-blood son of a pirate admiral. Perfect Christian courtesy, Francis thought, and chided himself. Young

498

Edmond Chü displayed perfect Confucian, perfect Chinese courtesy. Was that all, as his sinuous gestures and soft voice implied? Or was there steel under the cloak of exquisite manners? Did his slender height and his lean face with its wide eyes conceal a resolute spirit?

"I have suggested the Duke offer you parole while we await proof of your story." The young Colonel was, at least, forthright. "Will you swear by the Lord of Heaven that you will neither flee nor communicate with outsiders?"

"Of course, Colonel Chü," Francis replied. "And, of course, my secretary, too, will..."

"In that case, I can see no difficulties for the time being." The young Colonel smiled. "The Duke kindly permits me to take you on an excursion tomorrow. Less than twenty miles away lies a charming town called Anhai. It will, I am sure, interest you."

RIDING along the winding road to the sea, Francis pondered the abrupt change in the attitude of the young Duke of Changkuo, whom he had once known as Lucky Cheng. He was enchanted by the landscape, so different from harsh North China. Rice undulated in the silvery paddy-fields when the breeze teased its golden tasseled heads. Drying fish hung in fringes on the eaves of thatch roofs. Ducks waddled in single file along the dikes dividing the flooded fields; long-legged brown chickens with yellow tailfeathers scratched in the damp earth; and pink-bellied sows marshaled squads of grunting piglets. Fishing junks drifted under reefed purple sails across the placid channel between the mainland and an island green with trees.

"*Chin Men Tao*..." Edmond Chü pointed. "Golden Gate Island. Quemoy in the local dialect. A rich island for its crops... and for its sorghum spirits... as good as the *pai-kar* of Manchuria."

The young officer chatted pleasantly but offered no explanation for their journey or for the Duke's parole. Francis was content to let the mystery unfold in its own time. He had learned patience in China. Not because the Chinese were themselves patient, but because they were so provoking only great patience could endure them. Meanwhile he relished the idyllic scene. He had forgotten the abundance and the peace of South China.

The late-afternoon breeze was dissipating the humid heat

when they began their descent to Anhai, which meant the Peace of the Sea. The name was preternaturally apt when the junks hauled in their long nets to sail into harbor on the golden trail the declining sun cast on the water—and the tile roofs of Anhai glowed against the blue mist on the hills.

Edmond Chü let his reins hang slack while his horse threaded the narrow lanes, finally halting before a white-washed house. The black-tiled roof extended over the lane, while the door and windows of one low wing faced the busy street. The other wing was an open-fronted shop.

Even in Chüanchou, only the District Magistrate was sheltered behind high walls like those of Peking. The ways of South China were open and animated—untrammeled by the self-aware dignity that inhibited Imperial Peking. A prosperous merchant would not dream of secluding himself from the bustling life of the streets, where the people shouted and laughed. The house to which a casual maidservant admitted them obviously belonged to such a prosperous merchant. The signboard over the shopfront read: KAO-TENG MI—HIGH-GRADE RICE.

A young woman stood in the courtyard that separated the entrance hall from the family's apartments. She was perhaps twenty years old. Certainly no older, though perhaps younger, but it was hard to judge the age of Chinese women. Outlined by the close-cut tunic of orange cotton that ended at her blue-trousered hips, her supple body had probably not yet borne children. The face framed by a red-bordered blue kerchief was slender, fine-boned, and hauntingly evocative. Her skin was much fairer than one would expect in a daughter of South China, however loudly her mother scolded her to avoid the defiling touch of the sun. Her large eyes were light-brown, and her delicate nose was subtly arched. Altogether a face far too patrician and, somehow, too exotic for a rice merchant's daughter.

A premonition fluttered in Francis Arrowsmith's mind, a vague sense of great pleasure. He was virtually certain when the young woman knelt and bowed her head. He gently loosened the knot that secured the kerchief under her delicately pointed chin. The bright cloth fell away, and a curtain of shining fine yellow hair hung around her face.

"Maria...is it you?" He spoke unaware in English, the language he had occasionally used with the girl he had last seen five years earlier.

"Father," she replied awkwardly in the same language, "I am Maria."

Francis lifted his daughter and hugged her close. He could not speak, and tears clouded his eyes. Edmond Chü and Joseph King looked away from the unseemly display of un-Chinese emotion. Foreigners were different, Edmond realized, very different. Even Maria was different when her European blood was in the ascendant, as it was at that moment.

"Maria...my small Maria!" Recollecting himself, Francis spoke in Chinese. "I've missed you...missed you so much all these years."

"I longed to...but I could not come to you, Father."

"You are well, Maria? Well and happy? You know about your mother? No sign of her and..."

"Yes, I know, Father. I pray for her soul. And, yes, I am happy...very happy now."

Maria turned from her father and lightly embraced his secretary.

"Uncle Joseph," she said. "I am delighted you came too."

Joseph King returned her embrace fleetingly. His narrow face was red with embarrassment, but his eyes were liquid with happiness.

"SO you see, Sir, I could not possibly allow the Duke to lock you up." Edmond Chü's graceful courtesy smoothed their mutual awkwardness while the maidservant served tea. "I shall, of course, entreat you in proper form to grant me Maria's hand. But we are...except for your gracious permission...betrothed. I could not, of course, allow the Duke to imprison my virtual father-in-law. The Duke....He's a bit rough sometimes, but a gentleman for all that. He understood, of course, and....I hope I didn't tantalize you with my silence, but it was better for Maria herself to..."

"How could I have been so stupid?" Francis wondered alone. "The name...Edmond Chü...I should have known at once. But I didn't even suspect. It was as if my mind were blocked."

"I suspected, Arrowmaker." Joseph King was, as ever, omniscient. "But I didn't want to arouse false hopes."

"I am deeply in your debt, Edmond." Francis Arrowsmith responded gratefully to his presumptive son-in-law's anxious explanation, since he did not know quite how to treat the adult woman of seventeen he had known only as a child. "I didn't fancy spending weeks behind bars while you waited for reports from the north."

"As for that, Sir, it's really a formality. I don't think we'll worry too much about confirming your account. The Duke is in my father's debt.... And my father knows you as a true Christian and a true man, though you've met, he tells me, only briefly."

"And the Grand Secretary Thomas Chü, he is well?" Joseph King produced the obligatory inquiry.

"He is well, though terribly busy. We are not yet hard-pressed by the Manchus, but the gains of the past eighteen months are at hazard. My father is very busy...too busy, perhaps."

Francis could form no firm opinion of his future son-in-law. Edmond's patrician poise cloaked his true character. However, he spoke of both matters of state and his own affairs with quick candor.

Maria spoke little. She preferred not to intrude on the masculine discussion of politics, which warded off strained silences. The reserve of a Chinese lady was, however, pierced by flashes of spontaneous feeling. Nor did her eyes glaze—as her mother's would—when the men weighed the Ming Emperor's right to the Dragon Throne as the grandson of the Wan Li Emperor in the cadet line. While Edmond Chü cut through the thickets of Imperial genealogy closely pursued by Joseph King, her eyes were demurely cast down. But a smile teased the corners of her mouth. When the two scholars had temporarily exhausted their ingenuity, Maria offered a soft comment.

"*Ni-men wang-la, Edmond, wo pao-pei, Joseph Shu-shu.*" The European names rang oddly in the stream of lilting Chinese. "You're forgetting, Edmond, my dear, and Uncle Joseph. No other claimant can sustain their claims. So he is the true Emperor, since the Manchu claim is false. Besides, the Emperor is almost a Christian, isn't he? So he has every right!"

Francis was amused. His daughter's eminently practical observation that the Ming Emperor was entitled to rule because he possessed the power to rule had been followed by the wholly illogical conclusion that the Emperor had unquestionably inherited the Confucian Mandate of Heaven because he was almost a Christian.

Having found his daughter, the Englishman did not know what to make of her—or just how to approach her. She had, it appeared, been forced by hardship into the maturity her mother Marta had attained only in the last year of her life.

His own difficulty, Francis realized, would not be a failing of parental affection. His difficulty would be to avoid becoming too deeply attached to his daughter. But, he reflected, why should he not become deeply attached to Maria? He had spent too much of his life avoiding emotional involvement. His spontaneous feeling had too often been suppressed, frozen as hard as a Manchurian creek in winter. He could happily allow himself to love his daughter.

"The Emperor almost a Christian, you say?" Francis was glad of the continuing political diversion. "I'd heard something, but didn't..."

"*Almost* a Christian," Edmond answered. "Maria exaggerates a little. Her heart is too strong for her head."

"Not at all, Edmond. I know what I'm saying. His Imperial Majesty cannot yet profess himself a Christian. But just look at his family... all baptized... the Dowager Empress Helena and the Dowager Empress Maria, the Empress Anna herself. What more can I say?"

"More, my dear, if modesty did not intervene." Edmond spoke to an equal, a Christian lady of learning. "My father Thomas is Grand Secretary, while Commander-in-Chief Chiao Lien was baptized Luke years ago. And Achilles Pang, the Grand Eunuch, converted the Court Ladies. China *almost* has its first Christian Dynasty, except for the Emperor's reticence..."

"Christian fervor will endure," Joseph interjected, "at least as long as Christian guns sustain the Dynasty."

"Christian guns *and* Christian prayers," Edmond added. "Without our prayers, we could not have held Kweilin, the key to South China. Several hundred Portuguese gunners under Captain Nicholas Ferreira have been invaluable."

"So many?" Francis asked. "We heard some reports, but never of such magnitude."

"Even the Jesuits... even in Latin, they dare not send such news to Peking," Edmond explained. "Our Jesuits and the Jesuits of Peking are not in accord. Ours support the legitimate Emperor, the others the Manchu usurper."

"What says the Father Provincial?" Francis asked.

"That we must trust in the Lord.... His ways are mysterious." Edmond's cloak of perfect courtesy and perfect piety parted to reveal a puzzled young man. "What *can* he say to the stiff-necked stubbornness of Father Schall?"

503

"I should like you to meet Adam Schall." Francis warmed to Edmond's frank anger. "But, in fairness, he *is* in the north. God has kept Schall there to do His work . . . and the Manchus rule the north."

"For the time being, Sir. But I cannot believe . . . the Lord of Heaven cannot wish His priest to serve the usurpers . . ."

"As for that, Colonel Chü, any man . . . even a priest . . . can see his duty only as far as he can see," Joseph King pointed out. "Even with his telescope, Father Adam cannot see the Ming domain in South China."

"But to oppose a Christian . . . near-Christian, then . . . Dynasty and serve barbarian idolators . . . to make cannon for them. How can any priest?"

"Suppose you lose?" Joseph King murmured. "Is it not better for the Manchus to have their own Christian priests? Hope for the triumph of Christ in China would not die with the Ming."

"We will *not* lose, Master Joseph King," Edmond declared. "We will restore the Emperor to his rightful place on the Dragon Throne in Peking. With the help of God, of course."

"Of course!" Joseph echoed. "With the help of God . . . of course!"

JULY gave way to August, and the farmers stooped in the fields to shear the golden rice with sickles. Anhai offered little diversion, and Edmond Chü had returned to Chüanchou. But Francis Arrowsmith was content to unfold his rapport with Maria.

When the harvest was gathered and the sheaves had been spread on the roadways to dry, the people of Anhai saw in the glassy flatness of the bay warning of a typhoon. The air was still and heavy as men and women scurried to bring in the sheaves. The skies darkened, and torrents of rain battered at windows and doors. At evening, floodlets burst into houses—soaking cotton bedding and straw mats; pelting the bullocks, chickens, and pigs huddled in the courtyards; drenching the new rice. All night the people of Anhai were awake to barricade splintered shutters or doors. The typhoon ended shortly before dawn.

The sun rose on a land washed sparkling clean, and cloud tufts floated in an azure sky. Pronouncing himself a connoisseur of typhoons because his native city of Canton was so often assailed by those great winds, Joseph King declared that the center had passed a hundred miles away. Anhai had only been touched by the hem of the typhoon's skirt.

Late that afternoon four black junks, their slab sides pierced for cannon, meandered into the bay on the falling wind. Farmers spreading rice sheaves on the steaming roadways spared the dark craft only a glance. Edmond Chü, who had ridden frantically from Chüanchou to assure himself that neither his fiancée nor his guests had suffered, laughed when Francis asked what new threat to Anhai was posed by the ships that sent no boats to shore.

"There is *no* danger from the sea," Edmond explained. "The Duke's fleets command the China Coast from Hainan Island to the Shantung Peninsula. When they have repaired the storm damage, the ships will send boats for water and provisions. The crews will come ashore this evening, fifteen giant blackamoors among them."

"On what errand?" Francis asked.

"The crews seeking what sailors always seek... women and wine. The blackamoors, though, determined to hear Holy Mass."

"Blackamoors to Holy Mass?" Joseph King was incredulous. "A strange passion for half-heathens."

"These blackamoors are pious Christians, Master King. They were the bodyguard of the Duke's father, the Admiral of the Coastal Seas. He left them when he went over to the Manchus... afraid their piety would embarrass him."

"Have you talked with the Duke about how best I can serve the Ming?" Francis broke in.

"I have. He agrees you'd be best employed in Macao..."

"Doing what, Edmond?"

"Why, keeping our cause fresh before the Loyal Senate. And expediting shipment of the arms we've been promised. The Emperor is still in Chaoching in Kwangtung. He needs those guns to beat back new Manchu assaults."

"So be it, then. There is little I can do here, I think. Is the ordnance of your ships adequate?"

"Just adequate, Sir. The sea frontier is secure. But not the land frontier. I expect new attacks very soon."

"What of Maria, then? I would not happily leave her behind, Edmond."

"Nor I see her left behind. The coming months will be perilous."

"Then she must come with me to Macao. I'll have a word with her."

"EVEN if you're right, I don't like having my mind made up for me, Father." Maria's cheeks were flushed, and her nails picked at a strand of bubble-pocked seaweed. "I'd like to be consulted about my own fate."

"It's not your fate, Maria...just temporary prudence." Francis spoke over the hissing surf. "A father's concern merits some obedience...and Edmond agrees wholeheartedly."

"I'm too old now, Father, to start where we never left off." Maria's stress on the musical tones of certain words recalled her mother. "I want to be a dutiful daughter, but I'm not a child any more. As for Edmond, we're not married....Not yet."

"Whom will you obey, then?"

"Why, myself, Father." Her deformed feet sank into the soft sand at each step. "I am a Christian woman, not a slave...a play-toy to be passed from hand to hand."

"We only want you to be prudent. Those black junks are a portent. Anhai could become a battlefield. Do you long for the Manchus' tender mercy?"

"Then Edmond and I must marry now. Father de Caballero will return soon..."

"Will marriage vows protect you from the Manchus? Edmond will be in battle...fighting for his life and you..."

"You mean I would be a hindrance?"

"Not merely a hindrance. A weight around his neck while he swims a stormy sea. If he wanted to marry you tomorrow, this is no time..."

"As you wish, Father." Maria's abrupt yielding delighted Francis with her good sense—as he was already delighted with her spirit. "I'll go with you to Macao, but what I'll do there I don't..."

"You will learn something of your European heritage, Maria. You must be curious about Europe."

"Macao is not Europe....And, from what I've heard, offers little learning. Now if I wanted to be a courtesan, Macao would be ideal."

"Enough, Maria. That jest is too raw. And, I promise, you shall marry Edmond just as soon as he thinks it safe. All right then?"

"All right, Father." Maria smiled and dropped the tattered strand of seaweed. "But, next time, please consult me first....Not after you've decided."

506

Macao

THE silvery jubilation of trumpets soared to the groined roof, pursued by the soprano chanting of clarions. Bell-shaped skirts swayed across the mahogany floor as the ladies trod circles around their partners' uplifted hands. Deep-voiced viols caroled a joyful refrain to the harpsichord's chimed melody. Taffeta bodices rustled curtsies to velvet coats. The lace bullion on gentlemen's cuffs outshone the *broderie anglaise* cascading over ladies' bosoms. The musicians' black cheeks swelled in ecstasy when globular shawms and slender hautboys exultantly joined the minuet.

The files reversed and stalked toward the dais where Macao's Governor Dom Juan Peirreira and his entourage sat. The stately dance stumbled when seven gentlemen disentangled from their ladies' skirts the swords they should not have worn at the Gala Ball. Backs arched, young officers swirled their partners, and the crimson lapels of their forest-green tunics fell back to reveal the dull sheen of steel breastplates. Behind the Governor, bodyguards wearing helmets clutched their halberds and gazed warily around the Great Hall.

Suspicion between the Governor and the garrison hung over the Grand Ball that celebrated the sixteen hundred forty-ninth anniversary of the birth of the Lord Jesus in Bethlehem. That distrust was so fixed that neither gentlemen nor ladies were distracted from their concentration on each other. When the minuet ended with a shimmering coda, the couples promenaded through doors held open by blackamoors in white wigs. Their laughter swelled before the solemn joy of Midnight Mass.

Francis Arrowsmith squirmed on a spindly gilt chair and longed for the solid comfort of a Chinese stool. He longed also to exchange his confining breeches and his tight jacket of wine-red velvet for the ease of a Chinese robe. But he blessed fashion's caprice, which had recently replaced starched ruffs with wide linen collars.

White bosoms swelled provocatively from low necklines. Soft cheeks just filmed with powder and avidly open lips barely touched with rouge were indecently naked when he recalled the decorously concealing makeup of ladies in the Empire. Shrill female voices were raucous in his ears, and he marveled that respectable women should parade not only their persons, but their opinions. The perfumed air assailed his senses: the dark resonance of musk warring with unctuous attar of roses; jasmine and lavender, myrrh and sandalwood mingling in an oppressive fog.

His nostrils contracted in distaste at the sour-sweet fragrance of claret mulled with cloves and cinnamon. Having returned to Macao a week earlier after eight years, he shrank from the heavy smell of Europeans. Since most Portuguese washed infrequently and cursorily, stale sweat stank under the cloak of perfume. He recoiled from the fetid odor of men and women who devoured half-cooked meat and half-rotted cheeses. Francis shrugged in disgust, rubbed the ache between his eyebrows, and glanced at his daughter Maria, who was seated beside him.

Her expression was unreadable beneath the rice-powder coating her face and the pigments on her cheeks, eyelids, and mouth. Though he had told her Portuguese ladies did not paint so heavily, she had wisely applied her customary formal makeup. The disgust she felt would otherwise have been obvious to the eyes surreptitiously examining the curiosity the English artilleryman had introduced into their midst. He hoped the cavorting popinjays and their shameless jades could not read the revulsion their uncouth behavior aroused in a cultivated Chinese lady, since he needed Macao's good will to restore his fortunes.

Maria murmured an apology to the portly Jesuit, Giulio

di Giaccomo, who had been chatting with her in polished Officials' Chinese. When she turned to him, Francis was astonished to see her lips curved in a smile beneath their vermilion gloss and her eyes sparkling behind her kohled lashes. Maria gently touched his hand.

"*Ta-men tiao-wu-de....*" She spoke eagerly, and he realized she was a young girl despite her premature gravity. "They dance beautifully. I wish I could dance like that, but, of course, I..."

"Do you really mean it, Maria?"

Francis's surprise was succeeded by a pang of sadness. Her crippled feet would never permit her to dance a minuet.

"I do, Father. Truly. It's wonderful."

Maria impulsively removed her headdress of gilt wires clad with peacock's feathers. When her blonde hair shone in the chandelier's brilliance, Francis winced. He wished she would not make a spectacle of herself—not for his sake, but for her own.

Yet he had already made a spectacle of her. Her Court Robe of vermilion tribute silk set off her diamond-and-gold hairpins and her jade-and-pearl earrings—emphasizing her uniqueness. The appraising and envious stares of the Portuguese ladies paid tribute to her gorgeous costume and to her jewelry. Determined to impress by displaying the only wealth that remained to either of them, he had succeeded—perhaps too well.

"Father, you're not listening. I asked can you dance that...*min-yu-eh-teh?*"

"I could once, Maria. But it's been a long time..."

"Show me, Father." She coaxed like a small girl. "Please show me."

"Where would I find a partner? I'm sorry, but I can't."

"Not at all, Francis." Giulio di Giaccomo protested. "What about that lady...the one who's just come in?"

"Dolores! Senhorina do Amaral!"

"Not Senhorina Dolores do Amaral." The Italian priest smiled conspiratorially. "Senhora Dolores do Amaral de Albuquerque."

"Of course." Francis's spirits unaccountably sank. "She's married, naturally."

"*Was* married, Francis, but no longer. She lost her husband two years ago."

"I see, Giulio."

509

"She is hurt that you have not called on her. But I told her you had asked after her...were eager to see her."

"And who was her husband?" Francis asked casually. "A treasure-hunter, I suppose."

"By no means, my son." The Jesuit did not conceal his matchmaking fervor. "A young man of wealth, as the noble name tells you. His legacy doubled the sum her father left. She is the richest heiress in Macao."

"And hotly pursued, I'm sure."

"Naturally. But she favors no particular suitor. An independent lady, as always..."

"So she is," Francis laughed. "Remember how she defied her father to visit me?"

"But her independence cannot last much longer. Dolores is pressed by both the Governor and the Bishop. The Governor deplores her suitors' brawls and duels. The Bishop fears for her soul's welfare."

"But they cannot press her..."

"They can, Francis. Very soon she must either marry or enter the convent of the Poor Clares. The Lady Abbess yearns after her wealth."

"And Dolores? How does she feel?"

"She has not married.... And a nun's life is not.... But she is staring at us. Why not show Maria you can still tread a measure?"

Francis brushed past his old friend and former employer Manuel Tavares Bocarro with a smile. The hearty master cannon-founder clapped him on the back and whispered gruffly, "Godspeed! And good fortune!"

Even without that theatrical blessing, every eye would have followed Francis across the gleaming floor toward the lady who was attended by an African page in an archaic scarlet-satin doublet and green-velvet hose.

The Englishman and his half-Chinese daughter were the sensation of the hour. Maria's exotic splendor burnished the glamour of the only noncleric who had lived so long—and so adventurously—among the Chinese. Some men envied him and some detested him, but none was indifferent.

Dolores would have been notable if only for her independence. She would have been notable and, perhaps, shunned by proper matrons. But her wealth made palatable her disdain for convention. In commercial Macao, great wealth did not merely excuse breaches of convention, but virtually hallowed them.

Though Dolores's smile was a challenge, he gazed at her in silence. Her small mouth and her minutely snubbed nose were still deceptively childlike beneath her wide gray eyes and her arched eyebrows. But the passage of eight years had fined the rounded contours of extreme youth, molding her cheeks and her jawline to the delicate bones beneath her olive skin. She was twenty-seven, her former prettiness transformed into elegant beauty.

Her black hair flowed negligently over her shoulders, and pearls interspersed with diamonds encircled her neck with cool moonlight and white fire. Her hyacinth scent was fresh amid the miasma of perfumes. Her breasts pressed against the ivory lace gathered on the shimmering cloth-of-gold bodice that left her shoulders bare. Her bouffant sleeves and spreading skirt were slashed to display their lining of the same scarlet satin as her African page's doublet.

"Was it a pleasant excursion, Senhor?" she asked in throaty Portuguese. "You enjoyed yourself?"

"A delight, Senhora." He grinned at her mild acerbity. "A day's outing among the Chinese...always a pleasure."

"I am so glad, Senhor. But was it not more than a day?"

"Perhaps somewhat longer, oh thou perfect peony among pallid daffodils." Responding to her ironic mood, he parodied the labored gallantries of the *hidalgos* of Macao. "Each day away from you was a thousand days. I have been absent for an eternity. And I am overwhelmed at beholding you more radiant than ever."

"You flatter me, Sir."

"By God, that I do not, Dolores." Francis abandoned the heavy badinage. "You are radiant...a hundred times more beautiful."

"I want to believe that, Francis. But your English tongue is tuned to flattery."

"We English have a reputation for fulsomeness. I confess it. But, I swear, my tongue speaks only what my heart feels. No impediment lies between the organ of speech and the organ of feeling."

"Even your simplicities are ornate, Francis. Yet, somehow, I believe you. Perhaps because I want to..."

"Believe with all confidence, Dolores...believe in the truth."

"You need not fear. But, Francis, can you still dance a pavane?"

"Because it enforces silence, Dolores?"

Her fingertips brushed the gold braid twined on his wine-red velvet sleeve and they moved into the slow figures of the old-fashioned dance. The pavane was staid—unlike the daring minuet, which brought the partners so close their bodies almost touched. Amid the buzz of gossip, they glided across the polished mahogany floor. His tawny head inclined toward her dark head; his dark velvet jacket set off her gleaming cloth-of-gold ball gown.

FRANCIS ARROWSMITH did his sums on Christmas morning in the small house belonging to the Jesuits beside the Church of St. Paul. He assessed his past and plotted his future in a confined room that smelled of incense, ink, and piety.

Father Giulio di Giaccomo had ignored the reluctance of his brothers in Christ to lend the house to the troublesome Englishman. Some of the Jesuits were disturbed because the artilleryman had alienated the Manchus. More feared that his previous service to the Manchus was hateful to the Southern Ming. Most agreed that generosity to one in his equivocal position was unwise. The Italian priest wondered whom the former secret agent now served. But he felt the Society of Jesus was indebted to Francis, and the decision was his as treasurer.

"The Englishman has been back and forth to China many times—at our behest," Giulio di Giaccomo justified his decision to the Father Provincial. "He and his daughter should not in decency lodge longer with Master Antonio Castro, though the Marrano appears an obedient son of Holy Church. I have therefore offered him accommodation."

"Are you quite sure, Giulio, he will not bring odium upon the Society?" asked the grave Portuguese who was the Superior of the China Mission. "We must walk with care in these perilous times."

"Father, I am sure only of the Grace of God and the conversion of the Chinese.... But nothing else!" The Italian shrugged. "Yet Arrowsmith is no more deeply involved than many of our own foolhardy priests...less than some. I am also sure that we owe him a debt of gratitude."

"Yes, Giulio. And he may prove useful again. I concur. Give him lodging for as long as he wishes—or until his conduct dictates otherwise. But avoid any entanglement in his schemes."

Oppressed by the stuffy room, but loath to open a window

to the raw cold of December, Francis Arrowsmith knew nothing of that conversation. The Provincial's reservations did not figure among the liabilities he was noting. That list was already long enough.

Returning to Europe would be pointless. No merchant of Macao required an alien agent in Lisbon or elsewhere. Moreover, the wars of Europe, as fiercely embroiled as Asia, offered him little opportunity. Since they could find hundreds of artillery officers as skilled as himself, no Catholic Prince would offer high rank to a forty-two-year-old soldier-of-fortune who had been cut off for more than two decades from the rapid development of the military arts. Since he possessed neither influential friends nor wealth in Europe, he must seek his elusive fortune in Asia.

He was not, however, richly endowed with either friends or wealth in Asia. The commission of the Duke Koxinga—Adam Schall's former cannon-works foreman—to represent the Ming in Macao was supported by no commitment of gold either to purchase arms or to support himself. Though the prospects looked bright, the Ming Emperor was at the moment on the defensive. Francis concluded that he must start all over again. He was almost as poor as he had been twenty-five years earlier—and far less hopeful.

His military skills had, however, been honed by constant use, and he knew the labyrinth of the Empire's commerce as well as any European. No other layman could claim his familiarity with the Chinese language and Chinese customs, though Adam Schall and a few other Jesuits surpassed him. He also possessed an aptitude for espionage, a knack of surviving in that vicious demiworld, though a neophyte beside Chinese agents. Moreover, many Chinese and Manchu officers thought well of him.

Nonetheless, Francis concluded, the accounts of his past life were woefully unbalanced, and he could not live long in Macao by small-scale trade. The glamour of his exploits in forbidden China intrigued the ladies, but aroused envious animosity among most gentlemen. Besides, glamour was a wasting asset. In six months it would be waning; after a year it would have vanished. He must, he decided, realize immediately upon his glamour—and his other paltry assets. The market would not hold up long.

Francis Arrowsmith wrote one name on the last line of his balance sheet: Teresa Dolores Angela do Amaral de Albuquerque had displayed obvious interest in him. She not only possessed the wealth he lacked, but was compellingly attractive. And she would be an ideal mother for the European heirs he still craved.

Whatever love was that poets hymned, Francis realized he had never known love. This woman of his own world touched his being as his Chinese wife and his Manchu concubine never had. Dolores was, he imagined, past attaining the carnal skill that had been Marta's—and probably beyond Barbara's feral ardor. But he was no longer a lustful youth. Francis was determined that, this time, he would be the pursuer and Dolores the pursued. Moreover, no other—priest or Mandarin, prince or general—would interfere in this wooing.

WRAPPED in a cashmere kimono against the fog seeping through closed windows into the boudoir of her villa on Mount Guia, Dolores de Albuquerque watched the flames in the white-marble fireplace. Having coolly chosen her goal, she reviewed her plans. How, she wondered, could she flee so convincingly that the Englishman would certainly catch her? How could she manipulate that domineering man without also arousing his suspicion? He must never realize that she had dispassionately determined to rebuild her life around him, though to rebuild it to her own design.

Dolores de Albuquerque wanted a husband to free her from the restrictions that trammeled an unmarried woman in Macao, where she intended to remain. In Lisbon she would be another heiress of a nabob from the Indies. In Macao she was uniquely wealthy and powerful—and she intended to remain her own mistress.

Dolores had dutifully married Vicente de Albuquerque in 1645 because her beloved father wished her to give him grandchildren. Vicente was favored by Dom Sebastian do Amaral for his wealth and his descent from Duke Alfonso de Albuquerque, the Conquerer of the East. He was, further, willing to sign a marriage contract that gave Dolores much control over her own fortune. Vicente was accepted by Senhorina Dolores do Amaral because he was the least objectionable of the gallants who sought her hand—and her dowry.

She had put on mourning and hidden her tears behind a black veil after he was killed in 1647, when the long-unpaid garrison rose against the rapacious Governor. Her widow's weeds were worn for Vicente, but her tears were shed for Dom Sebastian, cut down by an officer's saber when he pleaded for peace on behalf of the commercial community. The bitterness of that quasi-civil war still divided Macao.

The same Governor was now eager to make the wealthiest—and freest—woman of Macao a ward of the state. Obviously, no woman could manage her own affairs, and acting as her guardian would satisfyingly plump his own purse. Her alternatives to that tyranny were to marry or to accede to the Bishop's desire to deliver herself and her gold into the hands of the Lady Abbess of the Poor Clares. Marriage was the least onerous choice. But she wanted a match that would leave her a free agent, and she wanted a man who was, at the least, not abhorrent to her.

The Englishman, Dolores concluded, satisfied her conditions—in part because he was not a Portuguese. An outsider in a foreign enclave on the edge of an alien Empire, he would not attempt to dominate either her or her business enterprises. His insecurity would diminish but not disappear in marriage to the greatest heiress of Macao. He was, moreover, too proud to demean himself by locking up his wife or demanding abject obedience of her. Like Marta and Barbara before her, Dolores marked Francis as an indulgent husband because his own welfare would depend largely upon his wife's standing among her own people, who were not his people.

Acknowledging that it would be a marriage of convenience, Dolores confided to her personal amah, who understood only one in four words of her rapid Portuguese, that she expected hardly more of Francis than a certain good humor and a certain assistance with her enterprises. She needed a man, since a woman could not command rough foremen or negotiate with haughty Mandarins.

"I believe all my expectations will be fulfilled," she added. "Not too much ardor...not too much self-will...not too much efficiency. And it might be amusing to have children with hair the color of butter."

Like Francis, Dolores concealed the finer part of her nature from herself. She was strongly drawn by his obvious need, which awakened her compassion. His air of mystery attracted her, as did his attitudes, which often appeared more Chinese than European. Not only did he walk with the curious light shuffle of one accustomed to cloth-soled Chinese shoes, he also had a peculiar habit of cocking his head and waiting patiently for others to complete their sentences that was Confucian in its courtesy. Because of that trick way of reserving judgment and his formal manner, the men of Macao no longer

515

called him "the lay Jesuit" but "the English Mandarin." Dolores was also drawn to Francis by his past suffering and the desperation she discerned beneath his assured air. He appealed to two chief traits of her complex nature: her protective—almost maternal—feeling and her desire for power. Refusing to be dominated, she instinctively sought to dominate. She could, she felt, shape the Englishman into an ideal husband and exercise her power through him.

Beyond the profound affection for the Englishman that had grown for some eight years, Dolores was titillated by her watercolor fantasies of sexual ecstasies. Francis had been taught by Oriental women, and everyone knew Orientals were obsessed with ingenious lovemaking.

SINCE she could talk freely with neither her female contemporaries (who were implicitly her rivals) nor her male contemporaries (who were intent upon seducing her), Dolores prattled to her uncomprehending amah. Since the amah could not reply, she made a confidant of her confessor, Giulio di Giaccomo, whose Jesuitical insight was tempered by Italian tolerance. He listened to her in comforting silence and encouraged her with impromptu parables. His Genoese soul delighted in intrigue, even the harmless intrigue of matchmaking.

Francis could not discuss Dolores with her cousin Manuel Tavares Bocarro, and he did not, somehow, wish to discuss her with his business partner, the Marrano Antonio Castro. Though he had resolved to be his own man, he was not so foolish as to spurn advice. Having made up his mind, the Englishman tested his purpose against Giulio di Giaccomo's worldly wisdom and gossip's knowledge of Macao. The Italian was both an old friend and the only Jesuit to whom Francis could turn, accustomed as he was to seeking counsel of the black priests. Giulio di Giaccomo blessed Francis's design, for he was as sentimental as an old woman.

"So it's off with the old and on with the new?" the Italian nonetheless twitted Francis. "New lamps for old, so to speak. A Dolores for a Barbara!"

"That is unfair, Giulio," Francis replied hotly. "You know I never wanted Barbara....But what could a slave do?"

"You always were something of an opportunist, Francis. From the Ming to the Manchus, then the Ming again, and, afterward, the Manchus again. Now the Southern Ming. That is quite a record."

"This is quite an era we live in, Giulio. Look at Adam Schall. He traded the Ming for the Manchus without a qualm, did he not? You Jesuits, too, change sides with alacrity, as you changed Holy Rites to accommodate them to Chinese preferences."

"But always for good reasons, Francis. A high tide of Christianity is sweeping China. Hundreds of prominent men and women of the Southern Ming have been baptized lately. Meanwhile, Adam Schall in Peking draws the young Manchu Emperor toward the love of Christ by his amiable nature."

"Amiable? Adam Schall? You're thinking of another man entirely."

"We *are* opportunists, we Jesuits." Giulio di Giaccomo ignored the taunt. "I acknowledge that, Francis, acknowledge it gladly. We are opportunists for the Lord...and for the conversion of the Chinese."

"And such sophistry justifies your opportunism? The Dominicans do not agree. The Franciscans draw aside in horror."

"The Dominicans...the Franciscans...pah!" Giulio di Giaccomo's upper lip protruded, and he expirated rudely. "Look here, Francis, we of the Society are opportunists for God. You are an opportunist for yourself...and your opportunism could destroy you."

"Giulio, I, too, seek a greater purpose...your own purpose: to serve God. But I must survive to serve Him. Not cosseted by a powerful brotherhood, I must survive alone. Anyway, I've taken no vows to sacrifice personal happiness."

"Francis, I wish for you great happiness in union with Dolores. Only take care that your devices do not supplant your purpose. You can find perfect happiness only in the unselfish service of God...vows or not."

Strolling along the Praya Grande toward the Rua do Chunambeiro, Francis meditatively twirled his umbrella under the persistent drizzle of early February and marveled at the priest's composure. Giulio di Giaccomo's good will had once again survived an exchange of truths a lay gentleman would have cut off with a challenge to a duel. The Jesuit had, however, clapped him on the back and seasoned his farewell with a final admonition.

"Francis, we're all fond of you," he said. "I am...and so is Adam Schall, though you may not believe it. You cannot cut yourself off from our affection...from everyone's affection. I hope you will marry Dolores. But you must not marry her unless you feel for her true earthly love, which is only less than the love of God. You must want...beyond all else in this world...to love her—and to care for her all your life."

"I think, Giulio...I'm not absolutely sure, but I think I do."

"Then, Francis, I give you my blessing with all my heart. But, remember, you must open yourself to the love of all your fellow men and women....And you must give them all your love in return."

The drizzle quickened, and raindrops bounced off the oiled-paper umbrella like pebbles. Rivulets rising among the cobblestones filled Francis's shoes, and the leather crumpled into soggy cardboard. His russet-mohair breeches were drenched, and his hair curled in soggy tendrils on his neck.

Francis Arrowsmith was hardly aware of the downpour. For the first time in years he was examining himself, rather than his worldly prospects—and he was not pleased by his discoveries.

He had, he confessed freely to the court of his own conscience, always chosen to be an alien. He had avoided committing himself totally to any person or any purpose by telling himself that they were not his own people or his own purpose. Obsessed by his own interests, he had valued others chiefly for their usefulness—and the approbation he could win from them.

He had, Francis saw, retreated into a borrowed shell like a hermit crab to escape the intrusive Chinese with their brutal plots and their cruel ways. But expedience had become habit. His carapace had isolated him not only from the Chinese, but from all mankind.

He had accepted the friendship of such men as Adam Schall and Giulio di Giaccomo, Antonio Castro and Manuel Tavares Bocarro, even Paul Hsü and Joseph King. Yet he had invariably taken more of their affection than he had given of his own. The same parsimony of emotion had beggared his relations with Marta and Barbara. He had even held his children, both Maria and Robert, at arm's length. To no man, woman, or child had he gladly opened his heart.

Having already resolved to be his own man, Francis formed a further resolution. He had helped himself to the influence and the goods others proffered, but had returned little, not even loyalty. In the future, he would give more than he received. He could only be the master of his own fate if he truly concerned himself with the fate of others.

He would begin by offering Dolores a humble, contrite, and loving heart, Francis concluded, instinctively falling into the language of the pulpit. The protective tenderness that welled in his heart might, he reflected wryly, astonish that self-possessed lady. Nonetheless, she required his loving protection. He would offer it, knowing she might laugh and spurn him.

He must break out of his carapace. And he must begin with Dolores, who was the most important person in his world. No, the most important person in the entire world, far more important than he himself.

Unaware that he was drenched, Francis was exultant when he heard the din of the foundry of Manuel Tavares Bocarro above the pelting rain. He resolved again to strive for the triumph of the Ming—and he saw God's will in the impulse that had turned his feet toward the foundry.

When it came to armament, Manuel Bocarro was the best man in Macao—and not only because he was the best cannonmaker in Asia, perhaps the world. The ordnance he cast for Portuguese forces in both the East and Europe had won him royal favor, which in turn gave him great influence in the settlement. Manuel Bocarro would not only know what weapons were available, but could also persuade the Governor and the Loyal Senate to offer those weapons to the Ming Emperor.

The smoky cavern of the foundry was lit by flames when furnace doors opened. Wearing only grimy leather breeches and wooden clogs, Manuel Bocarro was squatting to supervise the wedging of a mold-box. His right hand held a level against the box, and his left hand signaled his instructions. He glanced up when he was satisfied, and his teeth shone white amid the grime that blackened his face.

"Hullo, Francis!" he called. "Good to see you. Have a glass with me?"

"Gladly, Manuel," Francis shouted over the din and followed the cannon-master's sweat-runnelled back into the paper-strewn cubbyhole that was his office. The *haute bourgeoisie* were scandalized equally by Bocarro's working like a common laborer and by his slapdash business methods.

When the door closed behind them, the tumult diminished. Francis cleared his deafened ears with his thumbs. The master founder wiped his face with a damp rag, smearing sweat and soot into grotesque patterns. He lifted a silver pitcher with a ring of amethysts around its slender neck and poured the ruddy wine of Oporto into two aquamarine glass goblets. The rays of a hanging oil lamp streamed through the goblet he offered Francis, transforming the wine into a glowing ruby and the stem into a column of shimmering sapphire. His black beard bristling, his cheeks' swarthy parchment smeared with black swirls, the armorer was a genial imp in the half-light.

"*Saude, Paco!*" he smiled. "Just come to cadge a drink ... or do you have some business?"

Francis winced. His new sensitivity interpreted that genial sally as a reproach. Did all his friends, he wondered, believe he came to them only to advance his own interests?

"I need help, Manuel!" Francis said forthrightly. "So, I've come to you. Why, after all, have friends?"

"That's fine, Paco!" Manuel Bocarro looked at him quizzically; such straightforwardness—almost effusiveness—was unprecedented in his English protégé. "I hope your troubles haven't cooked your brain, though. Of course, you need help ... badly!"

"My troubles? What troubles?"

The armorer sipped his port. The gestures were delicate, almost dainty, though the goblet was enveloped by his tendon-corded fist.

"My lady cousin Dolores was here an hour or so ago," he said. "You know she's my partner ... or, rather, I'm her partner. She owns sixty percent of this broken-down foundry."

"I didn't know. On business, was she?"

"In a manner of speaking. Though the foundry's only a small part ... a very small part ... of her holdings. She's as rich as the Viceroy in Goa, almost as rich as King John himself."

"That's all very well, Manuel." Francis was dismayed by the broad hints. "But it's nothing to do with me. Now, I want to ask you..."

"By God's swine, I'd heard the English were cool and devious, but you surpass.... Of course it's to do with you. The poor lady, you've led her on for almost two months. How could she think anything else? You know, Paco, I may have to call you out for trifling with my lady cousin's affections."

"And make the biggest scandal Macao has seen in months?" Francis grinned at the rough humor. "Dolores is almost as clever as she is beautiful. She'd welcome a duel over her as she would the swamp fever. You don't expect me to take you seriously?"

"No, Paco, of course not. But still…I do have an obligation. Poor Dolores…orphaned and widowed in almost the same instant. I'm only her cousin, but there's no one else to look after her…."

"She may not require your protection much longer."

"Well, Paco, don't take too much time over it. There are others, you know."

"Leave it to me, Manuel, please. Now as to my real business…"

BY late February, Dolores de Albuquerque's pride had been battered by Francis Arrowsmith's dilatoriness in declaring himself, and she was hotly reconsidering her previous cool decision. Angry at herself for trailing her skirts so boldly before the unresponsive Englishman, she had impulsively ordered her sedan chair to carry her through the mud-clogged lanes to the Rua do Chunambeiro. There was one other with whom she could talk frankly. But she had not intended Manuel Bocarro to press her backward suitor when she pleaded business to lure him from his forges and his furnaces.

"I've made up my mind…finally." Dolores gazed into the ritual goblet of port and twirled the long stem in her slender fingers.

"And what is your decision, my dear?" From the eminence of his masculinity, Manuel Bocarro was amused equally by her passion and by the unaware disdain with which she gathered her full skirt of white samite interwoven with shining gold to keep from brushing the soot-filmed furniture of his cubbyhole.

"I was a fool, Manuel, ever to think of Francis. I've made a fool of myself…for an ice-cold Englishman. His courtship had been slow as a pavane…the partners never touching. And I thought … hoped … it would be a minuet."

"My dear Dolores, I don't quite understand. Are we in the ballroom, the drawing room, or the boudoir?"

"Never the boudoir. He is much too cold." Despite her anger, Dolores laughed at her cousin's blunt question. "And never again in the ballroom, either. I've made up my mind…definitely made up my mind. If he asked me this very afternoon, I'd tell him 'No, definitely no! Never have I considered marriage to you. Never would I consider it. Take your shopworn charm elsewhere!' That's what I'd say."

"Are you quite sure, Dolores? You've rejected almost... ah... every other possibility, you know."

"Of course I'm sure. I've decided I won't marry at all...ever. I'd rather take myself to the Convent. I'll have peace there...and no boorish men to make a fool of me."

"If that's how you feel, there's nothing more to be said. But your enterprises? Who'll run them for you?"

"The Devil take the enterprises—for all the good they do me. I'm a woman, not an accountant....And I'll do as I please."

"That you will, my dear...if you're absolutely sure, of course."

Amid the black-lacquered furniture of her drawing-room, Dolores recalled Manuel's last words before they had turned to business. Her gray eyes stared unseeing at the gold bas-relief figures trooping across the jet face of the credenza opposite the gold-veined marble fireplace. Her pink-enameled fingernails tapped the jade-inlaid table that supported a crystal decanter of Madeira. Was she quite sure, she wondered, absolutely sure?

Dolores reaffirmed her decision. The Englishman's milk-and-water wooing could only preface a milk-and-water marriage. She wanted an amiable companion, but also a lover, not a lap dog. No, she would not prolong the barren flirtation with the soldier-of-fortune. She stroked away the lines concentration had momentarily engraved between her black eyebrows, and she opened a ledger. For the time being, she would tend to business, forgetting all men.

The cream door vibrated under the scratching fingernails of her majordomo, José Rivera. The Japanese-Indian mixed-blood entered on felt-soled Chinese slippers.

"Senhora," he said, "Colonel Arrowsmith inquires whether you are at home."

"I've told you before, José, he does not use the title...does not wish to be called Colonel. But no, I'm not...not to him. Go tell him so."

The majordomo nodded and began closing the door behind himself.

"Just a moment, José," Dolores called. "Let me think a moment. No...do not send him away. Show him in. I'll have the pleasure myself."

The crouched leopard of a full colonel of the Ming Dynasty

on Francis's scarlet tunic bared its teeth as he tucked his helmet under his arm and bowed.

"Senhora," he said, "I am honored that you permit me to call on you."

"You are still free of this house, Francis." Curiosity diverted Dolores's anger. "But why the uniform? I thought you didn't.... If you don't want to be called Colonel, why wear the uniform?"

"Men change, Dolores. Yesterday...last week...I did not. But today I wear the uniform of His Imperial Majesty with great pride."

"The Governor will not like it.... Not when he's walking a tightrope between the two dynasties."

"He must abide it, Dolores. I am sworn to the service of His Imperial Majesty of the Ming. No other garment would honor this occasion."

Dolores leaned forward to stopper the decanter of Madeira, pointedly not offering Francis a glass. He was assuredly on the point of allowing her to revenge his failure to beg her hand earlier by begging her hand when it was too late. She smiled and waited.

"Dolores, my dear, I want...I'd like to..." Francis realized that he had never made a formal proposal of marriage. "That is, I realize it is unexpected, but..."

"Yes, Francis, what is it?" Dolores asked.

"It is simply that...I wish you to marry me," he blurted. "I know I have been...I am...deficient in gallantry. And I ask your forgiveness for my abruptness. But, my dear Dolores, I love you.... And I implore you to honor me with your hand. I shall guard you well."

"How could I ever have suspected? Your abruptness... abruptness..."

Dolores groped in her gold-threaded white bodice for a lace handkerchief. She could not contain herself. She did not wish to contain herself. She giggled like a schoolgirl, laughed openly, then chortled.

"By God, Francis, I am surprised...terribly surprised at ..." Another spasm of laughter shook her. "That is, I...I ...Oh God, it's too funny."

"Funny? Funny, you say? And that is all?"

"No, by Our Lady, it is not all. It is funny, though. What I wanted so badly...now...when it's offered, it's just funny. But that's not all."

523

"Senhora, will you have the goodness to inform me what else there can be to say after your laughter?"

"Gladly, Colonel," she flared. "Abrupt you have *not* been. I have been humiliated by your hesitation...your tardiness. Everyone had us marrying a month ago, but you...you couldn't bring yourself....Now, it's too late."

"In that case, Senhora, I shall bid you...."

Francis bowed stiffly and turned toward the door. Gripping the handle, he turned abruptly.

"No, I'll be damned if I withdraw in injured dignity. I would have...only yesterday. But not today. Now listen to me, Dolores. If you wanted me a month ago, you loved me then, did you not?"

"I suppose....Yes, I did...then." She nodded, then flared. "But not now...not *ever* again."

"Are you so inconstant? Four weeks later you no longer love me! If I believed that, I'd take back my humble proposal. But I don't believe it, and I'll..."

"You'll what, Francis?" Dolores despised the tremulous note she could not control. "You'll do what?"

"I'll force you somehow....Be damned to this palavering, Dolores. Now tell me plainly that you'll marry me...or that you will not. Tell me plainly without girlish giggles. Yes or no?"

"And if it's no?" she taunted.

"I'll be half-relieved, I suppose, and, then, half-desolate. No...utterly desolate. And I'll take myself off to the Ming Court...to serve the Emperor and to spare you the embarrassment of my presence. Duty will excuse my appearing to jilt you....But I shall be utterly desolate."

"Desolate, Francis...utterly, irreparably, and totally ...wholly desolate?"

"Of course, Dolores. I do love you deeply. Far above any other love I've ever felt or will ever..."

"I'm glad, Francis," she interrupted. "But you never said so. You never even hinted before that...that I wasn't just one among many...that you really..."

"Desolate," he plowed on, "is a mild word for how I'll..."

"Are you saying, Francis," she asked slyly, "that you cannot live without me?"

"Nonsense, Dolores!" He was emphatic, though cheered by the reawakening of her habitual humor. "I'll live without you....But I won't want to live."

"You leave me little choice, Francis. If that is so, how could I possibly say no?"

MARIA ARROWSMITH sat stiffly in the front pew of the Cathedral staring dully at the High Altar banked with roses, lilies, and carnations. Under the cover of sleeves that hung well below her fingertips, her hands were tensely inter-twined. Her long, lacquered nails clicked against each other as her fingers twisted, never still for an instant.

Uncomfortable in the green robe of a lieutenant, Joseph King studied her set face. He impulsively laid his hand on her embroidery-encrusted sleeve and squeezed her arm. Though he was virtually her uncle and thirty-one years older, his affectionate gesture scandalized Joseph himself. The admonition of the sage Mencius rang in his head: "*Nan nü shou shou pu chin....* Even when they hand each other presents, men and women must not touch." Nonetheless he squeezed the slender arm again. Maria needed what comfort he could give her, for she felt herself abandoned.

Half-Chinese and half-European, half-woman and half-girl, Maria of the shining yellow hair was forlorn within the gorgeous Court Robe she had worn at the Christmas Ball and wore again for the Nuptial Mass on April 18, 1650. She smiled gratefully at Joseph King while her thoughts strayed from the father who had found her after so long only to desert her again so soon.

She was thinking about herself, seeking her true self be-neath the divergent identities the world had imposed upon her. Was she, the unmoving figure wondered, Maria Arrowsmith or Hsü Mai-lo, baptized Maria? And the other essential questions: Was she European or Chinese? Was she both? Or was she not quite either?

Amid her bewilderment, one truth was fixed beyond question. She was, of course, a Christian. Her devotion to her mother's adopted creed, the Holy Catholic religion into which her father had been born, was the core of her existence. She could no more doubt her Christianity than she could doubt that she belonged to the sex that bears life and nurtures life.

The questions Maria pondered were not only spiritual or emotional. Her answer would have immediate practical con-sequences. If she were Maria Arrowsmith, she would, per-force, remain in Macao and attempt to fit herself to European ways. If she were Hsü Mai-lo, baptized Maria, she must rejoin her fiancé Chü Wei-wan, baptized Edmond, at the Court of the Emperor of the Southern Ming Dynasty. Despite endemic disorder in the Portuguese settlement, she would be far safer in Macao than in the entourage of the Emperor, who had again shifted his capital under Manchu pressure. But she would remain true to her essential nature, even if she must abandon illusory security. Besides, her father had prejudiced her choice by abandoning her for a woman only nine years her senior.

Recalled by the sonorous organ notes, Maria saw the Bishop of Macao standing tight-faced before the High Altar. Beaming impenitently, Father Giulio di Giaccomo stood at his right hand. Banks of candles spilled their light on the moiré silk of the Bishop's mitre and glowed on the embroidery on his Mass vestments. Maria smiled fleetingly, her amusement tinged with malice.

The Bishop, she knew, had vigorously opposed the marriage that would deprive the Church of the wealth of Dolores de Albuquerque. Finally forced to give his assent, he had flatly refused to marry the heiress to her soldier-of-fortune with a Nuptial Mass. But Dolores de Albuquerque and her powerful cousin Manuel Bocarro had compelled the Governor, who liked the alliance no more than did the Bishop, to bring the weight of the State to bear on the recalcitrant Church. The Bishop had finally consented with ill grace to give Dolores de Albuquerque the ceremonial wedding she craved, though the remarriage of a widow should properly have been modest. Getting what she wanted, Dolores cared no more for the discomfiture of the two chief personages of Macao than she did for the disapproving buzz of the settlement's matrons.

Maria saw *that* woman, Teresa Dolores Angela do Amaral de Albuquerque, mincing down the main aisle. Glowing in dove-gray samite shot with metallic gold, she was triumphantly erect. A pale-green cloud of bridesmaids followed her to the barrier of the Sanctuary, where Francis Arrowsmith waited with Manuel Bocarro. Groom and groomsman wore red-velvet jackets and breeches festooned with gold thread. The velvet hats under their arms flaunted golden plumes. Her father, Maria knew, had reluctantly agreed not to wear the Ming regimentals that would enrage the Governor. Manuel Bocarro had persuaded him that Chinese uniform would be out of place at a ceremony clearly European, as well as Christian.

When Dolores kneeled beside him, the pungent fragrance

of incense and flowers was sharply evocative to Francis. The memory of another marriage nineteen years earlier momentarily clouded his joy. But, he realized, he was for the first time truly giving himself without stint. The sacramental commitment was, as earlier, profound, but he had never before made a total emotional commitment. Bowing his head for the Bishop's blessing, Francis knew he had finally shattered the shell that cut him off from the world.

Diverted from her preoccupation, Maria studied her father's expressive features two yards distant. She was caught by the emotions of the man to whom she had again given her love during the past half-year. She could read his face easily. She had come to know him well, delighting in their long talks, which taught her so much about both her father and herself.

Her father's face was lit by self-abnegating love when he slipped a gold band on the Portuguese woman's finger, and Maria thought of her mother Marta. She thought again of herself and her future when the Bishop intoned in Latin: "Go in peace, and the Lord be with you always."

Her father, Maria saw clearly, had no need of her. She could only be an embarrassment to him and his new European wife. Besides, she could never live as a European. How could she, when her crippled feet forbade all the active pursuits of European ladies? Moreover, she would never find a European husband, even if she should break her vows to Edmond Chü, for whom she suddenly longed.

She was Hsü Mai-lo, baptized Maria, she concluded. She was Chinese, primarily and essentially Chinese, though tinged by Europe. She would, she decided, travel with the Polish Jesuit Michal Piotr Boym to Wuchou in Kwangsi Province, where the Ming Emperor held his Court and Edmond waited for her. Since Joseph King had offered to escort her, she would not be snapping all ties to her father's world. Besides, Francis Arrowsmith had sworn himself to the service of the Emperor as well as to his new wife, and she would see him frequently.

Wuchou

JULY 21, 1650

IN 1650, the first year of the second half of the seventeenth century, the seventh of the reign of the Shun Chih Emperor of the Manchu Dynasty and the fourth of the Yung Li Emperor of the Southern Ming Dynasty, Wuchou was eminent for its strategic position and its transient guests rather than any intrinsic quality. The amphibious town lay a few miles north of the Tropic of Cancer and a few miles west of the border between Kwangsi and Kwangtung provinces at the confluence of the West River and the Cinnamon River. Wuchou was nourished not only by the earth, but by the busy waterways as well. The inland port was the gateway to Kwangsi, a backward province remarkable for its otherworldly beauty, which had for centuries defied poets and painters to equal its splendors in ink or pigments.

Some two hundred miles by junk from Canton, Wuchou did not envy the wealth of that cosmopolitan metropolis of South China. Complacent, perhaps smug, Wuchou looked neither outward to the wave-dashed trade routes of the endless ocean nor inland to the tiered mountains, where green-clad rock spires towering above narrow river valleys into misty clouds dominated the classic landscape even the men of the North considered quintessentially Chinese. Wuchou was a small-minded provincial town of brick houses with skimpy umbrella eaves, and it lived by the small tribute it exacted for goods, services, and customs dues from every junk that passed its rough-stone quays.

In July 1650 the Ming Emperor was again temporarily resident in Wuchou. Should the Dynasty's fortunes revive, he would re-establish his capital at Chaoching, a hundred twenty miles to the east, or even at Canton, which was again under siege by the Manchus. Should his armies meet further defeats, he would take refuge in the western recesses of Kwangsi.

Blown by the winds of fate, the Yung Li Emperor had in March returned to Wuchou for the sixth time since his first entry in 1645, when he was a fugitive princeling. The weak Emperor, who attracted loyalty by his amiability rather than his talents, had been a fugitive for a quarter of his twenty-seven years. Settling in Wuchou again in the fourth year of his troubled reign, he eschewed the pomp of his ancestors to keep his Imperial Court on a fleet of barges moored in the muddy river. As befitted the Imperial Dignity, those barges were called *Shui Tien*, the Water Palaces.

The Grand Secretary who chose that name was the Mandarin Chü Shin-ssu, who had been baptized Thomas in 1623. He had been created Earl in Kwangsi in 1647, after valiantly defending Kweilin, the provincial capital, with the support of some three hundred Portuguese artillerymen. Thomas Chü had repeatedly rejected Manchu offers of higher rank, moved to desert his Emperor by neither the urging of the Jesuits of Peking nor his own pessimism regarding the Dynasty's future. Having scathingly criticized the Ming in its decadent glory in Peking, he was committed to the death to the Ming in its wandering exile.

Thomas Chü was diverted from his forebodings on the afternoon of July twenty-first by an occasion both joyous and portentous. The Emperor's direct command had brought him from beleaguered Canton to Wuchou, where his eldest son, Chü Wei-man, baptized Edmond after his birth in Peking in 1624, was to marry Hsü Mai-lo, baptized Maria after her birth in Tengchou in 1632. Thomas Chü had slipped out of Canton in the rags of a manure coolie too humble for his unshaven pate and his unbraided hair to attract Manchu wrath. At the age of sixty, he had traveled to Wuchou hidden under a cargo of dried fish in a river junk.

The wedding party's barges glowed with color. The damp

529

heat had not deterred the courtiers from wearing their magnificent robes of state, which symbolized the Imperial glory that should have been attested by acres of golden-tiled roofs with vermilion and viridian pillars. Maria knew her wedding would outshine the Nuptial Mass sung for Dolores de Albuquerque in the Cathedral of Macao three months earlier. True, no bishop presided, but two Jesuit Fathers, Andreas Xavier Koffler and Michal Piotr Boym. Yet the Emperor himself beamed his august blessing, and the Empress Anna wiped tears from her narrow eyes with a square of yellow silk. The palms bending their green-feathered heads over the river were, moreover, a living edifice more imposing than the cold stone arches of the Cathedral. Her wedding gown of shimmering scarlet tribute silk was, Maria concluded complacently, more splendid than the gold-shot gray samite the Portuguese woman had worn—and more fitting for a Chinese bride. More fitting, too, than the gaudy vestments of the Bishop of Macao were the Jesuits' black-silk cassocks cut like somber Mandarin's robes.

Maria felt herself triumphantly Chinese on the grandest day of her life. She was happy that Joseph King was among the congregation, awkward as ever in his green lieutenant's robe. Joseph was a living link to her father and her former life, but a Chinese link. Maria's breath caught when she glanced at her bridegroom in his colonel's scarlet robe. The poignant melody set to the love-lyric "The River-Merchant's Wife," by the supreme Tang Dynasty poet Li Po, floated from two-stringed Chinese violins and thirteen-stringed Chinese lyres. Big-bellied Chinese trumpets blared the refrain, and the smoke of tens of thousands of popping firecrackers cast a smoky-blue haze over the river.

Maria glowed in the radiance of the Imperial Couple, who were enthroned under a canopy of yellow silk on their own barge. No other bride not of the Blood Imperial had been so honored for centuries. No longer sequestered like his predecessors, the Emperor gladly showed himself to his devoted subjects to honor his Chief Minister.

The Emperor sat on a throne of gilt bamboo, and his gold-braided shoes rested on a golden footstool. The plum silk of his robe was embossed with the long-life ideogram and belted with gilt leather secured with a white-jade buckle. His soft face was unlined by the cares of state, and his dark eyes peered through lashes as sparse as the mustache drooping around his pursed mouth. His scanty goatee twitched when he bared his yellowish teeth to confer his Imperial approbation: "*Hau! Hau! Hau chi-la!*...Lovely! Lovely! Wonderful! We are all happy today!"

The Christian Empress Anna was seated beside her Lord. Her long face was framed by strings of jade hanging from her domed headdress set with rubies and pearls. Its orange lapels crossed beneath her pointed chin, her violet robe was embroidered with paired green-and-scarlet-plumaged parrots, the symbol of Imperial nuptial bliss. She fingered the rose-jade crucifix suspended on a silver chain around her neck and held the sticky hand of two-year-old Crown Prince Constantine.

The Austrian Father Andreas Koffler stood before the Holy Altar on the nuptial barge. At fifty he was thin, and his skin was sallow. Beside him stood the Pole, Father Michal Piotr Boym, ten years younger and exuberantly robust. Lacking a common mother tongue, the two Jesuits normally spoke Chinese to each other, and they recited the marriage service in the Officials' Language.

While Maria re-enacted the ceremony her mother Marta had described to her, her thoughts wandered to the pictures in her mother's pillow book. She commanded her wayward mind to concern itself solely with the Holy Sacrament. But before she closed the lid of her conscience on its chatter, an irreverent inner voice praised Maria for studying the pillow book.

Nothing, that voice asserted, nothing in Christianity required the marriage bed to be a joyless waste. A Christian husband merited not only many children, but sensual pleasure from his sole wife. A pagan chief wife who failed in the arts of love might still be happy presiding over the minor wives and concubines who satisfied her lord's needs. A Christian wife who failed could not possibly be happy. She would be tortured by her lord's violating their marriage vows with courtesans. Monogamy demanded much more of a wife than did polygamy, which had its uses, though Holy Church proscribed it.

"*Ho-ping-di chu-chü*..." The closing words of the service recalled Maria's meandering thoughts. "Go in peace, and the Lord be with you always."

The bride rose and bowed to her husband. They neither kissed nor touched, for the Jesuits sensibly realized that a Christian marriage was not, therefore, a European marriage. In China husband and wife did not display their affection. It

531

would have been obscene for them to kiss and lewd for their fingers to clasp. Maria nonetheless tingled as if she already felt Edmond's hands on her body. Her senses whirling, she bowed before the ancestral tablets of the Chü family and drank the ritual toasts from an antique rhinoceros-horn cup.

Myriads of firecrackers volleyed in the subtropical dusk. Rockets soared incandescent into the violet sky, and cannon growled a salute. The bullfrogs dived from the lilypads, and the Grand Secretary Thomas Chü frowned at the waste of gunpowder. The delighted Emperor smiled and fed the squalling Crown Prince a crystallized lotus stalk with his own sacred fingers.

Eunuchs poled the dining-boats toward the barge where the wedding party stood between the incense sticks smoking before the ancestral tablets of the Chü family and the candles burning before the Holy Altar of the Lord of Heaven. The guests were eager to toast the couple in pungent *mao-tai* spirits. Fingers itching for the winecup, stomachs rumbling in anticipation, the company resigned itself when Thomas Chü, Earl in Kwangsi, waved his bony hand for silence. Their convivial chatter subsiding, the guests waited for the doting father's address. Not even the eloquence of the Earl in Kwangsi could breathe freshness into the millennia-worn platitudes of hope and counsel.

Thomas Chü glanced at the Grand Eunuch Achilles Pang, who stood behind the Emperor holding a three-foot-round azure fan of ceremony. The Eunuch's square chin nodded, and his white hair trailed on his scarlet-silk shoulders. A moment later, his full lips smiled within a face still sleekly handsome at the age of sixty-four. Thomas Chü's eyes sought the open gaze of General Luke Chiao. The Commander-in-Chief nodded so violently his scarlet helmet trembled on his round head. The golden ideogram *yung,* brave, winked assurance through the twilight to the Grand Secretary, who was the leader of the Christian triumvirate that guided the Ming Emperor.

Thomas Chü set his horsehair hat squarely on his head. His long face, lean almost to emaciation, glowed pink in the light of spherical red lanterns emblazoned with the double-joy symbol of married bliss. He tucked his scarlet robe into his blue-leather belt, unnecessarily unclasping and reclasping its jade buckle. The silver unicorn emblem on his breast twitched its long horn, yearning toward the glowing orb that

532

symbolized dominion over the world. The guests saw that the normally self-possessed Earl was distraught.

Thomas Chü's face was cadaverous. His long, thin nose was set in gaunt cheeks, and his beard was white. When he lifted his hat to mop sweat from his high forehead, he revealed thinning hair striped with gray. The dedication that glowed in his eyes had survived decades of struggle against the enemies of the Ming.

The Christian Earl had shared the hardships of a generation of upright Mandarins, his fortitude and constancy not unique, though outstanding. His chief regret was for a private failure. Preoccupied with public duties, he had spared too few stolen minutes for his son Edmond. Only during the seven years of his suspension from office after his imprisonment for outspokenness in 1637 had Thomas Chü been able to give Edmond all his affection—as well as essential literary and moral instruction. Recalled to office after the fall of Peking in 1644, he had responded unhesitatingly, though both natural resentment and personal advantage counseled submission to the Manchus.

"Most Excellent Ministers and Most Valiant Generals, Noble Lords and Ladies, Gentlemen." Thomas Chü's sibilant Shanghai syllables whistled through his long teeth. "I have not come today to praise my beloved son and his gracious wife or to pray for their good fortune. I did not make the hazardous journey from Canton to overwhelm you with platitudes. Those who expect only formal pieties may depart."

The bright throng buzzed like a beehive stirred by a distant danger. No one moved, not one of the princes and the Eunuchs, the wastrels and the stalwarts, the time-servers and the zealots who, each for his own reason, remained true to the stricken Dynasty. None would affront the Grand Secretary of the Pavilion of Profound Learning, the Prime Minister of the Southern Ming.

"Marriage is an affirmation!" Thomas Chü commanded the attention of the few hundred men whose efforts would determine whether the Ming reconquered the Empire or perished. "Marriage affirms faith in mankind and our Sacred Ancestors. Marriage bespeaks confidence in the proper ordering of the world under the virtuous Emperor—and pledges obedience to the Lord of Heaven. Why else swear to cleave together to conceive and rear children?

"The best lies within us. Only our best can make marriage successful—or restore the glory of the Sacred Dynasty. The

Dynasty has *never* stood in greater peril. If we fail in virtue, the Sacred Dynasty will *assuredly* perish—and the godless northern barbarians will rule the Han race."

The throng whirred like angry bees. No Mandarin, not even the most courageous Censor, had ever affronted the Imperial Presence by declaring that the Sacred Dynasty stood in imminent danger of dissolution.

"As you know, Kweilin is besieged by the so-called Field Marshal Kung Yu-teh, the misnamed Virtuous Kung, whom the Manchu barbarians have given the ludicrous title Prince of the Pacified South," Thomas Chü continued. "Losing Kweilin would reduce us to landless soldiers-of-fortune, who can never overcome the enemy.

"The Lord has already struck down Virtuous Kung's henchman Keng Chung-ming, called the Halfwit. Together they revolted against the Sacred Dynasty at Tengchou in 1632—and caused the execution of those heroic Christians, General Ignatius Sün and Ambassador Michael Chang. The father of the modest and beautiful bride, Colonel Arrowmaker, who sadly cannot be with us today, was captured at Tengchou and delivered into captivity among the northern barbarians.

"The usurpers gave this Halfwit the false title Prince of the Tranquilized South. Some tranquility! Some pacification! But last year Halfwit Keng committed suicide rather than answer the usurpers' charge that his officers had virtuously harbored Chinese slaves escaped from Manchu captivity.

"The Halfwit's son now besieges Canton. If Canton, too, should fall, our prospects would be dire."

The courtiers shifted restlessly when Thomas Chü paused to sip *mao-tai* from an eggshell cup.

"These devils in human guise will succeed unless we take decisive action immediately. Heaven will tremble—and the earth will be rent asunder!" The Grand Secretary's voice rose, and Joseph King thought of an Old Testament prophet warning of doom.

"Who then is to blame? And what can be done?" The whiplash questions scourged the audience. "*You* are to blame...*all* of you...and *I* myself. Only we can save the Dynasty. The solution lies *within* ourselves!"

The Grand Secretary's eyes roved over the assembly. Joseph King saw contempt in that appraisal, but the Grand Eunuch Achilles Pang discerned anguished compassion. The courtiers squirmed when Thomas Chü resumed his address.

"*Hao jan chih chi shih Meng-tzu*... The Sage Mencius described the Moving Force that springs from utmost virtue within an individual. Without that Force, a man is starved in his soul—and cannot act effectively. In harmony with the Moving Force, all things are possible. But only rigorous self-cultivation can animate the Moving Force.

"The Sages counsel us that the rulers must be the model for all men. You must cultivate your own virtue, so that the Moving Force enters into you. Then all men will act as you do, and the world will be at peace under a righteous Emperor."

The Grand Secretary abruptly seated himself, leaving his puzzled son Edmond to lead their equally puzzled guests to the dining-boat. Joseph King shook his head despairingly. Of course the Ming required morality, but it required so much more.

Disappointment stabbed Maria Chü. Her father-in-law had neither extolled her goodness nor invoked blessings upon her marriage. It was her wedding, and she was not pleased by his using her day for an arid political speech. Her own father, she could not help feeling, would have done far better.

Maria stroked the bulge where she had pinned Francis's present to the lining of her robe and reproached herself for the timidity that had prevented her displaying a European brooch. She did not know that the magnificent sunburst of diamonds on golden rays had cost Francis all his sparse savings—and a large sum borrowed from his partner Antonio Castro. Practical as well as loving, Maria would have been deeply disturbed to learn that her father's extravagance had made him wholly dependent on the generosity of his Portuguese wife.

Nor did she know that Francis had bargained for days with the emissaries Thomas Chü sent to Macao. The matchmakers had finally agreed to accept the Englishman's services to the Dynasty as an earnest of the lavish dowry he swore to pay when his fortunes improved.

Maria Chü was preoccupied with annoyance at her father-in-law's inconsiderateness and disappointment at her father's absence. On this day of all days, both should have placed her happiness above all else.

Her irritation soon passed. She knew that Edmond loved her deeply, and that was all-important. Her father and her father-in-law loved her too, each in his own way, and that was almost as important. Besides, all eyes were watching her, and the wedding banquet was about to begin.

After smiling in wry sympathy with Maria's chagrin, Joseph King was picking over the Earl's exhortations strand by strand, like a bluejay choosing twigs for its nest. The reluctant audience had been bored—and, finally, resentful. They were no longer boys, those Ministers and Mandarins, to be patronized by moral homilies.

Joseph King was profoundly moved, at once exalted and depressed by Thomas Chü's admonitions. Having been a slave for many years, he marveled at the curious simplicity of the Mandarins of the Ming Dynasty, even those few who had risen from the common people. Thomas Chü and his colleagues had been cast out of the Northern Capital of the Great Empire without being cast down from their high rank and their great privileges. Having never suffered the indignities the lower orders endured, they could not possibly understand the soldiers and farmers whose enthusiastic support was their only hope. Nor could they understand that the arduous cultivation of virtue by a few hundred noblemen and Mandarins was almost irrelevant to the fate of the Ming.

The mission of driving the Manchus from the Empire required cannon and muskets far more than moral precepts and personal virtue. The mission further required much gold to reward ruffians who would fight desperately to seize the booty of an Empire.

Grand Secretary Thomas Chü, a pious Christian and a devout Confucian, might properly concern himself with his own conscience. For the rest, he should promise the rabble that the vast estates of princes, nobles, and gentry would be distributed among the soldiers when the Ming retook North China. Ordinary men would not hazard their lives to restore such magnates to enjoyment of their great possessions. Only immediate rewards—and the lure of greater wealth after victory—could raise victorious armies in Ming China.

Joseph King sadly concluded that the Grand Secretary was inept in modern warfare despite his tactical proficiency and his personal valor. Himself inspired by moral fervor, Thomas Chü could not realize that other men were moved by material gain. Detached from the common people, he could not comprehend the motives of those less noble than himself. He was therefore fatally disqualified from leading them to victory.

Only external intervention, the secretary concluded, could save the Ming Dynasty. But where, short of a miracle, was that intervention to come from?

"I'd rather show my valor this way." The stout Minister of Finance seated beside Joseph King laughed as his silver chopsticks pursued a minute shrimp around the green-jade serving bowl.

"And I'd rather cultivate inner virtue this way." The Minister of Public Works grinned at the shrimp wriggling in his chopsticks before popping it into his mouth.

Joseph wondered how anyone could govern—much less inculcate with virtue—a nation that knew ten thousand different ways to prepare pork. He was seated between the Ministers despite his low rank, because he represented the bride's family. While he brooded his silver chopsticks, crowned with minute rubies, joined the chase after the green shrimps, which were befuddled by the wine and vinegar in which they were served alive.

The Yung Li Emperor, the Lord of Eternal Days, had commanded an Imperial Banquet to honor the marriage of his Chief Minister's son. A fugitive in a provincial backwater, the Emperor could still command the finest dishes of every province of the Great Empire. Only one deviation was permitted in the ritual progression prescribed centuries earlier for the forty courses of several hundred dishes. The Eunuch headwaiters had first presented *mi-yo ping*, honey cakes seethed in oil, the perfect blend symbolizing the harmonious union of bride and groom. That common fare had been served under a silver lid adorned with a solid-gold bee, while a shrimp carved from rose jade crowned the green-jade lid of the bowl of drunken shrimp.

Maria and Edmond picked at the profusion, lifting a morsel from each dish to acknowledge the Imperial favor. They were seated beside each other, and one guest in every four was a lady. Just as the Emperor condescended to dine with his subjects, though on a separate barge, the convention of separate banquets for men and women that had ruled Francis's marriage to Marta was rescinded by the enforced simplicity of the Imperial Court in exile. The mingling of women's light laughter with men's gruff voices reminded Edmond of carousing in a Flower House. Though his propriety was offended, he chatted amiably with the Minister of Rites on his left.

"A very worthy point, your esteemed father's," the Minister observed, helping himself to the steamed conch after the Eunuch headwaiter lifted the silver lid by its gold conch-shell handle.

"We must all dedicate ourselves to self-cultivation," Edmond agreed politely, though his Christian skepticism distrusted his father's appeal to the antique virtues.

Seated on Maria's right, the Grand Secretary glanced quizzically at his son and asked: "Do you think, Edmond, cultivating the Moving Force is so different from the Spiritual Exercises of Ignatius Loyola, who founded the Society of Jesus?"

"No, Father," Edmond replied, "but I think we need Red Jacket Cannon more than moral self-cultivation."

"That too," Thomas Chü replied, "though cannon did us little good against the Manchus."

"But you do need cannon, Sir?" Joseph King leaned forward to ask.

"Yes, of course, Master King," Thomas Chü answered. "But the men behind them are more important than the cannon. Their spirits must be as one with the guns, and none of my people..."

"We shall see, Sir," Joseph King replied. "I understand your anxiety."

Francis Arrowsmith's secretary did not prolong his conversation with the Grand Secretary. There would be time later, and he was captivated by the dish the headwaiter placed on the table. A silver tureen chased with golden dragons and mythical birds was covered by a silver lid on which a golden cobra with extended hood reared. Porcelain side dishes offered chrysanthemum petals, chopped spring onions, shredded coriander, and tiny dried shrimp.

"Ah, the Dragon and the Phoenix!" Joseph breathed in delight, watching the Eunuch spoon individual portions into eggshell porcelain bowls in gilt holders. "A very long time since I..."

He sprinkled the condiments on the strips of white meat steamed with fragrant radish. Raising the bowl to his mouth, he relished each mouthful.

"A favored dish of your native province, is it not?" the Minister of Finance asked. "Chicken and snake, am I right?"

"Yes, Sir," Joseph replied. "But to me it tastes just like dragons and phoenixes."

Moonbeams filtered through palm fronds lit the barges with cool radiance, and paper lanterns glowed scarlet. From a barge that shimmered in the silver haze upon the water a flute cried to a zither in the haunting folksong "The Soldier's Return." Edmond Chü surrendered himself to the melody that celebrated his own return from the wars. He laid down his chopsticks and took Maria's hand under the table. His fingertips caressed her palm, and his mind leaped to the time when he would no longer have to go to war.

Maria closed her fingers on Edmond's and held them tight. The toasts had left her feeling strangely weightless, as if her body had dissolved into a golden mist. She clung to Edmond's hand, fearing she would float away. She no longer felt either alarm or longing when she thought of their bridal bed. It was as if that encounter, whether ordeal or delight, had already passed. It was as if they had been man and wife for years and she had just welcomed Edmond back from a long campaign. But a chill of apprehension warned her he must soon return to the battlefield.

For most of the company, neither past nor future existed. They were caught up by the present, with its unending procession of dishes: whole swans and peacocks, roasted and sliced before their plumage was restored; squabs, quails, and pheasants marinated in honey; clams, oysters, and scallops fresh on beds of snow from the mountains; camel's hump braised with wild garlic, a dish normally reserved for the Emperor; turtle stewed with fresh herbs; *ho-tun,* the delicious river fish that was poisonous if not properly prepared; and an abundance of fresh and preserved fruits to clear the palate.

Midway in the feast, trumpets flourished, and the Eunuchs presented boxes of carved-coral lacquer divided into eight compartments. Each section offered a different delicacy, their contrasting colors and textures delighting the eye as well as the palate: red-cured ducks' webs; powdered pork light as fluff; pullet wings in aspic; flaked icefish; a purée of glazed chestnuts; green lotus seeds; pickled walnuts; and sliced water chestnuts. The guests sighed, protested that they could eat no more, refilled their winecups, and devoured the delicacies.

Trumpets flourished again. On the musicians' barge, maidens in floating drapery performed a slow Han Dynasty ballet, as insubstantial as elves twirling on the silver river. The trumpets flourished once again and the feast resumed. Appetites restored, the guests ate eagerly, and the wines passed more rapidly.

At ten in the evening, five hours after the wedding party had sat down to the banquet, the Eunuchs brought in silver platters heaped with *pa-pao fan,* rice with eight treasures. As the guests moved that final ceremonial food around their

bowls, unable to eat more, Thomas Chü rose. His face glowing
with wine in the rays of the lanterns, he signaled for silence.

"I shall not trouble you again this night, except to offer
a toast to the beautiful bride and the gallant bridegroom."
Thomas Chü's words awoke a drowsy Maria to gratified delight. "His Imperial Majesty has been as lavish as the bride
is lovely. His Imperial banquet has been perfect as this marriage will be. Another grain of rice would be too much, just
as another fleck of powder on the bride's soft cheek would be
superfluous. The banquet is finished. Go with God!"

Macao

SEPTEMBER 5, 1650–NOVEMBER 3, 1650

"FRANCIS, my love, are you quite happy?" Teresa Dolores Angela do Amaral de Albuquerque Arrowsmith asked in early September over a breakfast of grilled sausages, fried garoupa, and roast pigeon. "Sometimes I think it's too perfect..."

"Of course, my dear." Francis abstractedly offered her reassurance. "I've never been happier. A loving and wanton wife who is a brilliant companion...and a beautiful home. What more could I..."

"Myself, I'd like a child soon. I'm not, you know, growing younger, and..."

"No more than I, my heart," he laughed. "But we're certainly trying hard. We could try again when you're through toying with the fish."

"Trying again right this minute won't make much difference, Francis." Dolores wrinkled her minutely snubbed nose in mock severity. "But I'm thinking of you. Will you always be happy living with no particular purpose? Only enjoying yourself?"

"Enjoying ourselves, my love...in a very civilized way. I am done with great affairs. Politics and doctrines only make plain men and women unhappy. Priests and princes, they are God's curse on mankind."

"And your pledge to the Ming Emperor?"

"Hastily taken...to fill my days before I found you."

"Francis, you cannot fill your days *only* with me. That's..."

"And I thought," he protested, "that was what every good woman wanted...the entire love of a reasonably good man."

"She'd have to be awfully good—or she'd be bored to death with a great mooncalf who did nothing all day but adore her. How utterly boring!"

"I bore you, do I?" Francis was almost offended. "What's the remedy?"

"Don't take everything so personally, my dear. I do, occasionally, have a thought that's not about you. I was speaking generally. But, nonetheless..."

"Nonetheless, what?"

"Nonetheless, you will bore me if you bore yourself. I can't carry the entire burden of amusing you...diverting you. And I shall bore you if you bore yourself. Besides, you did swear ...you pledged your service to..."

"...the Yung Li Emperor, the Lord of Eternal Days. Yes, I did. But you know Joseph tells me..."

"Joseph is pessimistic. All the more reason to remember your oath. If you are not true...if you back out because the Ming is in peril, what will you do when I grow old and wrinkled and crabby?...When we, perhaps, face poverty together? Will you desert me?"

"Feminine logic! God preserve me from such twisted thinking." Francis brushed his hair off his forehead, exasperated by Dolores's persistence and her implicit reminder that they lived on her money. "*What* do you want me to do, then?"

"Just talk to Joseph...seriously. Just hear what he has to say."

"I have, but I'll do so again...right now. It will be a relief to talk straightforward Chinese after twisted women's Portuguese."

Dolores's laughter at that preposterous sally followed Francis to the library that opened off the courtyard of the villa on Mount Guia. She could not believe he truly preferred the simplicities of Chinese to the intricacies of Portuguese. Like most Europeans, she was convinced the Chinese were the most complex people on earth and their language fiendishly complex.

Francis Arrowsmith had been annoyed rather than alarmed

by his secretary's gloomy assessment of the prospects for the Ming. Joseph King had been infuriated by his employer's sloth. He had not traveled in the hold of a salt junk with Thomas Chü, both disguised as backwoods peasants, so that Francis could listen to his report with obvious boredom. He had not pierced the Manchu siege lines around Canton carrying the stinking buckets of a manure coolie so that the Englishman could yawn in his face.

But Francis was engrossed by the bliss he had found in his marriage. Expecting little more than domestic security, he had discovered joy. Dolores was an eager and adept pupil in the *cama de casal*, the capacious Portuguese marriage bed. When she cast off her light stays, she cast off all inhibitions. Almost equaling the inventiveness of his Chinese wife and the ardor of his Manchu concubine, she gave him greater pleasure than either.

Dolores was also sensitive and responsive to him as no one else had ever been. For the first time, he enjoyed full emotional and intellectual communion with another human being. She also brought him the gift of laughter. For the first time he could relax from his constant struggle for survival and self-advancement. He rejoiced at having discovered the other half of himself, long lost but never missed until found.

Francis resented Joseph King's intrusion on his joy. He had been happy to fill the hours with long meals and lazy conversation. He had whiled away days talking with his cronies Antonio Castro, Manuel Bocarro, and Giulio di Giaccomo, and he had spent weeks refitting the junk *Maria*.

It would be some time before dissatisfaction with that aimless existence began to fester in Francis. But Dolores realized that she would not long be content with the gentleman of abundant leisure he had become. Having married a man of strong passions and strong commitments, she could not commend herself for transforming him into a gentle idler.

Aware that he was being gently manipulated, but unresentful, Francis sent José Rivera, the half-caste majordomo, to find his secretary.

"I have been instructed by higher authority to talk with you again about the Ming." Francis's acerbity was aggravated by Joseph's bland expression. "What am I supposed to do about it?"

"Well, you could always apologize to Dorgon, couldn't you?" Joseph drawled in his furriest Peking brogue. "Father

Adam is entrenching himself in the Manchu Court.... He'd probably be glad of your help."

"I'm serious, Joseph. Don't toy with me."

"And I am serious, too...couldn't be more serious. You obviously wouldn't give a copper farthing for the Ming—or for your oath. So the only thing is to make submission to the Manchus...and share their spoils."

"You're going too far, Joseph. I warn you that..."

"That what, Arrowmaker? If I am going too far, you are not going anywhere. If you want to sit here and rot, I'll take myself back to Wuchou...or to Canton. Times like these, the Emperor will be glad of even my poor services."

"You're free to go where you wish and do what you wish.... Of course, you are. But is that an ultimatum?"

"If you want to take it that way.... Then, yes. My poor country needs even my poor services. If the True Faith is to prevail, every Christian must serve the Ming. I cannot vegetate here. Of course, I'd rather continue to serve you, Arrowmaker, but..."

"I'm sorry I barked at you, Joseph. But what do you propose—precisely what?"

"Canton is the key. If Canton falls, the rout begins. We can't count on retaking Canton again...can't expect another miracle like forty-seven. And, if Canton is lost.... As Thomas Chü said, the Ming will be little more than landless brigands. So Canton must be relieved."

"It's the same story, isn't it? The Faith is imperiled...will be driven out of China unless we save the Ming. Exactly the same story it's been since I first came to China, isn't it?"

"Not quite, Arrowmaker. As I said, you can always go back to the Manchus and work with Adam Schall to..."

"That's impossible, Joseph. You know it. My marriage...Barbara would never forgive me. Anyway, I despise the Manchus. I couldn't go back to them, even if Dorgon didn't want my head."

"He will take your head...mine, too...if the Ming falls."

"All right, then. Let's talk about it.... What we can do."

Joseph King argued persuasively that the strategy that had inspired the earlier Portuguese expeditions was still valid. Only its bumbling execution had failed to expel the Manchus from the north. Operating in South China close to its base in Macao, rather than at the end of extended supply lines in the hostile environment of North China, a heavily armed, ultramodern striking force could drive the Manchus back. The situation was, Joseph insisted, ideal for a highly mobile unit with overwhelming firepower.

Both Chinese and Manchus used cannon and arquebuses for immediate tactical advantage. Since they distrusted modern technology, they had never planned grand strategy around those weapons. Besides, the Ming Court's interference had prevented the Expeditionary Forces' exerting decisive influence on the battlefield. Properly employed, cannon and arquebuses could transform the character of warfare in the Empire—and turn the tide of battle as decisively as had, in their time, the crossbow, the longbow, and firearms in Europe.

"I can see the Manchus rolling back," Joseph rhapsodized, his small eyes gazing into the distance. "Panic-stricken, the front ranks will trample the rear ranks. Terror of the invincible Christian battalions will defeat them...if we do it right."

Fired by his secretary's enthusiasm, Francis Arrowsmith forgot his own misgivings regarding the Southern Ming. Joseph King almost convinced him that the tide of victory would carry the loyalist armies to the Yangtze and, perhaps, beyond.

"A striking force of a thousand officers and men...Christian Africans and Indians commanded by Portuguese officers and stiffened with Portuguese sergeants under a veteran Christian commander....Yourself, Arrowmaker!" Joseph King dilated. "Operating independently, not subordinate to Ming generals...free of Chinese interference. Supplied from Macao, we would depend on the Ming for not a pinch of gunpowder or a handful of rice. I would call it the Invincible Force."

Francis was at the moment dazzled by Joseph King's eloquence. Later he confessed to Dolores that he was moved not only by the opportunity to advance the True Faith, but equally by the chance to prove himself. He added exuberantly: "You were right! I could not let my life draw to its close in slothful contentment. God requires this last, this greatest effort of me. Pray that it will succeed!"

The Englishman's fervor won over the temporal and spiritual rulers of Macao. The Governor heartily endorsed Francis's project in private, though he was circumspect in public. Fearing the Jesuits would otherwise reap all credit for victory, the Bishop blessed the enterprise. The Jesuits themselves were ambivalent. Adam Schall's growing influence in

Peking was a powerful argument for abandoning the Ming to invest all missionary effort in the Manchus. But so many priests scattered throughout South China were fervent partisans of the Ming Emperor that the Provincial could not withhold his support. Besides, the German was not universally beloved by his brothers in the Society of Jesus.

The commercial community was not enthusiastic. Antonio Castro contributed a hundred taels because he could, as a perpetually suspect Marrano, not withhold support for a quasi crusade. Manuel Bocarro lent his political influence, but told Francis, "If I were managing this enterprise, I'd let the Chinese pay. The Emperor must have warehouses full of gold....And look what happened to the Imperial hoard in Peking...all wasted."

Nonetheless Manuel Bocarro gave fifty taels, and his example spurred other merchants and manufacturers. None was, however, moved by Francis's eloquence to a substantial contribution. Dolores made up the deficit of two thousand taels, expecting to be recompensed manyfold by the gratitude of the Emperor.

By mid-October Francis had recruited seven hundred fifty Indian and African slaves and bondservants, as well as one hundred Japanese *ronin,* always eager to bloody their two-handed *katana* for a generous wage. The Duke Koxinga, who was moving his armies into Kwangtung Province to succor beleaguered Canton, promised the support of his fleets.

"The Manchus are land animals," the Duke exhorted Francis Arrowsmith through the mouth of his emissary Colonel Edmond Chü. "Drive them toward the sea, and I will destroy them!"

Francis chose a hundred unemployed Portuguese soldiers for his officers and sergeants. His deputy was Nicholas Ferreira, who had commanded the Portuguese artillery that earlier saved Kweilin. Finally, Joseph King mustered a thousand Chinese auxiliaries through his secret-society affiliations.

Cannon were, of course, the heart of the Invincible Force. Even Manuel Bocarro could not immediately provide the sixty-four field pieces Francis required. Instead, he made field carriages for every spare gun in Macao. Some were cumbersomely large, while others were ludicrously small, but the artillerymen could sharpen their skill while awaiting new guns from the foundry on the Rua do Chunambeiro.

In late October, Edmond Chü sailed into Macao on a war junk of the Duke's fleet. He came to place his wife Maria under the protection of her stepmother while her father and her husband campaigned. Nurtured in the solidarity of a Chinese family, Edmond could not doubt that Dolores would be delighted to shelter a half-Chinese stepdaughter nine years younger than herself. In any event, Edmond's business was too pressing for him to concern himself with women's feelings.

Canton's situation, he told Francis, was dire. The Manchus were tightening their noose, and even manure coolies were forbidden to carry their reeking buckets out of the metropolis. Food was running short, and the garrison's morale was plummeting. Finally Edmond handed over a smuggled letter from his father: "Esteemed Arrowmaker: Greetings in Christ! May His Love guard you all your life. Our situation is desperate. If you do not come now, you need not come at all."

Time had run out when the Invincible Force was half-trained and half-equipped. On November 3, 1650, the Christian battalions marched through the Siege Gate into the Great Empire. The few who watched at 3 A.M., the auspicious Double Hour of the Monkey, were shocked at its small array. More than one thousand men had assembled before the Cathedral when the Bishop blessed the colors and weapons. Under a vermilion banner emblazoned with a golden cross, Francis Arrowsmith, Colonel of the Great Ming Dynasty, mustered five hundred men and thirty-two field pieces. His main body marched toward Canton, ninety miles northwest for carrier-pigeons but twice that distance for gun carriages on the rough paths of the Peninsula.

The rest had already embarked in Duke Koxinga's war junks. The left wing was to sail one hundred sixty miles up the winding West River to Sanshui to attack the besiegers' rear. The right wing under Captain Nicholas Ferreira would sail a hundred ten miles up the Pearl River, forcing the fortified narrows the Portuguese called Bocca Tigris, the Tiger's Mouth.

Francis Arrowsmith disliked splitting his forces. A thousand men were, on the face of it, ridiculously few to hurl against Manchu units totaling fifty thousand. Even counting Chinese auxiliaries, the odds were twenty-five to one. But he would draw the Manchu riposte onto his main body while the two landing parties harried the enemy's flanks. Then the Ming army besieged inside Canton would sally out, while twenty thousand Ming irregulars in the countryside joined the assault.

Francis was content with neither that strategy nor the readiness of the Invincible Force. Though he swore to his men that victory was inevitable, he knew that name was vainglorious.

Francis had not planned to march for another two months, when he would hurl a battleworthy force at the Manchu army like a thunderbolt. Instead, he was compelled to split his unready command into three columns. He had planned to draw the Manchu army into a set-piece battle and allow it to batter itself against the rock of his defenses. Instead, he was compelled to attack.

"You are marching to your death," Dolores protested. "Why did I ever urge you to listen to Joseph? You're both mad!"

"What else can I do, my dear?" he replied, pressing her tear-stained face against his shoulder. "I cannot renege! Canton must be relieved now!"

"Don't go, Francis. Leave the Chinese to their own wars."

"Dolores, I must go—or be a laughingstock all my life. It is not the best way to commit my first independent command to battle, but it is the only way."

Francis crossed himself as the column marched through the siege gate. His men were shadows in the overcast night, and whips cracked to drive the overladen vehicles onward. He commended his soul to God, and he prayed that Divine Intervention would make up his earthly deficiencies. A bass murmur sighed heavenward as the entire Christian force raised the same prayer.

Wuchou, Canton, Macao

NOVEMBER 3, 1650–JANUARY 4, 1651

NOT all the lanterns that glowed like the orange moon on the Mid-Autumn Festival had been taken down from the Ming Dynasty's Water Palace in Wuchou. The Emperor delighted in their gaiety. Nor had all the round mooncakes been consumed. Children and greedy Eunuchs still hoarded a few sticky pastries.

The men of the Ming had fervently celebrated the two-hundred-eighty-third anniversary of the revolt against the Mongols that enthroned their Sacred Dynasty. If the present Emperor were as resolute as the Founding Emperor, if his followers were as resolute as the Founding Emperor, if his followers were as valorous as their ancestors, the new barbarian invaders would also be swept from the Empire.

The Dynasty that had lost North China largely because of the excesses of the Court Eunuchs was sustained in exile by the resolution of the Christian Grand Eunuch Achilles Pang. Yet Achilles Pang had almost lost faith in mortal men's ability to avert the Dynasty's doom when he watched the gaudy sunset of November 3, 1650, the day Francis Arrowsmith led his Invincible Force into the Empire. The Grand Eunuch's faith in the Lord of Heaven was, however, unimpaired, and he was determined to address his prayers for the

Dynasty's salvation to the One True God through His Vicar on earth.

The Jesuits Andreas Xavier Koffler and Michal Piotr Boym were delighted to assist Achilles Pang by drafting letters to Pope Innocent X and the Father General of the Society of Jesus. They were eager to win the support of the Catholic Princes of Europe for the Ming. They were also eager to enhance the prestige of the Society of Jesus, which was not universally beloved in Rome, by demonstrating that the Father General corresponded on terms of equality with the Imperial Court of China.

The Jesuits perceived an unparalleled opportunity in the plight of the Ming. Powerful European military assistance could assuredly restore the Dynasty. A grateful Emperor would then embrace Christianity, thus ensuring the conversion of all Chinese. Overwhelming success in the most populous realm on earth would not only silence criticism of the Society, but would also make it the most powerful force in the Church.

The Grand Eunuch Achilles Pang was, for his part, certain that the combined prayers of the Holy Father and the Father General would move the Lord of Heaven to smite the Manchus. The influx of new missionaries he also requested would assure the salvation of the Ming by bringing all Chinese to Christian virtue—and by their scientific and military skills. Because the Father General had already sent so many gifted priests to China, Achilles Pang believed he was the most powerful man in Europe. Once he understood the desperate plight of the Ming, the Father General would surely send many well-armed regiments. Achilles Pang did not ask for military assistance in his letters. But he had charged Father Boym, who would carry his letters to Rome, to make the Dynasty's urgent need clear to both the Pope and the Father General.

"It's not quite good enough, Master Achilles!" Father Andreas Koffler turned his drawn face with the tired blue eyes from the sunset.

"Not good enough, Father Andreas?" The Grand Eunuch looked up from the waterflies skittering around the gently rocking barge. "Why is it not?"

"The Holy Father and the Father General must be deeply impressed. But you cannot style yourself Grand Chancellor, can you? And Grand Eunuch is a title unknown to Europe, though greatly honored in China."

"If only the Emperor would consent to write directly." Father Michal Boym shook his heavy head theatrically, and his dark-brown eyes opened wide.

"He cannot...*absolutely* cannot," the Grand Eunuch replied. "Since the Emperor is not yet a Christian, he does not understand the Holy Father's transcendent spiritual power. My Lord cannot write to the ruler of a few Italian cities as if he were the equal of the Emperor of China."

"Then, I fear, your letters will not have much effect," Andreas Koffler prodded Achilles Pang. "If only..."

"The Empress, perhaps," Michal Boym suggested, as they had rehearsed. "The Dowager Empress Helena...if she would write to..."

"She will, I suppose.... If we suggest it." The Eunuch was puzzled. "But what good would that do? After all, the word of a woman..."

"Not the word of a woman, but the word of an Empress. In Europe, the plea of an Empress would command profound respect...and the additional sympathy due her sex."

"If you wish, I shall go to her," Achilles Pang agreed. "But I must go alone."

WHILE Francis Arrowsmith's Invincible Force was probing the first scattered Manchu skirmishers, Father Michal Piotr Boym left Wuchou for Macao by river junk. The Manchus, he knew, were tolerant of Jesuits because of Adam Schall's influence in Peking, and the Grand Eunuch's two ambassadors were dressed as servants. In his red-leather traveling chest Michal Boym carried four epistles in Latin, two signed by the Dowager Empress Helena and two by the Grand Eunuch. The tightly rolled Chinese originals were sewn into the hem of his surplice.

The voices of an Empress and a Great Minister speaking out of the silent continent would command an enthralled audience in Rome. Moreover, both those dignitaries addressing Christian Europe were themselves devout Christians because of the endeavors of the Society of Jesus!

Above all, the next Emperor of the Ming was already a Christian. Shortly after the Crown Prince's birth in May 1648, the Yung Li Emperor had yielded to the pleas of his Christian wife and his Christian mother. When he instructed Father Andreas Koffler to baptize the infant, the Austrian Jesuit had asked for a pledge that the child would never take more than one wife. The Emperor smiled but refused to indulge his women's religiomania to that ludicrous extent. Within days the newborn Prince developed a raging fever. When the Imperial physicians pronounced his heir on the point of death, the Emperor relented. After he was baptized Constantine, the Crown Prince quickly recovered.

Popes had raised armies to succor oppressed Christians in Palestine, Michal Boym remembered. Why not a new crusade? The greatest crusade of all would save a virtually Christian Empire from cruel pagan domination—and double the number of Catholics on earth!

AOCHI ISLAND, fifty miles northwest of Macao in the estuary of the Pearl River, was a gaunt silhouette against the dusk of November fifteenth. The salt junk carrying Father Michal Boym slipped past the war junks of the Duke Koxinga, which had on board the right wing of Francis Arrowsmith's Invincible Force. The anchored warships did not challenge the salt junk, which scampered into the dusk when the coxswain loosed the sheets and the matting sails filled.

The Jesuit saw men lounging in the glow of cooking braziers on the warships' decks. Smaller vessels were attached to the towering hulls like giant wooden barnacles.

Michal Boym assumed the warships carried the Christian assault force he had heard the Englishman commanded. He could not understand why lanterns lit the stationary flotilla for any Manchu scouts in the hills above—or why bamboo ladders of impressive solidity linked the war junks to the small craft. Outlined by the setting sun against the cliffs was a scene of settled ease rather than martial dispatch. Father Boym shook his round head sadly when he saw the gaudily painted sides of flower boats, the floating brothels of South China.

The war junks had sailed on the night of November 3, and the assault force was still sixty miles short of its objective two weeks later. Captain Nicholas Ferreira was weary of pleading with the junks of the Commodore of the Duke Koxinga to up anchor. The Portuguese was already sour, largely because he had been passed over for command in favor of the sinified Englishman. The Commodore only laughed when he threatened to turn his muskets on the warships' crews.

"Who would sail my junks for you then, Captain?" the Chinese asked.

The Commodore then returned to the unending mah-jong game on the poop, and the rattle of ivory tiles again assailed the shore. He would not dare the perils of forcing the narrows of the Tiger's Mouth. Ferreira knew the Commodore would lift anchor and make south toward safety if he disembarked his troops. Besides, he could not find draft animals to pull his cannon. The Chinese would not sail upriver to Canton; the Portuguese would not let them sail downriver to the sea. The assault party therefore did not move at all.

COLONEL FRANCIS ARROWSMITH with the main body of the Invincible Force had progressed no more than fifty miles from Macao on the morning of November 16, 1650. He had halted five days earlier when his scouts reported the flotilla anchored at Aochi Island and had sent his liaison officer to the war junks. Pale with anger, Colonel Edmond Chü returned to report that the Duke's Commodore had spurned his commands. The Commodore would not sail another mile northward, and he would not release Francis's men lest they bombard him from the shore.

"Now why would I do that?" Francis asked in momentary perplexity. "I only want to get to Canton."

"The Commodore would in your place," Edmond replied. "For revenge...to save face. He can't believe you'd act differently."

"And, of course, he won't relent, will he? I see it now."

"Hardly. Our men are his hostages...the only surety for his safety."

"Then I must offer a compromise...let him keep the guns."

"He'd enjoy haggling with you. Besides, we have nothing to lose."

Two days later, the Invincible Force resumed its march toward Canton some sixty miles away, and the war junks sailed downriver to the sea. Still on board were the sixteen field pieces of the right wing whose bombardment Francis had intended to break the Manchus' flank. Having surrendered their cannon to ransom themselves, Nicholas Ferreira's three hundred soldiers came ashore armed only with muskets, pikes, and swords.

Probing attacks distracted the Englishman from the loss of a large number of his cannon. But the cavalry the Chinese generals of the Manchu armies sent against the Christians were wary of the guns of the Invincible Force. Losing a few men each day, Francis Arrowsmith pressed forward. Through the twilight of November twenty-second, he finally saw the dun walls of Canton loom above the meeting of the West River and the Pearl River. He could cover the remaining five miles in a day despite the Manchu infantry massed before him.

But his recruits would have to clear the road with salvoes, then move half their guns forward under the covering fire of the stationary half. The forward echelon would then cover the advance of the rear echelon. The operation would have to be repeated twice before Francis could train his guns on the army besieging Canton. He knew his half-trained troops could not execute that difficult maneuver.

Reluctantly, Colonel Francis Arrowsmith ordered earthworks thrown up for an encampment. No matter how urgent was Thomas Chü's need for relief, it was imperative that his Christian soldiers prove to themselves that they could repel major Manchu attack. When the enemy had been demoralized by his shattering firepower, it would scatter before his renewed advance. *If* Thomas Chü's troops then sallied against the enemy; *if* the Ming irregulars in the countryside committed themselves; *if* his own left wing was then drawn to the thunder of the guns—*then* the four-pronged attack could break the besieging force.

Another commander, Francis Arrowsmith told Joseph King and Edmond Chü, might choose to preserve his forces by withdrawing from the virtually hopeless position. And another commander might be right. But he would not turn back from the mission he had sworn to carry out. There was, Francis added, some consolation. If he failed, he would have been defeated not by his own mistakes but by the haste Thomas Chü demanded and by the cowardice of the Duke Koxinga's Commodore.

"That may be some consolation...*if* we survive," Joseph said flatly. "When the Manchus execute us...when we die the death of a thousand slices, Arrowmaker, our virtue and our wisdom will be no consolation at all. I'm for running right now."

"I give you leave, Joseph. I'll send you to Macao with dispatches."

"I meant *all* of us running for it." Joseph was emphatic, his chin outthrust and his seamed cheeks set. "I'm too old to run alone. Besides, what would Maria say...or your wife?

If you're set on playing the fool, I'll keep you company. Some-body has to keep an eye on you."

"And you, Edmond," Francis laughed. "Would you carry dispatches to Koxinga?"

"I'd like to be there when the Commodore reports." Ed-mond smiled, and his wide eyes crinkled in his fair face. "But I couldn't face Maria or my father if I left you now."

"Then," Francis concluded, "there's nothing but to press on."

"You know, Arrowmaker," Edmond said lightly, "I never thought you'd do anything else."

MACAO'S certainty of victory was reinforced when the Duke Koxinga's warships sailed past on their way to the South China Sea. The right wing of the Invincible Force had ob-viously landed at the gates of Canton. Every gentleman was jubilant at striking a body blow at the unbelievers, and every lady burned with religious fervor. At long last, Christian Europe was intervening forcefully in the Empire. The inev-itable Christian victory would inevitably move the Ming Em-peror to gratitude, and the merchants of Macao would grow rich from the limitless commerce of China.

Rumor swept Macao: A sampan had landed a Chinese of-ficer on the Praya Grande at nightfall to explain that the warships were hastening to report a sweeping victory to the Duke Koxinga. The authorities awaited only Francis Ar-rowsmith's confirmation to order public celebrations.

The Governor drank jubilant toasts. The Loyal Senate pondered a fitting reward for the Englishman. The Bishop and the Jesuit Provincial offered prayers of thanksgiving. Each man believed the others were withholding the glorious news from himself.

Father Michal Boym told the Provincial he had only a few days earlier seen the war junks at anchor with the Christian troops still on board. The shocked Provincial hastened to cer-tify the letters of the Dowager Empress Helena and the Grand Eunuch, Achilles Pang. After the two Christian Mandarins who accompanied Michal Boym swore to their authenticity before the Ecclesiastical Notary on November twenty-third, the disquieting news came out—and Macao swung from ela-tion through disappointment to fear.

Although he knew no more certainly that the Invincible Force had failed to relieve Canton than he had a day earlier known of its triumph, the Governor declared that he had always distrusted the enterprise. Although Francis Arrowsmith was still encamped before Canton, the Governor despaired of defending Macao from the wrath of the victorious Manchus. Since the settlement had been depleted of field pieces and artillerymen to supply the Invincible Force, he could only hope the guns remaining in the forts would deter attack. If the Manchus ordered an embargo, he could do nothing. But he could prevent further hostile deeds further inflaming the Manchus.

The Governor forbade Father Michal Boym to sail on the caravel *Santa Catarina* for Goa, the first stage of his long journey to Rome. The Manchus would, at least, not be able to charge Macao with facilitating communication between the Ming and the Vatican. What he would do with the embarrassing Jesuit and his incendiary epistles the Governor could not say, but he was determined that Michal Boym would not leave the settlement.

The Jesuit Provincial was equally determined that Boym would sail on *Santa Catarina*. Even if Canton had already fallen to the Manchus, even if his English protégé had failed abjectly, the Ming cause was not yet lost. Even if the Ming were to collapse, his last remaining card was still worth playing. Time did not move so fast in China that a powerful expeditionary force sponsored by the Pope on behalf of the Society of Jesus could not reverse the tide of events.

The Provincial sent Father Giulio di Giaccomo to urge the Governor to reconsider. After four hours, the Italian returned. His plump cheeks were flushed with wine, but his enunciation was precise when he reported: "Reverend Father, the matter is hopeless. I begged and pleaded. But the blasted man is determined. He will not, he insists, repeat his previous mistake of indulging our friend Francis in his mad escapade. He is terrified of the Manchus."

"And less terrified of interfering with the correspondence of the Holy Father, Giulio?"

"So it appears. The Pope is in Rome, he said, but the Manchus are at Canton."

"We must try how terrified he is. Go tell him to present himself to me."

"He will refuse, Reverend Father. He is adamant."

"Not if you remind him this is the business of Holy Church."

Tarrying to demonstrate his independence, the Governor

finally presented himself at six in the evening, when the Provincial was at his prayers. The Jesuit kept his reluctant visitor waiting for an hour to demonstrate his greater power and then interviewed him standing in a vestibule.

"Is Father di Giaccomo's report correct, my son?" the Provincial asked gently. "Do I understand that you will not allow Father Boym to carry his epistles to the Holy Father and the Father General?"

"That is my responsibility, Father," the Governor replied hotly. "It's no affair of yours, but a temporal matter. I will *not* permit any action that further imperils Macao."

"But you *will* confiscate epistles addressed to the Holy Father and the Father General, will you?"

"If necessary, yes!"

"Then it is my business...my business as a humble subordinate of those two great prelates. It touches, too, on the welfare of your immortal soul, since..."

"You would make it so...this trivial matter?" the Governor asked.

"If necessary, yes! If you persist, I shall have no recourse. For presumptuous...blasphemous...interference in the affairs of Holy Church...I shall be forced to excommunicate you. Would you live all your days without the blessing of Holy Church, my son?"

"I'll consider it again, Father," the Governor blustered. "After all, I'm only thinking of the welfare of Macao."

"And I of the welfare of God's Church on earth."

Three hours later, Father Giulio di Giaccomo was summoned to receive the Governor's submission. When he returned, the six bottles of port he had shared to salve the Governor's wounded vanity emboldened him to ask the Provincial an imprudent question.

"Would you actually have excommunicated him, Reverend Father? It seems somewhat dire for his sin."

"By no means dire, Giulio," the Provincial replied. "This matter touches upon the honor...and the advantage...of the Society."

FROM his encampment five miles to the southeast, Francis Arrowsmith scanned the squat silhouette of Canton, the greatest city south of the Yangtze and the linchpin of the Southern Ming Dynasty. The Manchu cavalrymen surrounding his earthen fort were awed by his green-bronze guns, which they called the Red Jacket Cannon, the blood-red cannon. The cavalry rode wide of his cannon, and Colonel Arrowsmith watched the siege of Canton like a playgoer in a box high above the tumult of the groundlings.

The bright Cyclops-eye of his telescope scanned dun city walls scarred by the siege that had on November twenty-fourth already lasted eight months. The green tiles of the pagodas rising behind the walls were shattered and blackened. Red dust reared from the battering rams pounding at tiered gate towers, and giants' lacework of broken and twisted scaling ladders draped the walls. No sunlight flashed on armor to reveal the movements of the defenders. The Manchu archers had instilled a fearful discipline into the Ming troops, who bent double behind the pitted stone teeth of the battlements. Through the brass tube of the telescope Francis saw with terrible clarity the activity of the besiegers and the torpor of the besieged.

He knew why Grand Secretary Thomas Chü had enjoined him to desperate haste. Only five times that morning did cannon bark from the ramparts, and few arrows soared from the walls. The Manchu force prepared for a fresh assault virtually unopposed. The brick tunnels of tortoises snapped at the foot of the walls, and new scaling ladders were heaped in readiness.

The fitful defense was like the feeble twitching of a caterpillar brought down by an army of ants. The metropolis of the south was moribund.

A torrent of pennants poured from the Manchu camp, shinning green, scarlet, and yellow against the pale autumnal sky. Staff officers in silver armor surrounded two generals in golden armor. A hundred trumpeters lifted their brazen horns, and a hundred kettle-drums grumbled when mallets pummeled their taut faces. The trumpets' fanfare and the kettledrums' growl reached Francis's ears just as he saw the assault troops fling their scaling ladders against the city walls.

The Ming defenders showed themselves for the first time on the battlements to prise ladders loose and hurl down boulders. For every ladder that toppled, two clung. The royal-blue tunics of the Manchu troops swarmed up those ladders on legs scrabbling in white-canvas trousers. Ten minutes after the trumpets' command, the blue-and-white wave licked against the battlements. It hesitated, drew back for an instant, and then broke over the defense.

"We'll move out now!" Francis Arrowsmith handed the telescope to Edmond Chü and instructed his second-in-command Nicholas Ferreira. "A screen of musketeers first. Then half the guns. The remainder to provide covering fire....I want the forward battery firing in less than an hour's time. Otherwise it will be too late. Go quickly now, but not rashly. For Christ and Saint James! May the Lord bless you all..."

"Colonel, hold now!" Nicholas Ferreira shouted. "The cavalry...they're closing on us."

The noose of horsemen that had been whirling around the encampment just beyond cannon range was contracting. Stubby arrows defiled the sky, and muskets volleyed.

"Fire grape and stand fast. They'll batter themselves against our earthworks," Francis ordered. "All the easier to move out when they're broken and running. Fire grape...But do not fire until they are no more than a hundred yards distant!"

Francis clapped his white-plumed helmet on his head. Ostentatiously deliberate, he stepped onto the parapet beside the pole flying the Banner of the Cross. Left hand clutching the flagpole, right hand on his sword hilt, he stood unmoving.

Lead from the front, not the rear, he could hear Captain-Sergeant Miguel Gonsalves Texeira Correa speaking across the years. *Show the men there's nothing to fear.*

A second voice spoke to him, a shrill voice never heard before that moment: *Great arrogance this of yours, Francis,* it said with insinuating familiarity, *to oppose seven hundred men and a few cannon to fifty thousand Manchu troops. Now you stand like a coxcomb too stupid to be afraid...against the fiercest cavalry in Asia.*

"My men are untried. Only a rash example can feed their confidence, and I must..." Francis broke off, realizing with chagrin that he had answered aloud. He raised his hands to his ears under the rim of his helmet to shut out the whining reproaches. He closed his eyes, hiding for an instant behind his pink-lit eyelids the cavalry pounding toward the frail breastworks while his men held their fire.

The deep tones of the dead Portuguese Captain-Sergeant reassured him: *Nothing to fear, Francis, my boy. They're dead scared of the cannon...terrified. We saw it all at Chochou. Remember Chochou, where they scurried from unloaded cannon. A sprinkle of grapeshot...and it'll all be over. They'll be running again. Then move your guns. March to the city walls.*

Francis Arrowsmith uncovered his ears and opened his

eyes to judge how far the charge was from the breastworks. He raised his right hand to signal his trumpeter, who would blare the command to fire. Chopping downward, he wondered why his head had felt so hot to his icy fingers.

When the guns roared, a shudder shook him. He clutched the flagpole and peered through the smoke that obscured the sun and the cavalry. The day was growing darker, though the smoke and dust should have been dissipating in the brisk breeze.

Violent shudders gripped him, and he clung to the flagpole with both hands. His teeth chattered louder than the din of battle, and a mist covered his eyes. He was shaking like a marionette in an antic dance when an arrow found the chink between his cuirass and his shoulderplate. His bad leg gave way, and he crumpled like a marionette with strings snapped.

The cannon fired again, and arrows ripped through the gold-and-scarlet Banner of the Cross streaming above the black-powder smoke.

"...NEVER liked this enterprise..." The voice of Captain Nicholas Ferreira, harsh as pebbles in a sieve, penetrated the fevered visions of Colonel Francis Arrowsmith. "Cannon...for defense...invincible....But...madness to oppose....Only God's grace...gave us leave to withdraw."

"*Wu-chih-di*..." Edmond Chü's angry protest was translated into Portuguese by Joseph King. "Shameless! Shameless! We should have attacked. Now my father will die..."

A golden lattice studded with shining jewels fell between Francis Arrowsmith and the world. He was battered into unconsciousness by the swaying of the litter slung between two pack horses.

The Invincible Force plodded southward through a countryside aflame with the leaves of autumn. On the third day, the soldiers only occasionally glanced at the Manchu cavalrymen who rode just beyond their muskets' range. Chastened by failing to come to grips with the Manchus, the Christians had as little desire to engage the cavalry as the cavalry had to face their firearms. Having parried the Christian blow, the Manchus' generals were content to allow the Invincible Force to withdraw. Led by the dour Nicholas Ferreira, the Invincible Force was content to withdraw with minor casualties.

Francis Arrowsmith, Colonel of the Ming, was borne along

senseless. Alternately burning with fever and frozen by chills, he did not awake until the sixth day of the march.

"You'll be all right," Joseph King soothed him. "All is well...as well as can be."

Francis knew all was not well. Awakening again at noon the next day, he demanded an explanation. Nicholas Ferreira spat and turned his back. But Joseph King and Edmond Chü had agreed that they could not keep the truth from the Englishman.

"*Mei pan-fa, Shih-jen*...," Joseph explained. "We had no choice, Arrowmaker. We had to withdraw when the Manchus' generals gave us leave. It was too late to save Canton..."

"Too late?" Francis interjected. "Why too late? How too late?"

"When you collapsed, Arrowmaker, Ferreira countermanded your orders to advance," Edmond Chü said bitterly. "Swore we could do nothing...and he'd be damned if he threw the Force away. So we stood by...stood by and watched the city fall. But we could have saved Canton, I know it."

"Then the Grand Secretary Thomas Chü...your father, Edmond, he is taken?"

"We'll come to that in a minute, Arrowmaker," Joseph said.

"What happened to me?" Francis demanded. "What is wrong with me?"

"First an ague...an ague from *mal aria*. If you hadn't clung to the flagpole like a bulldog, we'd have had you down from the parapet. The arrow that pierced you...you wouldn't have been exposed."

"And now I'm useless again, finished this time."

"Hardly, Arrowmaker." Joseph forced a laugh. "We'll get the herbal doctor again.... You'll be fine."

"But the Expedition, it is finished, is it not?"

"I'm afraid so. You should know, I suppose, that the left wing never landed. Their junks grounded four times.... Then the Commodore turned and sailed south."

"So there wasn't any real hope, ever!" Francis was too weak for anger, but not for regrets. "I should never have split the Force..."

"You had no choice, and..." Joseph's sentence trailed off when he saw that Francis slept.

Francis woke again late that afternoon to demand news of Grand Secretary Thomas Chü, Earl in Kwangsi. Edmond's eyes locked with Joseph's, each pleading silently with the other to speak. Joseph stubbornly pressed his lips together, and Edmond finally spoke.

"My father, Arrowmaker, was not in Canton," he confessed. "He slipped away five weeks earlier...before we marched."

"And the letter...his pleading for assistance?"

"A ruse, apparently. The Ming general in Canton apparently thought a message from my father...an appeal in Christ...would move you as no other."

"And he was right, damn him! He was right! I would never have marched so soon...would never have flung away our chances if...Now we'll never know...could our weapons smash the Manchus."

"It's done now, Arrowmaker," Joseph counseled. "Time to think of the future, not the past."

"The future, Joseph? What can the future hold for me after this...this debacle?"

"The Invincible Force is intact. It's not over yet."

"Perhaps not....But what of Thomas Chü?"

"My father escaped to Kweilin, Arrowmaker. He did not desert Canton...did not desert us...but made for the position of greatest danger."

"Then he is alive! Kweilin still holds out?"

"As far as we know, Arrowmaker."

"Then there's still hope. You're right, Joseph. As long as Thomas Chü holds Kweilin there's still hope."

AT twilight of the same day, Field Marshal Kung Yu-teh, called the Virtuous, sat in his silken pavilion outside the broken city of Kweilin three hundred miles northwest of Canton. The fortress city on the Likiang River had fallen to his Manchu army on November 27, almost a week earlier. But the man who was a Senior Prince of the new Dynasty preferred not to move his headquarters into the gutted residence of the provincial governor until repairs had been completed.

The pounding of hammers and the whining of saws, he said, made him nervous, though the growls of kettledrums and the twanging of bowstrings were the sweetest music he knew. Besides, coal braziers kept his tent far warmer than the drafty residence could ever be.

Nor did the Virtuous Kung wish to flaunt the Imperial Regalia of the new Dynasty before the emaciated, frostbitten survivors of the siege that had for almost a year gripped in a ring of steel the city straddling the swift mountain river. The time had come for mercy, rather than the massacres that normally followed Manchu victories. He was determined to win over the adherents of the Southern Ming rather than slaughter them. Because of his great personal authority, the Field Marshal could make that decision without consulting distant Peking.

The Virtuous Kung walked slowly to the doorflap of his tent. He had grown stout by constantly feeding on success since his treachery at Tengchou. He gazed through the twilight at the summit called Wild Goose Peak because it resembled a bird in flight, then surveyed the surrounding peaks, which reared funereal black against the smudged sky. He shook his heavy head when he saw the spires of smoke still rising from the conquered city, and his bland features tightened.

Letting the doorflap fall, he returned to his couch. He removed his round hat crowned by a ruby and the black snake of his queue soughed against his waist-length blue-silk jacket. Having served the Manchus for seventeen years, he wore the distinctive uniform of their Dynasty as comfortably as he wore his loyalty to their Shun Chih Emperor.

His greatest disappointment, the Virtuous Kung reflected, was the brute obduracy of his fellow Chinese, their inability to understand what was best for them. They still called him the Hound of the Manchus. He longed to end the fratricidal struggle by persuading his intransigent countrymen that the Manchus had irrevocably replaced the Ming. He was determined to convince the so-called loyalists that the new Dynasty promised peace, culture, and prosperity for the entire Empire and all its people. The followers of the Ming were *sse yeh wan-ku,* stubborn beyond death. But the Field Marshal swore he would enlighten them.

The doorflap opened, and Grand Secretary Thomas Chü entered. The Ming Earl bowed to the Manchus' Prince. The caprices of battle—even bitter defeat—were no reason to stint the courtesies one gentleman offered another.

The four disastrous months since his son Edmond's marriage had gouged ravines in Thomas Chü's narrow face. His eyes stared above sagging gray cheeks, and his long fingers were a skeleton's claws. But his gray beard and gray-streaked hair were freshly trimmed, while his immaculate scarlet robe displayed the burnished silver-unicorn emblem of his rank.

He was no longer ravenous, though even the Field Marshal's hospitality could not assuage the hunger of months in a week.

"Have you thought well, my friend? Have you considered all the circumstances?" the Virtuous Kung asked softly after imploring his captive to be seated and offering a cup of *maotai* spirits. "You will now accept the trifling measure we discussed?"

"I'm afraid not, my friend. Your way is not my way. I cannot."

"It is so trivial....And you have acknowledged that this civil war is a disaster. Why not let us shave your crown and braid your hair? That is only a symbol."

"A symbol that encompasses the world...that means everything. You might just as well say the Imperial-yellow robe of the Emperor is only a symbol. The gesture means submission....And I cannot submit."

"I ask no more than the gesture. I do not require formal submission. Just that you wear the queue."

"I'm sorry, my friend. I cannot."

"Look you, then! I'm prepared to accept less...far less. Just let your head be shaved. Why not wear the tonsure of a Buddhist monk? Surely that would not offend your honor....And it will satisfy the letter of the decree. Surely that..."

"You forget that I am a Christian. How can I wear the tonsure of a Buddhist?"

"Then a Christian tonsure. I remember the old priest at Tengchou....What was his name?"

"Rodriguez...Juan Rodriguez," Thomas Chü answered.

"Yes, of course. That old fellow wore a tonsure. Why won't you accept a *Christian* tonsure?"

"Because, my friend, I am not a priest....Only a humble layman who loves Jesus Christ and the Lord of Heaven."

"Earl, you confuse me with your many loyalties. I ask only a gesture, call it what you will."

"Prince, my loyalties are my life. I can forswear neither my loyalty to the true Emperor nor my devotion to the Son of God. I would submit gladly...very gladly if I could...and buy my life. I know it pains you to think of commanding the silken bowstring to cut off my breath. I assure you, the prospect distresses me too. But I cannot."

"It does distress me...deeply. I am, therefore, striving to avoid the necessity. Only a few hairs. Certainly they're not worth your life?"

"The hairs are not what bother me. In truth I have few enough left. Prince, consider your own loyalty to the usurpers, misguided though it is. Surely, you must understand that I cannot surrender *my* loyalty, not even by what you call a gesture..."

"In your place, I would..." the Virtuous Kung sighed. "However, let us talk of other things. We still have time to talk...though the time allowed me is not unlimited."

Casually, almost negligently, since Confucian gentlemen do not parade their emotions, the Field Marshal had put forward his offer again—and Thomas Chü had again rejected it. The conversation was repeated a dozen times during December, ending always with Thomas Chü's refusal to accept even the semblance of submission to the Manchus. A dozen times thereafter, the Earl and the Prince discussed wine and painting, food and poetry.

Those conversations ended when the Field Marshal learned that his agents had intercepted a letter from Thomas Chü to the Ming General Luke Chiao. The warder who had been bribed with promises of a munificent reward to carry that letter preferred the lesser reward—and the greater safety— of delivering it to the Field Marshal's agents. Thomas Chü's proposals for renewed attacks on the Manchus forced the hand of the Virtuous Kung. If he did not act, his own agents would denounce his leniency to Prince-Regent Dorgon, and he valued his own life above his friend's.

On the bleak morning of the fourth day of January, 1651, the fourth year of the reign of the Yung Li Emperor of the Ming Dynasty, whom he still served, the Grand Secretary Thomas Chü, Earl in Kwangsi, was strangled with a vermilion-silk bowstring. Before facing the executioner, he thanked the Field Marshal called the Virtuous Kung for his hospitality and his solicitude.

After handing his captor a roll of rice paper brushed with exquisitely small ideograms, the Earl bared his neck and recited the *Pater Noster*. The manuscript the Field Marshal treasured until his own death was the poems Thomas Chü had written in captivity. It was called "*Hao Chi Yin*—Ode to the Moving Force."

Late that same afternoon, one hundred ninety miles to the southwest on the border between Kwangsi and Kweichou provinces, a Manchu outpost halted a river junk. Disdaining ineffectual disguises for his customary black robe, Father

Andreas Xavier Koffler was following the Ming Court to Nanning on the border of Vietnam.

Neither his cloth nor his threats, neither his quasi-Mandarin status nor his invoking the great Father Adam Schall moved the Jesuit's captors, who were Manchus, not Chinese. The Sergeant in Command had been warned to watch for the black priests who encouraged the Ming's resistance. A braided-cotton bowstring bestowed holy martyrdom upon the Austrian Jesuit. The soldiers threw his corpse into the Kwailo River, which flowed as swift as the narrow Danube at Regensburg, his boyhood home.

Neither the Field Marshal nor the Sergeant who ordered those executions on January 4, 1651, knew that Prince-Regent Dorgon had suffered a massive coronary infarction on the last day of 1650 while hunting in Manchuria. If the Field Marshal had known the vindictive Regent was dead in his thirty-ninth year, he would have spared Thomas Chü—for a time, at least. Even news of that portentous death would not have spared Andreas Koffler. Mercy to a European—or a Chinese—was as alien to a Manchu sergeant as was kneeling before the Holy Cross.

Macao

JANUARY 18, 1651–JUNE 28, 1651

"FRANCIS, do you sometimes think of Europe?" Dolores looked up from the leatherbound ledger that recorded her enterprises' accounts for 1650, the year just past. "It *has* been a long time for you, hasn't it?"

His wife's manner was casual. Her tone was more weighty when she asked what he fancied for dinner. But Francis could not reply as lightly. He did sometimes think of the distant continent he had not seen for a quarter of a century. His memories were at once hazy and glowing. But he did not think of Europe too often. Fear of the unknown cut him off from the land of his ancestors.

"Occasionally." He looked down from the terrace at the familiar spectacle of purple-and-tan sails impelling sandal-shaped junks across the muddy stream of the Pearl River in the cold brilliance of the mid-January afternoon. "Why do you ask?"

"No particular reason." Dolores was not herself quite sure why she had asked. "But, someday, I wouldn't mind seeing Europe again."

"Neither would I. But you've said you loved it here...never wished to leave. You're the uncrowned queen of Macao, and..."

"I'm so glad your tongue hasn't lost its English sweetness. You know I only married you because you flatter me."

"And, I was about to say, there is no lovelier crowned queen in Europe or the Empire. Lissome and slim, yet voluptuous and majestic...and just coming into the full flower of your beauty."

"You needn't prove you can still flatter me, Francis. Besides, I may not be quite so lissome and slim very long."

"Worried about your beauty's fading, are you?" he laughed. "Not yet in full bloom, yet fearing the bloom will fade. Now I know why you asked about Europe. You're thinking of your youth."

"That's not it at all. I was so small when I left I can hardly remember. I'm just curious, though I do love Macao."

To that self-contradictory remark, Francis sensibly decided, he could only reply with silence. He was in no mood for serious discussion. The pain of the new wound in his shoulder lanced him when he shifted in the cane long-chair. The old wound in his leg ached dully, and a small sore had opened beside the scar. He was also still a little lightheaded after the racking fever of his attack of malaria.

Songbirds twittered from the winding path beneath the terrace in counterpoint to the rhythmic flipflopping of the iron-mounted brush polishing the teak floor of the reception chamber. Dolores glanced over the parapet at two elderly Chinese gentlemen in padded blue-silk long-gowns. They were chatting gravely as they strolled among the scarlet poinsettias and the pink-flowered peach trees. Their liver-spotted hands held the brass rings of bamboo cages. The small birds perched inside were celebrating their daily airing with quicksilver trills.

"No, Francis, it's not that I'm longing for Europe." Dolores paused and was pierced by the longing she had just denied. "It's just that life in Macao...in the East...is so uncertain. ...And the dangers..."

"It was your notion that sent me charging into the Empire to rescue the Ming." Francis still suffered as much from the wounds to his self-esteem as his physical wounds after the debacle of the Invincible Force. "Otherwise, I would never..."

"You would have done something just as foolish," Dolores interrupted. "Or you would never have forgiven yourself. You had to try."

"I suppose that's true," he conceded.

"Of course it is. But, now, I'm wondering. . . . Perhaps it's time to think of a change. You need a rest, a long rest."

"I'm not that old and feeble yet, Dolores. I'm not ready to bask in the sunshine of a Lisbon plaza remembering ancient battles for other dotards. There's still some life in my old carcass."

"Oh, there's no question about that. But, I sometimes think, a *fazenda* in the Algarve, a small estate that would give us both more ease and security. . . . And for others, too, perhaps."

"There's still work to be done in China." Francis was vehement. "I am not ready to turn my back. . . . But what's this of *others?*"

"This is no place to raise a child, Francis. The climate, the turbulence, the diseases. I want no son of mine brought up like a halfbreed Macanese, not knowing his own land and his own people."

"When the time comes, we'll think about that, Dolores," Francis condescended. "But for the time being, there's no . . ."

"Francis, you are dense sometimes," she flared. "The time is now. . . . We must think about it right now. Can I tell you more plainly?"

"Dolores, a child? You're . . ."

"Yes, Francis. You finally understand, my dear. A child . . . sometime in June or July. A boy . . . I feel it."

"I *am* dense. But there's no question about it?"

"Hardly! Of course, Francis, it's nothing new for you. . . . But, for me, the first, the very first."

"The others were nothing to this, my love." Francis felt his conventional protest was true. "This will be the first for me as well, our first child, a European child who will be with us all our days."

"You *are* pleased, Francis?" Dolores was still unconvinced.

"Pleased? I'm overjoyed . . . exultant. This calls for champagne, a magnum of that new sparkling wine from France."

"A new wine for a new soul," Dolores gushed uncharacteristically. "And a new beginning."

"I see now why you were talking about Europe. But there's plenty of time. A boy, you think, my love?"

DESPITE his protestations, Francis could not wholly share Dolores's exultation. Paternity was hardly new to him, whose eldest child was already a married woman. Nonetheless he felt profound satisfaction at the prospect of a European heir who would not be bound to the Empire as were his half-Chinese daughter and his half-Manchu son. And he rejoiced over the delight of his wife, who meant far more to him than any child ever could.

Though he hotly denied such weaknesses to Dolores, he was, after forty-four hard years, feeling tired. Not only was his body depleted by illness and wounds, but his spirit, too, was weary. What, he wondered, had he attained in a quarter of a century of constant travel and constant battles—aside, of course, from his children and, above all, the late gift of Dolores herself?

He had learned a great deal about China and the Chinese. But he could, at the moment, use that knowledge neither to advance his own interests nor to affect the course of the Empire profoundly. He had, he supposed, finally grown into maturity. He was, at least, comfortable with himself.

Was it belated maturity or spiritual fatigue that made Europe much more attractive than he told Dolores? He could not parse the reasons. But he would not leave China so soon after his humiliating defeat at Canton. Nor would he happily leave while the struggle between the Manchus and the Ming was still undecided.

Despite the loss of Canton and Kweilin, the Ming was far from finished. The Chinese dynasty was vigorously exploiting fresh dissension within the Manchu camp. Despite the loss of Grand Secretary Thomas Chü, the Ming was again resurgent, and Adam Schall might yet regret investing all his hopes in the Manchus. Joseph King, incidentally, insisted the Ming was resurgent *because* of its loss of the virtuous Grand Secretary, who could not lead men in war because he could not understand that most men were less noble than himself.

Francis was distracted from the affairs of the Great Empire by his own business affairs. As Dolores let the reins of her enterprises go slack in her hands, he took over their growing trade with Manchu-held Canton. The Mandarins ignored his disastrous foray against the new Dynasty, apparently unaware that he had resumed smuggling firearms to the Ming. Above all, he was for the first time in his life wholly engrossed by a woman. His love for Dolores, he found, bred almost equal love for his unborn heir.

Watching her swell with that burden, Francis regretted her transition to motherhood. Her small nose and her gray eyes were still poignantly childlike despite her body's awkwardness in the oppressive humidity. She lost neither her sparkle nor her gift for laughter. Surprisingly, she gave in docilely to his insistence that a Chinese midwife attend the birth.

Altered chiefly by her affection for Joseph, Dolores no longer feared or despised the Chinese. Francis smiled when he recalled her horror at his summoning an herbal doctor to treat the wound he had suffered in the fight with the pirates at Hongkong. Besides, she was as anxious to please him as he was anxious for her well-being.

The midwife warned that it would not be easy for a pampered foreign woman to deliver her first child at the age of twenty-nine. Nonetheless, her time was still weeks away. Easy in their minds, Francis and Joseph sailed the junk *Maria* upriver to Canton in mid-June to buy silks, porcelains, and tea. When they passed Aochi Island on the return voyage, Francis remembered again the humiliating impasse with the Duke Koxinga's Commodore. He bitterly remembered the ignominious withdrawal of the Invincible Force from Canton, where he had just been received like any other foreign merchant, albeit one who miraculously spoke the Officials' Language.

When *Maria* approached Macao at midday of June 21, 1651, they saw the balconies of the pale-green villa on Mount Guia hung with bunting. Twenty-foot strings of firecrackers exploded as the junk tied up alongside the Praya Grande. Disdaining the sedan chair that awaited him, Francis pelted up the winding lanes to the villa. He was followed by a sweating Joseph King, whose wiry strength could not this once outpace his employer. Francis did not pause during the steep climb. He hardly broke stride for the congratulations of the half-caste majordomo, José Rivera, who called after him as he strode up the stairs: "It's a boy, Dom Francis."

"Look what I've...what we've done, Francis." Dolores's habitual humor was restored. "Only four days old...and he's almost talking."

Cradled in his mother's arms on the broad *cama de casal*, the dark-haired baby was naked except for the square of toweling around his loins. His face was smooth and unwrinkled; except for his fair skin, his face was a miniature replica of his mother's. His gray-blue eyes appeared to his father to sparkle with intelligence, and his small hands grasped his mother's breast tenaciously.

"A mighty warrior he'll be, Dolores," Francis exulted. "But you are well? Was it terrible?"

"No more tiring than a night spent dancing the minuet, my dear. Of course, he's perfect. But he'll even be a priest before a soldier."

"We'll worry about that later, my love. After all, we still have a year or two!" Francis joked, though he did not like to think that this child, too, might fail to pass on his name. "But should he be all naked.... Exposed to the air like that? Won't he catch cold?"

"Now, don't you start, my dear," Dolores laughed. "I've had enough protests from the midwife and the maidservants. He'd melt away if I kept him wrapped up as they wish."

"The night air, my dear," Francis insisted. "It can be deadly..."

"Not so deadly as suffocating, my love. Let me worry about him. You worry about the christening party."

"The grandest Macao has ever seen. Here in the garden with African musicians, Chinese fireworks, and a magnificent banquet."

"And vast quantities of champagne, Francis."

"Your Portuguese don't like champagne that well."

"All the more for us, my love. Of course, the Governor as godfather and the Bishop to baptize him."

"No, not the Governor. Manuel Bocarro."

"Manuel and the Governor, then. But, of course, the Bishop to baptize him."

"You had your way at the wedding, but the Bishop will not baptize my son. It must be Giulio di Giaccomo. And Antonio Castro as second godfather."

"A Marrano? Francis, how can you?"

"A good Christian gentleman and a good friend. You may choose the godmothers."

Replete with paternal emotion he might be, but not sated, Francis discovered when he stood beside the font on June twenty-eighth and watched Father Giulio di Giaccomo christen his son George Ignatius Francis do Amaral Arrowsmith. This infant, the Englishman exulted, would be the first among his children to bear the surname of his yeoman ancestors. Twisted and mangled though Arrowsmith might be by Mediterranean tongues, it would never be replaced by a Chinese or a Manchu name. The infant was George for Saint George of England; Ignatius for Loyola, the founder of the Society of Jesus; and Francis, not for his father, but for Francis Xavier, the Apostle to the East. Do Amaral, too, to honor Dolores's father Dom Sebastian, who had died before the birth of the grandson for whom he longed. But Arrowsmith for his father, and he would attend St. Omer's College to learn his English heritage.

THE pitch torches flaring in the breeze that flitted over Mount Guia from the sea leavened the tropical night with the tang of pines. Cherry-red suckling pigs roasted over bonfires, and an ox crackled on an immense spit. Popping champagne corks were echoed by volleys of firecrackers. Fiery fountains spouted from Roman candles to light the black hills of China, and Catherine wheels blazed like minor suns in the darkness. The sweet fragrance of jasmine mingled with the pungent scent of wild ginger.

Just outside the rectangle of fire that was a beacon for the fishing junks scudding across the South China Sea, a silver flute and a bamboo *sheng* like the pipes of Pan trilled a wild pagan dance. Between the measured merriment of Marenzio and Monteverdi, black musicians inside the palisade of torches spun their own haunting melodies. Despite the insistent rhythm, the minor key recalled both the melancholy *fados* of Portugal and the nostalgic folksongs of the Empire. When the orchestra paused, a gamelan of the Indies chimed a temple dance. From the foreshore along the Praya Grande, the drums of Africa throbbed in the Asiatic night.

A pair of stylized lions pranced into the light, their gaudy papier-mâché heads bobbing to the beat of a gong, their blue pop-eyes winking on golden springs. Brown feet skipped beneath their spangled flanks. Escaping with a prolonged sigh from miniature powder-kegs, six fiery segments joined themselves into a golden dragon and writhed across the hillside before sputtering out amid sparks. Flights of rockets reared a red-and-gold arch over Mount Guia.

Through that arch a stocky figure entered the square of light. A white egret plume soared above the russet yak's tail on the spike of his helmet. The cobalt-blue patterns incised on the helmet flowed onto the flap of mail that protected his neck, and a short Manchu sword hung in a scarlet-lacquered scabbard from his belt. His robe of plum-colored silk embossed with stylized blue clouds was cut in the Manchu manner, straight and narrow without lapels or collar. The officer stood unmoving, his palm shading eyes dazzled by the blaze of light.

"*Deus!* Who is this barbarian?" Dolores clutched her cloth-of-gold bodice. "Did you ask him, Francis? A Manchu?"

"*Wo tsai jer,*" Francis cried out. "I'm here, Robert."

The Manchu strode haughtily through the throng to kneel before his father. The cheeks under the helmet were smooth and unbearded, Francis saw, and the heavy gait expressed not arrogance but diffidence.

"*Wo liang-ko ehr-tzu...Meu dois filhos.*" Francis spoke first in Chinese to Robert and then in Portuguese to Dolores. "My two sons are with me tonight. I welcome my son Robert with joy!"

"You are welcome." Dolores greeted her stepson's intrusion coolly, but added warmly: "Very welcome indeed!"

Robert bowed perfunctorily. He would have liked to ignore his stepmother, as a Chinese would, but his inbred Manchu regard for women denied him that pleasure. He responded with rote politeness but did not smile. Turning from Dolores, he spoke urgently to Francis: "I must talk with you, Father."

"Can it not wait, Robert?" His son's brusqueness, Francis counseled himself, sprang from the awkwardness of a seventeen-year-old in outlandish company. "As you see, I am entertaining guests. Unless your errand is a matter of life and death, it must in courtesy wait."

"It can wait, Father," Robert conceded. "I am sorry if I intrude."

"My dear boy, you couldn't intrude." Francis threw his arm around the youth's shoulders in the rough caress a Manchu warrior could accept in public, though not a Chinese. "I am delighted to see you. And I am desolate that we cannot talk this instant. But here's Joseph King. He'll give you a drink and food."

Finally bidding his last guest goodnight, Francis, too, resented Robert's intrusion for an instant. Yet he could no more expect to keep the different parts of his life forever separate than he could keep himself from loving both his sons.

After promising Dolores he would not be long from bed, Francis sat beside his elder son. The torches lit Robert's round face and accentuated his arched nose. Despite his renewed pleasure in the youth's arrival, Francis was not displeased when Joseph King seated himself as by right beside his former pupil. He was amused when the ever-curious Giulio di Giaccomo joined them to give his blessing to the youth he had known only through reports before that night.

"Let me look at you, Robert." Speaking in Chinese, Francis

turned his son's face toward himself. "You've grown, of course. It is two and a half years. But you are not scarred by battle, I'm pleased to see."

"No, Father," Robert replied stiffly in Manchu. "Not scarred at all."

"What brings you here?" Francis ignored his son's coldness, which he still ascribed to diffidence, and spoke in Manchu. "I'm delighted, of course. How long can you stay?"

"No more than tonight, Father." Robert did not warm to that parental welcome. "I must return to my regiment tomorrow."

"Well then, my boy, say what you have to say." Francis cajoled his recalcitrant son no longer. "Tell me and have done with it."

"It was not seemly, Father, to desert us so." Robert spoke formally. "My mother sends her greetings to you, and I..."

"Did she send you to upbraid me?" Francis's temper rose. "If so, you may leave this minute."

"Mother bade me speak fair to you and tell you she has forgiven you. But, for me, Father, it is not so easy to forgive."

"In that case, it's between you and me, Robert." Francis was annoyed at himself for losing his composure with a balky adolescent. "You can say to me whatever you wish, even in the presence of our friends. But do, please, season your anger with civility."

"I regret my tone, Father." Robert's apology was emphasized by his speaking Chinese. "It was an unfilial act to talk so to you. I am appalled at my rudeness."

"Well, it's done... and forgiven. But tell me of yourself."

"I serve under my fourth uncle, Father. We ride out tomorrow evening to crush the renewed rebellion against His Imperial Majesty. The rebels who call themselves the Ming Dynasty are again presuming to threaten Kweilin. This will be my first campaign against those rebels."

"Well, Robert, keep your shield up." Francis ignored Joseph's angry movement when Robert repeated the word rebels. "And remember, not too much zeal. You have a long career ahead of you, a brilliant career. You must be in the vanguard, Robert, but not in the forefront of the van... not until you're blooded. No friendly words can instruct you. Only the enemy can teach you when to throw aside caution for valor. And a dead officer is no use to..."

"So my uncle tells me, Father. But those rebel hounds.

What can they do against Manchu warriors? How can they..."

"Those rebel hounds have kept your Manchu cavalry from taking South China for almost ten years, Robert." Joseph King spoke without rancor, a schoolmaster dispassionately correcting an unruly pupil. "They will certainly keep you from conquering South China for many more years. With God's blessing, they will in time set the rightful Emperor on the Dragon Throne in Peking."

"As for that, Master, I do not think so." Robert's tone was respectful, his firm denial dignified. "And, may I say it, I deeply regret your refusal to submit to the one true Emperor."

"There is but One True God, Robert," Francis interjected. "Earthly monarchs, even Emperors, are another matter. Men read the Mandate of Heaven differently. Only battle will decide between the two Emperors. But I assume you still follow the One True Faith?"

"I do, Father, though I cannot be open in my devotions." Robert leaned toward Francis and lowered his voice. "But my mother does not. She is apostate."

"I regret that, my son, deeply."

"No more than I, Father. Perhaps Mother keeps the Faith in her heart. She can confide in no one, not even me."

"Why is that?"

"Because she has remar...married an earl of the Green Banner. A pagan, of course. She said you would be pleased to hear her news."

"I am pleased, Robert. I wish her nothing but joy, though unable myself to..."

"Mother said you would speak those words. And she further bade me say that she forgives you...and wishes you much joy. But I cannot believe you will know true joy as long as you serve the Ming pretender."

"What would you have me do, my son? Return to Peking, perhaps?"

"Why not, Father? As you know, Prince-Regent Dorgon is dead. The Shun Chih Emperor has taken the government of the Empire into his own hands. Though just thirteen, he rules directly.... And wise men guide him. Foremost among those men is Father Adam Schall. The Emperor calls him *Mafa*, Grandpa. Father Adam asks you to consider returning to Peking. For that reason I came tonight...to carry his message. And, of course, to pay my filial respects."

"Be that as it may, Robert, tell us more of Father Adam."

Francis was excited by the thought of showing Peking to Dolores, for the German Jesuit held the key to the Northern Capital. "Is he truly so close to the young Emperor so shortly after Dorgon's death?"

"The Emperor admires Father Adam enormously. He behaves just like a grandson. He visits Father Adam in the Jesuit House and sits beside him as his pupil. When the Emperor holds court, Father Adam sits on a cushion beside the throne. . . . And he need not kowtow."

"No kowtow?" Joseph King exhaled in surprise. "I thought only six Grand Secretaries and Great Ministers were exempt from the kowtow."

"Well then, Master Joseph, Father Adam makes seven. Not only that, but much more. Father Adam does not present the reports of the Department of Astronomy through the Court Chamberlains. He is the only Mandarin who reports directly to the Emperor. Besides, he sees the Emperor at any time he wishes, night or day. That privilege no one else is granted."

"You astonish me, young man," Giulio di Giaccomo said. "We had not heard that news here."

"It is only true, Father Giulio," Robert replied. "I carry a letter to you from Father Adam reporting all this—and more. He believes he will soon bring the Emperor to acknowledge the One True God. Then I can profess Christianity openly."

"The Infinite Grace of the Lord God be praised," Giulio di Giaccomo exclaimed. "It was always Father Matthew Ricci's purpose to draw close to the Emperor and bring him into the One True Faith. When Adam Schall converts this Emperor, all China will become Christian."

"Converting Emperors isn't such an easy business," Joseph King observed. "Do not forget your fellow Jesuits' great hopes for the Ming Emperor. But, sorrowfully, he remains a pagan."

"Perhaps the Lord God wishes both Emperors brought into the True Faith at the same moment," Giulio di Giaccomo mused. "The entire Empire to become Christian at a stroke."

"Perhaps!" Joseph agreed wryly, while Robert shook his round head to deny the pretensions of the Ming Emperor.

Francis warmed again to his prickly son. Robert's pride was unabated, but he was learning to avoid gratuitously giving offense. Francis wondered whether Manchu hauteur could generally be tempered with Chinese courtesy, and he longed to see Peking again. Why, he pondered, should he not?

The Manchus had forgiven Chinese generals far worse offenses than his foray against the besiegers of Canton.

EARLY the next morning, Robert rode back to his regiment. Father and son parted with light good will, content to have joined hands across the chasm of resentment that lay between them. Both knew there would be time enough in the future to bridge that chasm. Convinced that his father would consider submission to the Manchu Emperor and a protracted visit to Peking, Robert casually waved his red-tufted lance in farewell when his horse cantered through the Siege Gate into the Empire. Francis did not grieve at their parting, but delighted in their partial reconciliation.

His wife was, however, pensive when he reported his conversation with Robert. She did not even express pleasure at Adam Schall's closeness to the Manchu Emperor. The imminent conversion of the Chinese apparently did not move the obedient daughter of Holy Church.

Dolores was determined that the casual parting between her husband and his elder son must be their final parting, rather than the prelude to closer affection. She saw in Robert a threat to her happiness second only to the lure China itself held for her husband. He was again talking of visiting Peking, though also talking of showing her Peking. But no European woman had ever been admitted to the Empire. He would, she feared, desert her for many months, perhaps years, rather than lose the opportunity to see his beloved North China again.

Francis would be wholly hers, Dolores realized, only when he was no longer drawn to the Great Empire that was her deadly rival. And he would no longer be lured by China only when he lived at a great distance from China.

Dolores finally smiled at Francis and agreed that the Manchu boy-Emperor's affection for Adam Schall was the greatest event since Father Matthew Ricci had penetrated Peking more than a half-century earlier. She congratulated Francis on the renewed affection between himself and his older son, and she listened with apparent sympathy to his prattling of their making a pleasure trip to Peking.

That same afternoon, she kissed her infant son George and ordered her chairbearers to carry her to Manuel Tavares Bocarro's foundry on the Rua do Chunambeiro. Dolores do Amaral Arrowsmith and her cousin sat for two hours in his cubbyhole office before toasting their common purpose in a final goblet of port. The scheme they had hatched would require some time to come to fruition. Haste could spoil everything. But Dolores could wait—as long as she knew she was moving toward her goal.

Peking, Macao

JOHANN Adam Schall von Bell stroked the bald scorch-scar on the trunk of the stunted plum tree. The scar inflicted in 1644, when all Peking burned, recalled the carnage One-Eyed Li had wreaked on the Northern Capital. Adam Schall saw also the outline of the Sacred Heart of Jesus, the mark of God's particular concern for the Mission to China.

All the trees in the courtyard of the Jesuit House had withered after the conflagration except the solitary plum, which bore a profusion of deep-pink flowers, though the meager fruit was sour. Only the plum tree with the heart-shaped scar remained of all the vegetation that had flourished in the time of the Ming. But the apple trees planted since the Manchus came were more fruitful each year. In late April 1652, eight years after the suicide of the last Ming Emperor to sit on the Dragon Throne in Peking, the scarlet maples and golden cypresses displayed his Imperial colors.

"In our endings are our beginnings," the Jesuit murmured. "The Lord forbids us to despair—and commands us to be hopeful."

The gravel path crackled under the Jesuit's felt soles when he resumed his stroll. The gravel grated when he turned in sudden decision and strode toward the moon gate of his study.

His deep blue eyes glowed with his new purpose, and he stroked his white beard, which hung almost to the white crane on the breast of his cassock that declared him a Mandarin of the First Grade. His sixtieth birthday was only a week away, and he had grown leaner with age. But his movements were still vigorous.

The Manchu Emperor, Adam Schall reflected, was an attractive boy any priest would be happy to instruct, even if he were the son of a shopkeeper. The Emperor was a pleasant lad except for the terrible rages no one else dared restrain. But it was hard at his age to respond to the shifting enthusiasms of an unfledged youth.

He was sorely tried by the architectural tasks the boy-Emperor heaped upon him. It had been challenging to strengthen the fortifications of Peking against rebels and Manchus a decade earlier. It was a distraction from his scientific studies to plan new fortifications when no enemy menaced the Northern Capital. It had been essential to cast cannon for the Ming, but it was a nuisance to cater to the boy-Emperor's desire for new cannon. And it was an infernal nuisance to indulge his curiosity regarding the wars of Europe. An aging Jesuit, mortally weary of tales of blood and glory, was no fit instructor in weapons and strategy.

The priest lifted the cloth-of-gold cover from his favorite armchair and folded it carefully. Similar swatches covered the seat of every chair. His majordomo had reverently laid that cover two hours earlier, when the Emperor rose to return to the Forbidden City. Any commoner's cushion honored by the impress of the Imperial posterior was thereafter decked like a sacred relic, never to be defiled by the buttocks of ordinary mortals.

Like any healthy youth, the fourteen-year-old Emperor had his moments of boyish humor. When the Jesuit told the Emperor that he could not sit down in his own house because every chair was taboo, the youth had laughed and asked, "What, you superstitious, Grandpa? By all means whisk them away. I give you my Imperial leave to rest your bottom on your own chairs."

Though he was tired, the priest could not relax his attentions to the Emperor for an instant. He was too close to the goal the Society of Jesus had sought for many decades. Only three weeks earlier he had surmounted the chief obstacle that kept the Emperor from the True Faith. The Dowager Empress had long been the protectress of the Mongolian lamas and the Manchu shamans—and the enemy of the True Faith. That patroness of aboriginal superstition now displayed a holy medal of the Lamb of God on her bosom. Yesterday she had presented the mission two stout oxen. He, Adam Schall, had been the instrument of the Lord's Will. The Dowager Empress had recanted after he cured a princess betrothed to the Emperor of an affliction of the throat that would not yield to native medicine.

So, close to the goal, he must redouble his efforts. Once the boy-Emperor accepted the True Faith, all his subjects, Chinese or Manchu, would clamor for instruction. The Emperor already accepted Christian doctrine intellectually, but had not yet been vouchsafed the gift of faith. Monogamy the youth understood in principle, could perhaps accept—but only for commoners. It was unthinkable to him that a monarch, who acquired allies by marriage, should be restricted to one wife. The Seventh Commandment, too, puzzled the youth who was barely a generation removed from the bloodthirsty nomads of the northern steppes.

"Your God, Grandpa, tells me I must not kill," the Emperor had taxed him only that afternoon. "How can I not? My enemies will kill me if I don't kill them."

Adam Schall affirmed his decision. He could at least share the tedium of answering such simplistic questions. The lad needed a confidant who was a little childlike. He needed a European who could discuss artillery bombardments and cavalry charges. In short, he needed a grown-up playmate to help bring him to the True Faith—and to share the burden that weighed upon Adam Schall.

The Jesuit smiled as he recalled the Imperial sanction he had received for the mundane act of sitting in his own chair. Crow's-feet crinkled around his deepset eyes, and lines seamed his high forehead. Meditatively stroking the tip of his long nose, he took a goose quill from a pewter inkwell. He squinted in concentration as the quill scratched the crabbed Latin script on the rice paper:

My dearly beloved son Francis,

I write to you standing between glory and perplexity. It is glorious that I am, as I hope and pray, so close to achieving the purpose that has animated the Society of Jesus since the blessed Father Matthew Ricci first stormed the walls that sealed the Great Empire from the world. I am in perplexity because my brothers in Christ are behaving more like apes with shaven pates and empty skulls than priests of the One True God. But more of them hereafter.

I implore you to join me in Peking. The Emperor is all but persuaded to accept baptism. Only some misapprehensions keep him from acknowledging to himself the Truth he already knows in his heart. He is also deterred by misunderstanding of the role of just war in Christendom. Besides, I tell you candidly, he requires converse with a Christian mind more direct than my own. My brothers in Christ are so complex in their reasoning and so subtle in their apologetics that they are fit only to instruct aged doctors of the Hanlin Academy.

What say you, Francis, to appointment as General and Master of Ordnance to His Imperial Manchu Majesty? The Earldom he has offered me can also be yours if you wish. Above all, I implore you in the name of the Risen Christ to lend your invaluable assistance to the greatest task—and the most glorious opportunity—given to Christian men since Saint Peter preached the True Gospel in pagan Rome: the conversion of the Chinese.

The Jesuit replaced his quill in the inkwell and read the words he had just written. What further inducement, he wondered, could he offer the restless spirit of Francis Arrowsmith? The truth was, he decided, the best inducement for that hotheaded and sentimental soldier:

I will not pretend that the task is easy or success assured. But I can promise that it will be engrossing. You, who have always been fascinated by power, will see from within the workings of the most powerful Court in the world, and you will instruct in modern warfare the Monarch who commands the most puissant armies in the world.

Also, Francis, I miss you. I would fain erase the memory of our strained parting with a joyous reunion.

Adam Schall went on to describe his difficulties with his fellow Jesuits, two of whom had been reprieved from execution for consorting with the remaining rebels only by his influence with the Emperor. Those Portuguese Fathers were now insisting that he require his converts to keep the Sabbath and the Holy Days without laboring, though a Papal indulgence had confirmed Father Matthew Ricci's original reluctance to impose such European customs on the Chinese. The old issue of prohibiting homage to Confucius and the Sacred Ancestors was also raised again.

Since the Chinese considered it a curse to be without heirs, the priest's letter continued, the Emperor had encouraged him to virtually adopt the young son of his faithful major-domo. The other Jesuits objected that his fondness for the boy was an occasion for scandal, as was his affectionate concern for his female converts.

Moved by envy, the German feared, his brothers in Christ charged him with worldly ambition because he still held the rank of a Mandarin. They conveniently forgot that he had refused five times before his Superior ordered him to accept rank, pay, and other honors lest he offend the Manchu Court.

Such contumacious charges [the letter concluded] are a distraction from my task. I would, as a weak human being, have the support of your stalwart good sense in my trials with my contentious brethren. Being always in the company of quarrelsome black crows oppresses me. I need a European layman, yourself, to laugh with.

For all those reasons, Francis, I implore you: Come back to Peking—and become a General of Ordnance and an Earl in Cathay, if that pleases you. Come back and ensure the glorious culmination of the Holy Mission you undertook almost two and a half decades past.

Yours in Christ,
Johann Adam Schall von Bell

Adam Schall smiled as he dripped hot wax on the folded letter and sealed it with his gold signet ring. This sprat should catch a fat mackerel—and the mackerel could catch the Imperial whale.

He must, however, find a perfectly trustworthy courier. He had to reveal his difficulties with his brother Jesuits to awaken Francis's sympathy. But he could not risk the further charge of exposing the Mission's internal quarrels to a layman. Though urgent, the letter must wait until he found a Chinese messenger who was as loyal as he was incorruptible.

"THE crude fellow whipped off his tunic and stood half-naked before the Duke Koxinga." Edmond Chü smiled fastidiously.

"This general then turned to show the four ideograms tattooed on his back: *Chih Hsin Pao Kuo*—Bare-Hearted Redeem the Nation. Now, I ask you!"

"Or, Edmond, if I understood the classical language properly: Whole-Heartedly Pledged to the Ming Dynasty!" Francis Arrowsmith interrupted his son-in-law.

"An admirable sentiment, but what a tawdry, histrionic trick!" Edmond's patrician disdain diluted his delight in the powerful recruits flocking to the Ming. "Still, I suppose, we must take all who wish to serve the Emperor."

"You are well advised to do so despite all your recent victories," Francis observed drily. "This general cannot defect to the Manchus with his loyalty tattooed on his back."

"That has not escaped the Duke or me, Arrowmaker." Edmond Chü's wide mouth smiled again in his fair, oval face. "If our new offensive is to drive the Manchus from South China, we must have generals who cannot desert at the first setback."

"Edmond, I am naturally delighted. But what brings you to Macao this glorious June day? Not only Maria's condition, I daresay."

"Arrowmaker, I could have sent Maria alone by sea." The Ming Colonel paced the balcony of the villa on Mount Guia, his quick movements revealing the wiry strength in his tall, slender frame. "I should be with the Duke's armies sweeping up Fukien and Chekiang. Of course, I'd rather be with the forces besieging the so-called Field Marshal Virtuous Kung in Kweilin."

"You'll soon have your revenge for your father's execution, Edmond. But what is this other matter?"

"Let me think how to explain," Edmond prevaricated, gazing at the crescent of lanterns that gleamed through the dusk on the channel between Macao and Lapa Island.

Francis was accustomed to the nightly display of bobbing sampans lit to attract fish. But the fire floating eerily on water still stirred him, as did the red flare of the declining sun behind the purple hills of Kwangtung Province. He sipped his claret and listened to the bustle of the household. His wife Dolores and his daughter Maria were hovering over his son George, who was almost a year old, while the infant's maidservants clucked their annoyance at the ladies' interference. Having won her battle to prevent the servants' stifling George with swaddling clothes, his wife was preaching her doctrine

585

of freedom for infants to his daughter in the mixture of Portuguese and Chinese they used.

Maria did not need to feign interest. She was distended beneath her loose robe, and her baby was due in late July, a month or so hence. Edmond Chü had brought his wife to her father's house for the last days of her pregnancy because South China was in flames. He wanted his wife safe in Macao when he rejoined the battles that would sweep the Manchus across the Yangtze. Edmond assumed that Dolores would not only welcome Maria, but would also watch over her with maternal love—as would a Chinese stepmother.

Dolores was actually behaving just like a loving Chinese stepmother. Listening to his wife and his daughter chat, Francis was astonished at their amity. If the women still resented each other, they were adroitly concealing their true feelings.

"Well, then, Edmond," Francis prompted. "What is it that brought you to Macao?"

"Arrowmaker, we are grateful for your finding us arms. Duke Koxinga says you have done as much for the Ming cause in the past year as lifting the siege of Canton would have accomplished. By the way, we captured those two Commodores last month, the cowards who abandoned their voyages with your men. Both have been strangled."

"I am not vindictive, Edmond, I think. But I shall not weep."

"We thought you'd be pleased. But consider the situation of the Ming. The closer we come to victory below the Yangtze, the more Manchu resistance stiffens. Nonetheless, we will soon strike north toward Peking!"

"Edmond, have you come to Macao to discuss grand strategy with a tired colonel in semiretirement?"

"And to put a proposal to that colonel, who, I see, is now full of vigor. The Emperor offers you appointment as Inspector-General of Ordnance and Musketeers over all the Imperial armies with a stipend of one hundred gold taels a month. To start, he'll also make you a baron."

"Beware of Greeks bearings gifts and Chinese offering patents of nobility," Francis murmured, half to himself. "What would my duties be?"

"Above all, to ensure that His Majesty's modern arms are used to best advantage. To train troops and to join in planning strategy. Also to command such troops in battle as you wish."

Francis was stunned by the munificence of the Ming proposal. He stared at the crescent of fire on the water, watching the two horns draw toward each other. If they joined within the next five minutes, he would accept.

"Is it not enough to tempt you?" Edmond asked anxiously. "Within reason, any other powers you may need..."

"Edmond, it is enough...more than enough. This is what I dreamed of when I came into the Empire almost twenty-five years ago. Inspector-General of all Ming troops equipped with firearms. In Europe I could never have become almost a field marshal."

"We can't offer you field marshal's rank just yet, Arrow-maker. I can tell you...as your son-in-law...that we had some trouble with the conservative generals about your appointment. Later, of course, your rank could well...just as an earldom could reward you for..."

"Edmond, I dor't want to be a field marshal or an earl. General and baron would suit me well enough."

"Then you agree? When can you join us?"

"In principle..." Francis watched the horns of the crescent of lanterns join in a circle of light. "In principle, I fully agree. But I must talk with my wife."

DESPITE his exhilaration, Francis wondered again at the dependence of the Chinese not only upon European science and warcraft, but upon Europeans. He had trained hundreds of Chinese officers, as well as many Manchus. Yet the resurgent Ming Dynasty, no more than the Manchus, possessed a senior officer qualified to command troops equipped with modern firearms. Adam Schall had taught cannon-casting to hundreds of Chinese, and Manuel Tavares Bocarro's Chinese artisans made the best guns in the world. Yet neither Chinese nor Manchus could produce their own bronze cannon three decades after the first Portuguese artillerymen had gone north to assist the Ming.

The Chinese response was the same to Western astronomy, which they needed as much as firearms: alternating enthusiasm and contempt, alternating dependence and rejection. The Jesuits had taught many Mandarins to use their astronomical instruments. But the Jesuits still manned the Imperial Observatory—and were repeatedly required to prove their skill by theatrically predicting eclipses. One moment entranced by Western science and warcraft, in the next the

Chinese disdained those arts as monkey-clever tricks unworthy of their uniquely superior civilization.

Would Christianity suffer the same fate, Francis wondered, being degraded to an intellectual plaything? Often appearing on the verge of triumph, the Holy Mission was still a great distance from converting all Chinese. Did the Chinese truly desire the inestimable blessing of Christianity, even the Christians among them? Did the Chinese truly desire Western science and warcraft, even the most enlightened among them? Would their insufferable pride not always reject those foreign gifts at the climactic moment? Worse, was there some deficiency in the Chinese intellect, however highly cultivated, that made it incapable of assimilating either Christianity or science?

Brooding on that paradox, Francis regretted impulsively accepting Edmond Chü's offer. He was no longer sure he wanted the high command for which he had yearned all his life. He was, above all, doubtful that he could carry out the duties of that command effectively hampered by obstacles like the opposition of the conservatives his son-in-law had rapidly glossed over.

Yet he had to know his own mind before he spoke with his wife. Having committed himself wholly to Dolores, Francis required her approbation of whatever course he chose. But he wondered how she would view his returning to the battlefields of the Empire.

Dolores had urged him to lead the Invincible Force to relieve Canton. But she had recently spoken of returning to Lisbon, perhaps soon. Motherhood had altered Dolores, directing her inclinations away from China and toward Europe.

Francis wavered in his own mind for several days and put off speaking to his wife. He finally concluded that he could conceive of no challenge more noble than commanding the Ming Emperor's troops—and restoring a nearly Christian dynasty to the Dragon Throne. Francis Arrowsmith's decision was hastened by Edmond Chü's manifest impatience. Though too courteous to press, the young Ming Colonel was obviously eager to report his father-in-law's acceptance. At dinner, Francis decided he would speak with Dolores in their bedchamber after the household had retired.

"Colonel Arrowmaker, a Jesuit lay brother is waiting in the vestibule," the majordomo whispered as he poured the wine. "He will say only he must speak with you."

The Chinese lay brother's face was haggard, and his cassock was worn. He offered a cloth-wrapped packet soiled by much handling.

"I am Brother Ignatius from Peking," he said. "Father Adam Schall urges you to answer as soon as you possibly can."

When Brother Ignatius refused a glass of wine, Francis returned to the table. He did not conceal the packet, but offered no explanation to his curious family. After dessert he retired alone to the study to open the packet.

"My dearly beloved son Francis," he read, deeply moved by that affectionate salutation. "I write you standing between glory and perplexity..."

Francis Arrowsmith read Adam Schall's letter three times, reading differently each time he came to the conclusion: "...ensure the glorious culmination of the Holy Mission you undertook almost two and a half decades past."

The English soldier was successively amused, indignant, and challenged by the German priest's once again summoning him to Peking after having sent him away so emphatically more than three years earlier. He was also moved to deep consideration.

The Ming's prospects were bright, but the Manchus held North China. The Manchu Emperor was close to conversion, but the Ming Crown Prince was already baptized. How did one weigh a virtually Christian Emperor against a Christian Crown Prince who was only four years old? The Ming might retake Peking, but the Manchus might yet unite the Great Empire under their rule. Though he was inclined to the Ming, Francis wondered which dynasty offered the greater prospects for Christianity. He did not weigh a Ming barony against a Manchu earldom.

Knowing he required Joseph King's subtle advice, Francis sent for his secretary. Joseph sat silent while his employer translated the Jesuit's Latin into Chinese. His closed Cantonese face was uncommunicative, and his tan robe lay unmoving on his slight body. From the hide seat of his folding chair Joseph's eyes glowed unblinking across the fireplace heaped with oleander blossoms while Francis knocked the dottle from his pipe and refilled the minuscule bowl.

"Well, Joseph," Francis finally demanded, flicking a spark from his blue lounging robe. "What do you think?"

"I am impressed, Arrowmaker, deeply impressed." Joseph's teeth gleamed like yellowed ivory in the oil lamp's light, and his bronze cheeks crinkled. "Truly munificent inducements from both the Ming and the Manchus!"

"You know of the Ming offer, Joseph?" Francis asked.

"It's no secret, Arrowmaker. Edmond told me...for his own reasons."

"What would you do, Joseph?"

"Arrowmaker, what I would do cannot decide what you will do...or should do. I am not proffered baronies and earldoms."

"You've never been so shy before, Joseph."

"I have not, sometimes to your exasperation, Arrowmaker. But I cannot advise you on this matter."

"I demand...require....No, I beg you to give me your advice."

"Put that way, Arrowmaker, I cannot refuse." Joseph was still irritatingly and uncharacteristically laconic. "For China, the Ming is best. What is best for the True Faith, I cannot say, but I believe the Ming. What is best for you I cannot say at all. You must decide yourself."

"Why such reticence, Joseph?"

"I would have come to you tonight if you had not summoned me, Arrowmaker." Joseph's face was grave. "Edmond made a proposal to me, too. Nothing as grand as yours. Just a district magistracy in reconquered Kwangtung Province. But I have accepted. I want to die among my own people. Before I die, I want to wear the Mandarin's robe denied me all my life."

"When do you leave, Joseph?" Francis's dilemma was overshadowed by the loss of his companion of almost twenty-five years. "When must we say farewell?"

"Tomorrow, Arrowmaker, I am sad to say." Joseph leaned across the oleanders and laid his hand on Francis's knee. "The Lord of Heaven knows how deeply it grieves me to say farewell to you. I hope we will be reunited from time to time, depending on your choice. But Edmond is determined to sail on the tide tomorrow evening. He can wait no longer for your reply, and I...I must go with him."

"I...I'm shaken, Joseph." Francis felt tears prickle his eyelids, and he saw that Joseph's dark eyes were wet. "We've been together a long time."

"So we have, Arrowmaker." Joseph King hesitated. "But we part in great friendship. And you have your wife and your new son. You will not be parted long from them, I know. Not this time. You won't flee again."

590

"At least I'll see you tomorrow." Francis clutched Joseph's shoulder, then embraced him. "To bid you a proper farewell."

The Englishman sat unmoving in his ebony armchair for ten minutes after his secretary withdrew. The marble backrest was cold through his thin robe. He felt naked and lonely when he realized how much he would miss Joseph's constant companionship and acerbic counsel. But he could not press his former slave to refuse the office of Mandarin for which he had longed all his life.

His secretary had forcefully reminded Francis that his personal decisions were no longer his alone. He would never desert Dolores as he had, he acknowledged, deserted both Marta and Barbara. He could wait no longer to speak with his wife, though, he suddenly realized, he dreaded the encounter.

Francis trudged up the stairs to the second floor of the villa. All the lamps were out, and the flame in his pewter candlestick gleamed darkly on the teak treads. He rapped on the paneled door and entered an empty bedchamber.

"Francis?" Dolores's voice drifted from a cane long-chair on the balcony. "Where have you been?"

"I come to you in some perplexity, my dear." Francis spoke in the words he had rehearsed in his mind to the slender figure in the white night robe. "I...we...must make a major decision."

"The packet you received earlier?" Dolores asked. "I wondered when..."

"Not only that, but another matter as well, my love." Francis saw how the shadows on her cheeks accentuated her minutely snubbed nose and her wide eyes. "A crucial decision."

"Don't stand there like a play actor, all solemn and stiff," Dolores laughed. "Nothing can be that crucial. Come sit by me and tell me."

Francis stretched out his legs in a long-chair, his eyes fixed on the circle of light on the water. As he watched, the yellow lanterns dispersed and flickered out. The fishermen were returning with their catches to the silent, dark shore.

"Two paths to glory have opened to me." His senses were caressed by her lightly astringent hyacinth scent when she stirred. "Both are great opportunities to advance the Faith."

Dolores lay silent until he concluded: "...and which path, my dear, do you feel I should take—the Ming or the Manchu?"

"This is not what I'd hoped," she said after some seconds. "Not at all, Francis."

"And what had you hoped, my dear?" Francis could not put off their inevitable disagreement.

"Manuel Bocarro and I have been talking about a grand plan..."

"Without me, Dolores?"

"You've been turning over your plans without me, Francis. But only listen before you..."

"I shall," he answered tensely.

"You can't see it, my dear," she said. "But you are not well. You won't be well as long as you live amid the miasmas...the foul air of Macao and China. There's also the baby. George needs a better climate for his body and his spirit. I don't want him growing up a wizened, yellowish Macanese..."

"And your plan, Dolores?" Francis interrupted. "What is it, this grand plan of yours?"

"Please don't take that tone, my love," she cajoled. "At least listen. You sound like a wheezy elephant blowing his trunk in a lady's kerchief."

"I'll try to sound like a healthy elephant." Despite his irritation, Francis smiled. "But, I assure you, I've never felt better. That ulcer on my leg comes and goes. But it's not bad enough to need a doctor. Otherwise, I've never felt better."

"You don't look it, Francis. Really you don't. But listen to my plan, please."

"I shall," he repeated.

"As you know, trade is slack. The Spanish, the English, and the Dutch are cutting into our markets all over the East. Manuel and I feel we must develop the European market. When Manuel becomes Governor, Macao will be in our pockets. If we can only open up Europe, the profits will be fantastic. But we need an aggressive representative in Lisbon and..."

"You'd do well in Lisbon, Dolores. You're surely aggressive enough."

"Not I, but you, you great booby. I have already have enough looking after you and George. I hope, too, there will be..."

"Are you hinting again, my dear?" Francis forgot his indignation. "Are you..."

"Not yet, but we can hope, can't we? But our plan, it's perfect. We leave Macao, but keep up the connection. And the excitement of Lisbon...the theater, the Court, the balls

...proper schooling for George and any other.... Can't you see it's perfect?"

"For you, perhaps, Dolores. And I've always planned George would go to St. Omer's. But not for me, this plan. I cannot leave China when the Holy Mission is so close to success...and the final battle for the Empire is near. Only a coward would desert the cause now."

"Francis, you'll always be torn.... Unhappy in China because you feel you should be in Macao...unhappy in Macao because you should be in China."

"I shall return often. I know I'll be torn by need for you, but I cannot refuse this opportunity."

"*Which* opportunity, Francis? You don't even know whom you want to serve, do you? The battle—not the cause—attracts you, doesn't it?"

"Battle? Yes, to an extent. But the cause is the conversion of the Chinese."

"You can do no more. You've already done more than enough. Regardless of who wins, Ming or Manchus, it will be decades, perhaps centuries, before the Chinese are converted. It's more than sixty years since Matthew Ricci..."

"Nonetheless, I must go.... And the Ming needs me more. Besides, I must prove..."

"My dear, you have already proved all you have to prove in this life."

Pleading for her happiness, for her future and her son's future, Dolores controlled her anger. Her husband, normally amiable and loving, was as stubbornly unyielding as a stone effigy of a Crusader knight on a tomb.

"You've proved yourself many times over," she resumed. "Why else should both the Manchus and the Ming want you if you were not the best soldier in Asia? Let us leave now. Otherwise, you'll die on some forsaken battlefield.... If you don't die of the fever...and I..."

"Nonetheless I must go," Francis reiterated. "This last time...until the issue is decided between the Dynasties."

"It will not be decided, Francis. Not in our lifetimes. Certainly not in your short lifetime if you persist.... You're not well, Francis. You cannot go campaigning again."

"I must join the Ming, Dolores. Duty commands..."

"...duty to your own vainglory!" Dolores gave her anger its head. "You're determined to kill yourself, leaving me and the baby..."

"I have no intention of killing myself, Dolores," he replied

593

stiffly. "And I promise you, after this one last campaign, we'll talk about..."

"We will *not*, Francis." Her voice crackled. "If you survive, there will always be another campaign. Even if you survive all the campaigns, I will *not* be here to..."

"Not here? How will you not be here?"

"If you join the Ming, I shall leave Macao." Dolores's voice broke, but she continued. "I shall leave you, Francis. Go and play at soldiers if you must. But I won't be here when you return."

"If you do, I'll know you never loved me. I was just a convenient..."

"And what am I to you, then? What am I that you'd desert me for a heathen emperor? I'm only good to warm your bed...to feed you and keep you."

"If you truly believe that, there is no more to say!" Stung by that reminder that he lived on his wife's money, Francis rose and paced the balcony. "Nothing at all to say!"

Neither could yield after that bitter exchange. Neither could yield, since Dolores, who affected to disdain false pride, was as proud as Francis, whose pride compelled him to the battlefield again.

After sitting silent for a time while Francis paced in silence, Dolores rose wearily from the long-chair. She doused the oil lamps and pinched out the candles. She ostentatiously turned her back to drop her night-robe before slipping under the sheets on the broad *cama de casal*. When the moonlight glimmered on her rounded hips and her delicate shoulders, Francis marveled at the sacrifice he was making for the True Faith and for China.

Macao

JUNE 30, 1652–SEPTEMBER 31, 1652

DAWN came early to Macao before storming into China on the last day of June 1652. Midsummer's Day had begun the protracted celebrations of the thirtieth anniversary of the Portuguese settlement's glorious victory over the Dutch invasion fleet, which preserved the Extreme East for the Universal Catholic Faith and Portuguese trade. When the Governor's Gala Ball concluded the festivities the preceding night, men with long memories recalled the decisive valor of Father Adam Schall. Without the Jesuits, there would have been no Macao in the beginning. Without that particular Jesuit, the enclave would have ended by falling to the heretics.

Francis Arrowsmith slept badly that night, awakening repeatedly to drink from a pitcher of water. His restless night exhausted him even more than had the Ball. Waking early, he felt not only his head, but his entire body ache.

Since they could not decline the Governor's invitation, Dolores and Francis had sat stiffly at the head table. They spoke only to sustain the illusion of public amity that cloaked their private quarrel. Half-reluctant, half-eager to dance with his wife, Francis found he could not dance at all because of the raw ulcer on his left thigh. To salve that pain he drank much champagne before the banquet, too much red wine with the few mouthfuls he could eat, and far too much brandy afterward.

When he stirred at dawn, Francis could dimly remember returning in his sedan chair to the villa on Mount Guia. He could remember neither throwing off his clothes nor lying down on the narrow cot in the dressing room, where he had slept since his bitter altercation with Dolores. The airy bedchamber with the white-marble fireplace was by unspoken agreement again her sole domain, as it had been before their marriage.

Striving to draw the cloak of sleep again over his exhaustion, Francis was stabbed into wakefulness by the spears of sunlight that pierced the slatted shutters. Magpies cawed in the garden, and seagulls mewed overhead like playful cats. The pink dawn suffusing the dressing room glowed red on his burning eyeballs, and his unsteady hand knocked the water pitcher off the side table. The porcelain shattering on the floor tiles resounded on his eardrums like a volley of muskets.

The brandy had done it, Francis realized. The pale Spanish spirit always disturbed his sleep and made him thirsty. But he was horribly thirsty this morning, and he could not remember his head aching worse. Brandy had never turned his forehead blazing hot and his hands clammy cold. Nor had brandy ever set his arms and legs quivering uncontrollably and his teeth chattering so frenziedly he had to clamp them together. If he had not drunk so much brandy he would have thought he was suffering another attack of the malaria that had plagued him since the coursing of One-Eyed Li eight years earlier.

Feeling his bladder taut to bursting, he swung his feet onto the floor tiles. They were scorching beneath his soles, but he was too eager to reach the minuscule closet room to wonder at that sensation or to draw on the orange-checked sarong lying at the foot of his cot. Clutching the furniture and leaning on the wall, he hobbled to the closet. The weight of his swimming head overburdened the stalk of his neck, and the outlines of the room danced like heat waves before his blinking eyes.

He convulsively swallowed the sour vomit that rose in his throat. Frightened by his heart's fluttering, he rested his forehead on the cool wall tiles and wondered why they were icy and the floor tiles blazing. With immense relief he felt the tightness lift from his belly as his urine tinkled into the glazed chamberpot.

A spasm seized him, and he shuddered violently. Leaning his hands on the wall tiles, he looked down. Horror pierced his half-stupor. The stream pouring into the chamberpot was neither white nor yellow, but dark, almost black.

Something was wrong with him, terribly wrong. Unwilling to call for help, wanting only to lie down again, though his narrow cot seemed a thousand miles away, he waited for the foul stream to stop.

Fog swirled gray around him, and lightning lanced his temples. Suddenly he felt much better, wholly in command of himself. His fever cooled, and his trembling ceased. An instant later his legs gave way, and his hands slid down the wall tiles. He crumpled and lay with his head beside the gaudy chamber pot.

"*KUIE HUIE HO*." A tantalizingly familiar voice was speaking in Cantonese. "He'll be all right...after some time."

Francis looked up into the broad face of the man Joseph King called *Daifoo*, Master Physician. The herbal doctor's eyes were slitted in concern, and Dolores peered anxiously over his shoulder. Francis realized that he was again lying in the broad *cama de casal*, their marriage bed. Beside his wife, his daughter Maria fingered her rosary. Behind the ladies stood Father Giulio di Giaccomo, his plump face grave and a crucifix in his hand.

"Is it...so...bad?" attempting a jest, Francis croaked. "So desperate...need Giulio's professional..."

"Be quiet, my love," Dolores soothed him. "All will be well if you don't exert yourself."

Francis closed his eyes. Hearing the majordomo José Rivera translate the herbal doctor's Cantonese into Portuguese, he felt a spasm of grief. Joseph King had always translated from his native Cantonese, but Joseph was gone, gone far away. Irritated by his own stupidity, he strove to remember where Joseph had gone, but could not.

"*Hak-niu-yit*," the Master Physician was explaining, his voice comically high and faint. "Blackwater fever. Not only the black urine....But, see how his flesh remains dented after I press it in. A great excess of the water element. Also, the yellow cast of the skin and the small bruises beneath it. A classic case."

Francis was troubled in his half-stupor. Something else was wrong, but he could not think what. Then he remembered: Maria! Maria was close to her time. She should be resting, not hovering over his bed. He tried to tell her, but no words emerged from the parched cavern of his mouth.

"He will recover?" Dolores asked the herbal doctor. "He won't...won't..."

"No, Lady, he won't. The Master Physician is certain the Colonel will recover...with rest and proper treatment." The majordomo reassured her. "He asks if he remembers correctly that the Colonel has suffered from *mal aria?*"

"Yes, though not recently," Dolores answered. "Is it *mal aria* again? I've never seen him so bad."

"No, quite different and worse than *mal aria,*" the doctor replied. "But how was he treated?"

"I'm afraid I don't know," Dolores answered. "Is it important?"

"Cincho...cin...cinchona," Francis quavered. "Father Adam in Peking...cinchona."

"Then my diagnosis is certain. With the racing, irregular pulse, it's unquestionably blackwater fever. I've seen it before in *mal aria* patients given this cinchona bark the Spiritual Fathers brought to China."

"And the treatment?" Giulio di Giaccomo demanded practically. "Do you have a cure?"

"Of course...from the ancient Chinese pharmacopoeia. Autumn crocus, dried and pounded with bat's blood. Also salves for that ulcer. It should not have gone so long untreated."

"Bat's blood and flowers," Dolores exclaimed in horror. "That's black magic, not medicine. How can you..."

"The Spiritual Fathers treat the miasma disease, the *mal aria,* with the bark of trees, do they not?" the Master Physician demanded. "Why spurn my crocus flowers?"

THE household of Mount Guia was further disrupted while Francis lay racked by spasms and fevers far more severe than he had suffered upon returning to Peking after the pursuit of One-Eyed Li, more severe even than the attack of malaria that had ended the Invincible Force's foray against the Manchu besiegers of Canton. Despite the flock of willing servants, Dolores was exhausted. Her golden-olive cheeks were haggard, and black circles dulled her dove-gray eyes. On July 5,

1652, when he had begun to enjoy a few lucid hours, Francis heard his daughter's shrieks thinly, as if filtered through innumerable layers of fleece.

Maria's agony was prolonged. She was even more slender than her mother had been, and the child's head pushed at her narrow pelvic opening for almost eighteen hours. The anxious midwife consulted the herbal doctor, who had virtually taken up residence in the villa. He would allow Maria only small doses of opium to take the edge off her pains, lest her muscles relax too much. At last, a dark-haired crown appeared between Maria's bloody thighs. Finally the head emerged, and the midwife hooked her fingers under the baby's shoulders. With her help, the enormous boy-child finally won his long fight to emerge from the womb.

The exhausted mother slept for an entire day while Dolores do Amaral Arrowsmith, briskly competent in her new role of step-grandmother, watched over the infant. She also sent for a wetnurse, since she knew Maria was too debilitated to feed the nine-pound boy herself. Despite the small difference in their ages, Dolores was anxiously maternal with Marta's daughter. The anguish of birth, which she had herself so recently experienced, erased the last of her resentment toward her husband's half-Chinese daughter for holding him to China. Whatever lingering hostility Dolores had still felt for her stepdaughter was transferred to the demanding infant who had almost killed his mother.

Wholly lucid by the week's end, Francis asked that his grandson be brought to him. He stroked the boy's round face with his fingertips, noting sadly that the infant's features and coloring were wholly Chinese. Except for a certain—perhaps fancied—wideness of his eyes, his Chinese blood had overwhelmed all trace of his European blood. Nonetheless, Francis rejoiced when he hobbled into his daughter's bedchamber supported by his majordomo a few days later and kissed her forehead.

"When they bring the red eggs to celebrate his birth, I shall tell them," Maria whispered. "I shall tell everyone he is to be called Francis Thomas for his two grandfathers. But Francis first."

That much more of himself he would leave behind him in China, Francis mused. Only a name, a common enough name, but his own. That reflection startled him. In his thoughts, he seemed already prepared to leave China, though Dolores had not pressed him again. Well, he would have to leave China some day, alive or dead, and he would be happy to leave something more of himself behind. Not only Maria and Robert, but this grandson, Francis Thomas, would carry his blood, mingling his small portion of Europe with future generations of the Great Empire.

Of course, he checked himself, it would be a long time before he departed. But he knew he was fighting a rear-guard action. It would be many months before he could even think of campaigning again, and the dynastic war was fast approaching a climax as the Manchus reeled back everywhere in South China. When Dolores brought the herbal doctor to his bed early in August and ostentatiously left them alone, he knew the rear-guard action was all but lost.

"*Tuen-jang Seen-sang...*" Francis strained to understand the Cantonese. "Colonel, you've been very lucky. I congratulate you on your recovery."

"*Jeeyeh-jeeyeh nei,*" Francis replied in his heavily accented Cantonese, and the herbal doctor smiled. "My thanks and congratulations to you, Master Physician. Without you..."

"Not necessarily, but very likely, Colonel. You might well have died. Without me, you could certainly not look forward to almost complete recovery."

"When? When can I get out of bed? When can I take the field again?"

"Quite soon you can begin walking...remain out of bed several hours a day. After a month, you should be fit to travel...by sedan chair or junk. But you will never take the field again....Not in China."

"What do you mean, Doctor? Not in China? Why?"

"You'll never recover fully in Macao. The climate is too fierce. As long as you remain in South China, I cannot rule out a relapse."

"Then I'll go north, and..."

"...and kill yourself on the journey. North China is also impossible—even by junk—for many months. Above all, you will always be in danger of a relapse as long as you remain in China. The virulent humors of the miasma disease and blackwater fever have spared you...just barely. But their evil essence lurks everywhere in China....And you are now their easy prey."

"So you say, Doctor," Francis conceded. "But it seems..."

"Listen to me, Colonel. After a few months you should be fit to endure a voyage in a great European ship. But only remaining away from China can keep you well. Your Lady and the Spiritual Father tell me that the climate in Europe..."

Francis heard that final verdict pronounced on all his hopes—all the ambitions of twenty-five years—with stunned calmness. It must, the thought flashed into his mind, be much like this to be sentenced to death. First, unbelief that this evil destiny should be yours. Then slow acceptance and, soon, utter anguish of the spirit.

Later, he knew, he would curse fate for snatching the prize of a lifetime from his enfeebled fingers. Later he would brood over the eternal glory he could have won by placing the Ming Emperor on the Dragon Throne with a crucifix in his hands. But, for the moment, he would take his foul medicine and try not to dwell constantly on his monstrous disappointment. For the moment, he could only strive to resign himself meekly to leaving that splendid triumph to others. God had decreed that he, like Moses, should glimpse the Promised Land, but not enter into it.

COLONEL EDMOND CHÜ returned to Macao in mid-August to cluck over his enormous son, to sit with his wife's hand clasped in his own, and to sympathize with his father-in-law's frustration.

"Arrowmaker, the great victory is already won," he comforted Francis. "Kweilin fell to His Imperial Majesty's forces on August seventh. I only regret that the so-called Field Marshal, the misnamed Virtuous Kung, escaped the torture he inflicted upon my saintly father...the alteration of hope and despair that closed with the vermilion-silk bowstring. The Virtuous Kung hanged himself as our Ming troops swarmed into Kweilin."

"Edmond, the Virtuous Kung tried to save your father." Francis recalled the Manchu Field Marshal's repeated pleas to Grand Secretary Thomas Chü to save his life by allowing his head to be shaved. "How can you, a Christian gentleman, be so vindictive?"

"As a Christian, I am a little ashamed of my vengefulness, Arrowmaker," Edmond Chü replied slowly. "As a son, I can only rejoice at the retribution inflicted on my father's slayer...and weep that he was not tortured."

"Do not tell your feelings to Father Giulio." Francis tried to warm with a jest that miasma of hatred that chilled the sun-filled room. "He will not take it well."

601

"I shall not make Confession until I can truly repent of my vengefulness," Edmond agreed. "Only the Lord of Heaven knows when that may be."

Francis wondered if the thwarted passion for revenge would ever leave his son-in-law in peace. But he did not speak of that grim contest between Chinese rage and Christian forgiveness to Giulio di Giaccomo when the Jesuit called on him the next day. His son-in-law had confided in him under the seal of filial love, which was as sacred as the seal of Confession.

After congratulating Francis on the recovery more apparent each passing day, the Jesuit revealed his own pressing concerns.

"Father Michal Boym should be almost in Rome by now." The Italian priest was excited by other events than the Ming's recapturing Kweilin, which he half regretted because he was still inclined to the Manchus. "I cannot in conscience or good sense pray that the Holy Father will raise an army for the Ming. But I rejoice that the influence of the Society of Jesus in China will be displayed by the letters Boym carries from the Grand Eunuch and the Dowager Empress."

"A remarkable concession from a Manchu partisan like yourself, Giulio," Francis laughed. "What would Adam Schall say?"

"I've come about Adam Schall. The disputes between him and those pestilential Portuguese Fathers grow grave...as do the protests of the pernicious Franciscans. Their letters attacking Adam have already gone to Rome. The Father Provincial feels he must submit the controversy to the Father General and the Holy Father himself. So dire have those unseemly quarrels become...so grave are the charges against Adam Schall. To rule on the dispute in Macao could divide the Mission to China irretrievably."

"What blasted nonsense!" Francis exploded. "Everyone knows Adam has been flexible, but never...never has he deviated from Holy Truth in word or deed. I doubted once myself. But now I know his is the only way."

"Then, Francis, you must assist Adam."

"Giulio, I am forbidden to go north. You know I am condemned to return to Europe. What can I do?"

"A great deal. Your testimony in Rome...the testimony of a faithful and valorous son of Holy Church. Neither Jesuit nor Franciscan, an objective witness, though a layman, could carry the day for Adam Schall in Rome."

"Giulio, are you bidding me to be gone soon? I remember once Adam Schall.... I never thought I would again be urged to depart by a good friend."

"I shall weep at your departure, Francis. But I am bidding you to be gone as soon as you possibly can. I do not urge you gladly. But I..."

"But you'll be glad to see my heels, Giulio, will you not? Even if I also plead in Rome for Father Michal Boym's mission...for aid to the Ming?"

"Even then, Francis, if that be God's will. But get you gone soon to plead Adam Schall's case."

IN the early evening of September 31, 1652, the twenty-gun caravel *Nossa Senhora de Vida* surged through the muddy stream of the Pearl River as the northeast monsoon filled her sails. In the luxurious stern cabin, the half-caste José Rivera presided over four tremulous Chinese maidservants who were laying out the belongings of Colonel and Senhora Arrowsmith for the protracted voyage around Africa to Lisbon by way of Goa. Two maidservants watched over George Ignatius Francis do Amaral Arrowsmith, who was at fifteen months a very small parcel of humanity to carry that grandiloquent name.

Though the caravel rode smoothly as the land swells subsided behind her rudder, the maidservants' faces were tinged with green. It would, José Rivera feared, be a messy voyage. Almost two years to Lisbon, a year and a half if they were fortunate, and the blasted Chinese women would be puking all the way. They were already seasick on a calm sea in a ship of five hundred tons, which hardly rolled but cut through the waves like a solid wooden castle.

Francis and Dolores Arrowsmith clutched the rail of the quarterdeck as *Nossa Senhora de Vida* quickened to the monsoon wind and white foam spurted from her prow. Their eyes were fixed on the pale-green villa atop Mount Guia, where an enormous banner flaunted the double-barred cross of St. Omer in the evening breeze. As they watched, the twenty-foot strings of firecrackers hanging from the balcony immolated themselves amid innumerable golden flashes. The protracted fusillade reverberated over the delta of the Pearl River, and startled fishermen looked up from the nets that harvested the South China Sea.

A cannon barked from the Guia Fort, then another and another. Francis counted the fourteen-gun salute due a baron and a general, though unshed tears obscured the black-powder smoke billowing across the hillside. He laid his hand on Dolores's.

She leaned against him, tendrils of black hair whipping from her scarf of golden tribute silk. Her gray eyes were clouded, and her lips were pressed together. Her olive cheeks flushed when the rough breeze touched them. She was just past thirty, and Dolores knew she had never been more attractive. She looked up tentatively at her husband.

Francis was again tanned. The sun had erased the white calipers etched by illness between his nostrils and the corners of his wide mouth. His long-muscled height was hardly diminished by the heavy shoulders straining against his fawn jacket. The declining sun lit his arched nose and taut cheeks, lingering on the silvered streaks in the tawny mass of his hair.

His face was set, but he looked so fit that Dolores wondered again whether their precipitate departure had been necessary. She was glad, she told herself, glad they were going. If they had stayed, he would have fallen ill again. The herbal doctor had warned that new attacks could make him an invalid—if he survived them. Content that they would now have many more years together, Dolores spoke slowly as Francis's arm encircled her waist.

"Edmond and Maria... Manuel Bocarro and Antonio Castro... Father Giulio." Sudden tears wet her cheeks. "They promised us a splendid send-off. It is bitter for you, I know, very bitter. But we *had* to leave..."

"I promised them I'd come back some day." Francis's voice was tightly controlled. "But I wonder..."

José Rivera appeared unbidden to offer them champagne. Neither husband nor wife spoke again, but gazed at the hills of Macao glowing beneath the broad scarlet-and-purple streaks the sunset painted on the Asiatic sky. Francis raised his goblet in a silent toast to his wife. Trailing crimson radiance, the sun retreated into the Great Empire. When the green hills of Macao were indistinguishable from the dark hills of China, Francis and Dolores Arrowsmith emptied their goblets and dropped them shimmering into the white wake of the caravel.

Francis knew he was parting forever from China, bidding farewell to the glory he had so long pursued, the glory he had almost attained when God snatched it away. For an instant rage choked him, but great sadness overwhelmed his rage. Yet there were still battles to be fought with words in Europe.

Dolores do Amaral Arrowsmith reminded herself that she was glad to be gone. Macao lay behind them, and Europe beckoned. A great future waited and great peace as well. Nonetheless, she wept for the Macao home she had known almost all her life. She wondered whether her husband would ever be fully reconciled to his premature parting from China. And she thanked God that not she, but his own body had forced that parting upon him.

Francis Arrowsmith told himself that he had rejected China by choosing to go when he could have remained, whatever the certain hazards. Yet he would always wonder whether China had at the end rejected him.

"Shall we go below, my dear?" he asked. "I promised the Captain a glass of champagne."

THRILLS * CHILLS * MYSTERY
from FAWCETT BOOKS

CURRENT POPULAR LIBRARY BESTSELLERS

☐ **THE SEEDS OF FIRE** 04672 $2.95
by Kenneth M. Cameron
The triumphs and tragedies of the Morse family, a mighty line of gunmakers, continue in this second volume of the Arms saga.

☐ **THE ENTICERS** 04678 $2.95
by Natasha Peters
While the Chinese revolution brews, four Americans struggle to find love amid the opulence and savagery of Shanghai during the thirties.

☐ **DUST DEVIL** 04667 $2.95
by Parris Afton Bonds
A saga of love and survival of the early settlers of the untamed southwestern plains.

☐ **MURDER IN THE WHITE HOUSE** 04661 $2.95
by Margaret Truman
A gripping novel of an unprecedented crime in the cloistered precincts of the highest office of the land.

☐ **FALLING IN PLACE** 04650 $2.95
by Ann Beattie
This is a novel about missed connections and accidental collisions—about couples who can never say what they mean, and more often say what they shouldn't.